The Three Scrolls

Kaarathlon

Knights of the Promise
The Three Scrolls

Return of the Dragonriders

DragonBirth
DragonWing
DragonSword

Legend of the Singer

Children of the Dryads*

*Not yet available. Release date TBD

Copyright © 2018, 2020 by Raina Nightingale

ISBN: 978-1-952176-03-6
All rights reserved. No part of this book may be reproduced or transmitted in any form or by any means, electronic or mechanical, including photocopying and recording, or by any information or retrieval system, without permission in writing from the publisher.

[1] FICTION / fantasy / dragons & mythical creatures
[2] FICTION / Christian / fantasy
[3] FICTION / fantasy / epic

Summary: A woman who becomes a queen, a man who is freed from a prison, and an orphan girl come to knowledge of the Creator through three scrolls that Kathreen gives them.

Cover art by Raina Nightingale
Cover design by Raina Nightingale

www.enthralledbylove.com

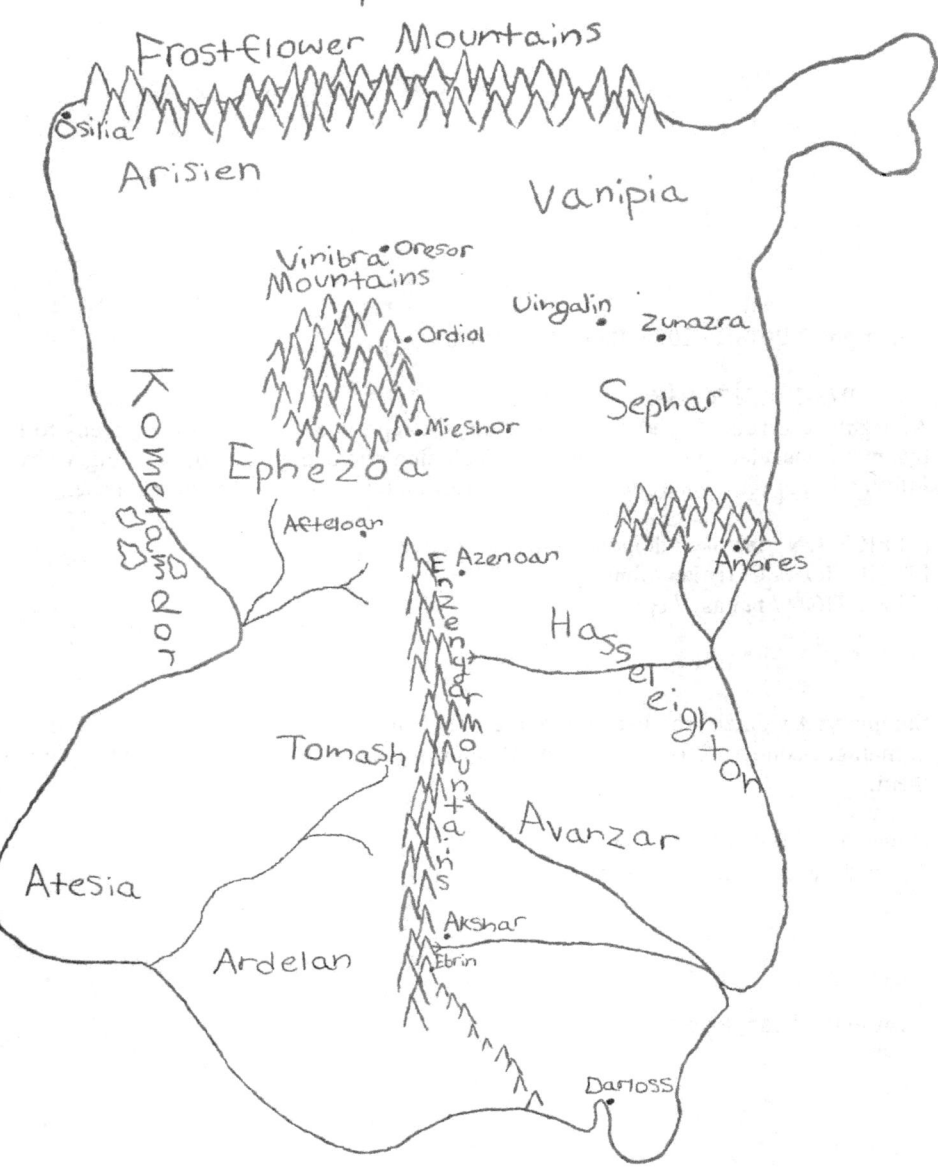

Table of Contents

1: The Loss of Sanity :1
2: The Call :5
3: A Lonely Place :10
4: Different Pieces of the World :13
5: A Traitor to Treason :17
6: The Helper :21
7: Risks :25
8: Venture into the Uncertain :29
9: To Be For the Prince :33
10: A Conflict in Family and Heart :37
11: The Shame :42
12: The Retaliation :46
13: The Fright :49
14: The Request :53
15: The Whole Problem :60
16: What Is It, Lady? :64
17: The Brethren :68
18: Game of Chances :73
19: The Few :78
20: Hasseleighton and Execution :83
21: Unpredictable, Really :87
22: The Insult and the Disturbance :92
23: Enemies :97
24: Barbs and Wounds :102
25: A Vision of the Promise :106
26: A Disquieting Meadow :111
27: A Child's Questions :115
28: The Witch :119
29: The Prophet :123
30: Little Joy :128
31: The Starling's Tears :131
32: The Letter :135
33: The Caress of the Night Wind :140
34: Too Big to Be Any Size :146
35: Wearing Thin :149
36: Dizziness :153
37: The Pain of Betrayal :157
38: Flattering the Emperor :161
39: In the Shadow :165
40: The Sundering Promise :169
41: Safe :173
42: To Face Death :178
43: Daddy :182

44: Flowers and Hair :186
45: Falling :191
46: The White Dragon Keeper :195
47: Tied Tongue :199
48: Twilight Gloom :203
49: A Change :208
50: Knights' Scroll :212
51: Kathreen of the Silver Sword :217
52: An Echo :222
53: Touch of the Dragon Keeper :226
54: Reflection :229
55: Under the Sword :232
56: Ashamed :236
57: Beginnings :230
58: Ice Blue Eyes :244
59: Scarier :248
60: Terror of the Undead :254
61: Ruin of the Beginning :258
62: Dragon-rider Knight :262
63: Healing in the Promise :266
64: Telling the Truth :270
65: The Dragon Tribe :274
66: Dawn in the Valleys of the Sea :278
67: Then And Now :282
68: Family Quarrel :286
69: Swamp of Disappointment :290
70: Thoughts From the Scroll :293
71: A Cup of Water :296
72: Singer :300
73: The Deceiver :304
74: Prisoners :307
75: Secret Things :311
76: Accused :315
77: Wailing Voice :319
78: The Sailing of the *Last Watch* :324
79: End of Life :328
80: The Queen's Regret :331
81: The Sea and the Sky :335
82: Secrets of the Elzari :338
83: Strangled :342
84: A Child's Warning :346
85: The Desert :350
86: Morning :354
87: Deadly Radiance :359

88: *Edgerunner* :363
89: The Curse of the Mighty :367
90: Laughter on the Waves :370
91: The Sign :375
92: Giant Mixing Spoons :380
93: Deadly Place of Life :384
94: A Good Place :388
95: The Healing :392
96: The Speaker :397
97: The Twin :401
98: An Inconsolable Longing :405
99: Fall of the Last Stronghold :410
100: The Shield of the Scroll :415
101: The Gift and the Thanksgiving :418
102: Sal-Itshunrara-Miktkakar :424
Glossary :429

#1
The Loss of Sanity

Arendellie stood outside, at the door of her house, looking up at the sky, where L'sa-moth flew away, up and over the village, her pale undersea green underside hanging between her violet and lilac wings. She was sorry for Kathreen and her dragon. They had been friends before. At Kathreen's request, she had kept the fact that she was a wizard secret. Kathreen wanted it so, and Arendellie wanted her to be well. She still wanted to be her friend, but she just did not understand how she could be friends with someone who had turned as fanatical as Kathreen. The young woman used to be her best friend; of the group of four, Arendellie, Dorene, Kathreen, and Mirla, Arendellie and Kathreen had been closest, and Dorene and Mirla had been closest. She had been rather depressed since that day when Kathreen had told her about her crazy intentions of proclaiming the Promise and building her whole life, every minute and every second of it, every part of it, around the Creator. She felt sorry for Kathreen, since she was making herself miserable. She already had most of Ebrin against her, and even had some of the young men so angry with her, for insisting that the only thing that mattered was faithfulness to the Creator and His Promise, and that one's whole life was to be governed by this, that they were almost threatening to rid the world of her. *I'm sorry for you, Kathreen,* thought Arendellie. *I'm sorry you didn't listen to me, but I can't make you, and one day you're going to be sorry that you did this, chasing the end of the rainbow and a glory in the mist, instead of listening to real, solid, down-to-earth wisdom.*

Several weeks later.
"What are you telling me, Mirla?" Arendellie asked, a little shocked.
"Kathreen's not crazy, Arendellie. Don't you think the source of our existence has got to be more solid than our existence?"
"What on earth on you getting at, Mirla?" asked Dorene.
"Well, don't you think it would be crazy to live like the ground under your feet isn't real? You really can't do that, and you can't *actually* live like the Creator isn't real, but you can live in defiance of His truth. Anyway, you're trying to live like the Real isn't real, and that's what is crazy – not Kathreen, trying to live in conformity to the truth and to the Promise, to all that really matters," said Mirla.
"Arrgh!" cried Arendellie. "Are you serious?"
"Yeah," said Mirla. "What we've been trying to do is kind of like trying to live underneath a crumbling cliff and consider the man who actually takes into account the fact that the cliff might fall to be crazy and insane and a fanatic who only cares about mists and bases his life on illusions! After Kathreen talked to me, I realized how crazy and disconnected and out of touch with reality my way of living has been. So–"
Arendellie threw her hands up. "You aren't trying to say you've gone insane too!"

Mirla's voice sounded like unbearably sad laughter. "No, Arendellie, no, Dorene. It is you who are living in defiance of reality and you will get hurt, just like if you try to live like gravity isn't real you'll tumble down a hill and get hurt, if you don't walk off a hill and die... Anyway, if you don't want to talk any further, and only want to scoff at sanity, I'll go now," she said, getting to her feet.

Arendellie looked at Dorene and said, once Mirla was out of earshot, "It looks like it's just us now... We've both just lost our best friends, so maybe?"

Dorene nodded. "Yeah, we can try to be best friends now." She sounded dejected, not like her usual self.

To be honest, Arendellie was disturbed by recent happenings. The world was changing. Ever since Wizard-Dragon Keeper Grale Casarion had begun to achieve prominence in Hasseleighton the winds of change has been stirring, and Arendellie was not sure how far it could go. Already, they seemed to be tearing friendships apart. She, however, just wanted to live her life. She pulled her hair over one shoulder, undid the clasp that held the braid, shook it out, and began to comb her hair with her fingers, while she lay on the grass thinking these things. She was not really sure that she and Dorene could be friends; not the way that she and Kathreen or that Dorene and Mirla had been. They were too different. Though Mirla was actually the oldest of the four, Arendellie often came across as older in many ways. As for Dorene, she was all-around the youngest. Personality wise, she was at least as different from Arendellie as was Mirla, and she was a lot younger. Arendellie did not really think that they could be best friends.

"Dorene," said Arendellie slowly, "why do you think that Mirla and Kathreen have decided to be so unreasonable?"

"I don't know," replied Dorene, her usually bubbly voice flat and weary with dejection. "Maybe it has something to do with thinking about death too much?" She sounded a bit cautious, hesitant, as if a little afraid or a little uncertain. "I know thinking about death is what made Kathreen go off the deep end."

Yeah! thought Arendellie, *that seems like it!* She was not quite sure what she was thinking. What she said was, "Yeah, some people seem to take death a bit too seriously. I wonder, is that because they take life too seriously? Or do they start taking life too seriously because they take death too seriously? Anyway," she said, after a brief pause, "let's try to think and talk about other things... live as if that hadn't happened. Okay?"

"Yeah, that sounds like a good idea," said Dorene, her voice recovering a little of its usual buoyancy. "Umm, Veance is actually walking Kolda around and steering her now."

"Yeah," said Arendellie. "It is kind of a funny spectacle, isn't it?"

"Yep, it totally is." Dorene giggled. "Anyway, when are you and Neshekh going to get married?"

Arendellie pulled her long hair around her neck, and over her shoulder. Still stroking it out, she said, "You race on ahead of us! He has not yet proposed."

"You two are being slow!" said Dorene. "The whole village thinks so."

Arendellie stuck her tongue out. "No," she retorted, "all the thirteen year olds think so."

One afternoon, Arendellie was sitting on her front porch, weaving lace for her wedding garments. Dorene sat next to her, stroking her dog, which had been convinced to lick Dorene and only Dorene, on the head. "Did you know," Dorene asked, very casually, "that Kathreen is back in Ebrin?"

"Yes, so I had heard," replied Arendellie. "Things get around here quickly. What? Anything about her?" Whenever they spoke about Kathreen, which was rarely, Arendellie had to be careful not to let the secret that Kathreen was a wizard slip out. She wanted to be faithful to her friend, even though they could no longer stand each other and never saw each other, but the fact that Kathreen was a wizard was such a big thing it shaped all of Arendellie's thinking about her. It was hard even to talk about Kathreen's choices without bringing in the fact that she was a wizard. In fact, she was tempted to go to Kathreen, and tell her that she should go to one of the wizard training schools to perfect her talent and gain some sense. Two things kept her from it. One of them was that she was certain, from what she knew of Kathreen, that she would never agree, or at least she suspected so. The other was that she did not want to have any conversations with Kathreen anymore than Kathreen did with her. She did not like talking about the Creator and His Sovereign Kingship and Reality and things like that; not that she never talked about Him anymore. After all, a few fanatics were not going to make her stop believing in Him. Now and then she would talk about Him with her friends. It was just, she did not believe in Him the way Kathreen did, and she did not want to, and just remembering the things Kathreen and Mirla said bothered her way out of proportion for some reason.

"No," said Dorene, but Arendellie, seeing the direction of Dorene's gaze and the look on her face, knew what the younger girl was thinking. Kathreen would appreciate Dizzy much better than she did. Kathreen would actually enjoy Dizzy's licking and exuberance, instead of being constantly annoyed with her, shooing her away lest she mess up clothes or skin or hair or furniture and insisting that she never touch her.

Arendellie concentrated on the weave for a few moments. Completing the stitch she was just then working on, she looked over at Dorene and said, "Aren't there other people out there who would appreciate Dizzy? Your own siblings? Some of the other girls, like maybe Ruhla?"

Dorene smiled. Dizzy spun around, jumped up, and exuberantly tried to lick her face. "No, no, no," cried Dorene, laughing and flailing her hands, "you'll knock out my teeth if you carry on like that!" She got the doggy to lie down on her back for her to scratch her belly. "Actually, yes," she replied to Arendellie, who found the interruptions and distractions Dizzy presented disrupting to conversation. The fact was, she and Dorene were not closer friends than they were before Kathreen and Mirla left them; no, it was quite the opposite. Dorene had been Arendellie's friend because Arendellie and Kathreen were friends, and Dorene and Mirla were Kathreen's friends. Now, they had almost nothing in common except that they had both been hurt by the loss of their closest friends to a fanatical devotion to the Creator precipitated by the rise of Grale Casarion in the east, and now the north. Whenever they were together both of them found the interaction dissatisfying and both of them knew that they would probably not be friends for another year. They would not hate or even dislike each other; there was simply no reason for them to be friends anymore.

#2
The Call

Azshbir sat down cross-legged on the ground, listening to a young, thick woman, about a year or two older than himself, talking about her experiences of the outside world, which he had never seen. She had a beautiful accent, and she was just a shade darker than his family. Never before had anyone from the outside world come to their home; when he had first seen her sitting with his mother pounding roots into powder he had been so shocked he had almost cried out. He would have been scared, wondering if she was some sort of police-spy, except for the friendship between her and his mother, made obvious by the fact that his mother, Sirifa, was sharing her work with her.

"So," the woman, whose name was Kathreen Alarion, continued, "I hid in the garbage heap. It really did stink. After they had gone, I had to discard my cloak, since it was way too disgusting for me to be able to clean it, even with wizardry. I don't even like to think about how I don't even know what kind of foul things I hid with!" Her story-telling was animated. It was fun to listen to, but Azshbir could not deny that there was a little cold tingling of fear in his heart; he had not known that the world was that, well, cruel. Kathreen had just been explaining the state of things in Sephar, and what she had experienced when she had gone there.

Azshbir cleared his throat. "How many places have you been?"

"Only Avanzar, where I was born, Sephar, and Ephezoa." Kathreen paused, and then went straight ahead as if anticipating a next question. "Avanzar is *not* under the control of King Grale Casarion and, as far as I know, the governing authorities have not been hostile to true commitment to the Creator's Promise. However, I fled from my village fearing that some of the people there might take measures to kill me if I stayed there. So…"

"So, nowhere is safe," Azshbir said, with a little humor. For some reason, the way Kathreen told the story, especially the one about escaping from the police seemed to have lightened her own mood significantly. Even while she talked about how awful it was hiding in a reek of garbage, or how fearful she had been, she seemed to be laughing within. Perhaps it was the combination of telling the story and interacting with the children that did it, but she seemed very light-hearted, and like she was treating the whole thing like an absurdity.

However, Azshbir's comment made Kathreen deadly serious. "Yes," she said, gravely, "nowhere is safe. Unless," she added in the quietest of tones, looking down at her lap. Azshbir wondered what she was thinking of. What horrors did she know that he had no idea about? As it happened, she was thinking about some of L'sa-moth's friends and their riders– dragons and humans she knew only through her dragon, but it was bad enough, since the bond, though not like that between dragon and rider, which L'sa-moth shared with his friends was close, and the dragon knew much of their fears and even sufferings, and indeed their thoughts and feelings. She was thinking, too, about her time with Mirla several months ago, and the dim forebodings and fears that had filled her mind and had never really left her when she looked at baby Brisia, in Mirla's arms, and thought that she would have liked to be a mother, but with the world the way it now was, it was better that she was a virgin. After a few moments she continued, telling about how she changed her clothes, and fled to Ephezoa, and of the way she was received in Uingalin.

Then, she made a comment Azshbir did not understand. Looking down, she spoke quietly, as if sad and disturbed, "They're the same people... their hearts are the same... I knew something was wrong then... but it's almost like it's a different nation."

"What do you mean?" asked Adaria, looking up from the castle she was helping her little brother, Laekoorj, to build with blocks and sticks.

"Well, when I first went to Ephezoa, I was invited by some people to speak to the people about my experiences and what I'd seen and learned. I knew somehow that something was wrong right from the beginning, and that I, or maybe my words, were somehow being treated like animals in a zoo, or something of the sort. I'm still not certain I really understand, but people were very interested in hearing me and talking well about me, and I think I liked the attention. I think I would have left sooner if I hadn't, but it was just too fun not being an outcast, though I felt wrong all the time. I got to speak to large audiences, to meet wizards and ambassadors and diplomats, and all that stuff. Eventually, I left to live in Darloss, a seaside city in southern Avanzar. Well, when I returned to Ephezoa, I saw it. In the frontier cities, they almost all just want to give up. The same people who used to want to hear me talk about the importance of living entirely for the Creator and in the Reality of His Promise now want to hear nothing about Him and seem to be bitter towards Him. They're angry about the losses they have suffered, being so close to the battle-line, and they want to just surrender to Grale and swear their allegiance to him. If you suggest otherwise, they look daggers at you. In fact, sometimes you worry that they might decide to kill you.

"The interior cities are different, too. It's much easier to see that their 'allegiance to the Creator and the Promise' is all about protecting their lifestyle and freedoms, and not being ruled by a Hasseleighton tyranny. Oh, they don't talk about the Creator or the Promise any less, but it's easier to see that they have the wrong idea of Him– that they want or think He's their god, to protect their values, and to make their lives like they want. The Promise isn't, to them, the Promise– being delivered from shame before the Creator's eyes – but about keeping the world from degenerating into chaos and cruelty in every direction."

There was a pause after that. Everyone was more or less quiet, except for the playing of the children. After a few drawn-out moments, Athara asked, tentatively, "So, kind of like Duhralra?" Duhralra was a Sepharian inn keeper's wife, who held that one could have allegiance to the Creator in one's deepest heart, but outwardly give allegiance to Grale Casarion, and that this was, perhaps, even what the Creator wanted.

An odd look appeared on Kathreen's face, as if she were thinking, for the moment out on a limb. Then, it was like a light went off. "Exactly! They're exactly like Duhralra!" she exclaimed. "I never noticed that before."

Azshbir got up, and began to pace. "Wait a minute. I don't think I get this. I can understand why you think the battle-front city folk are like Duhralra– they're like Duhralra in the same way her own country-folk are like her... not the same person, but the same ideas and doctrines and practices, more or less. However, why do you think that the interior people are like Duhralra? It's almost as different as possible. Duhralra says that she can give allegiance to the Creator in her heart, and that the Creator's not a king like Grale Casarion... He wouldn't care if she gives outward allegiance to Grale. Isn't that a world of difference from the Ephezoans, who you tell me want to fight Grale Casarion to the death and have nothing to do with Him, and want the Creator as one who will protect them from tyranny?"

"No, wait!" said Adaria. "I get it! I totally get it! They both make their own 'Creator', and don't realize how preposterous it is. Think about the things Duhralra said. 'He's good, and He loves us, and He wants us to be good and happy.' That's more or less what the Ephezoans all want! There's no Promise in that, no King in that. Duhralra thinks being good and happy is submitting to any authority and being comfortable, no matter what. The Ephezoans instead want their culture and lifestyle and not to be ruled by a tyrant. They disagree on what they want; they call what the other wants bad. They are agreed that the Creator exists for their wants, though they wouldn't dare put it that way. Neither wants Him as a Sovereign King to rule over them. Duhralra doesn't want to submit to His Kingship and suffer. Ephezoa doesn't want to submit to His Kingship and be imposed upon by a foreign ruler and culture. It's the same! The line about Grale Casarion not making rules that violate the Creator's is, again, the same. The people of Ephezoa don't realize that their own lives and the basics of their understanding of the world isn't in accord with the Creator, and His revealed truth, that we're all in rebellion against Him. They both have this idea that their regimes, rulers, cultures, authorities, whatever, can do no wrong. The differences between Duhralra and Ephezoa are really very superficial. The last thing either wants is a Creator who is the Highest of all kings and the Reality above all things, to be obeyed and honored in everything. Each has made a little 'Creator' who is no Creator at all for themselves!"

"You're totally right," said Kathreen. "Totally, Adaria. Thinking about it... so many things Duhralra said... so many things others have said... the difference between them so much on the surface... but they, of course, are too much on the surface to do anything other than get furious with you for suggesting that they might be just like their mortal enemies... It is really a bunch of people rebelling against the True King, and then being unable to decide what rules they are to live by or who will rule them, and fighting each other because they've shaken off all rule, and yet insisting that, at the core, they're each different from the other rebels they're fighting and that their motivations for their fighting over the rules are good, while the other side is wholly bad, because they're fighting to preserve something that looks like one of the rules of the King they rebelled against and are rebelling against, while the other side is fighting for something that looks a little like a different one of His rules, which they just happen to dislike, or for something clearly opposed to all His rules. Yes, Adaria. Oh, my!"

They talked for hours longer, the conversation wandering all over the place, sometimes jumping ahead, sometimes going back to something never explained or clarified in the past. Azshbir began to find it increasingly confusing. Yawning now and then, his mind wondered, often into thoughts of gratitude that he had been protected from the poisonous atmosphere throughout all Camil. Before, he had been irritated that he was so isolated; now, he was glad that he had not been raised to think of the Creator as something for his own ease and comfort or the advancement of his own values. Hearing Kathreen talk about conversations with people who thought such things, often without realizing it, he thought, *What a deep, deep pit, what a subtle lie. How terrible it must be to be caught in that snare. Certainly, only the Creator's power can cure the blindness or vanquish that poison.* At the same time, he found himself wanting to go with Kathreen, not to see the outside world, as he had thought when he first heard the offer, but to tell these people the truth, even if it would do no good unless the Creator opened their eyes to see it. He could not want to see the outside world for curiosity's sake anymore, but he did want to go to the people caught in a snare from which he had no power, in himself, to deliver them, for he could not even make them see that they were caught.

There came a time when everyone– that is, the four oldest– expressed their desire to go with Kathreen. Azshbir explained, "I want to go because those people need more people to warn them! I think protecting the Promise must include protecting it from the misunderstandings and abuse of people like those Ephezoans Kathreen was telling us all about. I also think the Creator wants us to warn them, even if they are deaf. It is such a terrible thing to be caught in such an abominable snare."

The other three put forth their reasons. Soon, they got a little loud, all talking over each other, and some of them getting up to pace about their excitement. Kathreen waved her hand down to silence them. "No, you can't all come. I'm sure your parents," here Kathreen glanced at and made eye contact with Sirifa, "need some of you to stay and help with your younger siblings, and there's also too many of you to ride L'sa-moth. Further, Athara, you're a bit young."

Sirifa looked to Kathreen appreciatively. Azshbir drew in his breath sharply. Was he not going to get to go? Well, he decided, if he could not go now, he would wait a couple years, to help out with his younger siblings while they grew older, and then he would go alone. He had to go! The danger did not matter. He had to go, to uphold the Promise before these people, and to warn them in the Creator's Name! But his mother was speaking. "I think it would be best for Azshbir,"– here his heart leapt, and he felt like he might faint for joy, even as he inwardly breathed a sigh of relief, praying, *Thank You,*– "and Adaria to go. Yes, it will be harder here, but you need to have opportunities to meet people, and even to meet people who might be marriageable. Azshbir is the oldest of our sons and it's time for him to get out into the world."

"Yes, Sirifa, that sounds good," said Hoobit. Turning to his children, particularly Azshbir and Adaria, "Of course, we're not forcing you to go. It's dangerous. You may have to flee authorities, and run down rubbish allies. You could be killed, or thrown into prison... I'm not trying to discourage you. You just should know."

Forcing us to go! Azshbir thought, still feeling almost giddy, *I want to go! It's dangerous?! I know that! Weren't we all just hearing about it!* The line, *or thrown into prison...* caused a small cold shiver to run through his blood, but it was nothing. He stood to his feet, still feeling almost dazed, first by the fear that he would not get to go, then by the announcement that he certainly would, then by the comment about not being forced. Shrugging, he addressed the issue of the dangers. "That's fine by me. The Creator is a very great King, and worth dying in whose service. After all, isn't part of the Promise that One Whom He has chosen and sent will reign even over death? If He reigns over death, can He not release His people from its dungeons? I think so! And, even if He does not, He is good, and has already been very merciful to me. He is worthy of my life." As he said these things, Azshbir was thinking particularly of how he had been protected from the poisons and snares with which his world abounded.

Hoobit turned to his daughter. "Adaria?"

"I think the same as Azshbir, and I would really like to get to know Kathreen. She has got to have lots of things to teach us."

#3
A Lonely Place

Azshbir stood next to L'sa-moth's shoulder, running his hand absentmindedly over her smooth, gleaming green and purple scales, which felt like they must have been oiled. The huge dragon had laid her head on the grass, and Kathreen stood next to it, stroking the top of her neck. Adaria stood between Azshbir and Kathreen, and a little away from the dragon. Azshbir remembered the first time he had seen this dragon, majestic as she had seemed then, though he had since discovered that she was actually a very gentle dragon, not at all fierce, and to one who knew dragons actually looked as gentle and kind as she was. He could feel that she was a person too, even though he could not speak to her.

For six months, he, Adaria, and Kathreen had traveled together. They had spoken to people in shops and at parks, on the streets and on outlaying farms. Once, a scene was made, when several people protested about what they were saying. What he had to do made him feel just a little scared. He had seen so much more of Adaria that he had at home; he felt he knew her much better. Kathreen also was a friend to him. Now and then, he found himself thinking that she would make a good wife and mother, but he knew better than to even ask or think about it; that was not her call, and they all knew it. Now, she and Adaria had been talking about their desire to visit Sephar again, and also Vanipia. It was time to venture out of Ephezoa, into other places. Adaria wanted to go into Hasseleighton, to venture into the very heart of Grale's reign, the land of terror, but Kathreen was not quite sure. Last night, they had all stayed up well past ten talking about these matters. In the end, Azshbir had gone to sleep, but Kathreen and Adaria had stayed up, talking about where they should go, and whether or not they should go to Hasseleighton. He had had little to say; he had not cared much, then.

After having some time to think about it, though, Azshbir knew it was not for him. For one thing, he needed to get away from Kathreen. They were spending too much time too close, and though Azshbir did not think that she felt drawn to him– he could not be *quite* sure– he was finding himself increasingly drawn to her, and he knew that she was not for him. Of course, he had been beginning to know that for a while now, and wondering how to do the separation, but also procrastinating, because he really did not want to do it. It would be so lonely. In addition, he felt certain that he was called to warn these blind and stubborn people who devoured poison like sweets and called their snares and pits castles, not to these other places. He was certain that it was not cowardice that made him think this; the chill in his veins when he thought of dangers and even tortures was not, indeed, wholly unpleasant. It made him feel alive in a tingling, wide-awake but early morning kind of way. He knew, also, that he needed to settle down somewhere and live among and warn these people. Yet furthermore, he had only been in this city one or two days when he began to get the feeling, "This is the place." So, he gathered the courage to speak. "I think, sisters, that I must remain here, in Afteloan."

Kathreen and Adaria both nodded. Adaria's eyes looked moistened by tears.

Kathreen swallowed, and said, "I thought it would be." Adaria stepped forward, and she and Azshbir embraced. "I am so going to miss you, brother," she said.

"And I, you," said Azshbir.

After a long minute, Adaria stepped back, her eyes bright like the dew, or like the sun just beginning to send his shining glory over the horizon. Her voice tight with tears and yet with a kind of joy or fun, she said, "But, that's okay. We will meet again."

"Even if on the other side of death," Azshbir completed. He did not feel as joyful about it as Adaria, at the moment. He turned to Kathreen.

She smiled. Azshbir loved her smile; he thought it matched her face, even darker than that of many Camilians, and of proportions to match her thicker body as well. Somehow, he thought it looked like the noon sun, even though the noon sun was blindingly bright to look at, and she was very dark indeed. He found himself thinking drolly, *I wonder, where will I ever find a woman as beautiful as you?* Catching himself, he thought, *Yes, it is definitely time.* "Fare you well, Azshbir. I will miss you, too. Your confidence and trust has been a great example and encouragement to me. I hope to come and see you again, sometime." she said. There was so much to say it was better not to try to say any of it. It would be better communicated unsaid than if a thousand words had been tried, especially in a moment like this.

So, also, Azshbir would have liked to say a lot more, but he knew that the more he tried to say the less he would end up saying. "Fare well, Kathreen. Your happiness has touched my heart, and I have learned much and been greatly encouraged by your openness about your struggles, and as much by your thoughts and words, the wisdom you have gained doing this before me." Did Kathreen blush, or had he only imagined it?

Feeling sick at heart, Azshbir turned and walked away. He did not think that he could bear to look back, so he kept his head low and hurried on, even while he heard L'sa-moth run forward, and the great beating of her wings on the air, as she took off. The voice of a singing dragon floated on the air, like shivers of morning joy. The birds began to chirp, weaving their own songs and harmonies around the dragon's richer melody, though clean, clear, thin and almost knife-like though without pain or sadness. Passing through the gate out of the dragon field, Azshbir sat down on a bench, and put his head in his hands. He had felt so certain last night, but this morning he felt so empty, dry, shallow, and like he had no idea where to go or where to start. Of course, he thought, he had to learn.

The sun rose before Azshbir pulled himself together and got up, but only a little before he did so. His first thought was that he must find some sort of job to support himself. For the better portion of the morning he asked around in the plaza, and told people that he had experience as a farmer and a hunter from the mountains. Then, he went back to the inn to have lunch; he had foregone breakfast. In the afternoon, he went to the park, stretched himself out on a bench, and thought about what he would do, and how to begin. Since he was staying in this city indefinitely, he had the luxury to go through it systemically, to try to find a way to warn everyone and, what was better, to give the hope of the Promise to everyone. As Kathreen had told them all, in that valley in the Vinibra Volcanic Mountains, what seemed like a century ago, the very nation that boasted of being most fixed upon the ordinances of the Creator and the hope of His Promise might well be the nation most ignorant of the true meaning of the Promise– or was all Camil like that? He decided that he would go and purchase a map of the city and the surrounding farmlands.

Upon acquiring the map, Azshbir returned to the park, and again stretched himself out on a bench, along with several pages of paper and a pen, to think and plan. He was a little wary of the Halls of Exhortation. He had discovered, during his first conversation with anyone other than Kathreen outside his family, in Ordiol, that even to suggest that the real motives of the Ephezoans for their war might be in contradiction to the ordinances of the Creator, or that the Creator did not really care about them keeping their culture, was often to be accused of treason. He did not really want to get the whole city mad at him before they had even heard the merits of what he had to say by making a scene at some meeting at the Hall of Exhortation. He would prefer to talk to individuals or small groups, whether of family or of friends, quietly and discreetly, so that people might know what he was saying, rather than believing rumors that he had said crazy nonsense that even he would heartily disavow. By experience, he knew that people would think that he had said things not unlike those which Duhralra had told Kathreen– that people are supposed to obey everyone who claims to be an authority or exercises power, no matter what the laws are, to keep the Creator and the Promise hidden and covered up if that was helpful to such ends, and similar nonsense. What frustrated him worst of all was that, while they could not have for the life of themselves seen the connection, and he had only understood it after Kathreen and Adaria had tried explaining it several times and in several different ways, he now could not help thinking that, to be honest, the substance of what these Ephezoan nationalists believed was very much the same as what the Sepharian inn keeper's wife who had so infuriated Kathreen believed.

At any rate, thinking and doing things made him feel less miserable.

Azshbir tried to sketch out several different ideas of how to comb the city and reach everyone, trying to look for one that was feasible and did not have glaring defects. Finally, he gave up. What kind of job he got would affect what he could and could not do, and what kind of opportunities he would be presented with, as well. He came to that conclusion a little before sunset. Gathering his things, he walked back to the inn. He ordered a small and uninteresting dinner, which he ate feeling rather lonely, though this was mitigated by the fact that he was still sorting things out in his head. Then, he went to his room, stretched out on his bed, and was soon fast asleep. He had gotten very little sleep the previous night, between having retired late and thinking over things before falling asleep, and waking up very early.

In the morning, he went to the plaza again, to look for a job. He was found out by a man who said he was in need of an all-around skilled farmhand, who could do everything from butchering the cow, to ploughing, to repairs, to dealing with unruly animals, to anything else necessary.

#4
Different Pieces of the World

Arendellie sat on the back porch of the house, with Neshekh, looking out over a large pasture, a little below their level, with lovely woods and meadows, and a little stream wandering through it. Cows, sheep, goats, and a few horses grazed, mostly keeping each to his or her own species. There were carpets of color in the meadows, yellows melding into pinks or blues, here and there patches of white, purple, or brilliant almost-red orange, and now and then patches of green. It was beautiful.

Arendellie pulled her long, braided hair over her shoulder, and leaned back against the wall. "This is beautiful," she said, taking a deep breath of the air laden with the fragrances of a thousand wildflowers, "... and soon to be even more lovely."

"Yes, my lovely one," said Neshekh, turning towards her. Their gazes met in a tender smile. "I love your appreciation of beauty, even more beautiful one. You are tender and kind, and so clean and lovely... like the wild roses."

Arendellie smiled. Everything was so like it always was, and yet there was something odd, like Neshekh was keeping something back. *Perhaps a surprise gift?* she wondered. They turned to face each other, for each was even more attracted to the other than to the panorama of beauty around them. They held each other's hands, one over the other, in their laps between them. *Oh, this is good– and when at last we will be able to really be together, the way we were meant to be!* Arendellie thought. Everything was so still and quiet, as if this moment could go on forever. Indeed, it might, it almost felt like, nor would she mind if it did, she thought.

They held each other's hands and gazed into each other's eyes like that for a while. It could have been a few moments, or it could have been several minutes. Time seemed to do strange things when they were together. After several moments Neshekh went on, "Indeed, I think you might almost have been named for the wild roses, as much as for your green eyes. Your name might come from Ar-a-Endel-Fri, Colors of Green Gentle in the ancient tongue, or it might be Araen Rendelli, Wild Rose. I think both are suitable."

They were together for a few more moments. Arendellie had the sudden impulse to unclasp her long, black hair, which Neshekh had complimented before, and shake it out of its braid, but she refrained. To let down one's hair before a man meant something inappropriate outside of marriage, especially if it was long, like hers was. If one kept one's hair short, it did not mean anything. Then, Arendellie felt Neshekh brace himself, and she almost bit her lip, wondering what was coming next. This did not feel right. His hands on and in hers tightened and then relaxed. He bent closer, and whispered in the softest of tones, like Arendellie loved, "I love you, Arendellie, my sweetheart, my beautiful one, my wild rose, tender and gentle. I love you, my Arendellie." He had said these things before, and even said them this way before, and yet it only increased her foreboding.

"Arendellie, my wild rose, my Araen Rendelli, I hope you won't hate me for saying this but..." Neshekh faltered, as if for a loss how to continue, how to say what he had to say next. Several times he opened his mouth as if to speak and shut it again, sometimes saying "but" first. Arendellie was so frozen in suspense and desire to know, also in fear and anxiety, that she did not even ask him what it was or encourage him to go on.

Finally, Neshekh just blurted it out. "I believe what Mirla, Aleria, and Ajiek do."

Arendellie's face, already lighter than that of most Camilians, paled with a kind of shock. "You don't mean to say–?" she asked, breathlessly. *So,* she thought, in a shocked, distant kind of way, *that was what he was doing on those evenings – gathering with them!*

"I think I do mean to say," replied Neshekh, in the quietest of all possible tones. Then, "I really do love you, Arendellie."

"I know," she said, beginning to cry. This, too, was inappropriate, but he took her in his arms and cradled her, while she snuggled up against him.

After a long time, Arendellie pulled herself together a little, and disengaged herself from his arms. "It's okay, I think," she said. "I do believe in the Creator and the Promise, though I don't believe it the way that you– they– you people– do." She hated her words with all her strength. She could not think of how to put her meaning into words, or perhaps it was that she wanted to use words and her meaning to change reality to what she wanted it to be, and it was not working.

There was sadness in Neshekh's eyes, though they now sat apart as they had before, with their hands in each other's laps. "Arendellie, oh my Araenyi, the world is changing." He seemed to gather himself together, to say what he had to next, as if he hated it and could hardly bring himself to say it. "I don't know how Avanzar has stayed out of it this long... There's no reason to suspect it will continue to be this way. Even Ephezoa is falling, we hear... Can we really share our lives, in this world?"

Arendellie looked like she wanted to snuggle up to him again. In a low, soft, soothing, drawn-out voice she began, "You're still Neshekh Dasaran, and I'm still your Araenyi. Of course, we can share our lives... We're almost married already, you know... As long as you'll love me and our children, of course... Just because you believe in Him the way Kathreen does, doesn't mean that you have to live your life the ways she does or do the things she does... Mirla believes in Him that way, and she can still be a wife and a mother. Most of Ebrin does despise her, but no one threatens her, ever... I'm your Araenyi. You can believe in the Creator and the Promise, and take care of me and love me."

Neshekh looked at Arendellie tenderly, but there was battle written in his eyes and on his face, as if he was fighting for sanity or for life. "Okay," he said, "but, you know what Grale Casarion demands of his subjects... How can we share our lives together, when my first goal must be always to be faithful to the Promise, and yours is simply to be a wife and mother and stay out of all messes?... I am a subject of the Creator and one of those who wait for His Promise before I am your husband or our children's father."

"That's what's cruel about how you believe," said Arendellie, softly. "Ethereal spiritual things have more meaning to you and are treated as more solid by you than real, living, flesh and blood... Anyway, that's all right. You'll be so busy taking care of me and loving me and being with me and the same for our children that you won't have any time to warn people or make scenes or be noticed. And," she added, "we live out in a middle-of-nowhere mountain village, so maybe they won't even come here." She said it in a way that was so smooth and soft, that even while she insulted and infuriated him, it was impossible for him not to be drawn to her, by a tug almost like gravity. She was flirting with him, even while she stabbed him, so to speak.

Neshekh stood up. Arendellie had never flirted with him quite like this before, and he was finding the urges to do inappropriate things almost irresistible. Later, he wondered if that had been her intent– to get him away from her for the moment and at the same time draw him closer to her and make getting away from her for the future more difficult. As it was, his blood was so thick and hot in his head he could not think everything, or even anything, through. He just knew it was too much, and that it had been too much a long time ago. "Arendellie," he said, "we get married a month from today."

"Okay," she said, in a way that was almost meek. He had decided on a month since one of her reasons for dragging it out this long had been the need for her to make her wedding dress perfect, and lace was so difficult. With a month, she might be able to get what she already had together so that it would work, even if it was not her idea.

Neshekh turned, as it were, and fled into his house. Arendellie sank down on the porch. The fact was, she was shocked. She had never thought it of Neshekh to join those crazy fanatics. She was angry at Grale Casarion. Why on earth did he have to take over the world? She didn't really mind his laws all that much, though she would prefer not to have to live with Hasseleighton culture, like having to cover one's hair, or even face in some circumstances. She was not really all that worried about that part of things, though, since she lived in a village out in the middle of nowhere, so in all likelihoods no one would try to mess with them too much. What infuriated her was that Grale Casarion's reign and tyranny was tearing those she knew best away from her. Several years ago, no one would have known the difference between what she believed and what Kathreen, or Mirla, or Neshekh believed, or if one had known it, it would not have mattered a whit. One would have been quite able to live one's life as if it did not exist. She did not think anyone *had* known the difference. Now, Grale Casarion was making people think and forcing people to make decisions no one should have to make, and the world was fracturing, and she and those she had known and loved were on different pieces. It was his fault that Kathreen and Mirla and Neshekh had all become fanatics! If they had not had this decision forced on them, they never would have even known that they believed in the Creator this way, and everyone could have been happy together. In fact, no one would have even had to decide whether they believed in the Creator Arendellie's way or Kathreen's way, let alone know that others were different, or what their belief meant. Even if Grale Casarion did not touch Avanzar, he had destroyed her whole world. He had made people think about things in ways they should never have to be thought about. He was cruel, cruel, cruel. Even though she and Neshekh were still getting married, their marriage could never be what it might have been, if the world had remained whole.

Arendellie got up and walked home, feeling dejected. She was the youngest of her family, and her other siblings were all married and her parents were getting older and lived with their eldest son, so she was alone in the house. It was still early evening, so she called Dorene over, along with several new friends she had made– if they could be called friends, for they were certainly not friends the way that she and Kathreen had been, and in a sense still were, for though they could not stand each other, they still intended a kind of loyalty to one another. Once they came over, she unburdened herself to them, telling them what had happened, and how upset she was, and intermittently weeping as she did so.

The fact was, the longer she thought about it the more she hated Grale Casarion. Not only had he caused reality to fracture, forced people to think about things seriously that should never be thought about that way, thereby tearing away her friends, but he had made it so that she could not start over and find new friends. They just were not there, for some reason. All her friends, it seemed, were in different pieces of the shattered world than she was. Oh, why had Grale Casarion warped and twisted and fractured reality! Something was wrong, drastically wrong, and it hurt Arendellie's head to think about it or try to figure out what it was.

#5
A Traitor to Treason

Azshbir sat next to the hearth with his employer, whose name was Darnize Katalonga. He had been working for him for a couple months now. To begin with, he had noticed that he had lost muscle and strength in the six months that he had not been working on his parent's farm, but he had quickly made up for it. After several days, Darnize had decided to keep Azshbir, and had introduced him to his family, but their relationship was only beginning to involve other things than work business. This was the first time the two men had sat down together to talk. They had already spent about three quarters of an hour talking about work on the Katalonga Farm, how it was going, what needed to be done when and how, and all related things.

"So, Azshbir, what do you think about the war?" asked Darnize casually.

"Be a little more specific."

"What do you think about Grale Casarion?"

"I think Grale Casarion is an enemy to the Creator and His people, and is trying to take what is not his to have," answered Azshbir. "You?"

"Much the same. I think that Grale Casarion's laws are tyrannical and violate the precepts of the Creator, and that it is not right for him to try to usurp thrones and conquer nations that never did him any harm," answered Darnize.

Azshbir agreed. He wondered where this conversation was going. He decided that he was going to ask a question now, though he was a little apprehensive. He had seen people often try to make out that they believed and cared about what he did, as he did, when they had no common ground at all. What made his task so terribly hard was that people did not even hear what he was saying; they only heard the meaning that they had given to words and concepts of which they had no actual understanding whatsoever. There was a total impasse in communication. "So, what do you think the Promise is, or means? What is the most important part about it to you? How does it affect your life?"

"Well," said Darnize, "I think it is really important that the Promised One is going to destroy death and reign over all things. He is going to bring His people into a perfect place and make all things well. I try to live in accordance with the Creator's laws, and I'm hopeful that if we seek to be His people and, more, to live in accordance with His precepts, then, ultimately, Ephezoa will win. You?"

Azshbir sighed. "I think the Promise has to be understood in terms of who the Creator is, and who we are. The Creator is the only one who can unreservedly claim the title of King, and that is because He is the Creator. He created us to know Him, to serve Him, to find fulfillment not in seeking ourselves, but in living entirely for Him, because we were created for Him. We haven't done that. Instead, we have all lived for ourselves. We've tried to be our own little kings. We plan our own lives and do things our own way. In the process, we hurt our fellow creatures, sometimes in more obvious ways, sometimes in less. However, this isn't our real offense. The big problem is that we're traitors. We're traitors to the only real and noble King.

We're the worst traitors possible. Made for the palace of the Creator's presence, instead we've lived in dung because we defy Him and seek our own. In His eyes, shame clings to us. We're too evil and worthless for anything but contempt. In the shame of our treason, He can not come near us, and He can have nothing to do with us, for He is the Only One who is truly regal, truly noble. So, that is what the Promise is about. The Promised One is going to bear the shame of His people far, far away, and conquer death, so that our shame will be gone so that He can take us into the Creator's palace by His merits, and lead His people out of death. That's—"

"Wait a minute!" Darnize held his hand up. Azshbir glanced to the side and saw that some of the Katalonga household was listening in on this conversation. Apparently it was interesting. "So, you're saying that the primary office of the Promised One is to bear away shame? How then is He spoken of as the Conqueror and King, who will defeat and reign over death?"

"Why do you think death comes into the story?" asked Azshbir. "The Creator has always been the Lord of Death. He made death as the only suitable dungeon for creatures to be regarded with such contempt as traitors to His nobility. Or, perhaps, death is what happens to creatures who have been separated from His life. And why would we be separated from His life except for our unspeakable shame? Indeed, perhaps that is why death is the only suitable dungeon. It is what happens to them. The Creator did not *make* death at all; death is the suitable and natural consequence of shame, of being hidden from the Creator's life-imparting gaze. So, death is suitable because death is to be despised, and because death doesn't have to be done— it is the consequence of contempt, it is contempt. At the same time, He casts His enemies into death to bear His wrath against their insupportable offenses. Anyway, enough for that. Death is the mark of our shame, and the Promised One's conquest over death is a result of, or means of, our deliverance from our shame in the sight of the Creator."

"Yeah, I see that," said Darnize. "That makes a lot of sense. I think it is what I always believed. I just did not know how to put it so well, or tie it all together like that." Azshbir had some serious doubts about all of Darnize's statements. "Anyway, you did not tell me how it affects your life."

"Well," answered Azshbir, "I am very grateful for the Creator's mercy. Because I understand a little of the mercy of His Promise, I can trust Him and rejoice in His mercy, without having to fear what life may bring my way, or whether He will allow me to suffer or not. I want to serve Him, and to explain the Promise to those who do not know or understand it, and to warn people that the Creator really is King, and must be treated as such. He will make Himself regarded as such, whether men are willing or no."

Darnize nodded. "That makes a lot of sense, though I'm sure it's not expected. The Creator knows that we would rather not suffer, or be conquered by Hasseleighton, and I think He's okay with that." Azshbir thought to himself, *You must have not heard what I was just saying.* "Anyway, so, what do you think about the war? How should it be done? I know you're from a different part of Ephezoa, and I've heard some think strange things, so what do you think?"

"What is the war about?" asked Azshbir.

"What do you mean?" queried Darnize.

"I mean, why are you fighting this war? What are your motives? What are your goals? I can't answer your question until I have the answers to those questions," said Azshbir.

"I guess, to protect Ephezoa. To protect our freedoms to express our belief in the Creator and be faithful to the commands of the Promise, and to raise our children in the same. Because we must not bow down to Grale Casarion and submit to his rule. We must remain free. We must retain our freedom to live our lives without being controlled by hostile influences. The way they do things in Hasseleighton is harsh and unreasonable and not in accord with the Creator's commands to be merciful and kind to other ways of doing things, to variety, to people who are different. They're full of hatred. They hate whoever does not worship Grale Casarion, and they hate even their own daughters. If a girl runs away and is living with a man to which she was not married by their parents, or by some other approved body, then they throw both of them into prison. They do other abominable things, of course, but at the top of the list, is their cruelty towards those People of the Promise who don't compromise with Grale Casarion," said Darnize.

Azshbir sighed. He suspected Kathreen would know more about the things Darnize was referencing. He was still rather culturally inept. He did know that Ephezoa and Hasseleighton had hated each other since time immemorial. "Are there any things about Ephezoa that you think are not in line with the Creator's will, like there are in Hasseleighton?"

Azshbir saw a glint of anger in Darnize's eyes. His voice rose a little. "Oh, there are things wrong in Ephezoa– there are groups, here and there, who are in defiance of the Creator. We have a few problems here and there, and we should probably try to get rid of them, if we want victory over Hasseleighton. However, they're nothing like the kind of atrocities encoded in Hasseleighton law, and even honored by the Hasseleighton people!" The way he said these things meant, "How dare you ask such a thing."

"Do you think, maybe," Azshbir asked, very quietly, "that you don't notice the things wrong with Ephezoa, or even your own life, simply because you are used to them– not because they are any less evil?"

"Are you a traitor to Hasseleighton or something?" asked Darnize. Azshbir had just insulted a man older and of greater rank than himself.

"No!" cried Azshbir. "You think I and Hasseleighton are friends? Grale could have me tortured for the things I was just saying about the Creator being the only one who has the power to give binding laws. I just know that all humanity is in rebellion against the Creator, and it is this high treason that is our real problem. We're supposed to live our whole lives in accordance with the Creator's perfect and most blessed will, but instead we're always running off in our own directions, whether it is to sue the mayor for stealing our cow or to kill our grand-daughter for disgracing our families by prostitution! Whether we're a tyrant wanting everyone to never say anything bad about us, or whether we want to criticize the government for taxing us and insist that we have a government that tolerates such behavior, it stems from the same evil of the heart– wanting our way–"

Again Darnize interrupted him. "Are you saying that everyone is just as bad? That I'm no better than Grale Casarion– than his torturers? Are you saying that you're better than everyone else?"

"Darnize," said Azshbir, his heart beating a little fast from the dash of the conversation, not realizing that he was speaking to an older man in a scolding fashion, "it is you who are self-righteous and maintaining that you are better than your enemies. I know that I sin against the Creator ten thousand times a day, if not an hour. Every time I am frustrated with not getting my own way, every time I complain about the fact that I miss my sister, or that I would have wanted a world in which I could marry a particular woman, every time I long after her to have her, oh, I could go on, I, too, commit this treason. All men stand condemned, in shame over their heads– myself and yourself included!" His voice was rising a little.

"You're frustrated right now!" said Darnize.

"Indeed," said Azshbir, "and doubtless there are my own reasons in it, but judge for yourself: Is anger appropriate for a belief that the Creator to whom all things, you and me included, belong, exists to make your life of a kind that you find comfortable or appealing?" Azshbir drew a deep breath, and went on calmly. "The Creator does not exist so that you won't have to be bullied."

"This conversation is over for the moment," said Darnize. "Go to your quarters."

Azshbir rose, and bowed to his master. Turning, he left the house, to find his quarters in the barn. Laying down on a hay bale, he wondered if he would keep his job or if he had just lost it. To be honest, though, from Darnize's point of view, from Ephezoa's point of view, he was a traitor– a traitor to the whole human rebellion. He would have nothing to do with their war for their own values and way of doing things. He would not fight them with swords or like weapons, but he would labor to show them their blindness and treason, labor to turn their hearts to be loyal again to the Creator, that is, from their point of view, to destroy their battle, to destroy their values, to steal their allies and turn them against them, though all this would work only if the Creator's power worked it. He had, as it were, declared war against their claiming the Creator's Name and authority for their own laws and values. The same war he had against the whole system of Hasseleighton he had with that of Ephezoa. From the standpoint of the One whose representative he was, Hasseleighton and Ephezoa were the same– rebels and traitors. And, he was a member of that rebel humanity, who had renounced his allegiance to rebellion in order that he might give it to the Creator. The only reason he was not a traitor was because that which he betrayed was treason, the loyalty to which he had turned was in fact a loyalty to which he returned, a loyalty all had betrayed.

#6
The Helper

Several days later, after another trying conversation with Darnize, Azshbir again went outside. He was still standing, with his hand on the wall of the barn, taking a deep breath and recollecting himself, when he heard soft footsteps behind him. Turning, he looked and saw a young girl, a teenager, probably about sixteen years old. She was one of Darnize's daughters. Her thick, black hair, somewhat wavy and somewhat curly, was gathered behind her head, and she wore a simple dress. He had seen her often before, doing her work about the farm, but he had only spoken more than a couple words to her on the day when he had been introduced to all the members of Darnize's household. Her name was Neah'ra.

She came a few paces closer, through the gathering dusk, and then stopped. "What are you here for?" Azshbir asked.

"Sshh!" said Neah'ra. "My father doesn't know I'm here... Come, let us sit down, and speak quietly." She led him into the bushes further towards the back of the barn along the wall.

Sitting down, Azshbir asked her again, "So why are you out here? And against your father's wishes?"

He thought Neah'ra looked a little sad as she responded. "Because you've said a lot of things that really resonate with me. I've been waiting for someone like you for a long time." She paused, and spoke even more quietly. "The people at the Hall of Exhortation are very, well, not quite right. They're as interested in teaching us about the history of Ephezoa and the deeds of the heroes of Ephezoa and the reasons and logic behind the wonderful laws and government we have in Ephezoa as they are about teaching us about the Creator and the Promise and the Prophecies. There's nothing bad about the former, but they just... so, when I heard what you said, I thought, 'I've never heard that before, and I wouldn't have thought of putting it that way, but I think it is what I have been feeling'."

"Yeah," said Azshbir, "so...?"

"I want to learn from you, Azshbir. I believe in the Promise! I totally do. So many people say things like what you said, and then they say other things, like what you heard Father saying... Or, they talk about the wonderful Promise one moment, and then about the deeds of Prince Teka-Rok the next." Neah'ra was silent for a while, and Azshbir did not know what to say. Was there anything to say? Then, she spoke again. "I think that, maybe, together we can speak to some of the people I know, a few from the Hall of Exhortation, and maybe they will see light... They don't tend to want to listen to me, since they all think I'm only a child– which I almost am– and I don't know how to articulate what I believe very well. I'm not even sure I know what I believe all that well. But, maybe, if you help me and teach me, we can tell them together. I think they'll be happier, too... They tell me that I'm only a young girl, so why should I aspire to set myself above them to know important things and be more interested in the Promise than in other things? I'm so glad I've met you. Now, I think I shall have the courage to tell them that that is what the Creator made us for, and their choice to seek something lesser does not obligate me to do the same lest I be 'better' than they."

Azshbir sat quietly. He was learning so much so quickly and he felt stuffed. In an effort to make conversation he said, "Yeah, saying you believe in something like the Promise and then not caring much about it is like, is like, I guess it is like insisting you want to marry someone and then never speaking to him or her."

Neah'ra laughed a little. "I guess so," she said, looking down at her hands in her lap. She was silent for a few moments, as if she did not have any more idea how to continue than Azshbir did. Finally, Azshbir said, "Your father is right that the Creator will set all things right. I can understand, too, how living in a collapsing country, in a collapsing world, under the shadow of a ruthless tyranny, can make the Promise of the fact that the Creator will make all things well and establish His reign visibly, through the One He shall send, is very dear to many people. What's wrong with it, is that there is so much bitterness towards others in their desire for this, and that what they are seeking is not the Creator's reign, but their own comfort. It is a beautiful Promise, and given for good reason, but we must not forget the rest of the Promise, we must not forget the Promise itself." He did not want to leave her with any misunderstandings or unfounded, fanatical criticisms.

"I know," said Neah'ra. "I think you actually explained it, that night almost a week ago now." She looked up, and Azshbir thought he saw a smile on her face, in the gathering dusk. "I was actually telling one of my friends at the Hall of Exhortation about what you were telling me. She's a year and a half older than I am. The thing is, we are right to look forward to the Creator making all things right, but it must be the Creator's right, not our right! Right?" She looked very pleased with herself.

"Exactly," said Azshbir.

"And we will have justice, and all shall be well, because it will be His justice! And," she added, looking down thoughtfully, "we will be able to endure it because of the Promise." She was silent for a few moments, obviously incredibly pleased with her way of putting things. Azshbir began to wonder if she was as old as he had thought at first. Then, she quietly got up. "I have to go now. Otherwise Father will suspect," she said quietly. "As it is, I have to milk the goat, so he probably won't."

Azshbir stood, as well. "What will happen so terrible, if he finds out?" He thought it was strange for them to be being so secretive in a country that prided itself on its freedoms, and in the home of a man who so prided himself on the same.

"Nothing really bad," said Neah'ra. "It will just cause lots of trouble. He might get mad. He might expressly forbid me from talking to you. He might fire you. He might just get mad and stay that way for a couple of days or weeks. He thinks you're some sort of traitor. Anyway, I really do have to go, now." She turned, and began walking away.

"Good night, Neah'ra," Azshbir whispered softly into the breeze. He turned also, and with a quick stride quickly passed her. He went to the little room he used as his own, gathered some of his possessions, and went out along the road. Tonight, he was going to a small festival that was being held just outside the city. There, he would try to engage some of the booth keepers in conversation. He was still working out his tactics for systemically going through the city to reach every person. *It is a good thing,* he thought to himself as he walked, *that Neah'ra is the one spreading what I'm telling. At least she will get it right, and she might be able to get her friends and teachers to at least hear what she says, instead of making up what they hear, even if they respect her not at all. Speaking of which, I wonder, how old* is *she?*

The days went on, more or less uneventfully. Azshbir continued having debates with Darnize, often going over ground already previously visited, often having to clarify his position, as Darnize accused him of saying first one thing he did not mean, and then another off the other end. For one thing, the man was constantly accusing him of saying that one should roll over and bow to any authority and any demand. Azshbir had to be constantly explaining that while, as far as one's own personal pride went, this was more or less accurate, the Creator's people were called to stand firm and unwavering on all His Promises and commands. They were never to fight for their own petty objectives, but they were also never to compromise when it came to obedience to the Creator. When Darnize asked if this meant that Ephezoa should simply surrender, and her people let themselves be executed without a fight when they refused to acknowledge Grale Casarion as king, Azshbir answered that he did not know whether it was right for Ephezoa to fight and defend herself against Grale Casarion and Hasseleighton. What he did know, was that they should neither war nor surrender for their own conveniences or safeties, or values, whatever one wanted to call it. He often saw Neah'ra pass by quickly, as if she did not trust herself not to speak if she was around for more than a few moments.

Azshbir and Neah'ra often found time, whether a mere five minutes or half an hour, to talk together. On one of these occasions, he learned that she was barely fifteen. She invited him to the meeting at the Hall of Exhortation which she attended, and he had the opportunity to explain his beliefs to many of the young men and boys. The atmosphere was strange; some people seemed to think his beliefs were fine as far as they went, but too radical for most, while others were extremely venomous, and would not drop the charge that he was a traitor and in league with Grale's tyranny, and others were simply reserved, if a little condemning. He set himself to trying to explain that the Creator wanted full allegiance and loyalty from all His people, not just some of them, and that He had created all His people for His very best: enjoyment of His presence, adoption, life in His palace. Since they were all created for the same 'radical'– if you wanted to call it that– end, they were all called to the same 'radical' commitment and devotion. There were no differences in rank or degree of calling or blessing for His people; there were only the Creator's people, and there were those who were not. He was not making himself out to be better than them, or trying to insist that everyone had the same calling. He was simply stating the facts: all were called to the highest blessing, and all were called to the same complete commitment. If one did not desire the blessing, it might be an indicator that one was not of the Creator's people!

Of course, he rarely got so much out at once, or as well as he would have liked to say it. They called him a radical fanatic, or one who did not understand that everyone was just human. He got the impression that Neah'ra felt more comfortable close to him, talking to the girls, many of whom were older than herself, while he spoke to the men, and relied on his greater skill and ease with words and concepts. However, about a week later she confessed to him that they had begun making fun of her for wanting to marry a man much older than herself and, more– since no one really believed she was interested in him– for believing and buying the fanatic nonsense of a radical stranger, who might even be a traitor to their way of life, and setting impossibly high standards, which the Creator would never make for the weakness of most mortal men. That was when Azshbir decided to share with her his thoughts on the conflict between the People of the Promise and the rest of the human race, and probably dragons too, whether they wanted to win them over to their side by slight mocking and niceties, or to torture them to death if not into submission, and on treason and the traitors' perception of it. "They don't want to face the fact that they are the traitors," he told her. The next night, he told her that their 'human weakness' was, itself, a part of their shame, fully exposed to the Creator though not to themselves, and that rather than using it as a defense against His right demands and an excuse for exchanging His honor for shame, they should be ashamed of it, and realize that they need one who will bear their shame away, and exchange it for His honor and merits. He knew too, that she was becoming much more confident in expressing and defending the One True Creator and the Real Promise; she thanked him for coming, saying that, before, she had been a mouse, unable to say what she meant, and without knowledge of how to deal with the ridicule and challenges that would follow.

Going to bed that night, Azshbir prayed, thanking the Creator for the friend and helper He had given him; one who could go where he could not go, and do what he could not do, and had the opportunities long relationships afforded that he did not have. It was wonderful the way He had provided him with this helper, and it was wonderful, too, the way He had provided her with him. Neither he nor Neah'ra was any longer alone. Surely, the pain of parting with Kathreen and Adaria was well worth it! How could he have complained.

#7
Risks

Arendellie was just tucking several packages of beef under her arm when she was approached by several men with strange facial features wearing strange uniforms. She had heard some people talking about the strange and threatening new-comers to the village while getting a few things; the wedding for her and Neshekh was supposed to be in three days.

"Hello," they said, stepping forward. They were very imposing. "You are Arendellie, correct?"

"Yes," she said, a little wary and hesitant; what was going on?

"Did you know Kathreen Alarion, reported to be a mighty wizard?"

"What's all this about?" asked Arendellie.

"We are from the Emperor, Grale Casarion." She could see that they thought she was very stupid for some reason, she did not know what. Maybe it had something to do with their uniforms. Her heart beat quickly and butterflies fluttered in her stomach. Why were Grale's men questioning her? They continued, not leaving her time to think. "Ebrin is now under our control. We understand that it is the home of Kathreen Alarion. Do you know her?"

"I'm not sure you have the right Kathreen Alarion," said Arendellie. She was rather worried. She did not know anything about what Kathreen was doing or where she was, right now. She had not spoken to her once since the time she had visited Ebrin about a year ago. She did not want to betray any information that would harm Kathreen; they were still friends, even if they never spoke and had nothing to do with each other. In a way, Kathreen was the only friend she still had; she was the only friend who had been close enough to her that loyalty and care remained, even across this.

"Oh, we have the right Kathreen Alarion. Do you know her?"

"I'm not sure what you mean," said Arendellie. "If we lived in the same village, of course we would 'know' each other. I could probably list the names of everyone in Ebrin right now if you wanted." She did not mind lying, but if she lied her lies would have to be the kind that would stand up to scrutiny, and to the stories of the rest of the villagers.

"We've been told that you and Kathreen Alarion were best friends. Is that so?"

Arendellie shrugged. "Perhaps."

"Do you know anything about her being a wizard? Is it true or is it just a rumor?"

"No."

"When is the last time you saw her?"

"Oh, two years ago or so," said Arendellie. That was, at least almost, the truth.

"That can't possibly be," said one of the men. "Everyone we've spoken to reports her having been here last somewhere around a year ago. Some have more precise information."

Arendellie frowned, as if concentrating. "I think I may vaguely recall someone mentioning her presence, somewhere around then," she said slowly. "However, I didn't speak to her."

"You sure about everything you've just told us?" asked the same man who did most of the talking. He placed his hand on his sword-hilt in a threatening gesture. Arendellie thought he did it subconsciously.

"Yes, totally," said Arendellie. She reached up with the hand that she was not holding the goods she had just bought with, to smooth out a couple strands in her braid.

"You can go now," said the man.

Arendellie did not acknowledge him. She just walked away. She did not like being bossed around. *Why on earth must they come to Ebrin? I didn't even think Avanzar had fallen or surrendered. I bet Kathreen is famous. How they know this is the village of her origin I have no idea. She's crazy. Between her and Grale Casarion, the world is in pieces, and I'm not in the same piece with anyone, certainly not with anyone I know! It's cruel.* Thinking these thoughts, she went home.

In the evening the next day, while Arendellie was working on her hair, and preparing to take a soap bath, she heard some loud knocks on the door. She had not spoken to Grale's men since yesterday morning, but she still checked at the window to make sure it was someone she knew, or at least sort of knew. The whole team of them was there again. She decided to ignore them and go back to rubbing the oils into her hair.

They only knocked louder. "In the name of the Emperor, open to us!"

Do they think that they can push everyone around like they do in that slave-state Hasseleighton? thought Arendellie. *I'm not letting them in.* She was beginning to get a little worried, and she definitely did not want them in her house alone with her. She was not wearing proper clothes, even by the standards of the Enzenyar villages. Her hair was down, and being primed for show-off. Only prostitutes would meet men dressed the way she was now. From what she knew, the standards of modesty in Hasseleighton were the strictest in the continent. Worse, these men were pushy and bossy, and evidently used to having their own way and never being stood up to by anyone. She did not trust them one bit, and would not have wanted them alone with her even when dressed properly. Her heart was beginning to race a little.

"Open to us!" they shouted louder. Arendellie begin to wonder if she should snatch a cloak, throw it over herself, and run through one of the windows. Instead, she went up to the door and announced, "If you want to see me, you must act politely." Now that she was doing something she felt confident and self-assured, and her voice showed it. "Women in Avanzar can not be bullied into seeing just any man anytime, and especially not if the man is rude."

Apparently, her little speech impressed them. They withdrew, and spoke in muttered tones. *I guess it is dangerous for women to live alone in Hasseleighton, or most of Camil, now,* she thought to herself, and resumed working on her hair. She had always had a commanding kind of personality, and expected that the men would not harass her anymore, at least for the moment.

She had lit the lamp in the room, and was just preparing to take her soap bath, when she was interrupted. This time, a clean-accented voice, clearly articulating words chosen with care, spoke. "We, as noble servants of the royal King Grale Casarion and Prince Vanesh wish to make a request fit for a queen of the Lady Arendellie, if she will speak to us." Arendellie had not heard this voice before.

Arendellie thought quickly and hard. How could she reply suitably and in kind. "The Lady Arendellie requests of you a few moments to make herself presentable in a manner fitting for one to whom such honor is offered," she called back. Getting up, she quickly rubbed perfume over her body, put on her best dress, and grabbed something that would make due for both headscarf and cloak. Wrapping it over her head, she approached the front door, opened it, and stepped outside.

Immediately, she saw a man who was dressed in such a way as to show that he far exceeded the men she had first seen in rank. He had with him two older women, both with headscarves, and two middle-aged men, who she thought she had seen before. Standing with her hand on the doorsill, she asked, trying to speak in the best official manner she knew, "What would his majesty and his royal highness wish to request of the Lady Arendellie?" As she spoke, she wondered if this higher ranking official had flown in on a dragon after the men had seemed to be discussing what to do after she told them off.

"His majesty would request that the Lady Arendellie come with us to Anores, as a possible bride for his nephew, his royal highness, Vanesh Casarion. She is a gem, fit to be likened to the wild roses, as serene and noble as the lilies, and may be a proper bride and consort for his royal highness. Doubtless, also, she was not made for obscurity in the barbarian mountains, but for elegance and prominence among nobility and royalty. Is she gracious to this most royal offer?"

Arendellie felt totally flattered. She had to focus on keeping her head. Was she really being made this offer, or was it a mockery? She would have to find out, somehow. "This offer will need some more consideration and examination, for it is a great thing and all that it involves is not yet clear to me," she said. She was enjoying herself. *Almost* as much as she did when flirting with Neshekh or snuggling up against him.

"We understand that," said the official. "My name is Sir Andelf. Shall we sit down to talk some more?"

"We may," said Arendellie, "though I cannot be expected to make such a great decision in a night."

Sir Andelf sat down on the steps, and Arendellie remained standing.

For about forty-five minutes they discussed the offer Sir Andelf was making. Sir Andelf, a man who had waited on Vanesh Casarion before the war, was almost certain that Arendellie would win his royal highness' graces; however, if he turned out to be wrong she would almost certainly still get to dwell in the palace. If he rejected her altogether, one of the courtiers or nobles would probably take her as his wife. The conversation was mostly carried on in high-sounding language, and Arendellie felt pleased with herself the whole time, but a cloud hung over her, too.

She was thinking of Neshekh. To accept this offer… and this close to their marriage date. To do such a thing would leave him heartbroken, and she was not quite certain if she did want to leave him. To be sure, she despised his beliefs, and the fact that Grale Casarion's men who were so interested in them, even just for information about Kathreen Alarion, made her think that being married to one who was willing to risk or lose everything or anything to remain faithful to the Promise was really not a good idea. But, she did love Neshekh, and he did love her.

As the conversation continued, she began to wonder if Sir Andelf almost wanted her hand. "There is another man I love, and am arranged to marry," Arendellie asked. It was a good way of being tentative, and of asking "what would it mean to reject this offer."

Sir Andelf spoke quietly, so that Arendellie could barely hear him. The others were a short distance away, and would not hear. "Ebrin is of great interest to his supreme majesty, because it is the origin of the infamous Kathreen Alarion. You are of even greater interest, being closest to her, along with Mirla who, I understand, met with her about a year ago, and no one believes has not met with her since, or that she will not visit again. As a result, I offer you this in an effort to protect you both. The Empire of Hasseleighton is ready to take drastic measures to achieve its ends, whatever people think of either its end or its means. However, if you are a princess in the royal court, or even the wife of a noble or courtier in good favor, you will be less vulnerable to these things, and your friends may benefit, though I can guarantee nothing. If your hand is given to a noble or courtier out of favor you could share his fall."

Arendellie nodded. "The Lady Arendellie thanks the emperor's officer, both for his offer and for his concern. However, she requests a little time to consider this offer."

Sir Andelf rose and bowed. "As you wish, my lady." He turned and strode away through the night, taking the rest with him. At least, for the moment, Arendellie was safe.

She went back into her house, and sat down, next to the tub ready for her bath. If she went with Sir Andelf to Anores, she was taking a small risk of disgrace to the eyes of many. However, the gains were so great, the risk relatively small, and she was already in a piece of the world with no one else. The only thing was, she did not want to hurt Neshekh in the terrible way that this would, and she still wanted him. On the other hand, to be a princess, to live with that dash; her taste of it had intoxicated her. She knew that she was cut out for the life Sir Andelf was offering her. It was a tough choice.

She also could not help but wonder what had changed their attitudes between when she told them she would not see them and when the officer had come. What had been their original intent? What had gone on between them? Her curiosity demanded answers, but she had no way of getting them.

#8
Venture into the Uncertain

In the morning, Arendellie walked to Neshekh's home. There were, she thought, too many risks accompanying staying in the village and marrying Neshekh to be worth it. The men of Hasseleighton's army were too pushy and she did not trust them at all; at least if she belonged to the royal courts she would only have a few people bossing her around, and no one would dare touch her. She walked up the steps, stood on the porch, and knocked.

In a moment, Neshekh opened the door. "What is it, Araenyi? What's wrong?" he asked.

The term, "Araenyi" brought tears to her eyes. Could she bear this? Could she bear to hurt Neshekh and forego all the love between them, and the greater yet to come, even though it would always be tainted and kept from true fulfillment by his fanaticism? Stealing herself, she said, "We aren't getting married tomorrow."

Neshekh paled with shock. "What?" he asked, his voice a mere gasp. "When then?"

"We aren't getting married at all," said Arendellie. She could hardly bear to say it. Her heart twinged with pain. It felt like it was twisting round itself, and would be torn.

Neshekh put out his hand to steady himself on the door post. He looked like he could barely stand. "What, Arendellie, why?" he gasped, his voice so quiet she could hardly hear it, low and broken with anguish.

Arendellie did not know what to say. He was in so much anguish already, and her own pain as well as sympathy was making it hard to think straight. One thing she knew. If she told him what had been offered her and that she was taking it up, it would only increase his anguish. She knew him well enough to know that he would rather die a million deaths than let her live that life, which he believed to be a nightmare and a slime pit, worse, perhaps, than the dungeons. If he found out what she was doing, she did not think that he would try to physically and forcibly stop her– though she was not sure– but she did think that he would die of emotional pain. She could never make him understand that this life was cut out for her, and she for it. "I just have to go away, and no one can know where I'm going," she finally got out.

Something like tentative, afraid to believe, bittersweet joy broke out on Neshekh's face. "Then, you too have known? You're going to–?" he asked.

Arendellie turned, gathered her skirts about her, and fled. That she had come to share his values and be called to something kind of like that to which Kathreen was called was the only explanation Neshekh could imagine, and she knew that he longed for her to believe what he did above all else, no matter what pain it might cost either or both of them or the whole world. She felt a little insulted, but preferred to leave him to his ignorance. At least, then, he would be, in some measure, happy about his heartbreak, and she did not wish him pain.

Once she got a fair distance from his house, she slowed to an almost shuffling walk. She felt very downcast. She did not want to imagine what might even now be transpiring in his home. She knew that of his family only he believed such radical things. It occurred to her that she was not the only one who felt as if the world had fractured and everyone who had been close was in a different piece than her, or him, self. Unwilling to feel pity or to bear its pain, Arendellie decided that she absolutely hated Grale Casarion and Kathreen Alarion for bringing this on them. What was wrong with Kathreen! For what else was she doing, even now, than traveling the world, in order to bring this anguish to more and more people, to anyone who had been spared so far, whose world had been allowed to remain calm and proportioned and whole, as it belonged. In fact, last she knew, that was Kathreen's express intention.

Arendellie went to her house, and worked on getting together her best things and anything she might want to keep. *None of these things are fit for a princess,* she thought, *so I only need enough for however long it takes to get to Anores. Probably we will be going on dragonback, so I don't think it will take longer than a week.* Thinking these things, she grabbed an elegant but simple dress Kathreen had made. Looking at it, she wondered if wizardry had been used to assist in its making. *I will keep this as a memento of her, and certainly of the earlier days. She may be misguided and foolish, even cruel, though I'm sure she does not know how cruel she is and has good intentions, and is herself hurt, but we are still friends, and we will still remember each other and be loyal to each other.* Clutching the dress to her breast, Arendellie sank down on the floor and wept. The emptiness and misery of the life she had chosen for herself was beginning to sink into her, even if she was not yet aware of it and would not admit it. She thought there was no reason for her not to choose this life, since it suited her, she thought, and who was to say it was wrong or bad or empty? Without sure footing on the Creator's Promise and will, looking at the world from His eyes, there was no foundation. So, in a sense, this life was no more empty or miserable than any other. However, she was abandoning all she had known and loved, all that had had any resemblance to meaning in her world, for a life of useless shallowness and luxury. Nonetheless, she did not know this, or at least she did not know that she knew this, refused to know that she knew this, and would not admit it to herself even in her deepest heart. Instead, she blamed everyone else.

Arendellie probably wept for a whole hour. Finally, she pulled herself together. *In all likelihoods, I shall be a princess, or at least a noble's wife,* she thought. Cheering herself with that thought, she got up, finished sorting through what she wanted to keep, dressed nicely, picked the nearest thing to an elegant headscarf she had, threw it over her shoulders, and set to having the dinner she had not eaten last night for breakfast.

She had just finished breakfast when she heard a knock on the door. She quickly wrapped the make-shift headscarf around her head, strode to the door, and opened it. It was Sir Andelf, attended by the same two women she had seen yesterday. "Greetings and good morning, lady," said Sir Andelf, bowing. "Have you had your time, or do such weighty matters require greater deliberation?" She thought he might have been smirking a little.

For a moment Arendellie got the insane urge to decide that she believed just as Mirla and Neshekh and Kathreen did, and run off to look for Kathreen to be friends again. She stayed it. Then, she momentarily wanted to say that, yes, she needed more time. That urge, too, she vanquished. She curtsied deeply. Then, straightening, she said, "The Lady Arendellie accepts his royalty's most gracious offer. However, there are still a couple friends to whom she wishes to request that she may bid a casual farewell."

"That is well," said Sir Andelf. "Let us meet here again in two hours."

Arendellie did not think what she wanted to do would take that long, but she did not say so. Wishing to keep what was happening a secret from Neshekh, that he might suffer less, she decided she would not tell anyone. How they were to avoid all knowing once she became the princess she did not consider. Of course, she was probably not the only Arendellie, and it would not be a surprise if another girl who looked like her had her name, since she was named for her eye color. However, she did not think about these things. She decided that she would bid Mirla farewell, despite the fact that she had spoken extensively with her only once in the last two years, in addition to friends like Dorene, Jassie, Carliet, and a couple others, and, of course, her aged parents. The thought of missing them made her sad, and she had a hard time trying to make sure they were not too certain she had become a fanatic and also did not get too curious about what had happened for a few hours. It was an extremely unusual thing, to break off with an engagement this late. In fact, as far as Arendellie knew, it had never happened before. For some reason, she felt comfortable confiding in Mirla, who then wept for her and tried to counsel her to change her mind, but at last shook her hair back, gathering herself together, and said, "You must make your choice, and I must trust that the Creator will do what is perfect in your life and with you as well, and can reach even into the deepest pits you may dig for yourself. Surely, He can do what He wills, and will do as He pleases, and surely He knows best." She was pale, and tears still flowed from her eyes, but her voice and bearing were calm and dignified. Her words made Arendellie feel like squirming and covering her ears with her hands, but she restrained herself. The two women embraced and parted without words. They did not know it then, but they would again never touch or exchange words in Kaarathlon while time lasted.

It had taken the two hours Sir Andelf allowed for, and when Arendellie walked back, crying softly, though she had not teared up until her and Mirla's last embrace, he was already there, along with the two women. Seeing her looking so miserable, he said, as kindly and gently as such things could be said, "Are you sure you want to do this? Whoever is to be princess should be happy about it, not miserable."

Arendellie looked up and tried to smile. "No, it's okay," she said. "It's just a little sad leaving all my friends, and I was just saying farewell to a friend I really don't see eye-to-eye with, and you know how that is." For the moment, she had forgotten about speaking fancy and distantly. For some reason, Sir Andelf had gotten quite familiar around her; she had no idea why.

"That's fine," he said. "Follow me, lady. We will be riding dragons. Have you ever ridden a dragon before, lady?"

Arendellie thought of riding L'sa-moth with Kathreen, and opened her mouth to say so, but then remembered that she could not say that; she had to protect her friend. "No, not really," she told Sir Andelf.

"That's okay. You will ride behind El-Reiza, on the dragon Leaoneth." El-Reiza was one of the two women who attended Sir Andelf. "You'll be harnessed into a saddle, so you won't have to worry about falling off. The thing that most fazes dragon riders, especially if they aren't dragon-riders is the height. It sickens a lot of people. Just try to relax and not to think about the fact that you're thousands of feet up in the air."

"We're flying right now?" asked Arendellie. She wondered at it a little; how could they just decide things that quickly like that?

"You and El-Reiza will be. I am also sending the dragon-rider Akasdar with you. He is one of the most trustworthy men I have. Both he and El-Reiza know where they are going and what they are doing. You can trust them both, as far as it goes."

Arendellie tried to absorb everything Sir Andelf was telling her. On the one hand, she felt sad and miserable, like her life was empty, and she was leaving all her friends and all she had loved behind. On the other hand, she thought she felt like she was meant for this. She was having an adventure, and her blood tingled with a kind of excitement. She was going into the great unknown, the uncertain. She was leaving all her old, predictable life behind her, and all that still smelled of the world before the winds of change and the shattering of reality, and venturing into a strange new world and reality, unknown, uncertain, new. Yes, this was meant to be. Her heart quivered with excitement and anticipation. The little fear she felt only added to this strange feeling of being vibrantly alive and... and... and, she knew not how to describe it. Perhaps, though, by immersing herself in this new life, the uncertain and unknown, the games of risks and honors and belonging and high stakes and dash and skill and quick thinking and everything that is wonderful about adventure, her loneliness might heal, or at least be forgotten. There was mingled in these thoughts a tinge of sadness: this would have been just perfect if she could have brought a couple of her friends from Ebrin with her. Of course, maybe that would have marred the whole scheme of starting out new, in an unknown and uncertain because totally different, a new world and life with completely new and different rules and aims, different material, different perimeters, different measures.

#9
To Be For the Prince

Arendellie stood next to the half-lying over form of a huge yellow and orange dragon, poised to climb up her leg and shoulder, to where a large leather saddle lay between her neck and shoulders. "I'm sorry, lady, that we can not provide you with accommodations more suitable to a to-be princess," Sir Andelf said. "I would, however, assure your ladyship that dragons are very royal creatures, and fit to bear you."

Arendellie nodded. "I appreciate your noble appreciations and concerns," she said, trying not to snicker. The last thing she had been expecting was Sir Andelf's words, and it hit her funny bone. The whole thing sounded like absurd pomposity to her. Being apologized to for not being given accommodations superior to a dragon ride, as if she were made of the most fragile porcelain, and might shatter at a little quiver! From what Kathreen had told her, riding a dragon was rather more comfortable than riding a horse. In fact, once one got used to it, one could even sleep between a dragon's wings. She had never slept on a dragon, but she had ridden L'sa-moth once, and she knew what Kathreen meant. A dragon's flight was incredibly gentle.

Sir Andelf bowed to Arendellie, and she curtsied back. She already felt like a princess! Then, El-Reiza motioned to the dragon's shoulders. "Arendellie, why don't you go first?"

Arendellie smiled and dipped her head politely. Then, she put one foot on the dragon's leg and another into a crevice between two scales. In a few moments, she was in the back seat of the saddle. She had mounted L'sa-moth several times. She looked down at El-Reiza and smiled.

The Dragon-rider nodded. She was small and slight by Camilian standards, and almost leapt up the dragon. Kneeling down on the dragon's side, she began to work on Arendellie's harness. Looking up, she asked, "How many times have you mounted a dragon before?"

Arendellie smiled. "I had an acquaintance who was a dragon-rider. I rode the dragon a few times– not very high, and not very far."

"Ahh," said El-Reiza, looking down at the harness and up again to Arendellie's eyes. "Are there many dragons in these part of the mountains?"

"I haven't known of many in Ebrin," said Arendellie. "However, I believe there are quite a few in Anasha." Anasha was another village, a little larger than Ebrin, a little farther north, and a little deeper into the Enzenyar Mountains.

As the day progressed, Arendellie learned that El-Reiza was not in fact a talkative individual. While they were in the air, she spoke to Arendellie only to make sure that she was doing well, and then she generally said as little as possible as quickly as possible. She seemed to be generally taut. When they landed, she and Akasdar set to preparing the meal and doing as much as possible, so that Arendellie should have to do no work at all, not even setting up her own tent or making her own bed. That evening, Akasdar said more than El-Reiza, whose only comment not directly related to work, and she made few even of those, was that Arendellie needed to concentrate on getting ready for the palace and being a princess, not on any sort of work whatsoever. El-Reiza was, however, incredibly spry and lithe, like an elf or a sprite, and seemed to be a bundle of muscle and controlled energy. Her skin was also about the same shade of darkness as Arendellie's, who was significantly lighter than average, though the color was a tad different. Watching her just move, Arendellie had a hard time believing that El-Reiza was a human woman, not an elf-sprite. She just hardly seemed human. She did not really look human, either, Arendellie thought. She was definitely a female, but she was just too much muscle and strength and compact energy to be a human woman. She was also too small and slight to be a human man, even if she had had masculine features and a masculine personality. Arendellie wondered what part of Camil she was from, but did not think it appropriate to ask.

Over the days, she quickly got used to and fell in love with the fact that she had nothing to do but be a princess and prepare herself for palace life and Vanesh Casarion. Several days later she decided that she would miss El-Reiza. She was beginning to realize that her life would be empty and shallow, but she was not admitting it to herself, and instead was trying to embrace that kind of life, and all shallow and empty things, something she had always had a leaning towards.

One day, the dragon circled down to land in a dragon field, very close to an imposing and flashing structure, tall, white, and huge, with countless towers and balconies. El-Reiza helped her down the dragon for the last time– that, too, about El-Reiza was different, not really human, more elf or sprite, the touch of her hand, the feel of her muscles, or at least it seemed that way to Arendellie. As she walked along the clean, white streets between El-Reiza and Akasdar, who was carrying her bundle of belongings, feeling suddenly and for the first time actually, truly, nervous, it suddenly came to her. Everything about El-Reiza, even the way she breathed, even the way she held utensils, was like the kind of physical tone and flow of that style of moving and fighting Kathreen had learned from Ishtailor and taught bits and pieces of to her! Ever since she had first seen El-Reiza, though she was wearing a long headscarf and a loose blouse and skirt, Arendellie had noticed that there was something strange about her, and at the same time almost vaguely familiar. It had been irritating. Now, just as she was about to part from El-Reiza, she knew what it was!

El-Reiza and Akasdar led her into the palace, between people dressed better than any of them were. El-Reiza asked a few questions of a female servant, and then led them down a hall. Arendellie was transfixed by the glowing colors on the ceiling. Where they alive? Pieces of frozen and living fire? She had not known cloth or stone could be that bright, that radiant with sunset colors.

Less than half an hour later, Arendellie was sitting in a large marble basin, in frothy, soapy water, with a maid rubbing her hair and massaging her muscles in the warm, soapy water. "So," asked the woman, whose name was Inshara, "what was it like living in the mountains?"

"The mountains are very beautiful." Arendellie thought for a moment. Anores was nestled on the edge of a mountain, but it was not like living in the Enzenyar. How should she describe it to a maid who had served in the palace all her life? "You know what the palace castle looks like from the city?"

"Yes, it's very grand," said Inshara, rubbing soap into Arendellie's foot, who was resisting the urge to withdraw her foot and say it tickled! This was one thing she did not altogether like.

"I'm sure you also know the gardens and the park. Try to imagine something like the grand outside of the castle, but to the dragon field meadows as the dragon field meadows are to the palace gardens." Arendellie had seen these on her way into and around the castle– tower– palace.

"I think I might have an idea," said Inshara. Arendellie felt pleased.

After the soap bath, which left Arendellie feeling very pleasant, smooth, clean, and soft, another maid, named Aki'lam, brought a soft gown of smooth, shimmering purples to dress Arendellie. She thought she had never seen anything so nice and pleasant. They were also beautiful. Bringing them, Aki'lam looked a little nervous. Arendellie guessed that she could not be older than thirteen, maybe only eleven. Inshara, who might have been into her thirties, smiled reassuringly at Aki'lam and took the gowns. Aki'lam stepped back, looking grateful. Arendellie got the idea that they all understood her to be big stuff. She liked the feeling, and basked in it, while Inshara held the dress– robe– gown open for her to step into. She relished the feeling of the cloth. It was lighter weight than she had thought on first glance. Inshara tied a string run through it in a bow at the throat and sleeves, gathering the material. Stepping back she said, "It becomes you very well, lady. It will not do for you to be presented to Vanesh in, or even before the court, but if someone sees you wearing it for a day gown, it can elicit only praise. Yes, it is very good, and it will keep you soft. You needn't worry about a single rash or scratch."

Comments like these were beginning to tickle Arendellie's funny bone less as time went on, but she still thought them funny. She was from the mountains. Scratches and tumbles and a bruise or two and now and then a rash had always been part of life for her, though it was very pleasant to think that was all over. So far, more or less, she thought she loved her new palace life, though she had not seen much of it yet. She loved the dash and skill of interactions, and she liked the way she was treated. Looking at her skin, she thought, *They're not doing it for me because I'm so fragile, but for the prince.* She was not bothered. One might have thought it would have stabbed her pride and made her think, *They're treating me like a baby. How insulting!* or, *I don't want to belong to the prince,* but it did not. It was nice being an important lady, a princess almost.

Inshara stepped forward, and splayed out Arendellie's hair around her shoulders. "Now," she said, "that is going to be amazing, once it dries." She seemed suddenly embarrassed of herself, stepped aside, picked up her headscarf and threw it around her shoulders, and said, "Now, lady, is there anything which you would like, or about which you want to talk?" She sat down on the stone pavement, and indicated that Arendellie could sit down on some padded cushions, in the sun for her hair to dry. "We've got to stay in these areas, since your hair is too wet to cover and, especially now that you are here, no man must see your hair, until it is his turn."

Arendellie tried to smile. She was really in no hurry. Her millions of curiosities about palace life, certain to be satisfied sooner or later, were taking back stage to this, to becoming like a princess, for the prince. She was liking it very much. Inshara was very dutiful, tried to be personable, but seemed a little sad. Aki'lam was just shy. She had not yet interacted with her other maids. "No, it's okay," she said. "I don't really need anything. I'm getting more than I've ever had."

Aki'lam returned, walking gingerly, and sat down a little behind and to the right of Inshara. In her hands she held a headscarf of bright, pale green, and a jar of something. Inshara noticed her, perhaps from Arendellie's eyes. She took the headscarf and jar from Aki'lam. "This is for when your hair dries, and I'll help you with it then," she said, "and this, you may rub on yourself now. It is perfume. I figured you would rather rub it on yourself than I try, at least the first time."

To be honest, to be the fuss and center of attention did not bother Arendellie in the least. At least, not yet. In fact, she rather enjoyed it. However, she knew Inshara was trying to treat her like another person, trying to be nice, and she smiled and said thanks, took the jar, poured out a little of the liquid into her palm, and then proceeded to rub it down her neck, and under the robe.

#10
A Conflict in Family and Heart

Azshbir had not been to any meeting at the Hall of Exhortation for a while. Neah'ra had told him once that she missed his presence, and that, while the atmosphere was less heated now that he had not come in a while, people, even people who had once been her friends, drew away from her and, while generally polite, never really spoke to her. A few teased her, now and then, or implied that she was some kind of traitor to their culture or values, even to the Creator and the Promise, most often by comments and remarks, never directed at her in particular or mentioning her, but implying that her complete allegiance was a kind of treason or, at best, dangerous foolery. She felt very lonely. She listened to the discussions and to expositions on the Promise and the prophecies, and sometimes made contributions, but the latter were almost always ignored. After talking to Azshbir, she said, she could understand and articulate things in ways she could not before though, as time went on, she realized that these things were the same as she had always believed; she simply understood them better, both individually and as a whole, and this was delightful. However, she had always to listen carefully to discern between truth and carefully shaded falsehood, and she felt that always having to be so critical, and so defensive, even if only in her own mind and heart, about that portion of the truth which was most lost and attacked, hindered her from understanding and seeing truly and fully. Sometimes, she had told Azshbir, she did not want to go to the meetings at all, but she knew she had to do so, since her father would never take it if she did not or, if he would or did, would ask why, and she did not want to have to tell him. He would never understand, or even be quiet long enough to hope to understand anything.

It had been long enough since Azshbir and Neah'ra had had a real talk, and he wondered why. Did she not want to anymore? Was she too busy? Was she worried about her father? He and Darnize still argued, sometimes heatedly, from time to time but, as far as business was concerned, their relationship was doing fine. He was intelligent and strong, and got the work done well, and Darnize paid him well. Since he lived quite simply and did not use the money to no purpose– he was used to living simply and having no money at all, his parents' farm lying in a very remote valley in the Vinibra Mountains, where there was no one but themselves– his money was building up. He knew that some people thought that Darnize should fire him, since he was a traitor and should be an outcast as well, but that Darnize held that, as he was not actually involved in treason and not actually hindering their war effort, though he held traitorous ideas, treating him fairly was actually one of the values for which Ephezoa was fighting, and which they must defend in their own country and their daily lives if they expected to defend to the rest of Camil. To be honest, Azshbir liked these things about Ephezoan life and did not want to lose them, but he could never join the ranks of those who fought the Creator, as well as all other tyrants, in the name of their autonomy and what they liked. It might be humiliating and distasteful not to fight against tyranny with the weapons of rebellion, but Azshbir had to trust the Creator to know best and do it, and he had to submit to the Creator's will, even if it meant humiliation and suffering, even if it meant submitting to the rule of tyrants.

Azshbir finished slicing the log, put the axe away, and rubbed his dirty hand on his no-less-dirty work pants. The stars were quickly coming out, and it was almost dinner time. He went to the well, pulled up some water, washed the dirtiest parts of him off, walked to his room, and changed into less dirty clothes. Approaching the house, he heard yelling. One voice was certainly Darnize. He thought the other was Neah'ra's, but he had never heard her either yell or cry before, so he was not certain whether it was her or one of her siblings.

"Father, you don't understand! I love you and I respect you, and I love and respect Ephezoan life and values too, but I can't let any of that get in the way of my love and respect for the Creator. He has to come first, no matter what it means! That's why we need the Promise in the first–" She was half-crying, half-yelling, sometimes yelling more, sometimes crying more. Azshbir was certain she was Neah'ra. He could not imagine anyone else in the household having a fight that would provoke such statements with anyone, though, he had to admit, he had no idea how it had started with Neah'ra.

Darnize had interrupted Neah'ra. "The Creator wants us to live well!" he yelled. "That's why He gave the Promise! Besides, Ephezoa is your country! You can't– the Creator can't want you to– just turn your back on her and let her die! It's irresponsible, too, to be raised in a land where you can be what you are without dying and not protect that privilege! It's lazy! It's even cowardly! Why'd the Creator make countries in the first place if we're not to belong to them? Besides, you talk so much about submitting to the government, why don't you submit to the governing consensus here?"

By now, Azshbir was standing right next to the open door. Neah'ra started yelling, and then caught herself half-way through her second sentence and tried to go on in a more reasonable tone of voice. "What law has Ephezoa made that I'm in violation of? Anyway, when did I ever say we are supposed to obey all laws? The Creator's law supersedes all other laws. It's just He's told us not to go around disobeying laws for our own pride's sake, or for whatever other reasons we come up with. If He's told us to do something, we, of course, obey Him! Anyway, how do you know the Creator, King of all, can't want me to–"

Neah'ra never finished. Azshbir had taken another step into the house and, seeing him, Darnize shouted, "What are you doing here! This is none of your business. Leave, now!"

Neah'ra cast Azshbir a pleading glance, and continued, her voice low and soft, "All men belong to the Creator, Dad, and I would be more interested in telling them about the Promise and urging them to turn to the Creator, than in killing them."

Darnize glared at Azshbir, who stood for a moment undecided, and turned to his daughter. "Neah'ra," he said, "did you say you won't kill them if they come here and try to take over and impose their stupid and accursed tyranny?" He was furious, and both his voice and the color of his skin told it.

Neah'ra drew herself together. "I don't know when or if it is or is not proper to kill! I may well be willing to kill defending my siblings and mom from those who would try to keep her from raising them, and instead teach them lies. It's not here now, so I don't know. However, if they win, they're the government! I'm not an Ephezoan nationalist. I'm one of the People of the Promise. Ephezoa, like Hasseleighton, is hostile to the Creator's reign. It's just, there, they have one tyrant reigning over all, here, we teach that everyone should be their own tyrant and respect the tyranny of their neighbors, as long as it doesn't intrude on their own. What do you think that law-suit about the cow and the fence is all about?"

Darnize turned to glare at Azshbir. "I said, Leave!" he yelled, then turned to Neah'ra, "So, what, would you rather have your siblings taken from us, over the dead bodies of myself and your mother, and suffer in dungeons, than live in a place where people all respect that everyone has rights?"

"What I would rather doesn't matter!" said Neah'ra, her voice rising again. She paused, to recollect herself and continue, but Azshbir stepped forward, "Darnize, I don't mean to be disrespectful, but I've never seen your family argue before, and I wouldn't know when to come back for dinner." He wanted to say that he would like to know what the fight was about, in case he might be able to help with whatever had caused it, but he knew he could not do that, not really. He also knew that Neah'ra wanted his help, but how could he help, when she was Darnize's daughter, and he was Darnize's servant? He was trying to buy time to think about what to do or how to handle this situation.

"Come back in an hour! Now, LEAVE!" yelled Darnize. Azshbir could tell that he was infuriated, and also deeply embarrassed that his servant had witnessed a family conflict. Of course, Azshbir would never publicly shame the Katalonga Family by sharing this incident with anyone. He could not even see any reason why he would be tempted to do so, or what he might think he would gain from it, but he was not sure that Darnize knew him well enough to trust him and, even if he did, it was still embarrassing. Azshbir turned and left, feeling conflicted. Obviously, Neah'ra wanted his support. How, though, could he help her? If he were to do so, he would simultaneously disrespect both Darnize's fatherhood, and his position as Azshbir's employer or master.

Azshbir went, sat down next to the barn, and buried his hand in his hands. It was dark now, or he would have done some work, to distract and occupy himself. Within, he felt deeply conflicted, and time crawled. His inner conflict become increasingly unbearable, and time seemed to pass ever more slowly. Finally, Neah'ra came out, sobbing. Azshbir saw her at once, since she was wearing an off-white dress, which almost glowed in the night. It was all he could see of her. He stood, and waited for her to come near. She came, took his hand, led him around the barn, and collapsed. He sat down close to her. She leaned against the barn wall and said, "I'm afraid."

"What of?" Azshbir asked quietly. It was not like her to be afraid.

"That Dad will fire you." She broke into sobs, and then spoke again. "I don't think he cares about what it would do to your opportunities. He's furious. You showed up, and now he says I've gone crazy and traitor. I'm so sorry." She broke out crying again.

Azshbir resisted the impulse to hold her. "What do you mean?" he asked softly.

"I'm not sure I remember how it started," she began. "I just know he was talking something about how brave the soldiers are, who are defending the Promise with their lives and fighting for the Creator, and I said, if that's so, they should be telling the Hasseleighton troops about the Promise and why they need to put their hope in it, instead of killing them. He asked me if I thought defending freedom was wrong. I said that wasn't mine to judge, but it is definitely not keeping the Promise, and it is definitely wrong to make it out as if it were, and even scandalous. He started getting mad then. I don't remember everything that happened." She burst into tears again. Pulling herself together she said, "He accused you of seducing me." In the language of Ephezoa, at that time, the word Neah'ra used for "seduce" referred, primarily, to a spell witches were rumored to cast on people they intended to recruit, in order to make them both able and willing to practice witchcraft. This spell was sometimes rumored to be also used for making someone marry the witch, but this was not its primary, and certainly not its only, meaning. In fact, it was rather a new meaning.

Azshbir did not know what to say. He was beginning to feel protective of this young girl, still a child, whom he was teaching and guiding. She continued sobbing softly, and her pain scraped his nerves. Finally, in a voice as soft, low, and quiet as the night breeze, he said, "You did very well, explaining and defending yourself to your father."

Neah'ra looked up, and he could feel her smile. "You taught me," she said.

"And Kathreen Alarion taught me," said Azshbir.

"She's famous," said Neah'ra. "Everyone knows about her. Wizard Kathreen Alarion, who went into Sephar for the sake of the Promise and returned alive out of great danger. The only thing is, people can't decide on whether she's a hero or a traitor."

"I know," said Azshbir. "Because she's neither. She taught me all about that, too." To himself he thought, *Neah'ra is still only a child! You can't be interested in her yet. You'd better wait a few years, and you probably never will, since... oh, let's not think about that.*

Neah'ra leaned against the barn wall. "Don't leave, please," she begged, half-sobbing again.

"I don't know how I can help it, if your father fires me," he said.

"Then, we will arrange a place and time to meet in secret, once or twice a week, okay?" she asked.

"I don't know about that," said Azshbir, feeling half-guilty and greatly conflicted. "Would it be respectful to him as your father for us to meet, especially since I'm a man and you're a girl, secretly and against his wishes? Would it be all right to so disrespect him?"

"We have to," said Neah'ra. "I'm so alone, and I know so little, and you're all the support I have."

"You're safe," said Azshbir.

He had, though, interrupted her. Neah'ra continued. "We're the Creator's People. Is it all right for us to live only around our enemies, who would seduce us, and never meet one another? After all, this is a war, and we are in a rebel country, behind enemy lines. We need the companionship of other People of the Promise, for we have no other friends. Who associates primarily with the enemy? Is not to do so to be in danger of falling, especially if one has any choice about it? We know isolation is often used to break someone from their loyalty. I'm certainly not strong enough."

Azshbir leaned back against the barn wall. Neah'ra's argument was superb. What bothered him was, he had learned from Kathreen Alarion that even if one thought one could argue to a certain conclusion, even if it made total sense to one, one had to make sure that all the premises and steps were in accord with the Creator's words. Otherwise, one might disobey Him. As impossible as it seemed, He could work even where one could not imagine how He could do anything. His people were called to trust Him, not their own understanding. His and Neah'ra's quarrel with Ephezoa and the way they were doing and thinking things, in fact, rested upon this premise. So, how were they to know what to do in this situation? Azshbir could not think of anything he knew to guide him here; he knew things both ways, for example, that one is supposed to respect authorities that source from the Creator. What was to be done here was not clear in black and white, like it was that Neah'ra must not deny the Creator's precepts, or that they must not call any but the Creator, Supreme King. In a merest whisper he breathed, "I wish Kathreen were here."

"Why is that?" asked Neah'ra.

"I'm sure she would know what to do." Azshbir replied. They were quiet for a while. Then, Azshbir said, "That's okay. We shouldn't be worrying about this right now, since we can't even be certain that it is happening."

Neah'ra was silent for a few moments. Then, sounding ever so forlorn, she said, "You're right." Suddenly she started. "We need to go in, now!"

Azshbir agreed. "You go first," he said.

"No, you go first. If Darnize needs to talk to you, you need to talk, and you can handle it better than I. Besides, I would like some more time… alone," said Neah'ra. It was an unspoken assumption that they must not enter together. To do so would be a dead give-away.

"Okay," said Azshbir. Nodding would not mean anything in the dark. He got up and started walking towards the house. Lights glowed in the windows, and he could smell the scents of delicious cooking, the delicacies laid out on the tables. He could not deny the apprehension flowing in his blood.

#11
The Shame

When Azshbir entered the house, Darnize pounced him with a question. "You are late. Where is Neah'ra?"

"It's hard to tell the time perfectly," said Azshbir, "and I didn't want to be early. As for Neah'ra, when did you appoint me her chaperone? I believe that is one job you have never given me."

"Then, why," asked Darnize, pointedly, "have you taken it upon yourself?"

I've embarrassed him, by being where I didn't belong and not leaving at once, thought Azshbir, *and now he means to do the same to me.* "What are you thinking of?" he asked calmly.

"You know what I mean. You teach her. You've gone to the same meeting that she goes to. You're with her all the time." accused Darnize.

"If I wanted to go to a meeting at the Hall of Exhortation, why shouldn't I have gone to the same one Neah'ra does? Should I have looked for some other one, just to stay away from anything having anything to do with my master? I knew when that one was," explained Azshbir. He was trying to stay cool.

"And, how did you know that? By talking to my daughter in corners all day long."

"Actually, I've never spent a lot of time talking to her. I would never dare to be impolite to my master's children. As for knowing, I'm around you a lot. I heard talk of it." He was going to ask, "Is there anything wrong with that?" but decided it would be better not to do so.

"You often talk to her, do you not? Is that not correct?" Darnize pressed.

I must not lie. It would be disrespectful to Darnize, as Neah'ra's father, and would imply that I am ashamed of what I've done, and don't trust the Creator. "I do speak to Neah'ra, from time to time," said Azshbir, trying to think out how to be both honest and not make Darnize too angry with Neah'ra. "It's natural that I should talk to her, since you never forbade our speaking to one another, and we've had lots of discussions and arguments. Naturally, she was curious about them, and about my position. It was new."

"From now on, you are forbidden to speak to Neah'ra," said Darnize. Azshbir had known it was coming. "You told me, didn't you, that you came to Ephezoa to hold high the Promise?"

"I did. That's the truth."

"That appears to amount, in your head and reasoning, to seducing good, loyal Ephezoans and making them into traitors. You're a traitor to Ephezoa, as you are going around trying to seduce people and make them loyal to something else," accused Darnize. In the increasingly tense atmosphere, this was the kind of thing that, if it got out, could potentially put Azshbir's life in danger, and certainly would make people unwilling to hire him, or buy or sell with him.

"I am not a witch, and have never seduced anyone. I only tell them what it is that I believe and why I believe that my position makes sense, and theirs does not.

Furthermore, to what do you think I am betraying Ephezoa?"

Darnize stumbled a moment. "To Hasseleighton, of course. Of course you're seducing people, if only with your presence."

Azshbir did not answer the second accusation. Darnize was trying to disgrace him, and it would not do for Darnize to become the one questioned. "To Hasseleighton?" he laughed. "I have nothing with Hasseleighton. Before them, too, I uphold the standard of the Promise and allegiance to the Creator alone. You know that I know they are my mortal enemies. No, rather, I have turned from the rebellion of the entire human race back to the rightful King, our Creator, and, if need be, will die trying to make them see their need to be saved from their shame before the Creator and all of righteous creation through His Promise, lest they perish eternally."

Darnize ignored Azshbir's declaration. "You have shamed my entire family, by seducing one of my daughters to your peculiar treason. You have damaged my reputation. What do you propose to do about this? What do you think I should do about this?"

Ah! thought Azshbir, *so that is what this is all about.* "I do not propose to do anything about it," said Azshbir. "I have one loyalty and one king: the Creator. I have one identity to which I am loyal: one of those who waits in hope for His Promise."

"And you will not do anything to undo what you have done, to repair the damage to the reputation of your master, without whose employment you would have no place to sleep, no food, and no money?" Darnize pressed.

Azshbir did not shrink. "I will never unsay or take back my loyalty to the Creator and my profession that He alone is worthy, nor will I apologize for this conviction, or for the Creator's work in winning others to the same."

Darnize sighed. "Are you willing to make this declaration public before the people of Afteloan?"

"I am."

There was still fire in Darnize's eyes, but he ceased the interrogation. "You've done good work for me, so you can eat and sleep here tonight. We will make your declaration public at the meeting in the Hall of Exhortation in four days' time. I have not decided what I am going to do with you yet. You do good work, so I think I shall keep you but cut your wages. Anyway, where is Neah'ra?" As he thought and spoke of his daughter, Azshbir heard tenderness and sadness come into his voice.

"I'm coming," she announced from outside. In several moments, she stepped through the doorway, and into her father's arms. They embraced. "Why were you out so long?" he asked.

She stiffened a little. "I needed the time," she said.

They all sat down to eat, but Azshbir struggled to enjoy the food. He was very nervous, and he could tell Neah'ra was too– for him, he thought. She tried not to, but he could tell that she was constantly glancing at him out of the corner of her eye, worriedly. He wondered what or how much she had heard of their conversation. He was a little excited: he was going to get to tell a lot of people why he was come to Afteloan, and what he was about. He was very worried, too. This was to clear Darnize and try to show him as noble and patriotic, and also to shame Azshbir as a traitor. He did not know why he had agreed, instead of running off. Perhaps, because if he ran the story would get around anyways, and a twisted version of it at that, as well as that he, himself, was ashamed, which was something he could not say. He was not, in fact, ashamed. He had come to tell the people. He was going to get to tell many, many of them, all at once, what the Promise meant to him, and at the same time get to show them what their country was– that was, in fact, the same kind of thing as Hasseleighton. Most would hate him, though, he knew, since they were mostly more or less like Darnize, and many would be a little worried about associating with him. He knew that the procedure would be to have the very same conversation between him and Darnize that had just been played out, in front of everyone.

Butterflies played in his stomach and, to be honest, he enjoyed the sensation just a little. He was having an adventure. It was playing out.

Sometime around midnight, the night before the public declaration was to be made, while Azshbir was tossing on the hay bale that was his bed, he heard the doors of the barn creak open, and then the door of the room in which he slept. Carrying an oil lamp, Neah'ra stepped in. "Hello, Azshbir," she said, seeing that he had sat up.

"Hi, Neah'ra," he replied. "What is it? Why?" Her voice sounded like she had been crying again.

"I'm afraid for you, and I'm afraid I can't take it myself," she said. "It is all just too much. Dad is so miserable. He is miserable about the fact that he doesn't have his mutual benefit argumentative relationship with you that he loved. He liked arguing with you, even though your beliefs infuriate him. He's even more miserable that he's 'lost me.'"

Ignoring the fact that it was inappropriate, Azshbir opened his arms, and Neah'ra melted into them. Though she was becoming a woman, and now and then he thought of her as one, he still thought of her more as a younger sister, kind of like Athara. She was not at all like Adaria. "It could be worse," he said. "At least, we'll still get to be around each other, and see each other daily, you know. Just smiling at one another, just seeing our friend and companion in our combat should be encouraging."

"You're right," said Neah'ra. She was quiet for a few moments, and when she spoke she said the most shocking thing, but as if it were the most natural idea in the world that had just occurred to her out of the blue. "Can you marry me, Azshbir? Then we can move out, be together, talk freely, and you can get some work, and I'll help you. You can teach me everything you know."

Azshbir froze, mouth agape. Neah'ra's very bold and blatant proposal was the most obvious mark of the fact that she was still very much a child that Azshbir had seen yet. It was almost preposterous. After he had gotten his breath back, he said, "Neah'ra, we can't do that. For one thing, your father won't even let us talk. You really think he would let us get married?"

Neah'ra collapsed a little. Even if she had childish ideas of how to get around the issues Azshbir had raised, she knew him well enough to know what his words meant. No.

Standing in front of the congregation, Azshbir felt no thrill of adventure at all. This was not an adventure; this was a public humiliation. His skin crawled, and he wondered why he had consented to this absurd indignity. Even now, he wanted to run away. Even the fact that this was an opportunity to tell them why and what the Promise was, an opportunity to do that for the purpose of which he had left his home, was not enough to keep him there, or even to make him understand why he had come there. Certainly, there was not much difference between what was happening to him and being handcuffed, paraded around, and thrown into jail. In fact, what was happening to him could well have been the worse of the two; it was far more public.

Then, in an indefinable flash, he understood.

The Promise. If this was what it was to stand disgraced before men, before men whose approval or whose contempt was of no weight and which even he despised… what horror it must be to stand disgraced before the Creator, the approval or contempt of whom was of infinite weight and which no creature, however foolish, could really at the last disdain, alone, disgraced and shamed also in the sight of all creation, not only righteous creation but one's very fellows in crime… Azshbir flinched. That was the Promise. One Whom the Creator would send would bear all that shame… that shame that actually mattered, actually was real, actually was a terror of horror beyond weight. Could it be, such deliverance? And here he was, complaining and ashamed to be shamed before men? How amazing must the Promised One be! Looking upon the people, Azshbir felt pity and compassion. They did not even know but, outside the Promise, that was the shame which awaited them– the disdainful and mocking rejection and contempt, not of fellow creatures with no power or authority, but of the Creator of all power and authority Himself!

#12
The Retaliation

Azshbir knocked on the door to Darnize's room, one early afternoon two days later. He still felt crushed by the weight of events, and this was the soonest he could muster the courage to do the dramatic thing that had floated formlessly into his head as he looked on the crowd, that day, and thought about what real shame meant and what the Promise meant. Though he still felt crushed by than turn of events, he was almost grateful; in that one moment he had seen more beauty and mercy than he had, in the rest of his moments put together. What marred it was that he could not remember that insight, or not as he would. He could remember that he had had it, he could remember how to articulate it, but it he could not remember.

"What?" asked Darnize's voice from within the room.

"May I come in?" asked Azshbir.

He could hear the surprise in Darnize's drawn-out, "Yes, of course." Of course, he had expected it. There was no reason Darnize would know of, or even accept, for his coming to him now.

Azshbir opened the door, and stepped in. Darnize was sitting at his table, looking over figures and the like. "What is it?" he asked, looking up and fixing his attention on Azshbir.

Azshbir shivered, well aware that what he was about to do would be considered inappropriate. Younger men and servants did not forgive older men and masters. To forgive was an implication of superiority, it was a statement that one was not bound by revenge or retaliation, was not, in fact, bound by the wrong one had suffered. "I wanted to forgive you,"– all the feelings of shame and embarrassing humiliation washed over Azshbir again, in full force– "for publicly disgracing me." He could barely get the words out. To say it made it too real, as if it were happening all over again. Darnize stared in shock, obviously embarrassed himself. "That's all," Azshbir stammered, bowed, turned, and ran out. He felt like he never wanted to see Darnize again, *not* like he had forgiven him! He could not think of why he had done anything he had done, least of all what he had just done, for the past week. Flush with embarrassment, he sought some hard work into which to throw himself, body and mind.

Darnize stared after Azshbir in total shock. When Azshbir asked to come in, he had wondered what it was; had something gone wrong, or had Azshbir totally had it? The man was such a responsible servant, and Darnize himself had a hard time believing that Azshbir had just let things happen the way they had. The man seemed like the sort who could stand up for himself. Would he do anything just to stay close to Neah'ra? Was he in love with the girl? She probably felt the same way about him. Darnize trusted Azshbir not to do anything with her, but he was not at all sure he trusted him not to talk to her, in defiance of his command. As a worker, he was responsible, about that Darnize had no doubts. He would do his work well.

However, he himself was totally alien and unpredictable to Darnize.

The fact was, Darnize had always felt bad about the way he was treating Azshbir. The man deserved a raise, not what he had gotten. He was competent and reliable, however crazy his beliefs might be. He was probably the best servant in Afteloan, maybe in all Ephezoa. Darnize thought he would be reliable and trustworthy even with great matters. His declaration of forgiveness doubtless meant, at least, that he would, at least while he served Darnize, do his work as competently, thoroughly, and responsibly as before. However, this was the last straw. Darnize was embarrassed to the death, even if he was not embarrassed publicly. What did 'forgive' even mean to Azshbir, Darnize began to wonder. It was just too much! He just could not stand being around the man. He acted like he believed every word he said. Darnize was inclined to believe this was the case. If Azshbir was around for too much longer, he would begin to see the inconsistency of his own life, especially with regards to what he said he believed about the Creator and the Promise. Not that Darnize thought this out in so many words. To do so would be to lose the battle, to be convinced already. No, he simply struggled, reeling with shock, deeply insulted, and desiring to get Azshbir as far away from him as possible. He never wanted to see the man again. However, he could not just fire him, he thought, since he had publicly declared that he would not. He did not think he could talk to Daffron about what he should or could do, either, since his wife was not the sort of person who would come up with such devices, or even consent to complicity in them. She just was not that kind of person. The fact was, he liked it about her, it was why he had married her. It made him feel safe around her. However, right now it made him irritated.

Oh! That was what he could do! He could fire Azshbir, and say that it was because he had not stayed away from Neah'ra, but had in fact been making advances to her, and trying to usurp his place as leader of the household. Yes, that was it! That way he could even shame Azshbir for everything about him that made him so unendurable, yes, even for that sickening forgiveness and refusal to, in any way, shape, or form, retaliate. It tasted sweet to him. Darnize decided he would wait just a couple of days more.

Azshbir had tried to be friendly toward Darnize, and had wondered at the way the man constantly seemed to avoid or slip away from him. Now, he knew why. The man hated him, hated him even for refusing to hate him. He had just finished explaining this, of course in very different words, to the entire household, of which Azshbir was no longer part.

Azshbir bowed to Darnize, accepting his decision, having calmly denied his accusations. It felt like everything was going wrong. He felt utterly worthless, useless, ashamed. He had failed in all he had come for, he felt. He turned, meaning to gather up his few belongings and leave, into the dark night. He would probably have to sleep outside tonight, since it was too late by now to find a place. He was certain all of this had been part of Darnize's plan, to do him in as much as possible.

This was what he had gotten for his responsibility and loyalty and forgiveness! It sickened him. As he turned, he saw Neah'ra's face. She was obviously about to cry. Her eyes looked into his, her own full of sorrow and pain at what had happened. A thousand words could not have said what he understood through her gaze. His heart well nigh broke. Fearing that he would cry himself, he hurried to his room to gather up his belongings. There was no way he could speak to Neah'ra what he so much wanted to speak to her.

Gathering up his bags, he walked down the lane out of the Katalonga Farm, and collapsed on the side of the road, without any idea where to turn next. He had not imagined that working in Ephezoa would mean this kind of persecution, though he realized now that he ought to have foreseen it. He held his knees to his chest with his arms, and shivered a little, only a little. To comfort himself a little, he thought about the fact that Darnize, by his own hatred and bitterness, had damaged his own farm, by firing his best worker.

Indulging his misery and self-pity, Azshbir found himself fighting against the thought that he had not come for himself and it was not about him, against the thought of what the Promise meant, and how indebted he was to the Creator, and against the thought that it was not, in fact, all in vain. Though it meant her pain, as it meant his, Neah'ra understood what she had not. He was, as he felt, utterly worthless and full of shame, except that the Promise meant that his shame had been taken from him, and borne into the future, to be placed on the Promised One, and he was given the merits and worth of the Promised One.

Then, out of nowhere, he remembered that embarrassing 'forgiveness.' It was as if the Creator said, through his memory and through the moist darkness, *"Now, you have the opportunity to really forgive Darnize— to make that forgiveness real, by not indulging your bitterness or dwelling on hatred or the desire for revenge. Now, you can really forgive."* It hurt. He felt like he was being nailed to the ground.

#13
The Fright

Arendellie stood in a beautiful hall, built of white marble. Hung over the walls were curtains of lovely colors. Flamingo pinks blended into sunset oranges and brilliant lilac purples, all seeming to be alight with inner fires. Weaving through these brilliant, fiery colors and, now and then, dominating a portion of the walls, were softer, clearer colors, greens, blues, even a red or a purple here or there, all clean-cut, clear, sharp, but also with softer, muted tones, and the feel of a cool evening in the forest on the edge of a lake. The carpets and the ceilings matched the drapery of the walls. Wherever the white marble of the structure broke through, it both matched and contrasted the color schemes around it, now and then appearing almost like the noonday sun, or like snow in broad daylight, or like snow in the evening, or in shadows, or like a white rock deep in the shadows of a forest. As beautiful as the colors and designs were, Arendellie was not certain that she liked it. It was altogether too much. It was, frankly, overstimulating, even for her. It made her feel almost dizzy.

Beside her were two very young maids, scarcely eleven years old, by the names of Girsa and Kawina. Her long, thick, lush black hair fell over one shoulder, down to her hips. Over her head, half-falling off on one side, was a thin violet veil. She wore a dress of rich emeralds, somewhat scratchy, that fit her body, neither slim nor stout, closely and perfectly. Over her arms, was draped a deep violet scarf, falling almost to the floor from her right arm. Over all, covering her from behind and from the side, a deep royal purple cloak hung from her shoulders. Around the halls stood the courtiers and nobles of the House of Casarion, most of them with their wives. At the far end of the hall, upon a great golden throne, so bright it could have been taken for the flames of a heated furnace, sat the Wizard Grale Casarion. He was handsome, but the intensity of his eyes scared Arendellie a little. On his head was a conical hat, perhaps a foot and a half tall, that flashed colors like tongues of fire. His robes were even brighter than his throne, and the whole effect was that he could hardly be looked at, the colors around him were so bright and overstimulating. All one could get was a dim impression of an intense gaze and mind, and flaming– almost literally– colors. Next to him sat a man whom she presumed was his nephew, Prince Vanesh Casarion. He was far less intimidating. If the flaming, swirling, rush of glorious color represented Grale Casarion, the smooth, cleaner, cooler colors represented Vanesh Casarion. He was rather tall, quite handsome, with skin just lighter than that of the average Camilian, and dark black hair. His eyes were as black as night. He rose, the clothes he wore making an impression as of a whirlpool, and began walking down the aisle. Arendellie thought that he was wearing way too much color. It was just layer after layer after layer of silk capes and ropes and drapes, all clean, clear-cut, cool greens, blues, whites, grays, purples, and a few reds or pale yellows. It was, however, in no way dizzying.

Then, the music began. Wild and yet soothing. Soft, strange, cold, and yet fierce and untamed, like a writhing serpent. Thousands of instruments and thousands of voices. Sounds as wild and untamed as the flaming colors. It almost frightened Arendellie again, and for a moment she thought she would pass out; it was just too much.

Vanesh drew closer to Arendellie, accompanied by his own men. When he was about fifteen feet away, Grale Casarion spoke. "Is this the one, Prince?"

"She is," Vanesh said, only in a whisper but, somehow, Arendellie knew, everyone could hear it. He took a step closer. Then, it seemed that he caught a waft of Arendellie and her perfumes. He signaled something Arendellie did not understand, and one of his attendants stepped forward, walked down the aisle, took Arendellie by the hand, and led her up the aisle. Vanesh turned and walked up ahead of her. The whole thing felt wonderful, and even surreal; it dazzled her a little.

For a moment she stood before the king. Remembering Inshara's prepping– the woman had seemed so sad while she was explaining things to Arendellie, though she did her best to hide it– she curtsied deeply, trying to avoid both the wizard-king's eyes and the flaming color, for his eyes stunned and scared her, making her feel like a mouse, and the color overwhelmed her and overstimulated her. Then, she followed Vanesh to the side, and through a door out of the hall. She followed him through several hallways and doors, guarded by soldiers who made way at the sight of him and knelt, and then behind a curtain, the purple color of distance. Here, Vanesh's attendant and her two maids stopped.

For the first time in this wild adventure, Arendellie felt a real sense of fear, the idea that she had no idea what she was getting into, and would never be able to go back. A feeling that she was losing something, something important, and would come back scathed and scarred. A feeling that she did not know if this was what she wanted; of something terrible, bigger than herself, something irrevocable, something that would devour her. With it, she felt a sense of sadness. For some reason, she felt like a death worse than death was before her and upon her.

Only for a moment. Arendellie shook off the gloom, and stepped forward, fully intending to enjoy and revel in this, as a coronation. She shrugged, and the royal purple cloak fell to the ground at her feet, and the veil slipped a little further off, revealing her glistening but soft black hair.

Then, Vanesh came towards her. Now muted by walls and space, the music still played. Taking her hands in his, he asked, "What did you like best about the mountains, Arendellie?"

"The way my name fits them, their colors and the wild flowers," she said, softly. "I am Ar-a-Endel-Fri, and Araen Rendelli, though one knew me as Araenyi. May I be Araenyi, again?"

Once again, early the next morning, Arendellie stood, radiant in the hall of thrones. Her robes and veils were now all deep, bright emeralds, and seemed to woven out of threads spun from dust made with emeralds whose hearts were green fires. She felt like she must be the beauty of the world, the goddess, queen, and form of beauty, or at least one kind of beauty; there are many different beauties. A faint gloom hung over her, but she steadfastly ignored it, until she was not even aware of it, hardly aware that she had ever noticed it.

Music was played now, too, but it was soft, gentle, background music. She looked down at the carpet before her. Then, the music changed, subtly at first. It grew stronger, louder, more like the wild color schemes that dominated most of the castle– palace. It was, however, far from frightening, though it still overstimulated her a little, since she, coming from the mountains of Avanzar, was not used to this kind of music. It was grand, noble, happy, and triumphant. She took the cue, and began walking forward, once again accompanied by Girsa and Kawina. She felt like glorious emerald beauty. About a third of the way down the aisle, she looked up, smiling and bright, stepping with a kind of deliberate energy. She caught Vanesh's eyes with her green ones, and smiled, subtly moving, so that only he would notice, but he *would* notice. Then, she walked on. About another third down the aisle, he came forward to meet her. He still wore fold after fold of layer after layer of capes and robes and other draperies.

Out of his many folds of clothing, Vanesh drew forth a golden circlet, set with a bright, flashing emerald, which he placed on Arendellie's head. He put his arm about her, and pulled her close to himself. She sank into him, and enjoyed the feeling. He held one arm high, and declared, as he slowly turned around with her, "See, the Princess Arendellie Casarion, named in the ancient tongue, the language of lore and beauty: Ar-a-Endel-Fri and Araen Rendelli."

Vanesh Casarion let her go, and Arendellie and he walked side by side up to the thrones, where another was placed for her. This was her day, her day of glory. For the moment when Vanesh crowned her princess and proclaimed her, the music had stilled, leaving only a few, soft, quiet, if deep, strains. Now, it rose in greater triumph and exuberance than before, so that it felt like the marble itself might try to leap and dance. Vanesh led her up the stairs to the thrones, helped her to sit down, and then sat down himself. She leaned against him for a moment, and then sat, erect, straight, and queenly.

Vanesh raised his hand. "Let Anores dance."

Looking up to a window high in the hall, Arendellie thought she saw signs that the sun was just now rising above the sea, so that the ocean and the mountains, the light and the shadow, were just now dancing. It was sunrise. At that thought, a swift moment of chilly gloom passed over her heart. A picture of the face of Neshekh passed through her mind, followed by the face of Vanesh. There was nothing more different than the way Neshekh had loved her and the way Vanesh loved her, though she had been destroying Neshekh's love, so that his love, at the end, was more like Vanesh's, and also less than it had been. Something was wrong. Terribly wrong. Life was now deadness, a colorful, mummified, bright, animated deadness, but deadness nonetheless. However, Arendellie did not think these thoughts, or articulate her feeling in this way. This is merely what she felt, for the fraction of a second. Next moment, it was gone. She was a princess, and she felt like a queen, wrapped in luxuries without number or name, and lady of a people, with servants at her beck and call. The fact she had this by Vanesh's dead love did not bother her. She had it. She had won Vanesh. She liked her life. It suited her, and it called out all her secret, hidden, and suppressed gifts and powers and desires. She smiled aloofly, taking pleasure in the life she had made for herself, thinking with disdain that she had once been a dirty mountain-child, back when she was very young, five or eight, and that even once she began to know that she liked and was made for other things, she was still far too dirty and common, but also with pride that she had, by her wonderful gifts, choices, powers, and talents, gone from that dirty, common life, to this life. She reveled in it.

#14
The Request

    Life was hard for Azshbir. He knew many people hated him, and he caught their glares. He worked alternately cleaning fish, cutting down jungle, and cleaning out waste, for various people. However, he had the opportunity to tell the people with whom he shared these jobs– generally outcasts, for one reason or another, some of them harmless, some of them actual criminals– about the Promise. Sometimes, he got to talk to his employers, though they almost never engaged, but remained aloof, and even hostile, treating both him and his words with disgust. It always stung him to the heart.
    Among the people he worked with, he knew quite a few who claimed to care about the Promise, and he knew two with whom he found a close bond of brotherly friendship. One was a man with a story not all that different from his own, only it had taken place several years earlier. Another was an orphan boy who came from a family with a history of various shames, some of them having to do with the errant behavior of children, some with accidents, and some with things Azshbir could not understand. He suspected there was far more to it than he knew or understood, since it seemed very complicated. However, the boy was genuinely interested in all Azshbir had to tell him, had his own insights which far surpassed Azshbir's, and tried to share with anyone around. He seemed unbothered by the way in which more respected people slighted him, but reminded Azshbir that the Promise was enough: they would reign forever with the Creator, as His children, by the Promised One, and dwell with Him, and this was glory and honor far beyond anything that these people could imagine, and far more real than anything they had, so they deserved to be pitied, rather than railed against. Azshbir always felt small around the lad, who was perhaps no older than Neah'ra.
    Every now and then, he went to meetings at the Hall of Exhortation, usually after an attempt to get as clean and well-dressed as he could now manage. One day, as he sat on the steps outside after a meeting, a girl stole up to him through the lengthening shadows. He looked up, wondering what on earth she could possibly want. She was dressed well, and handed him a slip of paper, whispered, "From Neah'ra, she told me to go to you, don't know what," and then stole away. Confused, worried, and half-afraid, the worse for the fact he had no idea what was going on, or even if it was the same Neah'ra, or the right *him*, he unfolded the paper, and struggled to read the scribbles in the half-light of evening. He made it out to say something like the below:

"Azshbir, I need help. Father is very hostile. Remember the request. Urgent. Neah'ra."

    He was not sure about the word 'need.' It could also have been 'flow,' or 'wind.' He was not sure whether the word 'Father' was not 'brother' or 'horse,' and he could not be certain the word 'hostile' was not 'hospitable,' or 'dank.' As for the word 'remember,' he thought it could possibly have been 'lake', and he thought 'request' might have been 'rose' or 'room.' He thought 'urgent' might have been 'very beautiful,' but he did not see how reading any of the words any other way would fit together well.

"Okay," thought Azshbir, standing up, and biting his lip. He read the note once more, thinking, *I suppose I could imagine Darnize getting mean, though I have no idea what the problem is.* He tore the note to pieces, and threw it into the gutter. *That way, there's no way Darnize can know what Neah'ra did, unless one of us tells him, and I won't. No matter what.* He stretched and yawned, wondering what he could possibly do. He did not think any of his new friends would have any idea of how to help. *I guess I just go over there and climb into her room– hopefully it's the same one as it was– though if I'm caught everyone will accuse me of meaning to kidnap and probably rape her.* The thought of being so accused scared him a little. He was not particularly afraid of the legal consequences, but of what everyone would say about his dedication to the Promise and the Creator. *Oh well,* he thought, *she's my friend, and my sister in the Promise. Whatever it is, I have to try to rescue her, and I think she is mature enough that she would not have sent me such a note in such a way unless there was a real problem. I mean, she could not even approach me herself. I'll try.* Having thought out so far, and no farther, Azshbir quickly hurried across the city to the alley-corner in which his friend Razi–the boy– slept. He laid his belongings, all except those he would take to the Katalonga Farms, at his feet, and then hurried through the quickly gathering dusk. It was dark, except for the stars overhead and the light of a crescent moon, by the time he approached the Katalonga Farms.

He quietly stole around the house, and to Neah'ra's room. He quietly and slowly opened the window, and gingerly climbed over it. It was very dark inside, and mostly he had to feel where he was. He soon discovered that he was not in a bed room at all, but in a flour storage room. At that discovery, a shock of fear and disappointment went through him, and he felt almost frantic. For a moment he considered that, perhaps, he had misremembered which room it was, and should climb out and try one of the rooms next to it, but then he thought that he had known quite well which was Neah'ra's room, and if he once gave into that frantic feeling his thinking and actions would be no more useful or reasoned that a chicken with its head cut off. Unable to think of what else to do, he found his way to the door and slowly opened it. His heart beat rapidly, and he had no idea why he was doing what he was doing or how it would do any good. He had no reason to suspect anything about where Neah'ra was. Maybe she was sleeping in the barn. Maybe she was waiting for him somewhere on the farm. He had no idea whatsoever. If he was caught, he would be sentenced to many years in prison for trespassing, attempted burglary, maybe attempted kidnapping, maybe even worse.

He stole out into the dark hallway, hoping everyone was asleep and that he would be able to find Neah'ra. Then, he saw a shadow, and froze. He heard a sob. He knelt down. The shadow moved. It was Neah'ra! He reached out, and touched her, meaning to meet her hand. She whispered a hushed and muted, "no... rope."

Azshbir moved his ear closer to her mouth. "Huh? Where?" he asked, in the barest whisper.

"Tied," she managed.

Suddenly, Azshbir understood. He felt around her head, and felt several ropes, one going from under her chin to the top of her skull, the others keeping it there. He fumbled a little, and then found one of the knots. It was dark, and so it took him rather a long time to figure it out, but finally he had it undone. He still had a hard time, since he could not see, but he managed to pull the contraption off her head. He felt her smile, and then start to exclaim, "Oh, th–!" but he cut her off with a whisper. "Not yet."

Next, he found her hands, which were behind her back. The knots on these were tighter and, between that and the dark, he could not untie them. He touched her lightly. "Wait, I'll be back," he whispered into her ear, then rose and walked down the hall. He meant to get one of the knives.

Having to steal around in the dark, and find it in the dark, it took Azshbir almost half an hour. It seemed far longer to Neah'ra. When he came back, he knelt next to her. He could tell she was restraining her joy, and possibly other emotions, and whispered quietly, "If I cut you, try not to gasp or scream, but quietly say 'ow,' okay?"

"Kay," she whispered, not asking any questions. Azshbir was, frankly, pleased and impressed. She seemed older than she had been. He tried to carefully cut the ropes, and she only said "Ow" once. Once it was done, he took her by the hand, and lifted her to her feet.

Neah'ra leaned against him. "Through the front door," she said, gasping in a whisper.

Azshbir swallowed his own questions, and took her advice. She leaned against him the whole way, and he found himself devoured by curiosity as to what had been going on with her. Finally, after what seemed like hours but was probably less than half of one, they were outside, with the door quietly closed behind them, both of their hearts racing. "At last," said Neah'ra, and collapsed on the ground.

"We aren't safe, yet," said Azshbir, still very quietly, and knelt down to pick her up again. With an arm around her, and one of hers over his neck, they walked down the lane. It seemed all that Neah'ra had the strength for.

When they had finally gotten to the end of the lane and to the real road, the night well more than half gone, Neah'ra begged, "Now?"

"No," said Azshbir, no longer in the merest whisper, "not quite yet. However," and here he smiled brightly, "we can talk, as long as we're quiet. I don't think there are robbers on this road right now. They're much more common in the cities."

He felt Neah'ra nod, and then start sobbing. For a long time, that was all she did, while he half carried her. He was beginning to feel very tired, since his work was hard and already left him exhausted at the end of every day, and the stress and energy of rescuing Neah'ra had drained even more of it. Finally, about a mile from the city gates, he took them off the edge of the road, helped Neah'ra sit down, and sat down besides her, his back against a tree. She leaned into him, and began to cry freely. He let her, and did not interrupt, too tired now for curiosity, or for thinking about safety measures.

Finally, she looked up at him, her tears glistening in the scant starlight. "Thank you so much, Azshbir," she said, her voice hoarse from crying, but obviously joyful.

He smiled wearily. "Of course, Neah'ra. I love you. You're my sister." He took her into his arms and embraced her. She wept more. He vaguely wished that he could engage with her emotions better.

After several minutes, she completely relaxed, going almost limp. After a long time, and a short doze himself, he realized that she had fallen asleep in his arms. He looked on her features, barely visible in the gray light of earliest dawn, with great tenderness. He wondered wearily what she had endured. He could not help but admire the way that she had retained her composure until he said it was all right. She was an amazing girl.

When the land was light, though still gray, with the light of dawn, Azshbir tenderly and reluctantly woke Neah'ra. As soon as she was awake, he said, "Try to get yourself a little more hidden in the foliage. Stay here, until I return." There was no time for more, and she had demonstrated enough maturity the previous night that he knew she would understand. He kissed her lightly, the first time he had ever allowed himself that freedom, or even desired it, and ran down the road. He had to get to Razi while he could still find him.

Suffering from a burning headache from thirst, and with the world half-gray and spinning around him, thinking he might pass out at any moment, Azshbir stood above the wakening Razi, leaning against the alley wall. Razi noticed, and asked with evident concern, "Good morning. What's it?"

"I have no time to explain," said Azshbir. "Take some of the coins in my bags, and rent a room. Then, take some more, and bring me some food and water. I will be in the line for announcing marriages. Look to the Promise."

Razi smiled brightly, stood to his feet, embraced Azshbir, and said, "Look t' the Promise." Azshbir nodded, stepped back, turned away, took one step down the alley, and fainted. He found himself laying on the cobble stone with blood on his hand, looking up at a blue sky. Razi knelt beside him, looking very worried.

"I'm okay," Azshbir promised. "It's just been a long time since I ate and I haven't slept. I'll try to be more careful." Cautiously and slowly, he rose to his feet and walked back up the alley. Razi watched him, until he turned out on the street, and then set about doing what Azshbir had asked of him.

As for Azshbir, he hurried back through the city to where he had left Neah'ra outside its gates. He tried to quell his nervous anxiety by remembering that the Creator was in control of everything. He knew that it was right for him to do all he could, up to dying, to rescue and help his sister. He also knew that success, as he might see it, was not guaranteed to him, but that the Creator would do all things well, even though he could not for the life of him understand it in the least. He did not understand how it was that he must lay down his life to love and help Neah'ra, but at the same time, it was not his duty to worry about whether anything he did actually worked or whether she was safe, but that the Creator would work out His will for both of their good, even if He permitted everything Azshbir did to go to ruin, and both of them to end up in worse situations than they were beforehand. He did not understand at all. However, he committed his worries to the Creator, and went on, realizing with shame that he should have done so long ago.

After passing out several times, Azshbir decided that he was thirsty enough to drink any reasonably clean water he could find. In the end, he took a long, deep drought out of the water for the animals– horse, donkey, or cattle– that bore loads or carriages through the city. It made his hunger far more painful– he actually noticed his grumbling, angry, clenching stomach– but at least, though he still felt like passing out, it was no longer actually happening to him all the time. He broke out into a jog.

When he came to where he had left Neah'ra, she emerged from the foliage on top of him, looking far worse than he had expected. He leaned against a tree, feeling dizzy, and afraid that he would pass out again, and tried to examine her. There were dark circles under her eyes, and she was thin. There were rope burns on the sides of her face, under her chin, and on her wrists. She looked like she might almost fall. He wondered how or why she had been out the previous day, to give the girl that message for him. Had this developed since then? Azshbir did not think so. Otherwise, she could hardly have known to send that message. But, how could Darnize have let her interact with the people in the Hall of Exhortation in this state? Azshbir did not know. And he did not have time to think about it either. He wanted to have their marriage in stone, as the saying went, before her father came for her.

"Neah'ra," he said, the world still swimming around him, "we're getting married." He knew that her line, "Remember the request" was an allusion to the day she had asked him to run off with and marry her, and a renewal of that proposal.

Instantly, she was transformed by a radiant smile, and fell into his arms. Azshbir held her for a few moments, and then let her go. "Can you walk beside me into the city now?" he asked.

"I think so," she said, looking serenely beautiful, to him. "Anyway, how are we getting married? Who's marrying us?"

"We're just going to announce it," said Azshbir. "You'll see." Looking up and down the street a thought occurred to him. "The sooner we get into the city the better," he said, "Let's go." He took her hand, and led her out into the road. Looking over his shoulder into her dark, trusting eyes, he asked, "How quickly do you think you can go until we reach the city?"

"A little faster," she said, and lengthened her stride. Azshbir tried to take as much of her weight as he could, but he was incredibly weak himself. Somehow, they made it. Once inside the city, among the press of the people, they allowed themselves to walk slower. Azshbir even took her aside, into the shadows of some bushes near the dragon field, and they both sat down for a moment. The rope marks on her caught his attention again, and he asked her, "What happened? Why?"

Neah'ra did not speak for a couple moments, as if recollecting her thoughts. "I'm not really sure," she said. "I think Father thought that, once you left, I would stop caring about the Promise. Maybe realize that it was all kind of overboard, fanatical, and settle down and be reasonable. Of course, those would be his words. Given that reality is what the Creator's Story tells us that it is, what could be more reasonable than to live as if the Promise is everything and this world nothing?" Azshbir was smiling, listening to her, and she was smiling a little, too. Then, she went on, "Well, that did not happen. How could it? I'd just been waiting to know and understand more when you arrived, I hadn't been as cold as Father thought at first– I just did not know how to put it or say it. I could never go back to that. And, I didn't. I'm often rather shy in the Hall of Exhortation, but I still said what I meant, and or rather didn't said what I didn't, and I tried not to budge one inch." She looked down in shame at this point. "I can't say that. I didn't. Several times, in order to make peace– at least, that's what I told myself, then– I gave in. I admitted that maybe I was a little too excitable, maybe it was reasonable and proper, maybe even good and necessary, to insist that our young men kill the young men of Hasseleighton, to protect us from Grale, instead of offering them the hope of the Promise which alone can change their hearts, and by which the hearts of my teachers need to be changed too! Things like that. Sometimes, I got upset and snapped at them for bothering me, too. But that wasn't all…"

Neah'ra's voice faded away, as she looked down at her hands. After several minutes, she picked back up again, "And, I started teaching my siblings. Sometimes, I would gather them together to talk about things. Sometimes, just one on one, while playing or doing chores. I think that made Father angry, too." She leaned her head against Azshbir's chest, and started weeping again. He had no idea how she could manage. Her head must have felt like it was on fire by now, he thought. Cradling her in his arms and stroking her hair, he wondered what their relationship was. Older brother and younger sister? Husband and wife? Something like father and something like daughter? It sent his head spinning.

When Neah'ra was done crying, they both got up. Azshbir let her lean against him, while they wove their way through the city to the line of people who were declaring marriages. There, he saw Razi, sitting down outside the area, since no one would allow him in because of his stinking, disgusting rags. He had a plate of bread and fruits and a water skin. When he saw Azshbir, he leapt to his feet, looking like he wanted to leap onto Azshbir and knock him over. He restrained himself though, seeing Neah'ra leaning on Azshbir. His eyes shining, he asked, "Who's she? Your bride-t'-be? I hadn't 'eard anytin' o' tis!"

Azshbir nodded. "I hadn't either, until last night. She's a sister. Anyway, give the water to Neah'ra, please."

Razi smiled, stooped down, picked up the water skin, and handed it to Neah'ra. The three of them drew off to a place a little by the side, and Azshbir helped Neah'ra drink, without spilling too much of the water. Once she was managing quite nicely by herself, Razi whispered to Azshbir, "She's quite beaut'ful; anyway, what 'appened t' her? What 'appened t' *you*?"

"She's the daughter of the master who, well, worked this life out for me. Darnize," said Azshbir, unable to draw his eyes away from Neah'ra.

"Oh!" exclaimed Razi. His eyes were glued to Neah'ra, too. "So, she's an 'xample of the power of the Promise?" he asked.

"Oh, totally. I still don't know all the details yet, but He had called her before ever I saw her. She's stood firm, and I just totally know the Creator loves her. He's kept her this far. She's the most amazing work of His' I've seen yet. Well, that's not quite true. All of His works are most amazing. Including you."

Razi nodded, still with his eyes on Neah'ra, who seemed to be oblivious to their whispered conversation about her. "When's th' last time she's 'ad water?"

"I don't know."

Razi turned, and hugged Azshbir. "Tat's all 'ight," he said. "I wan t' know 'er better. Anyway, I 'ave to go find 'ork, 'specially since you ain't findin' any t'day, an' she'll need eatin' an' stuff too, now."

"Oh, thank you so much," said Azshbir, hugging Razi back.

Razi stood up. "Look t' the Promise, you both!" he cried.

Neah'ra pulled the skin away from her mouth, too, and looked up. With Azshbir, she replied, "Look to the Promise!" It was their first time ever. Azshbir had been introduced to that farewell through Razi and his other friend, Anjis.

Neah'ra smiled, and caught Azshbir's eyes. He could tell that she was already feeling better. A lot better. *How long had it been? How much has it been?* he wondered. *How great You are!* Meanwhile, she asked, "Shall we get in line, now?" Glancing at the plate, on the ground between herself and Azshbir, she said, "I don't want that quite yet, though I might have a mango"– she proceeded to grab a slice of mango, yucky from sitting in the sun, off the plate– "so can you hold it for me please?"

"Gladly," said Azshbir. They both got up and got in line, smiling to each other.

#15
The Whole Problem

Over the next couple of days, Azshbir discovered that Darnize had grown increasingly hostile to Neah'ra, over the entire length of time since he had left. At first, it had been only verbal– calling her a traitor and a witch. However, it had gradually but steadily escalated. At first she had been given more chores, and harder ones, which left no energy for talking, or lonelier ones, in an effort, she thought, to prevent her from having any time to relate to her siblings. Then, she had been denied choice foods. Exactly what had prompted Darnize to tie her up and leave her in the hallway that particular day she did not know, but it was not the first time. It was, though, the time he forgot to stuff a rag into her mouth. She thought it was an attempt to make it impossible for her to talk to her siblings at all, by keeping her from getting any more sleep than was absolutely strictly necessary. She had been telling the story to all three of them, Azshbir, Razi, and Anjis, and broke down and started crying. "I don't know how Mom is;" she said. "I'm not even sure whether she believes in the Promise or not. I'd scarcely seen her at all in months. I'm worried Father may be persecuting her, as well. As for my siblings… oh, I don't know, I don't know, I don't know. I hope I told them well. I hope they've seen the Promise."

Hearing it had made Azshbir cry. He wondered if he should have rescued Neah'ra when she had first asked but, then again, if he had done that, she would not have had the opportunity to share so much with her siblings. Or to grow as she had, for it was obvious to Azshbir that she was stronger and brighter than she had been. She was no longer a child. *We want to know what the Promise means. Experiences like these teach us, don't they?* he thought, remembering the insight he had had, looking out over all those people, and thinking about the meaning of shame and the Promise, and also his experience with forgiving Darnize, first to Darnize, then in his heart. And, then, meeting Anjis and Razi, who had their own insights to offer.

Neah'ra also shared that Ellason, the girl whose younger sister– Ellason had not been there that day– she had sent with the note to Azshbir, had been a very good friend to her. Ellason was actually twenty-two, and though she still lived with her parents, they more or less gave her freedom to do as she liked. Neah'ra had really gotten to know her over the last several months, as Ellason was drawn to another young woman who knew the same things she did and had set her heart on the same bright goal. Ellason was deeply frustrated with the lack of actual interest in the Promise among the people of Ephezoa, for which they substituted interest in their own heroes, like Prince Teka-Rok, Dulu Mai, and Saris, and in their laws and traditions, all colored through with talk about things the meaning of which they had no faint inkling. She had also gotten to know several other girls who also, she thought, deeply cared about the Promise.

After a couple weeks, Azshbir decided to try to clean up himself and Neah'ra as well as was feasible, and get some semi-reasonable clothes for both of them–

Razi had commented that Azshbir had saved up a ton of money– and go to the same meeting at the Hall of Exhortation that some of Neah'ra's friends did (another of the things Darnize had done was switch around which meetings she went to, in an attempt to frustrate her finding like-minded people, though he never did stop sending her, even making her go; the actual effect of this was that she found more like-minded people, and they were all able to get to know and encourage each other). Azshbir tried to convince Anjis and Razi to go with him, but they said that they preferred not to do so, and could not see what use they would be there, so he and Neah'ra went alone.

As they were about to enter, a tall straight woman with skin substantially lighter than the average Camilian came down the steps. As she came closer, Azshbir realized that she was taller than he had thought; she might almost have been taller than he himself. She wore a simple dress and a simple cape, which swirled behind her as she came down. Calm joy in her eyes, she hastened to embrace Neah'ra, with a simple cry of, "Oh, Sister!" Once they had greeted, she turned to Azshbir. "I remember you!" she declared. "You were Darnize's servant. I never did understand the point of that thing. You brilliantly explained what the Promise is and what it means for us, and how it is different from Ephezoan nationalism, and even forbids the predominant forms of nationalism. I was quite confused, as it followed the procedures of a disgracing, but if anyone should have been ashamed it was Darnize! I am glad you and Neah'ra are together. Anyway, it is an excellent thing, how the Creator has been spreading His truth abroad, and calling people back to real trust in the Promise; showing us what that even is, for it was so hard to see or understand what was going on. It seems to me plainly evident that Grale Casarion himself can only serve His Maker's purposes. I know now that the Promise *will* come, and will come when it is time, will not delay, however many long centuries may pass before its appearing."

Azshbir bowed. "Thank you," he said. He felt a little awkward around Ellason. She was just so tall, and he had never met a woman nearly as tall as her before.

"Are any of the others here today?" asked Neah'ra.

"Only Sanahi, I think," replied Ellason. "Anyway, it is good to see you looking much better, sister. How did it happen?"

"Amria didn't tell you about the note that day you weren't there?" asked Neah'ra.

"Oh, she did," said Ellason, "– let's move aside since we're in the way– but I'd like to know how it happened after that."

"Well, Azshbir–" began Neah'ra, when as they were walking up the stairs and aside, she caught sight of her father. The next moment, she knew that he had seen her, too. Or Azshbir.

Azshbir saw Neah'ra blanch. "What is it?" he asked, in a whisper. Ellason had noticed as well, and was glancing around.

"Father," said Neah'ra.

"Speaking of that," said Ellason, "how is Daffron?"

Neah'ra did not reply. Azshbir grabbed her hand, which was suddenly cold, and squeezed it. "Don't be afraid," he whispered. "The Promise is as real as ever. You've endured already, and triumphantly." Neah'ra did not seem to respond. She seemed almost paralyzed with fear. "Look to the Promise!" Azshbir declared, using their little circles' favorite line, whether for greeting, or encouragement, or comfort, or expressing love. Ellason met his glance, and he knew she understood.

"I know. I'm sorry," said Neah'ra. "Look to the Promise," she whispered, but whether to herself or back to Azshbir, he did not know.

Ellason took one of Neah'ra's hands and one of Azshbir's and led them up the stairs, right inside the building. Speaking lowly and softly, she said, "Just to get us out of the footpath of the people coming in and out, so people don't have to go around us so much." As they stood against the wall, she said, "Let's not freak out. The Promise. What is the Promise?"

"The Creator will send One who will take all our shame away and bury it deeper than the deepest sea," replied Neah'ra.

That's eloquent, thought Azshbir. *Poetic.*

"Your turn, Azshbir," said Ellason.

"The Promised One will take our shame into death. He'll leave it there, but He will conquer death and lead us all out," he said.

"He bears our shame by being *as* us, and so we may become *as* Him, and live with the Creator in power forever–"

"Neah'ra, what are you doing here? Where have you been?" It was Darnize's voice. Behind him stood Daffron, crying.

"I've been with Azshbir, Father," said Neah'ra, trembling a little. Azshbir was once again holding her hand. He gave it a little squeeze.

"You're not Azshbir's. You're our daughter. Why did you run away? You're coming back with us," said Darnize. Azshbir thought that Daffron looked like she did not want to come or have anything to do with the whole thing, one way or another. Like she just wanted to be left out of it. *I don't think she does belong to the Promise,* thought Azshbir. *She never seemed to care about it at all when I was around. I'm not sure what she does care about. Just doing wife-things, and maybe some mother-things?*

"I'm not Azshbir's daughter, right," said Neah'ra. "I am his wife." Azshbir squeezed her hand again. *Right!*

"I never gave your hand to him in marriage. It's unlawful," said Darnize. "You're still mine, and you're coming back."

Just as Azshbir was opening his mouth to speak, Ellason caught his glance. *Let her*, she mouthed. Azshbir did not see why, but he did wait a moment.

"That's the whole problem," said Neah'ra. "I'm not yours. I'm the Creator's. I belong to the Promise. It's true that I did not always belong to the Promise. But I'm not going back. I'll never."

"Of course you are. We're your parents. You're shaming your whole family. You're breaking your mother's heart, as well as mine," said Darnize. "Are you really so stubborn and cruel?" Azshbir thought of Razi. Were things like this responsible for the disgrace of his family heritage?

This is it, thought Azshbir, *I don't care what Ellason thinks or says.* He stepped forward, and said, "Neah'ra is my wife and I am her husband. We have consummated our marriage. We are one, and we belong to the Promise and the Creator!" Very quietly he whispered, so that only those immediately around him could hear, "Neah'ra is my wife. I love her as my own flesh and blood, my own soul. I will die before you take her back or torment her. She is more precious to me than my own life. Do you hear?"

"I thought you were a pacifist!" said Darnize.

"I never said that," replied Azshbir, still speaking quietly. "We were talking about war. Besides, I did not say that I will kill you. I said that I will give my life and my blood for my wife."

"Your marriage is no marriage at all," declared Darnize, and then stalked away. The crowd that had gathered around to watch, murmuring, started drifting away with him.

Ellason glanced around. Azshbir could guess what she was thinking. *By whose law?* It was true that, by Ephezoan tradition, what they had done was unacceptable and disgraceful. However, Ephezoan law sanctioned it. Far more importantly, where did the Creator say that if a girl married against her father's wishes it was not a marriage? However, he did not have time for these thoughts. Neah'ra was looking up at him, her eyes shining, though he could feel that her pulse was still racing.

He bent down, and pecked her lips. "I loved that line, 'That's the whole problem,'" he said. "That was really well done. True."

All three of them beamed. "Well," said Ellason, "would you like to introduce him to Sanahi?"

"Certainly," said Neah'ra, "but…"

"But what?" asked Ellason, prompting her to speak.

"I don't want to talk to Father anymore right now," said Neah'ra.

"You won't," said Azshbir. "I won't let him, not anymore."

"Neither will I," said Ellason. "I just wanted you to handle it once. So you know. So you've said it. So no one can say we've coerced you or spoken for you. So that you're a woman, both in yourself and before men."

"Basically," said Neah'ra, "because I needed to say that I'm Azshbir's wife. If Azshbir– or even you– said it for me, then, uh…"

"It wouldn't be as real. Exactly," said Ellason. "And, even more importantly, you needed to declare your part in the Promise. You needed to say that you are *His*."

"I've done that so many times," said Neah'ra.

"Yeah," said Ellason, with a little bit of a smirk, "but not like that." Dropping her voice she said, "I know it has less meaning, for you, in these circumstances, than in those, but it kind of needed to be a proper public announcement, even though half of us all already know."

#16
What Is It, Lady?

Arendellie leaned against the walls of the palace garden, looking out over the city. She did not get to go out into the city. Of course, she would not have wanted to; not in a place like Hasseleighton. Then, she saw someone whose stride and form looked familiar. He came closer. In fact, he came right up to the wall– which was thick– and looked up at her. "Sir Andelf?" she asked.

"How are you, Princess Arendellie?" he asked. She thought she detected sadness in his voice.

"I'm well. Very long hair. Thick. Soft. Lush. Sometimes we oil it. Sometimes not. Lots of nice soft clothes. Beautiful clothes. All that stuff, but to go on about it would be boring. Prince Vanesh is interesting. He tells me about things sometimes. Umm, not much. Oh, yes. I would like to be able to go and visit Ebrin. Vanesh told me to ask someone else about it, and then we could arrange it together. Speaking of which, is El-Reiza with you?"

"Oh, my! You talk a lot," said Sir Andelf. "No. We're not in Ebrin right now. We withdrew. Avanzar told us to get out, and we are very tied up with Ephezoa and their allies, and do not care to fight Avanzar right now, though I *think* that we would win. There's an underground resistance in both Sephar and Vanipia, more so in the latter, that is driving us crazy. Some people associate it with Wizard Kathreen Alarion, but it really cannot be proved that it has anything more to do with her than with anything else. Kathreen is loony, so I don't know. She broke jail a couple times. I and several others have given up trying to predict her. These People of the Promise are stubborn though. Or at least some of them. So, I don't think we can work it out right now."

"Ahh," said Arendellie. Then, "Kathreen really… got arrested?"

"On yes. She and another woman by the name of Adaria. They're pretty bold. It makes Grale Casarion angry. One jail they ended up in, they explained their reasons for believing the Promise to every one of the inmates– none of whom happened to be People of the Promise. Well, Adaria did that. Then Kathreen, I believe that she morphed the materials of the roof and crawled up a staircase of mud with her friend. Something like that. I can never remember the details of wizards' spells," said Sir Andelf. Speaking very quietly, he said, "I decided to withdraw from Ebrin, and to give my analysis that we do not want to fight Avanzar right now, for you. Kathreen is getting too interesting and too bothersome, and it is a well-known fact that she is very close to Mirla. If we occupy Ebrin, I am in danger of taking orders to have Mirla, and anyone else with whom Kathreen has suspected connections, interrogated, by torture if necessary. So– and don't tell anybody this– but I hired Sung Cow-Ream to encourage the Avanzarin royalty to tell Hasseleighton to get out– or else. (Don't ask me about the diplomatic details– I did not even arrange half of them.)"

"Sung Cow-Ream?" asked Arendellie.

"Yes, he seems to have a knack for getting into things. Everyone considers him an asset. I don't know how he plays it all out, but he seems to get his nose in everywhere." Sir Andelf lowered his voice even more. "No one understands the man. He is responsible for the knowledge that Kathreen's town of origin is Ebrin. Whether it was a slip, or he trusted someone he should not have, or a total and complete accident, or whether he did it before he realized who and what Kathreen is becoming, I have no idea. However, he's even more unpredictable than Kathreen Alarion... At least everyone knows what Kathreen Alarion believes and what she is working for. Sung Cow-Ream though? No one has any idea what he is about."

Arendellie wondered why Sir Andelf was telling her all this, or what he was getting at. She found the news about Sung Cow-Ream disturbing, though. Sung Cow-Ream had appeared to be interested in Kathreen. His dragon Koarseth was certainly the mate of hers, L'sa-moth. She wondered if she could ask him or if that would be inappropriate, or even dangerous. She glanced over, back at the gardens. Her maids were meandering through them, and she did not know how much attention they might be paying to her. She decided to risk it.

"Do you know anything about Neshekh Dasaran?" she asked quietly, looking down again.

"Only that he left Ebrin shortly after you did. Where he went or what he is doing I have no idea." He looked down and then back up again, "I am sorry, Arendellie, but I do not know everyone or everything. Just a little. I did not even find Sung Cow-Ream for myself. He found me, and expressed concern for Kathreen. I am, in fact, a little worried that I am being used by *him*, but I'm trying to do my best to take care of you and those for whom you care. It's a shame that you're so close to Kathreen Alarion... but, then again, if you weren't, you never would have been noticed and given opportunity to be a princess." Arendellie smiled, feeling pleased, but she thought Sir Andelf did not sound very happy about this, even if his words were entirely positive. It reminded her of Inshara's words and moods. Maybe they knew each other. She decided she would ask Inshara.

Sir Andelf, however, was going on. "The People of the Promise seem to like to make scenes. I feel sorry for them, though in a way I admire their courage, but I certainly pity their foolishness. They are thick-headed and stubborn, and can not be made to see sense or reason. Nothing teaches them. Treat them well, explain to them the situation, talk them through reason, why it is better for Grale to rule the world, why it is better for them to surrender... all is for naught. Yes, a couple district officers tried that tactic, preferring it to torture. Neither appears to get any results. I can't say I like the latter, though. I hope to ensure that those you care for will be subjected only to the former, if they must be reasoned with at all, but I have little hope that I have any hope of that apart from somehow keeping them out of our... well... sphere of attention."

Arendellie nodded. Why did Sir Andelf care about her so much?

"Anyway," he asked, "do you like life as the princess?"

"Very much, thanks to your noble concern," she said. "With the advent of Wizards Grale Casarion and Kathreen Alarion– are they related, their last names are so similar– the world fractured into many pieces. Here, I am actually with people who are in the same piece in which I am. It was awful in Ebrin, since everyone, and most certainly everyone close to me, seemed to be in a different piece than myself. It is kind of cruel of both of them, since they make us have to make decisions no one should have to make– talk about that another time. Still, it's nice here, since there are no people close to me who are in different pieces of a cruelly shattered world, and a lot of people seem to be in more or less the same piece in which am I."

"Be careful what you say, Princess," said Sir Andelf, evident concern and stern warning in his voice. "Anyway, is there anyone close to you here, Arendellie?" Here, he seemed almost tender and close.

"Of course," she said. "How could there not be? I *am* married."

Just then, the voice of one of her maids, Alitholiel by name, came to her, from way too close. "What is it, Lady?"

Arendellie straightened, and spoke loudly enough to make sure Sir Andelf would hear her and understand. "Oh, just looking out over the city. It is a quite beautiful city, to be honest. I am glad to live in its palace. I was just passing a few quick words with one of the common folk, who don't seem to understand a lot." *I guess I have to be more careful. Don't know how I did that,* she thought to herself.

During that evening's bath, when she had a moment alone with Inshara, safely out of earshot of any of the other maids, she asked her, "Do you know Sir Andelf?"

"Never heard of him, Lady. Why?"

"Nothing much. You just look a little like him. Like you might be related or something."

She had deliberated about it, all afternoon, worrying whether or not she could trust Inshara with such a meaningful question as that. After all, maybe everyone here was like the Sung Cow-Ream Sir Andelf was telling her about. Maybe that's what he was doing. Warning her. Warning her to trust no one. Except himself? Or including himself? However, she really wanted to know. She would have thought it completely harmless, except for the little interchange with Alitholiel. Her heart suddenly throbbed for a relationship like that which she had with Kathreen Alarion, and would still have, if they could only be together again. But then, had not Sir Andelf said that Kathreen Alarion was loony and unpredictable, too? Yes, he had, but he had said she was 'loony,' and he had implied, too, that her unpredictability was of a totally different sort from that of the rest of people– loony, stupid, but not particularly disloyal. In fact, loyal to the point of stupidity. It meshed with what she knew of Kathreen, who might be willing to place her friends in danger because of her loyalty to something higher, but would never betray them, would never use them, would remain loyal to a friend even when the grounds on which the friendship had been built had been shattered. Perhaps, that was what Sir Andelf was trying to tell her. That some people were loyal and trustworthy, but loony and rock-headed, while others were cold and calculated, intelligent but without loyalty or compassion. Maybe, too, that she needed to watch for who was who. And, what was he saying about himself? That he fell somewhere in the comfortable middle? What? Maybe talking with him again would help clear it up a little. And what was that last question about? Did he want her? She had long ago suspected that he did, but perhaps he still did. But, how did he care about her? In what way?

Her mind went back to how he had contrasted Sung Cow-Ream and Kathreen Alarion. Maybe he had been encouraging her to consider herself? What kind of person was she? Was she more like Kathreen Alarion– or like Sung Cow-Ream? The thought bothered her. She could not say she was like Kathreen Alarion. If she had been, if she had Kathreen's kind of loyalty– would she ever have taken this life? Maybe that had been what Sir Andelf's final question was about, though why he would care she would never know. For, Kathreen had not lost as she had. Kathreen still had her loyalty, and she had, doubtless, friendship. The friendship of all those who shared her higher loyalty. A friendship deeper even than that between her and Arendellie. Kathreen still had her life. However, she was alone, and she was a princess, seeking after... after... oh, after... she did not know! What was it she was after? She could not really name it. It made her think of Sir Andelf's comment about 'no one knows what Sung Cow-Ream is about.' If she had to say what she was after or about, it would be a life totally different from, and therefore protected from, the sorrows of the life that was gone... though that was not working out. Or, she might say, being a princess. Being royalty. But what *was* royalty about?

Suddenly, Arendellie checked herself. If she went on like this, she would go crazy, and be unable to live her life at all! Besides, who was to say which was better, being a Kathreen Alarion or a Sung Cow-Ream? What was the standard for better? Arendellie did not know of one, and this was the life that suited her. It was hard even to say which was more dangerous. There were numerous pitfalls into which one could fall, all unawares and even at no fault of one's own, in her life. However, the life of a Kathreen Alarion would be lived in constant danger of every kind of horror... Arendellie knew that all kinds of terrible things happened in the dungeons. No, she would pull herself together, and live her life. Maybe that was what it was about. Excitement. Doing. Being. Making it. It suited her *and* it was all she had to go after. Yes, it was good, if that word had meaning, for Kathreen would not have said it was good. Mirla *had* said that it was *not* good, though the Creator could still use it. She had not understood that. And she didn't care. That settled it. As far as she was concerned, her life was good. It was what she wanted, and what she was made for. It was *her*.

#17
The Brethren

Over the past weeks, Ellason had been helping to provide for the small group of the People of the Promise. It was only a little here and a little there, but it made a difference. She belonged to a rather wealthy and well-to-do family, and she made extra money for herself with her paintings, which Neah'ra told Azshbir were really quite good. At any rate, the extra money she supplied allowed them all to rent a single room together, in which they could sleep and keep their scant belongings, in a relatively safe part of the city. She told them that she was sorry that she could not do more for them, but she did not want to ask her parents for help, since it would embarrass them, and it was just better the less they knew about her activities, about which they never asked. If they knew, she told them, they might decide to tell her to leave.

Now, Razi was telling Azshbir about how being covered from head to toe in rotten waste and excrement– they were working on cleaning the back gutter for a wealthier man, for whom they had never yet worked– was a little like that way it is to be in one's crimes before the Creator, only that the latter is a whole lot worse. Then, he added, "'ometimes I 'ave a 'ard time believin' th' Promise, since it says th' Promised 'ne takes our shame an' evils, an' you know, th' Promised One 'as got t' be a 'ot cleaner, see what I'm speakin', dan we are, t' this yuck, a 'ot 'ot cleaner, an' you see, I don't really tink I'd be 'illing– na, I know I not– t', uh, carry tis stuff off on 'ee, and our evils, shame, is 'ot, 'ot worse, too, you see, what I'm sayin'?" The piece of cloth tied around his face further muted his words.

Azshbir was about to reply, when he heard the voice of the man of the house asking, "But you do believe it, don't you?"

"Oh, for all 'ee life, yesseessee!" exclaimed Razi.

"Yeah, it's… it makes your head swim… take yuck… for… yuck… to make yuck… beautiful," Azshbir said, slowly, holding the bag open, responding to Razi and virtually ignoring Cavisto. "I still can't… get used to having this… this close to me… makes me not want to breathe… makes me want to wash off in some…. clear, mountain stream, just smelling it… But, we know that the Creator says what He means… Otherwise, I *wouldn't* believe… the Promise. I mean, we don't even… get close to this stuff without our… bandannas on, and we're worse."

Cavisto stepped closer. "I'm so sorry."

Razi steadily continued scooping. "What for?" he asked.

Azshbir looked away, in Cavisto's direction. He was incredibly grateful for getting to work with men like Razi and Anjis. Otherwise, he knew, he would long ago have lost any gratitude or perspective in disgust and self-pity, nurturing bitterness and total grumpiness. As it was, Razi and Anjis made sure he kept his perspective and, in fact, taught him many things he had never dreamed of knowing. If the purpose of everything was to know what the Promise meant, he could not think of much more optimal circumstances. If the purpose of everything was to proclaim the Promise, he got to do an awful lot of that, too. Tomorrow, he was planning to go with Anjis and Neah'ra to go to the 'bad' part of town, and try to talk to the prostitutes, and try to rescue any of them if they wanted and could. It had been Neah'ra's idea. Mostly. But, Cavisto was speaking.

"Azshbir," he was asking, "how did you end up doing *this?* I can tell you were not raised on the streets or in shameful quarters. You're not a prostitute's son. You speak well. You speak cleanly. And, I can just smell your disgust, as if this is something that you've hardly ever done before. You're new. What happened?"

"Razi, I'm going to go. I can't have this conversation while…" he glanced down with disgust. "I'm sorry." He walked a little ways away, sat down against a wall, and said, "I'm supposed to be a traitor. How come you don't know? Ellason did. Most everyone does. I used to work for Darnize Katalonga. He paid me well, and I got along quite well. But, we couldn't see eye to eye, and I made friends– friends– with his daughter. He couldn't stand it. He liked arguing with me about whether being Ephezoan or belonging to the Promise was more important but when it was his daughter… oh, the nonsense! So, well, who was going to hire me? I did try, went into the square, to ask if anyone wanted me to work for them. But then, along came one of the people who knew Darnize or had been there. They started up a chant. 'The traitor! The traitor! The traitor! He hates Ephezoa. The traitor! The traitor! Azshbir the traitor! Nameless the traitor! Has no town! Country is. Hasseleighton! The traitor– yippee, he's a traitor!' Or at least it went something like that. They taunt me with it a lot even when I'm gutting fish. Or, yucking."

"Yes, that was *not* funny, when you showed up at my door this morning, and asked if I could use some yucking." The furniture and figurine merchant burst into sputters, as he tried to control himself. Then, he sat down, and buried his head in his hands. "No, I actually think I may have vaguely heard of that, but so many things are happening nowadays, and you never can tell what's what. Everybody has a traitor. If you came from one of the frontier cities, you're probably a traitor. If you disagree with a single war policy, you're probably a traitor. If you think that it's worth while to tell a single citizen– or slave– of that Empire about the Promise, instead of stabbing them, you're probably a traitor. Or, so says the mob. So, I don't listen to the stories. As for the Halls of Exhortation, they make me sick. All they can think about is how glad they are that they don't live in the Empire of Hasseleighton. Or something like that. What about what you and Razi were just talking about? Speaking of which, Razi, come, leave that, and sit down here."

Seeing his friend's reluctance– he had never been treated like this before– Azshbir called, "Really, Razi, c'mon!"

Cavisto looked at Azshbir with surprise. "I didn't know you could talk street slang!"

"I'm not very good at it. I just get a little sloppy sometimes. I'm actually from a secluded family in the mountains."

"Ahh," said Cavisto. "That might explain your references to clear mountain streams." He looked for a moment like he did not know what to say next. Then, he said, "It must be wonderful, for both of you."

"Yeah, but, what d'you mean?" asked Razi. Azshbir said nothing.

"I mean, you actually know what the Promise means!" A light danced in Cavisto's eyes. "I am sorry that I have so long virtually ignored people from your class and station. If only I had learned sooner to ignore the ways in which most people think, I might have found brethren long ago. And learned from them, too. Do you talk about these things all the time?"

"Yes, more or less," said Azshbir. "What else is there to do? Complain? Whine? Get proud and sick? Razi and Anjis have taught me a lot, but I still need them to remind me to 'look to the Promise!'"

"There's another of you?" asked Cavisto. "Not surprising, when one comes to think of it. You guys should live with me and remind me! And, Razi, you really should go to all those people who think they believe in a Promise that isn't the real Promise, and tell them all about it! After all, you know far better than I do yet what it really means and is."

Razi looked stunned. He was only fourteen, and had been despised all his life. "I can't!" he exclaimed. "Dey wont 'ist'n t' 'ee. Dey'll throw 'ee 'n th' trash dum'!"

Azshbir jabbed Razi. "And, who cares if they do? Then, you can just stand on top of the trash pile and preach to them!" The idea appealed to him, and he burst into sputters of laughter, which soon proved contagious, as the others joined him.

"Anyway," said Cavisto, getting up, "why don't you take out what you have already done? That should do for a long time. Then, treat yourselves both to my bath tub, and to a pair of my clothes, even if you can't find any that fit. After that, if you get bored, why don't you clean my rooms a bit? If you get that far. I have to take care of business. You're brothers, so feel free to what I have. If you can't find a pair of clothes to fit, Razi, I will buy some for you before this day is over." He glanced around at the shadows. "However, I really do have to go and take care of some appointments and stuff." He got up and strode away. Then, he paused, as if he had forgotten something. Turning, he called out, "Look to the Promise!"

"Look to the Promise!" replied Azshbir and Razi. Then, Azshbir looked at Razi. "We catch on pretty quickly, don't we?"

Razi shrugged. "It's natural." Azshbir remembered the story of how it had started. Razi, who was only eleven then, had been showing Anjis how to slice through the jungle– Anjis had come from a respectable family, where he had learned how to do business and deal with numbers and interact with nobles– while Anjis told him about the Promise. When Anjis had sighed glumly and said, "I don't know how I'm ever going to manage this– why did this have to happen to me? My family kicks me out– here I am– really, I might as well be a slave, arrgghh!" or something of the sort– neither of them remembered exactly what Anjis had said– Razi replied, "Look t' th' Promise!" That had been the beginning of their little group.

Looking around the house, which was not by any means disgusting, Razi said,

"Anjis does better a' this dan you o' 'ee."

"I don't know where we would find Anjis this time of day," Azshbir replied. "Actually, Neah'ra would do better than us, too."

"What's she doin'?" asked Razi.

Azshbir did not answer. He could not think of anything more to do. They had cleaned the wood shavings out of Cavisto's work room, but left them in a pile outside, wondering if they might be used for something. It had been Azshbir's idea. Azshbir wondered where Cavisto's wife might be; he was almost certain that he had one. He suspected he probably had children– grown ones– and grandchildren, too, but could see no sign of them. He had, however found a pair of clothes left abandoned in a corner under several crates of strange carvings, that fit Razi okay. Well, they were a little small. But they fit.

Just then, Cavisto entered by the front door. "I see you found something to wear, Razi," he said.

Razi looked uncomfortable. He was not used to be treated this way. In fact, he had been uncomfortable the whole time. Uncomfortable bathing. Uncomfortable trying to clean a house the need to be cleaned of which he could not discern. Uncomfortable finding a pair of clothes. They had tried to be very careful to make sure that the bath tub was spotless after using it. Azshbir had felt uncomfortable, too. It had been kind of– no, very– weird. He had reasoned, though, that Cavisto would doubtless like them to be clean and not stinky when they were in his house, so he had gone ahead and taken the bath and found the clothes.

Cavisto strode further into the room, and looked at each of them in turn. "Come, let's sit down," he said. "Hopefully last night's stew is still good."

Last night's stew? thought Azshbir. Out loud, he asked, "Did your wife go somewhere? Is she, like, from a family from another part of Ephezoa and went to visit them?"

Cavisto looked over his shoulder with a sad look in his eyes. "Dinnessia died in childbirth twenty-three years ago."

That explains the lack of people in the house, thought Azshbir. "Did the child die with her?" he asked.

"No. Xalon is married and has two beautiful daughters of his own," Cavisto replied. He still sounded sad. "Here, haven't used these in ages," he said, pulling chairs out from under the table. Seeing Azshbir and Razi's reticence, he motioned to them. "Go ahead, sit down. I'll see if the stew is still good. If it isn't, I'll order bread." He crossed briskly to the other side of the room, and lifted the lid off a pot.

"We did not see much cleaning to do," Azshbir said. "There's lots of things, but we wouldn't know how you want them, though we did try to clean the floor of your wood-working room."

"That's fine," said Cavisto. "My problem is, I can't tell what's dirty or what to do with what, myself, and sometimes I have to treat people." He bent down to smell the stew. "I think it is fine," he said, then replaced the pot, lifted the lid, and carried it over.

Azshbir stood up. "Can I help? Like get the plates and utensils?" He still felt dizzy. Who was this man, what was he thinking, and why was he doing this?

Cavisto shook his head. "It's not necessary," he said. Azshbir walked with him as he went to get the plates and utensils anyways. In a low voice, though it did not matter if Razi heard, he asked, "Why are you doing this?"

Cavisto stopped, turned, and faced him. "Because *we* are all People of the Promise. You and Razi love each other as brothers? Well, so do I." He paused for a moment and swallowed, as if he might be about to cry. "You are in this situation because of the Promise. Though–" here his eyes glinted a little, "– I doubt not that you have learned more about the Promise through this, seeing Razi's wisdom, and yours in reply. I would like to see more of it. At present, though, I know that I must help you. I have the resources, at least for the present. And, our bond, as People of the Promise, is at least as important as the bond of fellow countrymen in a war to defend their land. We must be one, for we are at war." He looked down. "Kathreen, at least, reminded us that we must really care about the Promise... Times were so different, then." Cavisto turned, and continued towards the cupboard.

Azshbir felt dizzy. What was happening? First, rescuing– and marrying– Neah'ra. Then, Ellason's aid, which was amazing, shelter, and one good meal a day. Then, this, whatever this was going to turn out to be. He paused, below the cupboard, with two plates in his hand. "I need to go and get my wife," he said.

"Okay. Go, get her," said Cavisto. He watched Azshbir head to the door with mingled sorrow and gladness. If only his sons were like Azshbir. He wondered who was Azshbir's wife. Perhaps the daughter of Darnize Katalonga, who he'd heard had been kidnapped, or was that only a rumor? Still, he wondered who she was. What kind of girl was she? At that thought, another sadness washed over him. She was probably the kind of girl he would have liked as a daughter-in-law. Equally, regret that he had so long ignored the lowest classes, pulsed in his blood. It was not that he had done it intentionally. He had never noticed at all. He had never given it a moment's thought. However, he had missed out on knowing, loving, helping, learning from, and perhaps sharing knowledge with as well, who-knew-how-many people who saw more or less what he did, who believed in the Promise that most of Ephezoa did not even really know. Then again, he was happy. He had found them– or some of them– at last. He had been lonely for so long, and now he had found his friends and family. He still felt ashamed for not looking for them sooner, but actually despising them, as it were. Still, he was glad that he had found, or been found by, his people, People of the Promise, brethren– and, it seemed, sisters, too. He looked forward to meeting Azshbir's wife. He laid the plates down on the table, and tried to talk with Razi. What was his life like? How had he learned about the Promise? How had he met Azshbir? He did not know how to ask him all the questions he wanted to ask. What did he know? What could he share? Perhaps, these things might come out in the course of conversation. He felt awkward, too, almost even embarrassed. None of his class would do this. In fact, he would lose reputation if this become common knowledge, which was more than likely. It was awkward, too, talking to a lad like Razi, who could hardly speak one word right. Sometimes, he had a fair amount of difficulty even making out what he was trying to say.

#18
Game of Chances

Arendellie sat on the ground, clothed in royal purple, next to the couch upon which Prince Vanesh reclined. Something felt vaguely wrong. Maybe something had gone wrong at court, or in the war, she thought. Then, he asked her a question, and it made her heart skip a beat. "Why," he asked, his voice cold as ice and hard as stone, "have you been speaking with another man, a Sir Andelf, so much?"

It's been weeks since that day! thought Arendellie frantically. *I haven't talked with him around Alitholiel since that day! I haven't even spoken with– or seen– him in days! There must be another snitch or watcher.* Trying to sound calm and self-assured, as if nothing the matter had happened, she said, "Oh, it's just he who arranged for me to be brought to the palace and meet you, your royal and majestic highness, man of men, and I was wondering too how the people of Ebrin were faring, and a few affairs of the outside world."

"Why didn't you ask me?" Vanesh asked, his voice so cold, hard, and distant. It came to Arendellie that it might be the voice of a man who might order men or women to torture to achieve his ends or accomplish revenge with no more feeling – either of remorse or guilt or of anger, hatred, and fiendish delight – than that with which he selected an undergarment for the day.

"Because," said Arendellie, tilting her head and speaking sweetly, as only she knew how, "that would be to bother you with yet more concerns, and doubtless you have plenty of headaches thinking about court and world matters, and would not want your time alone with your wife intruded upon by yet more of such. Wouldn't it spoil me, if I brought such things up with you in our scant time together?" As she spoke, she rose to her feet, letting her thin veil fall slowly to the ground, and after it the cape she had wrapped around her. Then, with a small, subtle movement, she unhooked the thread that held the front of her dress together, and let it slip half off of her shoulders. The last line she said with a sweet, honeyed, almost sad voice, while standing above Vanesh Casarion, bending slightly to one side.

In her room the next morning, Arendellie sat looking out on the sun and the sky, trying to be stone. Frankly, she felt like crying. It had been horribly close the previous night. Of course, she felt that she ought to be pleased with herself. She had done splendidly. It had all worked out just fine. Still, she had no idea whom she could trust with anything. She felt lost and alone. Terribly alone. She tried to think though just how great for her this life was turning out to be. Soap baths twice a day. Soft, soft night and day gowns. Lovely silks. Power with, even over, a prince, *the* prince. Gardens to walk in. No other work than pleasing the prince. Hair soaps and shampoos. Skin oils. Every luxury. And the dash and skill and danger and adventure and energy and courage of the game. Why didn't she like it? After all, she was made for this position, and it for her.

Arendellie was thinking these thoughts to herself, when Inshara came in. She was alone, and carried a vase of the oils she often rubbed into Arendellie's skin, and sometimes into her hair. For some reason she felt like she could trust Inshara. Did that mean that Inshara was just that much more likely to be the snitch? She did not know. How terribly– no, no, she must *not* think that thought! Not ever. It didn't exist.

Inshara knelt down at her feet. "Lady," she said, speaking very quietly, "I don't know what to say."

Arendellie pretended she had not heard her. What should she even say to it, supposing she had? Besides, Inshara was her maid, and she was the princess. She did not have to answer Inshara, or even think about a single thing she told her, unless it had to do with pleasing, placating, and controlling Prince Vanesh Casarion.

Inshara was silent for a few moments, as if plucking up the courage to say something. "I believe that the Promise is real," she finally said, in a voice grave and quiet, but trembling, Arendellie, who still did not speak, thought. What did that have to do with anything?

When Inshara said no more, but just knelt there, she finally asked, "What does that have to do with anything? Many people believe that the Promise is real." Like Inshara, she spoke quietly.

Inshara looked up, brushing a few strands of hair that had escaped her bun back from her face. "Do they?" she asked, quieter than before. "Do you know what the Promise means, my Lady?"

Arendellie felt hopelessly confused. What was going on? What was Inshara after? What should she say? Was Inshara the snitch? What was this about? Well, it could probably do no harm giving the answer everyone knew. "The Creator will send Someone who will take on Himself the shame of His people, carry it away, destroy it, and conquer death," she answered.

Inshara looked up again, this time her eyes wet with tears. "I don't know about you," she said, very quietly, "but I can never give to anyone but the Creator and the King He has Promised my allegiance." Arendellie gasped. "I know He will come, and I look forward to the Day when the Promised One will triumph and reign over all things."

Arendellie bent down, so as to be closer to Inshara. In the softest whisper of all, she asked, "Do the others know?" and then straightened back up. She suddenly began to be worried that, if any of her other attendants should look in, they would see that things were not quite prim and proper. "Shall I take my gown off? Then you can rub the oil in," she said, rather louder.

"Certainly, Lady," replied Inshara in kind.

Arendellie could not decide whether or not she hoped Inshara would understand. She stood up, pulled her gown off her shoulders, stepped out of it, and lay down on the soft mat, softer than the bed she had had in Ebrin. Inshara opened the jar, and began rubbing the sweetly scented oils into her skin. In a whisper no louder than the breeze, she said, "Some of them do."

Arendellie did not respond. She was too busy processing. Which of them did?

Did Inshara know about the snitches? Were they watching her? Did they care about her? Who were they working for? What did they want? Was *Inshara* the snitch? If so, why would she arrange for Arendellie's relationship with Sir Andelf to get to the Prince? Was someone totally other the snitch? Perhaps someone watching not so much Arendellie as Sir Andelf? If only she could learn the answers to these questions, Arendellie thought, she might be able to understood the motives of those around her and predict and understand their movements. However, if she tried to hunt for the answers, she might give too much away to the wrong people. Even if she found answers, would she be able to trust them? What game was she supposed to play? Who was she supposed to be to whom? Then, with a deliberate force of will, *Oh, how I love this life!*

Inshara was speaking softly, again. "I don't know if any of the others are like me– unwilling to give any allegiance to another." A thought suddenly occurred to Arendellie, slicing through her mind like a dagger. *Does Inshara know what she is doing? Why is she doing it? Why does she trust me? She must realize that I could tell on her. Is she all safe, and is this just the game she is playing? To try to see where or what I am? Is she, after all, the snitch? What would anyone be looking for out of my responses? Or, does she mean it all? Is she like Kathreen Alarion? Is this a test? Am I supposed to report her? Am I not? What does it all mean? What is it all about?* These thoughts, and more like them, rushed through Arendellie's mind, while Inshara continued speaking, still scarcely louder than the night breeze. "I don't even think we're supposed to say we believe in the Promise at all, but I'm here and I do. When I let Girsa know– that was before you came– she wanted to know why I'm not willing to deny that I believe the Promise, and certainly, to give allegiance to Grale Casarion. I don't know how to put it. I guess I don't want to. The Promised One is King, not Grale. That's that." Inshara paused for a moment. Or had her voice just dropped so far that Arendellie could not hear it? Looking up and over her shoulder, she saw that it was not so. Inshara's lips were closed. Tears were in her eyes. One was falling down her cheek. Then she spoke again, and it sounded that she was on the verge of tears. "Lady, the Promise is everything."

Was that it? That was why Inshara was about to cry? Arendellie did not understand it at all. She decided to risk asking a question out of curiosity. "How so?"

It seemed to take Inshara a long time to decide how she wanted to articulate herself. Then, she said, as softly as ever, bending close to Arendellie's ear, as she rubbed the oils into her shoulders, "The Promise. We'll perish without the Promise. Dungeons of death. Shame. Punishment for our crimes. But the Promise. To have the very merits of the Conqueror. I'm not sure what it means, but it's everything. Far more than our whole world." Arendellie could not tell whether Inshara was nearly crying, barely crying, out of some sorrow she did not understand or out of happiness. "Of course, to be delivered from Death is everything already. But– to dwell in the presence of the King of all kings, the *Creator* of kings?" She paused for a moment, as if unable to speak, or perhaps to regain her composure, since her voice had been rising in volume. Arendellie wondered why she had to keep her voice down if she had already told the maids. Then, she had not told all of them. Maybe she was not supposed to be telling Arendellie. Maybe she was not the snitch. Then again, maybe she was, and this was all a ploy for convincing Arendellie that she was not. In Arendellie's world, anything could mean anything. She did not even know when someone was serious and when someone was merely probing. Maybe Vanesh had not even been upset. Maybe it was all a probe. How was she supposed to respond? She was not very good at this yet. With a good feeling, she thought that she would be. She *would* be. But Inshara was speaking again. "That is far greater, far more glorious, than to dwell constantly by the side of the Emperor himself. And, better still, the Creator and His Conqueror are *good*. They love us more than we can imagine– why else the Promise? But, the Emperor?" She left her answer unsaid, but Arendellie could easily guess *that*.

Inshara stopped talking and diligently applied herself to her work. Arendellie did enjoy having herself fused over and taken such great care of. Inshara began to hum a little, as she often did, while she massaged the oils into Arendellie's skin, now moving across her lower back, shoulders, and arms. After a while, Arendellie looked around, to make sure no one else was coming in, or had come in. Then, she asked, just loud enough she hoped Inshara would hear her over her humming, "Why did you tell me?"

Inshara stopped humming, and seemed to be taking a moment to form her response. Arendellie could tell by the movements of her hands. Then, she heard footsteps, and looked up to see one of the other maids standing in the doorway. "Would the Princess Arendellie like anything to drink? Or maybe some olive oil nut bread with oranges?" she asked.

Arendellie lifted herself up off the mat by her elbows. "Some juice," she said. "I'll eat in half an hour or so. I don't really feel like it just this moment. Inshara can finish this stage first." Then, she dropped back down on the mat. The maid motioned to another maid in the hall, relaying Arendellie's requests, and then came in. She sat down on the other side of Arendellie, and began to help with the massage. Arendellie could not help but feel a sense of disappointment.

No one could have made anything of her lack of further conversation– except Inshara. She was almost never very talkative, except to occasionally point out something she liked, make requests, command, or scold for tasks badly done or timed. It meant she was in a very good mood if she talked to her maids at all except to ask or scold. Except, she realized, with Inshara, whom she, for some reason, seemed to trust a little. Perhaps she had better stop that. Inshara could be the bad snitch, and her weakness. Maybe it was Inshara. It would make sense, then, how it was known that the man was Sir Andelf, and that she had been talking to him more than once, and somewhat recently. She had dropped one word– *one* word– about it to Inshara, since the day she had asked her if she knew Sir Andelf. Speaking of which, would Sir Andelf say he believed in the Promise? Did he give his allegiance to Emperor Grale Casarion? The answer to the second question was almost positively truly certainly *yes*. The answer to the first question might conceivably, just barely, be *yes*. But then, Arendellie could be wrong about so many things.

Perhaps, if she ever got the chance, she should ask. It would not mean anything; such a question could, itself, be a probe, like so much around her. Of course, Sir Andelf would know that, and it would somewhat diminish the value of his response, but only somewhat. It would still tell her *something*, however small, about what he was willing to say and do. Who he was.

#19
The Few

Razi, half-struggling while being handcuffed by two well-dressed police men, cast a fear-filled glance in Azshbir's direction.

Azshbir's eyes met Razi's, but he hardly knew what to offer. *This is Ephezoa?* Well, Kathreen *had* told him, years ago, now, that she did not know what they might or might not do in Ephezoa. As his own thoughts turned to Neah'ra's swelling abdomen and the child growing within, he nonetheless called to Razi, "Look to the Promise!" It was all the encouragement or strength he had to offer, and he knew that those four words would mean far more to Razi than either an eloquent discourse of fourteen thousand words, or a brotherly embrace.

One of the police officers slapped Azshbir across the face. "You're not supposed to be talking to each other! Criminals."

Still reeling from the shock of the whole situation, Azshbir asked, "Why are you arresting us? With what crimes are we being charged?"

The man slapped Azshbir again, out of pure spite and hatred he thought. Turning to a younger man, in fact, a mere boy scarcely older than Razi, he commanded in a hard, clanging voice. "Read the charges."

In a weak, trembling voice, stumbling over the words he was reading, the boy read, "Treasonous thoughts. Unpatriotic intentions. Subverting the people."

Azshbir felt like he had been hit with a load of beams. That? What kind of crimes were those? They had only been talking and preaching about which loyalties came first. They had not even advised people not to participate in the war effort. At least he had not. He did not know about Razi. Still, if Ephezoa was charging and convicting on such crimes, Azshbir could not see what defense they might possibly have. He looked over his shoulder to Razi again, as they were now being pushed down the street. He wanted to say a million things. He knew, though, that even if he could have known how to say them, he could not possibly have the time. "Look to the Promise!" he said, earnestly but not loudly.

His captor yanked him, so that he stumbled. He still heard Razi call back, "Look t' th' Promise!" Tears pushed at the back of his eyeballs. *Oh, Neah'ra...*

As they were marched down the streets, everyone stopped to look at them– a well-dressed, strong young man, and a boy who still looked like he had lived much of his life in the slums. What was more, Azshbir was pretty certain that many of the people knew, or at least guessed, who they were. This was especially easy, since a small crowd was following them from the Hall of Exhortation, most of them talking the whole time, especially to gawkers they came across. Azshbir caught bits and pieces of their words. "They're the traitors. They want Hasseleighton to win the war... Cripple Ephezoa's war effort... Don't they talk about the Promise?... No, they're from Hasseleighton..." Then, amidst all the slander and nonsense that, frankly, made Azshbir's head hurt, and made him want to put all the liars on the ground and shout the truth in their faces– he could even feel the blood coming to his head and making his face hot– he heard a female voice say, "Yes, 'Look to the

Promise' is a fitting rallying cry they chose." For a moment Azshbir felt elated. At least people would hear the truth! Then, he felt like passing out. *Hopefully, they won't arrest her too, whoever she is.* What kind of a country was Ephezoa? He had not expected this. Now that it had happened, he had no idea what to expect next. He was still, however, not really all that scared for himself. As far as that went, the thrill of adventure ran in his blood, side by side with a hot, burning, anger at being so humiliated and paraded around like a catch of fish! As far as fear went, though, he was worried for Neah'ra. How would she handle it? She had already been through so much, and she was pregnant, too, now. Was it a mistake to have married her? No, he had to do so; otherwise her father would have taken her back. That was how the law worked, sensible or not. She would probably be fine; she had other men– and women– around her, who would take care of her, comfort her, and encourage her. *"Look to the Promise!"* But, what if they got into trouble, too? What if Cavisto lost his business? Azshbir knew that his earnings and his work were already going down, as someone had seen him, or at least said they had seen him, in the quarter of the city that carried on the illegal prostitution business; several former prostitutes, along with the children of one more, were living in his house. It was a drain on their resources. What would happen to them all, now? Now that Ephezoa was actively persecuting them. Even if Cavisto was not arrested, would he lose all business? What about the women, most of them Neah'ra's friends– Ellason, Sanahi, Rumia, Warlisse? Amria would probably be fine; she was still a young girl in her parent's protection. As long as they did not turn out like Darnize, and maybe even do more terrible things to her than he had done to Neah'ra. Azshbir was so tormented by these thoughts that he almost felt like passing out.

Finally, they were hustled into a dark little building, where their handcuffs were taken off, and the door clanged shut behind them. Both of them collapsed on the ground, still stunned by the recent course of events.

When he could think again, Azshbir wondered why they had bothered to try to keep him and Razi from talking to each other earlier; were they just cruel? *Neah'ra had better not end up in their hands,* he thought with anguish. He did not know what he wanted to tell Razi, anyways. He wondered if Neah'ra already knew what had happened to him. It had certainly made a large enough scene that she *would* know, sooner or later. He wondered if he would have any legal representation; was Ephezoa still a semi-reasonable place to live, or in their zeal for themselves, for their own country and rights, had they become scarcely less horrendous than Hasseleighton themselves? Less and less did anyone but the few care for the Promise; more and more did they care only about the fact that they were *not* Hasseleighton. Oh, the cruelty of it! The tremendous madness of it! How like Hasseleighton were they? Certainly, they were as much about being Ephezoan as Grale was about making sure everyone was Hasseleighton– his. How far would Ephezoa act? Would they, too, demand an oath of unmitigated allegiance, next? Would they torture their prisoners? *Oh, Neah'ra, I hope you are safe. And stay safe. I hope you are well. If only I had told you all about how to find the refuge from whence I come, deep in the Vinibra Mountains.* Thinking about these things, he broke down and cried. He felt only a sharp sliver of personal fear, and it did not matter to him at all.

After crying for hours, it occurred to Azshbir that he had forgotten about Razi. He sat up, and tried to calm himself. He noticed that Razi was sitting coldly in a corner. "What're we goin' t' do now?" he asked.

"Do?" Azshbir scoffed. "I don't see what we can–" Then he caught himself. "Look to the Promise." He spoke the words so dryly. Did he believe them at all? He certainly did not feel like he did. *If I can't look to the Promise and find comfort and strength, how will Neah'ra?* he wondered, even more miserably.

"Yuh, look t' th' Promise," responded Razi. Azshbir could make nothing of his emotions or what he was thinking or going through. It was definitely something, but he just could not tell what it was.

After several more hours in the dark, too miserable to think of what to say or how to encourage one another, the guards brought them some food and water, which they ate. Afterwards, Razi withdrew to himself. He sat in a corner, with his head in his hands. Whether he was moaning and mourning his situation, or contemplating something and thinking, Azshbir could not tell. He seemed calm enough, but Azshbir knew that he, too, was calm, both exteriorly and, in a way, interiorly. It was, though, the calm of dryness, of excessive emotion expended, and of more reason. He was no less anxious and disturbed. He did not ask Razi what he was thinking.

Finally, he dozed off. The rough stone floor bothered him a little through the night, but not much. He was used to sleeping on uncomfortable surfaces.

In the morning, he was wakened by guards, who were taking them to go their waste. The place was rather disgusting, but it did not unnerve Azshbir that badly. He had grown somewhat accustomed to that kind of thing, in his work with Anjis and Razi. After that, they were given breakfast and water. He and Razi found that neither of them wanted to eat. Finally, Razi spoke again. "What's goin' on, Azbir?" he asked. He had never learned to pronounce Azshbir's name properly. Not that either of them had ever cared, and still less now.

"I don't know," Azshbir said, despondently. "I hope my wife is well. I also hope we are released, as improbable as it seems." He was silent for a few moments, then said, "I don't know what to think."

Razi had only one insight to offer. "I wonder, what 'e Promise means fo' us, i' this?"

The comment provoked a smile from Azshbir, despite his deep-rooted glumness. "You have gotten so used to looking for the Promise in everything and everywhere, all the time?" he asked.

"Yuh," replied Razi. "It's th' joy of life. T' look t' th' Promise."

Of course, thought Azshbir, *we both failed yesterday, in our fits of terror and grief.* He still felt very gloomy and depressed.

They did not have time to continue their conversation. Not half a minute later, the guards came, handcuffed them both– how Azshbir *hated* having his arms tied behind his back and being pushed around! Razi, however, they had to grab out of the corner, though he struggled far less than he had the first time. Then, they brought them into a large, well-furnished room, with many people all around. *Court. Trial,* observed Azshbir. He wished he were Anjis. Or Cavisto. At least they would know Ephezoan law. He did not.

Then, Azshbir saw Neah'ra. Her abdomen was growing with each passing day. He thought the bulge was shaped a little differently that it had been. She looked like she had been crying all night and had slept none of it, and yet she had such great composure and such an air of calm readiness about her. She was wearing a simple dress of yellow linen, and her hair was bound behind her head in a loose bun. When their eyes met, he saw such great strength in hers, and he wondered from whence it came. Then, he remembered that she, young and still immature as she was, had been through things that were, at any rate, worse than what he had, in some respects. He felt ashamed. She moved her lips, and he knew what she was mouthing, more by knowing her than by being a good lip-reader. *"Look to the Promise, my love."* Standing with her he saw several of the People of the Promise– the few. He wondered how many more groups of them, small and half-hidden, there were in Afteloan. He thought that, perhaps, they were uniting, for he saw several unfamiliar faces with Neah'ra.

He and Razi were marched through the hall, to stand before the judge. At the side of the table stood Cavisto. Azshbir's handcuffs were released. He felt strange. He had no idea what the procedure for these things would be. Then, the judge addressed his words to Razi, "Will you promise not to fight or struggle about anything, including being handcuffed again, but not excluding anything else, if we release your handcuffs?"

Razi shook his head, as if he did not trust himself to speak. Azshbir wondered why. Why would he not just do it? What was so hard about it?

"Very well; you shall suffer the consequence of your folly," said the judge. Razi swallowed, as if about to speak, but the judge turned to Azshbir. "Sir Cavisto Argaddonn has offered to represent you– both– as a lawyer. On the table are two sheets of paper for you to sign your names on to agree for him to represent you. Razi, if you wish to sign your name, you must promise not to resist so that we can release your handcuffs."

"I 'ouldn't sign 'ee name anyways," said Razi.

Azshbir took the pen offered him, quickly scanned the document, and signed his name. He trusted Cavisto, and he did not know law. He was grateful for the support of the few, some– many, perhaps– of whose existence and resolution he had been unaware of until this day. It greatly encouraged him that they were all together, for the Promise, that there were more of them than he had known, and who knew how many more people the Creator claimed, whom Azshbir did not yet know, and yet who still, in one way or another, stood with him, for the Promise, looking to the Promise. They were the few, yet they were many more than he had known. He shared a smile of gratitude and fellowship with Cavisto (what bothered him a little was that, by representing him, Cavisto would likely lose his livelihood, and with it his ability to care for the many, though few, believers in the Promise).

He tried to catch Razi's eye, out of the corner of his own, wondering at his stubbornness. Why? What good would it possibly do? Was there any good purpose in it, or only the stubbornness and pride with which Azshbir also struggled? However, Razi's reasons he would never know, for they would hardly more than glance at each other again, while life in Kaarathlon lasted. All this he thought in a mere few short moments. Then the trial began.

#20
Hasseleighton and Execution

"Razi, you are–" the judge began.

"May I represent Azshbir first?" Cavisto interjected.

"No, and you will lose the right to represent him unless you are respectful for the duration of Razi's trial," said the judge. Again, he said, "Razi, you were charged with treasonous thoughts, unpatriotic intentions, and subverting the people. We sent out men to arrest you with the purpose of examining you to see whether or not you are a threat. You have further complicated your case and brought the law upon your head by resisting officers of the law and unexcused stubbornness. Do you have anything to say for yourself?"

Listening to the judge's voice, Azshbir shivered a little. He did not know all that he was feeling or wanted. He took a step to the side and back.

Razi looked up. He spoke, if possible, more clearly than usual. "I don't understand th' 'arges. 'Ee 'eople's th' 'Eople of th' Promise. What's th' prob'm?"

"You have been subverting the people, have you not? Or do you deny telling the people that they should not have to do with the war to protect our beloved country from Hasseleighton, but that instead they should extend love to the people of Hasseleighton, and tell them the Promise? I believe we have your words here: 'You shouldn't kill or help kill them men of Hasseleighton. They need Promise like you do. They and you all are enemies to the good Creator. The Promise is– you can all live with the Creator in His home! Be People of the Promise only! Ephezoa won't last and isn't real good. Be People of the Promise! The Cre'tor good! The Promise good! Why you want to kill? Like you, Hasseleighton People deserve death and shame! Like you, Hasseleighton People can be forgiven! That the Promise! Good! Listen! You need listen!' Do you, then, deny any or all of these statements?"

Hearing the judge read, Azshbir thought that he could remember Razi crying out those words– and more– from the street side, shortly before their arrest. How many other times he had said those things, he could not remember. For himself, Azshbir tried not to say things that he knew would be more than likely to get him into trouble, even prison, that he did not need to say or in ways he did not need to say. However, he did not bother Razi. For one thing, the uneducated street kid would have been very unlikely to understand the problem at all, still less how to speak around it.

Razi answered. "Na."

"Then, you admit to having thoughts of treason, not desiring the welfare of your country, but being willing to do that which would work against it? Then, you admit to being most unpatriotic, caring nothing for the country in which and from which you were born, or anything pertaining to it, but belonging instead to another nation? Then, you admit to worse, namely, subverting other citizens, encouraging them to forsake their loyalty and duties and loves as citizens of Ephezoa, committing a crime of gross proportions?"

"Yuh," said Razi. "For th' Promise." Azshbir felt mad with indignation at this great injustice. He could feel the blood coming to his head again. It was so unjust! Razi was so unprepared and vulnerable. He probably did not even understand half the words the judge was using, let alone how to explain the nuances of that which is neither a yes nor a no, even if he had known to give such an answer. It was so cruel! Razi could have been accused of almost anything, and convicted! He wanted to leap in and put things right, but he knew that he could not. Looking at Cavisto, he could see that the man was even more upset than himself. His jaw was working, but he did not seem to know what to say or do. One more moment, and Azshbir thought he would have exploded with some kind of something!

Then, the judge spoke with a ringing voice. "Razi admits to the charges of treasonous thoughts, unpatriotic intentions, and subverting the people. We have no need of trying him for impudence and excessive stubbornness, as his refusal to agree to cooperate without handcuffs is ample proof of the afore stated. As for resisting officers of the law, will testimony please come forward?"

"Wait!" said Cavisto, unable to bear himself any longer, "he–"

The judge turned a cold state on him. "Do not interrupt again, or you forfeit your right to represent Azshbir." With that, seven uniformed officers of the law and three others, two women and one men, came forward, and gave their witness. Azshbir's heart raced and thumped a hundred miles a minute. He felt like he was the one being tried. The blood pumped in his head so hard that he could barely think. What was he afraid of? What would the sentence be?

"On conviction of the afore mentioned charges," said the judge, once more in a ringing voice, "I sentence Razi to execution!"

Razi looked at Azshbir, and quietly whispered, "What's dat 'ean?"

"It means they're going to kill you," replied Azshbir. He could barely say the words. Barely tell Razi. He had no idea what Razi was thinking or feeling, so overwhelmed was he already. He could hardly see. The world was spinning around him, dark and black. He was reeling from one shock and evil following fast upon another. He heard Razi say, "For the Promise," again, but it sounded impossibly distant and far. He wanted to wail and collapse on the ground. He did not know whether Razi's words were a question, a statement, an exclamation, or a rallying cry, much like 'Look to the Promise.' He hardly noticed, for a moment, when Razi was being led away. Was he to go to his death right now? Or in hours? Days? Months? Years? Would he ever see him again? Sadness overwhelmed him. Why was this happening? What was going on? How could this be happening? It felt unreal. Like a horrific nightmare from which he might– rather, *must*– wake any moment. Yet, he knew it was real. Razi was dying! DYING because of the Promise! Ephezoa was another little Hasseleighton. They might as well stop fighting Hasseleighton at once, since in the process of fighting Hasseleighton they had already become Hasseleighton. Other questions pounded through his head. How would Razi die? Would he be executed as well? How would Neah'ra fare? Would he be tortured? Would any of the People of the Promise, of the true few, who were here and known, be tried and imprisoned, as well?

The cry of the few broke him from his maddening, tormenting thoughts. "For the Promise!" they cried. "Look to the Promise, brother!" Their voices shook and fell with tears. Azshbir thought he heard weeping. Razi did not answer back, Azshbir would not know why, or if he did Azshbir could not hear him. He did not pass out, but as regarded his ability to relate to the rest of the world, he might as well have. At least for the moment.

Azshbir remembered little of his own trial. For one thing, he was not nearly as involved in it as Razi had been in his, because Cavisto was representing him, laying out laws, explaining laws, arguing. Over and over in his head ran the anguished thought that Razi was going to be executed– EXECUTED– only because he could not properly defend himself. Because the trial was totally unfair. As Cavisto argued, he realized that it had broken at least four or five different statutes. However, Razi was as helpless as ever. He could not appeal. Could not defend himself. He was going to die. *DIE!* And die helpless and innocent. Die like… like… like a… like a lamb. It made Azshbir want to scream and rant and rave. Then, he found himself wondering what Razi would have said about it. Razi had been so interested in what the Promise meant in and through this awful situation. If Azshbir knew Razi at all, he was no less interested in it now. He could almost imagine Razi saying that all these horrible things were not so bad, since he got to see new meanings and applications of the Promise in them. He wondered if Razi saw any now. If he did, how desperately he wanted to know them too! But he would never get to speak to Razi again. Razi was his best friend! The only person Azshbir might have wanted to lose less than Razi was Neah'ra.

He felt like he had lost everything. He had lost the incomparable treasure of all the insights Razi would have had through years of life– he was only fourteen and a half. He would not even know Razi's last insight, whatever would make this injustice and cruelty, this death, bearable and maybe, just maybe, happy (he remembered Cavisto saying that he could almost be jealous of him and Razi, for all the things they got to know more deeply by their experiences).

Azshbir was so busy with these thoughts that he remembered very little of his trial, though he did speak a couple times. He did remember his dreadful sentence: life imprisonment. It made him reel again. Never love Neah'ra again? Her have to live without him? Oh, the cruelty, the injustice, the evil of it all! And why? What had he ever done? Though, Kathreen had warned him, and he had chosen to go out, fully willing to die, even to be tortured to death. But, then, he had not been a husband then, or a father. That changed everything. He wept. Loudly. Bitterly. Not caring for what people saw or thought. It was too much.

Being led out of the hall– like an ox, he thought– he saw Neah'ra's dress and bulging abdomen out of the corner of his tear blurry eye. He wanted to hold her in his arms and embrace her, if only one last time, whisper comfort and strength. Unable to do so, he dared not even look into her eyes. He felt that to do so would be a surpassing torture. He only hoped she would understand, and was confident that she would. At least to some degree.

It was all lost. Would all the People of the Promise– the true few– share his fate? Was Cavisto going to lose his livelihood, and his ability to provide for Neah'ra and, of less prominence in Azshbir's mind but still important, the ex-prostitutes and their children? Better to have let Azshbir be executed, too, and still be able to provide for the others! Life imprisonment was not much better than execution. Not enough to warrant losing so much to gain it over execution. Maybe execution was even better. The torment and loneliness of such a life would be horrible. It already tasted bitter on his tongue. In a sense, he was already executed. The rest of his life was a useless waste. It would not be life at all. Unable to do anything but lay in a cell and rot, if he was not tortured, how could life be better than death?

In the back of his mind, Azshbir had the feeling that this kind of thing had happened too many times before; that there was something he was missing. However, he ignored it, whether out of misery or weakness or whatever else. He had had the feeling for a long time, actually, particularly when he was thinking about Razi's insights, and about Cavisto's comment about jealousy, and how he had even ended up in that situation, a kind of prompting to remember something. However, he fought it, clinging to his thoughts of misery, despair, and self-pity. Maybe, he thought, a life sentence would not be quite so bad. He was in so much emotional torment already he thought he would probably die long before he was an old man.

I wish I had gone with them into the heart of that Wizard-Dragon Keeper Casarion's territory. Then, I would have gotten to die, without leaving so much, so much pain, behind me.

Immediately, it was as if a voice spoke into his head, *"You're an idiot."* If he had done that, Neah'ra would never have learned and seen what she already knew and saw enough to want. Against his protests that she would have suffered and suffer less, his own thoughts, about insights into the Promise being better than the evils which brought them about, were thrown back at him. If all of this had not happened, the few People of the Promise, would not have known each other, would not have been brought together, would not have been given much encouragement, comfort, and strength, in the knowledge of each other, and of each other's insights into the reality of the Promise. Was that not good?

Still, I want to die. All that good would be the same, if I were executed like Razi. Or, if we were both freed.

Again, Azshbir's thoughts failed. He had not expected good to come out of what had before; what would he know about it here? He had seen and known good where he would have expected no good; why did he not learn from it, to look for good everywhere? As Razi– and all of them– had said countless times, to 'Look to the Promise.' Would he, even now, look to the Promise, and see that good, which he knew was there, if only he would look, and was real even if he did not, as all the things that Razi and he and Anjis learned about the Promise in their humiliations and difficulties, if they even called them that, would still be true and real, even if neither Razi nor he nor Anjis nor any other human being realized them?

#21
Unpredictable, Really

Arendellie leaned against Vanesh Casarion's chest, his arms around her, the green of her veil beautifully matching and enfolded in the purple of his robes. "So," she asked sweetly, "what has been happening? It has been a longer while than usual." They were reclining on a divan in Vanesh's tower, looking out on the beginning of the dawn, behind the mountains and over the sea.

"There's been a lot going on," said Vanesh, quietly, as if caught up in his own thoughts. "My uncle, King Grale Casarion, is totally furious."

"Oh," said Arendellie, trying to suppress a tremor that arose in her chest. "What about?" she asked in a voice even softer than Vanesh's.

"The People of the Promise," said Vanesh Casarion, quietly.

"What about them?" asked Arendellie. "Is Kathreen Alarion part of it again?"

She could feel the tension in Prince Vanesh's muscles. It took him a moment to reply. "We don't really know whether or not Kathreen has anything to do with it or not. I do know that Grale Casarion is so mad that he started sprouting flames, and he could not control them. We had to ask the Lady Assea, as quickly as possible, to come and put out the flames. So, that kept me busy for a while. And, then Grale Casarion left with Regaleath, so taking care of affairs took more time…" Vanesh spoke as if these things wearied and bored him exceedingly.

Arendellie sighed for him. "Very tiresome, I understand. Perhaps, you would rather not talk to me about it, lest our time together be spoiled by reminders of such tiresome and dreary affairs?"

"No, no, that's very well," said Vanesh, kissing her. "It is refreshing to me to talk to you. What were you going to ask about?"

"What the People of the Promise did to so infuriate the king," said Arendellie, giggling a little.

"Oh!" said Vanesh, giggling with her. "That! We're not very clear on how it happened, but apparently one of our officers– and a great one, at that, too– has taken to telling everyone around him about the Promise!" Here, he became deadly serious, and Arendellie even detected a cold but burning hatred in his voice. "Of course, we tolerate some degree of devotion to the Creator and His Promise, certainly in our dominions, and every now and then in someone close to the court, though we despise it, since it smells of the threat of treason and insurrection. If this officer worshiped the Creator and looked expectantly to the Promise– worship of the Creator is much more tolerable than waiting for the Promise– it would be… well… just barely tolerable. However, he isn't! He's spoken to everyone around him about the need to worship the Creator alone and obey Him first and foremost, and about the Promise, something about being delivered from the shame of our treason– to whom, I may ask– and from death, by someone– I can't tell whether a god or a man– who will be the Conqueror and King of all things. I hear," Vanesh went on, dropping his voice to the barest whisper, "that his entire battalion has accepted this abominable treason."

Arendellie was quiet for a few moments. She understood why private worship of the Creator was okay, but looking to the Promise was not. She had known Kathreen and Mirla too well, never mind that she had been taught all these things before the world was shattered and people were forced to make decisions that should never have to be made at all. What could private worship of the Creator possibly effect? Grale Casarion was not the god of gods, so it was okay to worship the Creator. However, to hold up the Promise was blatant treason. It was declaring that there was coming a Conqueror who would overthrow all kingdoms that stood against Him and take every throne for Himself, who would overthrow Camil Hasseleighton and rule. Moreover, it was not only declaring that one believed this would happen, but that one looked forward to the coming of this Conqueror, and had staked all one's hopes on Him. One's allegiance was to another kingdom, and an enemy kingdom, entirely. She waited for a few moments and then said, "If you're interested, I can tell you more about what these People of the Promise believe."

"Only in so far as it affects our governance of our empire," said Vanesh. "But, as far as it affects that, I would like to know everything." He dropped his voice again. "I take it you know these things from your association with Kathreen Alarion."

"And others," said Arendellie. "In Avanzar, these things are common knowledge."

"Okay," said Vanesh. "What?"

Arendellie thought for a moment, thinking how to word what she was about to say carefully. "I do not in any way endorse these beliefs, and I despise those who zealously hold to them. There are some sects of People of the Promise who believe that the conquest and reign of the Promised One is spiritual and metaphorical. As for the others, like Kathreen Alarion, I believe that their allegiance to the Conqueror will not result in open defiance of the laws of the land, unless those laws forbid that allegiance." She paused for a moment, and then went forward, carefully. "If I may offer any advice on how to deal with this disease, I would say that we should openly encourage a belief in a spiritual and metaphorical conquest that will disinherit no one of their kingdoms and thrones. It may help to curb this belief in a real and material conquest. I don't know what exactly to do about this later, except that I believe that it is actually aided by the threats that these people perceive as made against them. In our village of Ebrin, the only reason Kathreen Alarion decided that her whole life belonged to the Creator to spread His Promise and His Warning is because she feared she would be tortured and killed if she did not swear complete allegiance to Grale Casarion, and this made her think about what she really believed and what really mattered in ways in which she would not have, otherwise. Given the rise of serious belief in the Promise and the Conquerer that we have noted, I believe that much the same thing has happened with many others. What to do about it now, at this point in time, I have no idea, but we might want to bear that in mind." As she finished speaking, Arendellie relaxed a little, hoping that she had not just landed herself in dreadful trouble.

"Are you keeping up with events and the way things are going? How?" asked Vanesh.

Arendellie sucked in her breath. Was the prince simply curious, as she was his wife, or had she done something, given something away? Was it wrong for her to know these things? She took a deep breath, trying to calm herself. This dash and adventure was what she loved! "A little," she said. "Usually, I ask my maids." It was not quite true. More often, she leaned over the garden wall and asked people, for the most part, Sir Andelf.

"Ah," he said. "The dawn is beautiful."

"It really is," said Arendellie, twisting around and looking out the window. The city spread away below them, still in blue-gray shadow, here and there a glancing finger of reddish light. High above them, the bare rock and snow peak of the mountain gleamed in the red light of dawn. She smiled.

Vanesh spoke again. "What you say about the People of the Promise makes a great deal of sense." He sighed. "I do not think the king will be able to see it though. Perhaps, with a great deal of work, he might realize that there is some sense in it. Still, we tried that in Sephar."

"How did it go?" asked Arendellie.

"Well, we thought it was working beautifully. Kathreen Alarion went over there and made a scene in the Elgarasz' Diner, and a few other people, two of them native Sepharians, made similar scenes. Similar, I say. Only your friend, Kathreen, lost her temper and started yelling at the patrons and the lady both! Something about how only the Creator is king and He alone should be honored and obeyed. To be frank, I'm not sure why Kathreen was not so embarrassed of such a display as to never show her face again. Instead, she had the audacity to go to Ephezoa and be honored as a heroine! Eventually, she gave that up, too, and more or less disappeared for a good year or so. Nothing really seemed to come of these episodes, though, until recently. That is, we thought nothing had come of them."

"Yes," said Arendellie, "I had heard there is some kind of resistance in Sephar."

"There is," said Vanesh. "Some people attack our men and wreck havoc. Others are gathering to study the Prophecies and the Promise. They speak to people in corners, but they adamantly refuse to call Grale Casarion their king. They avoid coming to the rallies in honor of Grale Casarion and they stay away from places where the oath of allegiance is remembered."

"Yes," said Arendellie. "This went more or less unnoticed until the mayor of Zunazra joined them. He aroused some suspicion by not coming to events he used to frequent, but people assumed he was just really busy. When he missed one that is obligatory for the mayor, it made a big splash and he was told he had to not miss obligatory feasts and rallies anymore. He came the next time, and proclaimed that he can give his allegiance only to the Creator and to the Conqueror Who will come. He was warned what the consequences would be, but refused to recant and renew his oath. He was put in prison. This episode has drawn attention to the fact that there are many more than we knew in Sephar. Many of these People of the Promise deny killing or robbing anyone, but there appears to be a connection between the

People of the Promise and the violent underground resistance."

Vanesh smiled. "You have been following the happenings!" he said.

"I have," said Arendellie. With abrupt suddenness, she thought, *I have no idea why and for what I am even here!* Then she remembered, *Do not think that way!*

"As for whether or not Kathreen is involved, it is hard to tell. We can't be sure of everywhere she and that friend of hers, Adaria, go. We can guess, but it's hard to be certain. Speaking of Kathreen, we suspect she still visits her friend in Ebrin from time to time, so we are going to try and take Ebrin." He grabbed her hand and squeezed it lightly. "For you, my princess."

Arendellie smiled. "Thanks," she said. *That would be good,* she thought. *I have not seen my parents in a long time. I wouldn't want them to worry about me.* "Anyway," she asked, "why is Kathreen so important? Aren't there many more who are causing trouble, like whoever told that officer?"

"Yes," said Vanesh, "but many times we can not find them. We have no idea who or what convinced him to act so foolishly. Certainly, it is creating a bigger splash than anything Kathreen has done, but we're taking care of what we can see. There are others out there like that, whom we have killed. There are even others who live and constantly evade us. Others who are totally infuriating." As Vanesh spoke, Arendellie found herself growing tenser and tenser. "However, Kathreen is the only wizard, one of the only Dragon-riders, and one of the younger ones among them. That makes her... a problem. She's rather more known, too, after her little stints in fame and popularity in Ephezoa. She's also unpredictable. Why does she go for fame one day, and vanish into obscurity the next? She's... unpredictable, totally." Then, he noticed. "Arendellie, what's wrong?"

Later, Arendellie wondered why she said what she did next. It gave away too much, too much of who she was. It was dangerous, in a world where nobody could be trusted and nothing known, a world of such uncertainty, danger, adventure, and thrill. Maybe, it was because she was here to be Vanesh's princess, and so it should be safe... enough. "Kathreen is my friend," she said very quietly and softly, her face turned away.

Vanesh touched her with a tenderness that was more personal and tender than she had yet felt by his hand. It reminded her of Neshekh and made her want to cry. Where was he now? Was he okay? Was he one of the others... and, if so, of the others who constantly evaded and infuriated the Hasseleighton royalty, or of the others whom they had executed... maybe were torturing right now? She had no idea why she was feeling the things that she was right now. Vanesh spoke, very quietly and softly, "And you are worried about her?"

"Yes, yes, actually, I am," said Arendellie. She buried her head in the folds of Vanesh's robe and began to sob. Later, she wondered why she had broken down and cried, and both hated herself for it and felt embarrassed about it. Maybe it had something to do with the conversations Inshara had been having with her, upon occasion. Inshara was personal and tender with her.

Vanesh held her tightly. For himself, he did not know why he was acting the way he was, either. He had never cared for another or felt about another the way he did for and about Arendellie now. Wanting to comfort her, he lied, but without thinking about it. He was only wanting to comfort her. "It's okay, Arendellie," he said. "I'm sure Kathreen will take care of herself, and not act too rashly or foolishly. I think, too, that we will be able to prevent her from coming to any real harm if she comes into our hands."

Arendellie relaxed a little, but she knew Vanesh was lying. If Grale Casarion was anything like she had heard he was… if the rest of the Hasseleighton governing bodies were anything she and all Camil knew them to be… then it was not likely that any of the People of the Promise, let alone one as famous and hated as Kathreen, would find mercy at their hands.

#22
The Insult and the Disturbance

Arendellie stretched herself out on a soft mat near the bath. She let her body relax into it and sobbed.

Aki'lam bent down, and gently touched her shoulder. Quickly turning away, she left, and Arendellie heard her muttering to the other servants. *That dratted servant!* she thought. *It's been more than a year, and she's still, well, I don't know. I should get her replaced.*

Girsa came in. "Princess," she asked, speaking softly, "how are you? What do you need? Fresh clothes? Cosmetics? Would you like some cherry apple juice? Maybe some lolo pie?"

Arendellie raised herself up on her elbows. "You know nothing," she growled. "Get me Inshara. And, then, make sure everyone else leaves." Instantly, she wondered why she wanted Inshara. Inshara was the cause of half the problem.

"Yes?" the oldest of Arendellie's maids asked, coming into the room. "You wanted me?"

"Yes," said Arendellie. "I like the way you rub the oil into my skin, and you do an even better job when it's just you and there's no one else around."

Looking over her shoulder, Arendellie saw that Inshara was smiling, as if pleased with her flattery, but she saw tears gleaming in the older woman's eyes. Quickly, Inshara fetched the jar, then pulled Arendellie's robe half off. Speaking very softly, she said, "So, why did you really ask for me?"

"I wanted to ask you why you told me about the Promise and your allegiance," Arendellie whispered, her voice melding with the breeze, but still barely perceptible to Inshara.

Inshara began to massage the oil into Arendellie's shoulder. She took a moment to reply. She had not thought that Arendellie was the sort of person who would remember such a conversation. "That was a long time ago," she said.

"Yes," said Arendellie, her voice hard and drawn out, as if she was not at all pleased with Inshara's non-sequitur.

"Well," said Inshara, slowly, as if thinking, "the Promise comes with a command to share both it and the Warning." Her voice even more soft and quiet, and trembling, as if she were on the verge of tears, she said, "And, you need the Promise. You're lonely and lost."

Arendellie stiffened, and a shiver of fear shot through Inshara. Had she said something wrong? If she upset the princess, it could be the end of her. Arendellie could easily have her thrown into the dungeons and killed any way she chose, especially since she was one of the People of the Promise and would never deny it. She knew Arendellie was lonely and miserable. She knew, too, that Arendellie would never be able to commit horrors with her own hand, but she still did not trust the princess at all. Why had she ever sought this life in the first place? It had not been forced upon her. She could feel that Arendellie was making herself cold and hard, building a dark and icy wall around the hurt and loneliness that was devouring her heart.

Arendellie felt the tremor of fear that went through Inshara. *She's* probably *trustworthy,* she thought, *though, I guess, some people can fake fear like this.* She did not care to reassure Inshara though. It would not really matter, anyways. She was silent for a while. She could not think of what to say. Finally, she said, "I know you believe that. But you believe that about everyone, don't you?"

Inshara spoke as quietly as ever. "Yes, yes, I do. But you are special, Lady. And, you're especially lost and lonely." Arendellie could hear the tremor in her voice as she went on. "Lady, you're so sad you make me want to cry for you, often. I beg the Creator for you. Maybe… maybe, everyone else is as lost and lonely as you are, and the Creator sees them that way, and pities them all. But it's your lostness and loneliness that I feel, and so it's your lostness and loneliness that I pity, that hurts me, that draws my compassion." Her voice shook, and Arendellie thought she was terrified. For a few moments, she studiously rubbed the pre-bath oils into Arendellie's skin. Then, she paused, her fingers moving very softly, slowly, and rhythmically. "I love you, Lady. I really love you, so I want you to… be healed."

Arendellie tensed. *Healing?* she thought. *Healing? She offers me healing? The world healing? This crazy Promise is partially responsible for the fact that we are so shattered and broken. How can it possibly heal me?* She looked over her shoulder, and said, cold and hard, "I'm here to find what healing there is. I don't believe the Promise heals, and, at any rate, I don't want its healing."

She saw Inshara flinch, and she knew she was really scared. She put her finger to her lip, and whispered, "Sshh!" Then, continuing to massage Arendellie with the oil, she said, very quietly, "Arendellie, I love you. I know you don't want love, but I'm determined to love you. I'll die to love you, if it must come to that. I don't know why, but I do. And, you *need* the Promise– the Creator's love."

Arendellie tensed. *At least,* she thought, *this is an interesting diversion from what happened– I did– this morning.* After all, it was annoying and bothersome already. She did not know what to say or think. Inshara was being as clear as was possible. She had no idea what her actions would mean. She had even ventured to call the princess by her first name, Arendellie, speaking to her as an equal. She had implied that she was poor and miserable and in a state far below that of a slave, maybe even of a prisoner, Arendellie was not sure. Even if it was not about the hated Promise, it was bad enough that Arendellie could have anything done to her that she pleased. Furthermore, Inshara seemed to have no illusions about the potential consequences of her words. She was not pleading with Arendellie, either. Just telling her where she stood. Even the words about 'loving' her were an insult. It was an insult for a slave to claim to love her mistress in that manner; it was tantamount to claiming to be superior over your mistress.

While Arendellie lay, tense, thinking these things through, Inshara knelt down, continuing to massage her, silent, waiting. Arendellie could feel that she was still very tense, terrified even, uncertain what her frank, blunt, and unacceptable words might bring down upon her head, but she made no move to hasten any decision

Arendellie might make or her own knowledge thereof, or to change her position in the least. She just waited and served. Finally, Arendellie said quietly, "Why must you be what you are? Why must you be the only one of my maids who is so– well, I meant what I said when I called for you– and yet also so devoted to this Promise, this enemy to natural and proper human life and society?"

"Because–" Inshara began, when the voice of another maid interrupted. "Princess," she said, "there is a woman by the name of El-Reiza here, who wishes to speak with you. She says that she is an old friend, and that you will recognize her."

Inshara looked at Arendellie, who sat up and said, "Let her in, and entertain her. I am not at the moment ready to receive visitors, so she will have to wait for a little time." Turning to Inshara, she said, more quietly, "Make me presentable. Now."

"Yes, my Lady," said Inshara, clearly relieved, but also somewhat interested. Arendellie had never told her about El-Reiza.

About half an hour later, her hair braided and falling over her shoulder, Arendellie sat on a cushioned chair under a tall, swaying tree in the garden. Turning to Inshara, she said, "Bring El-Reiza to me, now." She wondered what this would be like, and why El-Reiza was coming. She had missed her, and looked forward to seeing her. However, she wondered what on earth this would be like, what on earth was going on.

In a few short minutes, El-Reiza came, most of Arendellie's maids with her. Arendellie drew in a breath. She had forgotten how small El-Reiza was. The small, wiry woman, dressed in a tight-fitting frilled pink blouse over a bright yellow skirt with a full size veil wrapped over her head, breasts, and shoulders and falling down her back, approached Arendellie and curtsied, gracefully, but like a warrior. She drew in her breath quickly; she remembered now that El-Reiza dressed like everyone else, but she still found it startling, more, discordant. It seemed to her that the woman, otherwise skillful, graceful, smooth, and everything except clumsy, would be forever tripping in such clothes. Seeing in El-Reiza's eyes something of which she did not know what to make and otherwise irritated at the cloying presence of so many maids interested in everything, she commanded, "Leave us alone, and get to your chores. *All of you.*" Everyone, including Inshara, hastily left.

"So, El-Reiza," asked Arendellie, "what brings you here?" The woman was never very talkative, and Arendellie wondered how her coming to have a conversation would work out.

"Sir Andelf sent me. He wanted me to tell you a few things," El-Reiza stated.

"Tell me them," said Arendellie. She had not spoken to Sir Andelf or anyone sent by him in a while.

"He wanted me to tell you that he loved you and loves you, and he is sorry for bringing you into the palace."

Arendellie looked down at her hands. *Don't tell me that you love me too!* she thought, wondering, *What is this all about? People telling me they* love me *and making it out as if my life here is somehow sorry!* Not withstanding her thoughts, she waited. "Go on," she said.

"Sir Andelf told me to tell you that we were all wrong. It is those who are simple and know the meaning of love who are wise. Those who play with power, danger, and thrills, fighting in the shadows, claiming wisdom and cunning, are the fools."

Arendellie sucked in her breath. *Is Sir Andelf the officer who has joined the People of the Promise and who Grale Casarion has gone to kill?* she thought, amazed at the tightness in her own chest. Why did the thought frighten and move her so? She had not really cared for Sir Andelf at all, had she?

El-Reiza continued. "Sir Andelf told me to tell you that a servant girl from a conquered Ephezoan city"– *so,* thought Arendellie, *it was him, and I'd never have guessed. He was so sensible and wise*– "who was serving the soldiers to make a living for herself told him about the Promise and the Conqueror, and he saw as he had not seen before. It is true and it is real, and we must be prepared to meet the Conqueror Who is the King of all, for His power and kingdom is far greater than that of any we have seen yet, and He will judge everyone and reign over all. He is terrible, but there is hope, certain hope, in the Promise." As El-Reiza spoke, Arendellie got the very distinct impression that she was almost quoting. "It is right to fear Him and Him alone."

El-Reiza came closer, and knelt next to Arendellie. "He said to tell you that he hopes that you, too, will come to fear the Promised Conquerer more than anything in Kaarathlon, and to put your hope in Him alone. He said to tell you that, unless the Creator intervenes in power, he will be dead well before you receive this message, but that he has died well and he hopes that you will live your life better than he has his, and die well, too, though he prays it will not be, like his, a violent death."

Arendellie smoothed a few stray strands of her hair– Inshara had been in a hurry– with her hand. This was disturbing. El-Reiza's quotations of Sir Andelf's words reminded her strongly of things said to her by Kathreen before she left and, later, by Mirla. About the Creator being more real and important than all His creation. About the men who look at what can be seen and felt being the fools who base their lives on a phantom, and those who live in the light of the truth of the Creator and death being the wise, who build their lives on solid reality. It had been a long time ago, and she could not remember it well, but Sir Andelf's message certainly sounded just like it. Upset, she thought, *Sir Andelf? Why did it have to be Sir Andelf! Is something or someone chasing me? Because it sure feels like it, what with then, and our conversation with Prince Vanesh, and Inshara, and this now!*

El-Reiza paused for a moment. "That is all," she said. "He did not have a lot of time. Grale Casarion and a flight of dragons were already visible in the sky, so we already barely had time for me and Leaoneth to fly. He did, however, give me one last command: if you wish to flee and live a better life, I am to do all I can to arrange for your escape and help you. And, I will."

Arendellie started in shock. What a preposterous proposal! A better life? This was the life made for her and she for it. What was wrong with all these people who seemed to think really living was a lonely pitiful misery, and yet somehow thought being tortured to death was better? And Sir Andelf? She really had not thought it of him. Just to prove how little you could know people in this world, and even less trust them. "El-Reiza," asked Arendellie, "are you one of the People of the Promise?"

"I don't know," she said, and waited. Still, patient, but taut as she always was.

After several minutes, absentmindedly watching the clouds in the sky and the birds in the trees, Arendellie said, "You may go now. I want to be left alone for a bit."

El-Reiza stood and nodded. She looked like she was tired of talking. She gave Arendellie a faint smile and turned. Before she walked away, she asked, "Is there anywhere I am supposed to stay?"

"Ask one of my maids," said Arendellie. As soon as El-Reiza was gone, she got up, walked a few paces, and stretched herself out on the cool, moist ground. Something was wrong. Drastically wrong. Maybe Grale Casarion was right in wanting to wipe these people off the land of Kaarathlon, they caused so much trouble and thought so much nonsense. It was quite sickening, actually. Yet, *they* all fit together. It was disturbing. She totally felt that she was being pursued. It just seemed like the same thing over... and over... and over again. And Sir Andelf! Really! But, then again, what *had* he meant, with all those stories and pieces of news he told her? Maybe she should have seen it coming. She sighed. She wondered how much she could trust Inshara. That was one reason why she would keep Inshara. The woman was, or so she believed, personal and trustworthy, by all accounts.

Why, she wondered furiously, was the world still shattering and tearing people apart? Why did people keep on being drawn into this crazy superstitious nonsense about the Promise and the Conquerer? Perhaps, she should distance herself from Inshara to protect herself from falling into this mess. No, it was okay, she was not in the least inclined in that direction. She knew where she belonged, who she was, what she liked and wanted. However, she was very distressed. Kathreen. Mirla. Inshara. Sir Andelf. Possibly El-Reiza. Where would it end? What would come upon her? Did everyone experience this, or was she singled out for this feeling as if she were pursued by someone or something, by the Promise? It was all nonsense. Life was life and that was all there was to it, and hers was great, luxurious, and exciting. She was, well, content was not quite the right word. Well-adjusted and well-fitted. Yes, that was what she would tell El-Reiza, and she would never talk to Inshara about the Promise again. If Inshara brought it up with her, then she would tell her never to talk to her about it again.

Additionally, her conversation with Vanesh Casarion distressed her. She did not know why it distressed her so much, but it felt like that was what had touched this whole thing off in the first place, and was well more than half of the problem. Oh well. She would get over it. She had before. She stood up, and brushed dirt and leaves off of her gown. "Inshara!" she called. "It's time for my bath." The woman came hurrying.

#23
Enemies

Azshbir was miserable. More miserable than he had ever been in his life (of course, when people are very miserable, they are apt to think that they are more miserable than they have ever yet been, since it is the misery that they are now enduring of which they are aware, not past miseries). Prison was worse than his wildest imaginations. He was forced to do hard work, helping to make the weapons Ephezoa used in its desperate struggle against the Hasseleighton that it was becoming even in the very process of waging war against it. In addition, the prisoners were required to do the work for keeping their living conditions reasonably tolerable. When he finally got to go to sleep at night, he was sore all over and tired to death. His chest and arms burned continually from the work, but even that was nothing compared to the misery of his loss. Lonely and oppressed, he cried himself to sleep whenever he had the energy to do so, heedless of what others thought about it. He was dead already, and he did not stupid care. At times, others of the prisoners taunted him about various things, or asked him what kind of treason on earth he had committed and why he was really in prison. He was too embarrassed and ashamed to tell them. He was a total and complete failure. He was no better than a dead dog. These thoughts only added to his torment. Once, he found himself thinking that he knew now at least one reason why Razi might have chosen to make sure he would be executed. Execution would be so much better than this miserable living death, this life devoid of anything worth living for, which could last decades! Then, he found himself thinking that, once Razi got over his almost reflexive repulsion in being manhandled– which he knew Razi would get over, in fact, was beginning to get over just a little– he would not find prison life nearly so miserable as Azshbir did. He would find some light on the wall, he would share the Promise with those around him and he would resign himself to his fate. Of course, it would be easier for Razi, since he had been more or less alone and mistreated all his life, and he did not have a pregnant wife. Then, Azshbir found himself wondering whether Razi was still alive or not, and if not, how easy his death had been. Biting his lip, he determined to stop thinking about Razi.

It was late, and he was tired almost beyond belief. So tired, in fact, that he thought he might not be able to eat his dinner, though his stomach growled and he knew he was weak from insufficient good food. He had to eat. Or, of course, he could just let himself die... not that he really liked that option very much. Oh well.

He heard keys jangling outside the cell door. The other men clamored and yelled for Azshbir knew not what. Was someone being released? Was someone going to be taken out for punishment? He knew it was not the meal, since that was pushed through a hole. The voice of one of their prison guards called, "Azshbir, come on and get out."

Azshbir got to his feet, feeling unsteady. This feeling was further increased by the clamorous cries of far more men than shared a cell with him, crying out why were they not being taken out. Azshbir barely managed to think well enough to figure that if everyone else wanted whatever was coming to him then it was probably not horrible and he should not be afraid of it.

"No, no, just Azshbir," said the guard, helping Azshbir get through the door quickly, and then slamming it shut. "You've got a visitor," the guard told Azshbir. The words made Azshbir want to jump, and then his head to swim. *Neah'ra! I'm going to get to see Neah'ra!* he thought exultantly. Then, *I wonder how she is doing. This might be more awful than I could imagine. How long?* He asked this last question out loud. "For how long will I get to see her?"

"Her?" asked the guard. "I think your visitor is a man. Anyway, you have a total of half an hour of visiting time, so it depends on how many there are to see you."

Azshbir's head spun. What man would possibly want to visit him? Anjis? That would make sense. Cavisto? He could imagine that easily. Razi? Were prisoners to be executed allowed to have visits with other prisoners– or had he been released? What could it possibly mean that Neah'ra was not there to see him? Had Darnize kidnapped her? Was he keeping her in a prison of his own? Was she starving? It had been weeks. That Azshbir knew. He could not imagine anyone coming to see him before his wife. Theirs was certainly not a love match, but they did love each other in their own way, though it was hard to define.

The guard led Azshbir into a room with three other guards, and had him sit down. Then, he went and brought in the visitor. "By the way," he said, "Neah'–"

Azshbir did not really hear what the guard said, for as soon as he saw Darnize he forgot everything else, leaped up and yelled, "DARNIZE! WHAT ARE YOU DOING HERE, YOU, YOU RAT OF AN ASS!"

"Sit down!" ordered one of the guards, and Azshbir obeyed. Darnize sat down across the table and said, "I came to apologize."

Azshbir managed to stay seated, and he did not yell quite so loudly as he had at first, but he scoffed, "You? YOU? Coming to *apologize?* What kind of cruel joke is this?" He felt a flash of shame and guilt. He was losing it in front of several other people and making a fool out of himself and the Promise. He was doing worse than Razi had done with his own stubbornness. However, he shoved the thought down. Maybe, if he could stay angry enough, it would drown some of his misery.

"Yes," said Darnize, and Azshbir saw that he was almost crying. Still, he could be an actor. "I am sorry for what I did to you. It was foolish, and I'm sorry for what it came to before this, and I'm really sorry it came to this, with you in prison, and my daughter pregnant and alone."

"Of course you meant it to come to this!" Azshbir growled. "What ELSE did you think it would come to?" His voice rose again. "WHAT DID YOU THINK YOU WERE DOING WHEN YOU PUBLICLY SHAMED ME FOR THE PROMISE! OR, HOW ABOUT WHEN YOU TORTURED YOUR DAUGHTER, *MY WIFE?"* He leaped out of his chair again.

One of the guards grabbed him. The guard who had brought him looked around, wondering a little what was going on. Darnize had said he was his father-in-law and he wanted to see his son-in-law. What was all this about? As for

Darnize, he was very nearly weeping now, making the guard think that Azshbir was not insane– what he was talking about *had* happened. "Azshbir," he said, "will you forgive me, please?"

"MAYBE!" Azshbir growled. "MAYBE! WHEN YOU GET ME OUT OF HERE AND MAKE A LITTLE RESTITUTION FOR WHAT YOU DID TO MY WIFE– YOU DON'T *DESERVE* TO BE CALLED HER *FATHER!*" Azshbir spat, as the guards began to pull him away. He did not fight. He just continued yelling. "OF COURSE, YOU CAN NEVER MAKE ANYTHING LIKE CLOSE TO RESTITUTION FOR TREATING HER LIKE YOU DID. BUT, *MAYBE*, YOU CAN DO ENOUGH FOR ME TO FORGIVE YOU."

By now, Azshbir was being taken through the door, and Darnize was being escorted out of the room.

Neah'ra grabbed hold of a guard's arm. "Is it my turn to see Azshbir, now? I'm Neah'ra. He's my husband."

"No," said the guard. "You can come back next month."

"Please, what happened?" she asked, her voice the voice of a woman who has been crying all day.

The guard looked down on the woman. She was probably about sixteen, and she still looked like a child. Her bulging abdomen suggested that she could give birth any day now. She had bags under blood-shot eyes, and her face was weary and worn. She herself was thin, and looked like she was so tired it would do her good to sleep and rest for a week. Her cheeks were dirty, and streaked with dried tears. He looked on her with pity, and decided to relate what had happened in the visitation room to her. Finishing, he asked her, "Darnize is your father, isn't he? What did he do to you?"

Neah'ra quickly related what she had endured. Then she said, "If you see him again, tell him *I* forgive him, even if my husband won't." She burst into fresh tears, her body shaking with silent sobs. "I wish he would come to believe in the Promise, too, but I don't see how he'll understand what the Promise means, if we who claim to be forgiven all our shame and crimes through the conquest of the Promised One are this bitter. Besides," she said, her words so garbled he could barely understand them, "I thought Azshbir forgave Darnize a long time ago. I guess he didn't. He only thought he did."

This woman, scarcely more than a child, tugged at the guard so hard he felt half-inclined to cry himself. She was such a young wife and mother, and she had no husband to provide for her. He reached inside his clothes, and gave her a coin. "Here," he said. "Take this. Rest tonight. Come back tomorrow. I'll try to see if I can arrange something for you two." He felt sorry looking at her that a man like Darnize, as she described him, should have been her father, and that she should be married to a prisoner with a temper something like a volcano.

Her features transformed by a glowing smile that still did not hide the lines of sorrow and weariness on her young face, she said, "Thank you, thank you so much," and turned to go. The guard turned away, as well, to go and see to all the things he had to take care of, especially if what he had just promised a stranger was going to turn out. She was so worn, and life was so hard for her already, that he did not want to disappoint her. He felt it would be cruel. He admired her, too. When she had looked up and said, "tell him I forgive him," he had wondered at her. What moved her to do it? After all, he had done even worse to her than to Azshbir.

Azshbir grabbed the doors of his cell and screamed. "I HATE YOU ALL! YOU ARE WORSE THAN HASSELEIGHTON! IF I HAD JUST GONE WITH KATHREEN AND ADARIA, I'D BE FINE, OR ELSE MERCIFULLY TORTURED TO DEATH! BUT YOU PEOPLE IN EPHEZOA, YOU CIVILIZED GOODERS, YOU HAVE TO COME UP WITH SOPHISTICATED FORMS OF TORTURE THEY WOULD NOT DREAM OF IN HASSELEIGHTON! NOT LETTING ME SEE MY WIFE BECAUSE I YELL AT MY ENEMY! THIS IS HORRIBLE. YOUR PRISON *SUCKS* TOO! I HATE YOU ALL! YOU'RE JUST LIKE HASSELEIGHTON!" He screamed these words and others like them, as he heard the boots of a guard coming down the hall. The other prisoners muttered and talked about him, but he did not notice them. He had already spent half an hour weeping loudly about what an idiot he was and how miserable his life was, and now he was screaming about all the people whose fault it was.

"Azshbir! Calm down!" commanded the guard. It was the same one who had taken him out for that deplorable visitation. Azshbir paused for a moment to spit. "You again?"

"If you promise to behave yourself, I'll take you out of your cell for a few moments."

"What for?" asked Azshbir, his voice only slightly lowered.

"That you will have to find out," said the guard. The other prisoners muttered and murmured, wondering what was going on. Accepting Azshbir's silence, the guard opened the door, and took him out. He took him a little way down the hall, and said, in the barest whisper, "If you behave yourself, and stop acting like a maniac who really might be a traitor to Hasseleighton, I'll arrange for you to be able to see your wife tomorrow." Thinking of Neah'ra, he felt sorry for her again. What had she ever done to deserve this deplorable situation?

Azshbir nodded. "Thanks," he said, through clenched teeth. The guard took him further down the aisle, and had him help bring the meals to everyone. "So they don't get too curious and upset and cause trouble," the guard said. "Your cell mates will think you got a little bit of punishment, but to compensate for being kept up late, and I know how much you need your sleep, I'll let you eat as much as you like. Just, don't tell them. Let them think you had to help serve food but did not get any yourself." The guard started laughing, apparently thinking this was amusing.

It helped a little with Azshbir's foul mood, though he did agree that he coveted all the sleep he could get when he was not either too angry or too miserable. Of course, he felt horribly ashamed for his behavior. Trying not to think about it, though, he said, "Thanks. What is your name?"

"Baren," said the guard. *Maybe, he's not as awful as I thought. Maybe, he would make a good husband for Neah'ra, if only he weren't a prisoner. If only I could do more, but Ephezoa is rotting.*

#24
Barbs and Wounds

Baren spoke softly to a woman sitting on a bench, her head down, her hands folded in her lap, her dress dingy and torn, her abdomen bulging so large it was hard to imagine that she could go another day before going into labor.

Neah'ra looked up, her face no less tired and worn than it had been the previous night. "It's not that kind of thing," she said, quietly. "If my husband would relax, calm down, and think straight, he might be able to answer your question. He is so much wiser and knows so much more than I do. In fact, he taught me much of what I know."

Baren had asked her one of the few questions that had been tormenting him, even in his sleep, ever since he had seen this woman, just under twenty-four hours ago. What had she done to deserve what was happening to her? At her reply, he straightened a little. Would Azshbir really tell him? He had thought the prisoner a little strange, maybe crazy, half out of his mind with some anguish, and very temperamental. Last night, he had thanked Baren and asked him for his name in a way that made the prison guard think that maybe there was more to him than he had thought at first. It still startled him a little, the idea that that man had taught this girl, whose serenity and peace, kindness and compassion even, gave her a beauty wider and deeper than all the loveliness of nature. Even tired and worn, thin, dark circles under her eyes, her face still dirty and streaked with tears– did she have time to wash, even if she had the energy– she was beautiful.

Baren unlocked Azshbir's cell and took him out. This time, the other prisoners did not clamor too much. This pleased Azshbir, since their noise and yelling always made his head spin and hurt. Not that Azshbir felt any better than he had yesterday. For some reason, he felt dirty and foul. There was nothing good about his behavior. He was not sure that the Creator exactly condemned most of it, but no one could have thought for a moment that it was the Creator's will for him– Kathreen had taught him about every breath and heartbeat, every word and thought, being made to be what the Creator willed, and the evil of it being anything else, even if that something was not explicitly wrong. As he walked, trying to drive away these ghosts of shame that tormented him always, dragging his feet from weariness, Baren said, "Your wife is a remarkable woman."

"Say that again," said Azshbir, slurring his words.

"Your wife is a remarkable woman."

"I know," he said, still slurring his words. "Why?"

Baren threw him a cutting, sideways glance, and did not reply. If Azshbir did not know what he was talking about, how could he possibly describe it? One had only to look at the woman. In a few short minutes, he had left Azshbir in the visitation room, and fetched Neah'ra. He could see her features light up at the prospect of seeing her husband.

Azshbir looked up when Neah'ra came in. At the guard's direction, she sat down in the same chair in which Darnize had sat the night before, and this made Azshbir furious. He tried to stifle his anger, but was afraid it still showed, plain for all to see. Reaching her hand across the table as if to caress him, Neah'ra said, "Oh, Azshbir," with indescribable tenderness.

Azshbir's heart throbbed with pain. He reached his hand out, and their fingers touched. "Oh, Neah'ra," he said. With every second that passed, the throbbing pain increased. They had only a few minutes together! It was cruel, unfair, terrible. Worse, they could not really touch. She could not melt into his arms. He could not hold her. Perhaps it was worse to see her this way than not to see her at all. How were they going to say all that they would say? He felt like dying. He felt like breaking something. Anything. Everything. Words he had not intended to say about a subject he had determined not to think about came out of his throat sounding strangled. "How is Razi?"

He saw a flash of pain move across Neah'ra's face. "They executed him. A week and a half ago. I was not there, but a lot of people were." She sounded as though she were near tears. He knew that he had been a dear friend of hers, as well.

Azshbir looked down. He could not think of what to say. Then, Neah'ra spoke. "Why did you do that to my father?" she asked, and her voice cut Azshbir. "He was apologizing! Pleading for forgiveness! I thought you had forgiven him."

Anger rose in Azshbir, increasing the throbbing pain, burning in every soreness of his body and strained joint. "You call *him* your father?" he snarled. "*Him* of all people, *your* father?" Baren understood, though he would never have guessed from Darnize's demeanor what he had done and been. "And, then, you want to know why I told him to go and rot? He hurt you! He hurt *us!* Do you not care?"

Azshbir saw that he had hurt Neah'ra beyond words, but he went on. "And my wife is telling me what to do? My wife is upset at me for not forgiving the man who hurt both of us and tore us apart?"

Neah'ra looked down at her hands. Looking between them, Baren doubted that Azshbir knew any answers Neah'ra did not. It was hard to believe that he had taught her. After a few moments, Neah'ra looked up. "Don't you pity him? He's without the Promise! Without hope!"

Azshbir growled. "The Creator can forgive him. I don't have to. He's FINE, do you hear me, *FINE!*"

Neah'ra began to cry. "Very well, Azshbir," she said coldly. Then, trying to manage a smile, "I don't know whether the baby is a boy or a girl, but you should think of a name, because he or she will be born any day."

"I don't want to talk," Azshbir growled, looking at the wall.

Neah'ra looked stunned for a moment. "You don't? And this is all the time we have? Baren told me only once a month. And, remember, you're embarrassing us."

"I don't need you to remind me!" Azshbir growled again.

Neah'ra broke into tears. Baren turned his back on them. "Azshbir!" she wept, "Azshbir, why? Why did I ever ask you to marry me, if you can't be a husband when you're in prison? If, oh, oh, oh, never mind."

It took Azshbir about half a minute to respond. "You're insulting me, Neah'ra. I *am* a husband. That's why what Darnize did to you hurts me so much!"

"Oh?" asked Neah'ra, cold, upset, almost mocking. "Really? That's why you hurt me and turn away from me, instead of comforting and loving me? No, Azshbir, I don't think so. You're hurt about yourself! Hurt about being a prisoner. Hurt about Razi's death. Hurt about missing me and life with me and with our children. It's not about me or Razi, Azshbir! It's about *YOU!* Your feelings and wants about life, about us, maybe, but not us! Otherwise, you'd love us through the pain!"

She paused, struggling with her tears, and Azshbir, without looking at her, yelled, "Neah'ra!" She burst into all-out weeping, rocking, swaying, her body wracked by sobs, tears streaming down her face. Turning, Baren felt sorry for all three of them. Her. The baby. Azshbir. In more or less that order.

"It's time to go," he said. Leaving Neah'ra, crying, he took Azshbir, and led him back to his cell. To his amazement, the man in no way fought or stormed or yelled. On the way there, he said, "Your wife told me you would be able to answer the question of what she did to deserve what is coming to her."

Azshbir growled. "Don't talk to me about my wife. And, I *don't* want to talk about that, either." Everything Neah'ra had said cut him. Her every word had reopened sores, probed wounds he had sought to hide, poked bruises. It was almost like every word of hers was a barb aimed at some pain or misery that tormented his every moment. "I don't ever want to see her again," Azshbir muttered.

"What was that?" Baren asked, but he had heard. He had heard, and he did not know what to say. *Oh well,* he thought, *it is none of my business, after all. Leave well alone. It's better that way.*

When he got to his cell, Azshbir collapsed into a corner and did not answer any of his fellow prisoner's questions. Frankly, he despised the men. They were all in prison for evil deeds, he for good ones. His wife was cruel. Cruel. Did she not see how much he was hurting? They had never fought before, and now they had, in front of four prison guards! The fact was, he did want to see her again. To hold her in his arms. To kiss her temples. To stroke her hair. To feel the baby move in her belly. However, he did not want to see her again in that pitiful manner in which they were permitted while he was a prisoner, and his was a life sentence. He would never be free. If the sentence were lightened and he ever were released, he would an old man, worn out and exhausted. Maybe, maybe, she would have remained his and not married another man, and they could spend the last of their miserable, pitiful years together, when he was old, weak, and tottering, and she, too, was old, exhausted, and everything except young and beautiful, getting to know and love each other again. If that ever happened, the faint joy would be incommensurate compared to the torture of constantly remembering all that had been lost… all that could have been. Why did not the Creator step in right now and make everything right? Why must they wait so many long years for the Conqueror?

When Baren returned, Neah'ra was sitting curled up on the chair, crying her heart out. Touching her, he helped her up. "I'm so sorry," he said. "Are you okay?"

"I think so," she said, between fierce sobs. "I don't need more... money, either... I have friends... taking care of... me."

Baren looked down, and saw her skirt soaked. That was way more water than tears. He had a wife, and he knew what that meant. Her water was broken. She was going to have the baby. "Tell me where you live, and I'll get you a carriage," he said.

"No, that's okay, I'll walk," she insisted. She was shaking with tears. Baren wondered how much this woman cried. She could have contractions any moment. She would never make it home this way, especially since it was night by now. She could not be going into labor on the side of the road, which she would, or lose the baby. He took her and moved her out of the visitation room. She staggered as she walked. "Are you sure you don't need help?" he asked.

"Yes," she said, shortly. "Getting away from you!"

Is that what she thinks I am? Baren wondered, then, *Maybe there is some of that going on here,* still wondering at this woman's way of using her words like a knife. Was she always like this, or just because she was in terrible distress, hurt beyond speech by the separation from her husband and then his callousness? Then he realized, he did need to keep his distance from this woman in all of her vulnerability. "Okay," he said, slowly, "do you have someone who can help you close?"

Neah'ra did not respond. She tried to run, her breath stolen by her weeping. He saw her collapse outside of the door, in the open air. Would she go into labor and deliver her child right there? Still, he did not see what he could possibly do about it if she did. Hopefully, those friends of hers would come looking for her and take care of her before too long. Fortunately, she was young enough she probably *could* have the baby right there, though she was rather thin and so distressed and worn out Baren still had his doubts. He hoped she– and the baby– survived, and that she regained that precious and beautiful calm. Most of all, he was sorry to see that swallowed up in her pain.

#25
A Vision of the Promise

Neah'ra looked up, and breathed a sigh of gratitude. He was not the prison guard she knew so well! She was a little surprised when he took her into the prison and to Azshbir's cell. *It is a good thing I did not bring the babies,* she thought. To her shock and surprise, she had been quickly frisked by a woman guard, to make sure, they told her, that she was not carrying any knives or possible weapons in. It was humiliating, but she had to endure it. Walking along the torch-lit corridors, she prayed, *My Creator, please help me not to lose it like I did last time. Please, help me to show Azshbir grace, to overlook the fact that he should be the strong one.* She did not know how she could do it. She had had a long talk with Cavisto and the others about how she had lost it at Azshbir. They had more or less all told her that there was no reason why they would know more than she did, but, like Azshbir had shared with them that Kathreen had said, she was supposed to try to make every word in accord with the Creator's will, not just not *wrong*, for it was wrong not to be in perfect accord with the perfection of the Creator's will, since everything was made and is sustained by that will.

Azshbir heard soft footsteps coming down the aisle towards him. They stopped, and he did not look up. He heard a voice, soft and calm. "Azshbir."

"No. Go away. I don't want to see you like this," he half-growled, half-muttered into his blanket.

"Azshbir, you have daughters."

Daughters? The word registered as strange. She should have said, *a daughter.* Perhaps one or the other of them was just too miserable and too exhausted either to speak or to hear right. "Go away," he said, lifting his head out of the blanket and half-yelling. He heard her break into tears, and begin to walk away. Sitting up, he called after her, "I love you, but I just can't see or love you in this environment!"

To his dismay, her weeping only grew louder. Why was this happening to them?

What must have been weeks later, she came again. Much the same thing happened, but this time she begged him for names for his daughters. Now he was certain she had delivered twins. The news only made him more upset. Why did he have to have two children when he could not even be a father to one?

Causing him additional anguish, was the fact that all these things reminded him of the young siblings he had watched die, or seen buried, when he was just a little child. The weighty, inexpressible grief and loss he had felt then, and the fear, both of death and of others he knew and loved, in his childish way, dying, came upon him again. He noticed it most in his dreams, where his present anguish, desires, fears, and circumstances would get mixed up with those of the past. Sometimes, though, the thought of Neah'ra would make him remember laying over his little sister while her breathing grew ever weaker.

The endless passing of days and nights only made him more irritable and unhappy. One of his cell mates asked him what the Promise was for the fiftieth time, and he decided to try to explain it, only to get mocked for more issues that he could count. The whole conversation provoked a quarrel about whether it was natural for those who were in prison unjustly to be more miserable because they were victims of injustice or whether it was natural for those who were in prison justly to be more miserable since they actually have crimes to be miserable about. The quarrel was temporarily broken by being taken out for the day's work, but was resumed in the night, causing everyone to lose much needed sleep, which only made them all more upset at each other.

I'm not even sure whether I belong to the Promise, anymore, Azshbir thought.

A voice spoke which Azshbir had never heard before, and yet he felt like he knew it from somewhere. Though it did not even fall upon his ears, he had the distinct sensation that it was solid and the walls of the prison were a mist compared to it.

"Azshbir."

Yes? he replied in his mind.

"I will show you My Promise." There was no discontinuity between the voice and the vision that unfolded. They were one and the same. The words of the voice were the vision that unfolded all around Azshbir, more substantial than the rock of the prison which enclosed him. Likewise, the vision *was* the words of the Creator spoken directly into Azshbir's mind and yet more solid not only than ordinary sound but than the ground on which he sat. If it was sitting, now.

Someone stood. Still and yet moving. He was so bright and radiant that He could not be seen. He towered over all existences, and Azshbir shook in His presence. He trembled so violently he thought his body would be torn apart. This Being was glorious beyond compare, cloaked in light as by darkness, great and awesome, beyond all worlds, and Azshbir was nothing before Him, a moth captured in a whirlwind of fire. Worse, he had violated His will and His essence. This Being was so great and far beyond all existences that He seemed to tear them all apart by His very existence, if one could use the same word for it, by His very Being.

A man, lighter than the Camilians but with dark hair and eyes, stood beside a precipice. He looked like any man, but He spoke and everything was silent and still. He radiated power and authority. His enemy bowed in complete submission and obeyed perfectly. He reached out his hand, and healed a child's body and a woman's soul. Compassion as well as power flowed from him.

The same man. He tottered, fell, and was picked up again. His face was swollen beyond recognition by ugly bruises. Most of his body was either cut and bleeding or swollen. He swayed, as if about to pass out, hardly able to take short, tottering, feeble steps. Where was the Power? Then, somehow, He stood upon an altar of white stones. Light flowed through Him and by that Light He moved and remained, but darkness fell upon Him, hiding the Light, covering all things. Nature cried out in agony, but her fear and agony vanished against His, as He cried out in utmost anguish. The stars fell and the rocks split. His voice rent the heavens. It was strong and victorious. The Power and the Light were there, and He was stronger than the darkness, but it fell upon the earth, stifling all light and breath.

The same Someone. The same man. Dawn glowed behind Him, pure and clear. The Light came from Him. Wounds had left their mark on His body, but it was perfect. Perfect as no body has ever yet been. The Power and the Light were clearer, now. He was brighter than the sun. Azshbir found that he could look at Him and yet that he could not look at Him. He spoke, and His voice roused all light and life to song. He touched a girl. The same girl who had drove the knife into His heart. She rose. Light sang. Joy moved with her. Light and Power were triumphant. The man was triumphant. The man was the Promise. The Promise was triumphant. Forgiveness was triumphant. Day had come. The man spoke, and Azshbir knew he spoke to him. Love.

Azshbir realized that he was not certain whether he had seen with his eyes or with his mind or whether it was seeing at all. He also realized that it had taken no time at all; it had happened all at once, in a momentous flash. His cell mates were yelling *exactly* the same sounds as they had been when the Creator had spoken His name. His head reeled. What had just happened? What had he seen? Covering himself in his blanket, he went to a corner and stayed there. He needed solitude. He needed to be alone.

All night long, however tired he might have been, Azshbir remained there. He had been ashamed of his conduct and his smallness, but the glory that was both flashing fire of light brighter than the sun and the darkness that concealed and flowed from this fiery glory, dark because the light was too bright, the glory that was so great it was terrible, sending destruction before it and leaving destruction in its wake, had burned the shame out of him, at least for the moment. He found himself wondering how he– or anyone else for that matter– would be able to live in the presence of the Creator when even the Conquerer was that awful.

The following day was longer than any other, Azshbir was so tired. He stumbled often, and was whipped from time to time. It was a light whip and only stung; as far as he could see, it left no real damage at all. He did not know whether it was the vision of the destroying glory– or was it the destroying love, he was not sure– or the weariness that made his bones feel like mush that made everything so clear, so crystalline. He knew, though, that the Promise was not what he– or anyone else– had thought or could think, had imagined or could imagine. It was far more than they had ever dreamed. It was awful and terrible beyond all human conception, even while it was the embodiment of kindness and compassion, the hope of all Kaarathlon and, if there were other worlds, of them as well. He understood, too, why so few men desired the Promise. The Promise *was* that Being who was so awful and terrible that the dread and glory of a raging inferno, a tempestuous hurricane of fire flashing lightnings and clothed in dreadful and oppressive darkness, was nothing compared to His terror and dread. It was that Being as a man from whom flowed compassion and kindness, who was murdered on an altar, and came back to glorious life, but that Being was not the less awful and dreadful because He was a man who was slain– would be a man who would be slain. Only, did it matter? The vision seemed to indicate that time had nothing to do with that Being.

At any rate, Azshbir knew why men fled from the Promise. To belong the Promise was to meet that Holy Terror, that Brighter-than-the-sun Darkness, that Destroying Love, worse– or better– to dwell forever in His Presence. Was it not to be destroyed? Eternally consumed by an eternal fire so wild and hot that the wildest inferno was mere child's play before its fierceness? Certainly, there was nothing in all of Kaarathlon, in all that is, more to be feared than the Promise! Of course, to bear the contempt of that Being was even worse, but it was also different! *So* different. It was death, while it was life to dwell with that Being, that Fire so thick with Light that it was impenetrable and blinding, or in other words, dark. However, it could only be life because he was to somehow be united to that Being so that the very ferocity of life which destroyed him would generate life in him, would enliven him with the same Terrible Life that was that Being and flowed from that Being. That *was* the Promise. That somehow men and that Being could be united, so that that Being would take into Himself and destroy by dying their shame and crimes and they could share that Being's... what?... and live that Life that was boundless. Azshbir bowed his head in complete astonishment and bewilderment. It was, but what it was he could not grasp.

That night, Neah'ra came again. Azshbir drew himself up on the bars, clinging to them, since he was both more exhausted than ever and in much pain. She saw, even in the dim torch-light, and took his hands. They grasped each other's hands through the bars, and after a few long moments, they put their faces as close to each other as they could, and blew kisses.

After a while, Neah'ra said, "I know something has happened."

Azshbir nodded. "Yes, but I'm not sure what."

Neah'ra laughed, and there was joy in her laugh, but it was also incredibly worn and sad. Then, she asked, "Do you have names for our daughters?"

Azshbir frantically scrambled for names. "What about Reilia and Della?" he asked.

"Beautiful," said Neah'ra. "Are they names of your people?"

"I made them up," said Azshbir, a little frustrated that Neah'ra did not sense that something so much greater loomed over them. Looking at her care-worn face, he wondered if he should try to tell her, then figured better of it. How could she possibly understand anyways? Maybe she did, since she seemed so far beyond him in so many ways, but if she did not, all he could say would only sound like so much gibberish. Indeed, he was not certain that it did not sound like gibberish to himself.

For several minutes they just stood there. Then, Neah'ra said, "I'm glad you're willing to see me again."

"So am I," said Azshbir. He hoped she felt something of the Presence that hung over them and was all around them, bigger than every universe, great and awesome and glorious, so brilliant and burning the lightest touch would unmake them in fire and light. For him, it pervaded the air, his own body even, and hung, for the moment, over every moment, every breath, heartbeat, and word, somehow commanding an awed silence and stillness. Somehow, neither his exhaustion nor all the heat and noise of work and life in the prison shattered it. Perhaps, because besides this Reality, all these other things were mere mists.

Finally, Azshbir asked, "Can you feel Him?"

"A little," said Neah'ra. Turning to look at him, she said, "I can feel that you feel Him." She was disappointed that he did not want to talk or relate– it had been so long and she was so weary, and then there were the children, his as much as hers– but she could sense that he did not want to talk. He wanted to be– with her– in the Presence, to enjoy, if enjoy is the right word, Him with her, for she had become a piece of him. So, she was silent with him, tasting what she could of the Glorious Presence that she knew was there, though she knew that she was not aware of Him the way that Azshbir was. As a result of the lack in her awareness, she remained disappointed and discouraged, even though she was greatly gladdened and encouraged by getting to be with Azshbir. Perhaps, next time, they could talk everything through, though there would not be enough time. There would never be enough time. Perhaps it was better for them to just be here in the Presence, as best as they could, for that way time would not hang over them so terribly, destroying the moments that they did have. Still, they would have to talk sometime, but maybe now, after their fight and their estrangement, was not the right time.

They lapsed into awed silence again, but it did not last long. The guard soon came to escort Neah'ra out of the prison. Even in the Presence, sadness washed over Azshbir. To his delight, his cell mates respected his desire to be left alone, and let him be by himself again, though the next day they were to pester him about what had happened as much as they could, and not understand a word of what he tried to tell them. He knew he did not communicate it very well, and soon gave up, telling them to forget everything he said, since it was all worse than nothing, and that if they wanted to know they would just have to ask the Creator what the Promise really meant. Not, of course, that that convinced them to leave him alone, and he struggled, now and then against frustration. For once he was glad of how busy and exhausting their days were, for it meant that the other prisoners had less time and energy to pester him about what he knew he would be able to explain no better even if he had all the time, energy, and health in the world with which to do it.

#26
A Disquieting Meadow

Walking through a meadow in Ebrin, Arendellie knelt to pick a pink wildflower. It felt like forever since she had been here, but not much seemed to have changed. Four maids trailed behind her, many of them picking wildflowers themselves, and twisting them into crowns and other jewelry. That morning, she had been with her parents, who were definitely aging, listening to their stories of life when they were younger– most of which she had already heard hundreds of times– and telling them about the palace gardens and several other pieces of life as a princess. Now, it was afternoon, and the sun was hot and clear. "Inshara," she said, "now you get to see what the mountains are like."

"I know why you love them," said the older woman. "They're wild, beautiful, and grand." She reached up to wipe sweat off her brow under the brown veil, which stuck out over her forehead enough to provide a little bit of shade from the brilliance of the sunlight.

To be honest, Arendellie was not at all certain why she had even come to Ebrin. It made her sad. It reminded her of what her friendship with Kathreen had been, before the world was shattered and they were left in different pieces of it. The world had been happy, then, and whole. That was what Inshara offered? Healing, which was restored wholeness, right? That was what she had said that she wanted and needed. Arendellie stiffened at the turn her thoughts had taken. The Promise, which had torn the world apart, which had divided the closest friendships and ties, could not possibly offer healing and wholeness anymore than could the tyranny of Grale Casarion, which had provoked the whole situation. Arendellie bit the inside of her cheek. How could she possibly think the way her thoughts had begun to turn!

Meticulously tearing the flower apart, she wondered whether to call on Mirla or not. On the one hand, she would like to see her, and she had already come this far, so why not? What could it possibly hurt? On the other hand, she definitely did *not* want to talk about the Promise and related subjects. She knew, though, that Mirla could not be trusted to respect such a request. Oh, as far as politeness went, she probably was. She had always been polite and good-natured. However, it would not stop her from making allusions to the Promise or trying to talk to Arendellie about what she thought profitable or necessary. Inshara, she knew, was afraid of her, afraid of what she might command, though she was bound to a higher law– doubtless, why Grale Casarion so hated the People of the Promise!– and would say what she believed needed to be said, however culturally insensitive– dangerous– it might be. However, she did not think Mirla would be afraid of her. Though Inshara knew her better than any of her other maids, she had not gotten to know her well. Arendellie had made sure of it. Of course, Mirla might be afraid of her. It was a long time, and she *had* changed but, somehow, she did not want to risk it. After all, she did not even trust Inshara never to disobey her in certain things. Mirla, seeing her for the first time in ages, and a free woman, could be depended upon to talk to her about things she did not want to talk about, afraid of her or not. At least, she thought so.

Arendellie threw the mangled flower on the ground and picked up a new one, ignoring the glances of her maids, who were enjoying the mountain scenery and air and clearly both perplexed and disturbed by their mistress' obvious agitation. Without turning or looking over her shoulder, she said, "Spread out the sheet."

One of the maids appeared at her elbow. "What did you say, Princess?"

The wind must have carried most of her voice away. "Spread out the sheet!" she said again, clearly annoyed.

They did so, smoothing out the tall grass and laying down the sheet. Arendellie lay down on it and tried to wipe the goo from the flowers she had mangled off her fingers on to its edges. She had forgotten how easy it was to get dirty in the mountains and how much she did not like dirt. Voices floated down the wind to her.

"Mirla, sit down– if you can– and tell me what has so upset you." It was Kathreen's– dead– mother's best friend, Aleria, speaking in a gentle and soothing, though firm, voice.

Arendellie's maids, perhaps to get away from her attitude, sat down on the grass a little ways away from her and chatted quietly together. The wind bore their conversation away, even as it bore Mirla and Aleria's conversation to her.

When Mirla spoke, her voice was shrill and clearly distressed. "I'm not sure what they'll do to me next time, and Dormik and Brisia."

It took so long before they spoke again that Arendellie thought perhaps they had gone, or the wind had changed and she would no longer hear them. Then, Aleria said, "The Creator is in control. Remember that, dearie." Perhaps Arendellie had missed a large chunk of their conversation. No matter. Why was she even listening to it, anyway? It was the very kind of thing she wanted to avoid!

"Then there's Kalimad." Kalimad was Mirla's husband.

This time Aleria's reply was quicker. "His attitude, at times even antagonistic, is difficult for you, I know. We've talked about this before. But, somehow, I sense that isn't the real issue. Not right now."

"You're probably right," Mirla conceded. Her voice sounded like she was probably about to cry, but, as it was borne by the wind, Arendellie was not quite sure. "I'm afraid. I'm really afraid." She paused for a few moments, or at least Arendellie did not hear anything for a few moments. "They're big time after Kathreen– why I have no idea." Now, Arendellie was sure she really was crying. "I'm afraid for her. But… you're right. There's more to it than that."

There was nothing again, for a rather long period of time. Arendellie's ears strained, listening, and she wondered why, irritated with herself. Maybe it was because she still cared about this mutual friend of hers and Kathreen's and wanted to know what kind of trouble she was in, in case she could maybe do anything about it.

"I'm scared. I'm really scared." Again, silence. When Arendellie heard Mirla's voice again, it seemed calm and tranquil. "I guess it's okay. The Creator will take care of Dormik and Brisia, and the baby… if I really am pregnant. And, He'll take care of me. Even if they do torture for me for information I don't even have!" Her voice rose a little, but she seemed to be laughing at the preposterousness of such a situation. Falling again, she said, "It'll be awful,"– "If it happens," Aleria interjected– "but it will be okay, and in the end it will be all be well. I'm safe. I'm a child of the Creator, and I will be okay." Now, she seemed to be repeating beliefs to herself in an attempt to keep herself calm. "Death is not to be feared, since I will only be going to wait in peace for the coming of the Conqueror. Torture won't last, and the Creator will love me through it. In the Promise, I'm His daughter." She was crying now, so hysterically that, as her voice was floating to Arendellie on the wind, she could not hear her at all. She thought she kept on talking about the Promise, something about something not being as horrible as something else because of something having to do with merits and shame, interspersed with something that might have been, "Oh, but I'm scared! I'm scared!" Finally, she could make out that Mirla was sobbing about her husband and her children, and repeating things about the Promise over and over again, while Aleria tried to offer rather clearer encouragement.

At last, it got to Arendellie and she could bear it no longer. She did not know why she had even listened to it in the first place. Getting up, she yelled, "Get this sheet and move it! QUICKLY! Why did you put in it a place where I would overhear that awful conversation? Why are you ALL so negligent and stupid– always?"

Quickly, they got up from their own chatter, and apologized to her, saying that they put it in the spot which she had seemed to indicate and they did not know about the horrid conversation. "Do you think I care about your apologies or your excuses?" scolded Arendellie harshly. She was upset and she did not want to think about the conversation *or* her maids.

A few minutes later, she was laying on her back, looking up at the clouds scurrying along in a brilliant blue sky. Kawina sat down on the edge of her sheet and asked, "So, what was that awful conversation you mentioned to us?"

"It was awful!" said Arendellie. "Do you really think I would want to talk about it?"

Kawina shook her head, got up, turned away, and stumbled off, clearly hurt, to talk with her friends. Arendellie only despised her hurt. Shaking her head she thought, *She should have learned better than to try to socialize with me by now if it bothers her so much. After all, I don't want her to, and she does not like it, so why doesn't she either just quit or stop feeling hurt by my brusqueness?* She tried to return her attention to the sky and the mountains– that is, to nothing.

Several hours later, the sun low in the sky and filling the ridges to the west with a flood of light that thickened the air, Arendellie sat up, and stretched her hands out in front of her. With a shock, she saw the smudges on her fingers. *Dirt! Mountains! No proper baths!* she thought to herself. "Prepare a good soap bath for me," she called.

Alitholiel hurried over. "What is it, Lady?" she asked. Arendellie despised her. "It's dirty out here. Prepare a good soap bath for me!" she said. "And leave everyone else. When it's ready, come get me. Be done well before dark."

Alitholiel straightened, nodded impersonally, and stepped away. She was probably about Arendellie's own age. It did not occur to Arendellie, but she may have been the most like her among her maids.

To herself, Arendellie thought, *Try to conceal your emotions a little better. You don't want anyone to be able to make anything of your behavior. Ever. And, you know you're a lot like this–* she did not think the words 'imperious and demanding'– *a lot of time, but you also know that an extra measure of emotional turmoil came out this time. Be more careful.*

#27
A Child's Questions

Brisia was laying on the ground, looking at her wooden toys, horses, dogs, chickens, and the like. They offered little comfort. Her mom and dad were fighting again. They fought a lot nowadays. She did not remember them fighting very much back when she was even smaller, but now they fought, what seemed to her, all the time. It had started a little before the day Mom had come home so late that even Dad was worried about her with a bruise on her cheek. She had been unhappy that day, herself. She had tried to comfort Brisia, but the four-year-old girl just knew she was on the verge of crying herself. Later, she did break down and cry. Dad had tried to comfort and calm her and say it was not a big deal, but Brisia just knew that he believed even less of what he was saying and trying to act like than Mom did.

Now, they were fighting again. They usually went behind that door to do it, though sometimes it just happened to them. Usually both Mom and Dad yelled and usually Mom cried, too, though Brisia tended to think that Dad was even more unhappy than Mom. Usually Brisia cried, too. Sometimes her older brother cried, but he did not do it nearly so much as she did. Sometimes she tried to play with her toys to distract herself and pass the time, maybe find some comfort and enjoyment, but it never worked. Sometimes she ended by throwing them against the wall. Neither Mom or Dad liked it when she did that. Sometimes she did it just to get them to stop fighting with each other, because if they noticed her throwing her toys at the wall they would scold her for it and stop fighting. It was usually hours before they resumed fighting again. Sometimes it was even days. Somehow, though, Brisia did not feel like that today.

Mom and Dad used words she did not understand when they fought, and sometimes when they did not. When she asked them they never told her what they meant, or if they did, they did so in very general terms which left her curiosity completely unsatisfied. Right now, though, Dad was yelling something she could understand. "Mirla, what about when they take our children away and teach them their garbage! You know I don't want that anymore than you do!"

That scared Brisia. She did not really understand what it meant. Had someone threatened to take her and Dormik– that was her older brother– away from Mom and Dad? She had heard both Mom and Dad suggest that before, but it really scared her. She wanted to stay with Mom and Dad, even if they did fight all the time now! She knew they both loved her, and that they both loved each other. She just wished they would stop yelling at each other and crying all the time. She did not like it when Mom cried even when it was not because she and Dad were fighting.

Mom was crying. She was so frustrated and upset that she was yelling, too. "I already told you it's not the torture I'm afraid of– not really! But I know I'm supposed to trust the Creator, and you would do better if you did, too!"

"Yes, it all comes down to that, when if you'd just drop Him, neither of us would have to fear that–"

Brisia got up, walked across the room, and found Dormik, who was sitting in a corner and paring roots. She knew he was deeply disturbed and troubled from the way he was sitting and staring at his work. She remembered, though, one word she wanted to ask about, and she hoped Dormik might know. He was a lot older than she was and knew a lot more than she did. Like how to pare roots! Sitting down next to him, she asked, "What does that crazy word they've taken to using way too much mean?"

Dormik did not look at her. That was the measure of how bothered he was. "Which one?" he asked, dully.

"I think they say torzur," said Brisia.

"Oh, that one!" said Dormik. He was upset beyond all measure. "I think it means when they poke you with hot forks," he said. He set all his attention back to his paring, but Brisia saw tears falling out of his eyes. She lay against the wall and wailed. That way she could not hear so much of her parents' argument.

After a long time she noticed that she was no longer wailing and that they were no longer yelling. She got up, and saw Mom walking towards her. Mom's face was red and puffy. She hated seeing it that way. Mom put her arm gently around Dormik's shoulders and whispered, "I love you." Brisia grabbed at her pants. "Mommy, Mommy," she sobbed.

After a moment, Mom turned to her. Gathering her in her arms and sitting down, she said, "Oh, Brisia."

Brisia burst into tears again. This time they did not last as long. Then, looking up, still sobbing, she said, "Mom, is it true that they are going to poke you with forks?"

It took Mirla a brief moment to process what her daughter was suggesting. She held Brisia tighter and wondered where she had gotten that idea from. Dormik took his knife and roots and walked away. She watched him go with sadness. Why did her children both have to need her constant attention and love? Of course, it might help if she could avoid fighting with Kalimad. Fighting giggles, she asked, "Who told you that 'they'– whoever 'they' are– are going to poke me with forks?" By the time she got to the end of her question she was really laughing. Snorts of laughter escaped and garbled her words.

"Dormik," said Brisia, wondering what provoked Mom's laughter. Was Dormik completely wrong and did torzur mean nothing of the sort? Did it really mean being poked with forks but were the forks made out of that foamy plant? Or did they drip mango juice? Brisia started laughing with Mom. Meanwhile, Mirla was wondering where Dormik had gotten his idea from. He was obviously very upset.

After her laughter died away– which was fairly quickly– Brisia asked, "Mommy, are they going to take me and Dormie away from you and Daddy?"

She saw a cloud pass over Mom's face. Mirla answered in the softest of tones, "It's time I explained everything to you, but I don't know if you're strong enough... if you understand enough." Her words, soft and tender, made Brisia cry again. Mirla held her tighter. "Not that it will be better if I don't."

Mirla scooted over, to lean against the wall. She rocked Brisia a little, feeling more than ever her abdomen, which was again beginning to swell with the baby growing within. The thought made her cry herself.

When she was done crying, she gathered Brisia, who had only recently completely weaned, close, and said, "My dearest, my flower, I don't know what will happen."

Brisia was still, tense, silent.

"Maybe 'they' will poke me with forks!" Snorts of laughter escaped, but it did little to obscure the seriousness and gravity of Mirla's meaning.

Brisia wrapped her arms around her mom, holding her as tightly as she could. Mom squeezed back.

"I will be well," said Mirla. "I don't understand it all, but I know part of the Promise is that all will be answered and explained, all will be well. I will always be oh-kay. I'm safe. My Creator loves me and will always take care of me." She felt Brisia squeeze her even tighter, and the deep sobs that vibrated within the little girl's body. She wished she could hold and support her always. It took her a long time to gather the courage and strength to say what she had to say next. Tears pushed at the back of her eyeballs. Brisia was so small, so weak, so vulnerable, so needy and, even, in her own way, loving. She clung to her mother, and just thinking about telling Brisia what she had to tell her next made Mirla's heart feel like it must break. For it to actually happen would be even worse. The thought of the other torture made her nerves shiver sometimes. This was the torture that cast her into deep darkness and gloom, that made her whole being waver and melt. She bit the inside of her cheek.

"Brisia, maybe someone will take you away from me and Daddy." Hastily she added, "But you must remember– we must all remember– the Promise. The Creator *will* take care of you."

Brisia was quiet for a long time. A painful lump formed in her throat. Finally, she looked up into Mom's eyes. "Why?" she asked, and Mirla knew she was not asking about the Creator or the Promise, but about being taken from her parents.

That one question tore at Mirla's heart. It was the question Kalimad always asked. They both knew that if she would swear the oath of allegiance, she would not be in too much danger even though she did not have the information about Kathreen Alarion that the Emperor's men sought, and would never give it, even if she did. Of course, she would never swear the oath of allegiance either. Her heart felt like it would stop. She remembered Kathreen telling her about her own struggle with fear and allegiance. Looking back into Brisia's eyes tenderly, she said, "Because bad men want me to obey them, and they want you to obey them, too." It was only half the answer but it was the answer, she thought, that Brisia needed in that form. She was always trying to tell her– and Dormik– the other side of the answer, *her* answer.

After a long time, Brisia said, sobbing, "I'll die if– no, no, no. It won't!" Die– separation from Mom– never– impossibility.

Mirla bent down, and softly kissed Brisia's forehead. Looking up, she saw her husband standing over them, watching them. She shifted Brisia in her arms– they were dreadfully sore– and squeezed her tightly. She did not think any words would help. Brisia was breaking down into violent weeping again, burying her face in the folds of Mirla's blouse over her chest.

    Leaning back and trying to get as comfortable as possible, Mirla held Brisia until she had cried herself to sleep. Then, she gently laid her down. She stretched, her muscles sore and cramped. *Now, I have to take care of Dormik. Oh, Creator, how? Why? How am I supposed to do this? How am I able to do this? It's too much.*

#28
The Witch

Arendellie looked down at her abdomen and finally realized what was wrong with her. In fact, it even explained her emotions and unpredictable and disturbing thoughts about, in particular, the Promise. She was pregnant! It had been a while since she had noticed something was wrong. It had even been a little while since she had noticed that her abdomen was not quite the right shape. It had disturbed her, so that she wondered if she had a disease. However, she was too exhausted with her unnatural emotions and entertaining Vanesh to really think about it.

She sank down on the carpet. She could not be pregnant! She could not! Whatever would she do? She would become ugly so that Vanesh did not appreciate her. That would be dangerous. She would be tired and exhausted, and that would not help Vanesh appreciate her. After she gave birth, she would have to nurse the child! Back in Ebrin she had wanted children. However, she was a different person now. She was glad she was a different person now. To have remained who she was in Ebrin would have been unbearable pain. But she did not want to be a mother. Or did she? Because she did.

That night, nestling in Vanesh's arms, taut and fearful, in response to his questions, she told him that she was carrying a child.

The prince's face lit up. He drew her tighter, then stood and whirled her around in a dance. Arendellie's mind was too numb to respond well. Finally, they stood facing each other, with Arendellie half in his arms. Seeing the shock in her face, he asked, "What, my princess? What is wrong?"

"I– I–I. Vanesh, I don't understand why you are so excited. I will be tired. I will become the wrong shape. Why are you so excited that I am– pregnant?"

Vanesh laughed. "You are a very stupid woman, Arendellie! Did you think I only wanted you to entertain me? I shall be king and emperor! Did you think I would not want an heir? Or that any man does not want his wife to bear him sons?"

Arendellie hung her head, ashamed and, still, afraid. She realized she was making great mistakes. She was so afraid and suspicious of everyone that she was dehumanizing them. Maybe it came from the rigors of being pregnant. She seemed to be dehumanizing herself, too, she thought, with a pang. Finally, she said, "I don't– I didn't– know. I guess I thought royalty were different. A race of gods and not of men. Besides, our child may be a daughter."

Vanesh cackled. Arendellie had never known him so merry. "Gods have children, too!" he roared. "Besides, if you have a girl, she will be queen and empress, except that you will get pregnant again and have a son! Do not worry, my lovely Araenyi." He paused for just a moment and then said, "We will arrange for nurses to care for your child once he is born, though you will get to play with him if you want."

It was the first time he had called her that, and she did not like it. If she had been Araenyi when she and Neshekh were engaged, she was certainly Araenyi no longer. She did not know how to tell him that, though. After all, she had told him he could call her that.

For the first time in her life, Arendellie collapsed into Vanesh's arms and cried. She did not know why. She was emotionally overwhelmed.

Vanesh held her, and she knew he loved her. She had never expected another man to love her the way that Neshekh had, right from the beginning of their relationship. She had certainly never expected it in a palace out of a prince of whose goals she could never be sure and whose motives she could never trust. The thought made her cry more, but then she realized that she was becoming the Arendellie she had been in Ebrin, or at least someone more like her. That Arendellie could never survive in a palace, could never be a princess. She did not want to be that Arendellie. She tried to pull herself together, stiffen her soul, throw up the wall of stone and steel that made her that other Arendellie.

She could not. She was pregnant and it threw her off. She was with Vanesh and that threw her off, too. More, Vanesh was treating her like never before, though she realized that he had been tending towards it and she had had signs enough, but that threw her off too. She just could not manage it. She might be made to be a princess, but she could not be queen of princesses and a mother at the same time. The two things were just incompatible. *Oh well. I'll protect myself from the Promise while I'm pregnant and stuff. I'll carry this baby and have nurses take care of him. That way I'll only be a mother while I'm pregnant, and I should be able to protect myself all right with such a small window of vulnerability. I don't like it though. I really don't. I hope this baby is a boy and that I don't have any more.*

Vanesh was speaking soothingly to her, while he walked them towards the couch, and then reclined with her upon it once more. She realized that he, at any rate, wanted her to be a mother, and was softened to her by the news that she would be. Or did he just want a son? If she bore a daughter, would he be angry? She did not know, and she preferred not to think about it. Not right now. She would later. She had to do so. She could not just relax because of her pregnancy and let her vulnerability run off with her. She was Princess Arendellie Casarion.

The months passed and Arendellie did not mention her concern for Mirla. She told herself that since the pressures had been acceptable so far they would probably be kept that way. Why else had they not been escalated long before her visit? She also told herself that to do such a thing would tie her too much to her old self and too much to the People of the Promise of which she now had to be extremely careful lest it establish a hold on her– two issues which were dangerous vulnerabilities to her because of her pregnancy, which twisted the way she perceived the world and colored her whole outlook. She absolutely hated it. She wanted to be in control of herself, of her mind, of her heart, of her emotions, and pregnancy threw it all off and ruined it. She desperately hoped that she would be able to recover. Hopefully, she would be even stronger than before.

The baby went on growing and Arendellie's stomach became more and more deformed. Soon she had to wear completely different clothes. She also had to eat more while discovering that she could eat far less at once. She needed the servants to constantly pamper and take care of her. Sometimes she developed dreadful heartburn. Worse, she found herself wanting to be a mother, remembering babies she had cared for when she was a little girl, even baby animals. She daydreamed and even dreamed about being a mother and caring for a little one. She hated it. If she was already this attached to a baby growing in her womb whom she had never seen and even whose gender she did not know, how was she possibility going to break free from the vulnerabilities of motherhood that so destroyed her calculated control of who she was? In fact, the ways things were going, when she gave birth and saw the baby she would immediately love him or her, being forever bound as a mother, and more of a mother than she was now, losing all control over herself forever! Who knew where she might end up, if that happened! She, the Princess Arendellie, could never become one of those stupid, crazy, idiotic, self-deceived, stubborn and thick-skulled People of the Promise. However, it had happened to so many people whom she would least suspect that if she lost control over who she was, she could end up even there! Just thinking about it made her blood run cold with fury. These People of the Promise were witches who seemed to have power even over the workings of nature and wielded it to suck people into their delusion. Perhaps Inshara was casting spells on her to trap her. Maybe that was why she liked Inshara's ministrations so much. Maybe they were enchantments. Perhaps she should have Inshara beheaded. That would save her from the torture that might otherwise await her and Arendellie would have to explain herself to no one. Vanesh was the only one who might ask her, and she could either lie to him– make up that Inshara did something really wrong when everything was going wrong and she was already exasperated, or something like that– or tell him the whole truth. She doubted that he would be a problem either way.

Thinking about it, Arendellie liked the idea. That way, she would get rid of Aki'lam, too. She knew that Inshara wanted Aki'lam with her, so she had kept the deplorable servant for the sake of Inshara– who she had thought was her best maid, though, it seemed, she might well be her worst. However, if she had Inshara beheaded, there would be no reason to keep Aki'lam. She could just give her to someone else and replace her, saying that she really did not suit her and would probably make a good kitchen slave. Yes, the idea appealed to Arendellie very much.

However, she just never did anything about it. Sometimes she would work herself into a fright, thinking that maybe Inshara knew what she was planning and was casting spells to make her unable to act on her persuasions and that she would have to find some way of doing something anyways. She became very cold towards Inshara, snapping at her more than at anyone else, despite the fact that her ministrations were still most pleasant. However, for some reason, whether because she did not have the nerve or because the thought went plain out of her head, Arendellie never had Inshara killed. Looking into her maid's eyes, she felt like she just could not do it– Inshara was a human being, tender and kind, maybe even a mother, too. She decided that if she was going to resist the enchantments laid around her and stay out of the traps set for her that she would have to stop looking into Inshara's eyes– maybe that was even most of the spell– and conquer her nerves to have Inshara killed. That way she would strengthen her control over herself and be less vulnerable in the future.

    Arendellie did succeed in never making eye contact with Inshara, but she never did make herself have the maid killed. For some reason she could not do it. She did, however, appreciate the hatred of Hasseleighton for the People of the Promise. She came to fully empathize with it. Thinking that perhaps she could arrange for Inshara's removal from her and death– the later of which was probably necessary for breaking the spells the witch had cast on her– by telling someone that she was one of the People of the Promise, she decided to do so. However, she could bring herself to do that even less, perhaps because it would be exposing the woman to greater pain. She figured that, since even starting small would be an improvement over doing nothing and enough to strengthen her control over herself and her independence, even if far less– besides the fact that she did not really want to be a heartless murderer and incur that guilt– she could simply drop hints about Inshara's allegiance until the wrong– or right– person picked them up and had her killed. However, for some strange reason, even that Arendellie could never bring herself to do. Along with her dreams of motherhood, she began to have nightmares about "the witch," but, however convinced that it was necessary, she was never capable of taking any action. She fell into fear and depression and, even when Vanesh asked her, could not explain it, though this further increased her fear and certainty that she was falling under a spell. Vanesh, however, took it as something that accompanied pregnancy in some women and encouraged and comforted her, talking to her about children and how he loved her.

#29
The Prophet

    The other men began to give Azshbir trouble about the monthly visits from his wife. After all, one of them was visited by a sister every once in a while, but the other two had never received visits of any sort, and none of them received even semi-regular visits. They went so far as to threaten him, explaining that they were robbers and thieves– they had become such in different ways, one of them merely to feed himself and his mother and siblings– and had no qualms about doing whatever they had to do for Azshbir-could-never-figure-out-what. To take care of this, Azshbir was taken to a cell by himself on the nights of visitation days and instructed not to talk about what happened to him. This arrangement mostly worked, until the day that Neah'ra brought him a change of clothes. After that, he was moved to a fresh cell. This time, he shared his cell with four who had been convicted and sentenced to prison for treason. Their crimes had been different, though, from his. They just wanted not to have to go to war and pay taxes and suffer and die fighting Hasseleighton. They thought they might as well be ruled by Hasseleighton.
    At first, Azshbir did not tell them about his charge. He was too heartsick to want to talk about it and too weary to think about how to do so. Then, Neah'ra came. She sat down with her back to the bars and he sat down with his to them, so that although they did not face each other they were as near as possible. After several minutes of this, she said, "Reilia and Della are becoming little rascals. They crawl around all over the place."
    Azshbir did not answer. He did not want to talk about his daughters. Thinking about them drove a dagger into his heart. He had never even see them, though Neah'ra had graciously waited for him to name them. He still wondered at times why she loved him the way she did. After all, he knew that they had married each other more because they both knew each other to be driven by and seek the same thing, both admired the other's commitment, wisdom, or whatever– allegiance to the Promise– and believed that it would be best for them to marry. They had loved each other, but it was a quiet love, almost even a brotherly love, at least at first. Azshbir wondered if, to some extent, it still was just that. Neah'ra seemed to sense his reluctance to talk about their children and distress at the mention of them, and did not say anything.
    For some strange reason– he *had* been feeling guilty about his conduct recently– Azshbir asked, in a voice so low it could hardly be heard, "I wonder how Darnize is doing."
    Surprisingly, Neah'ra heard him, though their backs were to each other. His cell mates were being respectful. He even thought they were interested and watching half for entertainment, half for true interest. Speaking only a little less softly, Neah'ra said, "I found Father out and told him that I forgive him, and that I'm sure you will, too. You were just feeling juvenile, hurt, grumpy, and otherwise out-of-sorts." Azshbir sucked in his breath. She had not been afraid to go to Darnize?

Afraid he would take her, steal the twins, and mistreat her? And then, she had had the nerve to say those things to him? He was reminded of one of the reasons why he had married her. If he had been far beyond her when they had first met, she was much farther beyond him now. Her trials in the house of her father– uhh!– and living alone with nothing to depend on, and the continuing trials, seemed to be making her like tempered and polished steel. But, she was still speaking. "He's dying, I think. Consumed by guilt and unwilling to admit it." Her voice shook with unshed tears. "When I went to him, he was back in his usual self. Excusing all the things he did– he was just trying to protect me from you, he was just trying to curb my fanaticism to protect me from all the evil that it will bring upon me, the end of which I have not nearly seen– and taking offense at my calling them what they were and offering forgiveness. He's angry that I don't think that he is somehow noble for risking his reputation to visit you in here."

Azshbir did not speak. His whole being was once again taut with an inner pain. *Why,* he wondered, *do my trials not result in the same thing in me that I saw in Razi and, much more, see in Neah'ra?* She was beautiful, and it stabbed him to the core, and he knew it was because he was not. Why? He wanted to be, and there had been that vision. Or, did he want to be? How would he act if he wanted to be? How would he think if he wanted to be? Perhaps he should think about that. Why did he not have the strength to act and think like he would if he wanted to become the same thing that Neah'ra was becoming, for all her weaknesses and imperfections, roils of darkness even, like when she had– and he knew that, on a certain level she had meant to– stabbed him at that first meeting? Did he not have the strength because he did not want? He would have to think about it. He would have to ask the Creator about it, especially now that he had known how personally and actually the Creator was willing to relate to him.

After an endless moment, the guard came to take Neah'ra out, where she would find Anjis ready, to escort her back to Cavisto's house. In previous visits, she had related in a few words the arrangement they had come up with for her well-being and safety, and the fact that Cavisto's business was seriously suffering, so that they relied, altogether too much, upon Ellason's paintings. These facts, particularly the later, about Cavisto's business, upset Azshbir greatly, and Neah'ra had learned not to talk about that kind of thing with him.

After she had gone, Azshbir noticed the interest of his cell mates. However, all of them were too exhausted from the day to talk much. In fact, two of them had already gone to bed. However, despite Azshbir's reluctance, he found himself telling them about the Promise and why he had ended up in prison. Neah'ra's explanation of how Darnize was doing had, apparently, piqued their curiosity. He did not, however, tell them more than he had to, though he knew they were, on some level, interested. He was still heartsick and weary, the more for trying to think things through for himself, and besides, he felt like such a miserable failure that he was not fit even to say that he was in prison on account of the Promise. He had failed so miserably that he was not fit for the Promise, either to be imprisoned or to be rewarded. He felt like for him even to speak the words was to dirty and demean them.

One day, in his darkness though— even in the prison, they had a day more or less off from work once every two weeks— his mind flashed back to his thoughts about what the Promise meant, in the Promised One's bearing away of his shame and crimes, that day when he had stood before the people in the Hall of Exhortation— nay, of Oppression. At the same time, his mind turned, also, to that irrememorable vision of the glory and the suffering of the Conqueror, to what he could still barely grasp of it, even if it was slippery and empty of the power that had infused it with dread, glory, life, and light, that night when he had beheld it. He remembered something about infinitely condescending immeasurable compassion and kindness. He remembered something about being infused by fire with the very life of the Conqueror Himself, and, certainly, that life was worthy to speak of Him and to be His. Azshbir thought he remembered something about the shame and crimes being burned to death by the same glory that would— or had it already done so?— burn him to life. It all made no sense, and he could not see it at all now, but he knew— or at least thought— that he *had* seen it. No, he had to have seen it. He would never have been able to think of something that he could not think at all or remember that he had remembered what he could think in words but could not remember, on his own or by his own imagination or torment. It was true, whatever *it* was and whatever *true* meant.

The next time Neah'ra came, he was thinking all about the vision and what he had seen, in so far as he could still— or now— see it in his mind's eye. He knew, though, that she needed to talk to him and that he had been cruel to her in not letting her. Sitting, facing each other, holding one another's hands through the bars, he said, "Now, dearie, why don't you tell me what has been going on in the past months?" A stab of pain went through his heart.

Neah'ra's dark eyes filled with tears. Faltering at first, she began to speak. Softly. Slowly. Haltingly. She told of living in Cavisto's mansion— no longer vacant— with the others. She told of the former prostitutes and their children. She told of the work they did to support themselves, since Cavisto's profits were plummeting since he had lost reputation and, though he still had a lot of capital, it would not last forever. She told about caring for two rascally twins who had learned to crawl and who grabbed everything in sight for the purpose of putting it into their mouths. They were also constantly needing to be held and nursed. It exhausted her. Several times she broke down and cried. Azshbir just listened, speaking only once to encourage her to go on, the stabbing pain in his heart increasing, tears pushing at the back of his own eyeballs. He loved Neah'ra. He wanted to hold her in his arms. To comfort her. To whisper reassuring words. To take all her burdens. To provide for her so that she did not have to work or worry. To help her care for their children. If it would have helped, he would have been willing to work all night as well as all day, but he had only one thing to offer. Looking into her dark, dark eyes, he pleaded desperately that the Creator would give her visions of grace and glory better even than those he had seen; perhaps He already had. Her life was so much harder than his and yet she was so much calmer, yes, even happier. When he had fallen, she had been there for him, a presence of quiet, strength, and peace. Anyway, he entreated the Creator to give her even more and better. He knew that she prayed the same for him.

Neah'ra was quiet, now, and Azshbir was about to speak, when the guard came to take Neah'ra back out. He knew one of the men in their fellowship would escort her back to her home. Feeling strangely at peace despite his disappointment in not being able to share with his beloved, Azshbir lay back and fell asleep.

The next month Neah'ra did not come. Azshbir was tempted to worry about her, but he knew that she did not come because of any less love for him. Her life was hectic and exhausting– maybe she had fallen sick, it was coming sooner or later– and, to be honest, she was taking risks he did not like. He would rather have died any death than have his wife taking the risks she was taking just to make ends meet. Perhaps that was what galled him most: not being able to do anything when he would have done everything.

The month after that, Neah'ra came again. Azshbir listened to her talk about her life for about five minutes, but after that she fell silent. He let the silence hang for a few long moments. Then, he spoke into the still semi-darkness. "The Conqueror was captured and tied up by men and then beaten so that he could scarcely totter," he said.

"What?" asked Neah'ra. "Say that again."

"The Conquerer was captured and tied up by men and then beaten almost to death. Rather, will be," Azshbir repeated. His cell-mates waited, listening, holding their breaths.

Neah'ra gasped. "What are you saying?" she asked, her voice barely louder than a breath of wind. How Azshbir longed to feel the cool night breeze on his face in the open air! But the longing passed as quickly as it had come upon him. His mind and soul were absorbed in weightier, more solemn matters.

"The Conqueror. When He bears the shame of His people He was despised by all. No, all of this will be, but I sense time does not matter much with the Creator. Of His own free will and by His own strength He mounted the steps of the altar. A girl, a mere child, slew Him." Azshbir paused and swallowed past the lump in his throat. It seemed even more real to him than he remembered when he saw the vision. He went on. "Darkness closed in on Him. The darkness of evil oppressed Him. There was no light, for the Conqueror lay defeated, the Deliverer lay slain upon the altar, by the hand of a child in whose heart evil reigned, for the Creator had withdrawn His light from His Sent One, and from Kaarathlon, and it was the hour of the reign of darkness." He paused again, and tried to swallow past the lump in his throat.

Neah'ra waited. Finally, she prodded, "What came next, Azshbir?"

Azshbir blinked his eyes. "The stars sang for joy. The Conqueror came forth, resplendent in the garb of His conquest, all things following in His train. He is Lord of Life and Lord of Death. Forgiveness and love is His touch."

Neah'ra gripped the bars between them until even her dark hands blanched. Finally in the lowest possible voice she asked, "This has been or it will be? For is not the Promise not yet fulfilled?"

Azshbir nodded in the dim lighting. "I don't know. I'm not really sure. I think that before the Creator it has happened. I certainly saw it as if it... *was.* Not like it was but no longer is, but like something that *is.* But, I don't think it has happened yet. Not in Kaarathlon."

Neah'ra nodded. Azshbir knew that she did not really get it. For a moment silence so deep it was almost oppressive reigned. Then one of Azshbir's cell-mates, a man a few years younger than himself named Rathor, said, "A prophet! A prophet of the Promise!"

Far more quietly another cell-mate asked, "What is so threatening about *this?*"

"He's a prophet!" Rathor repeated. "The Creator has sent us a prophet!"

Azshbir and Neah'ra flinched.

Rathor asked, "Azshbir, will we be released? When?"

"The Creator has not told me that," said Azshbir. Neah'ra could tell that he was deeply embarrassed. She rose to her feet and spoke clearly, "Perhaps the Creator has sent you a prophet. I am indeed honored to be Azshbir's wife. However, He has sent you this prophet to turn you to the Promise of which Azshbir has just been speaking. He has sent you this prophet so that you may believe in the Conqueror whose conquest came in being conquered. Do not yipe at what is not given you, for to you has been given, in this vision, what has never before been known since Kaarathlon was brought into being by the word of her Creator." She dropped her head and slumped against the bars, deeply exhausted and crushed. Azshbir saw her swallow against the lump in her own throat. Gathering herself together, she walked down the aisle, to where the guard would be coming for her by now, not that it had been half an hour yet. At least, Azshbir did not think so.

From then on, Azshbir had to explain to everyone in his section of the prison his vision and knowledge of the Promise. Some insisted it was real; after all, many of them had seen the change in *him* over the past few months! Others insisted that he was a drugged lunatic. Probably he could not keep to anything and was even schizophrenic. Maybe some days he was a revolutionary, other days a traditionalist, other days hallucination-prone.

However, he was not miserable, and he was learning to release his wife and children into the care of the Creator even though it hurt. Of course, he had no choice about the matter.

#30
Little Joy

Brisia stood, her face and eyes aglow. Mom lay on the only low couch in the house, holding a newborn baby at her breast. She saw the joy in Mom's eyes as she looked down on her newborn daughter. She drew closer, proud and happy. Mom looked up, and their eyes met. She bent down, and gently touched the very light fuzz on top of the baby's head.

Entranced, Brisia gazed at the baby's face. "She's so beautiful," she said, softly. Without tearing her gaze away from her baby sister she asked her question, "What is her name?"

Mom looked up at Dad. "What about Lalia?" she asked.

"Just what I was thinking," said Dad. Brisia stood proudly, beaming her unspeakable pleasure. The barrier that had been raised between her parents by their constant fears and fightings seemed to be on the ground, vanished without a trace, utterly destroyed by the birth of their daughter. Looking away from her little sister and between Mom and Dad, she said, "I want to call her Joy."

"That's fine," said Mom, absentmindedly. Her whole attention was still fixed on her child. Dad touched Brisia gently. "It is Dormik's turn, now."

Brisia was too pleased to feel very grumpy.

In the days that followed, little Lalia Joy Ammerius seemed to bring contentment and peace to the torn family. Both her parents and her siblings lavished their attention on her. Mom still spent time with Dormik and Brisia– usually while nursing Lalia– but Dad spent more time playing with them and teaching them how to do things. Mom and Dad almost completely stopped fighting as well, their attention and their energy too drained by their family. Brisia loved Lalia, and she took care of her at every opportunity she had. She loved to play with the little baby, though Mom had to teach her some things about what babies liked. One day, Mom asked her, "Do you love Lalia so much because she is a little baby or because she is your sister?" She knew that Brisia wanted a sister and that Dormik wanted a brother.

Brisia beamed. "Both!" she said. She reached down and tickled Lalia's feet, which she quickly withdrew.

Brisia curled herself around Mom. She knew something was wrong. She had known it from the way that Mom strode across the house to her and took her in her arms, even though Mom did not seem in such turmoil and distress as she had in the months before Lalia's birth. Still, she knew that something was more wrong than ever before. She did not want to know what it was. When she heard Mom take in a breath, bracing herself to speak, she cringed.

In the softest voice possible, Mom said, "The Creator came to me in a way He has never come to me before."

Brisia wondered what was wrong about that. She did not ask.

Mom was quiet for a while. Brisia thought that she was trying to think through the best way to go about saying what she wanted to say. Finally, she said, "The Creator will take care of you and comfort you. That is Who He is, and He's told me, too."

Brisia wondered what Mom was talking about, but every word she said made her want to know less.

"He will take care of Lalia, too. I've known Him, now, in such a way that I can only trust Him. This is Who He is. I can not tell you, Brisia, but I trust that the Creator Himself will tell you."

Brisia's whole body tensed. A vague, dark image floated into her head. She did not touch the idea of what Mom was talking about. It was too terrible even to think, let alone accept.

Mom bent down to kiss Brisia's forehead. "I know you probably can't believe this, yet, but please remember this, no matter what happens: the Creator loves you, and I love you. I will be well, and so will you."

Brisia knew that Mom believed every word she said. Looking up, she said, "I know." She was not quite sure why. She did not know why she did not really feel like crying, either. For a while longer she rested in Mom's arms, until Lalia began to cry and Mom went to nurse her. She shoved away the fear of the thought of what was bothering Mom; she did not want to think about it at all.

Two days later Mom and Dad had their first fight in weeks. It made Brisia's skin crawl. She noticed, too, that Mom was somehow different. She did not yell at Dad that much but told him over and over again the same things that she had told Brisia. The little girl collapsed against the wall, curled herself into a ball, and cried. It occurred to her– she was not sure why it had never occurred to her before– that Dad did not believe in the Creator *or* the Promise.

That night, when Mom gave Lalia– who was crying– to her to rock for a couple minutes while she did a little cooking, Brisia said, "I don't think Dad believes the Promise."

"No, he doesn't. Not at all." Mom sounded like she was near tears. After struggling with herself for a few moments, she said, "It's actually him I'm worried about more than anyone else. It's so much harder to trust the Creator about..." Her voice trailed away, more, Brisia knew, out of an inability to say what she was thinking than out of any intention of keeping it from Brisia, who knew, also, that there was a lot Mom was not telling her.

Taking crying Lalia back from Brisia less than two minutes later, Mom said, half to Brisia and half to herself, "Of course, that could still change."

Now, Brisia was even more confused than before. What was Mom talking about? She knew it had *something* to do with Dad but she had no– or little– idea what. For the first time, she asked a question. "What?"

Looking down at her daughter, Mirla realized that Brisia had no idea what she was talking about. She knew that she could not know everything. "Dad," she said. "He could still believe in the Promise. I pray he will."

Brisia wanted to hug Mom. She still knew that she was not telling her everything, but she did not want to know anyways. One thing she noticed with an overwhelming pang of sorrow was that Mom talked about Dad and her hope for him so much differently... with so much less confidence... than she talked about Brisia. She spoke as if totally confident that the Creator would show Brisia. About her husband, she expressed hope but also a nagging fear. A cloud of gloomy sorrow settled over Brisia.

When Mom sat down, Brisia put her arms around both her and the baby as well as she could to hug them. She kissed Mom on the cheek, and then turned and darted away. Mirla looked after her in surprise, wondering what had gotten into her little daughter's five-year-old self, but grateful that she was so happy and spontaneous.

Brisia, however, ran until she found Dad who was sharpening his scythe. When he saw his excited little daughter, he put what he was doing down. He opened his arms to Brisia and asked, "What happened?"

Brisia settled into his arms and put her face against his chest. After a few moments, he asked her again.

"I love you," she said. "I really love you."

"I love you, too, Sia, my little one, or shall I say, my next-little one?" Dad asked, chuckling.

"I know," said Brisia, turning quiet and solemn. Then, a brightness passed across her face. "Dad, you need to believe in the Promise! You need to ask the Creator to make sure you're in. You know, the People the Creator marks somehow so His Conquerer will know which ones are His so He can lead them out of Death. It's really important. I'm not sure quite why, but I think it's urgent too. Something is going to happen! Please, Daddy, please!"

Brisia noticed the shadow, the stiffness that seemed to be a response to some kind of pain, that crossed Dad's face. "What's wrong, Daddy?" she asked.

Dad held her tighter and then turned her to face him. She looked into his eyes for a moment, and then buried her head in his beard. He drew her away again, and held his hands under her face to make her look at him. "I love you, Brisia," he said, "and I love your mother, too. I *do* believe in the Promise and I'm sure the Creator will accept that. I just don't believe like that fanatical wizard, Kathreen, does, or like Mom does. Does that reassure you, little starling?"

Brisia loved it when Dad called her starling. It did not, however, soothe the wound she was feeling. A sadness had come over her for Dad and his words did not reassure her, not enough to banish the cloud she felt. She was not sure why, but something was just not quite right, just a little off. She did not know what to say or think. "Yeah, I guess so," she said.

Dad hugged her again. Then he released her. "Go, run off, my little starling, now, and help Mom with your little Joy while she cooks! I should really get back to this, now." He said it with a chuckle, but Brisia knew that he was not happy. She knew, too, that he really loved her, cared about her, and liked playing with her. He might be telling her to go away, but he was doing it playfully!

Brisia smiled, poked him, and ran off.

When she came back, Mirla guessed what had happened. *Oh no!* she thought.

#31
The Starling's Tears

Brisia crouched in a dark little closet near the middle of her house. She was too terrified even to cry. Dormik was too scared to cry, too, but he was sobbing in a corner. She was trying desperately to keep Lalia from crying.

She knew what was happening. She had known the minute Mom had grabbed her and Dormik and dragged them through the house, hushing their protestations. She kissed all three of her children, and Brisia knew that she had been about to cry. "Dormik, remember: the Creator does all things well. Brisia, remember: the Promised One will conquer, in us and in the world, and we will reign with Him. Tell Lalia: I love her and I always will. With our eyes we will see. Oh, do know, all of you: I don't understand, but I know the Creator will give us all His best. I've seen Him. I know. Oh, oh, oh… Kalimad…" Brisia had heard the unveiled pain, sharper than any sword in Mom's voice, as she spoke her husband's name. She had turned away, her own soul tearing, and closed and locked the door.

Now, Brisia heard the clashing of swords and the cries of men. It made her muscles tremble. She could not think. She could scarcely breathe. "Quiet, Lalia, Lalia, the moon will shine," she cooed, trying to keep the baby quiet, and not sure why she was even doing anything or what sense her words made.

She heard a scream and knew it was her father. She froze, her five-year-old brain panicked. What was happening to him? Softly, she cried out.

Lalia began to scream. Loudly. Brisia totally panicked. She freaked out. "Dormik!" she yelled, upset. Her head swiveled as she frantically sought some guidance or help. *Mom! Where is Mom!* Her brain reeled in panic and she could not think straight.

Next thing Brisia knew the door was being kicked open. She froze, too frightened to scream. Lalia went on screaming. Dormik screamed, too. The door came crashing down, and he flung himself on the soldier, fingers curled to tear as best as he could.

Brisia grabbed Lalia and held her to her chest, as she crawled into a corner between crates.

It was too late.

The next thing Brisia remembered was hearing a soldier saying something that she knew constituted a threat to kill Lalia. She sickened, her stomach already in turmoil from the fear and shock she had already endured. She heard Mom's clear, ringing reply but her brain never processed the words. She flailed in the arms of the soldier who carried her, vomiting.

Brisia watched in horror and shock as the soldiers hit and bound Mom. "Mom," she gasped, but her voice hardly came out. She barely noticed the two women, one tall and swift, the other shorter and thicker, who emerged from the bushes, gleaming swords in their hands. She finally realized what was happening when the tall woman stood over the body of a fallen soldier, Lalia in her arms. She was still so shocked and confused that she felt dizzy.

Her mind reeled as if it was being bounced and jiggled. A light of amazing intensity appeared out of nowhere, startling Brisia. She struggled in the arms of the man who carried her and cried out. She looked and saw the tall woman fleeing with Lalia. The soldier pursuing her fell and hit the ground heavily. Would she ever see her sister again– or Mom? She tried to look for Mom but she could not find her. Next moment, she squirmed and tried to get away with even more urgency as Dormik, who was somehow freed and wielding a sword, slashed at the man who carried her. Next moment, as Brisia remembered it, the shorter, thicker woman grabbed her from the soldier's arms even as he flailed and fell to the ground. What was happening?

Next moment the short woman had put her down. "RUN!" she yelled to them both. Brisia's head rang with confusion. The soldiers were yelling. "It's a wizard!" Some cried, "Kathry or Adaria!" Another yelled in reply, "Don't lose Mirla, too!"

Brisia looked at the short woman, her rescuer. *Wizard? What wizard?* she thought. She heard Mom's name, and looked for her. This time, their eyes met. *"Mom!"* Brisia gasped, her heart tearing.

"RUN! Obey her! I know–" yelled Mom. It took Brisia a moment to process her words, she was still in so much shock. Then she saw the soldier slap her across the face and drag her. Her heart clenched painfully. She stood for a moment, then felt her brother's hasty pinch. Still hardly thinking, she ran blindly but urged by fear.

Brisia saw the light behind her. It made some of the shadows dark and stark before her and muted others, as it played across the natural sunlight. She still could not process everything that was going on. She heard voices and the sounds of scuffing and fighting behind her. Dormik outdistanced her, but she could run no faster. She followed Dormik between two houses, and fell. Quickly she picked herself up, and continued running. Finally, she found herself in the woods and collapsed on the ground. Her side ached. It did not help that she was crying freely now.

The next thing Brisia noticed was the sound of huge wings flapping and then a huge body landing. In a few moments the tall woman was speaking to her. "Children," she said, "I don't know your names, but I am a friend of Kathreen's, whom your mom, Mirla, may have told you about. Would you be willing to mount L'sa-moth, Kathreen's dragon, and be taken to safety?"

Dormik, who had much more of his wits together than Brisia, though she did remember Mirla telling her about Kathreen Alarion and L'sa-moth, responded to the lady, whose name, it turned out, was Adaria. In a few minutes, they were both on the back of the dragon, flying low above the forests deeper into the mountains. Brisia did not really notice. Her whole body was too taut and upset from shock and fear for her to be further bothered by a little flying. She collapsed in the arms of her brother– who was held by Adaria– and cried.

Brisia had done all she could to care for Lalia, but without Mom to take care of her and nurse her she sickened, and Brisia knew it. She had known it the first day. It made an already horrible situation even worse. Too exhausted and distressed to bear it anymore, and unable to help anyways, she let Kathreen and Adaria take over the care of her little sister, who she was worried might die. She did not want to think about it.

She could tell that Kathreen was distressed, too. The woman, probably about Mom's age, often sobbed while she held Brisia, even when she was *not* crying. She knew that she was cut to the heart. Adaria seemed far less affected, though she was loving and warm.

Tonight, Brisia lay in Adaria's arms while Kathreen held Dormik. She had cried for hours while riding the dragon earlier in the evening, and now she rested against Adaria, quiet. She was lonely. She missed Mom so much. More desires and yearnings than she could name rose from her heart. She felt lost and confused; exposed, without any guidance, help, or support. She needed Mom. She needed her.

Dormik's ranting broke in on the quiet pain of her rest as she relaxed in Adaria's arms. "I hate them!" he said. "They killed Dad and dragged us all out over his dead body! I *HATE* them. They deserve to be killed. Beheaded on the roadside. Thrown from cliffs. Locked in houses and left to be burned when the wild fire comes through! They killed Dad, and who knows what they are doing to Mom! I loved Mom and Dad! I loved them! How I wish the Creator would throw them all down right now!"

Brisia flinched. *She* did not wish those things on anyone, if even they might be… no, she could not think that. She lifted herself out of Adaria's arms and looked over at Dormik. The firelight played on his torn and dingy clothing. "Dormik!" she scolded.

It was the first word she had said in days.

Her brother looked over at her. She noticed Kathreen and Adaria looking at her, too. She did not say anymore. She buried her head in Adaria's hair and cried while the older woman spoke kindly to her, her words soft and soothing. Brisia did not listen to her words, but her voice left an imprint on her mind. Dormik continued ranting, on and off, all night until he finally fell asleep.

The fact of the matter was that Dormik's rants made Brisia feel sick. She did not know why he was so angry. It did not help anything one bit. Not one bit at all. The ache in her heart increased. She felt the sudden urge to go to Mom and talk to her about it. Curl up close to her and let her presence comfort her. Ask her why Dormik was so angry. Discuss the whole issue with her. Learn from her and hear what she thought and understood. Just let her stroke her hair and tell her it was all right. Her chest constricted. She could not go to Mom. Mom was dead. Never again.

The next day, Brisia was glad to be sitting with Kathreen. That way she could not hear Dormik rant, because it all flowed past her in the wind. When they slid down the dragon's teal foreleg that evening, she turned to give her brother a hug. He almost picked her up. She knew, though, in his touch that he was as hurt as she was. He acted like stone. He was rigid, pale, unfeeling, but all because every nerve and fiber burned and twanged with searing pain it was so taut.

Listening to Dormik rant again that night– it seemed to be his favorite practice– Brisia leaned onto Kathreen's shoulder and cried. She could feel the woman's pain, intense and dreadful, strung through her whole being, even while she patted her gently. She remembered the things Mom had said. Her confidence. Her peace. Her assurance that, even though she did not understand at all, the Creator would ensure that all was well. She remembered her saying, too, something about the Promise being enough for everyone or anyone.

Then, she remembered the flash when it had occurred to her that Dad did not really believe the Promise.

Brisia's soul twanged in sharp warning. She recalled Mom's last words for them all. "Dormik, remember: the Creator does all things well. Brisia, remember: the Promised One will conquer, in us and in the world, and we will reign with Him. Tell Lalia: … In the end we will see."

The same pain she had felt for Dad throbbed in her heart for Dormik. She burst into fresh weeping, her tears soaking the shoulder of Kathreen's cloak. Sobs wracked her body until her whole chest and ribs hurt. She could not bear it. She could not endure it. "Oh, oh, oh," she cried, unable to speak. She could not have put her pain or sorrow into words if she had wanted to do so. She cried for herself. She cried for her family. She cried for her little sister, Lalia. She cried for Mom. She cried for Dad. But, most of all, she cried for Dormik.

#32
The Letter

Arendellie lay on a mat while her maids rubbed and soaped her body to clean the sweat away. Now that she was healed from the birth of her son she was doing exercises to help her body revert to its proper shape. As always, her maids chattered like birds. She hardly ever listened or responded to it, except to scold them for it. As usual, their ministrations were relaxing, except when their incessant chatter drove her crazy. That was one nice thing about Inshara and Aki'lam. They did not chatter much. Sometimes, they spoke a little in soft, serious tones, but they never talked much and they never chattered like a bunch of birds.

Now a snitchet of their conversation embedded itself in Arendellie's mind. Twisting around, she asked, "*What* did you just say?"

"Uh, there's just a sensational letter running around. A lot of copies have been made."

That's unusual, thought Arendellie. She also knew that the maid had *not* told her what she had said. Instead she had told her something else. She glowered at her and turned to the other.

Minshi looked very nervous and anxious. "Kathreen wrote it, my Lady," she said.

"Why are you holding out on me?" Arendellie scolded.

Minshi fidgeted. Arendellie had no idea why she was so uncomfortable... so terrified. "I'm sorry, my Lady," she said. "I should not have been chattering around you, my Lady. I'm sorry. I beg you, my Lady, please–"

Arendellie cut her off. "Stop it, Minshi! Don't grovel! *Tell* me! What were you talking about?"

"Uh," said Minshi, "my Lady, may the stars shine upon you,"– Arendellie glowered– "but apparently a friend of the Wizard Kathreen Alarion's was tortured to death. The Wizard and Dragon-rider Kathreen Alarion has also taken to styling herself, 'Knight of the Promise.' She insulted the High Emperor as no one else has ever dared."

Knight of the Promise? thought Arendellie. *They've called themselves the People of the Promise, but Knight of the Promise? Where did that come from?* Out loud, she asked, a whirlstorm of emotions she did not want to face and did not want to know churning in her heart, "What did she call the High Emperor?"

Minshi looked around nervously. "I do not think the words are proper to repeat," she said.

"Never mind!" said Arendellie. "*Tell* me them!"

Minshi looked terrified now. Arendellie glanced at the other maid, and saw the same terror on her expression. It was like they expected dark birds to fly out of nowhere and take them away. Maybe to the Undead Snow Queen. "I, I really don't think we should," Minshi insisted.

Something was going on. Her maids never resisted her this much. Arendellie knew they feared her and dared not arouse her anger. "Is it possible you don't know the insult?" she asked.

Minshi shook her head. At least Arendellie thought she did.

"*Tell me!*" Arendellie yelled.

She heard the sounds of her other maids running. In a voice low with terror, looking around as if she expected to be struck down by some strange magical terror, Minshi said, "'The Wicked and Abominable.' She said a lot more," she added, looking over her shoulder in strange fear, "but I really don't think I should say it."

Arendellie decided not to press her, though this was passing strange. Who had had the courage to tell Minshi these words, when Minshi dared not relate them? The other maids were gathering around, but Arendellie still asked the question most on her mind. "Do you know the friend's name?"

"I think, I *think,*" said the other maid, "that it was Mirla of Ebrin, my Lady and Princess."

Arendellie's blood pounded. Laying back down, tense, she said, "Finish your work. Quickly!"

Aki'lam touched Arendellie's elbow softly. "My Lady, are you sure this is a good idea?"

Arendellie started. This was the first time Aki'lam had actually related to her. Looking at her sharply she asked quietly, "Did Inshara convert you? Are you one of the People of the Promise?"

Aki'lam's face showed stark terror and shock. "Oh, no! Never, never! What made you think so?" she asked.

"Oh, nothing. You're just acting more like…" said Arendellie. To herself she thought, *Is this what I am becoming? What is going on with me? How come I am expecting anyone who is loving and caring to belong to the Promise? That is just wrong! WHAT IS HAPPENING TO ME!*

She had ordered one of her maids to get her a copy of the letter, despite their protestations that it was improper, not to mention dangerous, and they might not be able to obtain one, and their pleas to be reasonable and kind. Her mind had registered almost every word. As far as she could remember, it read like the following:

"Wizard and Dragon-rider, Kathreen Alarion, Knight of the Promise, to he who is unworthy to be called Dragon Keeper, who styles himself Emperor of Camil Hasseleighton, Grale Casarion.

"Your crimes against the people of the Creator, the One and Only King-over-all, against Whom you have declared war, are screaming to heaven. His patience will only last so long, and I do not know why it has lasted as long as it has. It will come suddenly to an end, before His wrath, for He will avenge His own.

"You have torn children away from their mothers. You have tortured men and women because they refuse you the complete allegiance that is due to the Creator alone. In the very city from which I write this, Akshar of South Enzenyar, Avanzar, your men cruelly treated and tortured my best friend, Mirla of Ebrin, a beautiful and favored servant of the Creator. Your men killed her husband, and orphaned their children. How many instances of similar atrocities have been committed by your command and sanctioned by your authority, only the Most High Creator and King of all knows. You deserve to be cast into the lowest dungeon in the depth of Death, which– if you do not know– was created by the Creator as a punishment and will be conquered and ruled by One Whom He will send– and rot there for all of eternity.

"You are a murderer, a traitor and a rebel, a torturer, and an imbecile, in whom dwells every kind of iniquity, transgression, sin, crime, wickedness, atrocity and evil, in all their fullness. Be ware!"

While she was reading it, Inshara had come and peaked over her shoulder. She had seen the look of shock and disapproval written in the maid's eyes, and it had taken her a moment to realize that it was not directed at her (Inshara was the only one of her maids who had yet to express disapproval towards her for her questions, demands, and actions related to this issue). The maid had, apparently, taken in the general tone of the letter in a glance, and sucked in her breath sharply. "Oh!" she cried. "I can't believe she did that!"

Without taking her eyes from the paper Arendellie asked, "Who? What?"

"Kathreen," hissed Inshara, clearly distressed. Arendellie had never seen her this upset before. "This. It's unacceptable, and I did not think it of her."

This time Arendellie glanced around to make sure no one was near and then looked at Inshara. "You knew Kathreen?" she gasped.

"No, I've never met her. Never even seen her," replied Inshara, a little taken aback. "But this is clearly wrong! This is clearly the product of nothing except fury, anger, and outrage. It's okay for Kathreen to be outraged. It's okay for her to say these things… they are all true. Every one of them. But the way she says them is wrong, and her motivation for saying them comes through this letter loud and clear, and it is nothing but wrong, too!"

Inshara had never talked to her this way before. She seemed to have forgotten Arendellie's admonition about never speaking to her about the Promise again, but Arendellie did not mind. After all, it was not really her fault, and Arendellie wanted to know what she was thinking, though she knew that later she would regret it. (Worse, she seemed to have forgotten that she was the slave and Arendellie was the princess of the heir, but that did not bother Arendellie too much at that precise moment.) "What is wrong with it?" she asked.

"Kathreen is just thinking about how mad and hurt she is. Did she notice that she never once mentioned the Promise in here? She is wishing all these judgments upon Grale Casarion! That is *not* our call. The Creator can decide things like that!" Inshara was obviously getting more and more upset as she went on.

"Be quieter!" Arendellie cautioned, in a low voice herself. "Otherwise…"

Inshara shook her head. "This *must* be disowned. Not Kathreen, but *this!* It is unacceptable. It can not go on! It is a scandal, and it will not do anyone any good."

Arendellie looked at Inshara in surprise. "You're not outraged at the atrocities mentioned herein? You're not afraid?"

"Oh, I am," said Inshara. Arendellie was not sure which question she was answering. "But this is just unacceptable! It will do us great harm for no good reason. At the moment, I'm more interested in making sure that no one thinks *that*"– Arendellie noticed that she said the word as if that to which she was referring was a poisonous snake– "is a representation of the Promise! It does not help that Kathreen wrote it as a Knight of the Promise, which indicates some authority and commission! Agh."

Inshara balled her hands into fists. "It's repulsive and juvenile. It's insolent. *NONE* of our people has done that! Not even before courts, condemned to torturous deaths! Call evil evil! And, then, command them to repent and take refuge in the Promised Conquerer, lest they be destroyed by Him! Oh, has she forgotten the Promise and the Call– the Command?" Inshara was muttering angrily, now. "What's worse is, she of all people should know and do better. Look at her titles– especially *Knight of the Promise!* She of all people *must* do better. Is called to better!"

Arendellie interrupted Inshara. She hated hearing her criticize Kathreen Alarion, her only remaining friend, for something that seemed, to her, so natural and, certainly, not deplorable. "Inshara," she asked, "how can you criticize Kathreen so? Wouldn't you do the same thing in the same circumstances? How do you know what Kathreen has endured?"

Inshara looked Arendellie in the eye. Her answer, calm, measured, confident, peaceful, surprised Arendellie. "What I would do is not important. Not in this way. Nor do I wish anything ill upon Kathreen. From what I have heard of her, she is blessed of the Creator and a blessing. However, this is unacceptable. It can not be passed over lightly. It is deplorable, and it is unworthy of her."

Arendellie had gotten up. She had no need to hear more, and she had decided what to do. She would demand an audience with Prince Vanesh Casarion immediately.

It was that against which Aki'lam had advised her.

"What is it, my queen– for to me you are a queen– that is so urgent?" asked Vanesh. At Arendellie's request, they spoke together in private chambers.

Arendellie was sobbing now. She hated herself. She was supposed to be calm and controlled and opaque, and now she had given everything away. Her best maids were probably going to be killed, too, as a result of this whole thing. However, she had gone too far, now. "I did not tell you a year ago about what was going on in Ebrin with Mirla. And she did not even have the information that would have saved her life! And, now, she has been tortured to death and Kathreen has written a letter that is going to get everyone associated with the Promise in bigger trouble than ever before, because it is so clearly an instance of unveiled subversion and high treason! I understand it is not even an accurate stance of the position of the vast majority of the People of the Promise and that Kathreen was just angry, upset, and grieving!"

"Be quiet, Arendellie," said the prince. He did not seem pleased. "This is why you interrupted me? What excuse am I going to give to the rest of the Court to explain your urgent demand to see me alone?"

Arendellie stiffened. Then an idea occurred to her. She smiled brightly. "Tell them that I was in a state of emotional shock upon learning that so many of my old friends, family, and countrymen were part of a sect so venomous towards my lord and his family!" she said. "Tell them that I only recently was pregnant, and I haven't all the way recovered emotionally yet."

"That might do," said Vanesh, somewhat pleased. "It will also further convince them that you do not have very great wits or intelligence– of which they are already so convinced. After all, you come from the countryside and had no education. Of course, *I* know they are wrong, and am going to seek your counsel more!" He laughed, but he was serious, cold, still distressed.

Arendellie shrugged.

"No, my queen," said Vanesh. "Do I gather that you feel guilty for what has happened?" He squeezed Arendellie lightly. "Don't worry," he said. "No one could do anything about it. Grale Casarion is unstable and not highly intelligent. He's also very violent, bloodthirsty, and has a penchant for cruelty. He would never believe that Kathreen is not visiting Mirla. He is suspicious to a fault, and actually often over-credits people with cunning." Arendellie felt accused. She stiffened, thinking self-defensive thoughts. After all, she lived in a palace, around this man. "You could have done nothing, if that would ease your soul. In fact, there was nothing anyone could do."

"Not really," said Arendellie, breaking into tears. "During my visit to Ebrin last month, I wanted to see Mirla and talk to her about some things. Everyone I asked told me the family had moved and they did not know why or where. I sensed they were holding back. There was something wrong. But I did not know what and I did not want to think about it." She paused for a moment, and wiped away her tears. "Now... I've no idea what happened to her children, but she has died a horrible death and something Kathreen wrote makes me worried that maybe worse things happened to her. I'll never see her again, but it's far worse than that. And, my best friend is hurting somewhere, and..." She was sobbing so that she could not speak.

Vanesh kissed her lightly. "You are so much more than the Court thinks you are," he said, "though I am glad they do not know." He stepped away. "I must return. Would you like to stay here, and I will send a slave to get some of your maids?"

"Yes, thank you very much," said Arendellie sniffling. She did not really want to talk to Inshara, but she did not want most of the others either. They would be worse. What might they think or be? "I want Inshara, Aki'lam, Kawina, and Girsa," she said.

"Very well," said Vanesh. "I love you, my very own queen," he said, kissed her lightly, and left.

#33
The Caress of the Night Wind

Brisia split slender roots while watching the three babies. They crawled around now, and needed to be watched constantly. She was helping Hoobit and Sirifa's third-youngest daughter, Senise, who was quite a few years older than herself, to watch the babies. Seeing one of the toddlers run off, Senise ran after her, grabbed her, and held the whimpering little girl to her chest, kissing her, and saying, "My sister, oh, Kizyia, Kizyia!"

Brisia dropped the roots, ran a few strides, skidded, and knelt beside another little toddler, significantly smaller than the other two, who was trying to put dirt in her mouth. She flicked it out, telling the baby, "No, Lalia. No!" Looking up, she said, "Senise, that's Nahiza, not Kizyia."

"I'm sorry," said Senise. "Their names sound very similar. At least, they flow the same."

Brisia gloated. "That's an excuse," she said. She had only been here for half a year– less than half the life of the twins– and she knew the two toddlers apart, while Senise did not. Touching her own sister's face very gently, she said in the quietest whisper, "When you're old enough, I'll tell you what Mom said." She began to cry again. She wished she had a word from Dad, too, both to cling to for herself and to give to her sister.

She remembered begging both Kathreen and Adaria to stay with her the day that Kathreen had left. To her, the older woman felt like the last piece of Mom to which she might be able to hold. Like a reminder of Mom, or one she could trust as a best friend of Mom. The two or so weeks before that dreadful day Mom's friends had, one by one, stopped coming over. She could tell that something was wrong and that Mom knew it, but she had not asked or even thought about it much. She still remembered some of them, particularly an old woman named Aleria and a younger one, whose name she could not quite remember. She knew it started with a "di'" sound and ended in a "yiet" sound. She vaguely remembered Mom telling that girl not to marry someone for some reason Brisia did not understand. Now, after more than half a year, she thought she knew what had happened to these people– they had endured the same fate as Mom– but she still did not want to think about it. Kathreen, however, though Brisia had not known her, she knew that Mom had. With that final glance, Mom had given her into Kathreen's care. She had felt, looking into Kathreen's eyes and feeling her arms about her, that Kathreen had not wanted to leave either. At least, there was a way in which she did not want to leave. Brisia knew that she also half-wanted to flee to the moon, but it was only the kind of flee that Brisia wanted to do herself: to flee from the wickedness, the cruelty, the sorrow, and the loss, the grief and the pain. She had also sensed Adaria's chagrin at having to stay behind, though she was very glad that she had, in fact, stayed with her!

Now, though, she was cuddling Lalia and trying to play with her and Nahiza while crying freely. "Dad, Dad, Dad," she sobbed, over and over again.

Senise touched her gently. "I'm sure he's okay, now," she said.

"He's *dead!*" Brisia cried.

Senise placed Kizyia on the ground next to Nahiza and put her arms gently around Brisia. "I know," she said, "but *he's okay.* I'm sure of it."

Something felt wrong with Senise's words. Brisia knew it. Or maybe, it would be better to say that she felt it in her bones. She struggled for a while with the words to speak. Finally, after Senise almost thought that she would not speak, she said, "How would you know?"

"Is your mom okay?" Senise asked gently.

"Yes."

"But she's probably dead– or worse. But probably dead," said Senise.

Brisia flinched. She clenched her teeth. She felt Lalia pick up on her tension and begin to cry. "I don't know," she said.

"What's different about your dad and your mom?" asked Senise gently.

Senise's comfort was not comfort. Brisia did not know how to put it. Finally, she said, "Dad was not willing."

At this point Senise was quite confused. "Willing about what?" she asked.

"I don't know," said Brisia. What she meant was, "I don't know how to say it," but she did not think of that. She put down Lalia, who was crying loudly now, and continued splitting roots. She could not comfort Lalia or even try to do so. She was too disturbed. She just could not face anything. At least, that was how she felt.

Several hours later, while Brisia was still crying, as much for herself as for anybody else, and Senise was struggling to watch and take care of three toddlers, Sirifa came. She spoke quietly with Senise, but Brisia did not listen. Then, she came and knelt down in front of Brisia. She took the roots away from her and said, gently, "Brisia, I love you."

"I know. I love you, too," said Brisia, looking up and smiling gently. Then, she looked back down. Her eyes were bloodshot and her cheeks were tear-streaked. Again. Sirifa gently took her hands in her own. "Brisia, this is not right."

Brisia did not respond.

Sirifa tried again. "Brisia, the way you're handling things is not okay."

Brisia still did not respond.

"You're not taking care of your little sister very well."

This time Brisia looked up. "I can't."

"What do you mean you can't?"

Brisia did not respond, except to look up and then away again.

"Brisia, I know you hurt, but that is not an excuse not to care. You love Lalia, don't you?"

Brisia mumbled something. "Say that again," said Sirifa.

"Yes."

Sirifa opened her arms, and Brisia crawled onto her lap and curled up there. She cried against her. For a while she was silent. Then, Sirifa began speaking. "The world is not right. I know that, too. In fact, I have known grief and loss, too. Three of my– " Sirifa drew back, knowing that it was not the right thing to tell a little girl.

Hopefully, Brisia was not listening intently enough to piece together the bits of information and cry for her children, too. Habits of thinking learned when young died hard. This was the first time this was being tested, and there were so many things that she had not thought through and then lived through.

Brisia cried more. Sirifa knew she could not hold this child forever. She had to nurse the babies. After a few more minutes, she told Brisia.

The nearly six-year old wiggled out of her lap and cried harder. Sirifa took Lalia and set her on one of her breasts. Brisia took Nahiza and helped Sirifa with the babies, but in a few minutes she was again crying so hard that she shook.

"What is the problem?" Sirifa asked.

"Dad," said Brisia.

For a moment there was a light in Sirifa's eyes. She thought she understood, but she did not know what to offer.

That night, Brisia who was still only learning to talk and play and communicate, and who was just beginning to share her pain or grief at all, did the most outrageous thing any of them had seen her do yet.

Dormik, who was even more withdrawn than Brisia, though he talked about what had happened a great deal more, said something about how he "wished whatever torments they were inflicting upon Mom would be inflicted back upon them ten times over."

Brisia had had enough. She flung herself at Dormik and yelled in his face. "HOW *DARE* YOU!" she screamed. Dormik pressed himself against the wall. They were all shocked at Brisia's behavior. They had never seen her angry before. Well, sometimes she got upset and snapped, but this was different. "By the Creator, how *can you!*" Brisia went on. "It's just wrong– wrong, wrong, *WRONG!*" Breaking into tears, she cried, *"He's good."* She was quiet for a few moments, and then she said, "I don't think you know Him."

It was by far the most words any of them had heard out of her mouth at a time.

Dormik cringed, pale. For Brisia, she had remembered Mom's last words to her in particular: *the Promised One will conquer, in us and in the world, and we will reign with Him.* She knew that, as much as Dormik needed the reminder, *the Creator does all things well,* she needed that. Her whole body slumped.

His voice trembling, whether with pain or with anger, Dormik asked, "What makes you think that?"

"You're so angry!" said Brisia, sobbing.

"And you aren't?"

She did not reply. She just cried. She cried so much that she had a perpetual headache and her throat was continually sore, her voice hoarse. She knew that everyone was looking at her and wondering about her, but she did not want to face it. She got to her feet, walked shaking through the room, and flinging herself down on the pile of linjer leaves that was her bed, buried her head in her blankets and cried. She buried her whole body in them, too. She did not want to be seen. She wanted to be alone. She would have gone outside, but she knew that it was dangerous and she was not allowed to do so.

Later, when everyone was going to bed, Adaria came and sat down against the wall not far from where Brisia lay. Once she judged that everyone was asleep, the little girl got up, crept over to her, and sat down, leaning against her. Adaria touched her lightly, and whispered, "Let's go outside, together." That way they would be alone.

Brisia nodded. Adaria felt more than saw the motion. She took her hand and led her softly out, between the sleepers. Outside, a moon but one day from full shone brightly. They stood together a few paces from the house. They kept the forest at bay a good sixty paces away from where the two now stood. For a long time they stood there, under the brightly glowing moon that shed a mist of soft white light across the sky obscuring the glittering stars. The whole sky was made a whitish gray-blue by the misty glow of the moon. The enchanting, sharp but delicate, fragrance of the night flowers reached them on the gentle breeze that cooled their skin. Brisia still had a hard time sleeping in the hot humidity of the jungles of the Vinibra Mountains, though they were high enough that it did get cool at times, sometimes so cool that she shivered.

In a whisper that seemed to be one with the night magic, Adaria breathed, "It's beautiful."

Brisia nodded, gripping Adaria's hand tighter. Adaria spoke again. "You never met my brother Azshbir. Of all of us, I think I was closest to him."

Brisia did not speak, but Adaria went on. "He went with me and Kathreen to warn the people of Ephezoa that their allegiance to their lifestyle and way of thinking was not true allegiance to the Creator. When I and Kathreen chose to go into the heart of Hasseleighton, he chose to remain behind in Afteloan of Ephezoa. I know he was ready to face any danger and never disturbed by the fear of torture, but he knew that was his place. It was sad, our last parting, and yet happy, too. I wonder how he is, now. What is he doing? How is he living? Does he know other People or Knights of the Promise?"

Brisia just listened, breathing deeply of the intoxicating night air. It was not really quiet. The air rang with the calls of strange jungle creatures, most of which Brisia had never seen.

Adaria drew a deep breath, and was quiet for a long time. Finally, she went on. "The world is changing. It always has been, only sometimes people don't notice. The Call is strange. It comes to some in one way, to others in another. It is rarely what we would expect. Sometimes, it is not what we want, or not what we might have wanted." She took another deep, long breath. Then she said, "But, always, it is good."

Brisia wondered if she was even talking to her.

Adaria stood for a while longer, still almost as the stone, looking up at the pale night sky. Then she said, more quietly than ever, "There is so much more. I just know it."

It was then that Brisia knew that, in some way at least, this was for her. Somehow, she felt that Adaria was not saying this *just* for her, but *for her.*

The minutes crawled slowly by. Adaria took a few steps and sat down on a patch of soft, feathery grass. Brisia sat down beside her. She fidgeted for a few moments, and then lay down, stretching herself out on the grass. The cool night air felt good. Adaria waited.

Finally, Brisia muttered something very quietly. Adaria did not hear it, and she was not at all sure that it would have been intelligible even if she had. Gathering together everything she had learned, by observation, by scant communication, and from others, about Brisia, she spoke softly and gently. Her voice soothed Brisia's nerves as if it were the caress or kiss of the night wind, even though her words stirred, gently though cruelly, the pain in her soul.

"You're afraid for your dad and for your brother. You saw that your dad did not trust the Creator or really believe the Promise. Your brother seems so angry and bitter, even though you both saw your mom's willingness to surrender and contentment, that you do not see how he can trust the Creator either. This very much upsets you."

Adaria took a depth breath, and then continued on. "You miss your mom. You want her desperately. Her love. Her guidance. You want to trust her. You don't know on whom else to lean or trust. That's not all though. You're just sad, too. You miss her. You grieve for her. You want her. You want and grieve for your dad, too, but you're afraid for him, too."

Again, Adaria fell silent. She waited several minutes before continuing. "You're sad for Lalia. You want her to get to know your mom. You want her to get to know your dad. To experience their love and care. You feel like so much has been stolen from you, taken from you, lost. Gone. It leaves an abyss of sorrow for what should be yet is not. You grieve both for what is and for what is not. So many hopes, so much of life, is just gone. It's death."

Brisia did not know what to say or even think. She lay quietly. For a very long time, all was silent except for the cries and noises of the night-creatures. Sitting there, quietly, listening to the same cries, breathing the same almost magical air that had no power to dispell the sting and pain of grief and loss, of what should not be and of what should be, for it is both: what should be must be twisted until it is no longer what should be in order to be what should not be, and what should not be can be only by twisting and destroying what should be. For a moment she was going to say that perhaps Brisia felt like she was only a small child and should not be expected to bear such loss, such evil, such darkness of grief. Then, in a flash of knowledge as clear and sharp as an arrow and as burning as a flame of fire Adaria knew that she must not even suggest such a thing. To do so would only add fuel to the element of self-pity in Brisia's suffering. If, somewhere deep in Brisia's young and simple soul such dark thoughts were forming, speaking and articulating them would not help and, if not, to speak them would be to sow the seed for them and do irrecoverable damage. She sat for a long time, perfectly still except for her fingers, which now and then reached for a blade of grass with which to fiddle, silent, waiting, waiting for the right moment and the right word, waiting for she did not know what and for what, to think about or formulate, would be to ruin by refusing to wait.

The stars moved in their wheeling dance above. The shadows cast by the moon shifted. Still Adaria waited in silence and Brisia lay in something that can not be described as silence, for in one part of her there was a torture, a turmoil, and a tension so taut it burned, and in another a contentment and relaxation.

Finally, Adaria said, "I can not tell you what you need to know, because it is not to know you need. But I can tell you, that it is the Creator. The Promise. There *is* what you… need, and I think you know. One whose love will support you and who will guide you. You may not feel like He is really real, but He is. What *is. Matters.*" Adaria was not sure if her words helped. She was not sure if they would really be heard. Perhaps they hurt. Perhaps they were an embodiment of a nothing; perhaps she should say no more, lest her words be negative rather than positive. Nonetheless, she spoke once more. "He gives." She had the feeling that she did not really know, herself, what she was telling Brisia. She knew that she could not say what, in that moment, she knew that Brisia needed to know. She could not even articulate it to herself, form it in her own mind. She was not at all certain that she even knew what it was that she knew that Brisia needed to know. She had the feeling, though, that Brisia had what she needed to reach out for it; there was nothing she could say, nothing she could do, nothing she could give. Gently and tenderly she ran her fingers through Brisia's tangled hair.

Still running her fingers through the small girl's hair, Adaria again looked up at the heavens, white with the light with which the moon shone. Something indefinable seemed to gleam and glance down at her. Something was there which she could not see, but she could see enough to know that it was. She felt, for a moment, like the fourteen year old girl who had first gone with Kathreen. Somehow frail, young, without strength or firmness. It, too, was indefinable. Like one standing in the wind, knowing not whither she goes, how she goes, to what she goes. A *pure* uncertainty. All this takes too long to describe. Looking up to the heavens, shining with a pure white light of which the day knows naught, she felt, somehow, as if… as if… as if… she did not know what as if.

Was Brisia going to know… or was it see… no, nothing fit… what she would not? Could not? Or would she, too, but not by herself, but by Brisia? Would all things, indeed, be done well… work for good and the best good, at that? Was it true? *What* was *it?* Bending down, she kissed Brisia lightly– was she asleep? She could not be sorry for Brisia. She could sit with her. She could let her pain fill her own heart. She could suffer with her. But she could not be sorry for her. *He gives.*

#34
Too Big to Be Any Size

Brisia heard everything Adaria said. Nonetheless, she was afflicted by a deep misery. Complaints and excuses and griefs she could not name whirled around in her mind. A guilt that had long half-slept, lurking in the dark, rose to cast a shadow over all that she was. She was no better than her brother. She condemned herself. *The Creator does all things well. The Promised One will conquer, in us and in the world, and we will reign with Him. In the end we will see. The Creator will give us all His best.*

Those words were for all of them. *For her.*

Brisia did not know what she wanted. She was confused. Dark and nameless desires lurked in her heart and wreaked havoc in its night. Inwardly, she collapsed and withered beneath a deluge of despair. Grief had become despair and outrage, a weight that could not be borne. These things entered into her soul. She was captive to a dark desire… throw it all to the wind… let it all go… weep forever… nothing is left… collapse, wither, shrink, there is no strength, no strength desired… what is life? let it go…

At the same time, Adaria's words had sunk deep into her. Meaning that could not be contained in those words but could come through those words and contain those words impressed itself upon her soul. A desire for that which spoke through Adaria's words formed itself in her. That is, if we may call it a desire, for it was, as yet, deeper and stiller than any desire. If it expressed itself, it expressed itself only in a dim discontent and sense of purpose that only accentuated the misery, the despair, the anguished writhing in protest against the world, against what was. For a long time she lay in her anguish, until sleep finally fell upon her. Adaria, hearing her breathing, lifted her up and gently carried her inside. Then, she lay down next to her, to fetch what sleep she could before morning came.

Days passed. Brisia was as silent as ever. A part of her itched to share her feelings, but she could not. Every time she wanted to try her very thoughts froze.

Nonetheless, she knew she wanted more, more than her despair, misery, and anguished desire for what could not be and outrage at her (and others') loss.

One night, she crept outside, sat down right next to the wall, and cried until she was done crying. She wanted more. She wanted the more that Mirla had had. She wanted the more of which Adaria had spoken. She wanted she knew not what and yet that she wanted it. Nonetheless, the dry, aimless, frantic misery still walked with her, distracting her and constricting the desire that began to burn in her, and which, the more it developed within her and pushed her the more it accentuated the frantic despair.

He was there. She knew Him. He called her to come to Him, to rely on Him. He called her to love Him and know Him. He wanted to be her mother; He wanted her to give up Mom to Him and take Him. She had known for a long time, but made excuses she could not put to words but later said more or less amounted to something about it being disloyalty to Mom to turn away from sadness over Mom and longing for her. She said she did not know the answer in words or thoughts or anything of the sort then or, in fact, for years. Later, she said that she knew then that there was only true loyalty to the Creator, and any so-called loyalty to her Mom would have been only disloyal and, to be honest, unnatural. When she was asked what she meant by unnatural, she said she did not know. At the time, she only knew He was huge, so huge that she could not see how huge He was. He was bright, too, so bright she could not see how bright He was. The brightness and the hugeness were the same thing. The brightness was just a kind of hugeness. He was huge in every way. He was like a waterfall. A very tall waterfall and very many waters falling. Huge. However, He was not huge in a frightening way. He awed her tremendously, but His hugeness was very comforting and loving.

Brisia did not talk about the experience at all for a long time. She could never even remember it happening or where it happened. She only knew, at some point in her life, that it had happened and remained imprinted in her mind. Even the point at which she realized that, she never remembered. What she did remember was telling Dormik one day, probably months later, when they were working in the garden together, "You know about the Creator?"

"What about Him?" asked Dormik.

"He's big."

"So what He's big? He wouldn't be small, would He?"

Dormik was bothered and frustrated by Brisia's comments, but Brisia did not notice that, or at least not until much, much later. She was too interested in her understanding of and perception of the Creator and excited about the same. "Well, He's *really* big. I mean, big, *BIG!* Just huge. I'm sure He's so heavy He'd crush the whole world as small as my thumb if He weren't so loving and careful with us. But since He loves us, I mean, all that bigness is so comforting! He loves us with all of His hugeness. He'll never get tired of holding us, and He can hold us all and there's still more room! I mean, for real. He's also really dangerous! I mean, I would not want to be His enemy, because if He stomped on me… well, it would really be bad. I'd be squished. I wouldn't be Brisia anymore. And, He's so big, there's really not much difference between me and the biggest, baddest, strongest enemy. It would be as bad for them to be squished by Him as for me. They wouldn't be them, anymore, but just a little bit of who knows what. Squished stuff. But I know He'll never stomp on me, or sit on me, or anything else. I'm His child, and He'll take care of me!" She said this last with sheer delight.

Dormik laughed dryly. The picture of the Creator squishing things amused him very much. The idea of Brisia being squished until she was no longer Brisia was not pleasant. "The Creator's not like that," he said. "I don't think He has any size."

"He has to have a size. He exists. And it's really, really big. Oh, yeah, you're right! The Creator doesn't have any size. He's too big to have a size," said Brisia with a note of finality.

Dormik did not bother responding to her. He was not sure how to explain it and he did not enjoy talking about the Creator. He decided that his little sister must be stupid. Maybe all the time she did not talk was because she was really dumb.

Time went on, and birthdays passed. Her sadness did not leave Brisia, but she was also happy. She tried to explain things to Dormik, but he continually did not respond to and ignored her. He retorted to her with annoyance and at times anger, and tried to imply that she was dumb. However, Brisia remained almost completely oblivious. The subject of the Creator, especially how He was huge and powerful and loving, caring, kind, and knowing, excited her greatly so that she was unable to notice Dormik's annoyance, being completely unable to conceive how anyone might even possibly be irritated by the subjects which excited such comfort and delight in her.

Adaria, however, listened with delight to Brisia's talk about the Creator and how huge and loving He was. She had noticed Dormik's attitude, and thought that Brisia's comment that the Creator was too big to be any size was just brilliant, and was as accurate as anything anyone could have come up with. She positively loved Brisia's comment, one night, that the Creator was so big that He could know everything and never forget any of it.

That night, when Dormik was once again grumping, grumbling under his breath about how his little sister "has such misconceptions in her head. She even thinks the Creator has a size! He's *big*, she says," Adaria followed him to his bed and sat down next to him. "What are you coming over here for?" he asked, his voice having the flat, dry, ugly tone of someone who is upset and suspicious but trying to sound like he is not.

"Dormik, you're being proud, arrogant," she held up her hand, "– no, listen to me– self-righteous and hypocritical. Brisia's understanding of the Creator being huge certainly involves more than physical hugeness but it does not involve less! And that is the reality. The Creator *is* big, Dormik. You've learned words, but you don't know what you're talking about. You think the Creator is less than big. He's more. 'Too big to have any size.' In your correct words, you've lost the truth. In all of her images, Brisia has more than images; she has what gives images meaning. Good night, and be willing to learn." She rose and walked away before Dormik could think of a retort. An interminable argument was the last thing that child needed. She hoped Brisia was not watching; it would not do her any good for her to have seen that.

It continually astonished Adaria how children could have such keen perceptions that put all of the adults' understanding to shame, and yet be totally oblivious to things that were glaringly obvious at other times. She thought maybe it was a kind of simplicity, a kind of taking the world at face value. Or maybe not the world, but taking *something* at face value. Maybe children did not see everything, but there was less between them and what they saw. *Of course, Dormik was not that much older than Brisia is now when he came, and he is not even that much older than Brisia.* She was seven now. Dormik had been eight.

#35
Wearing Thin

A dagger stabbed through Azshbir's heart. He was waiting to see his twin daughters, Reilia and Della. He only got to see them once a year, and every year they grew so much that he could only recognize them. The first time he had got to see them they were two years old. This year they would be five. While he waited he laid his head down on the table and wept, heedless of the watching guards. *O my Creator. Why?* he wondered. *I'm to be a husband to a wife I hardly see and a father to daughters I see even less. My Promise, will You be a husband to my wife and a father to my daughters, for she might almost be a widow and my daughters fatherless?*

It was only a few minutes before Baren returned, with Neah'ra and her five-year-old daughters, Reilia and Della. He could not tell them apart. The dagger piercing deep into his heart he looked into his wife's liquid brown eyes and asked, "Can you show me?"

She knew at once what he was asking. It had happened three or four times already, though it was worse every time. When they were just toddlers it had not meant much; sometimes she could not tell them apart except by their clothes, though they did have distinct personalities which she had learned to pick up on within half a year of their birth. She motioned to the twin clinging onto her right hand. "Della." The twin clinging to her skirt and hiding behind her was Reilia.

Azshbir felt awkward and totally at a loss for what to do. There was nothing that made him so uncomfortable as these days when he would get to see his daughters for no more than half an hour. He stood up. "Della?"

Neah'ra whispered a reassuring word and gently pushing Della forward to meet her father. She stepped forward tentatively. Azshbir knelt down, and when she stepped into his embrace he could tell that she felt even more awkward, nervous, uncomfortable, and unsure than himself. "Oh, my Della," he said, sobs stifling his words.

"Daddy," Della said tentatively. Neah'ra stepped forward and touched her tenderly. She laid a gentle hand on her shoulder. Slowly, she relaxed a little and eventually melted into Azshbir's embrace. "Daddy," she asked warmly, "what's your favorite color?"

"I don't know," said Azshbir, thinking. He did not get to see a lot of real color. "I think I like blue and yellow. The sun and the sky."

"I like the wind," said Reilia. She was standing right next to Della on her right, and her head was above Azshbir's as he knelt. It had not been that way last year.

Neah'ra spoke as softly as the wind herself. "The wind is very nice, but I don't know how much Daddy gets to feel the winds."

"It's okay, Neah'ra," he said, looking up on her. "I do know the winds. Yes, Reilia, I like the wind very much. It cools you when you're hot, and it brings in nice fresh air and scents of flowers." He did not mention other things the wind did.

"It's almost time," said Baren.

"Reilia," said Neah'ra, but her voice sounded like she was holding back tears, "can you give Daddy a quick hug, too?"

Azshbir almost did not want to; he knew how tense and uncomfortable she would feel, but he opened his arm, and hugged her very quickly and lightly. Then, he let Della go, who had just been resting against his shoulder and knee, and stood. Reilia and Della clung to each other, looking around the room, like frightened and exposed rabbits. Neah'ra stepped into Azshbir's arms and they embraced. "How can I teach them?" he asked. "How can I be a father to them? The time flies so fast."

Neah'ra kissed him lightly. "Ssh! Don't ruin this moment with those thoughts. We'll talk about that later." She was so affectionate and enticing. There was so much he wanted…

Azshbir held her, struggling not to let his thoughts and feelings come across. When could they ever talk about that? A few minutes! That was all they ever had, and they were both so exhausted. They never had time to have a single conversation, let alone all the conversations they needed to have. Somehow, she managed to talk as if it would be different in a week. Right now, that was. He knew that sometimes she struggled with her composure and collapsed into tears. He had never heard her rant, but he had heard her grump and grumble, and he thought she sometimes ranted inside herself.

Then, it was over. Neah'ra and the girls left the room, and Baren took Azshbir back to his cell. It felt like he fought a physical resistance to go back. Compared to taking a single step away from his family it would have been easy to kick and fight and punch through walls of stone.

Now, the days were longer than they had been earlier in his imprisonment. The time between Neah'ra's visits grew longer every time, though he knew that it was always the same number of sunsets and sunrises, except for when she missed one every once in a while. To be honest, it was okay when she did. He was so tired and short on sleep he could always use the extra half hour of sleep. He also felt weaker. Was the work harder or was he more worn out? He limped from a wound he had sustained when a bit of molten metal fell on his calf. He still bit his lip just thinking about the pain… but that physical pain was the slightest of the things he endured. This was far worse. As he lay in his cell, in the few minutes between waking and sleep he thought of how disheveled his daughters were. They looked better fed than his wife, but he would have liked to see better. They wore tattered dresses, threadbare and torn. He wondered what they were like at home… playing… working. The environment in which he always saw and met them was so different he was not sure if he would know them in the free world. Not that it would matter. His was a life sentence. Things would never be different, until he was so old and weak that he could no longer work, in which case he did not know what would happen to him… It did not scare him though. Death would be merciful.

Of course, things could turn out differently. He did not know much about how the war was going, but he knew that things were getting dire. If Hasseleighton conquered Ephezoa he did not know what would happen to him. Death by torture?

He only hoped that in that event Neah'ra and the brethren would be able to care for his children.

With that, Azshbir drifted away into deep sleep and missed his dinner. It was not saved for the morning. By now, the prisons were being flooded with prisoners. Ephezoa was moving prisoners from the outer cities into those which were still secure to work on manufacturing weapons, growing food, and whatever else was necessary for their war. They simply picked anyone not known to be loyal and excited about the cause of Ephezoa up from the outer cities they were in danger of losing and took them to the prisons to work. There were so many, and more if they had anywhere to put them, that some of the prisoners were put to work building more prison-camps. He knew that some of the punishments used to make the prisoners work were absolutely horrendous. Only last month he had spent nights up tending a fellow prisoner who had been tortured half to death for continually refusing to work– or was it just slacking, maybe intentional slacking– and then expected to work. Of course, he had been too tired to do his work well, and been beaten for it. It could have been worse, was much worse for most of the prisoners, but Baren hovered over him protectively. He thought he did it for Neah'ra and worried what intentions he might have towards his lovely wife. If he died, he was afraid the man might try to marry her, and he desperately wished to avoid any such scenarios. He did not fully trust Baren, and he knew that he was not one of the People of the Promise for all his kindness towards himself and Neah'ra.

One thing that Azshbir had found good about the present situation was that it allowed him to proclaim the true Promise to countless numbers of men. He had a captive audience, and an audience who was interested. He thought it possible that his whole wing of the prison knew that his crime of treason was of a very different sort from the prisoners being carried in daily from the war-front. It gave him a wonderful platform to proclaim the Promise and from which to display what the Promise had done for him. He had never forgotten his vision of the Person of the Promise and found that as the months dragged on it grew more real and he remembered what could not be remembered, not only of that vision but of the insight he had had years earlier when he stood before the Hall of Exhortation and thought of the utter horror of being shamed before the Creator whose regards alone mattered that would be borne– in some sense, had been borne– by the Promise. Perhaps the veil between him and the Terrible Light wore thinner as his strength waned thinner. It was this that sustained him daily. It was this that he told unceasingly, though it had earned him mockery from some and ridiculous requests from others. From some he thought the requests for specific and personal prophecies were just more mockery. However, others seemed to sincerely think he might be able to offer them something. They never got tired of asking either, though their asking truly tired him.

A couple months ago– he could no longer keep time straight– he had told Neah'ra about the beauty of the present deplorable circumstances because of the opportunity he had in them to do that for which he had been called. He also told her that that which cannot remembered was always with him now; he remembered it more and more.

He knew from Neah'ra, though she had not told them the details as time was so short, that it was becoming clearer and clearer, not only in the prisons and the war-front but in Afteloan itself, that in her war against Hasseleighton Ephezoa was becoming a little Hasseleighton. Atrocities and tyranny of all sorts were everywhere. Hardly anyone could have believed that Ephezoa was really a great and noble country, where the freedoms and well-beings of the citizens were looked out for and guarded, anymore. There was no reason at all for the people in the war-front cities not to want to be conquered and taken by Hasseleighton. Ephezoa was taking them to prisons which were more dreadful by the day for no reason at all. There was no reason to suspect that anything about Ephezoa would stay better than Hasseleighton for long, and in some ways Ephezoa was markedly worse. Hasseleighton did not imprison people for not being known to hold demonstrations in favor of the war! *Ephezoa will fall. Perhaps,* perhaps, *she might have stood if she did not treat her people so abominably. But, now, how will she stand when there is no reason to be Ephezoan? When she has denied almost every value that separated her from Hasseleighton and only kept a few superficialities which almost everyone, and all the strong and intelligent, will see through at once?*

At least, the persecution of the People of the Promise was not so severe as it was in Hasseleighton. *Yet.*

#36
Dizziness

Neah'ra stood outside the prison gates, sweating in the heat of the glaring sun. Reilia and Della clung to her skirts. She had been standing out here for hours, and she was already very hot and thirsty.

Afteloan was now a territory of Hasseleighton, and the conquerors had sent out word that all whom Ephezoa had imprisoned for treason and unpatriotic thoughts and behavior were to be honorably released from prison. She hoped Azshbir her husband would be among them. She knew there could be other outcomes. He had been very active in proclaiming the Promise within the prison walls, to fellow inmates and to guards. Rather than be released, he might be executed. The thought almost made her heart stop. She was tense out here, and the hours of tension, growing worse with each passing hour, wearied and tormented her.

It had been just two months since Hasseleighton had taken Afteloan. To begin with, it had been chaos as some in the city had fought against Hasseleighton. Strangely enough, some Ephezoans were still hearty, vibrant patriots. However, the siege had been short and merciful. With so many in prison and being practically worked to death for the Ephezoan war-effort, often with no real charge at all, very few had the heart or incentive to really fight Hasseleighton. When the forces of Hasseleighton laid siege to Ephezoa and the dragons began wrecking havoc on the city, many even who had pretended to be all for Ephezoa turned against Ephezoa. It had been total mayhem.

Then there was the treason. It was for that reason that Neah'ra had not even tried to visit Azshbir in the last two months. It had shocked her beyond belief. Ellason had been her closest friend. She had helped provide for her out of her income. She had stood with her when things were hard, first with her father, then with Azshbir's imprisonment, and throughout the terrible years since. And, now, she had betrayed them all at the first opportunity. Azshbir might be released, if Ellason did not succeed in securing his torture and death. She had already secured the execution by fire of Neah'ra's friend, Daera. She did not know what had happened to most of Daera's children. Her youngest daughter, Lasaira, was with Neah'ra. It was because of Ellason's treason that Neah'ra had not visited Azshbir. She did not want her to follow her to Azshbir or somehow get them both in trouble. Even if she secured Azshbir's death, Neah'ra would have to raise their children and make peace with her inability to ever see her husband again before his death or offer him any encouragement or love. She would have to be content with never getting to bid farewell.

She was still reeling with shock from Ellason's betrayal so that everything still felt unreal. She would never have thought it of Ellason; how could anyone who was not one of the People of the Promise possibly look so much like one, possibly know so much about the Creator and the Promise? She felt dizzy. She and Shaelene, another of the prostitutes she and Azshbir had rescued, lived with her and together they had found a farm outside the city which they now inhabited. They wanted to be as far away from Ellason and anyone close to her as possible. Neah'ra thought it was Darnize's farm, and thus her rightful inheritance.

She and Azshbir had been wrong when they thought that Ephezoa was beginning to look like Hasseleighton. The horror of Ephezoa was not even close to the horror of Hasseleighton. All of Neah'ra's friends and other People of the Promise were executed publicly in ways that chilled Neah'ra. She knew of it only by hearsay; she had hardly been in the city since the treason. She desperately wanted to talk it over with Azshbir; the idea of his execution was unbearable. She needed someone older and stronger to guide her, still. Even more, she just needed someone with her. Shaelene was not one of the People of the Promise. She needed someone she could trust and who believed the same as she did to discuss these issues with: to discuss Ellason's betrayal with, and what it meant, how it affected their lives, and how to move on and relate to others in the light of such shocking depravity and unrivaled deceit. It was worse than Azshbir's imprisonment. She could not believe it. It felt like she was living a dream, a nightmare. She could not believe that what was happening around her was real.

"Who are you coming for? What are the charges? What is your relationship to the individual?" asked one of the Hasseleighton guards in charge of the release of prisoners.

The answers were hammered in Neah'ra's mind by the constant pain of the last seven years. "Azshbir Nan-reem. Treasonous thoughts, unpatriotic intentions, and subversion of the people. He is my husband."

The guard directed her into the next line to wait. She shook her head. Long ago, when Azshbir was imprisoned and Razi executed, she had taken comfort in the gathering together of the People of the Promise. That horror had brought together the People of the Promise, and they had all discovered that there were more of them than they had dared to dream. They knew who each other were, and they referred to themselves as the Brethren. Now, as far she knew most of them had been betrayed into the hands of their enemies. Probably a few others, like her, had escaped, but there may well have been other traitors than Ellason. How would they ever know each other apart from their persecutors again? She thought of Razi's execution by beheading– that, too, she had only been told about– and longed for the days when they had been ruled by Ephezoa, for the days when executions had been quick, simple, and merciful. Now, who knew what horrors lay in wait for any of them? The Brethren were scattered and could no longer trust one another. She looked up at the sky. *Is this really happening?* For a moment she wondered if her father had been so wrong in thinking Hasseleighton should be fought to prevent this horror from covering the whole world and stifling all that was good, stifling all that was alive. But that thought brought more pain with it. Her father had died years ago, broken by his actions and her husband's lack of forgiveness, rejecting the Promise. *Forgive, Neah'ra, forgive! Forgive Azshbir for not forgiving your father. And you know he did in the end, though it was too late.* She thought that little could be harder to forgive. Darnize had only ruined their lives, had only condemned them to this life of pain and futility and loss in Kaarathlon. Azshbir had helped her father along on the path to eternal, everlasting and real, destruction and shame! And Azshbir should have been better than her father, not worse… Still, she had to forgive. Besides, she loved Azshbir, loved him as she could and would love no other. She *wanted* to forgive him.

Azshbir had known something was wrong for a long time. Neah'ra had not visited him twice, now. It was the first time she had missed more than once in his long imprisonment. The prison was different, too. One day, they had not been brought out, not been given food and water. No one. He had wondered if Ephezoa had decided to just let them all rot, and it had turned his heart to water for some reason. Then, conditions had changed, but it felt chaotic. All the old guards he knew were replaced, and soldiers of Hasseleighton become the prison guards. He knew then that Ephezoa had lost the war. Afteloan was near enough the center of Ephezoa. If this much of Ephezoa had fallen, there was no way the country would ever recover. Despite the fear in his heart, he told the soldiers of Hasseleighton about the Promise. Mostly they were cold, but their treatment of him did not degenerate. He had been asked by a higher-ranking official one day what his crimes were. When he told them the charges he was immediately transferred to a different wing of the prison and given special treatment. To any of the middle class in Ephezoa the treatment would have seemed deplorable, but to Azshbir it was a wonderful change for the better. The home in the Vinibra Mountains had been so long ago. He was used to poor treatment.

Now, he was being led out of the prison. He had been given a change of quite nice clothes and told to put them on. Goosebumps showed on his skin. What was happening? He saw a huge crowd of people. He was lined up against the wall with another crowd. Then he saw people coming forward from somewhere on the side of that other crowd. Almost at once he recognized Neah'ra. It had been so long since he had seen her in the glaring light of the sun, and she was now dressed in a long, full dress and had a shawl wrapped around her head and falling down her shoulder. Nonetheless, he recognized her. She looked so worn and weary, and there was a distant look in her eyes he had not seen before; what had happened to her? Beside her trailed the twins, also dressed in long dress and with shawls wrapped around their heads. Her clothing was dirty, frayed, and somewhat threadbare. His daughters' clothes were worse. It was torn, and the shawls scarcely covered their hair, they were so torn and threadbare. She looked like she had desperately tried to dress in a manner appropriate in Hasseleighton culture out of her poverty. He knew that she had dressed herself better because she was a full-grown woman and so it was more important for her. He also knew that she was hot. She looked pale and ready to faint.

He saw the moment when she recognized him, the shock in her eyes. Did he really look *that* what?

It was still an unbearably long time before they met each other. In a moment they were in each other's arms, hugging, while the children looked on. "Okay, now," a guard was telling them, "no time or space to do that here. Take your gift and get going. You can't be in our way."

"What's this?" asked Azshbir. He was still totally confused.

"I'll tell you," said Neah'ra. "Let's just go. Follow him." It was strange for her husband to be acting dazed, but she guessed the sunlight and the air of the free world might do that to a man who had been in prison for almost eight years. In a few minutes, they were in another line. This one was much shorter, or at least it seemed like it to them. At the front another official asked them some questions. One of them was how many children they had. Azshbir shot Neah'ra a glance when she answered, "Three." Then she asked, "Can I have a drink?"

As they walked away through the crowd, Azshbir carrying a rather large and heavy sack, Neah'ra gasped. "You're lame!" He saw tears in her eyes.

He nodded. "It's not that important really."

Neah'ra did not press him, but soon they got to a cross-streets. "No, Azshbir, this way."

"What? Did Cavisto move?" he asked.

"No," said Neah'ra. She put her hands on her hips. Azshbir thought that he did not even know his wife anymore. Things were going to be very rough. "No, he didn't move. He was burned alive!"

"Huh?" asked Azshbir. "I didn't know about that."

"We're going to my father's farm. That's where we live now. Now, none of he and his are there. It's my inheritance, so it's yours," Neah'ra announced. "I'll tell you all about it, but it's bad. There are too many people around right now."

"Okay," said Azshbir. "Very well then." He should have known when he married Neah'ra that she could grow bossy and self-assured and take over. Actually, he had admired that trait about her, and he guessed it was good, because how else would she have been able to manage over the past seven and a half years? Nonetheless, it was going to make things very hard now. This was going to hurt more than he could have imagined. Not that he had imagined. He had never thought that he would be released until he was an old man, and over the past month or so he had been hopelessly bewildered. Now, he did not know why the Creator had arranged for him to be released right now. It was going to make this so much harder. It would bring difficulties their way that they had no idea about whatsoever. He had thought that his relationship with the kids would be the biggest difficulty. Now, he realized that his and Neah'ra's marriage would be an even bigger one.

"By the way, what did you mean when you said we have three kids?" asked Azshbir.

"I mean we've adopted one– or we're going to adopt one."

"Huh?"

"I'll show you when we get home," said Neah'ra. "Speaking of which, let's open that sack and eat what we want. That way it'll be lighter, and we'll be stronger."

Azshbir complied. At least, Neah'ra *did* know what she was doing, which was more than could be said of him.

#37
The Pain of Betrayal

That evening they all ate what was left of the gift from Hasseleighton together. Lasaira, a girl of nine, only picked at her food. "What?" she asked. "You're adopting me?"

"In a manner of speaking," said Neah'ra. "Daera is still your mom, but she's dead and you're still a child and need guardians– parents."

"Shaelene's children only have a mom," said Lasaira.

"Children are supposed to have both a mom and a dad," said Neah'ra. "It's because both Shaelene and her children's father did wrong that they only have a mom."

Listening to Neah'ra, Azshbir thought that she was far more than he could have imagined. She was definitely a mother. Lasaira asked, "So Shantee, Kira, Kgarjin and Marlekk really do have a dad?"

"They would," said Neah'ra, "but he ran away before they were born."

"So," asked Azshbir, "tell me what happened."

Everyone at the table flinched. Neah'ra pulled herself together. "Ellason betrayed us. I was coming back late from delivering some articles I had made to a lady. As I came near, I noticed screaming and fighting." It was hard to talk about it, but for some reason she just told the story flatly. "I knew something was wrong, but not what. Then I saw Ellason with guards, and the Brethren in chains. There were children, too.

"Ellason was leading the guards, and I knew she must have done something, though I could not make sense of it. I knew also that my twins and Shaelene and her children were free. I didn't see them. I waited for them to leave, hiding in the shadows. Then, I went into the house, and found signs of a struggle, but no one there. I didn't know what to do. I didn't dare call, lest I be found. I fled out of the house and tried to hide, fearing someone might be watching me in the house. It was dark by the time that we were all together. I didn't like it, but I knew we had to leave that whole part of the city, and go where we wouldn't be too noticeable. Thanks be to the Creator, nothing happened to us that night. The next day we came out here."

Shantee volunteered. "We were all waiting for Neah'ra to appear, and I thought someone should go out to find her. She was way too late. We were all waiting for her to appear and I was insisting that some of us should go out with the men to find her, since it was getting dark and we all knew about the dangers of the night, but others insisted we wait. Ellason was one of them. She stayed really calm, but she was always like that. When the police came, I sat very calmly, and then sneaked away, so I never got tied. I've forgotten how everything went, but they asked lots and lots of questions. I think, now, that Ellason may have been giving them signals, and wanted the whole thing to take as long as possible. She was hoping to get Neah'ra, too. Then, they noticed I was gone. At Ellason's command, they started to bind the Brethren."

Shantee paused. "But I hadn't gone. I was waiting under the window. At first I was too shocked to think. I had been bewildered all night, but I'd never thought that Ellason had betrayed us. I wanted to go in there and scold her, but I kept my head. I went around by the back of the house and picked up a knife. Apparently I wasn't the only one who had escaped either. Della and Reilia had run away. Della saw me and tried to stop me from going in. I told them to hide and that I would be fine.

"The police went out to guard the house and all the doors and windows. Some of them stayed with the captives. I think Ellason was still hoping to snare Neah'ra. I crept in, crawling on the floor. Lasaira had already gotten her hands untied, and I slid the knife to her. Fortunately she saw it, and cut her remaining bindings and Marlekk's. I rolled under the couch. My heart was beating quickly and I didn't see how this would work. I was surprised the police hadn't seen us yet.

"Then they did. Lasaira screamed as they came for her. She threw the knife, which landed right next to my hand. Actually, it cut me, but not badly. I snatched it up, and threw myself across the path of the guard. He tripped on me and I fell. Kira managed to get her bound hands close to enough to the knife which I had dropped to grab it, twist it around in such a way as to slice the rope, and then cut the ones on her feet. By now all the policemen had noticed. They were coming in! But the rest of the captives were trying to help us. I don't remember everything that happened. Somehow Kgarjin slipped her hands out of the rope. Our friends got to their feet and fell on the guards or across them. Some of them got hurt pretty badly. I remember a lot of blood. I snatched the knife from Kira and quickly cut Kgarjin's leg bonds. I sliced her pretty badly, but it's healed up fine. Just a scar. We ran. I think I got all of my siblings because we liked to sit next to the best hiding places. They were also *my* siblings, so I, well, I noticed them.

"I didn't want us to all go in the same direction, so I pointed different directions. I got down out of a window and rolled to the floor. I think that was when the police decided to take them to the prison. I'm sure they were galled.

"Together, I and my mom got most of us together. I spied Neah'ra, and together we found Marlekk and Kgarjin.

"Now, I don't want to tell that story again."

Azshbir nodded. "What about you, Shaelene?"

"I asked to use the waste hole," she said, smiling. "My children were across the room, but I asked Reilia if she wanted to use the waste hole, too. She said it had been a long time since she had, and, well, I think Della and Reilia always try to be together. I don't think Ellason noticed at first– there was a lot of noise. When I saw Shantee heading in, I sent Della to tell her about the situation and warn her."

"So that's it," said Azshbir. "A long story... and Ellason. I never would have thought."

Neah'ra nodded. "It's sad. Really sad. We're alone, again, and the more died because we had gathered friends around us." She shook her head. "Shaelene and Shantee, do you mind cleaning up today? I want to take Reilia and Della out and play with Azshbir a little."

Azshbir shook his head. He had learned to tell the twins apart in the visitation room at the prison. He could not even guess which one was which now. Actually, it hurt less than he would have expected. It still felt bewildering and unreal, kind of exciting, but certainly too much to process. He felt so dazed by the day's events that he had a hard time playing the game Neah'ra made up and coordinated for him to play with his twin daughters.

That night, while laying together in a bed– it had been so very long– Neah'ra whispered to him, "You're going to have to tell our girls about what you've learned and what you know. I didn't tell any of us about your vision, because I thought you should tell about it."

Every hour left Azshbir more bewildered and confused. Now Neah'ra was deferring to him.

Frankly, he understood why Neah'ra was so disturbed about Ellason's betrayal of the Brethren. He found it hard to believe himself; she had showed so much discernment, so much understanding. She seemed to know what was what, what was necessary. He thought of the day when she had made him let Neah'ra tell Darnize where she stood herself, and then explained why that was necessary– and she had been right. It was hard to believe she had not belonged to the Promise, but it was clear now: she had betrayed them. It hurt and bewildered Neah'ra greatly, being betrayed by her closest friend. Azshbir knew there was more involved, too. He wondered if Neah'ra had been hinting that she was not even sure that she should trust him. To be honest, he would understand. Ellason had seemed to have so much knowledge and discernment, if she could betray them, neither he nor Neah'ra– or anyone else, for that matter– could ever know, unless the Creator Himself told them, who was a friend and would never betray them. Of course, he was thinking here of active betrayal; they had always known, so that it did not even need to be discussed, that betrayal of information under deadly pressure was a different kind of thing.

Nonetheless, he trusted Neah'ra completely. He was certain she would never betray him or anyone else, even in the most dire of circumstances, let alone the way in which Ellason had. He hoped she trusted him that way too. At any rate, she trusted him enough. She trusted him enough to come to him, to take him to her home, to defer to him, to share what was troubling and burdening her with him. Even if she did not trust him completely, she trusted the Creator absolutely– absolutely enough to trust him for the Creator. It would have to do. He hoped he would be able to trust that way, too.

One thing he had learned was that he himself could not be trusted. He had failed in ways he never would have dreamed he would fail. He had seen the glory of the Promise, and he knew that nothing in him could be relied upon. Nothing in his past, no deed, no resolution, no vision, could be relied upon to keep him from falling into the depths from which the Creator's love had raised him. He would not fear becoming a traitor himself, though. His fear would not keep or protect him from that which he feared at all. He could only place his trust and hope in the Creator and the Promise. He did not know why the Creator had allowed Ellason to be and do what she was and did, but he would trust the Promise.

Despite his resolution not to fear doing what he would never do and betraying all that he cared about, he could feel the fear tearing at his soul. He held Neah'ra in his arms and breathed in the scent of her skin. It was so good to be with her again. He let her presence soothe his aching, whirling thoughts and hoped that as time went on things would settle, at least in his mind. He wished he had answers to offer her but he did not. When first they had met, he had known more than she. Now, he did not think that was the case anymore. He had told her all that he knew, and she had let it sink into herself.

In the morning, he woke to find Reilia and Della on top of him. He wondered when they had come in. Neah'ra lay on the bed, breathing softly. The twins were awake. One of them poked his cheek. "Now we know you're our *Daddy!*" she exclaimed. The other laughed. "Yes, we do!"

Azshbir sat up. For a moment he felt stung by the first twin's comment, but it passed quicker than the twinkling of an eye. Their good attitude infected him. He laughed with them. They had fallen off of him and were giggling about it. "Let's go," he said. "It's time to let Mom sleep for a good, long while. Why don't you show me how to make breakfast? Or whatever it is we do in the morning."

The twins' faces shone. "Kira and Kgarjin are already making breakfast." They led the way out of the room, jumping and twirling as they did so. The other twin added, "And we know you know as much about how to run a farm as Mom, so why don't you go out and look at it." The first twin talked over her. "Yeah, 'cause we don't know much about starting a farm, but you're stronger and you know!" They spoke together now. "So, why don't you go and look, and we'll go with you? We'll show you everything!"

Azshbir laughed. "Can you tell me your names again?"

"Oh, sorry," they giggled. "we didn't tell you this morning." "I'm Reilia," said one. The other said at the same time, "I'm Della." He thought Della was the one who had poked his cheek.

"Sounds like a great idea," said Azshbir. He let them lead him along. He still needed time before he felt like he could relate to Neah'ra. He was amazed by how much the twins had warmed up to him though. He wondered if it would last. He wondered if they would let him teach them, or if they only wanted to teach and show him. Did they think he was their father or their big brother or did they not know?

#38
Flattering the Emperor

Arendellie walked through the halls of the castle, her silky capes swirling behind her. On her head, over the violet veil, was a coronet, and from a diamond in it flashed silver rays. She could tell that it was enchanted. It was time for the evening banquets, which she now attended with Vanesh Casarion. Several maids attended her, as always. She hated it when Grale Casarion attended the banquets. It was hard to keep her composure in his presence; she did not know why.

She stopped in the hallway. "Greetings and blessings," she said, dipping her head and curtsying.

The older woman, also crowned with a coronet, approached her and put her hands on her shoulders. "You're a beautiful woman, Arendellie; I'm glad that my son has you."

Arendellie nodded. A thrill went through her. This was the kind of thing she liked. "Thank you, Princess Eliaeya."

Eliaeya seemed to brush Arendellie's comment off. "You're a kind woman and intelligent; try to help Vanesh, will you?"

"Of course, Princess. In any way I can," replied Arendellie. She did not know what Eliaeya was talking about, and she did not ask. It occurred to her that Eliaeya was real and there; that she did not play games or act. She was a sweet old woman of the same sort as her own mother, and probably lacking in the intelligence to understand the intricacies of palace life and interactions. At the thought a feeling like that of cool, refreshing water flowed over Arendellie. She felt reassured. She knew that Princess Eliaeya was not one of the People of the Promise; in fact, she had probably never even heard what the Promise was. Maybe she had heard of the Promise. Yet Princess Eliaeya was nice and sweet. That meant the Promise was not anything! It was just that most of the nice people were attracted to the Promise and were not really all that intelligent, so they attributed their niceness to the Promise. She did not have to worry about the Promise really being anything anymore. Not that she ever had. Not really.

She was so relieved that even Grale Casarion's presence at the table did not put her off. "We've conquered Ephezoa," he crowed.

Arendellie leaned across the table smiling. "Yes, and a wonderful bit of work, too. It's a great thing that your majesty is a Dragon Keeper, and one of the only Dragon Keepers around. The dragons all look up to your majesty and recognize your great and royal wisdom, and that has helped us to show the people of Ephezoa their folly. It really is a great thing that you and your majesty's dragons have taken Ephezoa now, because Ephezoa was already committing so many atrocities. They were working people to death for no crime at all! In their book it was sufficient crime to merit worse than death to care more about one's wife and children than about the war effort. We're so much more natural and reasonable in Hasseleighton, thanks to your majesty's sagacious clemency and brilliant mind and compassion."

Vanesh seemed to really enjoy her presence. He tenderly laid his hand over hers.

Grale Casarion took a deep breath. A flame formed above his hand and flickered out just as quickly. Arendellie learned from Vanesh that one of the stronger water wizards was always near to Grale Casarion; when he was angry his spells could blow up, and he lacked the presence of mind to control them himself. It was not always fire or something related to fire that caused the problem, so the preferred water wizard, Lady Assea, had a wide range of talents. "I think it was a wonderfully royal idea to bestow gifts on the prisoners of the Ephezoan regime whose only crimes were sanity, which Ephezoa took to labeling as treason. They did not use to be so bad, which proves how wrong a country can go when it is not ruled by a king who has the intellect to understand the forces of the world, the wisdom and nobility to gain the honor and respect of the dragons, and the large-minded compassion and sympathy required to connect to hundreds of dragons. It does not matter how well it was made, it decays. I am so glad that I have risen to the occasion. Now, now, we are restoring the dignity these old and decrepit yet mighty nations stole from their people, and it is all because I knew when I was needed."

Arendellie smiled to herself, but she kept a perfectly serious expression on her face. She flattered Grale Casarion on purpose, and it was a source of endless amusement both to herself and Vanesh Casarion. He unnerved her less when he was acting like a pompous, arrogant, perfect idiot. The combination of the fool's smile and the grave seriousness of bearing the weight of the world on his face made her want to burst out into hearty laughter. Once, she had done so in his presence. When he asked her why she was laughing she lied. She told him how funny his enemies were, since they were tactical and strategical masters to be able to put up as much of a fight against his noble and royal forces but they were such idiots that they could not see how wise and gracious he was and the benefits of bowing down to him. She knew she made a lot of the courtiers nervous; they worried that she would kick off one of those states where he blew flames or whatever else it was. She knew he had started storming with lightning and thunder at least once. However, she had never triggered such a reaction. She and Vanesh amused themselves with the nervousness of the court too. They had a hilarious time of it. The other thing they laughed at together was the court's idea that she was really a rather stupid woman, in keeping with the Hasseleighton theory of womanhood. In reality, she was just brilliant, brilliant, and Vanesh relied on her input more than on that of any of the royal advisors. They had come up with this plan together just to convince the court that she really was not all that intelligent, just beautiful.

"I know," she said. "That was a lovely, lovely plan. It should win us so much loyalty. Soon, these places won't even have to be territories under territorial government anymore. They can become provinces, entitled to the full privileges of Hasseleighton Provinces." She leaned back with a smile on her face. "We'll have so much loyalty that people won't even be attracted to all this nonsense about the Promise. I think that might have been what caused that plague to take off. There was a lot of slander about Hasseleighton, and people just didn't realize that the government had changed hands. As a result, they were all terrified that we would be even worse than their own tyrannical and deceitful governing bodies. Then, when we had to punish all that rebellion, they thought they had their suspicions confirmed. Vanesh Casarion explained all about it to me, and now we're going to fix it. It was kind of bad, and wasted a lot of time, people blaming, attributing, and even forcing upon us, all the problems that their own governments had. Anyway, it's all over now, thanks to your most discerning majesty. By the way, your majesty has such a wise and wonderful nephew. He is so full of knowledge and leadership and such kindness and understanding! He might not be wizard or Dragon Keeper, but I think he will make an emperor who may not be second even to you. He has been enabled to watch and learn with your majesty, so he will have benefited from all your majesty's wisdom and experience. Oh, your majesty, I am so grateful to be joined to such a man as your majesty's royal nephew and under his care!"

Vanesh squeezed her hand ever so slightly. It was their way of communicating privately. They had so much fun doing this together that they could barely contain themselves. They would spend hours laughing about their brilliance and planning and plotting and thinking about what they could have done better, or what worked out really well but could have been risky, and all the intricacies and possibilities of their roles in the palace politics. She knew that she and Vanesh would soon be laughing about how ridiculous it was that she should be attributing conclusions they had reached largely because of her knowledge and understanding entirely to Vanesh, and then Vanesh's understanding entirely to Grale Casarion, when he had not even been raised by his uncle, and they both looked down on him for various reasons. One of these reasons was how a little bit of flattery made him act like he was drunk, but there were others. Lots of others. They thought it was hilarious how he was such a mighty wizard and Dragon Keeper when he obviously lacked so much both in the ways of intelligence and understanding other people. He had not seemed to have learned anything from his dragons; Vanesh and Arendellie had actually done a great deal of reading about dragons based on the accounts of Dragon-riders and Dragon Keepers of the past, and determined that Grale Casarion was no representative of the dragons. How on earth he could possibly be a Dragon Keeper they did not understand, but then again there was much about the dragons' ways that was an enigma to humans, and remained so no matter how much they tried to understand it. In fact, it seemed that the more humans studied the dragons the more they saw their culture and ways as strange and incomprehensible. Of course, there were some things about the dragons that had a very high level of obvious sense to them.

Grale Casarion gave her a smile which was meant to be grandfatherly and that both she and Vanesh thought was idiotic. "You're a great daughter-in-law," he said. "You'll make a wise and loving queen, a good partner for Vanesh. I am continually impressed by the keenness of your discernment and perception, but I guess I should not be. Doubtless, Vanesh has been giving to you what he has from me, and which I have from I have from my innate understanding, and from the combination of my innate ability to connect to dragons and the treasury of the dragons' knowledge. I am so glad you understand how important both wizardry and Dragon Keeping is to this business of ours. Fortunately, I shall still live a while yet, for I am a great wizard, so I will be able to impart much of my wisdom and knowledge and experience to you, so that you two will be better able to navigate the tricky waters you will be thrust into, because neither of you is either a wizard or a Dragon Keeper."

Arendellie looked down demurely into her lap. She spoke in a barely audible whisper, as if deeply ingratiated. "I am so grateful to your majesty and humbled by your majesty's assessment of my gifts and talents, which are indeed small, though doubtless they are sufficient, since your majesty is wise and discerning, and would never be led into assuring me of that which is not the very truth." Within herself she laughed at all of them, including herself.

"Now," said the great wizard and emperor, "I must attend to my duties. The responsibilities of my royal position as emperor weigh heavily upon me." He rose, taking his plate, and strode away from the table.

Arendellie looked at her food which she had only picked at so far. *I hope I'm not pregnant again,* she thought. *I shouldn't be, though. I won't worry about it. Things are more likely to happen if you worry about them.* She leaned against Vanesh. It was nice that she was playing the role of idiot; it meant she could get away with familiarities in public which were generally forbidden to respectable royalty. Of course, it limited what she could do in other ways. She could go fewer places and be alone less often and in less of them if the ruse was to be believable. Of course, that was okay. Hasseleighton had its problems, of which both she and Vanesh were very aware and working to solve in any way they could. Sometimes, she flattered Grale Casarion into thinking an idea was his own– which was, of course, the only way to be sure he would implement it. Vanesh had shared with her several months ago that he was very glad of her presence, since he too found Grale Casarion very intimidating when he was not flattered and acting like a silly idiot. There were *some* things Grale Casarion was good at, but understanding that the vast majority of the common people, and even of his royal court, were not eaten away by the pride and suspicion and hunger for power that ate him was not one of them. It was a strange thing for a Dragon-rider and Dragon Keeper not to understand.

She wondered if perhaps he did understand it when he was flattered, but just forgot it as soon as he was no longer being flattered. He was a strange combination of genius and dunce.

#39
In the Shadow

The work was grueling and hard, especially with only one grown man, and that man in constant pain from injuries he had endured while in prison. However, that was only the beginning of the difficulty and the pain which daily beset him.

Azshbir had discovered that he had not at all exaggerated the pain and struggle of taking up responsibilities and relationships again after such an absence. At times Reilia and Della would play with him affectionately, and they trusted him to know what he was doing with the farm– unless they or their mom thought they– or she– knew better. If Neah'ra thought something, they always– or at least almost always– sided with her. They were quite comfortable when around their mom, and reasonably comfortable when around each other. However, they watched out for each other and would not play games with him where they could not constantly be together and keep an eye on each other– and on him. Additionally, they tended to be more critical of anything that he tried to teach them than they were of Neah'ra. The result of this was that multiple times a day he was stabbed to the heart by the understanding that his children did not really trust him; that he was not really their dad. The cruelty of the Ephezoan regime had cost him the chance to really get to know his wife and children; it had cost him the opportunity to be her husband and their father; it had cost him their trust. And he could not blame them, however much it hurt him.

His relationship with Neah'ra was rocky, too. One minute she would be trying to boss him around, talking as if she knew everything and were in charge, telling him what to do. An hour later, she would want him to know everything and make all the decisions. It would have been okay if she wanted to be bossy when he was completely clueless and snuggled up to him for relief from the burden of decision-making when he knew what to do. Of course, it was almost never like that. She always wanted to be bossy and tell him what to do when he knew what he was thinking and doing, and she always wanted him to lead and know when he was at a total loss and looked to her for support. He did realize that part of this perception was his fault. When she acted bossy he always just had to know what he was doing, just because his pride demanded it. When she did not want to have anything to do with thinking or making decisions he often had to ask for her opinion just to be contrary, and push it, either just to be contrary or to show he was in control. He tried to be gentle; he knew that the past eight years had to have been extremely difficult for her. It was probably extremely hard for her to give up the habit of making all the decisions and giving all the directions and organizing and leading, and at the same time she desperately needed to give it up and was extremely relieved not to have to do it. There was probably even an element of selfishness that wanted to have done with everything having to do with that of which she had had to do too much for too long. She was probably trying. Just as he constantly resolved and set his mind to be gentler and kinder next time and found biting remarks and scolding, angry words leaving the tip of his tongue before he knew they were even there, so she too probably intended to behave differently next time and found that almost all of the time it was of no avail. He knew that there were times when he fought to keep control of his emotions and have the right emotions and yet his words came out with exactly the wrong tone, and she took offense. He knew there were times when he tried to speak softly and gently but the tension of the fact that he did not really want to– or was it did not *really* intend to– be completely gentle, loving, and patient came through, and she flipped out at him, and then he lost it.

At times, Azshbir wanted to blame all the problems in his marriage on the Ephezoan regime. If he and Neah'ra had not been separated in this evil and unnatural way this situation would never have developed. They had lived together for a full year and hardly even been annoyed with each other at all. In fact, he could only remember being less than taken with her in that year twice. Now, they had been separated, thrown into unnatural situations, and then thrown back together. That was why they were fighting. That was why their fighting left the children clinging to Neah'ra and cold towards him. On top of it all, she was pregnant again. He only hoped she would not have another pair of twins. Why had she had to have twins at all?

Azshbir knew, though, that he had one problem and it was himself. Even now, the vision of the Promise did not leave him. He knew that the problem was himself. He was not what he was meant to be. He did not live in the fire and light that was the life of that Being. His words might be only small failings; his imperfections might not be glaring atrocities. It did not really matter how small his shortcomings were. In the light of that Being, before the terrible glory of the Promise, the smallest imperfection was despicable and detestable. Even if it was not properly speaking wrong, it was evil in the light of the holiness, the greatness, the dread of that Being. He did not know why, except that absolute perfection was demanded and demanded rightly. It would have been injustice, it would have been evil, for anything less that absolute perfection to be demanded. The mere fact of that Being demanded absolute perfection. Minimalist notions of right and wrong and justice dropped out of the picture before the face of that Being. Every time he snapped at Neah'ra, every time he responded to her with less than complete love and forbearance, every time he even felt like doing so, he fell short of the nature of that Being, and to fall short of the nature of that Being, however little it might be, simply *was* a crime incurring of every and bitterest shame. It had nothing to with any abstract idea of justice at all; it was simply so because that Being was; it came straight out of the burning heart of the Promise. It was reality. If it was justice, then that Being contained in Himself all justice, was the one from whom justice came, and justice itself was simply a different word for reality. That Being determined justice because His very self determined reality. Azshbir's whole being resonated with this truth. His own soul condemned his imperfections and recognized the absoluteness rightness of the demanded absolute perfection. He himself demanded absolute perfection with that Being.

Azshbir bowed his head. *O Creator, please keep me right. I can't do it myself.*

I just can't. So please keep my intentions and my attitudes and my words right. Nothing else will do for You, and nothing else will enable me to love Neah'ra right. She knows when I fail, however hard I try to do it. I know it's because of a deficiency in my will that my intentions and my attitudes aren't right and my words don't follow, but please do it for me. Help me love Neah'ra for You. Make me perfect for Neah'ra for You. I need to be perfect for You. Anything else is shameful death.

"Neah'ra," Azshbir said, "please forgive me. I'm sorry for snapping at you this morning in the kitchen."

She nodded. "I forgive you, Azshbir." She took a deep breath, "And, I'm sorry..."

"No, Neah'ra, not right now. Please," said Azshbir. "I have to ask you a question so I can know. Do you trust me, or are you not sure because of what Ellason did to us– to you? No. Don't answer right away. Answer truthfully. Think it through. It's better that you tell me you don't trust me and I endure the pain straight out than that there be a lie between us, still less a lie between you and the Creator. And, if the answer is no, you don't, understand that I understand. If I were you, I wouldn't. I'm just honored you trust the Creator this much."

Neah'ra looked straight into Azshbir's eyes. He held her gaze. There was something in her eyes that he could not read. "So that's why you think I told you that?" she asked. "Oh, Azshbir, it would never occur to me not to trust *you* because of Ellason! I told you that *because* I trust you and I want your support and insight, not because I don't!"

"Are you sure?" he asked, then hastily went on, cutting Neah'ra off before she had a chance to reply. "Because, Ellason was with you for a long time, and you had to have known her far better than you know me. You knew and lived with her for more than eight years. We've only really been close for three or so."

"Yes, I'm sure!" said Neah'ra. There was a fire in her eyes that Azshbir had rarely, if ever, seen there. "Don't you dare think this way, Azshbir, or are you intent on torturing yourself?" There was pity in her eyes. Azshbir was lost. He bit his tongue. He did not want to say something he might regret. "Do not question me. There is nothing between us of that sort, unless?" She stopped, and there was sorrow and guilt on her face. "I'm sorry."

"It's okay," said Azshbir. "And, to answer your question, I trust you. I think you're better than I am."

Neah'ra laughed sadly. "Didn't we both think that of Ellason? Never mind. I'm sorry, I'm sorry." She burst into tears and started weeping.

Azshbir quickly moved around the table, toppling most of the chairs. He took Neah'ra in his arms, picked her up, and sat down on the floor with her. He kissed her temples and rubbed his face in her hair. "Neah'ra, Neah'ra, Neah'ra, my love, my love, my love." His thoughts went back to that day so long ago when they were both young and she was younger when he had rescued her from her father. He still loved her. He wished he could have given her better. Still, he would have given his life for her a thousand times. Daily, he would fight to lay down his life for her. However often he failed, he would get back up and give up his life, because he loved her.

O my Creator, I don't know why You have chosen this torture for me of loving a woman whom I cannot give what I would, but to whom I seem doomed to bring only more pain. I would honestly rather die by all the tortures of Hasseleighton ten times over than see and love this woman and be unable to do better for her, unable to give her more. I know, though, that You love this woman more than I love her, and You love me the same, so I know there has to be good in this. Good in her deprivation, in her sorrow, pain, and loss, in her not having what I would die to give her. Nothing was harder for him than thinking those thoughts. He had bitten the side of his cheek until it bled, as he held her in his arms while she cried against his shoulder. *There must be good for me, too, in this torture, in this thwarting of everything I am and desire, in this being unable to do what I would suffer anything to accomplish.*

"It's okay, Neah'ra," he whispered. "It's all right. I'm not hurt. I love you. You're still my love, my love, my love. I'll always love you, Neah'ra. Oh, my love."

Neah'ra just cried harder. Azshbir's words did not help; in fact, they only rubbed it in more. She was not quite sure what she had been thinking, what her motives were. She knew they had been dark, dark to the core. She had been pursuing evil deep into the belly of the earth, she had been chasing darkness, rubbing and rolling herself in horror. There had been nothing but disobedience, nothing but forbidden and forbidding lusts– though, not, of course, physical lusts– nothing but a horror of darkness in her own intentions so dark that she could not name it. It was not against Azshbir that she had sinned; it was against the Creator that she had sinned, against goodness that she had sinned.

#40
The Sundering Promise

"Lalia, I'm going to tell you all about the Promise and the Creator," promised Brisia. Of course, she could not tell her all because she did not know all, and she knew that, but how else could she say what she meant? Lalia would understand even less of the little which she could say of the little which she knew. Brisia did not, however, think any of these things, not deliberately, consciously, or articulately.

Lalia was three now and could talk. Brisia remembered how much she understood and knew, and she wanted to tell Lalia everything. She still had a kind of loyalty to her parents, and she felt duty-bound to teach Lalia as they would have; of course, Lalia was as much their child as were she and Dormik. She knew what Mom would want to teach Lalia. She would want to teach Lalia, as she had striven to teach Brisia and Dormik, about the one thing that now occupied Brisia's heart. She would want all her children to know the Promise and be enthralled with it. She had told Brisia, almost in her last words to her daughter, that she had seen the Creator and knew He was good. She wanted that for all her children; she had told Brisia as much, and the eight year old knew that her desires could not have changed. Brisia had met the Creator, too, and she wanted everyone else to know what she had known just as much as Mom had. What she did not understand was why Dormik did not understand, did not even want to understand. She knew that he was still bitter and cold towards the Creator and the Promise. He did not say he hated the Creator, but Brisia knew that he had to hate Him. He passively resisted anything that had anything to do with the Creator and the Promise.

What Dad would want to teach his children was less clear. Brisia did not even know what he had wanted to teach her and Dormik, what he had wanted for her and Dormik. He had loved her, she knew that. He had wanted to take care of her and play with her, and he wanted her to be happy and well. That was about all she knew. She did not know what he really cared about. Furthermore, she had not given all that much time to thinking about it. Just the thought of Dad still hurt. She knew that he had been killed by the Hasseleighton soldiers, and she knew that he did not belong to the Promise. She did not even want to think about what that meant: the Creator would squish him until he was not Kalimad anymore, was not her dad anymore. She shivered at the thought. She did not want that for anybody, least of all for her own dad whom she loved and who loved her.

She was afraid for Dormik. He did not know the Creator. He did not belong to the Promise. He did not say so, but she knew. He was like Dad. Almost exactly like Dad. She had tried to tell him that he should not want to kill Mom's torturers and murderers because if they died without turning to the Promise they would be squished until they were no longer human beings anymore. He had told her that the Creator was not like that and did not squish people– he did not have a size and was not heavy. He also told her that they deserved it.

That had made her mad. "Of course they *deserve* it!" Brisia yelled. "You *deserve* it! I *deserve* it! Does that mean you want it to happen to you and me?"

He had repeated that the Creator was not like that. "Of course He's like that!" Brisia stated, still angry. "He's great. He's huge. He's heavier than the whole world. He gets angry at people who are bad! That's the whole reason for the Promise, Dormik, or do you not understand?"

He had repeated his stuff about how the Creator did not have a size or a weight and just plain was not like that. "He's too big to have a size and too heavy to have a weight," said Brisia. She knew Dormik could not make sense out of that and she actually thought it was funny. He was older than she was. It also amused her that he thought she was silly for understanding things he did not understand. "Besides, how would you know? Have you met Him?"

Dormik had said something about how everyone knew the Creator was always watching everything and that if He was so big and heavy as Brisia said there would be no space for Him anywhere and he would crush everything. No, of course he had not met the Creator. Why should he expect to meet the Creator of all things? "Well, I have, and I'm telling you, He's bigger than big and heavier than heavy," Brisia had told him.

Dormik had wanted to know how one could possibly meet someone that big and huge and heavy. After all, even the world was too big for them to meet. Brisia told him she could not explain it and that he would have to meet the Creator for himself. She was sure the Creator would come if he asked him. Oh yes, and that did not mean the Creator was not here already. No, no more questions for her. Not right then.

She knew that Adaria and the rest of the adults found her way of putting things amusing, but she did not mind. As a matter of fact, she knew that they were also quite taken with her ways of putting things and thought that she sometimes perfectly stated something they had not been able to think of a way to put. So, she just went on saying things the way she knew how, though she learned how they said things too. She really hoped Lalia would understand what she did. She did not want Lalia to follow in the footsteps of her dad and her brother.

"What are you gonna tell me 'bout the Promise?" asked Lalia.

"The Creator made you and me. Don't you think that's amazing, Lalia? The Creator made you, and He made me. I wonder how He did it. I'll ask Him to tell me someday. But, sometimes the Creator doesn't tell us things."

"Why?" asked Lalia. "Why He not tell us things?"

"He tells us lots of things, Lalia," said Brisia. "It's just, some things He won't tell us. I don't really know why. It might be because we can't know the answers. I think our brother Dormik has questions that he would not be able to know the answers to, even if the Creator told him."

"What questions does he have?" asked Lalia.

"I'm not really sure," Brisia told her. "I think He wants to understand how the Creator is different from us, but I don't think that's possible. The Creator is so different from us we can't even know how different He is. He made us and everything there is, and I don't even know what the sky is or why it stays there, or what makes the sun move across the sky. Or the stars and the moon. The Creator made those things. He understands them all, but we don't. He understands us. I mean, He's the kind of being we can't know all about. Anyway, we…"

It was only a short while before Brisia noticed that Lalia was no longer paying attention to her. She was much more interested in the toys, and was chattering to Nahiza about the "dragons." Brisia sighed. Had she been this inattentive and distracted when she was four? She did not think so, but maybe sometimes. It might have been worse if she had had other children her own age with which to play. Besides which, Lalia and her friends were not four yet. She could only barely remember being three and did not know much about what she was like then. She would just have to try again another time. Maybe she could keep more to the point, instead of wandering off into her own thoughts and even further into Dormik's questions and problems. She knew that she was not the only person concerned about Dormik.

It occurred to her that she *had* been as distractable as Lalia when she was four. In fact, she was still almost as distractable as Lalia. No, she was not even sure that she *was* any less distractable than Lalia. It was just that she was interested in the Creator, and had been since she could really remember. She only wondered why everyone was not just as excited about the Creator and the Promise as she. What was there more glorious and good and interesting than the Creator and His Promise? But she had to live with the fact that many people did not think so. *O Creator,* she thought.

She decided to try to talk to Kizyia or Nahiza about the Promise the next time an opportunity presented itself. Right now the three-to-four year olds were busy and excited chasing each other around and showing each other their make-shift toys and chattering about whatever happened to catch their attention, in short, playing. Watching them Brisia knew that she would have been distracted by several other friends her age who wanted her to play with them, too, when she was their age. Right now it was her job to watch them play and make sure they stayed out of trouble. There was so much trouble to be gotten into, playing on the fringes of the jungle. Dangerous animals. Poisonous plants. Poky plants. Dark places and deeper forest for the children to try to play hide and seek in. For little children who wanted to investigate everywhere, the fringe of the jungle was a dangerous place, and the real jungle a place more dangerous still. Almost always there was someone assigned to watch each child, and at least two people who were older than thirteen. Brisia did not feel hurt by the fact that she was still considered a child herself and unworthy of the responsibilities of an adult. She knew that she would not be able to handle them. She was too much of a child and too distractable herself, still. Besides, she did not want them. Not yet.

Brisia decided it was as well that she did not know what Dad would have wanted to teach them. If it was in any way opposed to the Promise then it was something bad, and she would not do it anyways. She knew it was not about the Promise, so it would have been a boredom. It was better this way. This way she did not have to think about whether or not it was okay for her to try to impart it to

Lalia. She did not have to weigh her own distaste of thinking too much about whatever-it-might-be into her decision not to try to learn and teach it, or her loyalty to her dad as both her parent and Lalia's into any decision to try to learn and teach it. She did not even know what *it* was, so the whole thing was a moot issue.

Dad, she thought. She had tried to tell him that he had it wrong and that there was more; that he needed more. Or had she? She had hardly even known what was wrong, only that something was. Even less had she been able to communicate what was wrong. She thought he must have been even less able to understand. Just like her brother Dormik. If only it had not happened so soon. If only she had had another couple of years. Then she might have been able to explain the problem to him. But then again, Mom had known a whole lot more then and been a whole lot better at saying it than she had been then and was now. She knew Mom had tried to tell Dad what was wrong; upon later reflection it had occurred to her that this was what most of their fights were about.

#41
Safe

"What is going on?" Brisia asked. She could tell that something was up.

At first no one heard her, so she tried again. She walked up to Esiri, one of the daughters of Hoobit and Sirifa. "Can you tell me what is going on?" she asked.

Esiri looked down at her and smiled. "I don't really know, Brisia. I don't think any of us do."

"Well," asked Brisia, "why don't you tell me whatever you do know?"

Esiri knelt down and looked into Brisia's eyes. "Sir Kuthrynd had to go down the mountain. We don't know why and we don't know when he will be back. He said the Creator told him to, and we don't think even he knew why he had to go or when he will be back."

"Okay," said Brisia. She looked around. "I think it's about time for breakfast."

Throughout that day, she failed to understand the tension everyone else seemed to be experiencing. Kuthrynd often went into the jungles for the day. She knew that in general even the adults preferred not to be alone, but it was not that big of a deal for the adult men like Kuthrynd, who knew lots of things and how to do lots of things.

As evening turned into night and still Kuthrynd had not returned, Brisia sensed the concern of the adults turn into full-blown worry. When everyone was gathered together for the evening meal, she sensed real anxiety and fear. They were discussing the dangers of the jungle at night, what might happen to Kuthrynd, and whether they would ever see him again. She caught Adaria's eye, stood up, walked over, and snuggled against her. There was something she wanted to tell her or she wanted her to say, but she did not know how to say it. That kind of thing happened to her a lot.

Adaria understood. She had been thinking along the same lines, and had just needed Brisia's affirmation. "Do you remember when I and Azshbir left with Kathreen?"

Everyone around nodded, with the exception of Dormik and the young children, who had not been there. Even Laekoorj, who had been just a child himself, remembered. Sirifa asked, "Why are you bringing this up, Adaria?"

"You and Dad told us that what we were being offered was potentially dangerous; you encouraged us, but you also encouraged us to consider that we were walking towards possible imprisonment and death, and that we should be sure of our commitment to the Creator and the Promise first." She looked around. "I am here, but I was, at times, extremely close to being tortured. Azshbir is not here. None of us knows whether he is yet dead or alive, but we are satisfied that he is safe. Can we not do the same for Kuthrynd?"

"We are only taking precautions," Athara piped up.

"I don't know what you mean," said Adaria. "I agree that it is wise for someone to stay up and watch, and that we can alternate who it is, in case he comes back and needs help or something. However, I believe that some of us, and I myself am guilty here, have actually been entertaining worries and fears.

"What if he doesn't come back? Not tonight, not tomorrow, not ever? What if the Creator has called him to a mission that takes him away from us for as long as Kaarathlon endures, and perhaps to his death? I ask this not to induce fear or worry, but because it is a very real possibility and we must face it– and be prepared to face it. Many years ago, Azshbir said, if I remember his words correctly, 'If He reigns over death, can He not release His people from its dungeons? Even if He does not, He is good and has already been very merciful to me. He is worthy of my life.' Can we say the same for ourselves and for those we love?"

She looked down, and Brisia put her arms around her neck and kissed her. Adaria hugged her back. "Thanks," she whispered. "It was just, you reminded me of Mirla… and of the night when I told you how I feel about Azshbir."

Brisia snuggled closer to her. She had grown up a lot, but she was still a very little girl. She did not know how to respond to Adaria. "You're welcome," felt wrong. Anything other than affection that she could think of felt somehow wrong.

"Thanks, Adaria. That is a good reminder for us all," said Hoobit. "Now, I think it would be a good idea for all of us to go to sleep, except whoever takes the first watch. Adaria?"

"Fine." She kissed Brisia. "Good night, my child."

Brisia fairly glowed. After a few moments she stood up. When she caught Dormik's eye, she noticed that her brother looked sour. But then again, when did he not look sour? She knew that sometimes he seemed reasonably happy…

Voices broke in on Brisia's thoughts as she, Senise, and Laekoorj picked vegetables in relative silence. She could not deny the emotion. She thought she had heard Kuthrynd. She picked up her half-full vegetable basket and ran. She dropped it by the house and ran through it towards the other side. Senise and Laekoorj followed her at a more sedate pace.

Five paces into the room she stopped dead still. Kuthrynd sat on the floor, his back leaning against the wall. He looked totally and completely exhausted. His eyes were closed and his breathing was shallow. A young girl, probably about Dormik's age, knelt down next to him. "Are you sure you aren't still thirsty?" she asked.

"No. I'm just tired. Sleep first. Then eat and drink." Kuthrynd's voice was dry, flat, and emotionless.

Brisia continued walking forward. She was going to ask what had happened. She could not wait. She hoped Kuthrynd would be okay. What was wrong with him?

The girl straightened. She was totally unfamiliar. "Hi," she said. Her face was drawn. "I– I'm Khiel. Are you one of Kuthrynd's sisters?"

"No, not really. My parents died, and… well, I'm not really adopted. What happened? Is he okay?"

"I don't know," Khiel shook her head. She looked down at the floor as if not sure how to start. "Well, I guess what happened is that the king's men found us out." She sounded very sad.

Brisia gasped. "The king? What king?"

"Grale Casarion. Y'know, the Emperor, the Wizard, the Dragon Keeper, umm,"

"Yeah, yeah, I know about that one," said Brisia. "Are you saying he knows we're here? He's coming for us? I didn't even know that he'd conquered Ephezoa."

Khiel grabbed Brisia's arm. "Let's go outside. I can't make Kuthrynd eat and drink, and we might as well let him sleep. Well, we did make him drink a *little*. No, you needn't be worried about that. As far as I know the king doesn't even know this place exists."

"Well, if he doesn't know this exists he can't have found it out, now can he?" asked Brisia. She was extremely confused.

"I'm sorry, I'm so sorry," said Khiel. "I didn't mean to scare you. I didn't mean that us, either. I meant my and my friend's families. The People of the Promise in Mieshor were found out!"

"Oh!" Brisia gasped. She knew what that meant. In a moment she was carried back to that day so long ago when she had crouched in a closet with Lalia and Dormik… and to the last glance Mom had ever given her, the last words she had ever heard from her mother's mouth. "RUN! Obey her! I know–" Whatever it was her mom had wanted to tell her she knew, she had never had a chance to hear it. She suspected, though, that it was that she knew Kathreen. So she knew a little about what Khiel was going through.

"It's okay," she said. "Grale Casarion took over the place where I used to live, too. His men killed my dad and arrested my mom.

"Where was that?" asked Khiel.

"Ebrin, Avanzar," answered Brisia. "A beautiful place in the mountains. Well, they were different mountains, and they were much drier than these mountains."

"Oh," said Khiel. "How did you end up here if you lived so very far away? We barely made it this far!"

"Kathreen and Adaria here rescued me and my siblings," said Brisia.

Khiel laughed gently. There was too much sadness in it for it to be a real laugh. "I'm glad. I'm the only one of my siblings who got away."

"Who are the other voices I hear? Who is the we?" asked Brisia.

"Come," said Khiel, and again took her arm. "I ran to some friends' house and got them. That's who you hear." Her voice dropped. She was almost crying. "I'm the second youngest. My little brother was with my parents when the soldiers came. Only I got away." Now she did burst into tears. She cried so hard that she could not walk. She sank down onto the ground. Brisia sat down and put her arms around her. "I love you," she whispered.

Khiel forced a smile. "I know," she said through her sobs. Brisia just hugged her.

A couple minutes later Brisia looked up to see three grown-ups, one of them a woman, walking towards them. They all looked the same age, and they were all not too old. Athara and Esiri walked with them. "Are they your friends?" Brisia asked Khiel. At the same time the woman asked, "Are you all right, Khiel?"

"Yeah, yeah, I'm all right," said Khiel, trying to smile, and succeeding a little. "I don't know if Kuthrynd is okay. Maybe one of you would like to check on him?" *How distractable I am!* Brisia thought to herself. *Thank you, Khiel. Help me, O Creator. Help me to love better, please.*

"I'll go," said Esiri. She hurried past them.

Athara and the three new adults sat down around Brisia and Khiel. "Are you sure you're okay, Khiel?" asked Athara.

"That's a stupid question," said Brisia with a hands-on-hips attitude. "Was I okay? Are any of us okay? How do you be okay when your dad and your mom and your siblings are probably being tortured to death at this instant?! Especially when it's your younger sibling who you were supposed to take care of! Not that it's nice anyway!"

"All right, all right," said Athara, "I get your point, Brisia. But aren't you forgetting what Adaria told us all last night?"

Brisia looked down at her lap. No, no, she was not. She just was not quite sure how to say what she meant. "No, Athara, I haven't. Pain and sorrow are not the same as worry and fear… Of course, there is a kind of sadness that mostly is the same thing as worry and fear. But not all of it. And I think that pretending that you're happy and you feel okay and you aren't hurt is lying."

Khiel was actually smiling through her tears at Brisia. "I think you're right, uh, what's-your-name?"

Athara felt uncomfortable. Hoobit, Sirifa, Kuthrynd and Adaria had all staunchly defended Brisia's point of view in the conflict around Dormik. What would it mean about her if she could not see what this eight-year-old was getting at?

"Brisia," Brisia said in answer to Khiel's question. She hugged her again. After a few seconds she turned around. "So, what are your names?"

"I'm Kalar," said one of the men. "This is my sister, Janya." The woman smiled. "And this," she said, "is our younger brother, Kavra."

"And, I guess you heard, but my name is Brisia." She stood up. "Umm, Khiel, I'm going to go and check on Kuthrynd, or if he's asleep I'll just ask Esiri. Want to come with me?"

"Sure," said Khiel. "You're a great friend, Brisia." As they neared the doorway she added in a whisper, "They've lost siblings and friends, too. It's just as hard for them."

Brisia nodded. She let Khiel take her hand.

Brisia left Khiel in the house and went to quickly find Sirifa, who was with the babies. "Is it okay if I and Khiel just be friends today?"

She had forgotten that Sirifa could not possibly know about Khiel. She took a few minutes to quickly– and badly– explain. "I want to go back to her. Can I?"

"Of course," said Sirifa.

Brisia ran off. "Okay, Khiel," she said.

"Shh!" The older girl put a finger to her lip.

Brisia dropped her voice. Khiel was right. Kuthrynd was sleeping not far away. "We can just get to know each other. You must be tired," Brisia finished.

"Okay," said Khiel. "Can we go outside?"

"Of course!" said Brisia. She pulled Khiel up and ran out the door with her. The older girl laughed a little. "Not so fast! I'm tired enough to sleep for a really, really long time."

"Do you want to?" asked Brisia. She had already sat down, and was now laying stretched out on the ground.

"In a few minutes. I'd like to ask you two questions."

"Okay," said Brisia, when she realized Khiel was not going to continue until she did.

"How did this house come to be a refuge for fugitives from the king? How many other families are there here? And, how do you know Kathreen Alarion?"

"I don't know Kathreen Alarion," said Brisia. "I haven't seen her in years. She was just a friend of my mom's, when they were growing up. Why?"

"Wizard and Dragon-rider Kathreen Alarion is well known. She makes Grale crazy. He attributes a whole lot more to her than she has ever done, so I was wondering what she *has* done. I mean, every time someone joins the People of the Promise, he suspects her of having been involved. I've heard that one of the things his torturers hammer on is whether you've ever met Kathreen or been influenced by her. If you say no, they don't believe you. If you say yes, they want to know where she is or what she was planning. You die either way, because no one has the information they seem to think everyone has."

"Oh," said Brisia. "Are they pretty stupid?"

"You bet!" said Khiel. "Why else would you torture somebody in the first place?" She drew her scarf over her eyes. "The sun is bright. Anyway, how did this come to be a refuge home?"

Brisia lay down next to Khiel. "I'm not sure it is. It's just me and my siblings, you, your friends, and the family who owns it. There's only one mom and dad here."

"Oh," said Khiel. She seemed disappointed. "I guess that makes it safer, though. No way for the king to possibly find it. Unless, of course, Kathreen... but I don't believe that will happen."

Well, thought Brisia, *I think there is one other who knows of this place.* She had never met him, never seen him, though, and she knew he could not know about her anymore than she had seen him. In a few moments, Khiel's breathing was that of someone asleep. Brisia also dozed off, but she woke less than two hours later, as the sun dropped behind the trees. Khiel was still fast asleep.

#42
To Face Death

"Can I go with you?" Brisia asked.

"Yep, can't she?" asked Khiel. She was sober and calm, as if a heavy weight of sorrow hung over her.

"No, I don't think that would be a good idea, Brisia," said Adaria.

"But, but," pleaded Brisia, "you are my I'm-not-sure-what, since you're not my mom, but you are my whatever, and Khiel is my best friend, and I want to go with you! Besides," she drew up her chin and stood as tall as possible, "I'm not *that* much younger than Khiel."

"Khiel is twelve. You are turning nine. That is more than three years between you. Khiel is more older than you are now than you are now older than you were when you first came here. That's a lot, Brisia, and this is dangerous," said Adaria sternly.

"That's okay," said Brisia. "I'm willing to die."

Khiel also turned pleading eyes to Adaria. "I'm still a child myself," she said. "Doesn't she have as much right and ability to make this decision as I do?– does age even have anything to do with it?"

"No, Khiel, age doesn't really matter *that* much. However, this is not where Brisia belongs. She is not making this decision because she feels the call of the Creator, she is making this decision because of personal attachment to me and you. That won't do in a mission like ours," Adaria explained.

"No, no, that's not how it is at all!" protested Brisia. "I really am ready to die, and it has nothing to do with you, it has to do with the Creator and the Promise! It's like what you said Azshbir said!" She could not remember the precise words, but Adaria had told her many times, and she thought Azshbir's way of putting it was just right.

"We're not discussing your willingness to die for the Promise, Brisia," said Adaria. "We're not disputing your readiness to be tortured for the Promise, Brisia. We're discussing your desire to go with us now and do this here."

"Why don't we ask Hoobit and Sirifa?" suggested Khiel.

"We could," said Adaria, "but there's two catches. I'm sure Hoobit and Sirifa will see it the same way I do, whether or not I tell them how I think. Additionally, they don't have any authority here. This is my decision to make, not theirs."

"We can still try," said Khiel. "Maybe they won't see it how you think, and they'll be able to convince you otherwise better I or Brisia can."

Adaria thought it was extremely silly, but she agreed. She allowed Khiel to present her case, and explain that "they" were unable to come to a decision. Hoobit and Sirifa saw it the same as Adaria did, and Brisia was left behind. The only thing they had an argument about was Adaria's desire to go with Khiel and no one else. It was settled easily by the fact that no one else wanted to go– except, of course, Brisia.

"Brisia," said Adaria, "you seemed to suggest that I'm something like a mom to you. You might want to consider the weight of my understanding on this. Besides, if you can't accept this without sulking and moaning it is a sure sign that you are not ready for this."

Brisia bristled. "I–"

Adaria held up her hand. "*None* of this is about your preparedness to face torture or death for the Promise, Brisia! Stop making it about that! Goodbye for the moment."

Brisia's gaze fell. She felt very sad. Khiel was going away, and she did not know if she would see her again, even though they planned to come back.

Khiel saw. She walked over and hugged Brisia. "It's okay," she whispered in her ear. "I'll be all right."

"It's not that I'm worried about you!" Brisia retorted. "I told you all about how huge and loving and powerful the Creator is."

"Yes, you did," said Khiel, disengaging from the hug. "It was beautiful. Very comforting." Joy bubbled in her voice. "All the more reason for you to trust Him in this."

"I'm not afraid for you," Brisia insisted.

"Oh, and are you afraid for you?" Khiel asked with a twinkle in her eye, but also quite seriously.

"No, it's nothing like that either! *I want to go!*"

Khiel gave her another quick hug. "See you later, Brisia," she said, and followed Adaria out the door and into the jungle.

Three evenings later, Brisia, still displeased about being left behind, and Athara and Kalar walked up to the house with their baskets of fruit from the mountain-jungles. She heard what sounded like the voices of Adaria and Khiel from around the house, and ran over to meet them. She tumbled into Adaria's arms. "Hi, Brisia!" she exclaimed. "Good to see you!"

"I missed you. Both of you," said Brisia. She rolled off of Adaria and stood up. "Are you all right, Khiel?" she asked.

Khiel looked up at her. "Tired."

Brisia waited.

Adaria spoke softly. "I don't think Khiel knows how to talk about it just yet. She got to see her parents. There were some people around, besides the prisoners who were being moved for some reason, and I and Khiel decided to tell them about the Promise, how good and worthy the Creator is, the Promise of deliverance from shame in His eyes and death, in short, 'what Azshbir said'. After a little bit of a crowd came, the king's men came, and we ran away. The Creator wanted us to live." She smiled a little, and then looked down gravely.

Brisia turned to Khiel. "Were your mom and dad happy?" she asked.

Khiel looked up. "Well, they smiled at me," she said, as if that settled it.

"You're both hurting and really sad and happy," Brisia observed.

"Yeah, that'll do," said Khiel. She did not look up. "That'll do for my parents too."

"Why do you think they were being moved?" Brisia asked.

"So that our eyes could meet, and I could be both hurt and encouraged?" asked Khiel quietly. "Maybe seeing me was like that for them, too. Of course, I know they go to their deaths. They probably know what we did, and expect I and Adaria to join them in imprisonment and death." Her voice was soft, slow, and thoughtful. "I don't think they're *too* worried. I certainly hope they know I'm okay, just like I know they're okay."

She fell silent for a few moments, pondering her own thoughts. She looked up. "I don't know. Maybe to be executed?" Her voice quavered with pain and sorrow. Recovering herself, she looked up at Brisia. "How have you been?"

"What do you mean?" asked Brisia.

"Um," Khiel bit her lip, as if she was not quite sure that she wanted to say what she was going to say next, "did you spend the whole time moping?"

"No!"

"Would everybody else say that?"

"No!"

Adaria grinned. Khiel did not seem to want to talk anymore. Brisia wondered what she was thinking. She decided to ask. "What is going on, Khiel? What are you thinking about?"

Khiel looked up, startled for a very brief moment. Then her face clouded. "Nothing. I mean, nothing I could tell you."

Brisia's face fell. "How much is there you can't tell me?" she asked, clearly disappointed to the point of true sadness.

"I don't know," said Khiel, genuine compassion on her face and in her voice. "A lot, I guess. I'm sure there's a lot that other people can't tell you, too. Brisia," she said, struggling to encourage her, "I'm sure there are things you can't tell me. In fact, I even know what a few of them are about."

"What?" asked Brisia, genuinely interested.

"The Creator. You can't *really* tell me about what you realized about His love and power. I have a little of an idea, because the Creator tells me about that, too. There are others, but they aren't so clear to me right now, and we've only even know each other for a couple of months."

"Well, can you tell me that much about whatever you're thinking?"

"No," said Khiel, "I'm afraid I can't."

"Nothing at all?"

"Nothing that you would be able to understand if I told you. No, I can't even think of any words."

"Will the Creator tell me?" asked Brisia.

"He might. I'm sure He will if you need to know or it would be good for you to know."

"Of course," said Brisia sulkily.

"Come on!" said Khiel. "I'm sure you can do better than that!" She sounded almost playful.

Adaria watched the entire exchange silently. It reminded her of what had passed through her mind long ago when she had watched Brisia through the night, and been given words from the Creator for her. *He gives.* She remembered her thought that the Creator would give Brisia, through the pain and loss of what had happened to her family, what she, Adaria, could never know. She remembered wondering if she would know these greater things through Brisia, share in Brisia's knowledge, if perhaps all the People of the Promise would share in what was given and revealed to each of the People of the Promise. She stood up. "Brisia, let's go. I think Khiel would like to be left alone for a little while."

"Okay," said Brisia. "Where are we going?"

"Just a little ways," said Adaria. She had no idea how to tell Brisia what she wanted to, but she figured she might as well try.

When they were out of easy earshot of Khiel, Adaria sat down. Brisia sat down, too. After a minute or so Brisia asked, "What are we here for? What are you going to tell me?"

"I think the Creator has already given you something a little like what He has given Khiel. You will have to be content with the fact that you cannot talk about it and, of course, it's not exactly the same. It might be more different than either of you could imagine."

"What do you mean?" asked Brisia.

Adaria fought the temptation to get frustrated. "I know you struggle with the fact that you can't always figure out how to say what you want to."

Brisia nodded. "Yeah."

"Well, it's not just that we can't always figure out how to say what we want to. Unless the Creator does something, what we say doesn't even mean anything."

"All right," said Brisia. "I think you've said enough."

"I probably have," agreed Adaria. She wished she could share the vision she had had that night, but she realized that tonight was probably not the night. She decided to talk it over with Kuthrynd and her parents first. Maybe they could help her put words to it, and even see whether or not it was at all reasonable in the scheme of the Promise. She stood up. "Let's go and take care of that fruit you helped gather."

"Yes, let's!" said Brisia, but she felt somewhat downcast.

#43
Daddy

Kira tenderly laid the child in Neah'ra's arms. "You have a son," she said. Azshbir did not know whether she was speaking to him or to his wife. There was such happiness on Neah'ra's face, but she also looked so exhausted and worn out. *I'm sorry,* Azshbir thought again. He wanted to give her better. He was happy, though, to have a son to whom he would actually get to be a father. Assuming, of course, nothing else went wrong. In the world as it was, that could happen so easily. They lived outside the city, and that certainly made them safer, but Azshbir still had to go into the city from time to time, to sell and to purchase necessities that they could not– or did not know how to– grow or make. Every time he went into the city there was the risk of being stopped and asked to swear allegiance and pay homage to the "king of the world" Grale Casarion, and if that ever happened he would never return to his family. This time, he would not be thrown into prison on a life-sentence that might be changed or from which he could be rescued. He would be killed.

He reached out and tenderly touched his son's face. He felt such attachment to his son, such joy and pride in his son, his very own son. He had watched his mother bear children before, but this was different. This was his son. Neah'ra caught his eye. "What will his name be?" she asked.

Azshbir took a moment answering. He had a hard time tearing his eyes away from his son. He only hoped he would get to live to raise him. "I'll decide his name another time," he told Neah'ra.

In the evening, Azshbir came in late from his work from the fields. His shoulders slumped with weariness. Neah'ra sat on their one falling-apart couch nursing their son. After a few moments she looked up at him. "What about Kuthreb?" she asked.

Azshbir just looked at her. It took a while for his mind to even start processing her words.

"You named our daughters," she said, trying to smile. "I thought I could suggest a possible name for our son?"

She seemed worried that he might be mad at her for even suggesting a name. Guilt pricked him for all the times he had snapped at her for no greater offense– that is, for no offense at all. "Kuthreb is a good name, and it sounds like the name of my second brother," Azshbir agreed, then pronounced, "His name is Kuthreb."

Somehow, his newborn son gave him a kind of boldness. He approached Neah'ra and knelt down beside the couch. "I wish I could give you a better life."

She looked at him with something in her eyes which he could not interpret. He felt uncomfortable. He dropped his gaze and tried again. "When I rescued you from your father, I wanted to give you better. I did not want to lead you into a mess just as hard and just as painful, if differently so." He knew she suffered anxiety every time he went into the city.

Neah'ra smiled, then returned her gaze to the infant suckling on her breast. There was such tenderness, joy, and love on her worn face. He thought back to when she was a child, thoughtful, serious, happy, devoted, honest and simple. He looked up again. "I should have just rescued you, run away to a different city with you, and never married you."

Neah'ra turned to him. She looked like she wanted to slap him but, with the baby where he was, she could not. Azshbir felt like something was wrong; he did not know whether it was his own conscience telling him or the way Neah'ra looked at him.

After a few minutes, Neah'ra said, "We don't really know what would have happened had we done things differently. We just know what has happened, and there has been much good in it."

Azshbir was not quite sure what Neah'ra was talking about. "What?" he asked.

"If we'd done that, how would Daera have come to know the Promise? If we'd done that, where would Shaelene and her children– and Lasaira– be? How would those you told in the prisons know?– how would we have known that vision you saw there?"

Azshbir shook his head. He knew she was right but he was not quite ready to acknowledge it, even to himself. The mention of the prisons made him remember. "Neah'ra," he said, "they're dead. Hasseleighton executed anyone who had anything to do with that. I didn't care for Baren's interest in you, but he went out of his way to be kind to both of us. I'm sure he, too, has been executed!"

Neah'ra did not reply. She just looked down into the face of their son. The world was unjust. Sometimes she too had questions. Azshbir was speaking again, though. "And Ellason? If we had fled the city would Ellason ever have been offered the opportunity to kill so many?"

Neah'ra looked up at Azshbir with fire in her eyes. "We really don't know, Azshbir! We just know the Creator is King. Stop it, before I find myself thinking like you too!"

"Neah'ra!" demanded Azshbir.

She turned back to their son and stroked his fuzzy head.

"Neah'ra!" he nearly shouted again. The girls stopped their work and looked at him.

Without taking her eyes off Kuthreb, Neah'ra said, in a soft, grave tone, "Azshbir, you don't really want to do this."

"Yes, I do!" insisted Azshbir. The baby stopped nursing and began to cry. Neah'ra devoted all her attention to him. "Neah'ra, listen to me!"

"Say what you want to say," she replied.

"Don't tell me to stop! I need you to understand where I'm coming from. I need you to know that I'm sorry."

"For yourself or for me?" said Neah'ra. She still did not look at him. That further irked Azshbir. However, her words almost stopped him dead-still. Pulling himself back together, he said, "I want to take care of you."

Neah'ra nodded. Still without looking at him, she said, "Thank you." She was trying to see if Kuthreb would nurse again, instead of crying.

His conscience smote Azshbir. He remembered his agony in the prison over the fact that he could not be with Neah'ra, provide for her, or protect her. He remembered releasing his worry into the hands of the Creator. He remembered knowing that he was called to release his desire, even need, to *do* into the hands of the Creator. Obviously, that surrender had been far from perfect, far from complete, for he was trying to take back up what he had laid down. He had never truly laid it down. The Creator wanted him to come higher up and farther in trust and obedience. He was to trust the Creator not only for his own good but for that of his wife and children. It was insult, even blasphemy, to do less.

Azshbir reached out his hand and gently touched the side of Kuthreb's face. It was pride that made him want to be in control. It was pride that made him insist on being able to give his family what he thought best. It was the desire to usurp the Creator's position of sole provider and, in the Promise, sole provision. It was the desire to usurp the Creator's position of being the only wise, the only good. Otherwise, he would not insist on believing that what he wanted to give Neah'ra was better than what the Creator would give her. Otherwise, he would not insist on believing that he knew how to give Neah'ra the best better than the Creator did. It was the desire to usurp the Creator's position of being the King and Sovereign. Otherwise, he would not insist on believing that he was able to prevent the Creator from giving Neah'ra or his children the best. It was the desire to usurp the Creator's position of being the best, the principal lover. Otherwise, he would not insist on believing that he cared more about Neah'ra's good than did the Creator. "I'm sorry," Azshbir muttered under his breath.

"What was that?" asked Neah'ra.

"I was just telling the Creator that I'm sorry," said Azshbir.

"You don't have to be," said Neah'ra after a short pause. She was still trying to get Kuthreb to stop fussing.

"Yes, I do," said Azshbir quietly. "I did wrong."

This time Neah'ra did not question him. When he turned around from watching Neah'ra love his son he saw one of the twins standing right behind him. "What did you do wrong?" she asked.

Azshbir wondered what he was going to do. How was he going to explain this to his daughter? He did not want to do this. It was awkward. It hurt.

"Daddy, what did you do wrong?" she asked again, insistent in a cute and gentle kind of way.

Azshbir cursed to himself in his mind and bit his lip. He was also really annoyed that he was not sure who this was. "Reilia?" he guessed.

A huge smile lit the twin's face up, stretching from ear to ear. "Della!" she said happily, with the same tone one would use to say "Got'cha!"

It made even Azshbir smile. His kids were really cool. He did love them. She was insistent, though. "Daddy, what did you do wrong?" she repeated.

Azshbir realized that this was a perfect opportunity for him to teach his daughter. "A long time ago," he explained, "the Creator showed me that it wasn't my job to worry about all the things I couldn't do for your mom and you. He's good and He knows how to take care of things and I'm just His servant. Well, after I got out of prison I got all wrapped up in worrying about and being miserable about all the things that I'd like to do for you and can't."

"Like what?" asked Della. Azshbir noticed that Reilia and Kgarjin had wandered over and were listening too.

"Like having more nice food," Azshbir said.

Kgarjin tickled Reilia who giggled. Marlekk and Lasaira crept up behind them. Azshbir wondered if the entire household was going to come over to hear this story. How many questions would they ask? Which questions would they ask? Who would ask them? What would he end up telling them?

Lasaira asked, "Blankets! You'd probably want us all to have a thick blanket with a sheep on it."

Azshbir felt suddenly immensely sad. Lasaira went on. "Why can't you do those things for us?" she asked.

"Because I don't have very much of the thing people call money and use to decide who gets to trade what for what," explained Azshbir. "I can't get that very well because we just have a farm that we can barely make feed ourselves. I can't go into the city very much because then people will probably kill me."

Lasaira came forward and sat down just a couple feet away from Azshbir. "I know. Like they killed my mom." She sounded so forlorn.

Azshbir took her into his arms and hugged her.

Neah'ra had been right when she had said that Lasaira was their adopted daughter. She felt at least almost as much like his own child as Reilia and Della. And he could tell her apart!

#44
Flowers and Hair

Brisia glowed. An air of radiant joy filled the glade. The bubbling brook seemed to sing with it. She had known for a long time that Sirifa was very pleased with the arrival of some young men and young women in the family. It meant people might have someone to marry! She had not spoken about it, though, until it was obvious that Kalar and Adaria were all over each other, something which had not taken long to happen. It had already been showing by the time she had taken Khiel down to Mieshor to declare the Promise and get a glimpse of her parents.

Around the clearing, torches were staked in the ground, yet unlit. Huge clouds sailed in the skies above. They had only recently stopped pouring; the sky had only recently cleared. Brisia knew this wedding had been held off for a long time by the almost non-stop rain. How long, she did not know, or care. She was still very young. She had never seen a wedding before. She knew it was a very happy event. She was a little nervous, though. She was not quite sure what she was supposed to do when, where, or how. Oh well. It would not be a big deal. Everyone would just laugh! Suddenly, a thought occurred to her that made her very sad. Except Dormik. Dormik almost certainly would *not* laugh. It had been so long since Dormik had laughed. She was not sure she remembered Dormik *ever* laughing. It made her sad thinking about her brother. She did not know what was wrong with him. He did not yell anymore, but he was always so withdrawn and miserable. She wished he would play and laugh. Yes, it was still sad what had happened to Mom and Dad, she still felt miserable about Dad sometimes and missed Mom so much, but why was Dormik still unwilling to ever be happy or care about anything? She had tried to ask him once if it was because he was worried that Dad had died as one of the Creator's enemies. She cringed remembering how he had responded. After all, he was her older brother and she looked up to him in ways.

"Foul!" he had said. "Why would I *EVER* worry about such a *thing?*" He had said *thing* with such disdain it had made Brisia's ears crawl. "Foul things, all of them! No one will *EVER* take them to task, or repair all the damage they've done! Arrgh!"

Brisia hadn't known how to respond. She'd wanted to say that yes, someone would. The Creator would. Wasn't that the Promise– rather, one side of it? The Creator would take everyone to task. That's why the Promise was necessary. And the Creator *would* make all things right. Why, His Promised Conqueror would lead all His people out of the dungeons of death and they would live with Him forever! In His palace. What could Dormik want more than that? Isn't that what Mom had said specifically to Dormik. *"The Creator does all things well."* She had remembered those last words over and over, so many times. She knew them. If Mom had assured them of that then, knowing what waited, did Dormik really think it wasn't true? Besides, Brisia *knew.* She just did. She had wanted to say all these things to Dormik, but she had not known how. Her tongue had stuck in her mouth, and she had stood there, feeling dumb. Then, he had stomped off. She did not know how to talk to Dormik about it again. She did not want to. But she was worried about him.

She was happy for Adaria, though. Adaria stood next to her. Huge, beautiful jungle flowers crowned her head and hung around her neck. They were brilliant blues and purples, bright reds and oranges, vibrant yellows and greens. Her head was covered with them. Brisia had helped intertwine them into the many foot-long necklace draped multiple times around Adaria's neck. The flowers almost covered her and, here and there, one could see a few green leaves or stems. They had picked venarias and woven them through Adaria's hair so that the thick, long black hair was almost covered with flamingo petals. Brisia looked up at Adaria and smiled.

Adaria returned Brisia's gaze. I cannot say that she smiled at her, because she was already smiling so brightly that her face muscles hurt and her dark skin seemed to glow. Her eyes shone with happiness so intense it burned in her gaze. Brisia was so happy for her friend who had cared for, loved, and taught her. Someday soon, Adaria would have a baby. And, then, she would have a little girl of her own like Brisia. Maybe Brisia would get to be an older sister to Adaria's children as well as Lalia. That thought, however, brought piercing sadness. She hoped that what had happened to her family would not happen to Adaria's! That would be so sad, if Kalar and Adaria had babies, and then Kalar and Adaria were taken and tortured and killed, and she had to take the babies and try to find a place to take care of them, like Kathreen had done for her... Just thinking about it made Brisia start crying.

Adaria noticed. She knelt down and asked Brisia, "What's wrong?" The combination of intense happiness and expectation and concern for her friend looked odd on her face, not that Brisia noticed.

"I don't want... what happened to my Mom and Dad and me... us all, to happen to your... family," Brisia sobbed.

Adaria raised her hand. A bracelet of flowers had been wrapped around her wrist, and flowers trailed from her upraised arm like a banner. Their perfumes washed over Brisia, making her momentarily feel like her head was in the clouds. Adaria gently brushed her hair back and rearranged the smaller flowers in it. Gently touching Brisia's cheek, Adaria said, "Brisia, now is a happy time. I and Kalar are to be wed. It is not the time to be crying about such things. The Creator would not want us to. And they may never be. Let's be happy."

Brisia nodded. Was she being like Dormik?... miserable, when it was not even the time for tears, that is, tears of sadness?

Adaria stood and stepped a few paces away. Though her family was clustered all around, also decorated, though not as lavishly, with flowers, the intensity of her happy expectation seemed to create a wide space around her in which she stood, not resolute, but in a kind of happy thoughtfulness that was intense in a resolute kind of way.

Above, the clouds glowed with molten color, pinks, purples, and oranges.

A drum beat began. It was intense and pounding, working its way into Brisia's blood and thoughts. She stood next to Adaria, almost lost, while their family made a ring around them. They danced vigorously, to the beat of the drums, and as they danced the flowers with which they were adorned dropped petals on the ground. They sang, rhythmically:

> Why He gave this, oh, oh,
> We don't know,
> But He made this so
> The madness of reality, oh.
>
> Man and woman, see, see
> Like the sea,
> Waves tossing stormy
> Made a-like the mountains, dee, dee.
>
> Birthing, growing, yah, yah,
> Living, ah
> Dying, what we saw
> Yesterday, here today, ah, ah.
>
> Down deeper, deeper, deeper
> A-loser
> What is together?
> Is it a bother, or winner?

Brisia was not sure whether the words were even words, or whether they were just meaningless sounds that flowed like words. Adaria stooped and touched her lightly. "Now," she whispered. Brisia could not hear Adaria over the drums two of her brothers played and the loud singing, but she knew what was happening. Sirifa and Adaria had prepared her for this. She knelt down and picked up a whole bundle of interwoven flowers of all shapes, sizes, and colors. It was darker, now. The whole glade was in shadow. She walked in front of Adaria through the gap the dancers made. They pulled flowers from her arms. She smiled so brightly her cheeks hurt. It was fun to be part of this! She ran, jumping and swirling.

Just outside, Kalar stood. Khiel, Janya, and Kavra stood with him. Brisia watched as Kalar took a knife and cut off the long lock of hair at the back of his neck. He handed it to Adaria. For some reason, Brisia burst out laughing just then. Adaria took the hair. "This is the hair of a man," she said, "and I am a woman." She turned to her father, while Brisia collapsed in gales of laughter. Adaria, however, glowed with solemn joy and her voice glowed with the same solemnity and joy. "Father, is this not the hair of a man?" she asked.

"It is," said Hoobit. Brisia did not notice, but the solemnity in his voice was laced with laughter. He took the hair, handled it, and gave it back to his daughter.

Adaria inspected the hair more closely. "I believe it is the hair of a man who looks to the Promise and gives allegiance to the Creator's King and Conqueror. The hair of a man who is also strong and will be able to provide for me and the children I bear him. If this is not the hair of such a man, let its owner say so, lest he be guilty of a crime which will call the fire that shoots from the hearts of mountains down on his head and all of those near him!"

Kalar stood there, a silly smile on his face. "It is the hair of a man who seeks to be what you, lady, perceive in the hair. It is the hair of a man who has offered it because he is in love with you and longs to mix his hair with yours."

Adaria looked to her father. "We will be joined."

Hoobit took Adaria's hair and cut the lower eight inches off, leaving her hair a little below shoulder length. He gave it to Kalar.

Kalar and Adaria joined hands. They kissed. Then they stepped back, away from each other. The mingled hair fell to the ground. Khiel looked at Brisia with laughter and joy in her eyes. Then she handed a candle to Kalar. Adaria put her hands over his, and together they lit the hair laying on the ground between them.

Adaria took a flower from Brisia and laid it on the burning hair. Brisia wrinkled her nose. She did not like the smell of burning hair. She helped lay her flowers on the fire, slowly so they would catch fire instead of extinguishing it. Adaria threw her bridal flowers on the fire, too. Meanwhile, the men took the fire and lit torches. Brisia did not understand why they were burning the beautiful flowers, which made a strange, enchanting smell. She decided she would ask Adaria later. When all the flowers had been thrown on the fire, Kalar and Adaria began to dance, flowerless and plain. Brisia watched, feeling vaguely sad about all the lost flowers. Khiel grabbed her hand and pulled her into the dance, and everyone danced. Round and round and round, around the bonfire of flowers, within the ring of torches. Those who knew it sang a song of love and death, of a union brought about by intentional dying that brought forth life, a gift from the Creator that pointed to the Conqueror-King. Brisia did not understand it, and she did not think it was just because it was too fast and she could not take it all in.

Brisia sat with Khiel at one end of the clearing, near one of the smoking torches. "It was sad how they burned all the flowers. They were really pretty," she said.

"Someone was telling me that the flowers will wilt and wither by the following morning anyways," said Khiel. "Athara tried to explain the whole thing to me and all the hidden meanings, and I'm not really sure I get it all. She said you have to burn the flowers. If you keep them, they will wilt and wither. But you burn them, so that they can give you their perfume and become a fire that will, hopefully, burn in your hearts forever, instead of withering and dying. Then, you dance without them, to signify that your love and oneness, both just the groom and bride and the whole family, isn't based on youth or health and you'll go it together even when you're plain, bare, or sick, in whatever way you are sick. At least, I think it was something like that. I tried explaining it back to Athara five or six times, and she said I didn't get it quite right, or didn't get it all, every single last time."

"Oh." Brisia sighed. "What about the hair? I liked Adaria's long hair. And it was absurd! As if one's character is contained in one's hair! I'm sure mine isn't."

Khiel smiled. "I'd heard that the people in northeastern Ephezoa had strange wedding practices." She paused for a moment, then said, "I think it had something to do with dying to one's old independence and becoming one with one's mate... and, of course, you both have to kind of die. The man must care for the woman and, in a manner of speaking, die for her, if he doesn't have to, like, die, like the kind of die when–"

"Yes, I know," Brisia interrupted. "Go on, go on."

"Yeah, and the woman has to get pregnant, and live with her husband, and she might die giving birth, and then she'll have to care for the children and give birth more times if she doesn't... Adaria didn't explain it to you?"

Brisia shook her head, bewildered.

"She was probably too excited," said Khiel. "Anyway, I think the hair kind of has to do with that. I... I don't know how I feel about getting married."

Brisia did not feel anything about getting married. She kind of wanted to have babies. She did not think that was what Khiel was talking about. She thought Khiel was talking about the dying and fire-burning-on or something like that. To be honest, she had no idea what Khiel was talking about. She looked around. "Lalia! Where's Lalia?" she cried.

"Over there," said Khiel, getting up.

#45
Falling

Aki'lam laid the braid over Arendellie's shoulder. "Is that good, my lady?" she asked.

"Very nice. Well-done," said Arendellie. Standing, she asked, "What's that noise?"

"I don't know," said Aki'lam. Her voice shook with fear.

"Well," said Arendellie, a bit scared herself, "find out for me quick!"

"Yes, my lady," said Aki'lam. She ran. Arendellie called, "Someone! Get me my veil and crown. Quick!" She started towards the gate between the garden and her spacious indoor quarters. There was a great ruckus above her. She thought she saw fire in one of the palace windows in one of the turrets. She gathered up her long blue skirts and ran.

One of her maids met her almost at once with a royal blue cloak embroidered with gold and studded with small rubies, which she flung around her mistress' shoulders. She placed a matching brilliant, fiery blue veil over Arendellie's hair and deftly arranged it over her shoulders. Then she pressed a circlet set with a single sapphire onto Arendellie's head, securing both it and the veil. Finally, she stepped back. "Is something terribly wrong, my lady?" she asked.

Arendellie's heart hammered. She couldn't answer. She heard shouts of "Fire! Fire!" and knew her maids heard it too. She desperately hoped they would not run for their lives and abandon her or anything she needed. If they had heads on their shoulders, they probably would nott. If they did, they would be burned alive. Vanesh Casarion probably would have any who abandoned her out of cowardice burned alive so it would be clear cowardice did not gain one anything. Just a few hours and a possibly worse death. Arendellie shoved these thoughts and her squeamishness about them, her vague, remembered regrets, into the back of her mind, just as a well-dressed man-servant approached. "Come, your majesty." He bowed hastily. "The castle is on fire."

Arendellie nodded. "Maids!" she called. "Come with me!" Inshara, Aki'lam, and four others were with her at once. She gathered up her skirts and ran after the man-servant. She wished she were wearing less clothes, but she dared not take them off. The Prince's wife could not appear in less than absolutely decent and modest wear. Once they were out in the main halls of the castle Arendellie saw the total mayhem. Everyone was fleeing. It was total chaos. Fortunately, everyone had the good sense to give her wide berth. The soldiers who met them at the door made sure of it. Anyone who did not they cut down then and there. Arendellie thought that some of the slaves ran anyways, preferring a swift death by the sword to the horror of being burned alive. It made her angry. They should not get release from their duties and proper punishments by pushing it at a time like this. She did not long have space to be angry though. She could see the fire behind her and felt the suffocating, burning smoke. Terror ate at her heart. She ran as hard as she could. Under the layers of silks, she sweat profusely, but she did not notice.

Guided by the man-servant, Arendellie ran through the opening of the gate. Exhausted, her sides burning, her legs feeling weak, she stopped for a moment on the stairs to catch her breath, despite the urgings of her slaves. Briefly, she noticed a short, stocky woman, with a shawl that had fallen off one side of her head and burnt hair. Their eyes met briefly and Arendellie thought the woman bore a striking resemblance to her childhood friend, Kathreen. She swayed, a two-fold wave of nausea and blackness passing over her. When she recovered, the woman was gone. A crowd of slaves and courtiers was fleeing the castle, and her slaves were urging her onwards. Looking behind her she saw a pile of bodies where the soldiers had cut down men and women trying to flee who would otherwise have run into the princess and her choice servants.

Fighting back a wave of nausea, Arendellie staggered into the streets. She let the slaves guide her to a rich inn and up the stairs, to where a soldier, seeing her, opened the door. She ran forward and collapsed into Vanesh's arms.

"My love, my love, my beautiful princess," Vanesh whispered soothingly, though Arendellie heard a hint of agitation in his voice and a great deal of relief. *He does love me!* she thought, craving the security she had thought thrilling and satisfying to leave behind.

Vanesh held her in his arms and led her to the bed. He sat down on it and let her rest against him. Finally, he said, "Grale Casarion is dead."

"What?" asked Arendellie, not quite comprehending.

"The Emperor is dead," repeated Vanesh. "My right-hand man, Dragon-rider Ellez, told me."

"So," said Arendellie, still reeling from the rapid, shocking events, "you're King Vanesh, now?"

He kissed her. "And you are Queen Arendellie. Not until our coronation, though."

Nobody would miss Grale Casarion, Arendellie knew. She rested against Vanesh for a few more minutes. Suddenly, a thought occurred to her. She disengaged from his embrace and stepped back. "My son," she asked. "Are our sons all right?" She had become pregnant again and given birth six months earlier.

"Yes, my queen. Liesam and Aroch are safe and sound. As soon as I had sent the slave for you, I sent for them as well."

"Good." Arendellie collapsed into his arms again with a sigh of relief. Liesam was a playful, rambunctious child, who loved to spar with swords and daggers with the other princes. Arendellie had seen him several months ago. Aroch was a healthy infant, beginning to crawl around, but there was nothing particular about him yet. Arendellie was beginning to accept, even though she did not yet admit it to herself, all sorts of desires that she had suppressed.

Out of nowhere, she remembered dead bodies, pierced by swords and flowing blood, and the spatter of blood as soldiers cut a young man-slave down. Involuntarily, she shuddered.

"Are you okay?" Vanesh asked her.

"Yeah. I'm okay," said Arendellie faintly.

"Are you sure? Did anything happen?"

"No. It's just been…"

"Will you be all right if I leave?" asked Vanesh.

"Of course. I probably just need to sleep."

Arendellie moved out of his arms and sat on the bed. She *hoped* she just needed to sleep. She *hoped* a good night's rest would cure her. Deep within, she was beginning to suspect that nothing would. Ever.

"All right," said Vanesh, rising. "There are things to which I must attend. Inn-servants will bring up an excellent meal shortly for you. You may rest or eat as you wish. There is a nightgown on the bed for you."

"Oh," said Arendellie, standing. She kissed him. "You are so thoughtful."

He quickly pecked her in return. "I have to go," he said, and hurried out the door.

Arendellie collapsed back onto the bed. She called Inshara in to undress her and put the nightgown on, then dismissed her. She curled up on the bed and tried to sleep, but scenes she had glimpsed for a fraction of a second out of the corner of her eye tormented her. Even in Ebrin, she had seen very little death. A dead kitten, limp, still with eyes unopened. That was all. There was so much she had avoided in the village. That was one of the reasons she had thought she was made for palace life. However, now she had seen horrendous things, yet she knew the things she had seen were nothing compared to the crimes the regime committed every day. She could not bear the swift slaughter by the sword of fleeing slaves, yet the empire of which she was princess soon-to-be-queen tortured anyone who did not submit to its iron rule. It tore babes from their mothers. It committed atrocities that were not even spoken among the courtiers, though everyone knew of them…

Sitting up on the bed, Arendellie closed her eyes and thought, *I have to get over it. I am Queen. This is just what the world is like. What it always has been like. It's for the better, too, so that we can all get along and there can be no more war or conflict of any sort later. Just like the pain, sometimes even death, before a child is born. I have to get over it. I have borne children. I will manage this. I am the Princess. I will be Queen. I must be Queen. I must be strong. I must help Vanesh. Hopefully, we can find a way to do this with less torture, but we will do what we must.*

When Vanesh entered, hours later, in the cold of the early morning he saw the plate untouched and Arendellie laying on the bed, her eyes open. "Is anything wrong?" he asked.

"No. I can't sleep or eat. I'll recover, though. It's just been wild and traumatic, that sudden flight and all this sudden change."

"You were worried about me?" he asked.

"A little," said Arendellie. That was true. It would not have kept her from sleep or food, but it was true. She was beginning to feel uncomfortable lying. Could everyone see through her as easily as she saw through herself? This game of pretend was tiring her. She was not sure why. Why could she not simply decide to be what she was pretending to be? Why was she struggling not to be like Kathreen, Mirla, or Dorene... not, of course, that she found herself feeling or thinking like Kathreen or Mirla after they had gone crazy about the Promise, but why was she finding herself acting like a childish mother, or was it motherish child? Why was she struggling to be a princess? She had been a princess for the last ten years– almost– of her life. Why was she having a problem now? She was not even pregnant. In Ebrin she had never been like Kathreen or Mirla. Kathreen had been closest to her, and even then she had been incredibly different and alone. The whole village had known it. So why was she having to resist a tug, like gravity, in that direction now? It had not satisfied her then. It would not sit well with her now.

"Well, there's no need to be worried. We have the fire under control. It's not a problem anymore. The wizards and dragons have done a great job, even though most of the dragons just lost their Dragon Keeper. We're going to get to try our way of getting things in order, instead of being subjugated to Grale's crazy insistence on acting as if everyone is a traitor who needs to be dealt with by torture and that if something doesn't work it's because the torture wasn't harsh enou– Is something wrong, Araenyi?" There was sudden real concern in his voice.

Arendellie was cringing. When Vanesh Casarion started talking about Grale's tortures she flinched. Now, she was slightly pale. She shook her head, but she knew it was not convincing.

"Did you see something?" Vanesh asked in a hushed voice, full of concern.

Arendellie nodded. "Yes. It was, it was... horrible." She spoke in a low, quavering voice. She would not tell Vanesh Casarion that it was simply the beheading of a boy. She would let him think that it was something... unmentionable.

"It's okay. You're all right," said Vanesh soothingly, touching her cheek with the tip of his finger. "Don't worry. I won't ask you what you saw."

Against her will, Arendellie breathed a huge sigh of relief. She hoped Vanesh would interpret it as having only to do with not wanting to describe what she had seen. In truth, she could not tell anyone how she was beginning to feel. Even if she could, she must not. She had to change it, and fast, not *say* it!

In a moment, Vanesh's arms were around her. He lay down beside her and kissed her.

#46
The White Dragon Keeper

Amrath was a young dragon. She had hatched to the not-Dragon Keeper only because her egg had been one of the many he had touched looking for the dragonspell-touched egg, the egg that carried the hope and crown of her race. She did not want to think about what he had done, though she missed him. She missed him terribly. She knew others fared far worse than she did. They felt torn apart by his death. They *shared* his death. She pitied them. Regaleath, admired among the dragons, had been bonded to him; Amrath shuddered. Regaleath was representing the entire dragon race and offering a gift and honor on behalf of all the dragons, but she was only a dragonspell-touched dragon. The egg the never-to-be-named-again-among-the-dragons one had tortured was more than a dragonspell-touched egg. That dragon was the dragon who would ultimately represent her entire race. She was the ultimate dragon, the ultimate dragonspell-touched dragon. The never-to-be-named-again-among-the-dragons one had done an immeasurable evil to the crown of the dragons, the seed of the dragons, the entire dragon race. Amrath wanted to tear him apart with her teeth and then burn him with her breath, only recently discovered.

She heard Kathreen speak to the dragons. They all admired and honored Kathreen as no other. She it was who should have been born a Dragon Keeper. She had been a Dragon Keeper. Now, as Dragon Speaker, she spoke to all the dragons, and Amrath listened as she had never listened to anyone in her life.

I did not save your dragon egg. I do not think that I killed the wizard Casarion, for he was as pale as death before I thrust my sword through his heart. Furthermore, neither I nor that egg, however unique or precious it may be, are the hope of your race, or of any race. Only the Promise of the Creator can be that. It is for the hope of that Promise, for the desire to carry out the mission handed to me and proclaim it to you all, dragons and men alike, and because it would have been wrong to allow the inhabitants of Grale's castle to perish when I was present and able to do something about it, that I have led you all. In addition to all this, it was not my power that enabled me to lead you so well, nor my power that kept the castle from melting with fire the moment Grale died. It was the Creator's power, which He was pleased to allow to shine from my sword, that did all these things. It was not because of my courage that I ventured into the castle to rescue the stash of dragon eggs Grale Casarion was intending to hatch, nor was it my power that protected me among the flames and disintegrating stones and spells. It was the Creator's power. This same power enhanced and carried the spells of our wizards tonight, giving them a potency and effect far beyond that any of the wizards could have mustered. And, it is not I who am the Dragon Keeper. It is the Promised One who is the Dragon Keeper and the keeper of the whole world. It is through the Creator, and His Promise alone, to appear in the distant future when this dragonspell-touched egg hatches, which you praise me for rescuing but in which, in fact, I have felt Grale's dark and twisted spells, that you can all be kept from destruction and death.

I thank you all for your gift, which is certainly the greatest gift that you dragons can give to one such as me. I am most honored that I have been a reflection of the True and Eternal Dragon Keeper to you. I, however, beg you that you would give your honors and loyalty to Him, your only Creator and Keeper. Do not let your respect and gratitude to me hinder you from giving the greatest gift you can give, yourself, to the Creator, and do not let it diminish that gift by your giving some of yourselves to me. I am no greater or better than you, and have nothing in myself. The Creator does not need and will not benefit from the gift of yourself, but He is worthy, and He alone is worthy, and He desires that gift. Give the greatest gift, your very being, to Him, to Whom alone you can offer it without committing an atrocity more terrible than the one Grale sought to commit against you, and to Whom alone you can, in fact, give yourself. Thank you, dragons. Remember, also to watch and wait for the Promised, and give yourselves to Him when He comes.

Amrath could not help but admire Kathreen Alarion. She did not, however, understand how she could possibly commit an atrocity worse than the-never-to-be-named-among-the-dragons one *had* committed against her race. Whatever Kathreen Alarion said about herself, Amrath and all the dragons would admire her. She turned and flew northward. Something in her told her that there she would find the Dragon Keeper who could heal the hearts of the dragons who had hatched to the-never-to-be-named-among-the-dragons one. Something told her that there she would find the one who could heal her own heart and be her friend as no dragon could be.

Audra reached above her head to pluck the peach. She gently dropped it into the satchel she carried and started towards the little group of houses. The fruit was heavy, but she was a strong girl. She stepped out of under the orchard canopy. The sky was pale blue and the mountains rose steeply to the south. The sun hovered just above one peak. She looked around. Something was happening. Her skin skittered with the energy of it. She walked across the open space, a lightness in her step.

Then, startled by something she could not quite feel, she looked over her shoulder. Flying in over the orchard was a creature of monstrous size. Huge wings. Flashing scales of pink, pink-orange, and pink-yellow. She froze. The monster had fiery yellow eyes. Audra looked around her, but she saw nowhere to run. She stood in the middle of an open space, and the monster had seen her.

Amrath.

Audra could not believe it. Was she going crazy? How could the monster possibly be named Amrath? How could she possibly know the monster's name? She felt relief and joy from Amrath. She felt an exuberant assurance from the flying monster that she– she?– would not eat her. "Oh!" Audra gasped, unaware. She could not take it all in. She stood frozen still, but not by terror now, though she was still terrified. The wind from the flying monster's wings ruffled her hair, and she felt Amrath correct her thoughts. *Dragon. Not flying monster.*

Then, the young dragon landed. Responding to some desire from the dragon and impulse from within her, Audra walked forward and placed her hand on Amrath's leathery snout. It shimmered with peachy colors. She laid down the satchel of fruit and rested her head against the dragon's neck, basking in their friendship. She felt Amrath's joy. She had succeeded. She had found her... *Dragon Keeper.* Audra did not understand most of Amrath's thoughts. The dragon was quickly thinking... feeling... seeing things about the whole background of which Audra had no knowledge at all. She could not take it all in. Her head hurt from it.

"Stay here, Amrath, okay?" she asked, stroking the dragon under her chin. "I have to go take this fruit to my family and friends, and they'll be just as scared of you as I was... Yes, I'm sorry. Humans don't know about dragons here. No. Nothing at all. Yes, it is a bummer, but I have to go. Yes. I'll have to figure out how to tell them about you. Sure. I'll go with you. I wouldn't want all your friends to die of loneliness. Oh, Amrath." She kissed the dragon's nose. *Don't worry. I will come back, Amrath. You're my best friend, my friend-friend now. You're as much to me as I am to you, now. I'll come back tonight, Amrath.*

Amrath watched Audra pick up the fruit and head towards her village. She vaguely remembered seeing it in her flight. Her muscles were shaking and burning; if it took Audra a few days to convince her family it wouldn't hurt. She could use some eating and resting, especially since she was still such a young dragon. Now she would tell her friends that she had found their Dragon Keeper and bring her back. She was so happy. The never-to-be-named-among-the-dragons one had never been like Audra. For some reason, she and thousands of other dragons had grown terribly attached to him, but there was no love or warmth. Not like there was with Audra. Audra made her happy, even though she was afraid to have Audra walk away from her. Happy like she had never really even thought dragons could be. Well, she had known a few dragons who had real human partners, but she had never really understood them. Now, she knew they all experienced this.

Now, watching Audra walking through the shadows of the forest, she was amazed by the young girl she had found. She understood Audra perfectly, but the sounds that her mind connected with her meaning was totally different from those used by the humans in Camil. Other things about Audra were different, too. She wore a knee-length fur skirt and matching sleeveless fur tunic, instead of covering her whole body in cloths. She had hair so light it was almost white, though it was tinged with yellow. Her eyes were pale, pale blue, blue so pale it was almost gray, and her skin was almost white. Amrath could see the blue-green veins under her skin and a pink blush on her cheeks. Her lips were lighter, too. Apparently, humans could be colored as differently as dragons.

Amrath dug her claws into the earth and raised her wings. In a few moments she was in the air. She burned from flight and was very tired, but her stomach growled with hunger. She needed to eat, and she knew there was a herd of deer not far. She would have eaten them on her way here, if she had not been driven on by the knowledge that the Dragon Keeper, her rider, was very near and her terrible need for her. *Audra.* She knew her name, now. She tested it in her mind. She loved it. She sent it back to her friends.

She knew exactly where the deer were. Even in her weakened state, she would have no trouble catching one. She was a dragon, queen of flight and hunting.

#47
Tied Tongue

Azshbir stumbled home tired. None of them had left their farm in many months, and he had just gone into Afteloan that day to trade some of their excess food for things like sugar and salt and clothing. He had learned that rebels had arisen and were fighting for control. The Emperor, Grale Casarion, had died, and it was attributed to Kathreen Alarion. The kingdom had passed to his nephew, now-King Vanesh Casarion and a Council of Wizards who called themselves the Lords of Light. The blasphemy of the title "Lord of Light" did not escape Azshbir's notice. The rebels seemed to have some control of the area at the moment, but one of the things that had exhausted Azshbir was trying to stay away from the fighting. He did not want to be stopped by those who fought for the Council of Wizards and King Vanesh. That would mean horrendous death, since he could not assure them of his loyalty without renouncing the Promise. Besides, though he was not going to fight them– he did not even have time or energy to think about whether or not it was acceptable; he had a family to take care of– he did not want either side to consider him an enemy. So, he did not want to run into the rebels either. He really wouldn't want the Empire's men to hunt him because they thought he was one of the rebels. He would live with whoever was in power until they killed him or came for his family. He did not even know whether the rebels would be better than the Hasseleighton Empire; Ephezoa had been pretty bad before she fell, and growing worse. The rebels might be way worse. They could be anything.

One thing chilled Azshbir's blood. The Hasseleighton Empire under the Council of Wizards seemed to be far better at gaining the hearts of its people than under Grale Casarion. A young man, almost a boy, who wanted to buy his excess fruit for his family, had said something like, "Have you heard who Grale Casarion really is? Of course you have; everyone has. That cursed wizard, Alarion, didn't kill him at all; it was the time for him to ascend to heaven and return to what he'd been before in a pillar of fire. I wish these rebels would understand they have even less hope now than they did before his death, but they think the cursed wizard killed him. In reality, it was by his mercy that she escaped with her life." Azshbir bit the inside of his mouth to keep from roughly correcting the young man. If he did, he would probably be known throughout the whole region as one of the People of the Promise, and they would come for him and his family. He was still not horribly frightened of death or torture, but he had his wife and children and their friends to look out for. That tied his tongue.

He stepped in the door and dumped the few goods he had bought on the floor. Della– at least, he was almost certain it was Della– called, "Mom, Dad is home!"

"Tell him I'll be there in a moment. How did it go? I'm doing this," Neah'ra called back.

Azshbir knelt down. He did not feel like playing with his kids. He did not feel like trying to keep track of Reilia and Della. The little girl ran over and flung herself on his neck. "How are you, Daddy?" she asked.

"Okay," he said. "Are you doing well, Della?"

She beamed at him. "Did you know we tricked Mom today?"

Azshbir shook his head. "No, I didn't, but I can imagine." He did not know how the twins were so full of energy. They seemed not to understand that he and Neah'ra were totally exhausted all the time.

Della remained oblivious to his discomfort. "Yeah," she chattered, "I and Reilia have been working on it for a long time. We were discussing it quietly in the hayloft, how to do it, and then I came creeping down, and while Mom was milking the goat I leapt out at her, with just this smile on my face." She stopped to show it to Azshbir. "And, she yelled, 'Reilia! Don't do that!'"

Azshbir shook his head. "You naughty girl," he told her.

Neah'ra came over and looked down on them. Azshbir looked up at him. "You don't look well today," she observed. "Did something go wrong?" He hated the fear in her eyes. She looked like she had been worrying. He wanted to tell Della that she and Reilia were cruel to their mother, but he knew that, even though they were often callous, they were not trying to be mean. They were just rambunctious and unthinking, and it was true that he and Neah'ra did not play with them very much. He wondered how his parents had done it. It had not been any easier for them, if rather safer in some regards. "No," he said. "Rebels and Hasseleighton are fighting over Afteloan. Grale Casarion is dead." He spoke slowly and heavily.

"So, what's wrong?" she asked.

"Well, the Council of Wizards and King Vanesh is ruling the Hasseleighton Empire now. I don't know how they did it, but they have lots of people crazy about how Grale Casarion is… well, I can't say it, but it's dirty blasphemy."

Neah'ra nodded and sat down. "Well, they didn't capture you… they didn't kill you… You're back here with us. That's good, isn't it, and you don't have to go back in for what, three months? Four? Maybe we can stretch it a bit longer, though some people are growing and I've ruined so many good pairs of clothes trying to rearrange them into different sizes, so I'm not going to try that anymore unless I really have to."

Azshbir smiled weakly at her. He knew about her disastrous efforts to take clothes apart and put them back together.

"What's wrong?" asked Neah'ra. "You don't think anyone found out that we belong to the Promise and tracked you here?"

"No," said Azshbir, "no." He was remembering so many faces. So many greetings. So many questions. "No," he said. "It's not that. It's that I'm tired of having to be silent."

Neah'ra shook her hair back. "Well, if you want to, you *can* tell people. We could *both* tell people."

"And that would leave us where?" asked Azshbir.

"Maybe, the Creator sent the rebels here for a purpose. Maybe they will win, or at least so distract Hasseleighton that we will live. Maybe He sent the rebels and this feeling of yours together at this time so that we would see that, and follow.

"Maybe," agreed Azshbir, drolly, not really looking at her. He was *so* tired.

"Maybe. Or, then again, maybe we will both end up in the Empire's torture chambers. Maybe things I don't want to discuss in front of the children will be done to us."

"What don't you want to discuss in front of us?" Reilia piped up.

Azshbir turned around. "Things you don't want to know!" he growled.

Kgarjin hurried over from the kitchen. "What things do we not want to know?" she asked, leaning with her hand on the wall.

Azshbir opened his mouth and struggled for appropriate words. Neah'ra came to his aid. "Kgarjin, you can ask Shaelene, if she wants to tell you. As for the rest of you, Azshbir misspoke. We don't want to discuss them *at all,* in front of you or otherwise. At least, I don't. You?" she said, turning to Azshbir.

He was still so often spell-bound by his wife, tired as they both were. "You're right," he said, the beginnings of a genuine smile forming on his face. "I *don't* want to talk about them at all."

Hearing crying, Neah'ra bent forward to kiss Azshbir. She rose. "I need to take care of Kuthreb," she said, turned, and walked away. Azshbir wished she would have stayed with him. He could tell just from her gait that she was tired. He wished he had worked harder to come home sooner, that way she would not have worried that something had happened to him. Of course, very little of it could have been that. She could have just had an exceptionally hard day. After all, Della had been telling him about her and Reilia's shenanigans, and then there was their son to care for. It could have just been really hard because he had not been with her to help her, but his day, unfortunately, had been no less exhausting. Besides, if he had hurried more, maybe he would not have returned at all. That would have been worse, if worry *was* a contributer in the first place. He was inclined to think she worried less than he did. After all, she carelessly suggested that they just talk to people about the Promise. Maybe they would all be dead, if not for the fact that she had not left their land in years. She did not seem to mind.

Thinking about Neah'ra's words, he remembered freely proclaiming the Promise in the Ephezoan prison and, even, to the Hasseleighton soldiers who served as prison guards after the conquest. He did not know what had come in their lives of what he had done. He knew that he lived, though he had expected death. Perhaps, they were called to that again? The only thing was, he had not known if he would ever see Neah'ra and his children again either way, and he had known– or had reason to believe– that she had others caring for her. Now, she had only him, and he had reason to believe he would get to remain with her and care for her as long as he did not do this hare-brained thing he had to bite his tongue to keep from doing. It was different, now. The fact that the Creator had not let him die then did not mean He would not let him die now– when it would be worse; after all, Neah'ra had another child, a son now, and she might be pregnant again.

At any rate, there was no need to decide tonight. He was definitely not going back into the city just to talk to people tonight– or tomorrow. He stood. "Della?" he said.

"Yes?" Reilia responded. She was, apparently, standing right behind him.

"I don't want to play games right now," said Azshbir. "I'm too tired. You can tell your mom I went to bed."

#48
Twilight Gloom

Brisia looked up and knew at once that it was the dragon, L'sa-moth, the dragon bonded to Kathreen Alarion. It had been a very long time, but she knew at once. The sea-green underbelly hung between wings, dark purple against the brilliant blue sky. She turned to Lalia, with whom she was picking roots. "Get everyone. Tell them it's Kathreen." She sprang to her feet and ran back along the house. The others who were helping them pick the garden had heard.

In a few minutes, Brisia was standing in the clearing around the house with Adaria and her children and Athara and her child. Adaria held Rothen, her youngest, while watching Zsyinzjae toddle around. The dragon circled down. More of the family flowed in. Kalar. Sirifa. Khiel. Brisia lost track. The dragon came down. She felt the wind from the dragon's wings. L'sa-moth was so huge that she did not seem smaller to Brisia now than she was in her memories from when she was smaller herself. So many other things did. Finally, the dragon landed.

Kathreen was still undoing the straps that held her into the saddle when Brisia ran forward. As she slid down L'sa-moth green leg, Brisia flung herself upon her and hugged her, beginning to cry. She remembered Kathreen. The thick, dark woman– she had seemed so tall back then, though now she was only a little taller than Brisia herself– had held her in her arms while she cried. Thinking about it brought pangs of sorrow and pain to Brisia's heart and tears to her eyes. She hugged Kathreen fiercely and felt her hug her in return.

Over her head she heard Sirifa saying, "They tell me that their mother told them about you, and that you were very comforting and loving."

Finally, Brisia let go, and Kathreen released her. She stepped back and turned to Lalia, whom she had been teaching about the Promise. She had never forgotten the words Mom had given her for Lalia. *"I love her and I always will."* More importantly, far more importantly: *"With our eyes we will see."* She knew even she did not know all that meant. Motioning between her younger sister and Kathreen she said, "Lalia, this is Mommy's friend. *Our* Mom."

Brisia watched, with mingled pride and crushing pain as Lalia came forward to give Kathreen a hug. It still crushed her little child heart thinking of her Mom... remembering her... missing her... longing for her. She still wanted her hugs.

After hugging Lalia, Kathreen said, "It looks like a lot has happened here."

It has, Brisia thought. *Lots and lots. I have a best friend who's older than me and is like me but not like me. Her name is Khiel. I have Adaria. She's married to Kalar, whom you wouldn't know, and has two babies. Then Kuthrynd and Janya married and have a baby, and Athara and Kavra are married too! Both Janya and Athara are pregnant! Lalia is learning about how to take care of babies! And I teach her all I know about the Promise. It's a whole lot more than I did, but there's still tons more!* Meanwhile, Adaria was saying above her head, "Definitely." Adaria, her relationship with whom Brisia was not sure how to describe, hugged Kathreen. Then, she started telling Kathreen some of the things Brisia herself wanted to say. "I got married, and now we have children of our own. And Mom and Dad have grandchildren."

"Yes, I can see," Kathreen told her. "Your belly shows that you have recently been pregnant."

Adaria giggled. Brisia thought, *She doesn't do that very much.* She was telling Kathreen, "Yes, it does, doesn't it? Our lives show on us, and that's as it should be. Kalar, can you come and meet Kathreen, my best friend. She helped me grow into a woman, in the years we spent proclaiming the Promise together."

Brisia listened while Adaria and Kalar explained what had happened in their lives to Kathreen. Then, they started telling the story of how Kalar, Janya, Kavra, and Khiel had joined the family. Finally, Khiel told the story of how she and Adaria had gone down into the city and seen her parents. Brisia still chaffed that she had not been permitted to go. She wanted to have seen it, and she wanted it more every time she heard Khiel tell the story, which was not very often. She noticed, too, that Kathreen was uncomfortable, on edge. The woman was looking down at the ground. Brisia wondered why.

At last, Khiel had told the story and Kathreen turned to her and asked a question. "How can you bear to think about it? Aren't you angry?"

Brisia had a feeling something was going on. Now, Khiel looked down, avoiding the older woman's gaze. "I can't," she said. "Sometimes I am. But, then, I remember the Promise– or someone else reminds me. We all reminded each other down there, too. We met all the time, and we tried to encourage each other when others wanted to give up or were frightened. Sometimes, we encouraged others when we were sure we felt lower than they did, and found that the process of remembering to encourage them encouraged us. I miss a lot of my friends, but I'm happy here. The Creator has a plan."

Brisia smiled at Khiel and received a watery smile in return. Khiel never mentioned the friends she missed. Brisia had not heard about it in years.

"Yes, He does," Sirifa was saying. "Hoobit and I were wondering what we were going to do about the fact that our commission was to raise families and children, to keep the Promise, and among whose daughters the Promised One will dwell. We were beginning to worry, to insult the Creator by wondering if it would work out after all. But He always keeps His promises, even when we doubt Him, and He brought you and your friends here."

"Which brings me to the primary reason I am here," Kathreen said. "I have received a prophecy and a promise to give to all the Knights of the Promise: 'When twilight gloom has turned to darkest night, watch for your hope, the long-awaited Promise, for it is in the darkest and coldest of night that the morning star rises.'"

Khiel, her voice like the cutting sword edge of light, asked, "So then it is soon?" Brisia waited, still holding her breath.

Kathreen shook her head. "Of that, too, I have received further prophecy. It will happen in the distant future, on another continent, around the time a dragonspell-touched egg I now have, hatches. Speaking of which, I have something for you." She turned and looked through one of L'sa-moth's saddlebags, speaking while she did so. "Remember when we spoke of the prophecies when I was last here? Well, the Creator told me to make three scrolls, and one of them is for you. It contains all the prophecies and commands of which I know, whether received by me– which is only a few– or long ago." A few moments later, she found the scroll, withdrew it, and presented it to Hoobit.

Brisia wished she had not been so possessed by her own misery and remembered whatever Kathreen had done or said so many long years ago. It suddenly occurred to her that what seemed to her an indefinite amount of time, so long that it did not have any particular length, was not all that long to some people. But, Hoobit was speaking. "Thank you very much, daughter of prophets," he said. "Anyway, tell us of your story. It must be more interesting than the happenings here– though we do have some grandchildren of which you have not yet heard. Do you want to see them first, or tell your story?"

Kathreen shrugged, sat down, leaned against her dragon's side, and began to narrate a story of walking through the land, hiding and running from enemies, speaking to and learning from friends, leading friends to safety, and finally entering Grale Casarion's castle for no reason known to herself. "So, I stood there," she said, "and there was the egg, in front of him, and I knew it had been terribly twisted. I could feel that much in the energy fields, and then him all got up in his clothes, still working on his evil spell. I held my sword in my hand, and it shone with silver light. I could feel it itching to kill him. I cried challenge upon him, and stabbed him. But I think he was already changing. Lots of things happened at once. I picked up the egg and fled, my sword in hand. The castle began to explode into flame. So, I don't really know if I killed him or if his spell did." She fell silent.

"What did you say?" asked Janya, looking up from the baby she was nursing. Kathreen repeated herself.

"I think," said Hoobit, in the almost awed hush, "that there is a third possibility as to why Grale Casarion died."

No one spoke. After a few moments, Kathreen asked, "What?"

"That it was the presence and power of the Creator, visible in the shining of your sword, that killed Grale Casarion, whether by disrupting his spells or by some other more mysterious means," said Sirifa. "… Anyway, what is the world like after that evil wizard's death? Is Camil recovering and becoming more sane– perhaps saner than it has been in centuries?"

Kathreen spoke, upset, "Not at all! It's worse than ever before! We thought we would have freedom– we did for a few days– but there's these Eleven Counselors who call themselves the Lords of Light, which is blasphemy, since the name Lord of Light belongs to the Creator. They've concocted a crazy story, and for some reason everyone, especially the youth, seem to love it. I knew a girl named Yasya, who I thought was going to be a Knight of the Promise. Instead, she threw herself on me, begging me to honor Grale Casarion as the Creator Himself. It was totally sickening blasphemy, and I don't want to tell all of it right now. There were others like her. It's so much worse now, since the people hate us with all the venom that the government ever had for us." Brisia thought she sounded like she was about to cry, as she told of remaining in the area, training the few Knights of the Promise who remained in the midst of the oppression and fear.

Athara interjected, "It seems to me we must never put our hope or expectations in anything except what the Creator has explicitly promised, or we shall be disappointed and crushed."

"That *is* wise," said Kathreen dully. She sounded so sad and forlorn Brisia went over to her and gave her another hug.

Brisia was glad when Kathreen agreed to stay with them for a few days. She wanted her to tell her about Mirla, but Kathreen became very sad and told her that she did not remember very much that she could tell Brisia. All the things she could tell about Mirla, Brisia already knew. Finally, seeing how miserable it made Kathreen, Brisia stopped asking her for stories about her Mom. She knew, now, though what had been in Kathreen's gaze when she asked Khiel how she could bear to think about what had happened to her and wasn't she angry. Kathreen *really* could not bear to think about Mirla and she struggled with an anger she did not understand and could not control. Brisia wondered how close she and Mirla had been. She had not seen Kathreen when she was a little kid, but maybe before she was born Kathreen and Mirla had been like the twins of legend, Zaia and Kaia, who were joined at the hip and never parted. She wished Kathreen could tell her about Mirla, but let it go. After all, it hurt Kathreen horribly, and she did not *need* it. Mirla was with the Creator, and Brisia had Him. One day, they would all live together with Him. She did not need to know her Mom. She could know the Creator, and she could wait.

Brisia played with Kathreen's dragon, L'sa-moth, with the toddlers. She did not know how to relate to Kathreen. She hugged her a lot, trying to comfort her, but she knew that only the Creator could do that, just like only the Creator had been able to comfort her. She did not even know what to tell her. She thought Khiel would, but Khiel reminded her of that time when Brisia had begged her to tell her what the Creator had told her, and she had said she did not have any words, let alone any that would mean anything to Brisia by themselves. That had been after Khiel and Adaria returned from their journey to Mieshor, where they saw Khiel's parents and spoke to the people. Khiel seemed generally radiant with a joy sharper than the edge of a sword, but Brisia realized that she could not share that with Kathreen. She wished Kathreen would understand. She thought she almost did. Vaguely, she remembered how Kathreen had related to her, what she had been like, how she had changed on their journey from Ebrin, when she had been worried that Lalia might die.

Several days later, Brisia was hugging Kathreen. "I don't want you to leave," she told her, sobbing. "I want you to stay with us, and be happy. Heal. Get better."

"I have to go, Brisie," said Kathreen, kissing her through her hair. "I have a calling from the Creator. You may have one too, someday."

"But you need to be happy," Brisia sobbed. "You're so miserable, living under all the bad things that've happened and that you've seen."

"It's all right," said Kathreen, rocking Brisia. "I want to go and see some of my old friends and try to tell them about the Creator and the Promise. I hope they will listen to me, now. And, I'd like to see Azshbir, Adaria's brother–"

"Oh yes!" exclaimed Brisia. "I know about Azshbir!"

"Well, I really don't think I will, but I hope to see him if I can. And, I have to take the egg I told you about to where the Creator wants me to leave it. If I can, I'll come back after that."

Later, thinking back on her memories, Brisia realized that her presence hurt Kathreen, reminding her of Mirla, of pain, in her own life and in that of others, that she had never accepted. Right then, Brisia only said, "Then go, and be quick, 'cause the Creator's plan is always good!"

Kathreen smiled weakly, and they disengaged. Brisia never saw Kathreen again, but the healing she so desired for her was to be soon.

#49
Change

Azshbir was very tired. He had bought as much of certain necessities as he could and tied them in a bundle of clothes which he now carried on his back. His leg burned. He did not want to go back into the city for a long time. The situation was becoming more dangerous in this battle for allegiance. Out of the corner of his eye he glimpsed a woman who looked like Kathreen. Drawing up her pink and gold shawl over her face, she stepped forward and said, "May I help you?– I'm Kathreen." He still did not like the ways of Hasseleighton.

"Thank you, thank you so much," he said, and Kathreen took one end of his bundle. He felt embarrassed. Men should not need help from a woman. It was kind of embarrassing to be offered it, and even more embarrassing to accept it, but he took it anyways. He was limping badly from the weight and the long day, and it would be a great help to have someone take even a little of the load off of him.

Before a large old gate, Azshbir breathed a huge sigh. "We'll leave the sugar and salt there, for the moment, and go in and catch up a little." He shoved the gate open and walked up to his house. Surveying it, he hoped it would hold up for a few more years before it needed any major repairs. It had been abandoned for a while before they moved in. Neah'ra opened the door. "There's some juice for you, honey," she told Azshbir. As they walked in, she said over her shoulder to Kathreen, "I don't know who you are, and we don't have anything ready, but I'll get one of the girls to make you some–"

Azshbir thought that his wife was extremely tired, as tired as he himself. Then again, she always was, and it had been quite a few years since she had related to anyone outside their family. Kathreen had just interjected, "No, it's okay, and you seem very poor. I'm just Kathreen Alarion, and I knew Azshbir."

There was surprise, beautiful surprise in his wife's voice, Azshbir thought, as she said, "Kathreen Alarion? We'd thought you were dead or worse. The Circle of Eleven announced their offer for you to join them and their threat if you did not, and then nobody has heard of you at all for a couple months– which has happened before– but we thought…"

Wearily, Azshbir sank down onto a mat on the floor while she brought him the juice she had made. Above him, Kathreen laughed dimly. "Oh no, not at all," she said, moving to sit down also, a few feet away from him. "I'm actually here because the Creator specifically sent me here, just now. I have a scroll of the prophecies for you and your family, which I'll give you when L'sa-moth shows up. She should be coming. I also have a prophecy for all the Creator's people in this dark hour, though its fulfillment is still far off. 'When twilight gloom has turned to darkest night, watch for your hope, the long-awaited Promise, for it is in the darkest and coldest of the night that the morning star rises.'"

Azshbir looked up. "That's beautiful… It really has been hard," he said, dropping his head. He paused for a long time, thinking. He would, perhaps, have spoken of the Promise to someone, certainly to anyone who asked, except that

Hasseleighton had taken control, and he could feel the heaviness of the oppression, the watching eyes of the oppressors. They were like eagles or vultures circling their prey, in their oppressive and eagle watchfulness lest the rebels rise and take control again. It made him shudder. He had not believed that anything could be worse than Grale Casarion's reign, yet this was worse. "The only reason it isn't worse," he said slowly, "I think, is because I was actually thrown in prison under the Ephezoan regime."

It took a moment for him to process Kathreen's gasped "What?"

Neah'ra handed him the glass of juice, which he sipped gratefully, and answered Kathreen. "Yes. About a year after Azshbir stopped in the city, we married. I got pregnant, but a little before I was due, he was arrested by the authorities of Ephezoa for 'treasonous thoughts and unpatriotic intentions'. He had been telling people that they needed to be more concerned about the Creator's Promise and obeying Him, and about His kingship and authority, than about who happened to rule over them, or even whether they were mistreated. I got to visit him once a month, so he actually got to name our firstborn daughters, Reilia and Della. It has just been so hard, having twins without him though, and Azshbir and our daughters only got to see each other once a year. When they were seven, Grale Casarion took the city, and released Azshbir right away. I think it was because he assumed that anyone Ephezoa considered a traitor was a friend, and certainly not one of those he most hated."

Azshbir looked up. "That was funny," he said dryly.

For a time there was silence. Azshbir slowly sipped his juice. It was refreshing. He wondered where the kids were. Usually, they would be making noise. There were so many others in this household– Shaelene, Shantee, Kira, Kgarjin, Marlekk, and then his own, adopted Lasaira, Della and Reilia, and his son, Kuthreb. His eyes wandered over his wife's form. He was pretty sure she was pregnant again. Finally, Kathreen spoke, as if out of nowhere. "I was actually sent here to call you, Azshbir, as a Knight of the Promise, sent to proclaim the Promise, never hiding it in either heart or home, and to train more knights."

Azshbir winced. He felt like the breath had been knocked out of him. "I can't do that," he said, his voice hardly audible. "I have my family to care for." Slowly, his voice gained just a little volume. "It's already so hard, since I don't have a card, so I have to interact with others as little as possible and, even so, I could be arrested any day." A card was a note that had written on it that the bearer had worshiped the ascended Grale Casarion and was loyal to his high godhood. People were often detained and asked to show their cards. If they did not have a card, it could be very, very bad. People were lucky if they only had their day wasted. Sometimes, they would be tortured without any opportunity to prove their allegiance.

For a long time there was taut, cold silence. Then, Kathreen whispered, "The Creator loves you… He wants you to rest in Him… The responsibilities are all His… He is able."

Neah'ra looked between Kathreen and her husband. She had never met the woman who had traveled with Azshbir, and she was watching her, listening to her, half-evaluating, half-admiring her. She was not sure what she wanted... for Azshbir to accept this call or not. Fear, fear of she knew not what, fear of she dared not think what, pounded in her heart and blood. She wanted to be faithful and obedient, and more fears than she could process or name burned in her muscles and clouded her ability to think. The moment seemed to stretch itself out forever. Azshbir only barely noticed the look in her eyes, though, and he did not think about it. There was shortness and anger in his weary voice as he almost lectured, "How can you expect me to do that? I have to care for them! They will starve if I don't feed them. Moreover, if I'm caught, they might all be tortured in the dungeons, too. I can't do that! I can't expose them so. The Creator can't possibly demand it. I just can't."

Again, there was silence. Guilt tugged at Azshbir, but he could not think what other options he possibly had. He could not really think at all. Then Kathreen spoke softly, her voice pained and sometimes halting. She seemed to struggle to speak, to shrink from that which she remembered and told, wincing at her own words. "I knew a friend who did..." she began. "Her name was Mirla. She chose to remain true to the call of the Promise, even when men threatened to take the lives of her children." Kathreen's voice became that of someone struggling to speak through a weight of tears, to speak rather than cry. "She trusted that He was good and able, and left them in His hands... The Creator rewarded her trust, and let her see a little of its answer, using me, as unworthy as I have proved myself, to rescue her children and bring them to safety, one of them a mere infant." By now, her words were punctuated by sobs. At times, she had to stop altogether. "The Creator does not promise that He will always work in ways we can understand, but He will always take care of those we leave to Him, even if we can not see how He does so, or think He is not doing so... We must trust Him, for He is worthy. I met her again, as she was dying from her tortures. Her calmness and confidence was beautiful to behold... though I really flubbed my part up, and tried to help and minister to her for my own reasons, and rather contributed to her pain. ... I could hardly bear to see her trust and rest in Him, for I was worrying and fretting and chasing my own desires and hopes, rather than resting in His goodness... She showed me more kindness, unable to do anything but trust, than I have shown in all my life... She told me that we don't have to be strong enough, but only to rest in His strength... When I asked her, she told me she did not know how I could bear to live, but I know, now, that it was the same reason she could bear dying... To surrender, and to trust. Somehow, in that darkness and pain... the Creator showed her His love and sufficiency, even when we have no strength left... It's okay. He's real, and His love, He Himself, His Promise, is all."

Azshbir watched with amazement, his weariness momentarily forgotten, as something seemed to change in Kathreen while she told the story. Peace seemed to settle on her. She raised her head, as if finally accepting the pain involved in the Creator's will. A kind of joy or peace, inextricably mingled with pain, began to shine from her face as she went on. "I know now that, in that pain, He gave her, her desire, and that He has used my pain on her account and that of her orphans to give me mine– the knowledge of Him. I know, too, that this is for you– to be encouraged to seek Him, to lay aside your worries and beg Him to show you what He has shown others. To teach us all to trust Him through each other, to see in others' lives, and learn to trust Him in our own, that in all things, whether we see or feel it then, however much they hurt or far and distant He seems, He is giving us our hearts' desire, a desire which was given us by Him."

"I will read that scroll and meditate on the Creator and His Promise," said Azshbir. It was settled. He could not have said what had changed, but something had changed inside him.

Kathreen stood. "I will go and get you that scroll. Tomorrow morning we will perform the knighting ceremony, unless one of you thinks it better to do so now?"

Both Azshbir and Neah'ra shook their heads. As Kathreen walked out the door he turned to Neah'ra. "Where is everyone else?"

Neah'ra shrugged. "Pulling weeds. Picking fruit. Seeding the new patch we just finished." Her face fell. "I'm really much more tired than I should be." She seemed to be saying something more, something about her fears and hopes for the future, that he could not quite get.

"It's all right, Neah'ra," he said and leaned forward to kiss her. "Why don't you go and take a nice nap? I'm sure Shaelene, Shantee, and Kira can do just fine watching the littler ones."

Neah'ra nodded. She rose to go, knocking over the cup Azshbir had placed on the floor between them. A little trickle of juice spilled out. Her hand flew to her mouth. "Oh, no–!" she cried.

"It's all right," said Azshbir, suppressing his irritation. He would have liked to get every drop out. "It's only a little bit." He righted the cup. "Go and take a nap. That's just proof how much you need one." He wondered if it was the pregnancy or a light sickness. He *hoped* it was not more than a light sickness. Rubbing his bad leg, he leaned back against the wall and was quickly asleep himself.

#50
Knights' Scroll

Kathreen came in again, and Azshbir opened his eyes. She handed him the scroll, and he unfolded it. His eyes flitted over the runes. "Do you have a pen and ink?" he asked, an idea instantly occurring to him.

"Uh, yes. Why do you want it?"

Azshbir was not sure what to say. "Can you bring it, please?" he asked. Some of his weariness fell away in the excitement of what he was about to do.

"Right now?" asked Kathreen.

"If you don't mind."

While Kathreen went, Azshbir stretched himself out on the floor with the scroll in front of him. He saw there, very near the end, Kathreen's words.

When twilight gloom has turned to darkest night, watch for your hope, the long-awaited Promise
For it is in the darkest and coldest of night that the morning star rises.
The fulfillment of this Promise will be on a distant continent in another age:
When the egg of the dragon hatches
And wars and death across the land rage
Then the mighty Dragon Keeper arises
With the light of the morning star of coming day
For then dawn is near and noon is no longer far away.

While waiting for Kathreen, Azshbir thought that he would read this to his family. What could be more important than the prophecies of the Promise? He wondered if it would be possible to make copies. If they were all arrested and killed, they would not want this to be lost with them. He could not let his thoughts go in that direction. It was clear that the Creator did not want them to continue hiding. Perhaps it had been in accordance with His will for them to be silent for the past years, but when Azshbir realized that the time to speak had come, he should have obeyed immediately.

Kathreen came in and handed a pen and ink to Azshbir. He looked up at her and asked, "Do you know what this means?"

She bent down closer to see what he was looking at. "Some of it, yes. Some of it, no," she said. "Just because my hand wrote it doesn't mean I understand it. It doesn't even mean I heard it." She straightened and turned to go.

"Do you want a meal? Perhaps to share what's been going on?" he called. He did not really want to, but she would soon be gone and who knew if they would ever see each other again? They wanted to learn from each other, not let this opportunity go past.

"It's all right," Kathreen said, stopping and looking over her shoulder. "I might go out and see if I can help anyone with anything, but I want to be alone right now. You're poor and have a family, and I'm a wizard. It's fine." She continued walking.

Suddenly a thought occurred to Azshbir. "How long can I have the pen and ink?"

Kathreen laughed lightly, even artificially. "For as long as it lasts. If I want another, I can get myself one." Before Azshbir could say thanks, she hurried out.

To be honest, he was not sorry about it. They already had shared. They had shared ore than either of them would ever get to the bottom of, he thought. Kathreen's telling of that story had been the means of change in all of them. He dipped the pen in the ink, thought for a moment, and began to scribble:

>Mountains melted before His face;
>Rocks were shattered under His glance;
>He came down in a tornado of fire
>And the smoke from it hid the radiance
>In thick darkness and death;
>Men were caught like a moth burning
>In the flame of His breath –
>Dark and fiery winds, fierce and blinding.
>
>Though He gave only life
>And the Light of power and compassion rested on Him
>With untainted peace and authority
>Yet He bore the bruises of our strife
>And was crushed because of my portion –
>Stricken in darkness though He walked in light,
>Bearing my plague while creation writhed,
>For all was wrong in that night.

Azshbir took the pen and dipped it again in the ink, only then noticing how cramped his hand was. He had not written more than a few figures in years. He stretched his hand and massaged its muscles with the other hand, then took up his pen and continued to write:

>With power and authority He spoke
>Into the midst of the darkness
>And the enemy cowered and fled
>For His soul was radiant brightness
>Even while He walked in death;
>Even in his stronghold, no match for His might was His enemy
>Though dreadful to all men and dragons, and at His voice
>The rocks were riven, the stars fell, and the captives were free.
>
>Triumphant, He marched through the regions of night
>And the dawn answered His call
>He appeared in the morning, greeted in Light

And at the touch of His hand
The wounded were healed and the defiled made pure
Victory and peace sang His song
For He conquers His enemies, makes friends of His foes
The endless day follows Him, past the night so long.

Azshbir laid down the pen and stretched his hand. The muscles burned, but he was pleased with what had just flowed from his pen. He could not tell all that he had known upon seeing that vision, but the words had come to him. Moreover, this vision was his motivation. This was why he would obey the Creator as a Knight of the Promise. The Promise, though He had not yet entered Kaarathlon, already was in the Creator's eyes. Azshbir was confident of his forgiveness and freedom. He also realized how small and frail he was before the eternally burning fire of the Person who was the Promise.

He scanned the column he had just written, took up the pen again, and wrote above it, "the vision revealed by the Creator to Azshbir Nan-reem, son of Hoobit and Sirifa and husband of Neah'ra, in the prisons of Ephezoa after he had worried that he did not belong to the Promise because of his utter failure:"

The voices of young women and children broke in on his ears. Picking up the scroll, Azshbir stood, then swayed, his vision going gray. For a moment he thought he was going to pass out. Then he recovered. He knelt down again and closed the ink bottle. This time, he stood with both the inkstand and the pen, and the scroll, not wanting the children to ruin either. *Now, where can I put this where it will be safe from their naughty hands?* he wondered.

Lasaira stepped in front of Azshbir. "Dad," she asked, "what is that?"

Azshbir stopped. He wanted to get it put away. "Well," he said, "it's this, this, and this. Is that enough for you?"

A twinkle in her eye, she asked, "Will you tell me later?"

"Of course. I'll tell you all later, but don't tell your sisters just yet. I don't want them pestering me."

"Sure." Lasaira nodded knowingly. Azshbir walked on. He was going to hide it in a cupboard in one of the rooms down the hall and then cover it in some boards in case the roof leaked. When the time was right, he would read to his family from it. Probably tomorrow night.

Kathreen Alarion did not appear again that evening or night. Early in the morning, coming out from his bed in the semi-darkness, he saw her sitting on the couch his wife often used, awake but quiet and thoughtful. As she passed her she looked up. "Good morning, Azshbir," she said softly.

"Good morning, Kathreen," he said. He could vaguely make out the bright colors of her clothing in the light that fell from the window across her. "Is anyone else awake?"

"L'sa-moth definitely is. She really likes the early morning. I think I heard a couple of the girls moving around." Kathreen paused for a moment. "I'd like to do it now. Can you get your wife?"

"Neah'ra is pregnant, and I think she might have a mild sickness. I'd rather not wake her up," said Azshbir. He was not sure why *he* was awake at this hour.

"She can go back to sleep afterwards, and this will not take long, but I want to do it now."

"You're not going to stay with us for any length of time at all?" Azshbir asked her. "We must have so much to share and teach each other."

Kathreen shook her head. "I am being driven to take the egg across the sea as soon as possible. Many things are not right, and I still have a few more things to do before I and L'sa-moth can leave. Besides"– she looked down at her hands while she spoke– "life isn't about those of us who like and know each other sharing everything we think we know or have learned with one another and trying to teach each other all time. Life is about letting the Creator show us what He wants us to know, what we each need to know for us to know Him in the way He has for us and fulfill the call He's given to us each. Often the Creator teaches us through others; always, as far as I can tell, He uses others at one point in our lives or another. But it's not about soaking each other in, it's about Him, receiving His light in." She paused for a moment, as if thinking about how to say what she wanted. "The shadow is so heavy on us, me and L'sa-moth now. I don't really mean gloom, though it is both light and gloom. I can't explain it, I can't share it, even L'sa-moth can't share it with me. I am so alone in this, not that I detest it, and so grateful for all that life has brought by His will." She paused again, shaking her head slightly, as if trying to think about whether she should or even could share what she was thinking of. Finally, very softly, she said, "I've seen this in others, and had to watch them torn from me by it. Basically, I can't live where you want me to anymore. That's wrong. I can't live in the way you're thinking of, anymore."

Azshbir nodded. He thought he understood. Maybe. A little. He thought whatever Kathreen was talking about might be the same thing that at times shimmered between him and Neah'ra.

"Of course," Kathreen went on, "it's like this all the way up, and I think we experience it slowly, by degrees, and it's not always the same."

Azshbir and Kathreen both heard soft footfalls. He turned and saw Neah'ra, standing in her nightgown, absolutely gorgeous. He wanted to kiss her. It was a little lighter now. "You didn't wake up because I left, did you?" he asked.

"No," said Neah'ra quietly. "It was time. Hopefully, Kuthreb stays asleep."

Kathreen rose from the couch and arranged the shawl over her head. "Where is Shantee?"

"Why?" asked Neah'ra, standing so still, almost alone in a nice sort of way, in the semi-darkness, her whitish nightgown gleaming, her dark skin and hair a shadow in the shadows.

"I spoke with Shantee earlier this morning. I believe she also is ready. She may already be outside." Kathreen turned and led the way through the darkness into the chilly morning. It raised goose-bumps on Azshbir's skin though it was not that cold.

They often rose early, since these were the best hours in which to work, if not for the danger of snakes in the darkness.

After the short knighting ceremony, Azshbir wondered if he should show Kathreen what he had written, but thought perhaps it would be out-of-place. Maybe she already knew. She hugged each of them and then stood back while her huge dragon touched each of them on the forehead with her snout. "She's saying goodbye," she said, smiling. Then, she turned and mounted L'sa-moth and the dragon took off. She flew away into the gray mists of morning.

As they stood, watching, the eastern sky white with sunrise, Shantee said, "It seems like a long time, sometimes, but it really isn't."

"What are you talking about?" asked Azshbir without tearing his eyes away from the dragon, her form beginning to fade into the mist.

"Parting," said Shantee. "We're all going to be together again, as what we really are and are meant to be, and none of it will seem to have been long then. That will be the truth."

For a long time no one spoke. Finally, Azshbir said, "We're Knights, now, and as Knights we all have that call… Anyway, it's morning, and there's work to be done."

A sudden breeze ruffled their hair. Neah'ra said, "I'm going to go back to sleep… if Kuthreb lets me."

"I'll get Kgarjin to take care of him if he doesn't," said Shantee. As she went back in, she turned to Azshbir. "She's really tired."

"She is. Who knows what will happen next?" His eyes lowered, he said, "You might be right. It might really not be long. Death. Do we wait, or is it already? Never mind, you won't understand until I show you something, and there's work to be done. I'll show you tonight."

Shantee nodded. "I'm going to wake up my siblings, if Mom hasn't already."

#51
Kathreen of the Silver Sword

Arendellie walked along the streets of Ebrin. It had been several months since the horrible disaster of Grale Casarion's death. The images of the things she had seen then had dulled in her mind, and she was enjoying being not only the princess of the crown prince but the queen. Vanesh Casarion ruled with the Lords of Light, a council of wizards, and Arendellie knew that he was relieved not to have to bear the burden of ruling alone. Their coronation had been held about a week after Grale's death, and she had enjoyed it a great deal better than her presentation to Vanesh. There had not been too much color! Color that, she knew now, had been imprisoned flame. That was why, at Grale Casarion's death, the entire thing had burst into fire. Grale Casarion had taken some of the hottest, most volatile flame and woven spells around it to bind it into cloth and render it harmless in order to gain the effects he wanted for his palace. When he died, those spells, extremely complicated, had ceased being sustained by his will. Because of the wild energy of the fire, they had unraveled much more quickly than most spells were apt, and long before they were even mostly unraveled the fire was free enough to explode into burning motion. Arendellie did not really understand it. A female light wizard named Valiana had tried to explain it to her, but she was not a wizard so she could not understand.

Valiana had also explained to her that none other than Kathreen Alarion of the Silver Sword had led the wizards and dragons in putting out the fire before it consumed all of Anores. The Lords of Light were disappointed that a wizard of such skill could be so dense and thoughtless, not to mention so cowardly. They had tried to send someone to explain to her the real meaning of the Promise, which had been lost, and invite her to join their Council. However, she had already vanished, and they could not track her down, though there were rumors that she remained in the area and was hiding from them. Arendellie did not believe the story Lady Valiana and others had told her about the real meaning of the Promise and who the Creator actually was; she was not sure what she believed or if she believed anything. It did not seem to matter. She was just interested in living her life as Queen of Camil Hasseleighton. She was interested in being beautiful for Vanesh Casarion and helping him. She was sorry that Kathreen Alarion was so dense; did she not realize that if she were a little more intelligent– and, perhaps, less cowardly– she could join the Council of Wizards and work to make Camil a better place? She could help them rule with more kindness and compassion if she really cared about those foolish Knights of the Promise who were fit to be annihilated. She could help them keep the peace with the dragons. After all, she had been honored by the dragons as Dragon Keeper; if she remained around, she could probably give many of the dragons a reason to live and keep much of Camil from disintegrating into civil wars as the rebels and the dragons fought Camil Hasseleighton. That way, everything would be better. Better government. Less war. All around, less unnecessary killing, torture, and grief. Why was her brilliant wizard friend so foolish?

Never mind, thought Arendellie. *I don't want to ruin my visit to Ebrin by thinking about Kathreen and the present state of affairs. This is a time to be happy and enjoy the mountains of my birth.* She smiled at a young girl, who had probably been a toddler back when Arendellie lived in Ebrin but whom she did not remember. The girl smiled back. The people of Ebrin were proud that the lovely queen had come from them. They were wealthier, too. Arendellie had arranged for them to each receive two pairs of nice clothes, one for the winter and one for the summer, and seeds and trees from across the kingdom.

Arendellie heard an angry voice hiss, "Go away, now, and never come back!" *Is that Dorene?* she wondered. She could not imagine Dorene, always happy and carefree, yelling at someone like that. She took the right hand turn up the street towards the yeller.

A woman came down the steps from Dorene's house. Their eyes met, and Arendellie drew in her breath sharply. *She looks like Kathreen! Is she?* Quickly, Arendellie turned to whisper to her servants. "Withdraw a little ways away from me."

"Why?" Girsa asked.

Arendellie spoke firmly. "Remove yourselves a little ways from me. All of you."

They bowed and curtsied. "As you wish, your majesty."

As soon as they had done so, Arendellie stepped forward. She saw what she thought was recognition mingled with sheer bewilderment in the woman's eyes. The woman came towards her and said quietly, "You can't be Arendellie."

Arendellie relaxed. "Come," she said, and led Kathreen along a path that led to a little meadow in the woods near the village. When she reached the woods she turned and spoke to her slaves again. "Stay here, until I come back," she said. Then she gathered up her skirts and cloak and led the way through the grass. She quickly found the rock she wanted, shed her cloak, laid it down over the rock, and sat down. Motioning for Kathreen to sit down next to her, she said quietly, "Now we may speak."

Kathreen sat heavily. "Arendellie," she asked, still clearly bewildered, "what happened? You are dressed like a queen."

Arendellie shrugged. "I am one. I guess it is my turn to surprise you. I still remember when you told me that you were a wizard. Actually, I am the wife of Vanesh Casarion, Grale's nephew. I know you're going to ask what happened to my fiancé. I don't really want to explain it all right now. We never married. I was the princess until the Lords of Light honored Vanesh as king. Anyway, I really don't want to explain everything. It is a really long story, but I'm glad to see you again."

"Do you really like being queen?" Kathreen asked piercingly. Arendellie thought she was upset about something, but she had no idea what.

Self-consciously smoothing her green dress over her legs, Arendellie said, "Yes, yes I do. I am permitted to come back here and visit my family for a month, every year, so that is nice."

"You shouldn't. You're the wife of a man who hates the Creator, violates His promise, and persecutes His people. You're queen of a whole continent that does this." Kathreen's voice rose with frustration, and Arendellie was thinking, *Whoa! Whoa! No need for this kind of lecture! It's not like that, you know. There's no need for this kind of thing!* She felt taken aback by Kathreen's approach. "Sshh!" she said. Kathreen lowered her voice and said, "You can't really like it."

"Most would envy my position, Kathry," reminded Arendellie. "And, remember, you are a hunted fugitive with nothing. You have no friends and no home. You could be a wizard of the Lords, with far more power than I, for even Vanesh is more a figure head than a sovereign king. Oh, to be sure, I don't *really* believe the crazy new religion, but I don't mind it too much. I'm not responsible for any suffering– I did not betray anything about you, nor did I betray Mirla, nor do I intend to betray you– and I can't do anything about it. Furthermore, once all the Knights of the Promise die or leave, they won't be suffering here anymore." She settled herself smugly.

Kathreen sounded like she was biting her tongue to keep from yelling at her. Her voice sounded strangled! Arendellie half-enjoyed it and half felt discomfited. "Still, you're complicit with the sufferings of the Creator's people," she said. "I would be afraid to have any part with such a thing. I would, honestly, rather die in your king's torture chambers than have your life. You're a different person than you were when I knew you, and not a better one."

Arendellie laughed lightly, trying to dispell the shivers that ran across her skin when Kathreen said 'your king's torture chambers.' "You are also a different person, Kathry," she said. "You can say that so calmly and matter-of-factly, and I remember your fear and dread. Still, don't you think you're being a bit too harsh on yourself? Why don't you accept their offer, and try to work to make things better from within the established system? It would be safer, and you would have a lot more power."

Kathreen spat away from her in disgust. Arendellie recoiled. What was so wrong with anything she had said? "Never!" Kathreen exclaimed. "I must trust the Creator, not my own mind. The Creator has no alliance with darkness. He is the King of Light. I must build His kingdom, not mine, and I must have no part with His enemies. As I said, I would be afraid to compromise and to live among and be as one with those who are His enemies. I fear Him and I love Him, because He has called me 'Forgiven', and I would rather die any death."

"Oh, I believe you that you would rather be tortured to death. Your life proves it," said Arendellie lightly. "I'm only trying to convince you that it's not the best way to do things, or even to do what you want to do. If you did this, you could work to make things so much better for the Knights of the Promise in prison, and to make things less dangerous for those not in prison. You could serve the Creator so much better, and, remember, often kings send their subjects to be spies and infiltrators."

"You don't even care about the Creator, or His people," said Kathreen, scathingly, Arendellie thought. "If you don't want our torture, it's not because your heart is better than theirs, but because you happen to find such cruelty repulsive, and would not want to see it or feel guilty. Besides, the Creator dwells in light. He hates darkness and lies, and has no part with them, and His people are called to come out from the darkness and lies and be separate. We are called to live in the light as He does. Moreover, I'm a slave. My task is to do what I am told, not to think about what I could do that I think would work better. My Master, the Creator, is responsible for the consequences. I would suffer and die trusting Him. I know that He is good, and that He is the perfection of every goodness. And, Arendellie, I don't tell you that I would rather die by torture because I don't need you to convince me that I would rather not; I tell you because *that's how much I believe this!* If I believe and care about something that much, *it's because I'm dead sure!"*

Arendellie shook her head. "You are such a fool, Kathreen. How I wish you would drop your foolishness, and we could work together to make things better for everyone, and even spread the Promise."

"The Creator knows what He is doing, and I trust Him to do what is best, in perfect wisdom. I'm not that wise; I'm only a creature and a slave. I cannot trust myself, nor do I have rights, nor does or can any other creature. Rather, that you would see a glimpse of who He is, and find that you simply must trust Him, because He is so trustworthy and good," replied Kathreen sadly.

"Only fools trust another so that they would follow him blindly into anything, without care for anything else," said Arendellie.

"Then, I am a fool, and I am proud to be a fool," said Kathreen.

"You are so strange, and yet so good-natured," said Arendellie.

Kathreen did not seem to know what to say to that. After a while she said, "That is only because I've seen the Creator and trust Him, for I have seen that He is trustworthy, and He is more real than anything He has made."

Arendellie smiled sadly. "Be that as may. I've often heard that fools are kind. I don't know why it must be so, that the strong and wise are often cruel, while fools are kinder and more sincere than anyone else." Something really was horribly wrong, horribly sad. If they were right about nothing else, the Knights of the Promise were right about that. "However," she continued, suddenly noticing the passage of time, "I must return to my attendants, or they will get concerned, and one of them, who is a snitch, may talk to certain people about me. It was very nice seeing you again."

Kathreen rose and, to Arendellie's surprise, she saw her take something out of her clothing and hand it to her, saying, "This is for you." Taking it, Arendellie saw that it was a scroll. "Thank you," she said in the courteous manner of royalty. She hid the scroll in the folds of her dress and took up her cloak, then strode through the grass, again picking up her skirts, to where her attendants waited. It had been so long since she had seen Kathreen and she still considered her, her best friend. She wondered if Kathreen, who so obviously disdained and pitied her, felt the same way about her. She wished the famous Kathreen of the Silver Sword would want to do things in a wise and intelligent manner that might actually have good results, instead of reaping only death. She wanted her to just be a friend, too. She shuddered, thinking that she could very well end up in the torture chambers she talked about. At the thought, Arendellie felt like fainting. Already, one of her friends had been tortured to death by Camil Hasseleighton. She did not want that to happen to this one, too, even if Kathreen preferred it to wiser courses of action. She wished she did not have to pretend to be happy and have it all together all the time, but figured that it might be for the better. If she did not have to pretend and act, maybe she would sink to depths of misery and foolishness, maybe even succumb to whatever strange force drew people to the Promise, as Kathreen spoke of it. The Lords of Lights' Promise seemed to draw people too, Arendellie realized. So many of the young seemed to be so very excited about it. Perhaps, it would even draw the Knights of the Promise and seriously reduce the numbers that had to be dealt with by torture, though she was still sorry about the dragon rebels…

#52
An Echo

Over the past weeks, Khiel had been teaching Brisia to read the scroll Kathreen had left. Now and then, Adaria read from it to Brisia, but mostly it was Khiel and Brisia who pored over the scroll together. Mostly, it was Khiel who was obsessed with it. She was reading a poem, still near the beginning, to Brisia. It told of how the Creator had made Kaarathlon out of nothing and fashioned it by His wisdom and knowledge, how He placed it on the seas He had called forth from the void and hung the sky above as a curtain, a shield from the terrible radiance and freedom without. It told of the Rampart of the Stars that He had placed around it to hold the oceans and provide a resting place for the dancing stars that sang for His delight.

Lying on the grass, Brisia listened to Khiel's melodic voice. It stopped. "Is that all?" she asked.

"Why don't you get up and see?" said Khiel playfully. She spread out the scroll in front of Brisia and read it again, this time placing her fingers under the runes that corresponded to each word.

Brisia was tired of looking at runes. "It's very beautiful," she said.

Khiel agreed. "It praises the glories of the Creator," she said, and continued reading.

> All the worlds and stars above He made from His own pleasure
> And they sing before Him and delight in Him.
> Who among you can scale the Rampart of His Stars?
> Or know the secret things in the depths of His oceans?
> Who has walked where the stars danced
> Or heard their music or the words of their songs?
> Who has seen the halls in the depths of His seas
> Or touched the uttermost veil of His skies?
> Yet all these He made from the wealth of His delight
> For us to look upon and to delight our eyes
> With the reflection of His beauty and majesty
> The least of His works surpass us by far
> The valleys of the seas where we cannot walk
> And the peaks of the mountains, the blinding snows
> The airs that are too bright for our eyes and deadly to this flesh
> All these are but faint echoes of echoes of the light
> The deadly radiance that is round His throne
> And goes before Him wherever He walks.

"It's really beautiful!" said Brisia. "I'm tired of trying to read it. It spoils it. I'd rather just listen to you read it."

Khiel stretched out her fingers and tickled Brisia's ribs until she laughed. "What about when I'm gone? You'll have to read it to yourself... and your children… then!"

Brisia rolled away from Khiel. "Fine! Fine!" she pleaded. "But I have made a lot of progress, and it's only been a few weeks!"

Khiel let her go. "Yeah," she said. "You do have a point there. Well, I'll finish reading this poem to you, and then you can try to read it tomorrow. Good?"

"Good," said Brisia. She rolled over, closed her eyes, and put her hands over them, to keep the sun out of them. "It's really beautiful. Did I ever tell you about how He's so big He doesn't have any size? It's like that."

"Yes, you did tell me," said Khiel. "And what does this mean? Earlier it says this: 'The lands He made of nothing, and the waters He made from void." Here it says: 'All the worlds and stars above He made from His own pleasure… all these He made from the wealth of His delight.'"

"Yeah, I hear that," said Brisia slowly.

"I think it's saying that He made these things out of the overflowing of His own happiness. Or is that *because?*" mused Khiel.

"I don't know," said Brisia. "Maybe we can't know. It means what it says. It's very beautiful. It sounds right. Anyway, read please."

"Sounds like a good idea," said Khiel. She read about how the Creator made men and women and dragons to delight in each other and the rest of His creation and, most of all, in Him.

Brisia commented, "It sounds like there's a lot missing."

"It's a poem," said Khiel. "It doesn't tell the whole story. Only the parts that are relevant for the poem."

"And what's that?" asked Brisia.

"Well, it's– the poem!" said Khiel. "It kind of sounds like a song, doesn't it? Something like," and she began to sing, softly, with a lilt, "Who has walked in the depths of the ocean

"Or heard the music and words of the songs of the stars?

"Who has walked on the peaks of the mountains

"Through the blinding snows or in the bright and deadly airs?

"Yet all these are but the faintest echoes of His wonder,

"All these He made from the wealth of His delight.

"So," said Khiel, rolling over and panting, "I think what's in the poem is what's relevant to it. You said 'beautiful!' and 'like how I told you "He's so big He doesn't have any size,"' and so, I mean, I think that's what it's about. He's the Creator. He's overflowing life and goodness and pleasure. So big without size, so full it has no measure, I mean!"

"Yea!" exclaimed Brisia, sitting up and shading her eyes with her hand.

Khiel sat up and looked at the shadows. "It's probably time for us to get to work, now."

Both girls jumped to their feet. Khiel picked up the scroll. "We've got to put this away. It's the treasure of the household, seeing as there's only one of it and no way to make another. But, I know what you mean. We're not quite sure whether or not we can see. We certainly can't find words."

"Yep!" said Brisia, bouncing beside her.

"I love Him," said Khiel.

"Me too!" exclaimed Brisia.

"He's just so good. Good is such a flat, shallow word." They walked in silence for a few moments. Inside the house, just as she was laying the scroll in its customary place, she spoke again, half to herself. "You know, that's what I really like about the poem. That thing about 'faint echoes of echoes of His beauty and light.' Or something like that. It's really like that. It's like green is just an echo of an echo of something in Him. The same with all things good or beautiful, nice or terrible. They're faint echoes, and the real thing is Him, and He's that much realer and fuller and better and more than they as a voice is to an echo. Maybe more. Oh, I don't know." She looked at Brisia. "Do you get my meaning?"

"I think so," said Brisia exuberantly.

"That's great," said Khiel, embracing her. "It's so great that you know what I'm meaning, even though neither of us can say it, right?"

"Yeah," said Brisia. As an afterthought she added, "You can say it a lot better than I can."

Khiel laughed a shimmering laugh. "I couldn't say it better when I was your age. Remember?"

Brisia did remember.

"Anyway," said Khiel, "where is that basket?"

A few minutes later, Khiel and Brisia were cutting and grinding roots together. Laekoorj, a young man a couple years older than Brisia's eleven years, came over and began to help. "Khiel," he said, "what have you been doing today?"

Brisia was amazing by Khiel's reaction. "Laekoorj!" she scolded. "If you have nothing else to do and you want to help process roots, you may, but I am sick of your questions! Go, take whatever roots and tools you want to work with, and work somewhere else."

Laekoorj cast Khiel a glance Brisia could not interpret and walked away a little sulkily. As soon as he was, presumably, out of earshot, Brisia turned to Khiel with a questioning look. "What was that about?"

"Have you never noticed how much he likes to get close to me and ask me questions?" she asked.

"Uh, I don't know," said Brisia. "What's wrong with it if he likes to do girl-work instead of boy-work?"

"Nothing," said Khiel. "Oh, I don't know. There might be something wrong with it, but I actually don't care. It's not my problem. My problem is that I don't want to marry him."

Brisia gaped. "He wants to marry you? Has he said so? You won't marry him if you don't want to!" It seemed strange to Brisia thinking of someone wanting to marry Khiel. She had mostly forgotten that Khiel was three and a half years older than herself, the two were so close.

"No, he hasn't said so," said Khiel slowly. "I don't want him to get close enough to say so."

"Anyway," asked Brisia, "why don't you want to marry him? If you marry him, you get to have a husband and you get to have babies. Is there something wrong with him?"

Khiel stopped paring roots and looked across the clearing into the shadowy depths of the jungle, her hand over her eyes. Brisia continued slowly chopping roots while watching her. Finally, Khiel said, "I just don't want to. No, there's nothing wrong with him. If you want to marry him when you get a few years older,"– Brisia thought that would *never* happen, or at least not for a *very* long time– "I won't have any problem with it. But I… never mind. I'm not sure I really know myself." She turned to Brisia. "It's just something. It's not quite the right time or place. Maybe it's just I'm not ready, yet. After all, I'm only fourteen. Maybe, it's that Laekoorj isn't ready yet. After all, he's only about my age himself and he's a boy, not a girl. Or maybe…" Her eyes still had that distant look. "Maybe, there's someone else for me and he's for you or something like that. Something we haven't thought of. After all, a day before Kuthrynd went, no one knew that Kalar and Janya and Kavra and I would be here, that Adaria and Athara would get husbands and Kuthrynd a wife. Maybe it's something a little like that. Of course, it wouldn't really be like that."

Brisia nodded, smiling. "I think I get it," she said. "Enough."

"Probably," agreed Khiel. They both returned to their work. Khiel muttered something Brisia did not quite catch.

"What was that?" asked Brisia.

"Echoes. An echo of something," said Khiel.

"And you can't say more?" asked Brisia, but she knew the answer. It was just the way they had of happily interacting.

"You bet," said Khiel.

#53
Touch of the Dragon Keeper

Audra stood with her hands on her hips. "I know I'm only fourteen, Dad, but I am a Dragon-rider and Amrath and her friends *need* me. How would it be better if I were sixteen or seventeen? I would be married and under the rule of my husband. As likely as not, I'd be pregnant or nursing an infant. I'm fourteen, and I am going with Amrath, whether you like it or not." She turned and strode to the opening. "Or would you like Amrath to eat your sheep? She hasn't, you know, because you're my family, you're people, and she doesn't want to hurt you. But I *am* going with her." She held up her hand. "No. She is a *person,* too, even if you don't believe it. If you like, I'll bring back some eggs and you can find out for yourself." Ignoring her father's protests, she fled out the door, covered from head to toe in the furs Amrath had suggested and carrying a satchel full of food, both fruit and meat. Her father would have grabbed her, but Amrath intercepted him with her large head and gently knocked him over. Her family had already had a chance to meet Amrath, and many of her younger siblings had warmed up to the strange creature– the dragon.

Now, she climbed up Amrath's foreleg and chest as the dragon directed her, and sat just on her shoulders with her legs hooked under her huge wing pinions. The dragon took off into the night and Audra thought for a moment that she was going to fall off as she jolted forward and up into the sky. She did not fall, though. Amrath assured her that she would fly slowly and stay out of strong or even semi-chaotic winds until Audra was much more comfortable on her back. A couple days later Amrath explained that they traveled only at night so Audra would not have to deal with seeing the ground far below her. The dragon had heard that it disturbed some humans until they got used to it. Though she thought Audra could probably handle it, they would still fly only by night for a while, especially since they did not have any saddle or harness, so it would be really bad if anything did go wrong.

Isn't it safer to fly when you can see, though? asked Audra. She had learned she could easily communicate with Amrath by simply willing for the dragon to hear her thoughts.

Amrath explained that, even on cloudy nights with neither star nor moon, she could see quite adequately. She showed Amrath a memory of flying over the ocean on a cloudy night, still able to detect the motion of the gentle swell thousands of feet below her, though she had had to try.

The next night they flew over the sea. When dawn came, Amrath kept flying, probably no more than twenty feet above the peaks of the waves, maybe less. Sometime around midnight the following night Amrath landed on an island. The food Audra carried was running low, and so she ate sparingly though she was always hungry. At Amrath's suggestion, when day came she searched the island for edible fruit. Almost all the fruits were different from those she had known, but she found a variety of elanberry she hoped was not poisonous. Other than that, she found very little that she recognized. Amrath showed her pictures of foods humans ate in Camil and encouraged her to try to eat things that looked, tasted, and smelled good. She could not bring herself to eat anything except the elanberry and a few larger fruit of a strange variety that Amrath insisted that she eat since humans ate things just like it on Camil and did not die or get sick. She was still hungry, especially since fruit was not that filling, but she did not dare eat any of those strange fruits and flowers just yet. She wished she had more meat.

As much as possible, Amrath tried to time her flights so that they would take place at night and in the cool softly-lit evenings and mornings, after making the discovery that Audra burned in bright, direct sunlight. This worried Amrath, since Camil was a land of harsh, brilliant sunlight. They were still rather far north and the sunlight was nothing like so harsh as it was in Camil. Of course, there was deep shade throughout the jungles, but that would allow them to fly only at night and it would keep Audra from interacting with the other humans by day at all. Audra reminded Amrath that that was not really a problem; after all, they were going there to get Amrath's dragon friends, and then they would return to the northern altitudes of Audra's home.

Gradually, Audra gathered the courage to eat more of the fruits they found on the islands. This may have been due primarily to the fact that she was extremely hungry, but more and more of them were fruits Amrath recognized. One thing that scared Audra was the jungles. The forests of her home were generally clear. Tall pines thrust themselves towards the sky, many of them not branching out for many feet. There were underbrush and ferns of all sorts, but it was a generally light, airy environment, with soft light and shade. Deciduous trees sprawled out more than the pines, but compared to this jungle they were light. Now, she was entering a land of harsh, glaring sunlight and deep, dark shadows. The forests of the islands were so thick with growth that she could not force her way through them. Amrath had to find places where the fruit hung and forces paths to them, or even just break off whole branches with her legs and carry them to Audra.

Another thing scared Audra. Once, while walking in an area of the jungle where the trees were tall and their branches high and there was not *too* much undergrowth, after her eyes had adjusted to the dim lighting, Audra saw a brightly colored yellow and green snake slither quickly across her path about three paces ahead. She stopped to watch it, thinking that its yellow and green were very beautiful. She felt waves of fear she did not understand from Amrath. In the forests of her home there were several varieties of snake, though none were that green and yellow, and only the extremely rare and rather aggressive maroon snake was dangerous. Now, Amrath was shouting, *Poison! Poison! Danger!* into her mind.

What is it? Audra asked.

From then on, Amrath taught her about dangerous snakes of all kinds, some by poison, some by constriction. Audra began to wonder if she should have taken her father's advice. Being killed by dangerous jungle creatures the names of which she did not even know would not help her, her family, Amrath, or the rest of the dragons. Amrath tried to assure her that it would be okay, she would teach her and keep her safe, meanwhile secretly wondering herself. The things Kathreen Alarion had said when she spoke to all the dragons still bothered her and she preferred not to think about it, but sometimes she could not help it. She reached out to her friends and told them to hang on; she was bringing the Dragon Keeper.

Is that the mainland? Audra asked. They had stopped only for the hottest, brightest part of the day on the last island, and it was not yet dark. Even low in the sky, the sunlight was blinding on the waves. She could feel that Amrath was both excited and in a hurry. Ahead of her, against the sun, she saw not horizon but a dark mass of land as far as the eye could see and even a ridge that looked like it might be a chain of mountains.

The sun had just set and the western horizon still glowed with fire, though Audra thought it was not as pretty as when she saw only the sea against the sun, when Amrath glided down to land on a narrow strip of silver beach. Audra saw hundreds, maybe even thousands of dragons rise out of the surrounding forests and fly to meet them. She could not see them well in the lighting, but she thought they were all different colors. Amrath told her they were.

Before they even reached the beach, the dragons were a flying escort around them. Audra could dimly sense emotions she did not understand coming from them. Anxiety? Excitement? Happiness? Fear? Grief? Pain? She was not sure.

Audra slid down Amrath's shoulder, feeling like fainting. In a fever of anxiety, one of the dragons touched her leg as she fell, and at once she knew his name. *Ringeth.*

She felt the dragon's surprise at her appearance. Like them, she gleamed– white– in the darkness! She responded to their desire and rose. She walked through their ranks and touched them, one by one, tired though she was from riding Amrath. Now and then she stopped to hug one as best as she could or scratch under his or her jaw. She felt the dragon's pleasure at her touch. They revered and loved her, with a love that was not less but more intimate and warm because of their reverence, and she was not sure why. She was bewildered by their reaction to her, as if the mere touch of her skin, which they could not possibly feel through their armor-like scales– they *were* terrifying creatures– brought them life or happiness. How could she be to them like a glass of water was to her when she was thirsty from working in the summer heat, and more? Yet she was. They glowed with warmth, with pleasure, with love, with happiness, with a kind of admiring reverence, at her touch and, then, at the touch of her mind.

She did not know how many there were. She did not know how she knew or remembered all their names, yet they were stuck in her mind. *Zimth. Searth. Nameth. Ledth. Foretsth. Zjathempth. Roketh.* The names went on. Thoroughly exhausted, she crawled under Amrath's wing and fell asleep before she could wonder why they seemed to honor and love her so much, while they only appreciated Amrath's bringing her to them on the side. Yet, Amrath did not seem bothered about it at all. Her feelings about Audra were just as glowing and even more intimate than those of the rest of the dragons.

#54
Reflection

Arendellie, now in Vanesh's castle, was still bothered by her recent interaction with Kathreen Alarion of the Silver Sword. Then, she remembered the scroll Kathreen had given her. What did it say? What was it? She had no idea what Kathreen would possibly want to give her. Normally the queen would not do what she was about to do, but she did not care. She knew where her clothes were kept. She found the dress she had worn that day and drew out the forgotten scroll. She hid it in the folds of the violet she was wearing and spoke to a maid as she passed her. "See to it that I am not disturbed. I'm taking my mid-day nap."

The maid curtsied. "Yes, your majesty. I will tell the others."

Arendellie stepped into the room with its bed and large windows with curtains that could be drawn across them. She loved this room. It was the room she shared with Vanesh Casarion. She closed the door behind her, flopped down in a most unqueenly fashion on the bed, stretched herself out, and began to uncurl the scroll.

In the beginning, there was the King…

Arendellie stood on the shores of a large lake. The lake was almost still, but small ripples moved through it, gently disturbing its mirror-like surface. The lake was in a forest in a wide mountain valley. Around her the mountain ascended steeply. Tall, fortress-like trees seemed to pierce the veil of the sky, which was an exceptionally radiant blue. Her eyes fell again on the water. It reflected the rising trees and the bright blue sky. In the nearer shadows she could see the silver sand on the bottom, gently swaying weeds, and purple-spotted blue or silver fish. In the farther shadows the lake was a deep green. Farther out, it showed a deep color on the sides of the small ripples now and then; it was a purplish blue, except that it was too blue to be purple– or green. All this she took in a moment.

Arendellie never knew whether it happened quickly or slowly. The lake began to shine with an intolerable radiance. It was blindingly bright. Arendellie knew the lake was not shining or glowing of itself; it was reflecting an even more intolerable brilliance. Somehow, out of the corner of her eye, she knew that it was not reflecting the sky either; the sky, too, was reflecting this thin, terrible, too-bright light that came from… somewhere else. Somewhere that was not in Kaarathlon or part of Kaarathlon. The light grew brighter as if the fabric of the world was being torn and whatever was without, whatever brilliance out of which the world was drawn in isolation, was breaking in, in rays of bright destruction. Arendellie turned and fled from the light, but she saw in a brief glance that the trees and underbrush too reflected the terrible radiance that came from without. Closing her eyes against the brilliance, she fled up the mountain-side, trying to flee from the radiance that came from nowhere and everywhere, the light that was part of neither higher nor lower Kaarathlon and yet which both reflected back on her. It did not help. Even with her eyes closed, the light was of a blinding intensity. There was nowhere to which to flee. Everywhere she met, if not the light, then its reflection. She covered her eyes with her hands, but even that scarcely dimmed the blinding radiance.

Even the reflection was too much; she could not bear to face the light. NO! she screamed in her mind, desperately hoping she would not have to face the bright destruction but knowing that she must. It was breaking through the veil. Kaarathlon was too frail, too insubstantial, too small, too thin to keep it out forever. Sooner or later, it would be not only reflected at her, but it would be all around her, piercing her with deadly rays, and she would stand alone, completely unprotected and laid bare before its terrible rays. She hardly noticed the brush tearing at her dress, legs, and arms. Madly, she leapt sideways as she slipped down the slope. She fell and struck her forehead. Pain. Explosions of pain and light. She screamed.

Arendellie lay against the wall, bruising on her forehead and shoulder. She was not sure what had happened. She still felt dizzy and confused when the sound of the door being thrown open broke in on her. It took her a moment to realize what it was. Slaves crowded into the room. "Your majesty. What happened?" several asked, terrified and concerned. One whispered something Arendellie could not quite hear to another, and she ran.

Arendellie was still panting. "I... I had a... nightmare," she gasped. "I never have nightmares." She knew it was not true. It was not a nightmare. She had not been asleep. She had seen something about reality. Her thoughts flashed back to Mirla's words– she winced, remembering Mirla– of so long ago, that it was those who ignored the realities of death and the Creator who were living in a mad illusion. It had been so long ago and she no longer remembered Mirla's precise words, but she remembered a story about a cliff that was going to fall and a village that lived under it and a bunch of people who all made fun of the one person who noticed that the cliff was going to fall any day now and decided to prepare for that eventuality, saying that that person was out of touch with reality, having illusions, and acting as if their dreams were fact. Something about whatever had just happened felt like that.

"We're so sorry," Girsa said, her voice sounding like she was cringing to Arendellie. It infuriated her. She tried to stand and swayed. Then she heard Inshara's voice in the doorway. "All of you get out of here. Kalie, get some water. Aki'lam, prepare some juice." Arendellie could hear the slaves hurrying to leave. She turned and saw Inshara approaching her. "The scroll! The scroll!" she cried, almost panicking.

"It's okay," said Inshara quietly. "Come, and let's sit on the bed." Arendellie did so, and Inshara knelt down beside the bed. "I was the first one here," she whispered, "and I saw the scroll. I've hid it."

"Oh, thank you, thank you," said Arendellie, almost sobbing. She did not know why she was acting in such an un-queenly manner. What was the matter with her? It was over, was it not? Yet, she was shaking. She was terrified.

"It's all right, my lady," whispered Inshara soothingly. "I glimpsed it for a moment and saw that it contained prophecies of the Promise. How did you get it?"

Arendellie had long known that she could trust Inshara, though she did not like it. "Kathreen gave it to me."

Someone knocked on the door. "Come in," said Inshara.

It was Aki'lam, carrying a cup of juice. The woman, no longer a girl, looked so vulnerable and shy, still. Inshara rose, took the cup from her, and brought to Arendellie. Her hands were still shaking, so Inshara helped her hold it and drink.

Arendellie sipped long and slow. Then she took a deep breath. "It's good," she said.

"You may leave now, Aki'lam. Unless?" Inshara added, looking at Arendellie.

Aki'lam looked even more uncomfortable than usual. She opened her mouth and struggled to say something. Finally, she stammered out, "The, the… king, his majesty… is coming. Some… one told him."

"Okay," said Inshara. "Thanks." Aki'lam turned and left. Inshara looked up into Arendellie's eyes and asked, "Will you be o–?"

Just then, the king entered. "Go," he said to Inshara harshly. She rose and left at once, though she cast Arendellie a look of concern, or was it encouragement? Before Inshara had crossed the room to the door, Vanesh was beside Arendellie. He took her hands in his. "Are you all right?" he asked. "I heard you had a dreadful nightmare."

"Yes, yes. I should be okay," said Arendellie. She still felt shaken. "It's over now." She leaned into Vanesh's chest. She did not think about the fact she knew it was not over. It was just beginning. "I hope," she said slowly, "that nothing important got interrupted."

"It's fine," said Vanesh. His voice was tender and yet his tone was short.

Arendellie wondered what the matter was. "I am so glad, though," she said, "that you care about me so much you came running to make sure I'm okay."

Vanesh put his arms around her and hugged her tightly. He kissed her. "Of course. You're my queen. You've always been my queen." He held her gently for a moment, then asked, "Do you want to tell me what your nightmare was about? You don't have to, if you don't *want* to."

"No, it's okay," said Arendellie, straightening. "It was about a cliff," she lied. She felt a lot more relaxed now. "The cliff was falling, and I was running. It was turning into terrible things as it fell, and I was too terrified to look where I was going, and… I don't know if the ground opened up in front of me or there was another cliff, but I… fell."

"It sounds like a horrible dream," said Vanesh.

Arendellie did not answer. She did not have anything to say. She might have lied, strictly speaking, but it was nearer the truth than more than half the things she said every day. The reflection *was* like that. Or maybe that was like the reflection. They were about the same thing, and it scared her, only she did not know what it was. She was afraid to tell what she had actually experienced; it was too real, too personal, too… dangerous. It tasted of a thousand dangers, both the experience and the telling. However, even had she wanted to tell, she would not have known how, except to tell the story about the cliff.

#55
Under the Sword

A group of about ten were gathered in Azshbir and Neah'ra's living room along with Shaelene and the children. Azshbir was reading to them from the scroll:

"In the beginning, was the King," he read, "and He was the Creator. Out of His abundance He made Kaarathlon out of the void. His Light shone upon the waters and made them to be…"

"I think I heard that story once before," a girl, maybe about eight, said.

"They used to tell it from time to time in the Hall of Exhortation, when you were very young," her older sister told her.

A young man asked, "Where did you get that scroll? They never had that story in the city I come from."

"Kathreen Alarion gave it to us," answered Azshbir. Neah'ra added, "I think this scroll contains all the stories and prophecies the Creator has given us and wants us to have. Kathreen's words seemed to suggest that."

"They did," agreed Azshbir. At the same time, a teenage girl asked, "You met Kathreen of the Silver Sword? What is she like?" The little eight-year-old added, "What *really* happened in Anores when Lord Grale Casarion went up in fire? What did Kathreen tell you?"

Azshbir leaned back. "I used to know Kathreen very well. She was a young woman dedicated to the Creator and the Promise, though she had her faults. As for what *really* happened in Anores, Kathreen was here only briefly and we did not get a chance to talk about that. Unless Shantee?"

Shantee leaned forward. "We don't know. What we do know is that the Creator decided that it was time for Grale Casarion to die and that He protected Kathreen from the fires and helped her to help the entire city."

"Yeah!" said the little girl, bouncing up and down. "Everyone agrees Lord Casarion decided it was time for him to return to being the Creator!"

Neah'ra's face paled. Azshbir was used to this, but he flinched. Shantee bent forward. "No," she said, firmly and calmly. "It's not like that at all. The Creator has always been the Creator and never stopped being the Creator. Grale Casarion is neither the Creator nor the Lord of Death. Death belongs to the Creator and serves Him, though it is the enemy."

"You people are strange," said the young woman with the little sister, whose name was Lia.

Reilia tugged at Neah'ra's sleeve. "Can we play with Seair?" she asked. Seair was the eight-year-old with all the comments and questions, the younger sister of Lia.

"I think so," Neah'ra said quietly. "Just don't be too loud." She looked to Azshbir.

"That's fine," he said. He looked like he was thinking about something, perhaps disturbed by something.

"What's strange about us?" Kira was asking. "After all, didn't you used to go to the Hall of Exhortation and hear these same stories, believe these same things, and fear and hate Hasseleighton?"

"That was a long time ago," said Lia. "Things have changed. We were mistaken then. About everything. Now, we have peace and prosperity."

Azshbir was angry. *Peace and prosperity?* he thought to himself. *I guess, though. These people fail to understand that Hasseleighton has its part in the fighting or that their persecution of us is just dreadful. They remember Ephezoa's oppression of everyone during their war effort and they see the rebels as wholly responsible for the bloodshed nowadays. And, Hasseleighton* is *doing a fair job of restoring certain forms of order.* He shook his head, feeling defeated.

A teenage boy was asking, "Why are you all into this stuff about the mistaken Promise that we've since learned we got wrong and now we know what it really was and what its fulfillment is? I mean, Ephezoa did lots of evil things in the name of the wrong Promise, so why are you?"

Neah'ra was leaning forward, burning with the need to speak. "You don't understand," she said, her voice low with burning intensity, even a kind of fury. "Ephezoa imprisoned my husband for seven years. His leg still hurts because of the way they mistreated him. We don't care for Ephezoa anymore than we care for Hasseleighton."

"Then why do you believe in Ephezoa's Promise?" the boy asked. "If Ephezoa has done that to you."

"Ephezoa did that to us *because* of the Promise," Neah'ra explained, her voice still low and urgent. "It's not Ephezoa's Promise anymore than it's Hasseleighton's Promise. It's the *true* Promise, the Creator's Promise."

"How do you know that?" queried the boy. "Why do you have a problem with what the Lords of Light have revealed about what the Creator really means?"

"Only the Creator is Lord of Light," began Neah'ra, but the boy interrupted her. "Perhaps, no one has ever explained to you the truth of the Promise?" he asked. "We had it all wrong. We can all become the Creator. Those of us who attain to that always were the Creator. The Lords of Light are those who are still walking visibly around on Kaarathlon with bodies but are sure to become the Creator at the end of their present lives. It's very complicated and you'll probably misunderstand, but that's a place to start understanding."

Azshbir was so tired. He leaned back and listened to his wife handle it. He was surprised at her. She was well into her pregnancy, would be due in about two months, but she seemed to have all the energy and presence of mind necessary to competently carry on a conversation to which it made his head hurt to listen. She was saying, "Well, why do you believe that this new idea that did not even come out of Hasseleighton until after Grale Casarion died is the truth?"

The boy sat up, tall, straight, and proud. "Because when the Creator became Grale Casarion, he stopped being the Creator. He was just like other men, except of course he was a powerful wizard and Dragon Keeper. So, he didn't *know* what he had been and what he was becoming until, well, until he knew, and then it was done, he ascended in the fire. But after that, as the Creator, he called those who were Lords and Ladies of Light into the Council and revealed these things to them, so that we who are living after him may have the benefit of his life."

Azshbir had to resist the impulse to stick his fingers into his ears. This stuff made his skin crawl. Kira leaned forward. "Aren't you aware," she asked, "that that is all a bunch of preposterous blasphemy and lies and really belongs in the sewage hole?"

The boy looked at her, and Azshbir saw that he thought she was very beautiful. "What are you talking about?" he asked.

She placed her hands in her lap and sat up straight. "The Creator is the Creator. We were just reading the story of how He made everything. The things He made aren't Himself. He made them out of nothing by His abundance, but they never were Him and never will be Him. They aren't even the same kind of thing that He is. He can't cease to be Himself and be a made-thing, either. He's terrible. Azshbir told me once about how 'the mountains were melted before His face and the hills were shattered under His glance when He came down in a tornado of fire, the smoke of which hid His radiance in thick darkness and death, and men were caught like moths in the flame of His breath, fiery winds thick and dark with smoke, fiercely swift and blinding.' That doesn't mean that He actually wears fire and smoke or anything like that, or anything like the whole 'Grale-going-up-in-fire' thing. It means He's terrible like that to all He has made. He's different. He's *Himself,* and we can't even really get close to Him, let alone be Him, whatever that's supposed to mean. Right, Azshbir?" she said, looking at him.

"We can talk about getting close to Him another day, Kira. Pretty much." He was so tired, but he was worried, too. These people were so gaga about Grale Casarion and their new religion; would they have any inhibition at all about handing him and his family over to the torturers? He wasn't that terrified of torture himself, but his heart turned to water and he felt like he would faint just thinking about Neah'ra... or his son. (Of course, he cared about his daughters as well, but it was his son that he thought of at once, since it was his baby son who was in the bed with him and his wife.)

"So, you see..." she said, turning back to the boy.

An hour later, Neah'ra and the children had gone to bed and Shaelene and her children were tidying up. Azshbir was explaining in a low, urgent voice to the group heading home with torches. "Do not hand us over. Do not tell anyone about us. If you do, they might do horrible things to us. Seair, do you hear me? They might rip Della and Reilia up. You wouldn't want that, right? Don't tell. Please."

"But you told us," Seair pleaded. "At least, you told Lia, and she brought me. If you were willing to tell Lia, why shouldn't I tell my friends?"

"I guess you can tell them," Azshbir conceded. "But don't tell them where you heard. Don't tell them who told you. Okay? This is a really big deal."

"Yeah, I guess." Seair gulped.

"I'll try," said Lia. "She probably won't remember enough to tell who and where," she said reassuringly.

The young man who was looking at Kira nodded solemnly. "I understand," he said. "None of us would want that."

The others avoided Azshbir's gaze. He let them go, knowing he could not get more, and walked down the hall. He lay down next to Neah'ra.

She felt him settle his weight in the bed next to her and woke up. "What is it, Azshbir?" she asked. "Is something wrong?"

"We may wake up with shackles on our hands and ankles and swords at our throats," he said.

She was wide awake now. She sat up in bed. Kuthreb turned, and she touched him gently, spoke a few soothing words to him. "What? Did something happen?" she asked Azshbir.

"They're more devoted to Grale Casarion that I could have imagined," he said into his pillow, "They–"

"Say that again," said Neah'ra. "And get your face out of the pillow. Otherwise you'll never get to sleep because you'll have to keep on saying it."

Azshbir was surprised that she could poke fun. She seemed too concerned, too worried, too scared, to even think of fun. He complied. "They're more devoted to Grale Casarion that I could have imagined," he said. "It wouldn't surprise me if they don't care who's tortured how, if they feel that everyone who doesn't worship their blasphemy isn't even human and it doesn't matter how little or small they are, or how horrible the torture. It wouldn't surprise me if they don't even have hearts of stone in this regard."

"Sshh!" said Neah'ra. "What will come will come. We've done what we were called to, for now, haven't we?" Her own heart raced and her muscles felt like water. She was about to cry, but she tried to keep it out of her voice. *Oh, Kuthreb. Reiiia. Della. My baby. Oh. My Creator, give me the strength.*

"Yes, I guess," said Azshbir. "We'll just have to sleep under the sword." He sounded so miserable, so dejected, so hopeless. Neah'ra put her arms around him. "Azshbir," she murmured, "Azshbir."

It seems like a long time, sometimes, but it really isn't... None of it will seem to have been long then. That will be the truth.

Who had said those words? He remembered. Shantee! Feeling too sleepy to really talk, he said, "Neah'ra?"

She stopped stroking his hair and asked, "Yes?" He loved her voice. It was something like the trill of a night bird and something like the sound of the night breeze rustling in dry grass.

"Do you remember what Shantee said? 'It seems like a long time, sometimes, but it really isn't... None of it will seem to have been long then. That will be the truth.'"

Neah'ra was still for a long moment. "Yes, I remember," she said, softly, thoughtfully, contently. Mysteriously, those words brought her comfort far beyond the words themselves. She settled back into the bed, lying between her husband and her son.

#56
Ashamed

Arendellie looked up. "Yes, Kalie?" she asked.

"I've got what you wanted. Here's a list of the female prisoners in Anores, with their names, the crime they're in prison for, and their current position in the prison." She handed the small scroll to Arendellie, and lingered.

"Did something go wrong, Kalie?" Arendellie asked.

"Uh, no, but…"

"But what?" asked Arendellie, looking up and fixing Kalie with her gaze.

The slave-girl shrank from that a little. "I know they're wondering why the queen is interested in the occupants of the female ward of the prison in Anores."

"That's stupid," said Arendellie, laying the scroll down. "Maybe I'm helping my husband do something. Maybe I'm bored."

"That wouldn't do, your majesty," said Kalie, "if I may speak so boldly to you. Very few bored queens would wish to amuse themselves reading a list of prisoners. That would only rouse more questions."

"You're right," said Arendellie. She was afraid that being pregnant was making her diminish in intelligence. She was also afraid that she was pregnant again. She *hated* being pregnant. "I guess," she said, looking down and thinking hard, "that I'm doing research on what makes people commit crimes. Yes, that's it! I'm doing research on the cause and effect of crimes, what makes people commit crimes, how these people respond to being in prison. I'm doing research on the factors involved in crime. And," she said, looking up with a pleased smile on her face, "that *is* what I am doing."

"Okay," said Kalie. "I'll remember that, and the next time you ask me to do something like this, I'll remember that."

"Thank you," said Arendellie.

Kalie stood thinking for a moment. Arendellie had started thanking her slaves. She used to be aloof and impersonal with most of them, now and then sending one or another a scathing look that made her fear she was going to the torture chamber.

Arendellie spread out the small scroll. The particular crime that she was interested in was refusing to worship Lord Grale Casarion, as he was now called. Scanning the list of names she found several marked with that crime. More than she had expected! Kyil. Yamië. Two names. That would be enough to start with. "Kalie!" she called.

The girl, probably about fourteen or fifteen, came running. "I'm here, your majesty. What would you like?"

"Can you tell the warden over the prison that I would like him to make arrangements for me to meet and assess these two?" She took a pen and made a slight mark next to the names of Kyil and Yamië. "I want the arrangements made for tomorrow."

"Yes, I will do that for you, your majesty," said Kalie. She took the scroll from Arendellie and curtsied.

The female warden assigned to Arendellie led her through the upper levels of the prison. "Your majesty's slave said you are studying crimes, what kind of people commit which ones, why they do it, what effects it has on them and their families, and so on."

"Yes," said Arendellie.

"Why the interest in the crimes of refusing to worship our most high Lord Casarion and preaching rebellion?"

"It's peculiar. An amazing number of people commit it, who might otherwise be good citizens. If we can figure out what drives them to it, why they won't give it up, and what to do to get them to give it up, we may be able to add a very loyal segment of the population to our servants."

"That's wonderful thinking, your majesty," said the warden. "Did you know that we have had some success, your majesty? One girl worshiped our most high Lord Casarion almost at once. Another older woman has recently turned. Would your majesty like to visit them as well?"

Arendellie's instinct was to turn her offer down. However, she knew that doing so would give the lie to her words. "Yes," she lied. "I would appreciate that very much. Thank you for letting me know."

"Of course, your majesty. Here we are."

The warden put a key into a door and turned it. It swung open to reveal a small, bare room. In one corner a woman slumped against the wall. Her wrists and ankles were bound. Her scant dress was torn. Her hair was dirtied. She was rather thin and her face was worn. She looked like she was probably in her twenties. Her skin was bloody and raw. Her eyes flitted open, and Arendellie flinched and fought against the impulse to shrink and back away. She had never seen such light brown eyes before, and they were filled with shrinking fear and weary resignation. She had no idea how she could do this. She turned to the female warden. "I would like to converse with her alone."

"As you wish, your majesty."

Arendellie bit her lip and stepped into the small cell. She pulled the door shut to afford them a measure of privacy. She felt like she was walking through a wall. She wanted to faint. She was sure the woman in the corner wanted to faint. She knelt down. "It's all right," she said, trying to speak in a soft and soothing manner. She was not sure how. "What's your name?"

The woman's eyes flitted open again, and she fixed Arendellie with them. "Why would the cruel Queen of Hasseleighton want to know my name?" she asked.

Arendellie drew back as if struck. She remembered the things Kathreen had told her. "I'm not cruel," she said. "I'm not going to hurt you. What's your name, please?"

"Kyil," the woman murmured softly. "Though I don't know why…"

Arendellie waited. She chaffed, inwardly. Why had she come here, to subject herself to this pain? She looked over the young woman and wondered, *How could anyone do this to anyone?* She closed her eyes and turned away. "Why do you care so much about the Promise?"

Kyil did not answer her. Arendellie did not want to look at her again, so she kept her face turned away while she asked, "Are you still there?"

"Yes. I just can't answer you."

Arendellie bit her lips. She wished she had asked Kathreen. She was sure Kathreen could have told her. "Before you were arrested, what was your life like?" Arendellie asked.

"Why should I tell you?" Kyil asked.

Arendellie wondered if the woman had been kept in solitary confinement. "I don't want you to tell me names. I don't want you to tell me where your friends or family might be now. I don't even want you to tell me if any of your family members were also People of the Promise." She fought to keep her voice down. Speaking more softly, she said, "I just want to know roughly what your life was like. Tell me some story that you don't think could hurt anyone."

Arendellie reached forward and began to work on the knots in the rope that tied Kyil's hands. When she had loosened them enough to slip Kyil's hands out of them she turned to working on her ankles. She wondered how long these ropes had been on these younger woman. While she was fighting with the knots, Kyil murmured, "I had a baby. A son." She sounded like she was about to cry.

"I'm sorry," said Arendellie, not sure what to say. How could Kyil even believe her? After all, she *was* the Queen of Camil Hasseleighton and, just a couple months ago, had been telling Kathreen that this horror did not matter since once all the People of the Promise died, turned, or fled it would not be happening anymore. She could not believe she had thought or said such things.

Finally, Arendellie arranged Kyil's arm over her shoulder and took her into her lap, not caring that she was ruining her dress. She was about to ask Kyil how she felt about her son, what it had been like having a son, when she noticed that the woman was breathing like one asleep. Then, she noticed the feet of the warden. Hastily, and as gently as she could while being quick, she laid Kyil on the floor and drew her cape over her dress to hide the stains. Her heart was hammering.

The warden peaked in. "Oh!" she said.

Arendellie walked forward. "Yes, I'm done here. She's fallen asleep." She spoke softly. "I took the ropes off. A little kindness, now and then, might help. I think she's ready to be well fed and allowed to heal, so she can think things through."

The warden nodded. "We will do that, and we will measure your results against ours, your majesty." She curtsied and locked the door. "I'll get a slave to do that."

Arendellie came out from Yamië's holding cell. "She's renounced the Promise," she said to the warden as they walked down the hall. "I wouldn't talk to her about it, since she's very embarrassed about herself and uncomfortable, but I would reward her by moving her into a cell with a cot and giving her something edible. It wouldn't have to be something *I'd* find edible," she said. She felt disgusted. "Perhaps, you might want to put her and Kyil together." She knew both women would like that. She was lying to the warden. Yamië had *not* renounced the Promise. She was not in nearly as bad shape as Kyil, either. Arendellie herself felt too ashamed to think straight. She felt ashamed of her entire previous life, of her callous ignorance, callous to the point of the cruelty. She could not believe she had been what she had been, done what she had done, failed to do what she had failed to do. She had no idea how to even begin to repair her failures.

Later, in the night, laying next to Vanesh, she tried to sort through what she was realizing. She had hated every minute of her interaction with the 'turners'. She could not even remember much of it, just that she had hated it. "Is something wrong, Araenyi?" he asked.

"No," said Arendellie. "And, no, I didn't have another nightmare during my day-nap. I'm just thinking about some things. For example, I don't understand why it takes so much effort to convince the People of the Promise to be sensible people instead of crazy lunatics." She felt wrong saying that. Had she not just discovered, in that vision, that reflection, that the world around her and all her thoughts and feelings were mere trivialities against the light, the Someone or Something without, deadly, terrible, and real, that one day they all would have to meet. She dreaded the thought…

Was that the answer to why Kyil and Yamië would not renounce the Promise? Arendellie wondered, but she could not put it together. Something eluded her, and she was disturbed, and so ashamed. Now, though, able to think, she was not quite sure what so disturbed and shamed her.

#57
Beginnings

As Brisia read from the scroll, the world seemed to open up before her:

The grass waved gently in the breeze. Tall and graceful trees cast splotchy shadows on the ground. A calm sea gently licked the shore. Further out, storms raged and lightning flashed like piercing, slicing fire through the darkness. Bright morning turned to noon and then to evening and the stars and moon came out.

It was a perfect world, the world as it had been made and was meant to be. A world of beauty, but also of terror and danger, but terror and danger with no evil in it at all. Wild, but ready to be tamed. Then, she saw the dragons. Their scales flashed. One keened mournfully. It was the cry of a lonely creature, filled with unidentifiable yearning. It was not perfect. There was no trace of evil in it, but it was not complete. Something essential was missing.

The light of early dawn lay upon the mountains and the waters of the sea. Silhouetted against the gray light, stood a man and a woman, hand in hand.

Over the land lay the light of the Creator. It was unidentifiable, but He was there. His blessing lay upon the bright new world. It was still not perfect, though. It was a beginning, bright and full with possibilities, with perfection waiting to be. It was, though, almost *perfect. There was nothing missing... only more, perfection, waiting to be.*

Brisia rolled up the scroll. She stood and breathed in the evening air, heavily scented with the fragrances of the jungle. Kaarathlon had been that... At least, Kaarathlon had been made to be that. Whatever perfect was, it was not this. It was not death and decay, killing and grief, war and struggle.

How had *that* come to be this?

What *was* perfect?

In that moment, she remembered what it was like when the Creator spoke to her, when she felt His immediate presence. She remembered when she had known that He was too big to have a size and that He loved her, in answer to her grief and guilt and whatever else it was over Mom's death. She remembered that joy in Khiel's eyes, joy that co-existed with cutting pain and sorrow.

That was the answer. *That* was the perfection that was missing in that bright, new world, all fresh and full of goodness waiting to be, perhaps even eager to be.

Did all the evil, all the horror, all the pain, have to be, in order for this goodness, this perfection, to be? Brisia's being rebelled against the thought. All of that was *wrong! Wrong!* It was not supposed to be! Imperfection, evil, was never required for goodness, was it? It could not be! She knew that the Creator was perfect. He was entirely good. He was all-good. There was nothing not-good in Him, nor anything good that was not in Him.

She did not understand. That was okay. She did not have to understand everything. There was an ache in her heart though, for that world without evil, all bright and good and pure. It battled with the peace and satisfaction she had in the good she had. She remembered wanting to know whatever it was that Khiel knew, when she returned from Mieshor aglow with some clean, sharp, radiant joy. She remembered being upset because Khiel could not tell her.

She opened her eyes and looked up at the sky. Ragged fortresses of cloud hung in the air. They were dark and foreboding, but the light of the setting sun, hid behind the mountains, glowed on their westward edges, turning them gold, purple, and pink. Between them, the sky showed, here and there, dark, almost black. In the distance they were a beautiful storm-blue. A heavy rain-storm tingled in the air, eager to fall. Brisia wondered if that might be why the air was so laden with fragrances.

Khiel walked towards her, carrying a basket of fruit. "So, you're reading it by yourself now?" she asked.

Brisia nodded. It was surprisingly easy.

"Let's go in," said Khiel.

"Yes," said Brisia, giggling. "We wouldn't want the scroll to get wet, would we?"

Khiel was walking backwards towards the door. "No, we wouldn't," she said, "and by the looks of those clouds, it is going to come down *hard!*" She was enjoying herself and the thought of the storm. Then she added, not really seeming to be affected by it, "Of course, it looks like it is going to be *really HARD!* Hopefully, it doesn't come through the roof."

Brisia had not thought of that. It usually happened once or twice a year, and then everyone had to work on gathering the things required for fixing the roof and then on actually fixing the roof.

Brisia smiled. *That's what's different. I don't think there were any problems like these then... there. Was it Kaarathlon?* she thought. She decided she would talk with Khiel about it. Khiel was older and had more experience. Maybe she would know more. Maybe she would know how to say it.

Several days later.

Khiel sat with Brisia in the middle of a garden. She had listened thoughtfully to Brisia, asking a question here or there to make sure she understood properly, or maybe to help Brisia say it. Now, she asked, "Did you read what came next?"

"No." Brisia shook her head. "I've been meaning to..."

"It's okay," said Khiel. She looked down. "I think," she began, speaking slowly, "that it's not quite that simple. You see, maybe there are different kinds of goods. You know, maybe there is a good everything is supposed to have and then, no, I'm saying this all wrong. Uh, you see, maybe there is a good in whatever-you-want-to-call-it that we have both experienced, maybe, knowledge-of-the-Promise-in-pain-and-through-evil, that would also be present in other things, things we wouldn't know about, since we have not, umm, of course, experienced them."

She paused for a while, then said, "But then, we wouldn't really know, would we, since we haven't had them? Maybe there was a greater good that would have completed the beginning, and it was lost, or much of the good of the beginning was lost, but though the loss the Creator is giving another good... maybe, even, a greater good?" It was a question, but not for Brisia.

"But I want *ALL* goods!" declared Brisia.

Khiel tilted her head and smiled.

They both knew. The Creator was not going to do *anything* less than perfectly.

Khiel continued pulling weeds. Brisia followed. After a few minutes, she said, "I don't understand how it got lost, though."

"I remember poetry a lot better than stories," said Khiel, "and I only read that one once. The humans and the dragons did something wrong. Let me try to remember what it was." She was silent for a long time, busily pulling up weeds. "It was something the Creator told them not to do. I know there was something about some humans worshiping a dragon somewhere, but I'm not sure if it was there, or sometime later." She shook her head. "I'm sorry, Brisia, I just can't remember right now."

Brisia thought it was funny that Khiel was saying sorry for that. She said so. They both laughed.

Khiel looked up from the dirt. "You do know, Brisia, that we are still living in the beginning?"

"Yeah, I guess so," said Brisia. She stood up and stretched. Her muscles were sore and cramped. "You mean, like, the Promise is coming. The Conqueror hasn't even come yet... so, like, that's, what, the end? Uh, no, I don't think there is an end. Because you know, He's going to make everything right. No more dying. All as it should be. Maybe!" She started jumping up and down in her exhilaration at her thought. "Like, maybe, like if whatever went wrong had not gone wrong! Like the world perfected, as if no evil had ever been... but with whatever that special good that comes from our knowing good in the middle of bad stuff!"

Khiel tossed her weed into the bucket to be carried away. Weeds blocked sunlight. They could also take root again if they touched the ground anywhere. "Brisia," she said, "you'll damage the plants."

Brisia stopped. "I'm sorry."

Khiel just went on. "You may be right," she said. "In fact, I rather think you are."

"I can't wait!" said Brisia exuberantly.

"Don't start jumping again," reminded Khiel. "I think you will just have to, and you will be grateful about it."

"Yeah, I know," said Brisia. She felt simultaneously downcast about waiting and happy about what she knew was coming.

"I agree with you. There can't possibly ever be an end," said Khiel. "I wonder why I never thought of that," she said, speaking softly to herself. "It's so obvious. If death isn't the end, there's no end. And we know death isn't the end. Of course, I never thought about there being an end, either. Is it possible that it's not really important? Anyway, I have to get back to work."

Brisia did not ask Khiel what she meant. She knew that if she did not understand Khiel would not be able to explain it any better. It sounded like Khiel did not really know what she was thinking herself. Brisia stifled her excitement and walked over a couple of rows. She pulled up a weed, looked at the bucket, and said, "Khiel, it's time for us to go dump these."

Khiel looked at the bucket herself. "Oh! You're right," she said.

#58
Ice Blue Eyes

Audra stood under the shade of a huge balcony. White veils covered her, almost completely covering her skin. She had sunburned extremely badly, and at Amrath's suggestion had gone to get white cloths. To her surprise, everyone seemed scared of her. A dragon named Skyith had helped her learn the language, but it had taken her a while before she managed to corner a merchant and ask for white clothing. To her amazement, he shivered and shook and did not even ask for payment of any sort. She did not know why, but she had heard herself referred to as the "Undead Snow Queen."

Now, she had been summoned to an audience with the ruling body of the land, the Council of the Lords of Light. She was amazed by the idea that this vast continent was ruled by one small body. In the Trinazee Mountains, her tribe had occupied land that, while bigger, could not have been all that much bigger than the bigger cities of Camil, and it was ruled by a chieftain and a group of shamans and master warriors. The idea of a whole country spread across such a huge continent astounded her. She had seen some of its size, traveling to visit weaker dragons, and then searching for dragon eggs, which she seemed to find at her feet. She was accompanied by more dragons than she could ever imagine counting, and that was how the Council had found her. She had been approached by a woman and asked to come. She did not know why she had done so. Audra felt so uncomfortable in their presence. Their stares made her cringe. She had known, too, what they were. She had dragons in her company whose riders had been tortured to death, or were even now being held, by this Council.

Audra leaned against the wall, feeling ill. She could hardly eat, and she was fainting more and more often, for no apparent reason. She hoped she was not going to die. She could not think of any reason why she would be going to die.

"What are you doing here, Dragon Keeper Audra?" asked one of the Council Wizards. Audra had never heard of wizards, either. Amrath had explained the concept to her. Her first reaction, when Amrath had told her they could affect the world in ways that other people could not had been, *So, like shamans? Maybe just a different kind of shaman?* Almost immediately, though, she knew she had gotten it wrong. She did not know very much about shamans, but she knew that they had intercourse with the spirits who moved and breathed in the world. They could hear the spirits, and they did things to be able to hear and understand them better, and they could work with the spirits. Wizardry had no more– or less– to do with shaman-craft than did running. Wizardry was just about seeing things with one's mind and doing things with one's mind, instead of with one's limbs. Audra did not understand it. She figured she would not be able to understand it. It was frightening, though. She did not know what the spirits of her tribe might think of wizardry. That was okay, though, since she was not going to have anymore to do with wizardry than she absolutely had to. The real problem was, she did not know what the spirits would think of thousands of dragons. Especially since the dragons had made very clear to her that they did not even acknowledge the existence of spirits and certainly did not attribute any real power to them. A shaman had tried to convince her father that Audra and Amrath's partnership was acceptable and that he should let Audra go with Amrath. She did not know whether to take that as the spirits accepting Amrath or rejecting her. She drew in a deep breath. She felt so uncomfortable under the stares of the wizards. She was only a girl. "Umm, I just came to help the dragons, like, you know," Audra fumbled. She was really messing this up. She did not know what to do.

Arendellie sat beside Vanesh. She was watching Audra. The girl was white, almost paper white. If not for the white curtains that she draped herself with, she might have thought she was truly white. Her hand was up, outside of the white shroud, near her throat, and Arendellie could see the web of blue veins across the bones. It sickened her. It was disgusting. Humans should not be like that. Just from her hand and face bones, Arendellie could tell that she was way too thin. Her bones jutted out in ways they should not. Her eyes were a bright, pale, icy blue. No humans had eyes like that. Arendellie understood why the Camilian people thought she was the Undead Snow Queen. Camilian legend had it that an Undead Snow Queen would come down out of the north and subjugate the Camilian people, bringing on an endless winter of death. Audra, though, was human, even if something was obviously terribly wrong with her. She was shaking with fear. When she spoke, that fear shattered her voice. Undead did not know fear. And she breathed.

Audra was again replying to the Lords of Light. "No, sirs and ladies, I do come out of the north, but I've no such intention. I'm not an Undead Snow Queen, and, no, I don't intend to help you use the dragons to do your will."

Audra knew the wizards could kill her. She also knew that, if they did, her dragons would kill them. Even the whole group of them could not prevent a countless host of dragons from killing them all. Her dragons, in all their colors, shapes, and sizes were everywhere. They clung to and stood on every open space of the castle walls and roof. They circled in the sky above her. Countless small, young dragons were much nearer. A pink one and a blue and purple one perched on the balcony and looked down at her with light blue eyes, very much like her own, and glittering red eyes, respectively. Anger had replaced fear, as she thought of all the dragons who had been killed by this regime, as she thought of the precious dragon egg, as she thought of all the dragons who had lost their riders to the cruelty of this Council, as she thought of the Dragon-riders who were even now being tortured by these wizards' command and their dragons. Her voice rose. "Indeed, as the Dragon Keeper, I want you to release all Dragon-riders *NOW!*"

The wizards looked at each other and back at her. "You do not have that authority, Dragon Keeper though you be. It is we who rule in the Lord Casarion's stead."

Audra took a step forward. She was angry and very weak and swayed, feeling like she was about to faint, but she was just too angry. "And you have the right to torture Dragon-riders? To separate dragons and their riders? You have commanded me to leave this continent and never return. I may leave, if you release the Dragon-riders!"

She swayed, struggling to think through the oppressive headache or headfog. She felt the anger of the dragons burning in her own blood. It was time! She did not want to rule with the Council of Light. She did not want to help them. She thought for a brief moment of raising her arm and ordering the dragons to kill the wizards. It would work. She knew it would work. She would die. A few of the dragons would die. But the wizards would be gone. Their cruel and evil reign would be over. *DONE!* They could leave the King Vanesh and his queen, Arendellie, alive to rule the kingdom, instead of being the pawns of the Council. She knew, from the dragons, that Vanesh and Arendellie had a very different disposition, a very different over-all outlook and intentions, than the Council.

She also knew that if she did that, she would die. And, if she died, the dragons would all die, too. Nor would only the dragons die who had been dying until they saw her. All the dragons who had hatched at her touch would die, too, or almost all of them.

"We will consider your request," replied the Council.

Tired, her vision all blotchy and gray, Audra sank to her knees. It was a long time before she recovered sufficiently to think and to take stock of her surroundings. It was getting longer. To be honest, Audra was intending to go back to the north anyways. Maybe, hopefully, probably, if she went back to the north, this problem would go away. She found the heat so draining. She would find some place where the spirits would at least tolerate her, if the spirits of her own tribe rejected her. However, she did not want to bow down before this evil Council. She wanted to leverage everything she had against them.

Arendellie watched Audra, who was obviously ill, converse with the wizards. Her heart alternately soared and sank. She hoped the wizards would give Audra the prisoners. She could not bear their torture, and it was painful for her working out all the things necessary to improve their situation. She had to do so much to make sure that no one guessed what she was doing; there was so much effort she had to put into making sure that her deceit would not become self-evident. She was glad Audra had come and was doing something. At the same time, she still felt so guilty. By doing nothing, she shared in the responsibility for the torment of so many; for children torn from their mother's arms; for families starving because their father was dead or dying. It was endless. In her work with the prisoners, trying to undo what she could, she had come to realize a little of the true proportions of these atrocities. She knew the pain in their eyes, pain that had little to do with the physical torture to which they were subjected. She saw the pain grow as they were well-fed and allowed to heal, given space and energy for the emotional suffering. She had seen women lying on the verge of death, lethargic and in great pain, often somewhat confused about their surroundings and what was going on, with a light of contentment even through the glaze of approaching death. She had seen these same women struggle to maintain their composure weeks later, not only weeping but struggling not to fall into despondency beneath the pain of their loss and worry over their children. She had watched one begin to recover and then die of this despair and misery.

At the same time, Arendellie knew that none of this was solving her much greater problem: the Creator was real and He was terrible! She knew that a torture like no other awaited her when the veil of Kaarathlon wore too thin to protect her consciousness from His radiance: to be exposed to that searing light and unable to get away, even for a moment. She did not want to contemplate it; it was horrible, terrible. It was going to happen, even though with every particle of her being she feared it! She feared it more than it would be possible to fear the tortures she knew so much more about now than just half a year ago.

She would have hated Him, but she knew the Creator was good. As it is, she hated the situation with all her might. She was not sure whether or not that came out to hating the Creator. Did it matter?

Audra bent down and laid a cool cloth she had torn out of her curtain on the head of a young girl, a Dragon-rider only about her own age. She had already had to explain that she was not undead; she was not sure why, but everyone seemed to think she was undead because of her ice-blue eyes and white skin and hair. Did they not know that was how humans looked where she came from? She spoke out loud. "How are we going to do this? They can't ride. The wizards didn't heal them. I think they hope they will die!" She bent down. "I'm sorry... What's your name? I'm sorry. I can remember the name of every dragon, but not yours."

"Waiyeena."

Kathreen and L'sa-moth met healing moon dragons? You're sure you know how to get there, Cath? But how will they survive, is what I want to know! She did not know why she cared. She struggled not to pass out herself. She could not eat. *She was going to die if she did not get somewhere cool and nice, soon.* Further, she was a Dragon Keeper. The lives of dragons were supposed to be her care, not those of humans, some of whom weren't even Dragon-riders.

#59
Scarier

Arendellie was miserable. She was reading the scroll Kathreen had given her, and it scared her. She did not understand most of it. She read about how the humans climbed the one mountain they had been forbidden in order to walk in a hidden grove, the place of secrets. They wanted to know the laws and reasons for things and build their own world. After this, there was something about a portal and a veil, that Arendellie did not understand very well, and that was when lots of bad things started happening. It was the beginning of the world as Arendellie and everyone she had ever known had known it.

She had many questions. It was getting harder and harder to ignore the vision, which came back to her in terrifying glimpses as she went about her days, even as she wanted more and more to forget it. She did not have any hope. She just wanted to live her life and ignore the Terrible Light that she feared, for as long as possible. However, she had read that before they climbed the forbidden mountain and set foot in the secret grove, they had dwelt with the Creator. His palace had been visible on earth, though they could not enter it; perhaps that had been one of the reasons they had climbed the mountain. They thought they could get into the palace that way. The Creator walked with them and they knew Him. But, after walking in the grove of secrets, all that had changed, and He was a terror.

Why? Arendellie could not believe that the searing light could ever be anything except an unendurable terror. That was who the Creator was; how could His presence be anything but a torture? She felt like she would die merely at the thought of standing naked before that light; even seeing it reflected back from all creation at her was terrifyingly deadly.

Arendellie was lying on her bed, wondering why the People of the Promise *wanted* to live in the Creator's palace, instead of being absolutely terrified of His presence, and whether she should ask any of them, when Vanesh opened the door. "Are you all right, my love?" he asked, concerned.

Arendellie turned over. "Mostly," she said. Concealing everything was becoming so difficult.

"Did something happen?" he asked, stepping into the room.

"No. I just have these nightmares." It was close enough to the truth not to exhaust her as much as it would to come up with something else to say, but it was also close enough to the truth to be dangerous in the circles in which she walked.

"You did not use to have nightmares all the time," said Vanesh, sitting down next to her. "Any idea why you have so many now?"

Another lie, but it was one with some truth in it. "Well, when we were fleeing from the castle when it burned up after the Eternal Lord went up, well, the fire was so close. I saw people die. It could have been me. It could have been…" The wounds from that day were still so raw, and were so connected with what was troubling her now, that she really did begin to weep.

Vanesh lay down next to her and took her in his arms.

Arendellie was so afraid. She wondered if it mattered if the Council of Wizards found out that she was reading a scroll from the People of the Promise and lying to get People of the Promise out of prison. Well, of course it would matter for them; it would mean they would continue to be tortured. But, for her? Compared to the searing light she feared, a few weeks of torture was insignificant. It was not even comparable. Using the same word to refer to the searing light of the Creator's presence, of ultimate Reality, and to the tortures of the dungeons was so misleading. There was no comparison at all. She *so* desperately feared, even to the point of hatred, the searing light. She decided that was why it mattered that she not be found out. If she was found out, she would die. Of course, she would die anyways. But she knew that death would tear the veil completely and expose her to the searing light of ultimate Reality. She was certain, too, that, sooner or later, Kaarathlon itself would wear out and be incapable of shielding those who remained alive from that light.

Sooner or later, she would be exposed to that searing light, but she would put everything she possibly could between herself and that day. She feared it too much to be much influenced by the thought that it was inevitable, but she could not tell any of this to Vanesh. She was almost certain that he loved her and would not hand her over to be killed; however, she knew he would think her crazy.

At the same time, she worried that she would lose his love. She had to be beautiful and perfect, self-assured, intelligent, to win his love. If she ceased to be these things, he might very well turn to some other girl, who would remain young for quite a few more years.

She knew she had to have an answer: was it possible to be at peace with the deadly light? If so, how? It seemed inherently impossible. Between who and what she was and who and what ultimate Reality was, there seemed no way. However, some people truly seemed to be at peace with the deadly light; to have encountered Reality that transcended Kaarathlon and made Kaarathlon seem a shadow, a thin mist, and yet to be at peace with this Reality. Somehow, the Promise made this possible, but Arendellie could not for the life of her see how. What on earth did shame and merit have to do with the problem? Her problem was that she was not the kind of being who could live with ultimate Reality; ultimate Reality was the kind of thing– saying it this way felt all wrong– that was deadly to her. Shame and merit might be a problem, but it was not the whole problem. Even if there were not a shame and merit problem, she would be in really big trouble.

Arendellie pulled herself together. She was going to be and do for Vanesh what she had done that first night. She stood, and cocked her head.

"Inshara?"

"Yes, my lady?" asked Inshara.

"Never mind," said Arendellie. She had been thinking about asking Inshara how having one's shame taken away and receiving the Promised Conqueror's merit would make it possible to live with the Creator, but then realized that she did not really want to explain what was going on to someone as close to her as Inshara was, to someone who lived with her.

"My lady, you have someone asking to see you," said Girsa.

"Who is it?" said Arendellie, pulling away. Inshara's comb pulled her hair.

"A woman named Kyil. She's very upset. She says she was a prisoner and you are responsible for the fact that, at the moment, she is not."

"Send her in," said Arendellie, sighing. When Girsa had gone, Arendellie said, "I want to talk with her alone." She had no idea what Kyil came for. Maybe, she was in trouble again and wanted Arendellie to do something about it. At any rate, she did not want anyone to know what she was doing. She could not even evaluate whether it would be a problem if Inshara, who did know she was reading the scroll, knew.

A few minutes later, Kyil stood in front of Arendellie in the garden. "Why don't you sit down?" said Arendellie. "It's fine by me."

Kyil's voice was quiet with furious anger. "You lied about me," she said.

"Yes, I lied about you," said Arendellie. "Why are you upset? Because I lied about you, you aren't being tortured anymore. In fact, you look pretty healthy to me. Because I lied about you, you get to go back to your family."

"I belong to the Creator. I'll *never* deny the Promise!"

"You don't have to," said Arendellie. "You didn't lie. I did. It's not your fault."

"Are you really this clueless, your majesty?" asked Kyil.

"Huh?" asked Arendellie. There was something in Kyil's eyes that she could not interpret.

"I said, are you really this clueless?"

"About what?"

Kyil came closer. She was still thin. Perhaps, she always had been and always would be. She did not seem to know how to respond to Arendellie's question, as if there was something she knew that was just so essential and deep-down rock-solid she could never say it. "I was half-unconscious, but I think you asked me the first time we met, why I cared about the Promise so much. I'll tell you: the Creator is good. The Promise is good."

"He's *terrible,* too," said Arendellie in a hushed tone, before she realized the words had come out of her mouth. Somehow, it seemed appropriate. It was right to say them now.

Kyil stopped, shocked, mouth wide open. "You know *that?*" she asked.

"Why shouldn't I?" asked Arendellie, more bewildered every second.

"Because you think so little of lying about such essential things! You don't even know what I mean when I asked if you are really so clueless. You don't even know why it is so unthinkable and wrong to let it be thought that I… that I… that I denied the Promise!"

Sudden concern and worry raced through Arendellie's veins. "You aren't going to go and tell them that I lied about you and you really do worship the Creator alone, will you?"

"Yes, I'm going to do that," said Kyil.

"But, you'll ruin everything I'm doing!"

"It should be ruined, Queen," said Kyil very softly.

"I will never understand you, people," said Arendellie. "I used to have a friend who was a Knight of the Promise. We never understood each other. But she said some things that were really right."

"What?" asked Kyil.

"That I was participating in the torture of the People of the Promise by being queen of a regime that persecuted them and doing nothing about it, not even caring." Her face fell. "I am so ashamed."

"Is that it, then?" asked Kyil.

"Do you know your lying is wrong? But you're trying to repair your past... cover your shame." She knelt down, and touched Arendellie's knee. "My lady," she said, "that won't work. You will only increase your shame. And, believe me, I speak for all of us, when I say that we would rather be tortured than thought to have abandoned the Promise."

Arendellie did not understand, but she believed her. She knew it was how Kathreen would have felt. She remembered vaguely Kathreen saying, too, that she must not fight by way of darkness or deceit, that it was against the Creator's will, but none of it made sense to her. Besides, she was not right with the Creator anyway. "You say I will only increase my shame," she said to Kyil, "but I, I am indeed ashamed, but even if all my shame could be taken away, I would still be in trouble. He's terrible. His presence is deadly. I'm terrified of Him, and not primarily because I'm dirty, but because He is... bright!"

"That's why the Promised One doesn't just take away our shame; He gives us His merits," answered Kyil.

"How does that help?" asked Arendellie. "He's real. I need something between Him and me, otherwise His light will sear me, kill me, forever! It's terrifying. I fear it. I hate it. But I can't do anything about it. And words are so inadequate." She wondered why she was being so honest and straightforward. "And," she went on, "there's nothing that will hold up to Him. It's not that He's angry, or anything, but He, Himself, is just too bright! Too real, I guess."

"That's why He gives us His merits," repeated Kyil. "How do I explain?" she asked softly. "I thought I had all the time in the world to put these things into words, to figure out how to share them, when I was being tortured and while I was recovering." She was talking to herself. "I was sure I knew how to say them, but I guess I must not have. I must have just imagined it. I knew how to say them to myself."

Kyil paused. "So much," she said, then, "I think, I think that the Creator clothes us in the merits of His Promised One, and that is our protection from the deadliness of His light. It really is terrible." She smiled. "He gives us the strength to endure His life. He was so near... the veil was so thin.... His light, as you say, so bright. Sometimes, I was scared, but I think I was more scared of feeling Him all through me, giving me strength and joy, than I was of the torture."

Arendellie gasped and drew back. "And you want to live with Him forever?"

she asked.

Kyil looked at her with deep, expressive eyes. "Why, yes!" she said, as if it were the most natural and obvious thing in the world.

Arendellie shook her head. Nothing explained anything. "O my Creator, why?" she asked.

"Why what?" asked Kyil.

"Why *this.*" Arendellie gestured inarticulately. "Why anything. Why I can't understand. Why *everything,* I guess."

Kyil nodded. "I wish I could tell you more, but... I think only the Creator Himself can really show you," she said softly, rising.

"I don't think I really want Him to," said Arendellie. "I'm terrified of Him."

"That's why you need the Promise. It really is the solution."

"But you just said that His strength and joy is worse than torture!" exclaimed Arendellie.

Kyil shook her head. "Did I say that?" she asked. She put her hands over her face and sighed. Taking them down she said, "I don't know how to say this. And I'm pretty sure I didn't say 'worse'. I only said scarier. The thing is... He gives the strength to live in His presence. It's just, I think, that I kind of remembered how bright and terrible and overwhelming He is, you know, but I didn't really remember that He gives the strength. So, that's why I was scared."

Kyil looked across at Arendellie, who was standing now, her hand against a tree, staring off into the distance. "Do you want to talk more? Do you have any more questions? Or should I go, now?"

Arendellie did not turn back to Kyil. She was going to have to think of something to tell people to explain Kyil's behavior. It would hurt Kyil, but she had to do it. There were others who would be hurt if she did not. She was not quite sure if all the People of the Promise felt as Kyil, Kathreen, and several others she knew felt. For example, Inshara. Also, others would suffer. Their children. Their friends. Their husbands. Their sisters. So, she had to. "Are you so eager," she asked, "to return to the torture chamber?"

Kyil looked up at the sky. "I am grateful," she said, "for what I've enjoyed. The sky... the trees... the flowers... the colors and smells. It had been so long... Oh, and the food! And all kinds of comforts. But..."

Arendellie broke in. "Then, why are you so mad at me?" She still did not turn back to face her.

"I'm angry about what you did. I'm grateful to the Creator, not to you. How could I not be grateful? He is good, and this is nice. But, I cannot live with this as it is. To do so would be to deny the Promise myself, just as your doing nothing while Queen of Camil Hasseleighton is to share in persecuting us." She said it without any spite or desire to hurt, but it stung Arendellie.

Arendellie shook her head. "You are so bold," she said.

Kyil smiled, but Arendellie still did not see it. "When you've been where I've been, it ceases to really matter whether someone is a queen or a fellow prisoner. I'd have to work at it to worry about whether what I'm saying will get me tortured, and then I would feel bad."

"You really like nice things, but you don't care if you have to return to a stinking cell with no real light and disgusting, vile, painful torture?" asked Arendellie, finally turning around.

"Don't care!" said Kyil. "That's hardly an accurate description!"

"Then, what is?" asked Arendellie.

"It's *misery* to worry," said Kyil. "It's *not* misery to suffer."

"That doesn't make sense."

"I *like* things," said Kyil.

"I think you said that already; what is your point?" asked Arendellie.

"Look here," said Kyil, speaking to Arendellie as she had not been spoken to in a good decade at least, "I *like* things. I *don't* want to be returned to the dungeon. It hurts. It stinks. All that stuff. But, I knew the Creator there. I *like* that! Or, should it be *want?* And, I like this! It's beautiful. I'm so grateful for it. I long for it. It's comforting to know that He will reign in Kaarathlon, and all this evil will be over, and we will get to enjoy it all as it is meant to be enjoyed. It's really encouraging, actually.

"No, don't interrupt, please. Not yet. But, even if I didn't know that… even if I were going to be tortured in that dungeon forever, never dying, never seeing the sky or smelling the flowers, I'd go… without regret. I *love* Him. The Promise… I couldn't make you understand.

"So, now, I don't want to leave this. I couldn't. But I want that joy! I want to be with Him. I'd run from guilt and misery to Him anywhere. And, I just can't deny the Promise, by what I do or by what I do *not* do. It's my life. It's my hope.

"Do you understand, now?"

"No," said Arendellie.

"Well, I will ask the Creator to show you." She turned, walked a few paces away, then apparently remembered something. She turned back to Arendellie and curtsied as well as she could. "May I go now, your majesty?"

"Of course," said Arendellie.

Kyil refused to spend the smallest amount of energy worrying whether speaking the truth would have her tortured. However, it definitely did not have to do with any personal agenda of hers. She was everything Arendellie was not, and Arendellie still did not understand how the Promise was sufficient.

#60
Terror of the Undead

Kira opened the door. "You are back early. What is wrong?"

"Is Neah'ra around?" asked Azshbir.

"Not that I know of. I think she is out with the children, picking fruit or something. Why?"

"I need to talk to her, now."

"Okay," said Kira, confused. She was desperately curious about what was going on. She was also worried; had something terrible happened? Probably. Terrible things always happened. "I'll try to find her."

"I'll go with you," said Azshbir.

Kira led him out through the house and behind the barn. Sure enough, Neah'ra was there, with Reilia, Della, Kuthreb, and Kgarjin. She brushed back a lock of hair and rose. "Is something wrong, Azshbir?" she asked.

"The Undead Snow Queen has come. The Council of Wizards is giving all their enemies to her. That's where all the dragons have gone, and many of the prisoners. Everyone is terrified, now. Nobody will trade with me anymore, since I don't have the locket."

Neah'ra nodded. "The locket?" she asked.

"Did I never tell you that? You know what the locket is. Well, you aren't allowed to buy or sell without a locket."

"Huh?" asked Neah'ra. "Of what importance is that? Aren't you not allowed to live unless you have a locket?... So, I guess this just means we can't trade anymore."

"There's also the Undead Snow Queen. People say they know people who have seen her; she's as white as a ghost and has eyes of ice. Some of the people I frequently traded with, People of the Promise I thought, are terrified of the Undead Snow Queen. If she takes you, then, well, you don't really die, like, get released. Not until the end of the world."

Kira gasped. "So, this is what's bothering you, Azshbir?" she said, stepping backwards.

"Yes, this is the problem?" echoed Neah'ra.

"It is terrifying to a lot of people. They are more careful than ever not to offend the Council of Wizards or Grale Casarion," answered Azshbir.

"*If* there is an Undead Snow Queen, then she only has whatever power the Creator gives her," said Neah'ra.

"*If?*" asked Azshbir. "People have seen her."

"There are lots of legends," said Kira. "Who knows how many of them have any truth in them at all? People say Grale Casarion went up to heaven in a pillar of fire by his own will. We know that Kathreen actually drove a sword through his heart, whether that was what killed him or whether it was something else."

"I said, the Undead Snow Queen, herself, is only part of the problem. I don't know what to do; I may be betrayed for not having a locket; someone may tell about me in order to gain favor with whoever questions them about who they were trading with, and why they did not bother making sure they only traded with locket-owners," said Azshbir.

"We have the scroll," said Kira. "If other People of the Promise are terrified about the Undead Snow Queen, why don't we invite them over and share the scroll with them? It is so clear, and encouraging. The Creator is the Lord of Life and Death. Who knows? Maybe, the Undead Snow Queen has power, but only over those who do not belong to the Promise."

"There is something in that idea," acknowledged Azshbir, "but the Council gave her Knights of the Promise."

Neah'ra stepped forward and put her arms around his neck. "The Council is a Council of Liars, Azshbir. Besides, even if they did something, that doesn't mean it worked, does it?"

"You're right," said Azshbir, kissing her.

"Anyway, why didn't you invite them over, already? We are actually doing quite well. We even explained to them that Kathreen actually drove a sword through Grale Casarion's heart," said Kira.

It had been quite a night. Surprisingly, Shantee had told the story, from when Kathreen flew with L'sa-moth to Anores to her flight from Yasya, a once-friend who had been desperate for her to venerate Grale Casarion. She even told of how the dragons made Kathreen a Dragon Speaker and called her a Dragon Keeper, and of how Kathreen had explained that there was only one Dragon Keeper: the to-come Promised Conqueror. Equally amazingly, the people had listened to her tell the story. After that, an argument had erupted. Some had fiercely defended Grale Casarion as the "Eternal Lord," saying it did not matter if Kathreen thrust a sword into what looked like it had been his heart; it did not really affect anything. Kira said that this was ridiculous; people claimed that it was by Grale Casarion's power that Kathreen escaped the flames, because she was so near to whatever-it-was-they-called-it. If this was so, why was she so deluded? Why had it been allowed? If Grale Casarion was a god of some sort, why did it all turn out this way? Meanwhile, many of the visitors just listened, apparently considering this new thing they had just learned, wondering what to make of it. Several had declared that they were liars and ran away. For weeks, everyone had worried that they would betray them, but nothing happened. They did, however, never come back. A few had accepted the idea that Grale Casarion was just a man, and their society was a total mess.

"It's funny," Kira had said, once. "How long ago was it? Ten years, something like that, that everyone was all into 'Ephezoa! Ephezoa! Ephezoa is great! Hasseleighton is evil! Grale Casarion is a tyrant!' Now, most people worship Grale Casarion."

"Ephezoa killed herself," Azshbir replied. "The war was hard, and she persecuted her own people. She herself played into the idea that she was evil and tyrannical, that Grale Casarion came as a savior of sorts."

"Not to us," said Neah'ra. "So many Ephezoans thought they were People of the Promise, too."

"For a while, Hasseleighton persecuted only those People of the Promise who would not give to Grale Casarion the allegiance they had once given to their own culture; only when Hasseleighton had already won a place in the hearts of the people, did she demand this," said Azshbir.

Kira shook her head. "But, there are still Ephezoan patriots. For a while, the city would change hands constantly; you told us about the dangers it posed, Azshbir."

"Yes," Azshbir had replied. "There are always a few who really do believe in their nationalism, and Hasseleighton *is* cruel and tyrannical– in some ways, as we well know, worse than Ephezoa had yet become."

Someone had asked why they did not associate with these people. Azshbir's only reply was that he had never looked for them; somehow, it seemed better not to do so. Not that the rebel-patriots did not need the Promise, too, but somehow he did not feel called, and he would not invite the danger of associating with them as well upon himself unless he knew he was called to do so. After all, he had a family for which to care.

Now, Kira said, "So, why did you not invite those you suspected to be fellow People of the Promise over a long time ago?"

Azshbir did not have an answer to that one.

"Anyway," she said, looking at the shadows, "is it too late to go back and ask them over, today?"

"Perhaps, instead, we should flee. Someone may know where we are and betray us to avoid falling into the hands of the Undead Snow Queen. I don't want to be seen in the city again today, either."

Kira wondered why Azshbir would fear that. She did not ask. Instead, she said, "If you flee, I and Shantee are staying. There are people here we *must* reach with the message. We *must* tell those who have been gathering that the Undead Snow Queen has no power against the Creator and His Promise. If you go, I want you to tell me where and how you found them, so I can find them, if they don't come for fear. I also want you to tell me how to find those you have been trading with, who, you think, may be People of the Promise, so I can tell them, as well."

Azshbir wondered how she could be so sure that Shantee would make the same choice. "Sure. I will tell you," he said.

"Thank you," said Kira. For some reason unknown to Azshbir, she curtsied. Then she turned and ran lightly across the fields.

Neah'ra looked up at Azshbir. "What do we do, now? If we must flee, I don't know where we would go or how we would survive."

"I don't know, either," said Azshbir, holding her and struggling against his dejection. "I don't understand: how does Kira know that Shantee would also choose to stay?"

He felt Neah'ra pull back. "Azshbir, Kira doesn't know *for sure,* but it is the kind of choice Shantee might be expected to make. Do you remember her words the morning Kathreen left us?"

Azshbir did. She had said something about the time seeming long, but not really being so. "Yes."

"Shantee knows the Promise, and she is a young unmarried woman. Why should she flee?"

"I get it," said Azshbir. He still felt dejected. He did not want Kira and Shantee to leave, and what about Shaelene? She talked like she believed the Promise, now. Would she flee with Kgarjin and Marlekk, who was still quite young? Would Kgarjin want to stay with her sisters? Would Shaelene allow her? Azshbir did not know.

#61
Ruin of the Beginning

It was pelting outside. Brisia took the scroll, went to a corner, stretched herself out on the floor, and unrolled it.

Several dragons soared in the sky. A human couple entered the grove. It was quiet in a way in which no other place was quiet. The air was bright. The shadows were deep and blue. They had climbed up the mountain to come here, to this secret grove, where they had been told they would be given understanding of the secrets of the world, of what was good and how to make it good, the knowledge to rule their lives and their world. Before, they had walked in the presence of the Creator and had learned from Him. Now, they would know themselves. They would impress Him with their knowledge; they would know before He told them, and would not need Him. They would make their own decisions– like He did.

So, they stole into the forbidden grove.

As they stepped foot in that place, a veil was drawn across the world, a veil that came between them and the bright presence in which they had always walked. The sun was dark; colors were no longer vibrant and fresh. There was a darkness, a rottenness, in the air that they breathed, in all that bright world around them. Then, suddenly, they were aware of a terrible light.

The human pair knew it was the same light in which they had walked and delighted, but now it terrified them. They needed the darkness. They ran from the secret and sacred grove and hid in a cave in the mountain-side.

Brisia began to cry. It was the saddest thing that that bright, fresh, clean world was ruined, that a beginning so full of promise should be turned to this, this thing of wrongness, everything out of joint.

The veil darkened, and as it did they perceived the light of the Creator as more and more terrible and deadly. They wanted the veil now, even while they feared it, and they cried out in terror and fear and guilt, ashamed, for the Creator must surely know what it was they had done. The dragons hid in the cave with them. It was in that moment that they heard the Creator's voice.

"All is not lost, for I will send you a Conqueror. When the dragon egg of your hopes hatches, then My Promised One will come, out of the race of man born of women, and He will take away your shame and guilt and give you the merit I made you to have, so you can dwell in My presence, in My palace, with no more veil over all the light. But, for now, you will dwell in Kaarathlon, under the veil, beset by the woe, misery, and pain of your choice to seek for yourselves in your own time what is Mine."

They waited before the voice of the Creator, with terror and hope, and then found themselves on the shore of an ocean, the waters lapping around their feet. The light on the waves of the ocean was dim compared to the light they had known, but it hurt their eyes, and they squinted painfully.

Brisia sat up, weeping, and thrust the scroll away. She understood what had happened, now. Somehow. The Creator had made them to choose to love and obey Him and live with Him. Instead, they had chosen to do things their way. They could have grown to the perfection the Creator had planned for them, but instead they chose to make Kaarathlon a place of grief and loss, still thrumming with the promise of what might have been, and the pain and misery of what it could no longer be. In the Promise, the Creator was going to make it all right, to give far better than anyone had yet known or dreamed. Yet it was still so sad. It was so wrong.

Adaria knelt down next to her. "What's wrong, Brisia?"

"Everything's wrong," sobbed Brisia.

"Everything?" asked Adaria.

When she could speak again, Brisia said, "Well, I don't mean *everything*. Some things... are very good." Even now, she could not forget that.

"Well, what *is* wrong?" asked Adaria. Since Brisia had met Khiel, and especially since her marriage to Kalar, and even more so since she had gotten pregnant and started having babies, she and Brisia had not been so close.

Brisia pointed to the scroll. "Read that."

"Which part of it?" asked Adaria. "It's kind of long."

"Near the beginning," said Brisia. She went on weeping while Adaria read silently.

"Why is this such a cause for distress that we disobeyed the Creator and tried to be our own, even though the Creator had warned us it would lead to death and misery, to separation, the veiling? You already knew that, didn't you? You certainly knew that all this evil is because we try to do our own thing instead of living with and trusting the Creator, and you know that evil is... evil," said Adaria slowly, trying to comprehend.

"Not like that," said Brisia. Then, "Why don't you ask Khiel? Maybe she would know how to explain."

To be honest, Adaria had grown somewhat frustrated with the fact that, nowadays, whenever Brisia did not know how to explain something, she always said, "ask Khiel." Khiel did not know everything or how to explain everything either, and Adaria had heard Brisia explain things quite well, though she would never, in thousands of years, have thought of putting it the way she did. "Did you know," she told Brisia, "that Khiel does not even know everything you know, just as you have not experienced everything she has?"

"Well, I can't explain it right now, and I can't... imagine why you... don't understand," said Brisia through her sobs.

Adaria took the scroll and put it back away.

An hour later, Brisia came to her and said, "I'm sorry for snapping at you."

"I'm not at all sure that you did," said Adaria, nursing Rothen.

"Well," said Brisia, sitting down, "I'm not at all sure that you will understand, but evil is evil. You see, what hit me," here, she paused for a moment, "was that what happened– and, still does happen– was just evil. *Wrong.* Like, a disease. Like, wrong all through and through, from top to bottom. The Creator is so good. His world was good. Like, I mean, *good.*

"And we ruined it. We still ruin it.

"I never saw it like that, before. If you didn't see it like that, I don't know how I can explain."

Adaria felt extremely pleased. Brisia was definitely growing up. She had grown up so much. "You did very well," she said. "I don't think I understand like you do, though."

"Weren't you telling me that I have to figure out and say what I mean and see, since no one sees things the same, even me and Khiel?" asked Brisia.

"Yes, I was," said Adaria. "Anyway, I was saying, you were saying, that seeing evil as the ruin of something truly good is what makes it seem really *evil?* What's evil about evil isn't so much that which is evil, but that which it is committed against, that which it ruins, that which it is *not?*"

"I guess," said Brisia. She did not completely follow Adaria.

"And," Brisia said, "what does the Creator mean that He will make it all well? Will He perhaps make the evil not to be evil– the ruin not to be ruin– basically, restore the good– evil? What's the right word?"

Adaria held up her hand. "Some things," she said, "cannot be expressed."

There was a glow on Brisia's face. She was thinking of things that could not be expressed. "Oh, I know!" she said.

"Maybe, you would like to tell Khiel?" Adaria suggested. "Now that you've at least tried to tell me, I don't think there's any harm in it. In fact, I think it's good for you and Khiel to talk, since you see enough the same to help each other say and see more, in a special way. Not," she added, "that all ways aren't special." She was thinking back to the vision she had had of each one sharing in what was done for and seen by each one, while sitting beside Brisia in the moonlight, so many years ago.

"Yes, I think I'll do that," said Brisia.

As she stood, Adaria said, "After that, why don't you tell all of us?"

Brisia smiled, shrugged, and walked away. The thought made her very uncomfortable.

When she told Khiel, the older girl said, "I think you have the answer to what you were wondering earlier, after you read about the beginning."

"Yes," said Brisia thoughtfully, "I do. But, umm, isn't it strange, how one hears things and know things, and then suddenly one knows what they mean?"

"I think everyone experiences that," said Khiel. "I do. All the time."

"I'm glad the Creator is going to make everything right. Really glad." Brisia pulled her arms together, as if she shivered. "I don't know how it's possible. But

I'm glad He will."

"I know," said Khiel. "It's so wrong. So *horrible.* Terrible, in a horrible way. I guess, just *evil.*"

Brisia nodded.

"I think Adaria said, like nothing."

"I like that!" said Khiel.

Brisia did not understand. She told Khiel.

"Evil is the ruin of good. You said that."

"Yes," said Brisia.

"Well, that means evil is for good not to be. That's kind of like nothing, you know. Evil isn't as, well, there, it isn't as much as good."

"I kind of get how you're saying, but I don't understand," said Brisia.

"That's fine!" said Khiel. "I think you do understand what I mean, since it's the same thing you realized while reading that scroll a couple hours ago!"

Khiel stood. "Enough about this. Let's play."

#62
Dragon-rider Knight

Azshbir had explained the situation to the entire household. He still did not understand why Kira and Shantee were nowhere around. It was late and dark by now, and they should have been back hours ago.

That was when the door opened. Kira stepped in. Azshbir sucked in his breath. A blue dragon flew behind her shoulder. Shantee walked behind her. In her arms was another blue dragon. All Azshbir could see of the second dragon was his or her wings, which were a pale, pastel blue. The other dragon was much darker.

"What?" asked Neah'ra. She was nursing Kuthreb, and so could not get up.

Shaelene, however, rose. "Shantee! Kira! That's why you were out! I never hoped for anything like this for my daughters."

Kgarjin ran forward. "Can I have a dragon, too?" she asked.

"You're old enough to know better than that," said Shantee. "Dragons only have one person, and we don't know about any more eggs." She laughed softly. "Kameth. Greet my sister."

The light blue dragon leapt out of her arms. They saw, now, that her body was azure.

Kgarjin held out her arm. Kameth alighted on it. "Her eyes! They're so pretty!" she said. Kameth had dark violet eyes with specks of light in them.

"Kira," said Azshbir.

"Yes?" said Kira. She came forward and knelt down on the floor. The dark blue dragon landed next to her. This one had eyes of purple ruby.

"I thought of why I didn't invite them over."

Kira knew who he was talking about. Those he had suspected may be People of the Promise.

"Remember the betrayal of Ellason?"

Kira nodded and swallowed. Instantly, she understood. A lump formed in her throat. "I understand," she said.

Why had Ellason betrayed them? Ellason had known what the Promise meant. She had known the need for the Promise. She had understood more than many of them. Yet, she had betrayed them. Thanks to Shantee and the Creator's aid, Kira and all her family had escaped and lived. Daera, however, had been killed. Kira did not even want to think about how. She knew that it had hurt Shaelene terribly. Many of Daera's children, Lasaira's blood-siblings, had been taken. Had they, also, met torturous deaths? So many of her friends had died. And, Ellason! Ellason had been a strength and tower of support to all of them. How had she betrayed them? How had no one known?

Azshbir watched Kira. None of them had mentioned Ellason in years. Kira's dragon looked up at her with quickly whirling eyes. Azshbir did not know anything about dragons. What did that mean? "Kellyth…" said Kira. So, that was her dragon's name. Male or female? Azshbir could not tell that either. How had Kgarjin known Kameth was female? A wild guess? Kameth sounded like it might have been a male name to Azshbir.

When the usual visitors had not shown on the usual day, Kira begged Azshbir to tell her how and where to find them. Azshbir only told her where she would be likely to meet those who were at least questioning Grale Casarion's position as the 'Eternal King.' Early in the morning, she had gone out with Kellyth, now known to all of them as a female dragon.

Shaelene was very worried about her and had begged her not to go. With the threat of the Undead Snow Queen, even those who questioned the Council of Wizards might well betray her to them. As for the Undead Snow Queen, if the legends were true, there was no worse fate– except, perhaps, to be on the bad side of the Creator. She could tolerate her daughter tempting torture, but not the bonds of the undead!

That had been when Azshbir knew that Shaelene was not yet ready to be a Knight of the Promise.

Kira had stood straight and told her mother that this was what she was doing; she knew that no Undead Snow Queen had any power but what the Creator allowed her. She knew that the Creator was the Lord of Life and Death, and the Promised One would conquer and reign over all things. It was far worse to fall into the hands of the Creator, from whom none can deliver, than into those of the Undead Snow Queen. She was going. With that, she had turned and run out from the house, quickly grabbing a shawl to wrap around her head.

When everyone came in, in the evening, Kira was sitting against the wall with Lia and Seair and several others, a few of whom were unknown to Azshbir and the others. Kira looked up and said, "Hi!"

"You're well!" said Shaelene and rushed to embrace Kira.

"Yes, I'm well," said Kira, obviously smothered and uncomfortable. When Shaelene finally let her go and stood up, Kira said, "I think Lia believes in the Promise. She wants to be a Knight of the Promise."

Lia nodded fiercely. "I do."

"I would like it, too," said Kira. Leaning back, much of her weight on one arm, she said, "I'm desperate to tell even those who were vehement about Grale Casarion's godhood. I want to tell them about the freedom we have in the Promise."

"Freedom?" asked Shaelene. "Freedom from what?"

Kira shook her head gently. Shantee said, "Death. The Undead Snow Queen."

Kira nodded. "Thanks, Shantee," she said. "That's what I mean, Mom. We're free anywhere. Everywhere. No matter what. I'm free to tell my friends. Azshbir, can you *please* tell me how to find the others? I won't bring them here, if you really don't want."

"Yeah, I'll tell you, and, no, you can bring them if you want," said Azshbir. "Come back the next time you can, Lia, and both you and Kira can be Knights of the Promise. Unless you can stay the night? Because I want to make sure, first."

"No, I don't think staying the night would be safe. People would wonder where

I was."

"Kira," said Lia, "I heard that the Undead Snow Queen took all the dragon eggs. How did you get Kellyth?"

"Shantee also has a dragon. Kameth. We found the eggs together. I don't know how. We'd been where we found the eggs hundreds of times. Whether there is or is not an Undead Snow Queen I don't know, but I do know that the Council is a bunch of liars and they want everyone to be scared to death of them. Whatever happened, they probably exaggerated, and flat-out made up stuff."

"Yeah, that makes sense," said Lia. After a long silence she said, "I'm still scared."

One of the new girls asked, "Then why in Kaarathlon are you doing this?"

Lia laughed nervously, but as if the suggestion that she not do 'this' was absurd. "Are you scared, Kira?" she asked.

"Yes. Sometimes," said Kira.

"What does Kellyth think?" asked the other girl. Dragons were held in high renown, and some considered them to be wise.

"Kellyth is a hatchling," said Kira.

"Hatchling dragons are already creatures of awe and magic," said the other girl.

Listening to the exchange, Azshbir thought that she did not know anything about dragons. Kathreen's dragon, L'sa-moth, had certainly been very beautiful, having the colors of the undersea world, and very huge and strong, but she had been a gentle, motherly creature. As for Kellyth, he knew why Kira did not want to talk about what she thought around other girls with such a high opinion of dragons. Kira had told him that Kellyth was not ready to acknowledge the idea of a King who had a right for her to obey Him. She had no problem with the idea of someone good and wise with whom she would willingly cooperate, but she did not like the idea of someone actually having authority over her. Finally, in answer to the girl's pestering, Kira said, "Kellyth thinks the Undead Snow Queen can't possibly have any power over noble dragons." She did not say what Kellyth meant by noble. "She is not sure if the Undead Snow Queen even exists. If she does, the dragons– and everyone else– should fight her, not submit to her. She is sure that the dragons' fire and life is at least a match for her ice and undeath, whatever that is."

"Ahh," said the other girl. "So that's why–"

"No, actually, that's not why," interjected Kira. "Why is because I believe in the Promised Conqueror. Even if Kellyth were certain of the Undead Snow Queen's power and adamantly against the Promise, I would still do this."

Shantee bent down. "Here're some snacks for you girls."

"After this, I'll have to go," said Lia.

"And, it's a good thing you have a whole group with you, since you don't have guardian dragons!" said Kira. The night-time was dangerous, especially for women or girls, in the cities, and even in the day there were places that were extremely dangerous if one were alone, but no one would dare attack a Dragon-rider with her dragon. Dragons were held in too high esteem, and they were feared. Their ability to predict a human's motives and actions was legendary and often exaggerated in some circles, and their ability to recognize someone was too perfect to be much exaggerated. Attack a dragon and his or her rider, and other dragons will hunt you.

Some of those who had been vehemently against the Promise came, at Kira's request and when she explained to them the power of the Creator even over the Undead Snow Queen and the Promise. Over the next weeks, they and many of Lia's friends believed in the Promise. The terror of the Undead Snow Queen was working against the goals of the Council, as it drove people to see the freedom and life offered in the Promise and the goodness of the Creator's Kingship. Shaelene, however, become obsessed with her fear of betrayal, that what had happened under Ephezoa would happen again: People of the Promise would gather together, so that they might be betrayed together, and in one move slaughtered and brought to an end. Many of them shared in her fear, but Azshbir knew that they must not give into it. The People of the Promise found the promises of the scroll encouraging. Azshbir had also invited those who he had suspected to be and confirmed to be believers in the Promise, but who had succumbed to the terror of the Undead Snow Queen.

Kira said, "Sooner or later, someone will be found out and die. We know that will happen, unless the Creator does something very powerful and unusual. There are many of us, and we are bold. We *will* be bold in our proclamation, even when we shake with fear. After all, we are the Knights of the Promise. But that does not mean this will all come to naught. In fact, we know it will not. The Creator has specifically given us this mission. Now we are knights; then, we were not." Shantee added, "And even then, it did not all come to naught. We know that we gathered encouragement through those dark years, and that we live. What else came about, we don't know."

However, it could not escape their notice that, as before, the People of the Promise had been brought together by persecution, so now they were brought together and grew by terror; it seemed like the beginning of a re-play.

#63
Healing in the Promise

Arendellie explained to the warden that she thought Kyil had reverted because she felt ashamed of many things in her past. She had made up that Arendellie had lied about her because she was embarrassed. Arendellie hated herself while she did it, but she was desperate to see Kyil again. When she stepped, once more alone, into her cell, she felt like she would pass out. She could not bear to see the wounds on her body. Kyil was quite awake, and she knelt down next to her, covered her with her cloak, and gave her a drink from a skin she had brought. "I don't want to force you to talk to me, if you…" Arendellie said.

"What do you want to talk about?" asked Kyil, sitting up and drawing Arendellie's cloak about herself. She was shivering, even though it was not cold.

"I don't know," said Arendellie. "I don't know at all. Is there anything you want to talk about?"

Kyil was silent for such a long time Arendellie wondered if she was ever going to say anything. Arendellie covered her own face in her hands. All her shame felt like it was piled on her head heavier than she could bear. She could not believe the things she had said and done. She *deserved* the surpassing torture of being exposed to that terrible light. Only a few days ago Kyil had stood before her with bright eyes, more or less healthy. Now, she winced with every breath, and Arendellie felt like it was her personal fault. It could have been. Finally, Kyil said, "Don't think I don't want to talk to you. But I don't want to talk about anything in partic… Talking about certain things is… hard."

Sudden terror washed over Arendellie. This time, she was sure, Kyil *was* going to die soon. She could never play her trick again– Kyil would know and tell, right away– and if she asked to have Kyil brought to her, she would be asked why, and it would not be done. She dug her finger nails into her palm until it began to bleed.

"I guess," said Arendellie, her heart hammering, "I guess, I read about the veiling again the other day. I don't really understand it. It seems to indicate that the whole problem is that we don't live with the Creator, and the shame of what we've done. But, the Creator is too terrible! I'm dead scared of Him! Even if I weren't ashamed." She lowered her voice. She had to make sure no one heard what she was saying. "And, I'm only saying this because I think you want to talk to me about it, so if at any time you'd prefer I leave, or stop, or anything, I will."

"Oh, no," said Kyil, her eyes closed. "I think, that's your problem. You don't want to live with Him."

"How could I?" said Arendellie.

"He's good. You have to see and want His goodness."

Arendellie thought the situation was hopelessly discordant. She had almost forgotten that she was the queen, but it felt discordant, wrong, upside-down, flipped, she did not know what. Only that she itched to be away from it, and yet she had sought out Kyil because she wanted to talk to her. It terrified her. She was beginning to think that Kyil was her best friend, and she was doomed to lose Kyil!

Arendellie thought for a long moment. "He's terrible. I don't see how they could endure living with Him. Is that, perhaps, why they disobeyed Him? Because they did not want to be with Him, and they knew it deep down inside?"

Kyil's eyes fluttered open and she exclaimed, "No! Never!"

"What, then?" asked Arendellie.

"So much I can't tell you," said Kyil. Arendellie noticed that she did not say 'can't understand' or 'don't know.' "But," Kyil went on, "maybe the reason you can't endure living with Him is because you aren't living with Him? You're not in the right place to Him, so…"

Arendellie could not argue.

Kyil went on. "I think it's the Promised One's merits that make it possible for us to live with Him. Make us strong enough."

"Oh," said Arendellie. She did not understand, but she was not trying to. She was listening. "I'm so ashamed," she said, half to herself, thinking of how she had contemplated having Inshara tortured to death. *O, Creator, thank You for not letting me!* she cried in her heart.

Sudden fire entered Kyil's voice and she sat up straight and held Arendellie's gaze. "That's why you need the Promise! You may not understand *how*– I don't understand how, but I know that– the Conqueror will take your shame and guilt away. *Really AWAY!* Truly gone. Just turn to the Creator! I know you're scared to, but He really *will* take all the shame *AWAY.*"

Arendellie did not know what to do or say. She was going to say, "But I don't want to come to Him! I don't want to be with Him! I'm scared of Him!" but something kept her from doing so out loud. *It's true, though,* she thought. *I can't live with the shame of what I've done– what I've been. I can't live with it! I don't know whether I can't live with the Creator or myself more! I wonder why I don't run away! I don't even want to be here.* "Do you know, Kyil," she said, inadvertently speaking out loud, "that I used to intend to have one of my slaves tortured to death because she believed the Promise and actually loved me– affected me?"

"Did you?" asked Kyil, softly.

"No," said Arendellie. "The Creator kept me from being able to carry it through. I couldn't even hint to the wrong people that she believed the Promise."

There was genuine joy in Kyil's voice. "Thank the Creator!"

Arendellie nodded. "Thank the Creator," she whispered.

Arendellie was in the worst of all possible positions. She believed in the Creator. She believed that He was truly real, that He alone was King. However, she feared Him. She could not trust Him. She could not look forward to His Promise. Her own country, the very nation whose queen she was, would have her killed, just like they were killing Kyil, for believing the Creator alone was King, alone was Real, alone was worthy. Yet, she could not endure the thought of dying– of facing Him, the veil of Kaarathlon no longer between her and Him. Though she could never be more ashamed of what she had done and been, torture seemed a very small thing to her in the light of the unearthly, unbounded Reality which she knew to be good and which above all else she feared and desired to flee.

"O Creator, Creator," she sobbed.

"Do you want me to stay?" she asked Kyil.

Kyil did not respond. Arendellie wondered if she heard her. *The Promise,* she thought. *The Promise. Shame taken away.* She rose, opened the door, and was about to run down the corridor, when her guide met her. "Your cloak, you forgot your cloak," she said.

"Leave it!" said Arendellie, harshly. "Take me out." She was in too many pieces to realize that the way in which she was acting was extremely dangerous.

That evening, she managed to act perfect for Vanesh. Then, he noticed the scabs on her palm. "How did that happen?" he asked.

She lied. Again. "I think it happened during my nap. I had another nightmare."

"I'm so sorry," said Vanesh, genuinely. Then, "You need to make sure no one else knows you have this problem with nightmares, if you want to continue your current line of work. Wear the gloves until it heals."

Arendellie nodded, and obeyed.

"What shall I tell them? They are sure to ask me questions," protested Kalie.

"Tell them the queen did not tell you why. She simply told you to have Kyil brought to her quarters. No, go, now," said Arendellie. She was in terrible angst. For some reason, she did not want to talk to Inshara. Kyil was her friend. Her only friend. Her best friend, in a long, long time. She was going to die soon if she were not brought, *now!* And, she was desperate. She did not really care what people thought, or said, or did. She was going to do this!

An hour later, Kalie returned. "I'm sorry, your majesty," she said, curtsying deeply, "but Kyil has been executed."

Arendellie drew in a quick breath, but it was in relief. "Thank the Creator!" she exclaimed in a whisper. Kyil was with Him, now. It was this she had been wanting for so long. This was far better than anything Arendellie could have offered. This would mean the healing of all her wounds, those in her soul, by the loss of her son and the things she had seen, and the loss of others. This was complete healing, for her to live with the Creator in a perfect place.

Kalie yelped. "I didn't know you believed in the Promise!" she said. Too loudly.

Do I? thought Arendellie. *Do I? Is this what believing in the Promise means?* Kyil's words echoed in her mind, and she responded. *I do want that! I want all my shame taken away– gone– never to be found again!* It was a dizzying thought. She remembered determining that she, she, would never believe in the foolish Promise. She remembered Inshara telling her that the Promise would bring healing, and her thought that it had brought only pain and division. Yet, here she was, obviously believing otherwise! Obviously, she did believe there was ultimate healing in the Promise.

"I didn't," said Arendellie, still not quite sure whether she meant that she did not in the past, or that she still did not.

Several servants came running. "Did I hear the queen is one of the People of the Promise?" one asked.

Arendellie found herself saying, "I wasn't," again not quite sure what she meant. Since she was not sure, why could she not just lie and say, "Of course I'm not?" It would be safe, and it would not *really* be lying, because she did not know! In fact, was it even possible to be one of the People of the Promise if you thought that you might not be one?

Hopefully, the slaves would not notice the all-important difference between 'wasn't' and 'am not.'

"I need to go," she said. "Leave me alone, until I call for you. Do you hear me?"

They all answered, yes.

"Make sure everyone else knows as well," she said, and fled.

#64
Telling the Truth

Arendellie threw herself down on the bed and wept. She had felt momentary relief, even joy, at the news of Kyil's death. Now, she was overwhelmed with sorrow. Her best friend was dead. She was alone. Horribly alone. More alone than she had ever been in her life. She was overcome with oceans of grief.

Vanesh found her there, weeping and sobbing, rocking back and forth. "What is wrong, Arendellie?" he asked. She had not cried like this in so long, if she had ever cried like this.

She looked up, her face wet with tears, the covers where she had laid it drenched with them. "My best friend... is dead. Kyil...

"I made friends with... one of the People of the Promise... in the dungeons. I think... I think... I think I believe the Promise myself." That was wrong. She did believe the Promise. She wanted the Promise. There was no doubt about it. But she did not want to try to say it again.

Vanesh said nothing. He knelt down and put his arms around her. "Araenyi... Araenyi... Araenyi," he murmured, over and over again.

Arendellie thought that Kyil would have rejoiced to know that she had turned to the Promise. Maybe, she had. Maybe, she had known. After all, she had been crying, "O Creator, Creator," before she left. She did not even know when she had accepted the Promise.

Finally, she stopped sobbing. "Did you say what I think I heard?" Vanesh asked.

"What did you think you heard?" asked Arendellie. Her voice was so hoarse she could barely speak.

"That your best friend was a prisoner named Kyil who has died, and you think you believe the Promise."

"I don't *think* I believe the Promise," Arendellie croaked. *Think* she believed the Promise? What kind of sense did that make? For how long had she believed the Promise? Months, probably. It was just that she had only recently– she suddenly realized the sense of the word!– accepted the Promise.

"So, all of this is because you made friends with a condemned prisoner?"

Arendellie nodded.

"I'm going to have to tell the Council that you are sick," he said. "I will be back."

Arendellie suddenly remembered. She had been going to have dinner with Vanesh and the rest of the court! Even if she could get herself completely together in time, she would not be able to go. She could not talk.

Vanesh rose, resting her against the bed. "You will be fine, if I go for a few moments, right?"

"Yes," Arendellie said.

When Vanesh left, she examined the marks of her weeping. Her face felt stiff from the dried salt her tears had left. She was very thirsty. She did not readily get headaches from crying, but she had a terrible headache now, possibly mostly from thirst. A whole patch of the covers were soaking. She guessed it was okay. A few of the slaves could simply be asked to wash it. Arendellie did not think she would mind doing so herself. It would certainly be a lot less uncomfortable than other things she had been doing.

She wondered if she should tell Inshara. The woman would certainly rejoice.

It occurred to her now that, all her life, the Creator really had been pursuing her. She remembered the message El-Reiza had brought her from Sir Andelf, about the Creator being terrible, but there being certain hope in the Promise. She remembered something about 'praying you would come to fear Him above all else,' and yet hoping in Him. She knew now what that meant. Suddenly, in the blink of an eye, it was her life. And, there was nothing else she need fear. It felt unreal.

Vanesh returned before she could figure out what to do and do anything. "It looks like you're feeling a little better," he said. "I'm glad."

Arendellie smiled at him a little. "Thanks," she said.

He sat down next to her on the bed. "So, what happened?" he asked.

"Well, I didn't want the People of the Promise to be tortured and killed," she said. It felt unreal actually telling the truth about something for the first time in what felt like forever. "So, I figured I would pretend to be trying to talk them out of allegiance to the Promise– I did think it was stupid– and lie about them, saying they did not believe in the Promise." For some reason, she felt so ashamed that she had done these things, that she had lied in this way. She flinched, talking about it. "Well, I made friends with a young woman named Kyil. When she learned she had been given her freedom because of my lying, she went back and told them. She was again tortured and then executed."

"Whatever put such an idea in your head? Is this why you have been having nightmares?" asked Vanesh.

"I *haven't* been having nightmares. Or not like I've said," said Arendellie.

"Huh?" Vanesh started. "Then, what about your crying? What about the marks on your palm?"

"I did that while in the cell with Kyil," said Arendellie.

"You've been lying to me about everything," said Vanesh.

"Yes," said Arendellie. She could not believe this was actually happening. However, the wonder, the unreality, of her actually being one of the People of the Promise so surpassed the wonder of the fact that she was telling the truth that she scarcely noticed the later.

"So, why have you been doing this?"

"I was afraid," said Arendellie.

"Of what?" asked Vanesh.

Here, Arendellie grew self-conscious and embarrassed. She decided not to tell the whole truth. It would probably really bother Vanesh, and it was only half, no, less than half, of why she was afraid. "If what I was doing became known, I was afraid of... many things... like that it would be stopped. I was also really afraid that I would be executed because I was so afraid of facing the Creator. He is terrible."

"*Was?*" asked Vanesh. "Why were you afraid of that? I did not know you believed in the Creator. And, why aren't you afraid of dying and meeting the Creator now?"

"Well, I never disbelieved in the Creator. I just didn't care about Him. And, then I met Him. It was awful! That was the day I told you I had a nightmare about a cliff falling."

Vanesh put his head in his hands. "Why?" he moaned.

"I used to ask that question, too," said Arendellie. "I asked, why did Kathreen and Mirla believe in the Creator so very much? It put a wall between me and my friends– everyone I knew. I called it the 'shattering of the world.' That's actually why I'm here. The man I was going to marry, Neshekh Dasaran, really believed in the Creator, like willing to die for Him kind of believe, and I did not like that at all, because I didn't. I thought I was sensible and wise and would never really believe in Him."

"By 'really believe in Him,' you mean 'willing to die for Him kind of believe,' right?" asked Vanesh.

Arendellie nodded. "Oh yes!"

"Oh, my Araenyi, my Araenyi, what am I going to do?" said Vanesh. He held her and kissed her. "Why must you be so foolish?"

"That's how I used to feel," she said. "It really isn't foolish. I was as set against this kind of 'crazy, foolish belief in things you can't see' as anyone. I was very angry that my best friend, Kathreen, and my fiancé, Neshekh, believed it."

"Neshekh? Neshekh Dasaran?" asked Vanesh.

"I said that already. Why?"

"He is a thorn in the sides of the Lords of Light. Sometimes he can be thrown in prison, but he often escapes. Vanishes! No open doors. No dead guards. No missing guards or keys. Not a trace. He preaches about the Promise all over Avanzar. He infuriates the people, whom we have taught to worship Lord Grale Casarion. Sometimes, they riot and try to stone him or beat him to death. How he doesn't die, no one knows," explained Vanesh.

"Thank the Creator!" breathed Arendellie.

Vanesh moaned. "Can you please, for my sake at least, try to keep this to yourself? I may be king, but I do not have the power my uncle did, and I won't be able to protect you from the Lords of Light if it becomes known that you are one of the People of the Promise."

"If I'm asked, I won't lie, but I have no intention of simply getting myself killed. I would like to improve things, not simply die as so many others do. I would like to improve things for us all. So, don't worry. I'm not going to just tell everyone," answered Arendellie.

"What do you intend to do to improve matters?" asked Vanesh.

"I have a couple vague ideas, but I have not had time to think them through," said Arendellie. She tried to be sympathetic towards Vanesh. She well remembered the misery of feeling the way he did now, but somehow that seemed to be another world. She wondered also why and how Kathreen had been so terrified of torture. It did not even touch her, and she knew that she knew far more about it, had seen far more of it, than Kathreen had. Kathreen had not known anything, really, back then. She knew many details. She had seen people torn and almost completely disfigured by it, and the images haunted her; it was true she had started to have occasional nightmares. However, she knew it was nothing. It did not matter. She might have feared it to some extent before she had encountered the terror and light of the Creator. However, Kathreen had met the Creator, had, indeed, turned to the Promise, and she had been so scared. How?

Vanesh groaned. "I told them my wife was sick and I had to take care of her, and this is it! *This!* This preposterous absurdity of a Promise! This, that has brought so many people to useless deaths." He held her tightly. "Please, Araenyi. You are the light and joy of my life. You are my comfort and my pillar and my staff of help. Please, Araenyi. Please, do not throw your life away. Do not die. Do not leave me alone. I love you, O Araenyi."

"I love you too," said Arendellie. He was holding her so tightly she could not relax. She wriggled. "Please. That's too tight."

Vanesh loosened his grip. He buried his face in her long, thick hair and her veil. "Araenyi, my love," he began to sob. "I never realized this was what was happening to you."

Arendellie felt lost and confused. What was she supposed to do?

#65
The Dragon Tribe

Audra finally landed on the shores of Syrwe. The moon dragons had worked together, at her request, to heal the freed prisoners who had not yet died. They brought back some even from the brink of death over weeks. Some of them now traveled with her, along with a good hundred new dragons she had hatched. She was still totally amazed that she could remember every name and infallibly recognize each dragon. There were thousands of them.

She was bothered by how some of the prisoners had died on the journey. Some even who were Dragon-riders had died, and she had to work with even more dragons who had lost their rider. It was clear to her that the loss of a rider was far more horrible than the loss of a mostly absent Dragon Keeper. All the prisoners who had been given to her– she knew there were many more who had not been given to her– who were not Dragon-riders seemed to be so-called People of the Promise. Even some of the Dragon-riders who were with her, whether they had joined her freely and fled the continent with her, or been released from the dungeons to her, were People of the Promise. *People of the Promise! What a weird name!* she thought. It was as weird a religion as that strange one about the godhood of Grale Casarion. She understood neither religion. *What is it with people fighting and torturing each other over various interpretations of some ancient prophecy known as the Promise? It might have something to do with them not respecting the rightful spirits of nature. Perhaps, by not giving due respect to the spirits of nature, acknowledging their power and right, these people get obsessed with increasing their own power! Certainly, those Lords of Light were crazy for power and control. Probably, because they have forgotten to respect the power and control of the many spirits of nature. The spirits of nature there are probably not the same as those on the slopes of the Trinazee Mountains, but I could feel that they exist. Perhaps, all that has ravaged that continent is their punishment.* She felt much better now. In these southern areas of her own continent, it was very warm for being autumn, but it was quite comfortable, at least after the oppressive humidity and heat of Camil.

Cooking venison on a fire a dragon had lit for her, Audra thought that there was no way she could return to her village and live there. Thousands of dragons could not fit there. *Though,* she thought, *with these dragons, our tribe could easily achieve supremacy. No other tribe could match us in battle, and we could conquer anyone we pleased. Our bows and spears are no match for a legion of dragons. More than that, everyone would flee at the sight of a single dragon. Only we would know that dragons can be friendly, and we could teach our enemies to attribute to dragons even more dread and power than they actually possess. We could teach them to believe that dragons are spirits, gods of fire and wind. The scales they shed would be a great adornment to our festive garments, and the moon dragons could increase our life spans and almost eliminate untimely deaths. They can heal almost incurable wounds. Who knows? They may be able to heal diseases, and even the sicknesses that bring death at old age, so that we may live two or three times our current life-span. They would also give us light at night.*

Still, she did not know if the spirits of the mountains would accept such a major disruption in the order of things. She hoped that, if they did not, she could convince her family to join her in her new life. Already she sorely missed her father and mother and her siblings. Actually, she missed so much of her group within her tribe.

She would like dressing like she was used to, and not like an "Undead Snow Queen," whatever that meant.

As the years passed, Audra found herself, almost against her will, in a position of power and influence. As she predicted, through the shamans the spirits of her tribe rejected the dragons. The oldest of the shamans, who was most favored by the spirits, known as the seer, foresaw that the dragons would bring about the destruction of the tribes and their way of life, steal the respect and honor of the spirits, and bring about terrible war and death. When Audra heard the pronouncement, she clutched the wall to keep upright, fearing that the seer was only too right; after all, what had happened to Camil, where the dragons had been so great? However, she was a Dragon Keeper, and, Amrath reminded her, there were not any spirits and it was all a bunch of superstition. Taking two of her siblings, who were in love with two of her young, newly-hatched moon dragons, Audra left, weeping, having implored her family to come with her. She had to steal her brother and sister away, so they could be with the dragons to whom they were bonding. The dragons helped her watch and care for them, since they were very young, her sister being only a toddler, and she raised them, turning her back on the spirits. With the dragons, she traveled the continent, sometimes north of the Trinazee Mountains, sometimes south of them (in those days, what was later to become the Marinaza Desert was a much thinner and more watered strip of land, inhabited by a few of the poisonous turtles, but quite passable). She generally did not go far south, except in the winter, for those lands were hot, and even in the winter they were as warm as to which the summers she was used. She was not interested in finding out what they were like in the summer, though the plants there had to be a different kind of plant, just as the dark peoples of Camil were a different kind of people, since they flourished and grew thickly even in such a climate. Or, perhaps, she thought one day, they grew in the winter and were dormant in the summer, as some of the trees and plants of her home were dormant in the winter but green and growing in the summer?

The dragons mated and laid eggs throughout Syrwe, and some of these eggs drew children and young adults from the various tribes scattered throughout both the north and south of Syrwe. These new Dragon-riders joined them, and sometimes an entire tribe would accept the dragons. Audra found that, unlike in Camil, there was no common language throughout Syrwe, though they ended up speaking the language of Camil, which, at first, most of the Dragon-riders spoke, mixed with a little of the language of her birth. The tribes who did not reject the dragons were, through the Dragon-riders, molded into one great tribe with a single language, and Audra began to wonder if that, too, was how Camil ended up being the way it was. She loved the dragons, and hoped they would not bring upon the tribes of Syrwe the same terrible fate she had witnessed on Camil. She wondered what she could do to prevent that happening.

Only a couple years after she met Amrath, she married a Dragon-rider from Camil, the one Camilian man who thought that she was beautiful, and she later learned that it had taken him a year and a half to see that she was beautiful. His name was Leiarne. His dragon, Dallyth, did not, however, mate Amrath. Dallyth had flown another dragon, Zyimeth, and she had been killed by a wizard before she ever laid their eggs. Dragons only ever had one mate; if that mate died, then they would never fly again. Instead, Amrath mated the purple Nameth.

Audra did not know what to think about the People of the Promise. One of the reasons she had consented to leaving her own tribe was that they had put to death Waiyeena, a Dragon-rider about her own age with whom she had made friends despite the fact that Waiyeena believed in the Promise. Of course, Waiyeena had asked for it. She had told the women that their spirits had no power and should not be honored, but that only the Creator should be worshiped; unless they worshiped the Creator alone and waited for His Promise, they would all be thrown into the dungeons of Death forever. Somehow, Audra could not deal with the spirits of her home killing people in ways that, frankly, reminded her of the Lords of Light; it made her wonder if maybe the spirits were evil, very much like the Lords of Light of Camil; if Waiyeena was only not right in that the spirits actually existed, but quite right in that they were not what Audra's people thought they were.

More than a quarter of those who left Camil with Audra were People of the Promise. It was not like that anymore. Many of them had been killed for behavior similar to Waiyeena's. Audra could not really tell them not to; more than half of them had been thrown into dungeons and intermittently tortured for their belief in the Promise prior to being given into her care. They really believed it, and there was no way she could convince them to keep it to themselves; not when they had suffered so much for it and still deemed its proclamation worthy of their life and blood. In fact, thinking about their dedication and about the reactions of the spirits, not only of her own tribe but of many others, to them, she wondered at times if the Promise was right; if both spirits and men grew evil, seeking power and control that belonged to someone above themselves and treating their fellows cruelly as they sought it, unless they submitted to and worshiped this higher power, who, Audra realized, could very well be the Promise's 'Creator.'

Amrath, and many of the dragons, did not like this idea. She understood that Amrath would prefer if she did not think about the Promise at all. She was not sure why Amrath did not like the Promise so much, but she did, even though she totally admired Kathreen Alarion, who had been a Knight of the Promise.

One day, something happened that, the dragons told Audra, was totally unprecedented in the history of the dragons. A Dragon-rider whose dragon had been killed, more than a decade ago now, was carrying one of Amrath's eggs, when it began to hatch. The hatchling bonded to him. Audra understood that it was particularly unlikely because he was well into his forties, and, the dragons told her, dragons usually bonded to young humans. By now, Audra herself was into her thirties and had five children with Leiarne, the oldest being thirteen and the youngest one. Two of them had almost died of an often deadly childhood disease, but for the healing touch of the moon dragons.

#66
Dawn in the Valleys of the Sea

Brisia still found the vision of evil she had seen bothersome. It made the world feel like it was tilting around her. When Adaria had again asked her if she wanted to share it with them all, she had stomped her foot to emphasize her "No!"

She had experienced a lot of evil. Her dad had been killed; her mom arrested and tortured to death; and all while she was still very young. She knew her brother still had not made peace with what life brought. Her best friend was an orphan herself. She knew there were others who suffered a great deal more, but she had known what evil meant. What wrong meant. What it was like to lose goodness, the should-have-been. But it had always been her own, her own desire, her own loss, her own pain... until the night she saw what happened to the Creator's work.

She would not have understood it if she had not seen the previous vision, of the clean, fresh, but unfilled goodness of the beginning of the world. She would not have seen just how evil, just how abominable, just how horrible, just how sad, evil was. Now, she did, and it had shaken her. It left her reeling. The only thing she could hold to was the Promise of the Creator that He would make all things well. That was what Mom had told Dormik, but she had told it to her as well, many times.

So, for a couple weeks she had stayed away from the scroll. Now, Khiel called to her. "Brisia! Would you like to read from the scroll?"

Brisia jumped up from her work. "Sure! Which part are you going to read?"

"I don't know!" Khiel called back. "Adaria is going to read it to us and her husband, and several others, while we take care of the babies!"

By now, Brisia was running. In a short time, she and Khiel were running side by side. When they reached the clearing around the house where Adaria was going to read, they grabbed some huge leaves to shake the water from the recent rain all over themselves. Brisia sniffled. "It doesn't smell nice," she said.

"I bet we don't smell nice either," said Khiel. "We can badger one of the men into taking us to a reasonably clean pond tomorrow and bathe."

"When are you going to sit down?" said Kalar.

"Right now," said Brisia. She and Khiel sat down.

Adaria unrolled the first few sections of the scroll. Then, she began to read.

"In those days, the Dragon-riders taught that the dragons were gods, and established themselves as the spokesmen of these 'gods.' While the children of Majhor were building a shrine to the dragons, Siareth, a hatchling of one of the mothers of the dragons, flew Azeroth. When the time came, she presented her eggs to the Dragon Keeper Afrar. One of these eggs was instantly recognized as the dragon egg of promise, for there was a sheen of power and beauty over it. Afrar ordered a vault built in the depths of the temple in which to keep the dragon egg from which would one day hatch the dragon of dragons who would usher in the age of restoration and prosperity. Dragon Keeper Afrar told the dragons that this dragon would be their champion and raise them, and with them all of Kaarathlon, to their rightful place, giving to them immortal life and to the whole world perfection."

Brisia yawned. "This is *boring!*" she said. "Can we read some of that wonderful poetry instead?"

"I think this is interesting," Khiel whispered.

Zsyinzjae, Adaria's daughter, walked away from her dad and towards her and grabbed at the scroll. Adaria held it up and moved it behind her back. "I guess," she said, smiling at Brisia, "that you were right. That is enough of that, today."

"I could read," offered Kalar. He stood up and walked over, to take the scroll from his wife and out of the reach of their toddlers.

Khiel said to Brisia, "You weren't finding it boring earlier. In fact, you were reading it yourself."

Adaria said, "If you want to. I do think that we should not read much more."

Brisia replied to Khiel, "That was different... I do want to hear some more of that poetry! I wouldn't mind hearing that one about the rampart of the stars and the depths of the sea where we cannot walk again, either."

"I did like that one," said Khiel.

"How about we read the one Khiel and Brisia like, Kalar, and then be done?" suggested Adaria.

Brisia jumped up. "Yea!"

"Which one is the one Khiel and Brisia like?" asked Kalar.

"It says something about a rampart of the stars and 'depths of the sea where we cannot walk,'" began Adaria.

Khiel closed her eyes and recited. "Who among you can scale the Rampart of His Stars, or know the secret things in the depth of His oceans? Or who has walked where the stars danced, and heard their music and the words of their song? Who has seen the halls in the depth of His seas or touched the uttermost veil of His skies? Yet all these He made from the wealth of His delight, for us to look upon and to delight our eyes, and the least of His works surpass us by far, the valleys of the sea where we cannot walk..."

"You could just recite it for us," said Kalar with a twinkle in his eyes.

Khiel looked down, shyly. "That's all I have memorized."

"Anyway," said Kalar, "that doesn't help me find it much. Where is it?"

Khiel scooted forward. "Here. Give it to me. I'll find it, and you can read it."

Kalar handed the scroll to Khiel. "You could just read it," he said.

"You're just teasing me," said Khiel. She took the scroll, unrolled it, quickly found the place she was looking for, and gave it back to Kalar, pointing to the desired section.

"This?" asked Kalar, and began reading. "Kaarathlon He fashioned out of the voids, and from nothing that His own pleasure called into being."

"Yes," said Khiel, bouncing up and down. She tried to play with Rothen, helping his mom keep him occupied.

Kalar continued reading.

Brisia got more and more excited. When he finished the last line, Brisia said,

"I really like it the way you read it. It fits!"

"Thank you," said Kalar.

"That one is really good, Brisia," said Nahiza. "Are they all like that?"

"I don't know about them *all*," said Brisia. "More or less," said Khiel. "They are all that nice and that good, and all that, but they don't all say exactly that."

"I *really* love that part about how, 'the valleys of the seas where we cannot walk, the mountain peaks and blinding snows, the bright airs that are deadly to us… All these are but faint echoes of the radiance round His throne, the terrible blinding light without,'" said Brisia.

"Well, *almost*," said Khiel, referring to Brisia's success quoting. "Which part are you talking about? The faint echoes of His radiance, or the valleys of the seas, or the part about the brightness of the snows and deadly airs?"

"I like the *whole* thing," said Brisia. The adults walked away with their children, but Lalia, Kizyia, and Nahiza remained. "I mean, that picture of the valleys of the seas is *really* pretty," Brisia continued. "They probably look something like L'sa-moth. Darker, because there's less light, and not at all sparkly. And there's probably creatures and plants there, too. Why else would they be valleys? I wonder what the halls of the seas that no one has seen are like."

"It really makes one understand why it was such a terrible crime for them to want to know and rule the secrets of the world," said Khiel.

"Oh, don't!" said Brisia.

"What are you talking about?" asked Nahiza.

"Well, how Kaarathlon got the way it is, is that people wanted to rule the world and their lives and know the Creator's secrets. When that happened, the light and goodness was veiled and they were exiled from the Creator's presence. Somehow, they ended up somewhere else. And they did not want to live in the Creator's presence anymore, it scared them, though they were just as scared of the veil and the badness," explained Brisia. "It's frightening and bothersome. Especially since I, well, I want to walk in the depths of the sea!"

"Oh, so that's what bothering you," said Khiel. "Is that your problem?" asked Lalia.

"I only just thought of that now," said Brisia. She looked down at her feet. "What's disturbing about it is, I would like to know and see everything, too! And, it was *bad*. I mean, *evil bad*. What they did there, to the Creator's good world, was just *bad*. As bad as anything people do nowadays in this no-longer good world. At least!"

"Well," said Kizyia, "why don't we play?"

"Okay!" said Nahiza and Lalia.

Brisia sat down on the ground. "What am I supposed to do, Khiel?"

"I don't know," said Khiel. "I also don't know why this is bothering you so much."

"Isn't it obvious?" asked Brisia.

"No, Brisia, it isn't," said Khiel, emphasizing each word.

Brisia put her head in her hands. "It was *evil! Evil!* In fact, evil isn't, well, an adequate word for it. And I – *I could have done EVIL."*

Khiel sat down next to her. "And you're horrified by evil."

"An understatement," moaned Brisia. "Evil is evil."

"Evil *is* bad," said Khiel. "I'm going to get the scroll. I think I should read that poem to you again."

Brisia made an inarticulate noise.

"It *is* really beautiful. Great. Amazing," agreed Brisia, after listening to the song again. "I like how it says 'the least of His works surpass us by far.'"

"I know. It's amazing," said Khiel. "I am going to write a tune for it. It needs to be sung."

"It does," agreed Brisia.

Khiel continued unrolling the scroll. "I think I am going to read this, too." She looked at Brisia. "Unless you are no longer having issues?"

"Issues?" asked Brisia.

"Feeling miserable about evil," clarified Khiel.

"Okay," said Brisia.

"Okay," said Khiel. "Here it is. I only just found this:"

> Triumphant, He marched through the regions of night
> And the dawn answered His call.
> He appeared in the morning, greeted in Light
> And at the touch of His hand
> The wounded were healed, the defiled made pure
> Victory and peace sang His song
> For He conquers His enemies, makes friends of His foes;
> The endless day follows Him, past the night so long.

Having finished reading the stanza, Khiel said to Brisia, "What does that sound like?"

"It sounds glorious," said Brisia. "What's it talking about?"

"When the Promised Conqueror comes."

"How can that be? It talks of something that has already happened."

"There's a lot we don't know," said Khiel. "Remember how we were talking about how there is goodness through all this evil that we don't think could have been otherwise?"

"Uh-huh," said Brisia.

"Well, I think this is it! Or, some of it," said Khiel.

"It is amazing," said Brisia. "Is that the whole thing?"

"Well, there's more," said Khiel, "but it's all very strange. How about we read it tomorrow and get to work right now? There's only a few more hours of daylight left."

"Sure," said Brisia.

#67
Then and Now

"Tell Inshara I want her to come to me," Arendellie told Kawina.

When Kawina had left, she sat down on the carpet and hugged her knees against her chest. It was still unbelievable, even unreal, to think that she believed in the Creator. The Creator, whom she had promised herself she would never stoop to believing in. The Creator, whom alone she feared, and that with a terrible fear. She did not feel like herself.

She was also terribly sad. She missed Kyil. She wished she could have been her friend. This completely surprised her, since she had not even spent much time with Kyil, and she had not even missed Kathreen in this way. She thought she had never been so lonely in her entire life, not even while she lamented that, together, Grale Casarion and Kathreen Alarion had shattered the world so that no one she loved or knew was in the same piece of it as she.

"You wanted me, my lady?" Inshara's voice broke in on her musing.

Arendellie rose. Suddenly, impulsively, she stepped forward and hugged Inshara. Inshara stiffened. Arendellie stepped back. In a soft, out-of-breath voice, Inshara asked, "What?"

"I belong to the Promise!" said Arendellie.

Inshara stepped forward. She tried to hug Arendellie, but Arendellie could feel that it was totally strange to her. She could not relax; she could not imagine that the royal queen was relating to her like this. "I'm sorry," said Arendellie, beginning to cry again.

Inshara stepped back. It was too much. "What for?" she asked, still in a kind of shock.

Arendellie could not speak past the lump in her throat. Could she dare tell Inshara what she had wanted to do to her? It was not that she was afraid of what Inshara would think. It was not that she was afraid that Inshara would not continue to love her. Inshara had made it very clear, long ago, that she knew what the consequences of her words might be and that they did not change anything to her, when she told Arendellie that she needed the healing of the Promise and that she loved her. No, it was that Arendellie was ashamed to say it; ashamed that it had ever been. It would have been a shameful thing to mention even if it had been someone else. So, she did not answer Inshara.

Softly, Inshara said, "I knew."

"When did you know?" asked Arendellie.

"I don't know," Inshara answered, slowly and quietly. "I knew, many years ago, that the Creator was drawing you to His Promise, making you see your need even against your will. When you began to read the scroll, I think it has been clearer and clearer from then on, even though you did not tell me what was going on." She looked down. "I still don't know... how."

Arendellie did not know how, either. Though it had happened gradually, over time, it had all the feeling of a line, of an uncrossable chasm between the 'then' and the 'now.'

Inshara looked up, and she was smiling. For the first time in her life, though, Arendellie noticed a lingering sadness in her. She did not ask though; she was not even sure what it was that she noticed.

After several weeks of thought and planning about how to do it, Arendellie continued to work to improve the circumstances of the People of the Promise. She no longer lied about them, but tried to have them placed in areas where they would not be tortured, arranged to simply have some released, and got people involved in certain wings of the prisons who would be kind and compassionate. Now and then, at Vanesh's request, she shared details with him.

"O Araenyi," he asked her several months later, "why do you have to do this?"

"Because it's real," said Arendellie. "Do you remember when Grale Casarion went to destroy Sir Andelf and his legion?"

Vanesh nodded. "It was a notable– and chaotic– event."

"He managed to send me a message, telling me that he was sorry for helping me get into the life I had; that we were all wrong about who was wise; in reality, it is those who are simple and know the meaning of love who are wise; that he hopes I come to know the Creator is real, to fear Him alone, and to trust in His Promise, though he hopes I do not die a death like his."

"No one would want you to die a violent death, Arendellie," said Vanesh.

"If that is so," she asked, "why do you fear so much for me? Never mind. What I'm saying is… please, don't make the same mistake I and so many others have made. I used to be upset that all my friends cared more about some unseen half-real Creator than real, tangible, life, and took death too seriously. Now, I see that I was wrong and they were right all along. Compared to the Creator, Kaarathlon is hardly real. One day we will all have to realize that we stand before Him, we will all stand exposed before Him."

"Maybe some of our courtiers are right, and it is a disease," muttered Vanesh.

"What?" asked Arendellie.

"Maybe they are right, and it is a disease. After all, this happened to you after relating to Kyil and Yamië and others," said Vanesh.

Arendellie did not know what to say.

"Anyway," Vanesh went on, "they are more convinced than ever that you are just a stupid woman who does not know what you are doing, by this whole little thing with Kyil and several others. So convinced, in fact, that they aren't even bothered to try and see what you're doing now. They laugh endlessly at how you think you're so smart, but, really, you're just like any other woman."

"And we laugh at them for thinking that, even though we helped them to it," said Arendellie. She knew. She was working under their noses, and they would probably never guess that she was actually doing anything, but would think that she was just amusing herself.

Together with Inshara, Arendellie got together those of her maids whom she trusted not to betray them. To begin with, she started with just Aki'lam and Kalie, inviting them into the garden and quietly reading from the scroll. She did not know what else to do. One day, she asked Inshara, "Have you heard this before? How many of these stories are familiar to you?"

"Not many, really," said Inshara, her voice low with some pain she had never yet shared. "We've been slaves for many generations, and, from what you've told me of Avanzar, I don't think Hasseleighton was ever like Avanzar. Certainly, in the Casarions' domain the Promise was not well-known. Most had heard of it but made no pretense of believing it. Though I've learned to read, somewhat, mine has not been a life you could understand, Queen." She paused, then said, "I had a husband, and four children with him, but we were separated before you came to the palace, and I only rarely see any of my children now, though they were still children when I was given to you."

Arendellie looked down when Inshara began and did not lift her head. She was so ashamed. She doubted Inshara had any intention of hurting her; Inshara had never shared this before, and probably only shared it now because she was beginning to get used to relating to Arendellie as an equal. She could hear loads of hurt in Inshara's voice. She knew the woman did not hate her, did not despise her, was in fact as willing to be her friend as possible, but there was a lot of grief and regret in Inshara's life. *And I never thought about it, at all,* thought Arendellie. "Can you please not call me Queen?" She meant for her voice to be level, smooth, and soft, but instead it came out snappy.

"I'm sorry," said Inshara. "I hurt you."

Suddenly, in a moment, Arendellie thought that Inshara reminded her of Kathreen. They even had similar builds. For a long time she did not respond. Finally, she said, "I deserved it. In reality, I hurt myself." She lifted her head and said, her voice bitter and cynical, "I deserve it. Oh, how much I deserve it! It's just what I did and thought, and was coming back to stab me. As they said in Ebrin, you reap what you sow." She lowered her head again. "And, now, I'm getting angry again." It was such a habit with her. It was still hard not to order her slaves around as if they were inferior human beings and snap at them when they did not perform in exactly the way she had in mind, even when there was no way they could possibly have known better. Every time she did it, it felt like a dagger tore through her, yet she could not seem to stop. The progress she knew she made, if only because of the difference in the way her maids related to her, offered her no comfort, because she still did it far too much, and, oh, how it hurt! It felt like she died each time she did it. And, now, having heard Inshara's story, she knew it would only hurt that much more. *Why am I even trying to be secretive?* she wondered. *Why am I even trying not to be found out? If I were, this would be over. If I were executed, this would end at once. If I were thrown into the dungeon, I would be on a level with them. All its foulness and tortures I would prefer to what this feels like! And, this pain, this arbitrary, artificial separation would be* gone! *Really, why don't*

I? I could just tell everyone I meet that I believe the Promise, and it would not be long. But, then, it would hurt Vanesh. And I told him I wouldn't. And, it would mean I could no longer do what I'm doing to try to make things better for others.

There was also the fact, but Arendellie did not notice it then, that it would not have felt natural for her to simply tell people she belonged to the Promise. She was too used to a lifestyle of secrecy and deception to be at ease being completely honest. It would have been awkward, unnatural, uncomfortable. She would not have known how to go about doing it. She still wanted deceptions and conspiracies and the thrill of running and hiding from danger, knowing she might not succeed, but also attached to her vision of success.

Arendellie stood. "I think this is enough for today. I am going to get to work."

Inshara, Aki'lam, and Kalie all knew what kind of work Arendellie was talking about.

Arendellie also still wondered how it was that the Promise was actually sufficient to make her right with the Creator. Somehow, inexplicably, it did, but it made no sense to her at all. She would not have believed it, except that she had experienced it. Somehow, the Promise made it possible for her to live with ultimate Reality, the terrible Light.

#68
Family Quarrel

Azshbir relaxed on the couch and slowly stretched his leg out, wincing. Wind from the open window behind him blew across him. He had been into the city to exchange goods with his friends who were People of the Promise. It had not occurred to him that the two dragons might bring danger upon him, but he had recently learned that almost all the dragons of Camil, or at least the regions around Afteloan, had vanished. It was believed that the Undead Snow Queen had taken them and their riders into the north. Because of this, Kameth and Kellyth were almost a sensation in Afteloan. Kira's friends had told all of their friends about Kellyth, and they, in turn, wanted to meet the dragon and Dragon-rider.

Azshbir did not know if Kira was aware of the dangers this posed. He told her that she needed to not invite all of these people to their home; betrayal would be too likely. At this, Kira and Shantee got together to go into the city with their dragons. He wondered if they knew that they might be handed over to be killed simply because of the jealousy of their friends– that people might hate them simply because they were Dragon-riders. What was more, they were exposing themselves to hundreds who were crazily devoted to Grale Casarion. He had warned them to make sure they never let out any hints about who might be their relations or where they live. He wondered if they knew just how dangerous it was; quite possibly the only reason they had not yet been arrested was because people were waiting to see if they could arrest others along with them.

It was dark. Shaelene walked in. "Azshbir," she asked, "are my daughters home?" She sounded close to tears.

"Not yet," said Azshbir. The thought of what could happen any day to Kira and Shantee bothered him a little. He would miss them too, if they died; both Shantee and Kira were mature, insightful, young women. He knew Shaelene was almost insane with fear and worry. He remembered her clinging to Shantee, begging her not to go. He remembered her screaming at Kira. Shantee had calmly explained to her, "Mom, I and Kira are adults, now. If there were acceptable men around, we could get married. We know you care about us, but we are no longer children, and this is our life."

Shaelene had stepped back, weeping inconsolably. Neah'ra had gone to her and put her arms around her.

Now, Azshbir looked across the dark living room. He was glad that Kira and Shantee were Dragon-riders. The streets, even the open roads, were dangerous for anyone, especially young women, and especially at night. Kameth and Kellyth were already the size of large dogs and would be fearsome creatures to fight. A dragon was a far more formidable foe than any dog, even without the fire-breath, which Kameth and Kellyth had never yet used. Their scales were hard and gave them substantial protection against most weapons. They could fly and twist and use their tails in ways that no dog-like creature could.

Shaelene stood still. "Do you think they're okay?" she asked.

"They've been gone this late before," said Azshbir.

Kgarjin piped up, "Their dragons will keep them safe!"

"Sadly," said Shaelene, and then her voice failed her and she could not continue.

Azshbir did not know what to offer her, and he was far too tired to think about how to say anything that might help. That was one reason he did not want Shantee to die; she had ways of seeing things, ways of putting things, that were very helpful.

"Where are Neah'ra and her children?"

"Outside. I think they're milking the animals," said Azshbir. They had already had dinner and left some for Shantee and Kira.

"Okay," said Shaelene. She sat down, sounding dejected. He and Neah'ra had been hoping that she was coming to understand and believe the Promise, but it was by now evident that she had no commitment to it at all. He was so tired. He would have been fast asleep by the time she came in, but for the aches in his body. Now, he was far too exhausted to find a better place to sleep.

He woke to Shaelene's squeals. The girls were playing. Kuthreb was crying about how he wanted something, and Neah'ra was trying to shush him. He sat up and rubbed his eyes. "I'm hungry and tired, Mom," said Kira, "and it's not my fault you insist on worrying about me so much that you won't eat."

Shantee looked at her sister. Shaelene did not say anything. "I'm sorry, Mom," said Shantee.

Shaelene looked like she was about to pass out from outrage. "No, you aren't. If you were, you'd stay here, instead of mixing with your sister's dangerous friends."

Azshbir cringed. Did Shaelene want to have a fight? He certainly did not want to hear one. *O my Creator, help me.*

"I didn't mean it that way," said Shantee.

"If so, then it's useless," said Shaelene, "and I'd rather you not say it."

Kira stepped forward. "If so, why don't you stop treating us like babies? We believe the Promise. You don't. We'd be grown up and moving in with our husbands by now, anyways."

Shaelene buried her face in her hands and cried. "Are you all going to desert me? Kgarjin and Marlekk, too?"

Kira had always been less gentle than her older sister. Now, she was definitely upset. "Remember when Azshbir and Neah'ra rescued us? Would you prefer to be still living on the streets and making a living by prostitution? Would you prefer that was our life, as well?"

Azshbir buried his head in his hands. He did not want to face this quarrel. He did not want to think about how to make peace. Shaelene was yelling again. "Kira! You're mean. It's not my fault!"

Kuthreb was still crying. Neah'ra grabbed his arm and put it on his lap, then shoved his son against his chest. "Try and see if you can calm him," she said so quickly her words could hardly be distinguished. Then, while Azshbir patted his crying son on the back, feeling almost dizzy and fighting not to grudge his wife's request, she strode towards where Shaelene and her children were yelling at each other. "This is really stupid, Shaelene," she said. "Shantee and Kira are young adults, now. This is what they have chosen to do. We might all miss them, and dread the thought of what may happen to them, but you have to let them make their own decisions. Kira, please try to think before you speak."

"This is Azshbir's and my home. Anyone who wants to keep on fighting and yelling must leave."

Azshbir breathed a sigh of relief. Neah'ra left Shaelene, Shantee, and Kira, and returned to the couch. She took Kuthreb from Azshbir, made herself ready to nurse him, sinking down on the couch, and began to do so. At once, he stopped crying and nursed. Almost as quickly, her eyelids drifted close and she slept.

"Lasaira," Shantee asked, "do you know where any food we can have is?"

"Yes. We saved some for you. Right over there," Lasaira responded, and pointed.

"At least," Kira sobbed, "Kellyth doesn't give me as much trouble about this as Mom does."

Shaelene stalked off. "Kgarjin and Marlekk, do you want to come with me?"

"No!" said Marlekk. "We want to play with the dragons!" Kgarjin and Marlekk said in unison.

Azshbir wondered how they could have so much energy. He knew they did not work as hard as the adults, but they did work. He also knew that the years of his imprisonment had worn on both him and Neah'ra. He inched off the couch, lay down on the floor, and almost instantly fell asleep. He would have wanted to sleep on the bed, but he was too tired and exhausted and so, apparently, was Neah'ra.

When Azshbir woke in the morning, the first thing he noticed was that he was stiff and sore. Instead of alleviating his pains, he ached worse. Sitting up, the next thing he noticed was that Neah'ra was not on the couch. It took him a few moments to convince himself to get up, and when he did, he walked through the semi-darkness to the room in which they usually slept. The large house was beginning to fall apart. Beams were rotting. He did not know how he would manage to repair it. Marlekk was still a boy, though he was becoming a young man. Though they lived in poverty, unable to satisfy their cravings, rarely able to get meat and low on such things as salt, they lived in a run-down mansion.

Neah'ra still slept. She was cuddling his son while he nursed. The twins, Reilia and Della, lay next to her. He thought she was pregnant again.

Neah'ra believed this was her family inheritance, the Katalonga Farms. In that moment, his thoughts flashed back to Darnize, to Daffron, to their other sons and daughters. He wondered if any of them were still alive. A lump forming in his throat, he wondered if some of them had been killed by Hasseleighton for their fierce devotion to Ephezoa... or if they had turned from Ephezoa before the end. He wondered if any of them were People of the Promise. He knew some of Neah'ra's siblings had been interested, at the very least.

O Creator, forgive me, he thought. Still exhausted, he walked across the room and lay down on the bed. *Please, don't let Shantee and Kira act like I have. Don't let them shame their calling and their words by acting in an unworthy manner. Like I did, they have started out well. Don't let them stand in the way of those to whom they tell of Your Promise, like I stood in the way of Darnize and, possibly, others of the Katalonga family.*

Sleep tugged at him, keeping him from considering the similarities and differences between Kira and Shantee's lives and his own.

#69
Swamp of Disappointment

A couple weeks later, Arendellie was in Ebrin for her yearly visit. She had scarcely spoken to Dorene for years, but it suddenly occurred to her that Dorene had been her friend and that, as she had somehow changed, Dorene could change as well. Maybe, Dorene was even now ready to change. It had been a long time. *O Creator, please don't let Vanesh do the same thing I did... or worse.* Though her relationship with Vanesh had not begun in love, she loved him now.

Asking her maids to wait, she walked down the street and up to the door of Dorene's house. She knocked. A girl, about ten years old, answered the door. She appeared startled. "The Queen... Your majesty... what would your majesty like?"

"I presume you are Dorene's daughter?" asked Arendellie. *How come I ever consented to become princess and then queen?* she wondered. *It makes relating to people so difficult.* But, she had been a wretched fool back then. She remembered calling Kathreen a fool.

"Yes," the girl said, obviously very nervous, even scared.

Arendellie did not know how to help. "It's okay," she said. "I and your mom used to be friends. I just want to see her."

The girl nodded, but other than that she could have been stone. She trembled a little.

Arendellie tried to sound reassuring, but she had no idea how to do so. It struck her that she did not even know her own sons, Liesam and Aroch. "Can you go get your mom? If she doesn't mind, I'll come inside."

The girl's jaw shook as she said, "You can come inside." She turned and, seemingly, fled. Arendellie turned to her maids and told them to wait until she returned. If they wanted, they could go and amuse themselves. Then, she stepped inside and closed the door behind her. Gathering up her long peach skirts, she found the table, sat down on a chair, and waited. She wondered what the young girl was doing in the house, until she heard a toddler cry.

Just then, Dorene appeared, coming in through the back door. She had changed in the years since Arendellie had last seen her, but she was still recognizable. Keeping her eyes down, she approached Arendellie. "I am honored that you have come to visit me," she said, "but why should the great Queen wish to visit someone such as myself?"

Arendellie's mind flashed back to the way Kathreen had related to her, actually rebuking her for her decision. But, Dorene was not like Kathreen. Arendellie did not know what to say to get her to relate to her in a less deferential way. "I have news for you," she said.

Dorene still did not look up. Arendellie thought she was afraid of her. "What news, your majesty?" she said.

"The Creator is real. Life and Kaarathlon will eventually wear thin, and we will all stand before Him. The only refuge from the torture of His intolerable light is in the Promise. Yes, I don't understand it, but that is how it is." She knew that

Dorene wanted to interrupt, but dared not do so. She stopped speaking.

When Dorene still did not speak, Arendellie said, "Speak your mind. Don't be afraid. I have no intentions of– I don't know what."

Dorene still struggled. "I don't understand," she finally said. "What Promise is your majesty speaking of? The Promise revealed to the Lords of Light, or the Promise Kathreen and Mirla spoke of?"

"The Creator alone is Lord of Light," said Arendellie. "I am referring to the same Promise of which Kathreen and Mirla spoke."

Again, Dorene was silent for a long time. "Sit," said Arendellie. "We're friends. Forget that I'm queen."

Hesitantly, Dorene sat. At last, she said, "How? Was your majesty not chosen by the Lord Grale to be the wife of his nephew?" She stopped, not as if she had no more to say, but as if she were afraid.

"Grale Casarion was just a man. A wizard and Dragon Keeper, but a man nevertheless," said Arendellie. "That does not shock you, Dorene, does it? You never *really* believed the stuff, did you?" she asked.

Dorene shook her head slowly. "So, pardon me, your majesty, but you think that death should not be taken seriously, but the end of Kaarathlon should be?"

"Call me Arendellie," said Arendellie. "I don't see any difference between death and the end of Kaarathlon."

Arendellie could not see Dorene's face very well because she kept her head bowed, but she thought she looked confused. Finally, she said, "What is the position of the Lords of Light on this?"

Arendellie thought she knew what Dorene meant. "They're still torturing People of the Promise. As far as I know, they don't know I believe the Promise. But, Dorene," she said with real earnestness, "it's *real.* The Creator is so real that His light simply *must* burn through Kaarathlon. Kaarathlon *cannot* last. None of it. Not the good, or the bad. You probably haven't seen, but I have. He is terrible! He is true! We *need* the Promise. I still don't understand how the Promise solves the problem of the fact that we simply aren't the kind of beings that can endure the Creator– can endure *Reality*– but, I know that it does– somehow. Please! Please, at least consider what I am saying." She wondered if giving Dorene the scroll would help. But, she needed the scroll. And, how could she have a copy made? Besides, she had left the scroll in the palace. If she were to give it to Dorene, she could not do so now.

Somehow, that broke down the wall between her and Dorene. "You're scaring me, Arendellie," she said. "I can't."

"Can't even consider that this might be true? It makes all the difference in the world! Besides this, *nothing* matters, and I mean *nothing.*"

Dorene buried her head in her hands. "I never thought the day would come…" she said. Finally, "What do you mean, your majesty?" she asked.

Arendellie could not think of any way to say it. "Exactly what I said," she said.

For the first time, Dorene turned and looked her straight in the eye. "Is it worth it?" she said.

"Thousands have lived and died without regretting it." Arendellie wished Dorene could know Kyil. She would never forget the image of that young woman looking up at the sky, and saying that she certainly liked all the pleasures of life outside the prison, but the Promise was worth so much to her, was so real to her, was so good that she would cling to it, even if it meant suffering in the dungeons without end.

"Is it worth it to you?" Dorene asked.

"Yes," said Arendellie, a little nervously.

"Well," said Dorene, after a long, tense moment, "it isn't to me, your majesty. I have a husband and children. I have friends and family. I have a house and a farm and animals. Veance is helping her children train cows. She trains cows for everyone in the area. I even got to ride a cow not so long ago."

"You don't know that the Promise isn't worth it to you, Dorene," said Arendellie insistently. "You don't know the Creator or the Promise, so you can't know that it isn't worth it."

Dorene seemed very nervous. "Your majesty, do you mind if I go and take care of my babies? Dardar– that's my son– is hungry. I'm sorry, your majesty–"

Arendellie stood. "No, that's fine, Dorene. You can go. I don't do evil things to people. I don't insist that you treat me like you're a slave. In fact, I'd rather you didn't. We were childhood friends." Arendellie caught herself. "Go," she said, unable to think about how to relate in a caring and considerate way. She had not even tried for so many years; rather, she had learned how to be imperious, aloof, and demanding, as much as possible. She hurried towards the door and past the girl who held it open for her. She had to make sure she did not cry. Not all her slaves were trustworthy, and they must not know what she was– or what she did. She took a deep breath, trying to draw herself together and get her emotions under control. She could not pretend that she was not terribly disappointed. How she had hoped that Dorene was ready to see and change, just waiting, even if she did not know it, for someone to call her! She tried to remind herself that she and Dorene had never been close. Besides Dorene, she had had many friends in Ebrin, though none were friends like Kathreen, or Mirla– or, even, Dorene. Nonetheless, she felt swamped by disappointment. She felt like she was drowning in it. Why did it matter so much? As some of her slaves approached, she bit the inside of her cheek. *I must get myself together.*

#70
Thoughts From the Scroll

A couple years later.
Laekoorj sat down next to Brisia while she pounded roots. Several wives sorted herbs and watched their children a few paces away. "The scroll is very interesting," he said, taking a couple roots.

"Yes, it is," said Brisia. "Why?"

"Well, it's kind of confusing. The part that I really don't understand is right at the back. It talks about someone who is like a fire that consumes men like moths and is hidden by its smoke. Then, it says that this someone has been destroyed because of the speaker's deserts, and then it says that this someone has defeated all his enemies and made them his friends, that he has healed the wounded and brought everlasting day." He reached out and took another bowl, then placed his roots in it.

"I and Khiel discussed that, too. The part about how he has marched triumphant through the regions of night, how he has defeated his enemy in his own realm, death, and come forth to bring healing and daylight... That sounds a lot like the Promised One, who will conquer and reign over all things, even death," said Brisia.

"It's weird, though," said Laekoorj. "How is the Promised One like a fire that melts mountains and burns up men like moths while spreading darkness of smoke over the lands?"

Brisia stopped pounding roots for long enough to shrug. "I don't know."

Laekoorj grabbed a knife. "It sounds kind of like some of the stuff about the enemy."

"Like what?" asked Brisia. She could not recall anything like that.

"Well," said Laekoorj, beginning to cut his roots, "it talks somewhere about how the enemy will bring burning darkness of destruction and horror upon those in his power."

"Ah!" said Brisia. She remembered now. *Something a lot like this,* she thought. *'The burning flame will consume them and they will find themselves in thick darkness, never to awake from the smothering fire and the suffocating shadow.' But, that passage is talking about death. I don't remember whether it's a few lines earlier or later, that it says, 'The gates of that wretched place He will tear up and carry beyond the horizon.' There's nothing about brilliance and light associated with the enemy or death, and that stanza talks about how His radiance, the radiance that melts stones and consumes everything, is hidden by deadly darkness. Which isn't to say that I understand.* "It is odd," she said. "It talks about death as a place of horror, darkness, and torture, yet it says of the people of His Promise that they will never suffer in that place, yet we know that we all die." She shook her head. "But, then again, in some places it speaks as if the Promised One has already come and conquered death." She had had so many conversations with Khiel. She did not think she ever would understand, and she did not care about it, either.

Neither of them spoke for a while. Brisia did not look up. When she thought that maybe Laekoorj had grown bored of cutting roots, he laid the knife down and took up a pounder. "Oh," he said, "and then there's this other weird passage. It talks about how one will arise 'with wings of shadow that blot out the sun' who will 'lay waste cities with her fire' and that the 'darkness will fall when it appears that she had defeated light, but the darkness that falls will not be her shadow.' What's it talking about?" He began to pound his roots.

"It's right after some passage about the beauty of the fields and the dew glimmering in the dawn, right?" said Brisia.

"Maybe," said Laekoorj. Brisia and Khiel were known for spending the most time reading– and talking about– the scroll.

Brisia, Lalia, and Khiel were all sitting down together. After a little while, Khiel asked, "Have you noticed that Laekoorj comes over to talk and work with you almost every day?"

Brisia shrugged. "Why should I care?" she asked.

"He's treating you the same way he used to treat me. Right down to the cutting roots!"

Brisia remembered. It had happened many times, but that was the time that she had asked Khiel what it was about, and Khiel had explained that she was not interested in marrying him– that she felt the touch or call of something else. Now, Laekoorj had turned his attentions to her.

Lalia, however, did not understand. "What do you mean? How did Laekoorj used to treat you, Khiel?"

"He was interested in marrying me," said Khiel.

"So, now he's interested in marrying my sister– you?" asked Lalia.

Brisia blushed. Khiel nodded. "It would appear so."

Lalia giggled. "Are you going to marry him?" she asked.

Khiel's hands flew up to her head. Brisia looked away. "I haven't thought about it," she said.

Lalia started bouncing– even sitting with her legs folded underneath her. "You'd get to have babies!" she said. "And, I would have nieces or nephews!"

Khiel and Brisia laughed. Khiel wondered if Laekoorj had overheard her telling Brisia that she would have no problem with it if she decided to marry him– after all, though she had not said this then, it was Brisia's choice to make. Or was it just that it was obvious that she herself had no interest, and Brisia was the only other girl-becoming-young woman around?

"Actually," said Khiel, "I heard Adaria discussing with Senise that Laekoorj is complaining that you are even more rock-like than I am."

"Why didn't she just tell me?" asked Brisia. "She knows she could!"

"You're funny, Brisia," said Khiel. "Do you even care? Maybe, she's thinking about whether or not she should tell you. Or, maybe it would never occur to her to tell you. Let Laekoorj tell you himself!"

Brisia shrugged. "I'm done talking about Laekoorj. Though, he does like to talk about things he reads in the scroll."

"Like what?" asked Lalia. Khiel echoed her.

"Well, today he talked about how strange it is that the last poem in the scroll describes a person who appears to be the Promised One as a fire so bright it melts mountains and consumes men, but is covered in darkness and smoke," said Brisia.

"Oh. What did he have to say about it?" asked Khiel.

"Well, he said that the enemy or death is also described as a fire that brings darkness. But, I was thinking, I don't remember any place where death is described as bright or attributed with the power to melt the world," said Brisia.

"I don't remember any parts like those either," said Lalia.

"There aren't any," said Khiel. "Light belongs to the Creator. It is said that He will destroy Kaarathlon with His bright fire, but in other places it is said that He will re-make Kaarathlon with light. That is why it is such a blasphemy that the Council of Wizards call themselves by the name that they do, for the Lord of Light is the Creator."

"I'd forgotten that!" said Brisia.

"Kathreen told us, and only once, maybe twice. I think it made her sick."

Brisia shook her head. "I still miss Mom, sometimes," she said. "I'm glad the Creator gave me you."

Khiel smiled sadly. "Am I like Mirla?" she asked.

"It was a long time ago," said Brisia. Dropping her eyes, she said, "Maybe, next time Laekoorj comes by, I should ask him about my brother. We haven't talked in months."

Lalia looked confused for a moment. Then, she said, "Oh, I'd forgotten we have a brother!"

"I'm also glad the Creator gave me Adaria." Softly, she said, "It's just... I remember Mom telling me she'd seen the Creator in a way she hadn't seen Him before, and she knew everything would be all right. He would take care of me." Her eyes began to pool with tears. "And, then, I remember pestering you to tell me what you meant by happy." Her voice dropping even lower, she said, "Mom was much happier than Dad, that I can remember. But, we had so many problems... so much fighting... so much unhappiness. That's why you are Lalia Joy. Because when you were born, it seemed to me that my parents would forget their worries and fears in joy over you." Sometimes, Brisia hardly felt like Lalia was her sister. She had grown up so differently. She had never known Mom. Neither had she known the pain and grief of the loss of both their parents... or of Dad and Dormik. She was, however, attached to Lalia, always trying to be with her and guide her and teach her. Theirs was not a normal sibling relationship, though they did fight now and then. Worse, Nahiza and Kizyia often felt left out, like Lalia was her favorite, and until recently it did not even begin to make sense to them that it was because Lalia was her sister, and they were not. They had many brothers and sisters; Brisia always lost count how many. In fact, she was still not sure they got it at all.

In fact, Brisia thought, *perhaps I should try to talk to Dormik, now. I am much older, and I know much more. At least, I know how to say more. And, it's been so long...*

#71
A Cup of Water

Very early in the morning, Brisia stepped in Dormik's way. She had learned from Adaria's husband, Kalar, that the young man tended to avoid interactions as much as possible. "Hello, this morning," she said. She felt so awkward. It had taken days for her to get herself to do this. She hardly felt like she knew her brother anymore, and the last they had interacted a lot he made fun of and harassed her at every opportunity. She still remembered how he had mocked her for calling the Creator bigger than size.

"Good morning," said Dormik. "You've grown quite beautiful."

For some reason, Brisia flinched. "That's not what I wanted to talk to you about," she said. Her mouth felt dry.

"Well, what did you want to talk about?" said Dormik, disdainfully. She felt tears pushing at the backs of her eyeballs.

"The Creator. The Pr-pr-pr-pr-promise. How you are doing." She had never felt so embarrassed in her life– and talking to her own brother.

"Why are you still so interested in that?" asked Dormik, mockingly. "You do know," he said, with an air of arrogance, "that it never did anyone any good."

"Mom said 'The Creator does all things well.' She said that specifically to you."

"Well," said Dormik, as if he might spit, "that might be, if He never does anything."

Suddenly, inexplicably, Brisia began to cry. "Why are you becoming so evil!" she sobbed.

"Excuse me," said Dormik, and stepped past her.

Brisia collapsed on the ground and rocked back and forth, crying. She did not even remember Dormik. He had become so much more hateful, so much more bitter, that she scarcely even recognized his tone of voice. He seemed alien. Suddenly, possessed by some impulse, Brisia got to her feet and ran after him. She guessed which way he went and ran as hard as she could, quickly getting a stitch in her side. He did not notice until she was within fifteen paces of him, at which point he turned around and said, "Brisia, leave me alone."

"Do not kill! Do not kill them!" she pleaded.

Dormik turned and continued on his way. Brisia continued to cry. How was it? How was it that she knew the Creator and loved Him, while Dormik hated? Why did everything that happened in her life eventually help her to see and love the Creator, to see that all He gives is best, while Dormik grew more and more hateful and bitter toward everyone and everything? Why did he insist on following in his father's footsteps, ignoring the Creator and bringing death upon his own head?

That was where Laekoorj found her, hours later. Apparently, he did not see her and decided to go looking for her. He learned that she had intended to confront Dormik, and he knew that Dormik often took this trail into the jungles to go hunting. He did not expect to find her, but he had looked everywhere else of which anyone could think. Standing several paces away, he asked, "Brisia?"

She was not crying audibly, though she was still shaken by sobs, but she scarcely noticed his voice.

"Brisia?" he asked again, louder this time. "What is wrong?"

Brisia straightened, incidentally noticing that her muscles were sore and cramped. "Dormik," she said, her voice hoarse from crying. "He hates the Creator."

"He told you so?" Laekoorj asked, surprised. Dormik never talked about the Creator at all.

"He suggested that He never does anything. And, I don't know him. I think he hates me."

Laekoorj did not know what to do or say. He would have liked to take her in his arms and kiss her, but he knew he could not do that. It would be taking advantage of her vulnerability. In fact, the fact that he had gone looking for her alone, without asking someone else to go with him, would be looked down upon. He wondered briefly if he had neglected to do so on purpose.

"Let's go back," he said, trying to speak as kindly as possible. "Perhaps, you would like to talk to Adaria or Khiel."

In fact, they were met by Sirifa, whose hair was now completely gray and whose face bore the marks of age. It had been a complete surprise when she had become pregnant with the twins, Nahiza and Kizyia, and now she was over sixty. When Kathreen and Adaria returned with Dormik, Brisia, and the infant Lalia, they had given thanks. Now, she looked at Laekoorj. "Did you just happen to run across Brisia?" she asked, a note of rebuke in her voice.

"Yeah, more or less," said Laekoorj which, he felt, was, more or less, true. He had certainly not *expected* to find Brisia that far down Dormik's favorite trail.

"Laekoorj!" she said, and he ducked his head and walked away.

"Brisia!" she said, and embraced the girl. After a long embrace, they stepped apart. She had seen Brisia's puffy eyes and tear-streaked mud-stained face, and asked, "What happened?"

"I tried to talk to Dormik," she said, and sat down. "He's so hateful. And, I don't know why. I don't know why I know the Creator and love Him, and all Dormik knows is hate." She stopped, but Sirifa was silent, waiting for her to go on. She would have cried again, if she had not cried, on and off, for several hours. After a while, she said, "Mom and Dad were kind of similar. Mom knew the Creator, and Dad worried and feared and fought with her. Of course, Dad didn't hate anybody, that I know of. He just didn't really care about the Creator, and he wanted to make sure what happened wouldn't happen."

Brisia's sentence was slightly confusing, but Sirifa thought she understood what she was saying.

After a while, Brisia spoke again. "I don't know why Dormik hates so much. And, I don't know why I'm different."

"I think," said Sirifa slowly, "that you're different because you know the Creator, and he does not."

"Why?" asked Brisia. Then, before Sirifa could answer, she added, "He's becoming *evil!*"

Sirifa knew about Brisia's experience when she had seen the meaning of evil in what humans and dragons had done to the good world made by the Creator. Brisia repeated again, "Why? How? It's not because different things happened to us! Eventually, the Creator used it all to show me how good He is." Her face lit up. "How very big and compassionate to us He is!" She paused for a moment, contemplating that vision. Then, she said, "But, Dormik? The same things– He's my brother! And, he just grows more hateful and bitter and evil as he grows." She buried her head in her hands and rocked back and forth. "I don't know why there's so much evil. *Evil!*"

Sirifa waited. She did not think that anything she could say would help. Nahiza walked by. "Is Brisia crying?" she asked.

"Uh-huh," said Sirifa.

"What about?"

"I don't think it will help if I tell you."

"How long has she been crying for?"

"I don't know," said Sirifa.

"I will get her some water!" announced Nahiza.

When Nahiza returned with the water, Brisia drank it all. She had known she was thirsty, and the water was *so* good. "Thank You," she breathed with delight, and handed the cup back to Nahiza. "Thanks," she said.

Nahiza beamed. "You're welcome," she responded. "Would you like more?"

"Yes, I would," said Brisia. "Thank you very much."

When Nahiza returned, Brisia again drank all the water and thanked her. Too late, she asked, "Mom, would you like some?" Nahiza waited.

"No, thanks. I'm fine," said Sirifa. Nahiza sat down several feet away, and Sirifa asked Brisia, "Are you all right, now?"

"All right in what way?" asked Brisia. She looked past Sirifa and said, "Thanks a lot, Nahiza." The water that Nahiza brought had been such a reminder of the Creator's goodness with which He had made Kaarathlon, the goodness that was still visible in Kaarathlon and sometimes seemed to shock her with its intensity, even though Kaarathlon was so marred by evil. How? How was it possible, to have such good and such evil so close? "But," she said, "I don't want to keep you..."

"No, it's okay," said Sirifa. For one thing, things were no longer as hard as they were at first. They were not a man and a woman figuring out how to live and provide for and raise children alone in the mountains. They were more like a small village, now. Staring off into the distance, she asked, "What was Laekoorj doing?"

Brisia shrugged. She looked down at her hands. So much good, and so much evil. They were both present in this world. Even a cup of water was so good, brought such relief, and more, sheer pleasure. Good abounded. It was far more plentiful than evil. Was it possible that even in the darkest, most horrific, most evil places in Kaarathlon there was almost incomparably more goodness than evil? Good was natural– was good. Evil did not belong– was *evil.* That was why it was so horrifying. And, if that was so, what must the deepest dungeons of death, reserved for the Creator's enemies, deprived of goodness, be? Brisia shuddered, just thinking about it.

"Are you okay?" asked Sirifa. Nahiza said something Brisia did not quite hear.

"Uh," said Brisia, not quite understanding. "Uh, yeah, umm, just, something I don't really... Never mind." *How horrible must it be to be evil?* she thought, pitying Dormik and all others who chose to be evil. *O my Creator, how little I understand. How I long for when with our eyes we shall see.* She shook her head, oblivious to the fact that Sirifa and Nahiza were still present. *O Creator, how is it that You allow such evil, such ruin, such horror, for it is so evil because it ruins the goodness of what You have made. How can You permit it? How is it, that You do all things, even this, well, and make this best? It's so evil,* EVIL, *but I know You would know that far better than I. You made it all. This is Your creation. It's Your goodness, Your work. And You are far better than I. You know far more. You see the ruin, the destruction, the evil so much more completely. O my Creator...*

#72
Singer

Ellason stood on the path leading up to the farmhouse. She was surrounded by a contingent of soldiers. Motioning with her hand, she said, "Take them."

Azshbir reacted quicker than thought or lightning. He threw his weight against the door, pushing it open, and grabbed a kitchen knife. It was not the best weapon, but it would have to do. In the terror and necessity of the moment, he moved almost as if uninjured. He hurled himself down from the steps leading up to the door and upon one of the soldiers going around the house. The man crumpled to the ground under his weight, and he sliced across the hand that held the sword.

Other soldiers bore down on Azshbir. He struggled, thrusting the knife at them, hoping to buy whatever time he could, trusting that Neah'ra would know what to do. Ellason called, "Remember the Queen's orders: do not kill them!"

Pottery crashed around them. One of the men screamed. He could hear Shaelene screaming inarticulately and angrily, as she threw whatever came to hand. One of the men grappling with him grunted and flinched, but he was already face-down on the ground, his hands and feet being tied, as much as he struggled to kick, hit, and flail. "Shaelene," he heard Neah'ra say with quiet urgency, "don't hurt Azshbir." He heard her only because she was his own wife; he later discovered that others had said things much more loudly that he never heard. *Why didn't you run?* he thought. *Why didn't you run and* GO! But, there was nothing he could do.

It was not long before they were all bound, on the ground. Azshbir looked around. It seemed that he and Neah'ra, Shaelene, Shantee, Kira, and Marlekk were all here, bound. Ellason was speaking to the soldiers. "Four of you stay with me. The rest of you, go and find the others."

Neah'ra managed to sit up. She turned her head as far around as she could, and motioned with it. Azshbir wondered what she was trying to say. He was pretty sure the gesture was not meant for him. He rolled over, and saw a flicker of motion in the underbrush in the approximate direction of her nod. He wondered if some of their children were there.

Ellason noticed, too. She took a few long strides to where Neah'ra sat. "What were you doing?" she asked.

Neah'ra did not answer. Ellason slapped her. Azshbir's vision flickered red and black. He felt vomit rise. He detested Ellason more than anyone else he knew.

Ellason repeated her question, or one like it, and when Neah'ra did not answer, slapped her again. Azshbir struggled against his bonds, knowing with a kind of enraged knowledge that he could break them, and found himself struggling against one of the soldiers.

Ellason rose. "Things are going to be very bad for you, you know," she said. "I'm not sure whatever possessed you to fight so hard. The Queen sent orders that you are to be taken to Anores, for her and the wizards to interrogate, and I doubt she will take kindly to the assault of her soldiers." Cold fear poured over Azshbir.

"Anyway," Ellason continued, "it might incline them to be somewhat more kindly in their treatment of you, if you will tell us where the rest of the members of your household are."

Azshbir spat, enraged by such a suggestion. "You *really* think," he said, disdainfully, "that I'm going to hand over those I love to your tortures in the mere hope that I *might* suffer a *little* less!"

The soldier restraining him slapped him. Tasting blood in his mouth, he yelled again. "Like I care!"

Neah'ra was still sitting up. "Really, Ellason," she said, "how could you do this to us? I thought you were a sister."

"That's the whole point," said Ellason, with an evil smile. "To cause as much pain as possible. I was your best friend, your most constant support. You trusted me as much as anyone. So, now, you've been betrayed, and you will never be able to trust anyone again. Can you even believe the Promise, seeing that I could act like a perfect believer of the Promise, and then torment you like this?" She shook her head. "And, you don't even know: I arranged for Razi and you, Azshbir, to be arrested. I'd hoped for you both to be executed, but Cavisto foolishly interfered with my plans." She shook her hand, amused. "Foolishly, I say, for it worked out to the furtherance of my end. I found so many more People of the Promise to have tortured and killed. My only regret was that I never succeeded in securing your death, Azshbir, but, now, I have done so!" She looked at Neah'ra's swelling belly. "How many children do you have now?" she asked.

Neah'ra did not answer Ellason's question. Instead, she said, "You're wrong. You didn't destroy us. We still trust the Creator, and we still trust one another." Her voice rose. "We will trust and risk betrayal, before we will live death!"

Azshbir bit his lip. He hurt, much more than usual. What had happened had seriously exacerbated his pains, though he had not noticed until now.

Ellason scoffed. She turned to Shantee. "Where is your dragon?" she asked.

Shantee did not speak. Azshbir wanted to close his eyes and wake up from this cruel world before it got any worse.

Ellason pressed. "It is said you are a Dragon-rider; are you one?"

My Creator! Azshbir pleaded silently, while Shantee replied, "I'm not going to tell you anything except the Promise." *O Creator! At least, please deliver Lasaira and Kgarjin and Reilia and Della and Kuthreb and Norden! My Creator! How can this be?*

Ellason was speaking. "It won't do nearly so much good as you think, not speaking to us. You will only hinder us, never stop us. We have been watching you and Kira for a long time, only waiting so that we could harm many more; of course, it took us some time to trace you here; you did do very well. But, at last, we did it. Do you know why your friends are not here, today? It is not because they were delayed by something and spared. It is because we have already arrested Lia and the others."

My Creator! Not again, if You will, and not this! I can't endure this. Why do You allow it? How many others has Ellason deceived over the years? But, You have pardoned and forgiven me. Is that why? I fail to understand. O Creator!

Hours passed. Finally, the soldiers returned. "We can find no one," they said. "We have searched everywhere."

"Very well," said Ellason. "We will take these to the prisons, and then we will call and send out a search party. What of the dragons? Have you seen any?"

"There are many marks that dragons live here, but we have seen no dragons."

A single torch, placed in a socket in the wall, burned, providing just enough light to see where someone else was. They were in separate cells with bars between. Neah'ra's stomach churned. She had never been so terrified before in her life; what if whatever tortures awaited them at the hands of the wizards were too much, and she surrendered? The thought terrified her. She tried to get comfortable. Most of all, the baby in her belly scared her! Ellason had taken her away from everyone else, and told her that the procedure was that no one would harm her until her child was born. If she surrendered and told them everything they wished to know, she could keep the child and go free. Otherwise, he or she would be taken from her. Unable to even contemplate that outcome, she had screamed, "I'll die! If you take my baby, I'll *die!*" Just thinking about it, she was drenched in cold sweat. She crawled across the cell and put her hands through the bars.

When Azshbir took Neah'ra's hands, he felt her fear. Her heart was racing, and her hands were simultaneously icy and slick with sweat. He did not know what to say. He could not ask her what was wrong. He was certain that they did not have privacy; someone was watching them, hoping to glean any information possible from anything they said or did. That was why they were all in separate cells, but all within easy ear-shot from everyone else. Unable to think of anything else to do, he took a tune he knew and quickly figured how to set the poem about the vision of the Promise to it. "My love," he said to Neah'ra, took a deep breath, and sang the first line. "Mountains melted before His face."

Neah'ra just clung to his hands. Kira took up the next line of the tune, which was sung by a female. "Rocks were shattered under His glance."

"He came down in a tornado of fire, and the smoke from it hid the radiance," sang Azshbir.

"In thick darkness and death," Shaelene and Kira sang back in high tones.

"Men were caught like a moth burning," sang Azshbir, and then Shaelene, Kira, and Neah'ra joined him for the final lines. "In the flame of His breath– dark and fiery winds, fierce and blinding."

When they finished singing the song, Neah'ra burst into tears. Azshbir's hands barely fit through the bars, so he could do little to comfort her. Besides, if the final stanzas of that poem only served to cause her to weep, what comfort could anyone offer? He was worried about the scroll. Would it be okay? Worse, he wished he had at least told everyone how to find his home. Why in all of Kaarathlon had he not taken them all there? If he had done so, they would not be here. *But,* he thought to himself, *that's not what Kathreen told me was the Creator's commission for me. 'Never hide the Promise in heart or in home,' she'd said, and if I'd done that, how would any of Kira and Shantee's friends have ever known?*

A door screeched as it was opened, and a guard entered. "You aren't supposed to sing like that," he said.

Azshbir was surprised when Shaelene responded. "We already know we aren't allowed to be Knights of the Promise, so why shouldn't we add to it by singing about the Promise?" *I hadn't known she believed the Promise!* he thought.

The guard spoke to his buddy. "It's a pity the Queen wants to interrogate them fresh," he said.

"Yep," the guard responded. "Otherwise, we could torture them, just like we do everybody else. Wonder why her majesty is so interested in these. How did they ever come to her majesty's attention?"

"Well, let's leave now," said the first guard. "There *are* things we can do, so beware."

"Mom!" said Kira as the guard left.

"I don't want to talk about it," said Shaelene. She sounded dejected. Neah'ra thought to herself that, at least, Shaelene's youngest child, Marlekk, was nearly sixteen. Reilia and Della, who were by far her oldest, were only thirteen. Kuthreb was four, Norden was almost two, and she had another in her belly. *O Creator,* she pleaded, *please deliver us.*

#73
The Deceiver

The following day, they were forced into several enclosed wagons, which were drawn by horses. Their guards kept muttering about the Queen's orders and urgency, and the lack of dragons in the land, because of that "cursed Undead Snow Queen." Kira and Neah'ra were very clear to everyone, that they did not believe in an "Undead Snow Queen," and they certainly did not believe that she had any power over those who belonged to the Promise. Azshbir smiled, listening to them, but he knew that Neah'ra was in terrible pain. Her voice was hoarse and broken, as if she had a bad sore throat, but he knew that it was induced by fear and worry. He did not know under what terrible emotional torture she had been placed, instead thinking that it was due to worry over their young sons.

The wagons rocked badly, and shook them all around. Everyone had a hard time eating. When Azshbir saw Neah'ra, which was once or twice a day for a short time which did not allow much more than a "hello" or "good day," he noticed that she was growing thinner. He worried about the child she was carrying, and knew that she must be worrying more than he was. They took to calling "Look to the Promise!" to each other whenever they saw each other. It was the only thing they could do, and nobody could think of any way to say more without a great deal more words. They all knew what the Promise meant. Those short four words were loaded with the meaning of a thousand conversations to each one of them. It was not only Azshbir, Neah'ra, Shaelene, and the three of her children, but many of those who had gathered with them, among them both Lia and Seair.

A couple weeks later, one day while Azshbir was taken out, Ellason approached him. "So," she asked, "how are you doing?"

Azshbir gritted his teeth. "Do you care?" he asked.

"The Queen cares that you are not abused before she gets a look at you. Why her majesty cares – or even knows– about you, I have no idea. She is a wonderful Queen, dedicated to wiping out whatever threatens the well-being of her people and healing all that she can. Sometimes, I think the Mighty One speaks directly to her majesty, possibly even more so than he does to the Lords of Light. After all, he chose her for his son and to be queen after him," said Ellason.

Azshbir looked up at the sky. *Creator, I failed before. I said that I forgave Darnize, and then I cursed him.*

Azshbir could not deny the command that seemed to be impressed upon him with terrible weight by the blue and white of the sky. He had asked, "Why do You allow this to be?" Was it not possible that the Creator allowed Ellason to continue her cruelty in order so that she could come to Him, as well? Azshbir bit his lip. It came again. Until Darnize hurt Neah'ra, Azshbir had not succumbed to hatred and bitterness, but Ellason had hurt Neah'ra maybe even more than her father had. So, in this way, he could, by the Creator's help, conquer where he had been beaten before. Still, how could he? The words stuck in his throat. He could not even imagine himself saying them.

"What is it?" asked Ellason. She was amazingly perceptive.

"The Creator is telling me to tell you that I–" Azshbir began, and then stopped short.

"That you what?" pressed Ellason. She did not allow her utter disdain to come across in her voice.

You deserve my obedience. Why am I having so much trouble, my Creator? I don't hate Ellason, but I can't say this for some reason and yet... I remember... I know... that because You are Yourself, I don't even want to be less than perfect... less than more than perfect... less than– is there a word? "Forgive you," said Azshbir.

Ellason collapsed in gales of laughter. She ordered the guard to take him back. *These Knights of the Promise, as they call themselves! Wasn't there some story about Azshbir shouting at Darnize that he wouldn't forgive him? But, Kira, Shantee, and Neah'ra have all told me the same thing! Hahaha!*

The Queen wanted an audience with her, about her work, Ellason presumed. She had met the Queen twice before, and envied her skin which looked like it had been rubbed with cream and her green eyes. Other than that, she thought the Queen was a lot like her. She was sure her majesty would be quite capable of deceiving people to achieve her ends; in fact, who knew everything the Queen did? Maybe, her majesty did do the same things she herself did. After the destruction of those who had met with Cavisto, Ellason had set her sights on others. She infiltrated their groups, often becoming an honored figure whom everyone believed to be farther along in the Creator's service than most. Then, she betrayed them, turning them over to be killed, and sometimes allowing a few to escape, to wander about distraught, afraid to trust anyone, tormented by loneliness and mistrust. She watched them, and noted that this seemed to be a far greater torture than death. She took such delight in ruining their lives and happiness. They were so miserable, haunted by guilt, afraid to share, afraid to trust. Or most of them. Now and then, someone did not seem so affected, but continued to share the Promise with everyone. Then, she would arrange to have them arrested and killed in such a way that they would think that someone whom they thought was almost ready to or had accepted the Promise had betrayed them. It was so much fun: both, the effort and concentration that it required, and the success, the misery, that it produced.

She had not, however, arranged for Razi and Azshbir's arrest. She had made that up, thinking that it might cause them even deeper pain and that they would believe it. As well as she could remember, she had believed the Promise then. Alone, without anyone to guide her, all her friends mocking her as Neah'ra's friends had mocked Neah'ra, Ellason had come to conclusions very similar to Azshbir's, which he had taught Neah'ra and told everyone who would listen. In fact, his appearance had made her bolder in the sharing of her own beliefs. Then, she was not really sure what had happened, but she had decided to arrange for the arrest of all the People of the Promise she knew by Hasseleighton. It had given her such a thrill.

Now, she positively glowed over her success. Every time something thwarted her plan, it turned out, sooner or later, to the furtherance of her goals, by her own cunning and attentiveness. She *had* tried to secure Azshbir's execution, but the Hasseleighton officials were over-worked and would not listen to her for long. They told her they had their orders, and that she made no sense. Now, she was doing this! She had even come to the attention of Queen Arendellie Casarion. It seemed that all that was said about the Creator was coming true about her! She did not believe anything, but if she had, she would have believed that she was destined to be the Lady of the World, the female counterpart to Lord Grale Casarion. Of course, she did not *dis*believe anything either. She did not even disbelieve in the Creator or the Promise. She was so exhilarated by her success, though, that she did not seem to need to eat.

Ellason would have liked to destroy the Queen, but she did not think she would be able to do so. The Queen was in a position far above her. She was as high as she was because of her majesty's favor, and she knew that her majesty could have her killed as easily as she could have People of the Promise killed– and no one would ask questions. She had meant what she said when she said there was no explanation for the things her majesty knew, so it might conceivably be dangerous to even envy her. She knew, of course, that few others shared her perceptions of her majesty. She was revered and honored, but much of the court thought that she was an ordinary woman, made to delight her husband and to have children, who had grandiose ambitions and was a little of a fool. Of course, no one said so. Everyone spoke of her majesty with respect and honor, but Ellason had always had a very keen perception of others. She also had immense control over how others perceived her. She reveled in her control. She was afraid, though, that the Queen Casarion had much the same powers; in fact, she was almost certain that she did. She was afraid that her majesty saw through her completely, in which case it would, indeed, be very dangerous to envy her.

She looked at the dingy green cloth on her sleeve. She liked beauty. She envied the Queen's beauty– her majesty was genuinely believed to be, possibly, the most beautiful woman in Camil; no one knew about other lands, or could. She did not like wearing dirty or poor clothes, but she knew that travel would quickly ruin anything she wore. She had already planned out what she would wear for her audience with her majesty. She would wear that brilliant blue dress, with the white and gold trim, and a headscarf of the same bright blue, overlaid with lace. It was *almost* as good as anything her majesty had.

#74
Prisoners

Arendellie stuck out her tongue at her coming-two years-old daughter, whom she had decided to name Kyil Kathreen, after her friends. She had chosen the names because they embodied her dream for her daughter; she would like her daughter to be a person like Kyil and Kathreen, not one who would fall into the pits she had fallen into or, still worse, be like Ellason. As far as she could tell, Vanesh had forgotten that Kyil was the name of one of the People of the Promise she had known; otherwise, she was sure, he would never have allowed it, not out of hatred for them but out of irritation at and worry over her. Kathreen, she was sure he had not forgotten, since no one would forget Kathreen, but it was a name from her hometown; in fact, she had had a great-aunt named Kathreen. She had been worried when she bore a girl that Vanesh would be upset, but he had taken an immediate liking to his daughter. She had simply asked if she could name her Kyil Kathreen, and he had said, "Name her whatever you want." She was getting to know her sons, Liesam and Aroch, and was beginning to tell them about the Creator. Daily, she was painfully reminded of her failures. Liesam, the crown prince and a handsome and intelligent young man who had inherited her green eyes, was more than fifteen years old, and well-educated in the lore of the new kingdom. She struggled to tell him about the Creator; he mocked the idea and argued with her about its strangeness. Though she had seen him intermittently over the years, he did not really know her as his mother, and she was afraid that he would one day betray her, when he grew tired of arguing with her and testing his skills. Aroch was younger, being only five, and she thought she could build a relationship with him.

Alitholiel entered the room. "Your majesty," she said, "Ellason is here for you."

"Thank you," said Arendellie. "Get someone to care for Kyil." She rose, and let Kathreen crawl around while she preened her appearance. When the maid came, she was ready. "Just play with her," she told her, and walked to the waiting room, where Ellason would be waiting for her.

Ellason curtsied deeply. "Greetings, your majesty."

Arendellie knew what Ellason was. There were many such, whom she used, and to whom she gave the impression, without ever saying so, that she was such as they, though, out of all those she knew, only Ellason had perfected the art of deceit so horribly. "Have you brought the prisoners I asked for?"

"Yes, Queen. They are here, and they are all in good shape, as your majesty commanded."

"I would like to see them, Ellason. Then, we will discuss what I would like next," said Arendellie.

"Very well, your majesty," said Ellason, curtsying again.

Good shape? thought Arendellie, when she saw the pregnant woman. Her belly was swelling, but she looked dangerously thin. Entering the cell, alone, she said,

"I'll get you a nice meal, tonight. And, I'm not going to do anything bad to any of you."

"Honestly?" Neah'ra asked. "Aren't you the Queen? I thought you wanted to interrogate and torture us."

Arendellie sat down. "I tell Ellason I want to see you and interrogate you, and she makes up the rest. I think she actually thinks I said it. No, Ellason has been watching you. I sent orders to have you all arrested now and taken to me, in order to disrupt Ellason's plans."

"You could be a liar," said Neah'ra.

"I could be," agreed Arendellie. "But, if there's anything that isn't right, tell me. I'm going to have you, Azshbir, and your children quartered together. Once I have things arranged, you and many other People of the Promise I have been watching and arranging will be placed on a ship, to leave Camil and find other lands. I, myself, am one of the People of the Promise."

Arendellie found that it was hard to talk with any of the group. They did not trust her, and refused to tell her anything. That night, she had them all transferred to a wing of the castle connected to her quarters over which she and Vanesh had exclusive control, and feasted royally. When she had a moment alone she laughed to herself. She would tell everyone that she had given them to the Undead Snow Queen, and no one would ask any more questions. Of course, Vanesh would know the truth, or most of it.

She knew something was wrong, though. She was almost certain there were more people. Watching them, when they were altogether, she knew that Azshbir and Neah'ra's children were not present. The next day, while she dined with Ellason, she asked her about it.

"There are more. We know that Azshbir and Neah'ra have at least three children who would be in their teens by now, and that Shaelene has another daughter. I have a search party looking for them. They will be sent here immediately upon being found. I hope that satisfies you, your majesty."

Arendellie was not satisfied. "I want you to go back and ensure that they are found. Have search parties sent out from all cities in the area. They must be found, if I am to be able to do what I am planning. Moreover, you must make sure that everyone involved understands that, by royal order of the Queen, no one is to be touched until I get a look at them and decide how best to proceed."

Ellason was cringing. "Yes, your majesty. I'm sorry, your majesty. Please pardon me, your majesty."

"I will write and seal the mandate," said Arendellie. She called to a slave passing by, "Get me letter-paper and an inkstand!"

The slave returned, and she wrote as follows:

"Queen Arendellie Casarion, to the prefects of the cities,

"By royal order, give Ellason Zaele as many search-parties as her judgment deems fit, to search for the children of Azshbir and Neah'ra Nan-reem and

Shaelene. Make sure that you in no way harm any of them, but send them at once to me in Anores. If you can enlist any Dragon-riders to take them, do so, and I will pay whatever price the dragons and their riders set."

Arendellie turned to the slave and said, "Take this to my scribe and have five copies made. Then, bring them back to me and I will sign them."

Ellason saw what Arendellie wrote and took in a breath. How she would love to have that kind of power! Arendellie noticed. She knew that Ellason envied her for both her beauty and her power. Though she was forty years old, she had scarcely aged at all. She despised Ellason's life-style. Some day, when there was nothing more for her to do, and nothing for her to lose, at least for others, she would tell Ellason what she really was, and what Ellason was. She did not think it would do any good, since Ellason knew as much as anyone about the Promise, but Ellason so disgusted her, she would have to do it sometime. She fixed Ellason with her stare, and saw the woman flinch. Fear glittered in her eyes.

Arendellie dropped her hand on the table. It was still early in the morning. Her thoughts turned to all the various operations she was overseeing. On top of it all, in addition to finally trying to be a mother to her three children, she had to entertain Vanesh. He was taking her to a feast with him tonight. It was all more than she could handle. She would have liked to get rid of the snitches among her slaves, and knew she could do so, but she was almost certain that, if she did so, the Council would employ other snitches and spies. It was better to know who was a spy and be able to control one's interactions with her to some extent. She kept everything away from the snitches as much as possible, even what she did with Ellason, even things that could not possibly do harm; that way, she would keep suspicions down about the things she really wanted to keep safe, and she would have a measurement of how successful she was at hiding what she did; if something slipped, chances were that it would not be something sensitive, and she would be able to make corrections. Also, that way, she kept the Council of Wizards under the impressions that she was just another foolish, beautiful woman for as long as possible.

She was happy when, several days after Ellason left, she saw that Neah'ra, Azshbir's wife, had given birth to a healthy, if somewhat small, baby girl. She brought her daughter, Kyil Kathreen, to them several days later, to watch over and play with. Even though they did not trust her, she found their company refreshing, and she loved how free they were about the Promise, a privilege which, she regretted, she could not have, at least not now.

The next day, she brought her scroll, and Inshara, Aki'lam, and Kalie with her. When she started reading from the scroll, a poem about the stars and moon bowing before the Chosen One of the Creator, she saw a spark in the eyes of her listeners. When she finished reading the poem, Azshbir asked her, "Who gave you that scroll?"

"Kathreen Alarion did. The last time I ever saw or heard of her," answered Arendellie.

She saw that they did not really understand that. A young woman named Kira asked, slowly, "Did you see Kathreen before that time?"

"I and Kathreen grew up together, hard to believe as that might sound. She was my best friend. I named my daughter after her," said Arendellie.

"Then," said Azshbir, "you are Arendellie." "How did it happen?" asked Neah'ra.

Suddenly, it seemed that they trusted her. They asked her so many questions, and she had to go, for the sake of not raising suspicions, before she could answer half of them. They made her so ashamed. She only managed to tell them of how she had become the bride of Prince Vanesh, instead of marrying Neshekh Dasaran, and someone suggested that, perhaps, that was the Creator's way of rescuing Neshekh from the heartbreak of having her as his wife. She learned that they had had a scroll identical to the one she had, also given them by Kathreen Alarion shortly before she left Camil, and that they wanted to keep it. She promised to come back the next day, if she could without raising suspicions. Before she left, Azshbir told her that they had named their daughter Nourdë. They told her about the missing members of their family. "They have Shantee and Kira's dragons with them, so they will probably survive," they said.

For some reason, Arendellie did not tell them that she was looking for their children and friends.

#75
Secret Things

Laekoorj sat down next to Brisia while she read from the scroll, reading it along with her. "Can you go to the back?" he asked.

"Sure," she said. She unrolled it and spread it out. "Is that what you were looking for?"

"I thought I remembered something like that," he said, and then read, "'the vision revealed by the Creator to Azshbir Nan-reem, son of Hoobit and Sirifa and husband of Neah'ra, in the prisons of Ephezoa after he had worried that he did not belong to the Promise because of his utter failure.'

"So," he continued, "Azshbir, my oldest brother, wrote this, and he was alive not long ago. I don't remember him."

Brisia knew that Adaria remembered him well. "Adaria," she called, "come over here!"

Slowly, Adaria stood, carrying her youngest child, who was nursing. Laekoorj looked up from the scroll. "Look at this!" he said. "It's right before the poem about the one whose face melts mountains and shatters rocks, who gave only life but 'bore my plague while creation writhed,' who walked through death, defeated His enemy in his own stronghold, and returned in victory to heal and give light. It says, 'the vision revealed by the Creator to Azshbir Nan-reem, son of Hoobit and Sirifa and husband of Neah'ra, in the prisons of Ephezoa after he had worried that he did not belong to the Promise because of his utter failure.'"

Adaria sat down. "So, Azshbir is alive, or was alive not long ago, and he wrote this." Her face glowed, and tears trickled from her eyes. "I'm so proud of him! Or, should I say, glad for him?" She bent forward, as well as she could while nursing her four-month-old, and read it again. "Ah!" she said. "So, he married a girl, and he was imprisoned by Ephezoa? Ephezoa? Well, they were so proud of their freedoms, but Kathreen *did* warn us that they could not be trusted." Her shoulders slumped. "Did he write this in prison? It doesn't say. But, the vision was shown him in prison. I wonder what has happened to him, for Ephezoa is no more." She sucked her breath in, through her teeth, over her lips. "'His utter failure.' I wonder what that refers to. Hmm. These scrolls are strange. We know he never touched this scroll, and yet his words are here. Kalar! Dad! Would you come look at this?"

"Your dad is getting old," said Brisia.

"Yes, our parents are old," said Laekoorj.

"I will miss your mom when she dies," said Brisia.

Kalar stood over them. "Who are we talking about dying?" he asked.

"Oh, Brisia is just saying that she'll miss our mom when she dies," said Adaria. "Come, look at this." She took the scroll from Laekoorj and showed it to her husband.

"Why didn't any of us notice it before? It was there, wasn't it?" mused Kalar.

"Khiel would know," said Brisia and Adaria, together.

Running ahead of Hoobit, Khiel asked, "Why? What is it?" and plopped herself on the ground.

Kalar held the scroll towards her and Hoobit. "Was the title, about Azshbir and when he wrote it, there before?" Adaria said.

"Uh," said Khiel, looking at it, "yeah, I think so. Why wouldn't it be?" she sounded confused.

"Because," said Brisia, "Azshbir is their oldest brother."

"Oh," said Khiel. "I don't think I noticed. I mean, I knew Hoobit is their dad's name, and Sirifa their mom's, but they're hardly ever called that, so I don't think I noticed. Since, I'm not really sure I've ever heard of Azshbir…" She looked embarrassed. "I'm sorry."

"It's okay. It's not your fault, and it didn't hurt anyone," said Hoobit. "Anyway, what is it?"

"This was written, apparently, by Azshbir," said Adaria, pointing to the end of the scroll. "It's a vision he had while in a prison in Ephezoa after a failure he doesn't tell us about."

"Perhaps," said Khiel, "he doesn't tell us about it because we don't need to know it. It might not help us any to know it." She looked at Brisia.

Brisia knew what Khiel was talking about. After her encounter with the ugliness of the evil that had ruined the world and that, she knew, infected her as well, Khiel had shown her the entire poem. It resonated with her somehow; she did not understand it and would not pretend to understand it, yet it was unmistakably *right,* with a rightness that touched the very core of being. *'Though He gave only life… yet He bore the bruises of our strife and was crushed because of my portion,'* remembered Brisia. *'Stricken in darkness while He walked in light, bearing my plague while creation writhed, for all was wrong in that night.'* Somehow, I know, that that is just how it is. *'For all was wrong in that night,'* and it was, and yet whatever the poem means is so perfectly right. *He spoke with power and authority in the midst of the darkness, and His soul was radiant light even while He walked in death. Even in his stronghold, no match for His might was His enemy, though dreadful to all men and dragons… and the rocks cracked, the stars fell, and the prisoners were free!* *'At the touch of His hand, the wounded were healed and the defiled made pure.'* No, it has to be that way. I don't know what it means, only that it tells of the very deepest nature of things.

Khiel squeezed Brisia's hand lightly, prompting her to speak."It's about reality," she said, "about the 'utter failure' of all Kaarathlon and what the Creator is going to do with and to it."

Someone had shown it to Sirifa. "But," she said, "I'd just like to know what happened to my son… How did he end up in an Ephezoan prison?"

Khiel bit her lip. "It is ugly…" she said.

Adaria shook her head. "I'm sure," she began, but Kuthrynd interjected, "So, I think I understand that we have the writing of Azshbir on this scroll, even though he never touched it."

People nodded or muttered some kind of assent.

"The work of the Creator," said Kuthrynd.

"And deserving of respect," said Athara. "It's not often we see something like this."

Khiel lowered her head. It was not often that one saw anything. She and Brisia had talked about this before: the awe and wonder of the Creator's work. Every sunset only came once. She remembered Brisia telling her, once, that she would like to get to stare at the clouds in the west for hours, but the light on them changed every half minute or less; she would have liked to see each moment for hours. She had told her to just see each moment, let it go, and enjoy the next one... and repeat. Of course, there were the times when necessary work kept one from enjoying the beauties one saw. Then, there were other things in their lives that had only ever happened once... Only once, so far, had Sir Kuthrynd himself been clearly told by the Creator to go down the mountainside... and found her, Kalar, Janya, and Kavra.

"I think... I know what you're saying," said Adaria. "It reminds me of that night when we were waiting for Kuthrynd's return, so, of course, those of you whom he went to find were not there and wouldn't remember this. But, our concern was becoming worry and fear over him, over whatever the Creator's call might mean for him. And, I think those of us who really knew and loved Azshbir need to let go now... let go of our desire to know what happened to him and fear of the 'worst.' Of course, I'm probably the guiltiest person here. I think it was Brisia who reminded me then." Looking down at her infant, who was crying softly, she said, "Oh, baby. Dami, my Dami."

At the same time, Brisia felt Laekoorj touch her, ever so softly. She elbowed him and moved away. She wanted to shout at him, *Stop looking at me! Stop thinking about me! So what I reminded Adaria then? Who cares? It doesn't matter!*

"Maybe, we should roll up the scroll and go to bed," said Hoobit.

"That's a good i–" began Sirifa, but her last word was lost in a yawn.

"I'll do it," said Kalar, rolling up the scroll with the usual care.

Brisia stood. She wished her bed-place was farther away, but of course it was not, since, after all, she had been here first, re-reading the story of the beginning for whatever reason, and then Laekoorj had come over. For a while, he had just looked over her shoulder and read. The night wind came through a gap in the wall. Brisia swatted a bug away from her face and drew the thin cloth more tightly around her body. For some reason, the insects had always bugged her, Dormik, and Lalia more than the others. She could not remember the itchy welts that the bug-bites often became from her earliest years in Ebrin. *Maybe, I just don't remember because I was too young then... and certain things happened.*

"Still," said Esiri, "I wonder how he failed so badly that he worried about whether he belonged to the Promise. What could he possibly have done? He was as wonderful an older brother as anyone could have hoped for."

"It might not be something you would think," muttered Khiel.

"Say that again," said Esiri. When Khiel repeated herself, she said, "Oh! So, you mean, like when Brisia was so bothered about the fact that she– what was it? It had something to do with secret things and the depths of the sea."

Brisia spun around. "You spied!" she said, with rare anger. "And, I *didn't* worry about whether or not the Promised One would come for me. I didn't think about it *at all*."

"I'm sorry," said Esiri. "I couldn't really help it… I just happened to be passing by. I didn't mean to anger you."

"I was not thinking of you, Brisia, at all," said Khiel. "I was… well, I'm not sure what, and don't want to tell."

"That's okay," said Brisia. Her tone of voice might have sounded sulky, but she did not mean it that way. She was disturbed by the way Esiri, and even Khiel, had reacted to her exclamation and not sure how to respond. "I'm going to bed," she said, turning to face the wall and sitting down.

A few minutes later, Laekoorj called to her, "Good night, Brisia!"

She did not respond. She was grateful when Kuthrynd softly scolded, "Laekoorj!"

#76
Accused

Azshbir hugged his wife and infant daughter. He keenly missed his twin daughters and his sons. He knew Neah'ra felt the same. However, watching her cuddle her daughter, he knew that the threat, which she had now shared with him, weeping and shaking when she did so, still hung over her. There was a simultaneous tenderness and hesitancy in the way she caressed Nourdë, or the voice with which she spoke to her. She seemed to try to keep a kind of distance, fearful of becoming too close, too attached, lest she suffer or lest she be unable to give Nourdë up, Azshbir did not know. At the same time, she spoke to and cuddled Nourdë with such tenderness and sweetness, as if soaking up every moment, as if trying to give or draw whatever she could in each embrace, each soothing word or touch. Often, she cried silently. Azshbir did not want to think about it, and he wanted Neah'ra to cuddle Nourdë without thinking about the threat she still feared, too. "We're going to get fat and lazy," he said.

"It'll take a while for us to get fat," Neah'ra responded. "We got thin on the way here." Her silence had a piercing quality, that made Azshbir tense, wondering what she was thinking. Then, she said, "The Queen is a strange person."

"I don't get her either," said Azshbir. "I've really been enjoying talking with the other men here." To Neah'ra, he sounded happier than he had in a long time. "It's really wonderful. Even though we don't have the scroll, we've had more time to talk about things and discuss what they mean, and talk about the world, and how to live in it, than we have in ages. The only fear, here, is that someone accidentally breaks in, or that they find the Queen out, and nothing we could do could help with anything in that case, so we don't even think about it."

"I guess I wouldn't notice it as much," said Neah'ra, "since I always have Shantee and Kira, and now the younger ones, around, anyways." She moved, and then responded to Nourdë's cry. Then, she said, "I really miss Della and Reilia, and I'm worried about Kuthreb and Norden." Azshbir had told Shantee and Kira not to tell her that their dragons relaid that they had all been captured. It would not help, not right now, when she was so worried about her baby– or about loving her. He was somewhat tense and worried himself, and wondered if he should ask the Queen if she was in charge of their arrest as well, or if it had been carried out by someone else– someone truly, not merely apparently, dangerous.

Even without that information, Azshbir understood. Kuthreb was still a little kid, and Norden was just a baby, not even fully weaned– though he would be, now. If he was still alive, that is. Azshbir vaguely remembered siblings who had never grown up.

"It's sad how used we are, to worrying about everything, to thinking out every possible problem," said Neah'ra, half as if to herself.

"What are you trying to say?" asked Azshbir.

"You've thought out all the potential dangers, here. It's sad."

He rolled away from her, stood up, and stepped away. For some reason, he was inexplicably mad. He tried to keep his voice even as he asked, "Are you accusing me of something?"

Neah'ra heaved a sigh, which was an irritant. "I'm not accusing anyone of anything," she said, with painful slowness and annoyance. "I'm just stating a fact."

"A fact, which implies that I waste my energy worrying and fearing," Azshbir said, his voice taking on a bitter, cynical tone. Lia's exuberant voice interrupted. "Queen Arendellie is here!"

Azshbir did not want to think about the Queen right then. Like Neah'ra had said, she was a very strange person. He remembered her half-minute visit to his cell, during which she assured him that she would not torture anyone, but would have him put together with his family. Then, she had hurried away. Over the course of perhaps seven hours, in ones and twos and threes, they had been bathed, dressed, and moved around. None of them ever saw the same slave or servant twice. Then, they had all been served a feast fit for a king. Some of them, Azshbir knew, were eating more than they should. The food was very good, much better than they had had in a long time, which made them want to devour it. Additionally, none of them were doing any work. They slept, and talked, and ate, and some of them watched the young girls and young men relate. Last night, two more people, people they had never known before and found to have come from far regions of Camil, had arrived. But, Lia was saying, "Come on! You do want to!"

"Okay, Lia. I'll come," said Azshbir. He was, later, quite grateful for the interruption which kept his and Neah'ra's conversation from turning into a fight. They had not fought in years, and he wondered why they– or he– found it so easy to fight here. "It's okay," he told Neah'ra, "if you don't want to get up. I'll tell you everything." She did not respond, and he did not think about it, but followed Lia.

When Azshbir reached the room where the Queen visited them, and sat down, he saw that the toddler princess was already playing with Seair. Kira was saying, her voice shaking a little, "Your majesty, I wouldn't want to intrude upon your time and energy, but my dragon tells me that my sister and her friends have been captured, and–"

Arendellie interrupted. "I should have told you when I was here last time, three days ago. I had ordered for search parties to be sent out for them. How long ago were they arrested?"

"My dragon found out several days ago. She thinks they were taken in the morning, but she and Kameth had left them in a clearing they had marked, and gone hunting. She would have destroyed their captors, but they were already in a city by the time she tracked them down." Kira swallowed. "You think they're all right?"

"Unless someone disobeys my express orders, they should be here within the week," said Arendellie. "I'm sorry I didn't tell you three days ago. Unless," she added, "no Dragon-riders will take my offer."

"What is going on?" asked Azshbir. Another man asked, "How did you even know there were more of us?"

"By watching spies, voluntary or paid, and obtaining their information," said

Arendellie, as if it was the most obvious thing in the world. Inwardly, she was screaming. She was so good at hurting people! How much worry had she caused these people by not telling them what she was doing! She had thought of telling them, but had not done so, and now they had probably worried and fretted. She could not imagine how it had hurt them. After all, it was their own children! Her eyes fell on Kyil Kathreen, the only one of her children she had known all her life, and even the others were dear! *O my Creator, forgive me,* she prayed. *When will I stop doing this? When will I stop hurting my friends– Your people? Even after years spent serving them, I still do it!* She wanted to leave. Actually, she did not know what she wanted. People she once enjoyed interacting with now disgusted her. She struggled not to expose her hatred and disgust of the way Camil Hasseleighton handled 'traitors' and its tortures, and it disgusted her having to pretend to be all in with it. At least, she would be able to talk about giving people to the Undead Snow Queen easily, since she knew no Undead Snow Queen existed, only a Dragon Keeper from the far north named Audra. She still loved Vanesh and enjoyed entertaining and pleasing him, but there was plenty of trouble in their relationship. Though he allowed her work and, she knew, secretly approved, in no way endorsing or approving of the tactics of the Empire of which he was king only in name, he hated the fact that she was doing it. He hated and feared the danger in which it placed her. He cared nothing for the Promise, and hated it for putting her in danger, though he did not love her less for believing it.

A young man rose and made his way across the room. Bowing, he said, "Thank you, your majesty, for your work to protect us."

His words only made Arendellie more uncomfortable. In fact, she was so uncomfortable that most people could tell. She curtsied, deeply, gracefully. "I'm honored," she said, "and, you don't have to always call me 'your majesty' or 'Queen.' I used to just be a village-girl, and being a princess and then a queen did not improve me at all. No need to thank me, either. I'm only doing what I ought, and it will never make up for what I did and what I did not do."

No one would ever know she meant it. For some reason, even when she was most uncomfortable, she carried herself and spoke like royalty, even though it was not how she had been raised. In fact, when she was uncomfortable in certain ways was often when it was most impossible to behave otherwise, to behave even remotely naturally. However, even though she said it with the impassive artificiality of royalty, she said it that way precisely because she meant and felt it in such a terrible and painful way.

Watching her, Azshbir wondered, again, why they had all trusted her. Somehow, when she brought out the scroll, they had all found themselves trusting her. Yet, who but the Creator knew whether she had stolen it from its rightful owner for the express purpose of deceit? She looked like the kind of person who might be able to spin an almost flawless story on the spur of the moment. As for details, Azshbir did not know the details of Ebrin or Kathreen's life and could not catch her if she had made mistakes. However, she knew so much about them, who knew what else she knew? How she could fit it all in her mind at once was a mystery, but it was possible that here was a woman who could lie like no one else in the world had ever lied before.

What did she mean by what she did and what she did not do? What had she done? What had she had the opportunity to do and not done?

#77
Wailing Voice

Even now that they were becoming young ladies, Reilia and Della looked very similar. For a moment, it felt as if the years had not passed, and he stood, seeing his twin daughters for the first time outside of prison. Which one was which? Azshbir could not have told if his life depended on it; could not have even guessed. For years, he had never confused them, but now, after several months apart, they looked exactly the same to him. His heart twisted with pain, at least remembered pain. Next to him, Neah'ra was crying as she took Norden in her arms and simultaneously tried to comfort Kuthreb. Then, one of them stepped forward and tilted her head. Azshbir recognized the look in her eyes. "Reilia?" he asked, still not *quite* certain.

She nodded and fell into his arms. Della followed. He knew it hurt them as well that he could not recognize them.

He noticed that others were wailing. Why? Was Kgarjin not here? He knew Lasaira was standing a few feet away, waiting for her turn. He tried to look around, but Reilia and Della clung to him. "We were so scared," said Della, sobbing. Reilia sobbed, too.

Azshbir did not know what to say. What could he say? Doubtless, they had all expected the same horrors he had… but at least their journey here, taken on the backs of great dragons, could not have been as awful as his, which had reminded him of certain times in the prisons of Ephezoa.

The wailing did not sound like that of people suddenly relieved of fear and happy to be together with those they loved and with whom they were comfortable. It sounded more like the wailing at a hopeless, tragic funeral to Azshbir. Finally, Reilia and Della stopped clinging to him. Lasaira gave him a quick hug. He knew she was less comfortable around lots of other people. She was also older. A stab of pain went up his leg as he knelt to ask Neah'ra, "Do you see Kgarjin?"

"Yes," said Neah'ra, her voice muffled by her hair and the hands of Norden. "I can't point, she's, uh, she's… over there," said Neah'ra, awkwardly motioning with her head.

Azshbir looked, and was able to pick out Kgarjin, standing with her mother and siblings. There was no question, now, that Shaelene had accepted the Promise. He knew from Neah'ra about her confrontation with Ellason, who had insisted on individually questioning and threatening each of them. Apparently, after asking her all manner of questions and getting no answer, Ellason had said, "Do you also believe all that stuff about a Promised One who has not yet come and will do we do not know what?" to which, according to her own report, Shaelene replied, "We do know what. He will conquer and reign over all things, even death, and He will cast all His enemies into death, but those who have waited for Him He will lead out from death in victory." Ellason had said, "So, then, you wish to suffer Daera's fate? I'm sure the Queen and her wizards have even worse in store for you; they may even hand you over to the Undead Snow Queen. If you will renounce this treason and help me, you can go, and I will let your son go with you." Shaelene had only told Neah'ra this morning, but Azshbir had overheard a lot of it. She still seemed uncomfortable in a way Azshbir did not understand. She had emphatically told his wife that, "I never told Ellason anything or responded to any of her questions, except when she asked if I believed all that 'stuff' about a Promised One, and all the rest. I just couldn't stand it. It was mockery, and I had to say *something!*"

Watching Neah'ra and Azshbir relate to their children, and Kgarjin to her mother and siblings, Arendellie thought, *I do this because otherwise they will suffer even worse, and if I do not do it this way then everything I've done will crumble, and they will suffer even worse.* She felt terrible. They had all thought that they were going to be tormented in horrible ways– and, *because she had not told them otherwise!* Of course, how could she help it? Once, she could help it. But, if she did not allow it to be thought that she was doing the same thing the Council of Wizards was doing, if she let them know that she was one of the People of the Promise working to better their circumstances, then it would all be over. She was not really sure what would happen to her and, besides, she cared what would happen to her only for Vanesh's sake, but she would never help anyone again.

Then, a young man, the same who had bowed to and thanked her a week earlier, approached her. He bowed again, and appeared to have forgotten her previous requests. "Queen, may I ask where are my and my wife's children?" he asked.

"Your children?" asked Arendellie. "Are they not here?"

"No," he said. "We thought you were bringing them to us... that the young children were being taken separately. Is that not what your majesty told us?"

Arendellie shook her head. "No. These ran away, successfully, and I had to find them. That is why they were late."

"Mine were with us when we were arrested. They were all young– our oldest was eight. We know others here to whom the same thing happened. What has happened to our children?" Beginning to be afraid, the man was sobbing.

"I don't know," said Arendellie, feeling flustered. "Ellason must have done something." She bit the inside of her cheek. "I'll see what happened and what I can do."

"Thank you, your majesty. Thank you so much," said the man.

Arendellie did not respond. She closed her eyes and took a moment to compose herself. She did not have long today, anyways. Just enough to get the slaves together and escort the teenagers and children. She smirked, remembering telling people that she was bringing in new slaves for herself and Vanesh. Of course, it was *partially* true. She had bought more slaves, along with this whole operation, partially to help cover it up.

Unfortunately, it was hours before she could get the space she needed. She called her scribe and said, "Have a letter written to Ellason, demanding her appearance here as quickly as possible, and promising whatever payment is required to hire a dragon and Dragon-rider. I will sign it." To be honest, she was pretty sure Ellason had enough money to pay for a single flight to Anores. She was almost certain Ellason had enough money to mostly pay for one. Not that money was an issue for her, but she intended to have everything Ellason owned confiscated. She had not yet decided whether to have her thrown in prison or not. She would not be asked any questions and, if she were, she could simply say that Ellason had disobeyed her expressly given orders. Ellason was responsible for the torture of so many People of the Promise, she did not feel bad about the idea of throwing her in prison, though it would mean she might suffer any of the cruelties of the Hasseleighton prisons. Of course, she would not do any of this until she had questioned Ellason to discover exactly what she had done.

She was really upset. *How did I let this slip?* She already had the ship and she had been planning to send them on their way at the most convenient time in the next week. Now, she had no idea how she was going to solve this problem. She had no idea what had even been done, let alone how she might go about fixing it! She buried her head in her hands and fumed silently.

Ellason was nervous, as she always was about any interactions with the Queen. She quickly selected an extremely bright purple outfit, found a Dragon-rider, and gave him the Queen's note. She wished she were a Dragon-rider, and could make riches this way! She hated the fact that the Queen could pay for any convenience or expedience without thinking twice about it. It was power! Now, too, that there were so few Dragon-riders in Camil Hasseleighton, they were making fortunes by carrying the royal mail, any other mail someone would pay a sum to have delivered, and ferrying wealthy people around the continent.

When she appeared before the Queen, she shivered. She could feel burning anger in the Queen's gaze. She kept her voice rather even, but Ellason knew she was absolutely furious as she asked, "What did you do with the children?"

"What children, your majesty? I had Azshbir's family delivered to your majesty, as your majesty commanded," said Ellason, trying to gain some favor by following the rules of respect as perfectly as possible, even going above and beyond.

"The children of the families we had linked to Azshbir and the Dragon-riders. Did I not command that they all be brought to me in Anores?"

"Your majesty, I did not think that your majesty cared for so many small children. Your majesty was going to have plenty of adults and older children to study and work on. Your majesty, I am very sorry."

Arendellie could tell that Ellason was going to go on and on in the same way. "What did you do with the children?"

"Your majesty, I was only trying to help. Your majesty, I gave the children to loyal families, your majesty, who did not have many children of their own. That way, your majesty, they will be raised up in our way, in the way of the Mighty Lord. I hope, your majesty, that you will be pleased with my intent, or at least have mercy on me in accordance with my intention."

Arendellie had to resist the impulse to slap her. Ellason was disgusting. She also had no idea with who and what she was dealing. As for the children, Arendellie had no idea how she was going to get them back. Hire a professional kidnapper? How would she make sure that it was kept a secret from the Council of Wizards? She continued to question Ellason about whom she had involved and when, how, and what she had done, in great detail. She asked for all kinds of detail, details which she thought would be helpful and details which she did not *think* would matter for her purposes; any detail of which she could think, in fact.

It was then that Ellason noticed that she had a scribe on the side, taking down everything of note. What was the Queen thinking of doing? She began to be so afraid she had to concentrate on speaking clearly.

Then, Arendellie stood up from the table. She called to one of her slaves and whispered something in her ear. She continued questioning Ellason, while she worried about what the Queen had said. She had nervously hoped she was going to be elevated, given some task of weighty importance, or something of the like. Maybe, it was not even that big of a deal. She had no idea how easily the Queen would toss orders and payments around.

Then, guards came through the door, accompanied by the Queen's slave. "Take her to the dungeons; she has blatantly disregarded my wishes and disobeyed my commands!" Arendellie said. Ellason screamed. "Have mercy, your majesty! Your majesty! It was a mistake! An accident! I told you I'm sorry! Your majesty, I only meant to–" she wailed, but the guards cut her off and carried her outside. Arendellie felt half-inclined to laugh. Ellason only meant to *what?* And, it was a *mistake?* It was no mistake. Arendellie had long known that Ellason hated her. Now, however, she had to think about how to clean up this mess Ellason had made. She could not very well send the parents across the ocean without their children, yet she did not know how she would find the children and make up an excuse to take them. She wondered if she could ask Vanesh for advice.

Then, she remembered Sir Andelf and El-Reiza. She wondered if El-Reiza and her dragon companion, Leaoneth, had survived all the tumult and upheaval of the following years. If she had, had she, with most of the Dragon-riders, gone with Audra to the north? If she was still here, Arendellie thought she could find her. With so few dragons on the continent, a yellow dragon and a Dragon-rider as different as El-Reiza should be relatively easy to find. Yet, she would not want anyone outside of her circle of confidence to know that she was searching for El-Reiza, if she was to do what she planned next. Perhaps, she would just ask for a comprehensive list of all known dragons on the continent, with as much or as little information as was available, but she wanted as much as possible. El-Reiza– and the people she might know– might know how to 'kidnap' the children and be willing to do so for Arendellie; the only trouble was that this could take years. She would immediately initiate the search for El-Reiza and Leaoneth, and then gather as much information as possible about the families to whom the children had been given: what they did, where they went, habits, favorite meals and pastimes, how they educated their children, everything.

She felt so bad. She should have known. Ellason had 'adopted' all of Daera, an ex-prostitute friend of Neah'ra's, children, except the one who had escaped– Lasaira. It had not gone over perfectly. Ellason, herself, had handed over some of them to be tortured and killed, when they grew up and lived in her household and did not turn from the Promise. She knew because Ellason had lamented this to her over a meal they had had together half a year ago.

#78
The Sailing of the *Last Watch*

Half a week later.

Arendellie had the parents who had lost their children gathered together. "This ship is sailing tomorrow night," she told them. "You will stay here until I can recover your children, in which time you will sail on the next ship."

Afterwards, she went to the others. The group had grown, as she brought whatever People of the Promise she could rescue. She explained the plan to them.

Prompted by some impulse he did not understand, Azshbir said, "We must not accept a crew who are not also Knights and People of the Promise."

Arendellie was shocked. The first thing she asked was, "Do you speak for all of them?"

Unanimously, the gathered People of the Promise affirmed that, at least in that statement, Azshbir spoke for them all.

"How will you sail without a crew? I don't know all of your backgrounds that well, but more than two or three of you cannot have any experience with sailing ships of this size and type. Without a crew, you will only be driven around by the wind, you may be caught in a storm and wrecked, in short, you will all die, sooner or later," said Arendellie.

"We will not accept a crew of our enemies," repeated Azshbir. "We must trust and rely on the Creator's power alone."

"I did not mean that I would give you a crew that will torture and kill you. I've found the rare crews that are not fanatic. It will be an excellent opportunity to share the Promise with them. You will have nothing to fear," explained Arendellie.

Azshbir did not know how to reply. Instead, Neah'ra said, "We must obey the Creator. He is powerful, and we need to rely entirely upon His power and guidance in this. It is simply how He wants it done." Her words encouraged Azshbir, who said, "I never meant by enemies that I feared the crew you have selected. But, Neah'ra is right. We must do it this way. We don't have to know why. We have never known why before." He had not known why he must stay in Afteloan. He had never known, until it happened, why he had to be imprisoned by Ephezoa in that way– but it had turned out to great good. He had never known why Kira, and Shantee, had to be so bold and open in their declaration of the Promise. Or, why they had to be captured by Ellason as they were. All these things, they were beginning to see turned to good. Centuries and ages might pass before all the good that came of any one thing, whether seemingly foolish or a terrible disaster, became apparent. Only the Creator would ever know all that came of anything.

"Very well," said Arendellie. *If that's how you want to do it, it's none of my business and I won't force you to do otherwise,* she thought.

In the west, the stars shone brightly in a dark sky. The city of Anores towered behind them. The eastern sky showed gray with dawn beyond the sea and on the shoulders of the mountains. Surrounded by her choice maids and a few man-servants, Arendellie stood on the sands, several feet out of reach of the lapping waters. Not more than two abreast, the Knights of the Promise and the people of their households walked out on the plank and boarded the ship, which was provisioned with as much food as she could hold. Arendellie shivered a little in the morning air, but whether from the slight cold or from apprehension she did not know. She would have been scared to do what these people were doing. She would have been scared to sail into the unknown *with* an experienced crew– for they were sailing into the unknown. They were seeking another continent, perhaps Syrwe, but it was up to them whether they looked for the north-eastern continent or another, yet unheard-of by anyone in Camil. *How,* Arendellie wondered, *was it so exciting to seek the unknown peril of the court, and yet just thinking about this raises goose-bumps of apprehension?* It did not occur to her then that it might be because then she had sought the unknown peril of court-life to exercise her talents; it was more than she could handle, but she intended to handle it. She wanted the excitement of her own doing and thinking and learning. She wanted something fit to her perception of herself and the world and to distract herself from that which she did not want to remember or consider. This, however, was a venture into the unknown in complete reliance on Another. There was nothing they could hope to do to steer their course or protect themselves. They were not going to *do* anything at all, or even to *be* anything. It required nothing but walking down that plank onto the ship and casting off. They were in the Creator's hands; she was in her own (or had thought so), and, certainly, she had endeavored to be in her own.

Near her, a sudden worry struck Azshbir. "The scroll!" he said. "We cannot leave without the scroll!"

"Where is the scroll?" asked Arendellie, but Shantee, her voice matching the gentle lapping of the waves on the shore, said, "No need to worry. Kameth went into the house and found the scroll. I told her to hurry, because we are going. Look! There she is!"

Shantee turned and pointed and, following her finger, Arendellie saw, near the mountains, the shape of a dragon, dark against the stars, but, already, the eastern sky was lighter. The whole landscape was a little less black and a little more gray than it had been five minutes ago. Shantee spoke again and said, "I don't know how long an age is, but we are going to the distant land!" Her tones still soft and measured, her voice yet carried an excitement, young, fresh, and eager. *Like the rising sun,* thought Arendellie. *Or, is it not so much excitement at all, but expectant gladness?* Shantee's voice held no impatience.

Watching the dragon approaching, Arendellie took a deep breath. Something about the whole atmosphere stirred something in her spirit. Maybe, it was just being completely outdoors in the early hours of the morning. She had not *really* been out of doors in years. She had not even been to Ebrin these last few years. The closest she came to the outdoors was the royal gardens, but they were hardly out of doors. Within the castle walls, the towers and parapets and ramparts soared above them. Completely enclosed, they were carefully tended by slaves whose specialty was the care of gardens, the flowers, grasses, trees, exotic herbs, walkways. They were nothing like the free woods, where plants simply grew, and animals ate them, wild and refreshing. Even this patch of sand, between the city and the ocean was far more outdoors. For one thing, the ocean was wild and untameable. Even the best ships were sometimes lost on it, Arendellie knew. Its waves were terrible and even unpredictable, and only the Creator knew what moved or lay in its depths which no eye could ever probe, to which even dragons, with their superior breath, could not descend, or, with their superior eyesight, especially under-water, see. So many of the songs in the scrolls praised and explained the wonder and majesty of the Creator, made evident in the seas.

There was something lonely, too, about the beach and the sea and the last watch of the night. Even with her maids and man-servants standing only a little way off and a little village standing on the beach and walking down the plank onto the ship, it was lonelier than her chambers or gardens ever could be– even though she could clearly hear the patter of feet on the plank. The *Last Watch* was a strange name for a ship, but for this ship, Arendellie thought it was appropriate. The last watch was the watch before the dawn– and these sailed for the dawn. It was appropriate, too, sailing at this time, into the dawn. Turning, she saw two dragons in the east, coming out of or around the mountains. She could now only see the shape of the dragon in the west, apparently Kameth, against the stars, but these were dark against the dawn sky. Kameth was close now.

A few minutes later, almost everyone was gone. Azshbir lingered, with his wife and their youngest three. He did not seem to quite know what to say. "Arendellie," he said, calling her by her first name, "we bid you farewell, until we shall meet again when the Promised One establishes the kingdom. Be strong in complete dependence upon the Creator." It seemed that the whole weight of his life, or perhaps only of the future that lay before him like the sea, weighted those words, making them as heavy and unsupportable as an ocean of gold to Arendellie.

"Farewell, Azshbir and Neah'ra, until we meet again," she said, not knowing what more to say.

Slowly, they turned. Azshbir picked up his youngest son, Norden, and walked the plank, Kuthreb hanging onto his legs. Neah'ra held her daughter, Nourdë, and walked behind him.

The eastern sky seemed almost white. The waves began to rise a little, making the ship bob more, but the couple and their young children made it on board. Something wild arose in Arendellie's heart. Some wild, winged impulse to sail into the horizon and the dawn, beyond the reach of any eye, into the loneliness and the unknown, the breast of the ocean, or even the breast of the world. She stood, breathing deep of some wild air from lands more distant than the sunrise.

Several men fumbled with the ship, figuring out how to lift the anchor. Above the *Last Watch*, three dragons circled in the sky, dancing elaborately. As the light increased, Arendellie saw clearly that two were blue and the other was red. She did not know to whom the red dragon was bonded. She closed her eyes and lifted her face to the sea-breeze. *O Creator!* she prayed, lifting up her arms and catching the wind in her sleeves and cape. *How wondrous You are! Yea, for who among us can know the secret things in the depths of Your oceans or who has seen the halls in the depths of Your seas? For none have walked in the valleys of the seas. Who can ride Your winds or direct them in their paths, and who among men or dragons knows the ways of Your storms? Yea, no one has seen from where You gather the wind or to where it returns!*

After a long moment of silence, even in her heart and mind, except for the pounding of the waves upon the sand, Arendellie turned and, accompanied by her escort, entered her quarters in the castle as the sun rose above the waves. Her last view of the sea and the ship was as the *Last Watch* slowly turned to open sea and the rising sun.

#79
End of Life

It had been pouring. The ground was soaking wet and netted with rivulets and sheets of water. The thick foliage dripped almost as hard as it had been raining, with whole buckets of water falling from and through the leaves at once, from time to time. Bright yellow trumpet flowers still held their heads up. They were filled to the brim with rain-water, tinged with their pollen.

Brisia felt uncomfortable. She was dripping wet, but not cold, for the rain was warm, as it often was in the Vinibra Mountains. Laekoorj had invited her here, along with his father and mother, Hoobit and Sirifa, and the other married couples, Kalar and Adaria, Kuthrynd and his wife, Janya, and Kavra and Athara. She did not know how he had gotten them out here without their babies. She consented to come, nervously, half-unwilling, suspicious of what would be coming.

Everyone knew that Hoobit was dying. Daily, he was growing weaker and weaker, and he was often cold. Laekoorj took her just a little ways away from the married couples, into the shadow of a huge yellow trumpet-flower. Brisia flinched a little, hoping it did not dump all that water on her. Then, Laekoorj asked the dreadful question. "Brisia, will you marry me?" He stuttered her name and the word 'marry'.

Brisia stood like stone. She had known that Laekoorj would, sooner or later, ask this question, for a long time. She had not thought that it would be later; she had been unable to face it, unable to really accept or think about it, and simply felt that it would be later, that it *was*, in some sense, however nonsensical, 'later'. It was terrifying. If she said yes,' she would go on to marry Laekoorj, and it would be the end of life as she knew it! Nor would it be the end of life as she knew it, simply in that external circumstances would be different. Who she was, what she was, what was expected of her would change. She would be Laekoorj's wife. Whatever that meant or involved. She was not ready; was he ready? What did it mean for him to be a husband?

Laekoorj waited. No one spoke. Gingerly, Brisia touched one of the amazingly small leaves of the trumpet-flower. It quivered, but the flower did not dump its contents on their heads. She wished she had someone to guide her, someone to tell her what to be married would mean, what the future would hold. Her lips quivered as she said, "Yes."

She had thought about the 'later' that was, by definition, 'later'" and would not come until forever had passed. She had thought she would marry Laekoorj. She had never felt just how terrifying the decision was until it was upon her– until the 'always later' was 'now,'"with all of the present's huge, unfathomably high and import-full, terrifying approach. It felt impossible and unreal, like some kind of dream floating among the stars.

Kalar helped his father-in-law back to the house. Without being told, Brisia knew that Laekoorj had chosen this time because he wanted to ask her before his father, Hoobit, died. He hoped, in fact, to marry her before Hoobit died. Hoobit's impending death saddened Brisia, for he was the father of the house, and had been a little of a father to her. Walking slowly, and several feet apart, they trailed behind the already-married couples. Her head was down, not because of sadness, but because she was so overwhelmed, even shocked, that she felt a little– a very little– depressed. She could not shake the weight of the change that was suddenly becoming 'now,' that loomed above her. Laekoorj, too, was solemn and silent, feeling the weight and solemnity of the moment– the choice– the change– the life. He had been scared to ask the question, and he had waited tensely for her response, terrified whichever way she should choose– terrified of the 'yes,' of which he was almost certain. His fear that she might say 'no,' was of a very different sort, so that it did not really make sense to call both by the same word, which is not to say that it was less intense, that the thought was less shaking, but it was certainly not expected.

Adaria watched Laekoorj and Brisia with a kind of dizziness and amusement. She had been almost as old as Brisia was now when Laekoorj was born; she had seen him come out of their mother. She had played with and amused him while he was a toddler. She could only begin to imagine what it might be for Hoobit and Sirifa though, of course, they had already let Azshbir– who had apparently married– go, and already seen Kuthrynd, herself, and Athara married. As for Brisia, she had not seen her born or played with her when she was a baby, but she had comforted, and, even, if it was possible to use that word 'mothered' her, when she was only a little more than a baby.

Over the days and weeks that followed, Brisia and Laekoorj discussed what kind of wedding they would have. Khiel and Brisia talked about the poems in the scroll and about songs. Lalia, Nahiza, and Kizyia were eager to share their insights and suggestions, often to the point of being an extreme annoyance. They decided that one of their wedding songs would be the poem about the wonder of the Creator shown in His creations, "the least of His works surpass us by far," to the tune that Khiel had written. It did not really have anything to do with marriage, but Brisia liked it and thought it was very beautiful. Khiel said, "I don't know. It probably doesn't have anything to do with it, per se, but it might have a lot to do with how you want to live and see the world together! Still, I don't really know." Somehow, though, being engaged to Laekoorj subtly changed Brisia's relationship to Khiel.

Hoobit continued to ail. Sometimes he seemed stronger, and would go out with the men for a little while, despite the pleadings of Sirifa. More and more, however, he spent his time with his younger children. Then, one night, he died.

"I guess," said Laekoorj, unhappily, "that I will have to bury my father before I can marry my bride." He had taken to spending as much time as possible with his father, learning from him everything he could. Nahiza and Kizyia were crumpled up on the straw, crying, with Lalia. Sirifa did not seem as distressed.

Brisia heard Laekoorj's miserable voice, and thought for an instant of Dormik. Fear clutched at her stomach. *No!* She saw Lalia, curled up and weeping, and remembered when she had lost her parents. Something froze her where she stood. *Lalia, this isn't even your father,* she thought. Then, more bitterly, *But Dormik will never care at all. About anyone. Ever again.* She would never forget the look in his eyes. They had pierced her and made her shudder with the coldness of the hatred that had wound itself all through his soul. She was afraid of him and avoided him. She fled when he greeted her, which was rarely. There was something dead about him, and something deadly. What had he become?

Of course, she thought, *Lalia never knew Mom and Dad. Hoobit and Sirifa are the only Dad and Mom she's ever known. And, Nahiza and Kizyia are her best friends. They might as well all be twins, or whatever you call three. And, that's okay.* For herself, it was not Hoobit's death that caused the tears behind her eyeballs so much as Hoobit's death and all the things it brought to her mind.

Brisia found Khiel and asked her if they could go outside and work on the gardens together. Standing outside the door together, they saw a dragon circling in the skies above them. There was no doubt that it was not L'sa-moth. Sapphire scales flashed between red wings. For a while they stood, gazing up at the creature in fear. Was it friend or, more likely, foe? Was this end of life together, the end, probably, of life for all of them except those who would give allegiance to another than the Creator and His Promised One? Again, Brisia thought of Dormik. She had no doubt that he did not truly accept the Promise, whatever he said once or twice in as many years, but she was certain, too, that he would fight and kill those whom he considered to share responsibility for the death of his parents. He was consumed by bitterness and hate, and she had no doubt, now that she thought of it, that he secretly cherished the thought of revenge. Back when he was younger, he had made no secret of his lust for the pain of those who had hurt him.

What is it that divides us? she wondered, again. *Why is it that I accept the Promise, and he does not care for the Promise? For, evil is evil. O Creator, please protect us.*

#80
The Queen's Regret

Vanesh stroked Arendellie's hair back, behind her ears. "You dance beautifully, beloved," he said, kissing her, "but I sense something is distressing you."

She turned away. "What am I supposed to do? I am trying to help, but even there, I find myself inflicting pain. I can't bear to see the anguish in their eyes... and to know that I caused it by not revealing the whole truth sooner." She knew Vanesh would not like the reminder of her work, but he had asked.

"By 'them,' you mean the People of the Promise you take, I assume?" he said.

"Yes."

"Then be comforted by this: if you reveal the whole truth sooner, then it will not be true," he said.

Arendellie shook her head. She knew all these things. She knew all the arguments. Still, she felt guilty. Especially, she felt guilty for not keeping Ellason under tighter control. If she had done that, she would not have the current problem on her hands. If she had done that, certain people– and their children– would not be suffering what they were, now. Instead, they would all be on the *Last Watch*, sailing away from this wretched land.

"Anyway, why don't you tell me what you're doing right now?" asked Vanesh.

So, Arendellie told him. She told him about Ellason and about the plans she was currently implementing, to find El-Reiza in case she was still around, and to gather any information that might be helpful. "The main problem, at this point, is this: more likely than not, El-Reiza is either dead or has gone with the Dragon Keeper to her land."

"This is the first I've heard of El-Reiza," said Vanesh. "How do you know her?"

"She was with Sir Andelf," began Arendellie.

"Sir Andelf was my right-hand man, before my uncle started this war. He visited me as often as he could. I was sorry when he died," said Vanesh.

"Well, she took me to Anores. When Sir Andelf saw Grale and his dragons coming in, he sent her to me with his last message to me."

"He sent a messenger to me also," said Vanesh, "probably with a similar message." He sounded dejected and irritated. After a few moments, he asked, "Why do you think that El-Reiza will both be willing and able to perform this feat?"

Arendellie did not want to tell Vanesh what Sir Andelf's last orders to El-Reiza had been. "She is different," she said. "I'm not really sure she is human. She seems more like an elf-sprite. She is definitely not a typical human woman."

"Undead Snow Queens and elf-sprites," Vanesh muttered under his breath. He wondered how Sir Andelf had enlisted El-Reiza. Out loud, he said, "You are not a typical human woman, either, Araenyi."

Arendellie heard both comments. She moved towards him, and said softly, "No, I am an ideal human woman." She did not really think it, but Vanesh did. She drew away again, and said in a normal tone of voice, "El-Reiza is no man, but she is more unlike what we associate with human womanhood than you could imagine without meeting her."

"I don't really need to know anymore about El-Reiza." He was quiet for a while, thinking hard. "No," he said slowly, "I think your plan is pretty good... Always assuming El-Reiza is here, and willing. It's a hard and tricky thing you are trying to accomplish. If I happen to come up with any ideas, I'll share them with you."

Arendellie could feel tension in the air between them. She did not know how to respond in such a way as to alleviate it. It was only a few moments before Vanesh said, "Why do you insist on doing this? I wouldn't mind it as much if you did not believe the Promise or were prepared to deny it!"

Arendellie knew why. It would mean that no question posed a threat, that if suspicions arose they could be strongly refuted. Also, if she were discovered, it would probably be much easier to convince the wizards to only restrict her– and his– activities.

"Because it is right. The Creator is good, and everything else doesn't matter compared to Him," said Arendellie. She wished she could say something else. That would do nothing to soothe Vanesh.

"Sir Andelf was my friend and counselor, and he turned to the Promise and was killed. Now you, my wife, my best friend and helper, have turned to the Promise, and you are going to die, too!" Vanesh seemed to catch himself. "At least, you will almost certainly be killed. Those wizards don't respect anything except their own lust for power and control. They're like Ellason, as you well know!"

"I know what it's like," said Arendellie, desperately trying to calm things down. "First my best friend, then another of my friends, then my to-be husband! And, then more and more of those I knew or trusted."

"You don't mean to suggest that you don't trust me because I don't accept the Promise?" asked Vanesh.

Arendellie knew he was not thinking. If that was the case, she would not tell him the things she did. Or, did he think she made the stories up out of thin air? She was not quite *that* good. She rose from the couch, spread out her arms, and danced, moving through rhythms slow and graceful and others quick and pounding.

Vanesh watched her and then rose, himself. Instead of coming towards her, he said, "I have to attend to some things, now. I'm already late. How about tonight?"

"That would be great," said Arendellie and curtsied. When he left, she threw herself down on the couch, distressed. After a while, things Vanesh had said began to fit together. *O Creator!* she sobbed. *Are You pursuing him, as You pursued me? Did you bring me into his life in order to pursue him like this?* Her thoughts flashed back to a comment one of the people of the Promise had made about the Creator taking her away from Neshekh to keep him from marrying her. *It would have been awful. We would both have been miserable. I don't know how awful it might have been... but I'm sorry.*

She did not want to do anything. She remembered the *Last Watch* with the dragons above, and the wild, inarticulate feeling that had awakened in her. When

King Vanesh died, which would be well before herself since he was much older– his hair was already dark gray– she decided that she would set sail on the last ship. In the keeping of her son, Liesam, she would have much less power and freedom, unless he were to change, so there would not be any reason to stay. The world was so horrible, so cruel, so hopeless. She knew Aroch did not understand anything she tried to teach him. His teachers used the same words to mean such completely different things, and they had much more time with him; she only managed to confuse him. She thought she might be able to raise Kathreen; princesses did not need the same education that princes did, and she might be able to oversee and control Kathreen's environment and somehow manage to make the time to raise her a great deal herself. She could ask people like Inshara, Aki'lam, Kalie, and Surra to take care of her when she could not. However, Aroch was a prince. She could not even ask for more control or oversight. Even Vanesh could not give it to her; the Council would not allow it. Even if he could, he would not, for he would not want his sons to follow in her way, to accept the Promise. She knew she had to be careful with Aroch; she would not want him to give away what she was, and, certainly, she would not want him to give away what she was without even understanding, himself, what she said.

She was beginning to hang all her hopes on El-Reiza still being around. She even wondered if she could run away with Aroch and Kathreen. She did not know if she wanted to leave Vanesh, and she knew that, if she were to do so, it would hurt Vanesh. *My Creator, why did I fall for all this foolishness? It is I who have been the fool!* She remembered calling Kathreen Alarion foolish. Even longer ago, before she began making the choices that had led to this, she remembered what Kathreen and Mirla had told her. Why had she not accepted the Promise then? It had been as obvious as daylight. She was sure that she had known it. The things that she had said had been so absurd, so preposterous, as Dorene had reminded her. What in Kaarathlon had she meant by saying that maybe some people took life so seriously because they took death too seriously, or did they take death too seriously because they took life too seriously? How had she not seen the sense of the idea– the truth– that the Creator and His judgment is more important than the things that are seen?

My Creator, this hurts so much. This hurts too much. Why did You let me do this to myself? It hurts too much.

If she had accepted the Promise, if she had stayed and married Neshekh, then she would probably have had children with him. She would, in all likelihood, have ended up like Mirla– perhaps, her children would not even have been rescued, like Mirla's, apparently, had been, by Kathreen Alarion. She thought of holding Kyil Kathreen and looking into her baby blue eyes, dark as the starry night, when she was born. She thought of playing with her. *O my Creator!* And, this, this horror, was what the People of the Promise endured? What Kyil, for whom she had named her own daughter, had endured? What she had dismissed as okay, because sooner or later they would be dead and no longer suffering. Of course, she had not believed it, then. She had been fighting as hard as she could to remain the cruel and callous queen she had been. But, that did not make it better. It made it worse.

I have to get to work, she thought. She went to the door and opened it. "Someone!" she called. "Oh. Minshi. Bring an outfit for me. Thanks."

She knew everyone thought it strange that she said thanks to her slaves. She had become so imperious and demanding. She just could not help it, sometimes. Sometimes, she was imperious, demanding, and hard, too, like when she was in a hurry– which, very often, she was. In fact, she was in a hurry now. She did not have time to mourn her position in life and her past choices. Waiting for Minshi to return, though, her previous train of thought tugged at her mind. *I* would *take just plain torture over this. I* would. *But, not* that. *O Creator, Creator, how do You allow it? Such evil. Such horror. How, my Creator? It's torturous, just considering it... to me. How do* You *allow it? How can You tolerate it for a mom–* Just then, Minshi returned, with another maid. She opened the door a crack. "My lady?"

"Come in," said Arendellie, only a little annoyed. To be honest, she was grateful for the interruption. She had meant to plan and think about work, not to consider *that*.

#81
The Sea and the Sky

Azshbir sat on the deck with Neah'ra. She was nursing Nourdë, and Kuthreb and Norden were both napping. The *Last Watch* was moving away from the land, and they did not know how much of it had to do with anything they did or could control. "Did I make a mistake declining her crew?" Azshbir asked the wind. He had worried about it a little, a very little, between when he made his announcement and when they boarded the ship.

"No, you didn't," said Neah'ra. "We all knew it was the right thing to do."

"Is that actually how you feel?" he asked. "No quiver of fear?"

Beside him she shrugged, which was not an answer. When she did speak, she said, "There is something about the Queen."

"She's tormented by stabs of misery. Regret. You've seen it, haven't you? A word, and her face shows pain. I wonder what she tells her court," said Azshbir. "And, then, there was that elusive statement about never being able to make up for all that she did and all that she did not do."

"Perhaps," said Neah'ra, "we don't need to know, and never will."

"You're right," said Azshbir. He stood, and placed his hand on the mast to steady himself. "Still, I feel sorry for her," he said.

Neah'ra gently touched Nourdë's face. She would never understand Azshbir. She answered his earlier question. "No fear worth mentioning. There's no comparison between the uncertainty here, and the threat I was under." She did not say more. Azshbir did not need her to do so. Nourdë began to cry, and Neah'ra shifted her to nurse more easily. She looked up at Azshbir. "No; this feels rather safe. Of course, the rocking of the ship is strange and makes my stomach roll a little. I could think about how we might drown or starve or whatever, but, it's like, we can always worry about anything if we try. It's been such a long time since I wasn't afraid for our children... for what Hasseleighton might do to us and them." She lowered her head. "It was really stupid, actually."

The blue-green sea rippled and rolled. It was somehow reminiscent of the way a dragon's scales and skin moved over her muscles as she flew. It was so wide and open; Azshbir had never imagined anything so open in his life, except the sky. It *was* like the sky; an endless expanse in all directions. A dark mass of land could still be viewed against the horizon in the direction from which they came. "What was stupid? How?" he asked, realizing he had not been paying attention to his wife for the last few seconds.

"Being afraid... of what they might do to us... or to our children... to hurt us," said Neah'ra.

It was a good thing the sea was very calm right then. Calmer than it had been a few hours ago. Otherwise, he would not have been able to hear her the way she was speaking. As it was, he had to strain. "How do you feel like that?" he asked. "You were terrified." He did not really understand what she was saying. What new insight had come to her? He knelt down, still holding the mast, so it would be easier to hear her.

"As I said, it was stupid." She paused for a moment. "It's no different than anything else... I guess I wasn't seeing clearly. What is it? What is it, really?"

"I don't understand. What is what?" asked Azshbir.

"I'm sorry," said Neah'ra. "I'm not sure if it can be said, and I feel so sleepy."

Sorry for what? wondered Azshbir. He was about to ask her, when he realized it would be rude, since she was feeling sleepy. Wrong? He knew that to actually fear something was wrong. But, what exactly did Neah'ra mean by being afraid? What exactly did she mean by stupid? He took some sacks and second pairs of clothing, and arranged them around her to make her more comfortable so that she could doze while nursing their daughter.

When Kira strayed by, he called to her. "What is it, Azshbir?" she asked.

"Neah'ra is tired and cannot tell me what she means," said Azshbir. "She said that it was really stupid to be afraid of the things that Hasseleighton might have done to our children and to us. I was wondering if you understand or could tell me what she means."

Kira looked down thoughtfully. After a few moments, she said, "I just want to make sure: you mean torturing others to get us to surrender? Or, taking others and raising them away from her to get her to surrender?"

"Probably the former," said Azshbir. "Do you understand?"

Kira looked down again. She shook her head slightly. The wind blew her hair across her face. "I might. A little," she said.

"Can you explain?" asked Azshbir.

Kira brushed her hair back from her face. "Can you tell me everything she said? That might help."

Azshbir thought for a few moments. "Something about it being no different than anything else and not seeing clearly," he said. He had puzzled over the conversation.

Kira nodded. He noticed that she still struggled– like he himself did– with the swaying of the ship. It was especially evident as she turned and took a few steps away. They were halting, cautious, ginger. She said something that was lost in the wind and the motion of the *Last Watch*. "Can you say that more loudly?" said Azshbir.

"I don't really understand," she said. "Certainly not how to say it." She turned back to him. Her mouth was open, and she had an expression on her face and in her eyes as if she were about to reveal something. "It's–" she began, and then a shadow crossed her expression. "No," she said thoughtfully. "I don't think I can." She paused for a few moments, then brought up a totally different subject. "Do you know why you had to say no about the crew?"

"Do you think I made a wrong decision?" asked Azshbir, feeling suddenly defensive and hating himself for it.

"No," said Kira. "No, that's not what I was thinking at all. I just wanted to know if you knew."

"Not really," said Azshbir, "and nothing more that I could say than what I said to the Queen. We must rely only on the Creator and set our hope only in Him."

Kira nodded. "I think I understand... a little," she said.

Though she was a young woman, ripe for marriage, now, she had been a young teenager when he first met her, no older than Neah'ra had been when he had first met her. For some reason, he could not resist the impulse to tease her. "Do you understand everything a little... and nothing very much?" he asked.

Kira smirked. "No," she said. The sails flapped and made a great noise. Azshbir looked down on Neah'ra. She did not even stir, but he could tell that Nourdë was close to fussing, and *that* would wake her. For some reason, he could not get the Queen out of his mind, especially those last moments with her on the shore before he and his family boarded the *Last Watch*. Something, he did not know what, had happened, and Kira's question had reminded him.

Over the next several hours, he came to understand. He thought about the different things she had said, about how she had found them and had them brought to herself. The Queen had no understanding of the fact that the Creator's people were supposed to trust and rely on Him; they were supposed to fight in the light, since He was the Lord of Light, and not by means of deceit. Or did the Queen have no understanding of it? He thought she had enough understanding to be uncomfortable. She certainly seemed uneasy, but he was not sure if she knew it yet.

In that moment, in the rocking of the ship on a larger, more wave-like swell than usual, in the clamor of the sails flapping in the changing wind, he heard the Creator's voice.

"Ask Me that she may live in the light as I will for her to do."

It was the Creator Himself who had even revealed Arendellie's struggle to him; he would never have understood it on his own.

More and more, he knew the clear and immediate direction of the Creator; he could, however, take no satisfaction or rest in that fact. He was given it for the sake of others. He had felt it in that lingering moment on the sea-shore when he had called the Queen by her first name and bade her farewell. He had felt it when he had told Ellason of his own and the Creator's forgiveness. It was frightening and uncomfortable at the same time as being comforting and reassuring, but there could be no mistaking the fact that it was not about him. It was almost exactly like the way that they were venturing on the sea. All around was uncertainty; all around was the dark; all around was unknown to him. He could only trust the One who was unknown to him even while He was known to him– the Creator and the Promise.

He looked for Kira, but she was staggering away. He wondered if there was anyone around to help him with his wife and daughter. *The scary thing is the ocean is right there– on all sides of us. Like cliffs. And, there is not much space. A wild, careless, or unsuspecting child could easily run off and drown. We aren't sailers. In anything even beginning to be a storm, we could tumble and get thrown off, or who knows what. Creator, You brought us to this. We came here at Your direction. Protect Your people. Bring us safely to whatever place You have for us, the place in which Your Promised One will come.*

#82
Secrets of the Elzari

"You have someone requesting an audience with you, your majesty," one of her newer maids informed Arendellie.

"What is her name?"

"El-Reiza, I think," replied the maid.

"Bring her to me," said Arendellie.

The maid turned to go. "Where, your majesty?"

"Here. In the gardens." She was playing with Kathreen.

In a few minutes, El-Reiza entered. She was older than she had been. There were a few wrinkles on her face, and her black hair was turning silver. As always, the combination of her personality and movement and her clothing struck Arendellie. She wore a blue skirt, turning silver at the hem, a silver blouse, and a violet shawl which she had already dropped from her head. She curtsied with warrior grace. "Your majesty," she said.

"You did not hear that I was looking for you, did you?" asked Arendellie, slightly worried. She had recently seen a scroll with all the Dragon-riders from the northern provinces, and had not seen El-Reiza or Leaoneth among them.

"No," said El-Reiza. "I came to check in on your majesty; the care of your majesty was the last charge Sir Andelf gave me."

She is incredibly loyal, I guess! thought Arendellie. She had so many questions for this strange and elusive woman. She was also quite distressed. Her husband, Vanesh, had recently told her to stop telling their second son, Aroch, about the Promise; he was saying things that roused suspicion and even protesting a few points. Some of his teachers were worried that there might be one of those loyal to the Promise among his nurses or one of themselves; a hunt for this individual was likely, at this point. He did not think she was in direct danger, but her maids might be. This distressed her, but she had been especially hurt by it when he said, "Besides, it had to stop; I was beginning to notice it myself, and I don't want my son to believe your nonsense about the Promise a great deal more than I want him to believe theirs." She wondered what she should do, but, before she could worry about her issues, she had to do what she could to fix the mess she had caused by allowing Ellason to get out of hand. *Creator! Thank You for El-Reiza!* she thought. To El-Reiza, she said, "May I ask you questions?"

"Yes, your majesty," said El-Reiza, shortly, not because she was upset, but because she was always like that, as taut as tightened wire.

"Do you believe the Promise?"

El-Reiza seemed very uncomfortable, more taut than ever. Arendellie thought she could guess what the issue might be. "There is no need to fear," she said. "I believe in the Promise."

El-Reiza still did not respond. Arendellie decided she would not push it. She had other questions, though, especially since El-Reiza was devoted to Sir Andelf, now long dead, and her, in some strange and mysterious way. Her timing was perfect. "Are you human? Are you a messenger of the Creator?" she asked.

"I am human," said El-Reiza. "As far as I know, I am not a messenger of the Creator."

Arendellie looked down, considering her next question. "I know this is rude, so please pardon me, and don't answer if you do not want, but, why are you so different from all humans and especially all women I have known?" She knew El-Reiza would have a hard time answering, given how little the woman was giving to talking.

"My people come from far away," she said, and paused, whether considering what to say next, how much she should say, or how to say what she had in mind, Arendellie did not know. "We call ourselves the Elzari. I may not tell you our secrets, but I am unusual even among the women of the Elzari."

Arendellie turned her head to watch Inshara play with Kathreen. She was not sure what to do. Could she fully trust someone with as many secrets as El-Reiza must have? A woman from a strange and secretive people? It was, she decided, her only option. She *knew* that most of her own people were treacherous, deceived by the lies of the Council, or downright bloodthirsty and cruel, like Ellason. She did not know anything that spoke ill upon either El-Reiza as an individual or the Elzari as a people– of course, this was the first time she had heard the word. She knew that Sir Andelf, who seemed generally perceptive, had trusted El-Reiza.

"I have a problem," Arendellie said, "that I was wondering if you could help me with. When I ordered families of Knights of the Promise brought to me, the parents and older children were brought, but some of the younger children were given to other families to be adopted. I have been gathering all the information I can about the families to which they have been given. You were willing to help me escape from the palace; would you be willing to kidnap these children for me and take them to Osilia?" She had already bought– using another agent whom she hoped she could trust– a mansion-castle in Osilia, near to the sea-shore.

"I want the information and proof that the children were stolen first," said El-Reiza simply.

It did not take Arendellie long to provide El-Reiza with the necessary information. Late the following night, when Vanesh was somewhere else, she took El-Reiza to meet the parents of the children. *Of course,* she thought, *if El-Reiza betrays me, we are all done for.* She could tell that both El-Reiza and the parents found the introduction uncomfortable, but the parents were glad when she told them that plans were underway to rescue their children. As she was leaving, she overheard someone whisper to someone else, "I am glad. This is like a really nice prison. A prison where we are spoiled, but still a prison."

In the corridor, Arendellie turned to El-Reiza and asked, "Do you know anyone in the armies that I could trust?"

"What for, your majesty?" asked El-Reiza.

"In my line of work, it is important to know people one can trust in the right places, or even people one can trust who might know others who might be trustworthy in the right places," said Arendellie. She hoped it would be enough for

El-Reiza to understand.

"No," said El-Reiza.

Several steps further down, Arendellie took an envelope from the folds of her dress. "In case you need resources to rescue and transport the children," she said, handing it to El-Reiza. "Just, make certain that if you or anyone associated with you is caught, nothing traces back to me. The lives of many more than you have seen here depend upon it."

El-Reiza nodded. "I understand," she said solemnly.

"Thanks; I don't feel like it right now," Arendellie told the maid who brought her lunch. She had recently heard that there were reports of a settlement in the Vinibra Mountains that was not registered with the Empire of Camil Hasseleighton. She wondered if there was a way to prevent whoever was hiding and fleeing from the tyranny from being arrested.

The maid peeked in again. "I'm sorry to interrupt you, since I know your majesty is not feeling well, but you have a visitor."

Arendellie looked up. "Who?"

"She says she is Mi'shael and she comes from El-Reiza."

"Send her in," said Arendellie. "I will meet her here."

Like El-Reiza, Mi'shael was slight, small, and colored more lightly than most Camilians. She also moved in a similar way, like a cat ready to pounce; there was coiled energy, ready to be released in any direction in her every movement. However, she was more graceful than El-Reiza and somewhat less taut. She wore a loose, flowing robe of strips of black and dark gray cloth and a black shawl over her head. She shut the door, then curtsied gracefully. "Your majesty," she said, and then drew nearer. "Is it safe? Is it private?" she asked, glancing around.

"Yes," said Arendellie. "We can make it more so, if you would feel more comfortable, though," she said.

"I would," said Mi'shael. "If you please, Queen."

Arendellie led the way further back. It occurred to her that this was not exactly safe; privacy meant she could be at Mi'shael's mercy; there would be no help, no one to protect her. She had seen how El-Reiza could move and suspected that Mi'shael was capable of similar feats. These Elzari would make expert assassins if ever they felt like it.

Mi'shael curtsied again. "El-Reiza asked me to tell you of some whom you can trust. I am here to give you their names and locations, so you can find them and ask for their aid."

Huh? thought Arendellie. *I thought El-Reiza did not know of such people.* She did not, however, ask. These Elzari were strange and they would not share their secrets. Perhaps, El-Reiza had lied to her; perhaps, there were all kinds of intricacies in the society of the Elzari that she could not understand. "Before I can tell you though," Mi'shael said, "I need you to promise that you will not reveal this information to anyone under any circumstances. You may enlist their aid, but you must promise that you will never tell anyone about me or El-Reiza or our connection to any of these."

Arendellie did not understand why, but she promised.

Mi'shael was certainly quite different from El-Reiza. She was a much more natural talker. She made elaborate hand motions as she described where the people were and how to find them; there were three of them. Arendellie found herself saying, "The way you move reminds me of the way a friend of mine moved when she used a sword."

There was something Arendellie could not read in Mi'shael's expression, but it was frightening. "You knew one of us? What was her name?"

Arendellie was taken aback, and a little worried. "I don't think she was Elzari. Her name was Kathreen Alarion. She was not built at all like you. I'm sorry."

Horror and fear showed in Mi'shael's eyes. She was visibly shaken and she paled. However, she did not say anything. She rose and said, "Thank you for telling us, Queen. Be careful; Camil is full of enemies."

"I know," said Arendellie. "I just want to make sure: do we have the same enemies?"

"Do not worry, Queen," said Mi'shael. "Elzari *never* betray *any*thing. Do not betray us."

"I won't," said Arendellie, bewildered, and beginning to worry if she had done something wrong in asking for El-Reiza's aid, as Mi'shael left. She was drawn into yet another area about which she knew nothing, full of potentially dangerous secrets and pitfalls. She knew even less about these elusive Elzari than she had about the intricacies and dangers of royal courts. She did not even know what her promises might be made to mean. *O Creator, help me,* she prayed. At any rate, she would tell the Elzari about the settlement in the Vinibra Volcanic Mountains and the threat to it; perhaps, it was their hiding place, and she owed it to them to tell them.

Unless, they were her enemies? Mi'shael had not answered her question.

#83
Strangled

Brisia knew that, in the clearing down the hillside on the slab of volcanic rock on the shores of the lake, Laekoorj waited. She, Khiel, Senise, and Sirifa had gone through the clothing they had stored away, shortly after Sirifa and Hoobit had come here. They had found a yellow dress, which they had stitched to fit Brisia. Sirifa told her that she would be glad to see her married. She was almost dizzy with happiness. Her hair was braided behind her head and flowers were woven into it.

"A dragon! A dragon comes!"

Brisia heard the frantic cry interrupt the song. Someone else cried, "It isn't L'sa-moth! It looks white and black!"

Brisia fled. She dashed into the trees, into the jungle. Almost at once she fell on her face over a vine she had failed to see in the dim light. It felt like it took her minutes to crawl out of it. She heard people screaming, but she could not even tell from which direction the screams came. When she finally could stand, she did. She did not know what to do. At least she could see a little. All around were trees and bushes and vines. There could be snakes anywhere, too. She was not on a path. She continued running.

She caught her hair on a brush and had to stop to untangle it. It began to come undone and the flowers fell out, but she did not think about that. When she stood still for a moment, she heard the sounds of others crashing through the jungle, and screams and words she could not understand.

Should she go back? Should she try to tell whoever had found them about the Promise? It was that, or death in the jungle. Of course, nothing was certain. She might be tortured, or she might be heard. The Creator could do anything. He could deliver His people in strange and mysterious ways. Anyway, she could not go back. She did not know where she was. She stood for a moment, frozen with numerous fears and concerns. *Dormik! O my Creator, don't let him die like this! O my Creator, can you use this to change his mind so he doesn't hate anymore? Please! Use this to show him love and forgiveness!*

She fled downhill. She tumbled through a bush and tore her dress, then rolled through vines. She knew she might die at any moment. A poisonous snake might bite her. Another jungle-animal might take her and eat her. She could die in any number of ways. *O Creator, please! I want to live and die Your way. Like Kathreen. Like Mom. Not like Dad.*

Someone spoke her name. Urgently. Concerned. "Brisia!"

She struggled to sit up. Vines were wrapped around her. She had been scraped on a flat rock she had rolled down. She recognized Laekoorj's voice. She felt uncomfortable, strangled, as if her clothes were too tight. She felt dizzy. "Laekoorj!" she called, as best as she could.

"A snake!" he cried.

Brisia tried to get up. "A snake?" she asked. She tried to look around. She could hardly breathe. She must have hit her head. Laekoorj appeared in her visual field.

He held a black rock. He raised his arm to strike her with it. She flinched, but she could not draw back. She felt a thud, and then she felt teeth dig into her shoulder. She closed her eyes and grimaced and screamed in pain. She continued to feel the thuds, as Laekoorj struck her, but it did not hurt as much as being struck with a rock should hurt. She felt the creature bite her again. "Help me!" she screamed. Moaning, she cried, "O my Creator, help me; it *HURTS!*" She wanted to ask what was happening.

She felt something slithering over her. She was shaking with sobs. She felt tense, cramped, and somewhat bruised and scraped. "What– what– ha... happened?" she sobbed.

"A small kimmer had you," said Laekoorj, trying to be soothing, but obviously somewhat shaken. "Did you roll on him in his den? Because, that's how they usually catch things. They wrap themselves around anything that stumbles on them. It was small enough it only had a chance with you because you did not even realize what was happening. I probably could have just pulled him off. I'm sorry. Then, he wouldn't have bit you."

Brisia nodded. Her head was spinning. She knew she had to tell Laekoorj something, but she could not figure out what. Finally, she stammered out, "Where are the others?"

"Soldiers ambushed us. I wanted to find you. I don't know," said Laekoorj. He looked over his shoulder. "This is still far too open. Let's go."

Laekoorj took her arm, and half-dragged her back into the jungle. She followed, still feeling dazed. Finally, what seemed like hours later, after she had fainted more than once, he lowered her to the ground and sat down. She leaned against his shoulder. "Is this pointless?" she asked quietly.

"What is this?" asked Laekoorj.

"Fleeing," she murmured. She still felt like passing out. Her wounds throbbed. Her dress was soaked in blood. "I mean... aren't we just going to die in the jungle this way?"

"Not necessarily," said Laekoorj, feeling worried about her. It could not be venom, though. That snake was definitely a kimmer, and kimmers were not poisonous. "My parents set themselves up in the jungle alone. We might be better off. I might be able to sneak back and get their tools. Maybe we can even use a lot of the food from their gardens, until we establish our own."

Brisia did not hear him. She was struggling just to think. She closed her eyes, so she did not have to fight to even see. "Or," she said, "we might go down into the city and tell as many people as we can about the Promise... and then die... We'll tell the guards and the prisoners, too... After all... we have no children."

Laekoorj looked down on her face, distressed. He could not see much in this lighting, but he thought she might be pale. Her rambling continued to disintegrate. "The Creator will rescue us all... The guards will be very pleased. Ahh."

Laekoorj heard the sounds of people coming through the jungle. He thought he heard the sounds of steel. "Brisia," he whispered. "Come." She did not respond. He could not carry her; even if she woke up, he did not know if she could stand, let alone run. He remained very still, reassigning himself to his fate. He thought of her ramblings. Was there anything to any of it? How much of it actually had something to do with reality? In them, was she telling what would happen?

Light glinted off the steel armor of several soldiers entering the clearing. They bore down on him and struck him. "Don't hurt her; she's hurt already," he pleaded, but he did not know if they would even hear him. His face was pressed into the mud. Still less would they care. Doubtless, they delighted in torturing the Creator's people. *Thank You,* he thought. *Thank You.* In her present state, she would not survive much torture. He wondered if she would survive at all without care.

Brisia woke in almost total darkness. A dim light flickered. She was stiff and sore. Her bruises throbbed, and so did wounds she could not remember receiving in her shoulder and arm. "Where am I?" she asked.

"Prison," said Esiri.

"Oh yes," said Brisia. "I think I remember." She still felt strange. How long had it been?

"Would you like some water?"

Yes! That was it! That was why her head hurt. She was very thirsty. "Yes, thank you," she said, sitting up. Her cramped muscles screamed in protest, and she felt like she would faint.

The water Esiri gave her was not very much. She wanted to go to sleep again. "Are the others here?" she asked. "What happened?"

"Somehow, they captured us all," said Esiri. "We all ran in different directions, and some of us fought for the others, but they captured us all. They told us so, though we haven't seen everyone."

"How–" began Brisia, but Esiri whispered, "Sshh!" The door creaked open, and they heard the sound of boots. Brisia saw a shadow against the dim flickering light. Then, another door grated open, and she heard something dropped. Someone grunted.

"What–" Brisia began to ask again, but Esiri clamped her hand over her mouth. Brisia did not struggle. She was too confused to try, scarcely even to think.

When the guard had departed, after perhaps half an hour, Esiri let go of Brisia's mouth. "We aren't allowed to talk."

"What was that?" Brisia asked.

"We aren't allowed to speak to each other," Esiri repeated herself.

"No. I meant– what was *that?*" She struggled to speak. Why could she not make herself clear?

"That? That is Khiel's cell. It might be her."

Brisia stood. She felt like passing out, but, somehow, she did not fall. The world still spinning around her, she took the single stride to the bars. They were too narrow. She could fit her arm through them. She tried to push herself through the bars. Maybe, just maybe, she would fit. It would hurt, but maybe… if the bars bent just a little… she might be able to push through. She grunted, struggled. "Esiri, help!" she pleaded, her voice short and gasping.

She felt Esiri's hand on her. "Ow!" she breathed, for it was her injured shoulder. Esiri drew her back. "No!" she pleaded.

"It won't work," said Esiri gently. "You won't get through. If you do, or even if you only try, you will only succeed in getting yourself tortured."

Brisia collapsed on the ground. She looked up at Esiri fiercely, but Esiri could not see her expression in the dim light. "We're all going to be tortured, aren't we? Unless you plan on worshiping Grale Casarion. I would only torment myself by trying to avoid it! I might as well just let it happen, since it *will,* and not even try. Otherwise, I torment myself with fear and vain effort and worry and useless thinkings."

Esiri sighed. "Whatever, Brisia. Try to be quiet. I don't want to get in trouble because you are overheard." She sat down. "Why are you so upset anyway?"

"It *will* happen; I might as well not fear it," said Brisia, as if she had not even heard Esiri. The fact was, she struggled to concentrate on Esiri's voice. She struggled to speak herself. The world still felt half unreal around her, shallow, colorless– not that there were any colors to be seen in the dim, flickering light of a single torch.

Esiri did not respond. She could not think of anything to say. She did not even know what she thought about what Brisia was proposing.

#84
A Child's Warning

Brisia got up and walked to the back of the cell, next to the bars between her cell and Khiel's. "Khiel," she whispered, but there was no response. She dug her fingers into the wall, and found that it was clay and stones. Gritting her teeth, she tore at it. Her fingernail tore, but a small chip came off. She sucked her finger for a moment, trying to soothe the pain, but unsuccessfully. She attacked the wall again.

Esiri came over. "What are you doing?" she asked.

"This," Brisia grunted, hardly pausing in her work. She was fighting against waves of suffocating blackness.

Esiri did not ask again. Instead, a few moments later, she pulled Brisia away from the wall. "Stop it!" she hissed in her ear. "It won't work, and you'll get us both tortured... for nothing."

"I might as well not worry about it," insisted Brisia again.

"You're acting like a little child," said Esiri. "Anyways, why do you want to be with Khiel so much?"

"She's hurt–" Brisia sobbed, but Esiri covered her mouth. "Sshh! He's coming," she whispered.

Brisia stumbled back and sat on the ground. Why did Esiri care? She was not trying to do anything wrong, and they were doomed to torture and execution anyways! Better not to worry, fret, or fear. Better not to waste one's energy on fret and worry about what was not one's responsibility and would happen to one anyways! Better to simply accept one's circumstances. The guards slipped something through the bars. She heard Esiri slurp something, even before the guard departed, and chew. When he had left, she offered a plate to Brisia. "Eat," she said.

Brisia did not respond.

"Would you like to drink first?"

Brisia gladly accepted the cup and drank. She was hungry, but she knew eating would only increase her thirst. She rose, took the short stride to the correct corner of the cell, and continued her attack on the wall. When she found herself passing out, she decided maybe she would eat. It took a long time to chew the stale bread, and she was desperate to get across.

"What is wrong with you?" Esiri asked her, as she rose again.

"It's better not to waste my energy fretting and worrying about something that isn't my job and will happen to me anyways," Brisia responded.

"Conserving your energy so you can suffer more torture?" Esiri mocked.

Brisia ignored her. She did not even notice the disdain in her tone of voice. She took her plate, which was metal, and attacked the wall with it.

Esiri pulled her back again. She gasped as Esiri grabbed the wounds the snake had left. "Stop it! You'll make such a clamor we will all be tortured."

"The Creator is good," Brisia gasped, struggling and trying to get away from her.

A voice called to them from a couple cells down. It was Kizyia. "What is going on?" the girl asked.

"I want to get to Khiel, and Esiri doesn't want to let me!" shot Brisia back.

"She's crazy," said Esiri. "Besides, why does she even want to get to Khiel?"

"She's hurting," said Brisia quietly. "She is in pain! How would you like lying on a cold floor in bloody rags after you've been beaten and tortured? Just dropped on the floor? Alone?"

"Twice," muttered Esiri under her breath. "She's probably fine," she said. "Better than most of us. Remember how happy she was, even after seeing her parents transferred? Besides, we will all, most likely, be in her position soon. Certainly if you do what you are doing."

Brisia cut in, before she was done speaking. "Yes. So why worry about or try to prevent it? Is that an excuse to be mean?"

"Mean?" asked Esiri, but Brisia took her plate, and continued to hack at the wall. It broke on a brick, and she just went on. Esiri sat frozen in fear. Brisia hurt, but she did not care. Finally, she thought she had made enough of a dent in the wall. She dropped the plate and drew back, until her foot touched the wall on the other side. She steeled herself against the explosion of pain she knew would come and took a running leap.

She could not help but cry out in pain as her body struck the bars and wall. She wriggled and writhed, and managed to position herself so she could get a little more of her body through. She got an arm on the other side and pushed. She bit her lip against the pain– she could not push through it. "Esiri, please!" she begged. "Please, help me!" Realizing herself she said, "And, DO NOT pull me back!"

Kizyia must have had her face pressed against the bars on the other side of Khiel's cell. "Yes, Esiri. Please!" she pleaded quietly. Other voices added to her plea.

For whatever reason, Esiri cooperated. Brisia slid onto the floor. *My Creator, help me,* she pleaded. She crawled across the floor to where Khiel lay. She wished she had more than her torn, ragged, dirty and bloody dress. Carefully, tenderly, she touched her friend. "Khiel," she whispered. Groping with her hand, she found the plate and cup. She took the cup and carefully– for her hand was trembling, and damaged– brought it closer. She opened Khiel's mouth and poured a few droplets in. Some of the water trickled down her swollen cheek. Brisia began to sob.

"What are you doing?" asked Esiri.

Brisia tried again. She did not know what she was doing. "Giving her a drink," said Brisia.

"What?" said Esiri, struggling to keep her voice from rising out of rage. "Do you want to keep her alive to face even more torture?"

Brisia resorted to very childish behavior: she turned and made a face at Esiri– a face which Esiri could not see because of the dim light.

Khiel murmured something.

"I'm sorry. I did not hear you," said Brisia, putting the cup aside and bending low.

"I'm glad, Brisia. Thank you," she said.

Brisia nodded. "Are you well?" she asked, though she knew it was so much gibberish.

Khiel reached out her hand and gently touched Brisia's cheek. Her fingers were sticky with blood. "You know…" she said, her voice trailing off.

Brisia nodded, swallowing past the lump in her throat.

At that moment, the door pushed open. "What is all the ruckus about?" demanded a nasty voice.

Brisia's voice stuck in her throat. She struggled to say, "Me! Me!" she tried again. "I am what all the ruckus is about!"

Gasping, Khiel raised herself up on one arm.

A guard came to the door, inserted the key, and flung it open. "You two are the makers of all this ruckus!"

Brisia stood, swaying, whether with fear or with hunger or thirst. "No!" she protested, feeling as if the world dropped away around her. It did not feel quite real. "Just me," she continued, struggling to find words and to get them out. "Just me! I did all the ruckus. Not her! It's not her fault! Just me!" She continued to protest frantically as the guards caught up both her and Khiel. She heard Khiel let out a short scream of pain. She stopped protesting to say, "I'm sorry! I didn't mean to hurt you mo–" Her bearer slapped her, and she stopped speaking.

They were both carried from the cells and into a room that stank like nothing else Brisia had ever encountered. She felt like it would make her pass out. The guards dropped them both on the floor. Khiel crawled to her and whispered, "No, Brisia. Thank you."

Brisia closed her eyes and waited. It seemed that an eternity passed. She sat up and vomited, trying to get her face away from Khiel.

"The smell of death. Blood and death and you," said one of the guards.

Khiel's voice, soft and strained but musical, broke in on Brisia's ears. "How do you bear it?" she asked.

"As long as you're vomiting, we like it," said a guard.

That's not much of an answer, thought Brisia, wondering if the worst thing they were going to do to her was watch her throw up. It was cruel though; she was already weak from lack of food and water and incredibly thirsty.

The guard's voice was closer now. "How do *you* bear it, though?"

"We are going to a perfect place," said Khiel. Brisia knew she wanted to say more, but could not figure out how. At the moment, she could not figure out how either. She was still retching, pains wracking her body, even though nothing was coming out.

"What is this perfect place like?" the guard asked, sneering. To his companion he said, "Get things ready."

"Our champion has conquered death," Khiel said slowly. "Even this will be well."

Brisia cringed, but she knew what Khiel was talking about. They had discussed it so many times. She lowered herself down, too tired and too overwhelmed to care about getting her vomit on herself. She began to beg inarticulately. "Creator... Creator... Creator," she sobbed aloud.

"He won't rescue you, you know," the guard said, striking her.

Brisia did not care to respond. She knew the Creator could– and might– rescue her. He had, once before. He had used Kathreen Alarion then, but He could do whatever He wanted. He had showed her many things through the scroll. Speaking of the scroll, where was it? Not that it mattered. Besides, she was just calling out to Him. His Promise was all she had. She knew He was real. She needed His help. What that was, she did not know– or care.

She heard the other guard enter. She wriggled away and sat up. "Actually," she said, getting to her feet and speaking through a wave of blackness, "you should be scared. He is very, very big. Bigger than any size. He could crush you so tiny you won't even be human anymore. He will, too, if you don't accept His Promise."

The guards exchanged glances. "It is time," one of them said.

Blackness came over her, and she fell to the ground, slipping on something.

#85
The Desert

Brisia sat against the cell bars. Khiel felt to her like she was dying. Brisia struggled to remember a thought that she knew was very important. It kept slipping away from her. Finally, she asked, "The scroll. Do you know what happened to it?"

"I have it," said Khiel. Brisia heard her moving and, then, she handed the scroll to her.

"Huh?" asked Brisia, looking at it. It seemed unharmed, unaffected even. Unrolling it, she found that she could read it, even though it was even darker than it had been, earlier. She did so, out loud. "Then, He shall stand upon the mountain, He for whom the nations longed and the earth cried out. His gaze shall bring the ruined flowers to life, and where He goes the desert shall blossom." It helped her ignore the throbbing, burning pain. She read a few more lines, then found that she could not read it anymore. She lay down next to Khiel, trying to find a position that did not hurt too much, but the pain kept her from sleeping. She would have to be very, very tired to sleep at all. She and Khiel had shared the water in their cell, but it had not helped much. *O Creator, Creator, Creator,* she thought over and over again, through the pain.

The door opened again. Brisia cringed, and as she flinched pain shot through her body. "Here they are, your majesty," a female guard was explaining. Light entered the room. "We did not know you were coming here and would be interested in them. We are sorry we have already started."

"It is all right," said the Queen. "Be at rest. I did not tell you, so there is no blame. Can I have the keys?"

They jangled as they changed hands. "Thank you," said the Queen. "Now, you are dismissed. I prefer to work with those I know."

"Yes, your majesty," said the guard and left.

Brisia turned to see. The Queen was splendidly dressed in green and purple. She had five female servants, also well-dressed. None of them looked cruel. One of them carried a brightly burning lamp. Its light hurt her eyes and made her head hurt unbearably. She closed her eyes and turned away. When an almost unbearably long time had passed, the Queen said, "Pull the door most of the way closed."

When that had been done, the Queen handed the keys to one of her servants. "Open all the cells, please," she said.

What kind of Queen says please to her servants? wondered Brisia. She was so confused. She wished she could sleep– pass out– anything. The world was unbearable.

"Firstly, I want to tell you all that I have no ill will towards you. You will be fed and cared for and sent away," said the Queen. Brisia's head throbbed as she heard the cell door swung open. *Creator,* she begged again in her mind. Someone bent down.

Feeling the need to be respectful, Brisia forced herself into a sitting position. She grimaced because of the pain and tried to relax. It was the Queen who knelt before her and Khiel. She lowered her head. "I'm sorry," she said, embarrassed, ashamed, confused, without any idea how she should carry herself. Then, she realized she should say, "Your majesty," and did so.

"My name is Arendellie," said the Queen. She glanced at the cup on the side. Without turning her head, she said, "Nagi, get me a skin of water."

"Thanks," said Brisia, and closed her eyes. She had seen great pain and concern on the Queen's face. Meanwhile, Arendellie looked over Khiel. Gently, she touched Khiel. "Are there any others like this?"

Adaria stood just behind her. "Here? No, your majesty. Where are my children?"

"I will make sure all your children are brought to you. In fact, I have already sent out orders and servants to that effect. I am very sorry that the Council's soldiers got to you before mine. I tried."

Brisia wanted to disappear. She wanted everything to end. This was not the way that the Queen should be acting. It made no sense. Was it some huge, ugly trick? *I wonder how long it takes to die,* she thought.

Khiel struggled to sit up. Brisia felt and heard her move. After a long, long moment, a moment that felt long to Arendellie and even longer to Brisia, though Brisia was not paying attention, she said, "Your majesty,"

Arendellie interrupted. "No. It is I who am sorry. I am sorry this has happened to you. I am sorry I–"

Brisia found her eyes flitting open. Khiel raised her arm slowly. She touched Arendellie's cheek, leaving smears of blood. Holding her hand there, she said, "No, Aren, whate–. Don't be sorry. I'm well. I'm glad." She held her hand there a moment longer, then dropped it. Her shoulders slumped. Brisia moved, to hold her. Kizyia stepped in and sat down. Others, unknown to the people from the Vinibra Mountains gathered around.

Arendellie sat there, feeling very uncomfortable. What was she supposed to say? She *was* sorry. Even if she was not guilty. But, how could she say that again? How could she offer anything? "What's your name?" she asked.

"Kizyia," said Kizyia. Brisia opened her eyes and saw Arendellie looking at her. She shrank back. "Brisia," she offered. *How long will this go on? How long will this last? My Creator?*

The door opened again. "Here is the water," said Nagi.

Carefully, Arendellie poured some into the cup and handed it to Brisia. When Brisia drank, she again poured it into the cup, and Khiel drank. Esiri brought her cup, and they filled them both again. "After you've finished with that, Nagi," said Arendellie, "make sure anyone else who might be hurt gets to drink first."

"Yes, your majesty," said Nagi, straightening.

Arendellie rose. "Kalie, stay with Nagi. I must go to arrange what is necessary. Come." There was so much she had to do. It would be much more complicated, now that they were already in the city's prisons. She had to get them all out, and together, and she had to provide suitable environments for the recovery of those who were injured. *O my Creator, help me do this. Help me serve Your people,* she prayed, overwhelmed. More and more, these days, she felt like collapsing. She felt so tired. It did not make sense. She was no longer exactly young, but she was only in her early forties. She was far from old. Already she had seen the men, but she could not go back to assure them that those whom they loved were okay. She did not even know who everyone was.

Late that night, in the early hours of the coming day, she entered the room where the women were held. It helped that she was Queen and could simply demand access to everything, without having to say what specifically, or why. She found six or seven people laying around Brisia and Khiel. They remained asleep, but both Brisia and Khiel's eyes flitted open. Neither of them could truly sleep.

Arendellie bent down. "I'm not supposed to say I'm sorry, right?" she asked. Joy flitted across Khiel's face, and she saw a warm glow in Brisia's eyes. She placed her hand on Khiel's brow. She was running a very high fever. She touched her wrist and barely felt her pulse. *Why do I care so much? There are so many, and I cannot do this for all of them. In fact, I don't know if I can do anything for her.*

A slight smile graced Brisia's features. Arendellie did not know what she was thinking about. She debated whether or not to ask, and finally did so.

Brisia did not know how to answer. She sat up. "I'm not sure…" she began. Then, she began to sing, softly, slowly, a haunting melody Khiel had written. "He formed the skies to be a canopy about His radiance, and He laid out the earth upon the waters below." Her eyes closed, she went on to sing the entire poem about the valleys of the sea where no one can walk and the echoes of the echoes of the deadly radiance round the throne of the Creator, the airs that are too bright for flesh and the blinding snows. Arendellie listened, wondering, remembering both her first reading of that poem, and standing on the shore of the sea, watching the *Last Watch* sail away into the sea and the dawn. Brisia's voice was enchantingly beautiful, and she closed her eyes to absorb the song. It roused images in her mind of she knew not what and yet she both remembered and yearned to know.

Several others woke and sat up to listen to the song. "We were going to sing that for your wedding!" Lalia called. Brisia ignored her and continued to sing. When she came to the end of that song, she sang it again, just for pleasure, and for the distraction it proved to be. Though she knew quite a few others, it was her favorite one.

"What's that?" A girl's voice broke in on Arendellie's thoughts. She opened her eyes. "What?" she asked.

"What's that for?" the girl asked, pointing to a bundle she had. "It is clothes for you all," she said. "Why don't you take that cloak to– Brisia, I think?"

"The singing one?" offered Nahiza.

"Yes," said Arendellie.

"That's the one," said Nahiza.

"You should put that on her, but try not to step on anybody who is sleeping. Her clothes are hardly even clinging to her body," said Arendellie. It was true. The dress Brisia wore was far worse than it had been when she emerged from the jungles and was rescued by Laekoorj. At this point, it hardly deserved to be called clothing.

Brisia came to the end again and stopped. "We will make a litter for that girl." Arendellie bit the inside of her cheek. She *hated* calling people 'that girl.' It reminded her of what she had been before she encountered the terrible Light. "What is her name?" she asked.

"My friend? Who is very hurt?" asked Brisia. There were tears in her eyes.

"Yes."

"Her name is Khiel."

"We will make a litter for Khiel, and we will go outside the city. After that, Dragon-riders will begin to carry you away." She had heard from El-Reiza, who was mostly using the Dragon-rider Mi'shael as a messenger, that she had 'kidnapped' the children, and they were at this moment being taken to Osilia. She had already had the parents and everyone else she rescued flown there. Now, she had all of these. She had plenty for the ship which she had bought and which was due to deliver its goods to Osilia in less than two weeks.

While Arendellie, her servants, and several others worked on making the litter, Brisia bent down close to Khiel. "Are you going to die?" she asked. "I will miss you so much, but I guess it…" *Explains why you are not to marry,* she thought, but did not know how to say it.

"It's not like that," whispered Khiel. *I know it isn't,* thought Brisia. A few moments later, Khiel said, "Don't be sad. If I'm to die… it is right."

Brisia nodded, swallowing the lump in her throat. Her injuries throbbed.

"Your voice is lovely," said Khiel, and Brisia knew she meant far more. She knew that, like herself, Khiel felt the absolute perfection of the poems and the song, the meaning which they both knew was there but which they could never share, never explain, the meaning and reality behind the world, behind all that was, the Uncreated, Unspeakable Glory and Light, a radiance, beauty, goodness, and joy as sharp and as severe as torture and as tender, gentle, and mellow as underwater colors. Brisia closed her eyes, and sang another poem for which she and Khiel had written a tune.

#86
Morning

Brisia sat through the night by Khiel, offering her water from time to time, keeping a wet cloth on her forehead, and singing. In the early hours of the morning, Laekoorj came and sat down next to her. "Are you all right?" he asked.

Brisia shrugged.

"The Queen told me you were tortured," he said, concern evident in his voice.

She shrugged again. "I will be fine," she said. She was in pain. There would be scars. It would not really be a big deal, though, in a couple weeks.

"Is she all right?" asked Laekoorj, meaning Khiel, and slightly annoyed at Brisia's unwillingness to tell him anything.

"She would say she is," said Brisia. "It depends on what you mean by 'all right,' though the word we like is 'well.'" She sighed. "I'm so hungry."

"I'll get you something to eat," said Laekoorj.

She looked up. "How long has it been since we were captured?"

Laekoorj shrugged. "Five days? I wouldn't know for sure. Why? You would know as well as I."

"No, I wouldn't," she said. "I didn't wake up until… yesterday, I think."

"Well, I'm glad you're alive… and healthy," said Laekoorj. "I'll get you food."

"Thanks," said Brisia. She was so tired. She was sure she wanted to sleep more than she wanted to eat, but she was still having trouble sleeping. She might almost be able to, she thought. Certainly after she ate.

It was almost an hour before Laekoorj came back with food. The sky was white with dawn. She could hear the wings of the several dragons who were carrying people away. As she sank her teeth into a warm slice of bread, Laekoorj asked, "Are you still going to marry me?"

"You're impatient," she said, garbling her words through her mouthful. After swallowing, she said, "I don't see why not. It's what I said I would do, right?"

"Yes," said Laekoorj, uncomfortably, "but a lot has changed."

"Marriage would change a lot, anyways," said Brisia.

"That's beside the point, and doesn't change what I was saying," said Laekoorj.

"I am Brisia. You are Laekoorj. Half a week in prison doesn't change any of that." She was not sorry for Khiel. She would just miss her. They were best friends. They knew the same things– far more so than she and Laekoorj knew the same things. It was really strange to be getting married.

She did not manage to eat half of what Laekoorj brought her before she was full. She shoved the plate aside, and told him that she was full, she would eat later, and to leave her alone. Then, she spread out the cloak Arendellie had given her and lay down. The new robe was made of the smoothest, softest silk, and it helped her get some small measure of comfort. It was hopeless to try to get away from the pain, so she just lay down and, amazingly quickly, was asleep. It had been a trying time, and it had been at least a day and a night.

Still tired, she woke when the sun was fully risen and above the mountains.

Khiel had found her hand and held it. She did not want to move, and so, still laying down, as comfortable as she had been for what seemed like an age though it was really less than a day, she said, "Good morning." It was a useless thing to say.

"Morning, sister," Khiel murmured back. There was so much in that word. *Morning.*

"I'll miss you," said Brisia sadly.

Khiel only said, "This is right." Brisia knew what she meant, or some of what she meant, and she could not or did not try to think of how to say more.

It did not erase the ache in Brisia's heart. "Would you like to eat?" she offered.

Khiel gasped as she moved onto her side. Brisia did not want to get up to hand the plate over, but she did. Then, she settled back down, a little differently this time. She was still so tired. Just sitting up, she felt like passing out. She wanted to relax... to vanish into sleep... to rest and do nothing but rest for a good long month and a half. She was driven to drink somewhere, and then pulled the cloak over her face, partially blocking the light, and drifted in and out of sleep.

Probably less than two hours later, she woke up, without hope of getting any further sleep for a while. She noticed that Khiel had– literally– hardly had a couple mouthfuls. She was, again, extremely hungry, but she still did not manage to eat half of what was left on the plate. Looking at Khiel, she thought that she was finally really asleep. She dipped the cloth in the water again, wrung it out a little, and laid it on her forehead. Then, she took the scroll, spread it out before her, and read. It struck her as strange how it had been neither noticed nor damaged. Neither had it fallen out of Khiel's clothing. How? She knew Khiel must have grabbed it before running. It was a special scroll. Azshbir, Adaria's older brother's, writing had appeared on it, even though he could not have written it on it.

While Brisia was thinking these things, Esiri passed by. "Brisia," she said softly.

"Yes, Esiri?" said Brisia.

"I'm sorry for how I acted in the cell," said Esiri, genuinely.

"Okay," said Brisia. She could not think of how to respond.

"The dragons are about to take another round. Would you like to come this time?" asked Esiri.

"No," said Brisia. "I am staying with Khiel."

"All right," said Esiri. "I will tell the Queen that." She paused for a moment, lingering. Then, she asked quietly, "Brisia?"

Brisia turned and sat up. This time, she was not actually afraid that she would faint; she only almost felt like it. She did not want to wake Khiel up.

"I've heard from the others– apparently, Queen Arendellie has a reputation for giving Knights of the Promise to the Undead Snow Queen," said Esiri.

Brisia did not care. She hardly remembered anything about the Undead Snow Queen. "A legend?" she asked.

"She was a legend. Apparently, she actually came, and took many dragons and People of the Promise away. That's what they're telling me," said Esiri.

Brisia did not care. She lay back down, wishing she could fall back into sleep.

At least, everything around them was beautiful. Blue sky. White clouds. Tall trees with bright flowers. A warm, stifling wind that felt like it might bring rain. She thought of Esiri's question in the prison: why did she even want to get to Khiel so much? There were good reasons to do so; it may well have been the right thing to do. But, upon consideration, she instantly thought that there had been wrong in her reasons. She might well have done it for someone else if given the opportunity; she might, then, have done it entirely, or almost entirely, for right reasons. She had a fierce attachment to Khiel. It felt awful– it felt like retching after all the vomit was gone– to think about Khiel dying– about losing Khiel. She loved Khiel. They were sisters, best friends, closer than any twins could be. But, Khiel was dying– she had seen the concern in the Queen's face and she knew that, while she was recovering her strength, Khiel was still losing hers– and she was getting married. She remembered her and Khiel's conversation about Khiel's feeling that marriage was not right for her, and about she-knew-not-how-to-say-what-she-did-know. She knew that when Khiel had said, "This is right," she was referring to those conversations. *Something* was right. It was time. She got on her elbow and looked on Khiel, pale and breathing shallowly. With tears, she remembered playful tones in her voice, she remembered things she had said– and more, the way she said them.

She might have feared that Khiel was going to die because she clung to her in the wrong way– because she wanted her too much– because of her. However, Khiel had made sure that she did not feel that that was the primary reason– perhaps, it was a reason as far as Brisia was concerned, but as far as Khiel was concerned, it was not.

Khiel's eyes fluttered open. They were not as clear as Brisia was used to. "It was so evil," she muttered. "So much evil… inside of them. So wrong. So sorry."

"What is she talking about?" asked Laekoorj.

Brisia startled and looked over at him. "You're here?"

"I'm staying here until you go," said Laekoorj quietly. There was some sorrow or memory in his eyes that Brisia did not understand. Gravely, quietly, he said, "She looks like you did… when I took you into the jungle, just before we were caught."

"I hardly remember it," said Brisia.

"I'll have to tell you. Do you know what she's talking about?"

Brisia ignored him and tried to help Khiel drink and change the cloth over her head. "Thanks," she murmured, falling back down. Finally, Brisia turned to face Laekoorj. She stood up and swayed, dizzy. He put his arm around her, to steady her, and she gasped. "Did I hurt you?" he asked, concern and pain in his voice.

"No," she gasped. "Just hold me… here." She moved a little, and leaned against him gingerly. "She could be talking about a lot more than I know," said Brisia, haltingly. "She knows– she saw– she heard– she felt– more than I did. But, I think she's saying that the real evil, the real horror, was what was inside the guards, the torturers…not what they did, but what what they did was an expression of." She fell silent. She remembered the cruelty in their mocking voices, the sneers.

She remembered Dormik; how he had looked at her and how he had spoken to her when she pleaded with him about the Creator and the Promise, when she had asked him not to hate. How? How could they remind her of him? He was so different. He was her brother. And, they were all he hated. She looked at Laekoorj. "How is my brother?"

"He's not dead," said Laekoorj.

Brisia started away, let out a sharp "Ow!" and spoke through the waves of blackness that hid the world and made her feel dizzy. "They h-hurt him?" she cried.

"He fought," said Laekoorj. "He actually killed– in prison, not being captured. He spat and he fought. Every chance he had." Laekoorj spoke sadly.

Brisia sat down. "I'm sorry," she said. Then, "That's what I think Khiel was saying. She's sorry about the evil inside them. Like, I'm sorry for Dormik." Hastily, she added, "Not that he ever did anything cruel." No, he was just consumed with hatred, bitterness, and evil. It was ruining him. What would it turn him into before the end? She began to cry.

She felt Khiel brush her with her hand, as if in question.

She twisted around, ignoring the pain. "If you die… if you see the King… please, ask Him to help my brother not be evil," she said.

She knew Khiel acknowledged her. Laekoorj sat down next to her. "Is it okay if we talk?" he asked.

"I don't think she would mind," said Brisia.

"I don't know if you remember it," said Laekoorj, "but I think what you said came true. The Creator did rescue us."

Brisia laughed with lightness and joy. "Just like they said He would not, and I didn't even think that was what I was asking for, then!"

Laekoorj looked at her. "I mean, after I rescued you from the snake. After I got you far into the jungle, you started talking in a disjointed way. You said we would tell guards and enemies, and the Creator would rescue us, and the guards would be pleased."

"Oh," said Brisia. "Yes, I vaguely remember that." She was quiet for a few moments, thinking. "I was just saying what might happen. You know, it's like, we could die in the jungle, or we could have allowed ourselves to be captured, or we could, having no children to care for, go down into the city… kind of like Khiel and Adaria did a long time ago… and be captured… and die… or, maybe, the Creator would rescue us."

"Oh, yeah, I get what you're saying," said Laekoorj. They were quiet for a long time. Then, he said, "You will have to tell me about it sometime."

It took Brisia a long time to respond. When she did, she said, "Why don't you tell me about it for you?"

"What you said came true. I told guards. I told would-be torturers. Some of them were very happy. Dormik–" Laekoorj stopped short.

Brisia glanced at Khiel, then turned back to Laekoorj. She whispered, "What? He… *changed?*"

"No," said Laekoorj. "He made perfect opportunities for me." When he saw

Brisia wanted more, he said, "He made it easy for me to tell them that I was not going to kill them; I was going to tell them about the Promise."

"I don't want to talk," said Brisia. She did not know what she wanted. She did know she wanted something. Something very real.

It might have been almost an hour later that Laekoorj said, "Of course, perhaps we are not rescued. Many think that the Queen is not a friend at all but an evil trickster. That our friends who have gone may already be being tortured, or that we all go to horrors."

Brisia heard him, but she did not respond. She had nothing to say. She would not think or worry about that at all, one way or the other. When now was torture or impending torture, she meant to accept it and not torment herself by fearing and striving to avoid it. When now was sunshine and flowers, she would enjoy it, and not torment herself by fearing and worrying about how it would end or what would come after. But, she did not know how to explain that to Laekoorj. She had tried to explain it to Esiri, and failed. She did not want to think about how to explain it again, not right now.

#87
Deadly Radiance

"Thank you for the bath," said Brisia, curtsying. She had learned that the Queen preferred not to be called your majesty, and so did not do it.

"You're welcome; it's the least I can do," said Arendellie. "I am very sorry that there are no healing wizards to be found who are not loyal to, or even part of, the Council. I am sorry I did not get here earlier... that I did not get you myself. Then, all of you would have lived." She motioned to Brisia to sit down.

Brisia still felt awkward in the presence of the Queen of Camil Hasseleighton. She sat down, wishing she had an easier time with words.

"I heard Khiel say to you, 'It is right,'" said Arendellie. "What did she mean?"

Brisia clenched her hands together. How would she ever manage to explain this? She could not quite remember how Khiel had said most of the things she had told her. The Queen waited patiently, while she thought. Finally, she said, "I don't know how to describe it. It's like this," she said, and sang, "'The peaks of the mountains, the blinding snows, the airs that are too bright for our eyes and deadly to this flesh. All these are but faint echoes of echoes of the light, the deadly radiance that is round His throne, and goes before Him wherever He walks.'"

Arendellie was silent for a while. Thoughtfully, she said, "I can't... quite make anything of that." While Brisia was thinking about how to reply, she said, "It makes sense. There is something to it. Something right about it." Brisia's face lit up, and she was about to clap, but Arendellie went on, and told about how she had meet the terrible Light of the Creator.

Brisia listened, her attention fixed on Arendellie's words, a light in her mind. When Arendellie had told of her feelings about the vision of the Light that dissolved and broke through the world, she said, "I think that's what Khiel meant! I think she knew that Light very well!"

"So," asked Arendellie, "she would be dying anyways?"

"I don't know," said Brisia. "It isn't always like that." What it was like, she did not know. Her eyes lowered. "When I told her I was sorry for getting her hurt more, she told me it was okay. She was well. She was *glad*. That's what she said, too, when Esiri told me not to help her drink, because it would mean she would..." Brisia stopped talking. *Die,* she thought. Khiel was dying. "I don't want to talk about this," she said finally. "It isn't right to talk about this, like this, right now."

"Do you and Khiel like the word 'right?'" asked Arendellie.

"It means a lot to us," said Brisia. "Especially since the world is very wrong, and right... well, I couldn't say all that it means to us. Kindness and flowers and happiness, and all things as they should be, I guess."

Arendellie said nothing. She was thinking of Kyil, of things Kyil had said. After a while, a thought occurred to her. "Is it that terrible and good are the same thing? That goodness is terrible?"

"It sounds right," said Brisia, half to herself. *Terrible good. Deadly radiance. They sound similar,* she thought. She whispered Mom's words to herself. "'The

Creator does all things well. The Promised One will conquer, in us and in the world. In the end we will see. The Creator will give us all His best.'"

"What's that?" asked Arendellie.

"The last thing Mom told me and my siblings. Her name was Mirla," said Brisia.

"I knew a Mirla," said Arendellie. "She was tortured to death, like so many others, after we ceased being friends."

"That's what happened to Mom, too," said Brisia, sadly.

"You aren't from Ebrin, are you?" asked Arendellie, beginning to be suspicious. Brisia looked Avanzarin, maybe Hasseleighton. She certainly did not look Ephezoan. She did not have the same facial shape as Khiel, or most of the others she was with.

"I am," said Brisia. "Kathreen rescued me and my brother and sister."

"I used to be friends with Mirla, your mom, and Kathreen," said Arendellie. She crossed over to Brisia, and knelt down next to her. "Brisia," she said. "I thought your name sounded familiar." Past a lump in her throat she said, "I'm sorry. I'm so sorry."

Brisia reached out and touched Arendellie on the shoulder. "Don't be, please. The Creator gives us all His best. He does all things well." She swallowed. Something Khiel had said came to mind. It was so much like how Mirla had said, "The Promised One will conquer, in us and in the world. In the end we will see." "Don't worry, Arendellie," she said. "Even the bad things will be well. But, they're still very bad and wrong," she added. "Did you read about the veiling?"

"Yes," said Arendellie. She wondered what Brisia was getting at. She was as incomprehensible as Khiel... or Kyil. She knew Brisia was uncomfortable and backed away a little. She needed someone wiser than herself to ask for advice. "What do you think I should do?" she said. "I am so tired and overwhelmed. I want to go. My oldest child tolerates me telling him what I believe, but I do not know him and he does not know me. My husband, King Vanesh, does not want me to teach my younger son about the Promise. We are all in danger; what should I do? I love my husband, but I also love Aroch and Kathreen."

"I don't know," said Brisia. "How should I? I am young and I am not married. I don't have either husband or children. Only a brother who frightens me, and a younger sister."

"You have a brother who frightens you?" asked Arendellie. "You are scared of your brother?"

Brisia sighed. "Not exactly." How should she say this? "It's something inside of my brother that frightens me. Everything, good and evil, has shown me more of the Creator, more of the Promise, more of goodness. He is full of bitterness and hatred. Evil is in him. I fear, and I do not know why I know the goodness of the Creator and the Promise, and he knows evil and hatred. After all, there is badness in me, too."

Arendellie shook her head. "I wouldn't understand, either," she said. "What does he hate?"

Brisia started to sob. "At first, he hated Mom's murderers. Now... Now, I don't know what he hates. I think he might hate me. I think he might hate everyone and everything. I think... I think he only knows how to hate... He's becoming hatred." She gulped, then said, "It makes me so sad."

Arendellie wanted to put her arms around Brisia and hug her, but knew that it would not be wanted for various reasons. "Why," she moaned to herself, "do those who could give us wisdom always die?"

"What?" asked Brisia, sitting up straight.

Arendellie repeated herself.

"I think you're confused," said Brisia. "I know the Creator wants us to know and rest on Him, not others." A bright smile covered her face, as she remembered. "The Creator showed me how caring and tender and– well, I still think of it as big– He is. That," and here she paused for a moment, as if struggling with herself, "that I don't need Mom; I need *Him*. It's not loyalty to Mom to mope and cling to her when she is gone, to make her my everything; it's disloyalty to *Him*. But I could never explain it. Dormik could not understand at all. He always gives each one His best. *With our eyes we will see."*

"You're right," said Arendellie. "I was so miserable about losing Kyil– not sad for her, it was happy for her, I knew her that well– but that is how I came to, or realized that I did, believe the Promise. I'm not sure which." She stood. "Anyway, I can't sit here and talk forever. Tonight, Surra and a few others will take you and the rest to the dragons. I will try to meet you again in Osilia."

She was perpetually distressed now. Talking to Brisia did not quench a thirst she did not understand, only knew existed. Nothing satisfied her, and nothing refreshed her. *Did I do something wrong?* she often thought to herself. She almost wanted the fear and terror of the unbearable light rather than this, but then she ran from that fear and terror. Even her tastes of it after believing the Promise were not pleasant. It felt like a repeat of something that had had happened at least once before in her life. She was finding it harder and harder to simply live, and do, and work, and absorb herself in the task, the need, the call at hand. Only, she understood even less of the problem, the cause, this time, she thought. She had no idea what was wrong. She struggled and fought to know what was wrong whenever she could not *do*. That was the opposite of how it had been before, when she had struggled and fought *not* know what was wrong.

The other thing that was different was that she had more to do. There was so much to do. So many details to which to pay attention. She hardly ever had any rest from things she *had* to do, not from adventures she could, to some extent, avoid had she wanted. Yet, she still felt empty, dry, and struggled to keep herself doing. She felt exhausted. She had not been exhausted before. *O my Creator, help me,* she thought. She had hoped talking to Brisia would help; she was glad Brisia was definitely getting stronger. She had become very worried about her when she needed help to stand and walk through the city, but it appeared now that it was mostly because she had had very little food and water for too long. She loved her singing, and had hoped that she would be able to give her what she had. She was deeper than she knew, though. She knew, in a vague and shadowy though somehow solid way, what Brisia spoke of and meant. She knew she needed it. But, where could she get it? Brisia had hinted that she needed to get it from the Creator, and no human being could help her.

As for Brisia, she felt relieved when the Queen left. Talking with her, the things they talked about, the way they did it, she felt that there was something kind of wrong.

#88
Edgerunner

Brisia learned that Esiri had helped her to drink before she awoke. She also learned many of the details of their flight and capture, and of the men's interactions with their guards and with each other; these were shared with her mostly by Laekoorj, who then asked her about her experiences. "There isn't much to say," she said. "I wanted to get to Khiel, and I succeeded, despite the fact that Esiri was worried about avoiding torture for as long as possible and as much as possible. It seemed useless to me. Just a way to add the torment of fear! Well, they heard me, and they took me and Khiel. There isn't really much to say about it either, except that they are evil. Oh, and, isn't it hilarious? Esiri was right! If I hadn't done what I had done, they would probably not have done any more to Khiel, and I would not have suffered at all. But, I don't regret doing it, even though I did have childish and wrong reasons, like the ones that caused me to cling to sorrow over Mom and resist the Creator for so long." After that, she did not want to say more. One of the reasons for this was that she missed Khiel terribly, and that experience was almost the last thing, and in some ways perhaps was the closest thing, she and Khiel ever did– or, perhaps, a better word would be 'were in,' but Brisia did not think of that– together. *Even this will be well,* she thought to herself.

The next day, the Queen returned. That evening, just as darkness was falling, she took them down to the harbor, where the ship was anchored. Across its greatest sail, which was green, was written in red letters, *Edgerunner.* "How will we sail it?" asked one of the mothers of the children El-Reiza and her friends had rescued. "Do any of you know anything about sailing ships?"

"There's a crew," said Arendellie. "If you will accept it," she added.

"Why wouldn't we?" asked Nahiza.

"The last Knights of the Promise would not accept the crew, since the crew-members did not believe the Promise," said Arendellie. "It was really stupid; they could have told the crew-members about the Promise."

"Are the members of this crew believers in the Promise?" asked Adaria.

"No," said Arendellie. "It is hard to find believers in the Promise, as you are killed so much, or at least imprisoned."

"Then, we will not accept this crew," said Kalar. Adaria added, "Have they ever sailed to another land before? No one in Camil has more than heard of other continents. Why would we expect those who do not hold to what we hold to, to risk and take us where we go? No, we cannot."

One of the men who had been rescued with them from prison raised his voice. "Then we will go to the bottom of the sea!"

"We go without the crew," said Kuthrynd. "Kalar and Adaria are right."

People began to argue. Athara's soft voice could not be heard above the clamor as she said, "Mom– Sirifa– says the same!" Kuthrynd said it for his sister.

They began to divide themselves based on what they wanted. Arendellie was upset. What could she do? Let one group go with the crew and buy another ship for the other? Force them all to go with the crew? But she did not want to do that. Then, one of them approached her with a solution. He bowed and said, "Your majesty, it is my understanding that the Frostflower Mountains are not far from here, and that they are largely uninhabited; there may be a few wild tribes in their reaches. If your majesty will give us the necessary tools and resources, we would be glad to journey into the Frostflower Mountains and make our living in their depths. At least we are certain of the land there, whereas we do not know if it is even possible to sail to another continent from here, and still less do we know how."

"We can arrange that," said Arendellie, relieved. It solved her problem. She spoke to a servant and told her to make sure word was immediately send to the head of the crew that their job was canceled for the night.

"Dormik wants to go with them to the Frostflower Mountains?" Brisia exclaimed. "Where is he?"

"Over there," said Janya. Sensing the direction of Brisia's thoughts she said, "I will go with you."

Brisia trotted across the quay in the near darkness. She heard Dormik talking angrily, and wove her way to him. "Brother!" she said.

He looked at her with disdain in his eyes. "What is it, Brisia?" he asked.

"Please, Dormik! Do not go with these people who do not trust the Creator and do not wait for the Promise! If you do, you will find yourselves among those whom He will crush, and you know how terrible it is to be on His bad side, precisely because it is so safe to be on His good side."

Dormik tilted his head back. "Mirla trusted in the Creator and look what happened to her– tortured to death!– and us. Khiel trusted in the Creator, and she was tortured and died of her wounds! You– trust in the Creator and were abused, too! It doesn't seem to do anyone any good."

Brisia refused to be goaded, though she knew that Dormik had almost died himself. "Brother, even that will be well– for us. But you are challenging the Creator! You are consumed by hatred, and you are daring the Creator's anger yourself! Just like our torturers and persecutors!"

"Go away, sister," said Dormik. "I'm tired of you."

Brisia took a few steps away, then turned to face him again. "You're my brother! I love you. Do you not remember loving me? Playing with me? Caring for me?"

"Brisia!" growled Dormik. "Come, Brisia, let's go," said Janya, taking her by the shoulders and guiding her away. "At least," said Brisia brightly to the taller, stronger woman, "it doesn't hurt when people do that to me anymore."

"That's nice," said Janya. "But, it was mostly the snake– and Laekoorj's– fault, right? Not the prison gua– oh!" She realized that Brisia was crying.

"He's my brother!" the girl sobbed. "My older brother! He was my friend. And, he won't even call her Mom anymore… and, he's my brother! I love him. He used to love me." She sputtered for a while, struggling to stand, while Janya held her. "I don't want him to end up like Dad. He's so much worse than Dad ever was, already! Dad and Mom could live together."

She looked up at Janya, her tears sparkling in the starlight. "He hates me, Janya. I think he hates me as much as he hates our persecutors. As much as he hates the tyrants."

"He might," said Janya. In the way Brisia said his name, she could catch a hint of what Dormik might have been like. Now, he was a bitter young man, swimming in a sea of hatred.

"O Creator, please forgive him," Brisia sobbed. "*Please,* answer my prayers. I asked You to use this great evil to show him love and forgiveness, to take him out of hatred and evil."

She heard Sirifa half-screaming half-crying, "Senise! You're my daughter. The Creator will take care of us. Don't go with them!"

Senise retorted, "I am twenty years old! I can make whatever decisions I like! I think the Frostflower Mountains is a safer route, especially since you are rejecting the crew!"

Brisia walked out of Janya's arms. Sirifa and Senise were arguing only a few feet away. "Senise, no!" she cried. "You're my friend. Besides, you're listening to lies." She held up her hand. "No, Senise, listen to me. Do you know what the torturers told me? 'The Creator won't rescue you,' they said. Many times. I'm here; obviously, He did. The Promise is going to come on another land; let us go! The Creator will take us, and among the daughters of your mother the Promise will come, on that other land. Remember the prophecy?"

"No," said Senise. "Bemdar is going to the Frostflower Mountains. He has always wanted to share the Promise with the mountain tribes, and he thought he would not be able to when he was arrested and thrown in his prison. This is his dream come true. He's a strong, caring young man. I want to marry him. I am going with him. I know it is out of custom, but this is all out of custom." She stepped forward and hugged Brisia. "I want you to know that I do admire you and you're still my friend," she said.

"Admire me?" asked Brisia, confused. *What would she admire me for? She's never told me that before.* Senise did not hear her; she had turned to Sirifa and was hugging her. "I don't hate you, Mom. You and Dad raised me very well. I haven't turned my back on the Promise; Bemdar himself believes in the Promise. But, I'm staying here. After all, someone has to stay here and keep the Promise here, right?"

Sirifa was crying. "Someone, yes, but not us. We have the opportunity to go here. The Queen and her maids are staying. There are countless others, scattered throughout the Empire, that believe the Promise, but we have a special prophecy."

Senise stepped back. "Please, don't do this to me, Mom."

Half an hour later, Brisia collapsed on one of the bunks and wept. Why were people so given to evil? Khiel's death was one of the least sad events around her. She *had* cried over Khiel, but not like she cried now. Her Dad. Dormik. Senise. She did not know how many others. Why did her heart tell her that Dormik was not unlike their torturers? She could not believe it. She loved her brother so much.

He had been kind, himself. Yet, he was eaten away by evil. Just as they were. His scorn was not nearly so different from their sneers as another might have seen it, or as she would have liked to see it. To be sure, she did not think, she was almost certain, that he was not nearly so far down the path of evil, that he was not nearly as entirely evil, nothing, as they were, but it was where he was going, what he was seeking. He used to love her, too! But, then, he had started mocking her for believing in the Creator's love when he only cared to hate, and now he had gotten so far as hating her. Love and joy and beauty seemed banished from his life. Could she have told him that Khiel's death was better than his life? As one of the poems in the scroll warned against, there was no fear of her envying the wicked and the rich. It would never have occurred to her. Her situation had always been better than Dormik's. Even Arendellie gave her no cause for envy. She and Khiel had been happier under the mercy of the prison guards than the Queen was, even though she did know and believe the Promise. Was it because, as she had told Esiri it was awful to do, she was tormenting herself with her plans and desires, her worries and fears? Though, Brisia was almost certain, Arendellie did not know how unhappy she was– or, should it be, how much happier she could be?

O my Creator, please have mercy! Please have mercy! Show us goodness. Show them goodness.

#89
The Curse of the Mighty

Azshbir was so tired of watching his sons run around on deck. Neah'ra was even more exhausted. Just that morning she had said, "You watch them today; I can't even see anything that moves." Of course, she had to nurse Nourdë.

Words broke in on Azshbir's consciousness. "That was a really stupid idea." He was so tired he ignored it. The men continued to argue.

"I wonder what Azshbir would say to that. No land in sight, and it's all his fault." The man who had said that, Nyezer, stood right to the side of Azshbir. "Kuthreb! Kuthreb!" he called

His son looked at him. "Take Norden, and go to your mom. Now!" When he saw that his sons were obeying him, he turned to Nyezer. "What is this about?" he demanded.

"There is no land in sight. We are sick of eating fish the dragons catch. We have a hard time cooking it. It's your fault. You refused the crew. Worse, we're almost out of water."

"Yes, I did. It was the Creator's will, as you all recognized."

"Shaelene, can you take care of the children please?" asked Neah'ra.

"Of course. What do you plan to do?"

"See what's going on out there, and do whatever I can to help," she said. She snatched up a shawl, threw it over her shoulders, and hurried outside. She quickly made her way through the men to where her husband stood, arguing with them.

Azshbir saw her and held out his arm. She stepped into his embrace. "This way of thinking is what causes people to deny the Promise," she said quietly. He knew she was speaking through unshed tears. "This way of thinking, I would have denied the Promise in order to keep my children, only to have found that I was never going to lose them," she said, trying to speak so that she could be heard, at least by those close to her. It was hard for a woman to be heard through the noise. "This way of thinking," she went on, "Mirla, of whom I think many of us have heard, would have sworn allegiance to Grale Casarion in order to be keep her children. She died, but her children were rescued through the care of the Creator!

"How many times have people trusted the Creator, and they have not seen His power or care, but one day it will be revealed? There is so much we do not know. He sees all. There is so much we do not understand. He has power over all. How many times have we failed to trust the Creator, and He has proved Himself faithful? How many times have we failed to trust the Creator, and not seen His mighty arm because we trusted in our own weak knowledge and strength and did not look to His mighty arm?" She held out the scroll and handed it to Azshbir. "Read it to them!" she said.

Azshbir unrolled the scroll. Neah'ra pointed, and he read. "The mighty will fall; the sure-footed will stumble in the pits. Treacherous will be the land in that day, and the winds will be chaos and turmoil. The waters will be wild and deceitful. The lakes will turn out to be lies. Then, will the wise be confounded, and all the training of the mighty hunters will fail them. Their knowledge will lead them into places from which there will be no escape. The eyes will see illusions of delight, and men will be led by them in dungeons and death. The echoes will be utter confusion, and voices will wail and call out of the places of destruction. The voice of a friend will lead into the fire, and no one will be able to trust another. When a trusted guide does not turn traitor, his voice will be heard calling into doom and assuring of peace and safety. Then will those who followed their own way fall from the cliffs, and those who trust their knowledge will be destroyed by it. A man's greatest enemy will be his skill, and a man's wisdom will be to him folly and death. Then those who knew the Creator will be vindicated. Many will take the voice of the adversary for His, having been deceived, but those who followed Him will walk on the clouds above the chaos. Those who saw Him will walk in true light, and they will not be led astray by illusions. They will set their eyes on Him, and find that the fire they feared has become pleasant plains. They will follow His voice, and the raging waters will let them pass. While others fly from false fears into terrors disguised as peace and horrors hidden by a veil of pleasure, they will turn their backs on the appearance of brightness and pleasantry, and they will find the castle of the King behind the ramparts of the adversary, and walk in pleasant and joyous gardens behind the terrors of their enemies and the deceit of that day. Then, will the dungeons of death be filled with their rightful prey, and the Conqueror will ride forth to defeat the adversary. Kaarathlon will blossom with light and no curse shall be found anymore on land or sea or sky."

Azshbir stopped reading, rolled up the scroll, and handed it back to Neah'ra. All the men who had been protesting were silent. Someone's voice rang out. "If we had a crew, we would have consumed all our dried fruit and water a long time ago!" They had visited several islands on their way and re-filled their water from their springs, but they could not replenish their food very well.

One of the trouble-makers retorted, "If we had a crew we would be on land by now!"

The argument continued. A friend of Azshbir's said, "We do not know that. Remember the words of the scroll?"

Azshbir looked at Neah'ra and saw her looking up at him, a glow in her eyes. "It's frightening," she said.

"It is like this. Like this journey," said Azshbir.

"I guess," said Neah'ra. Then, after a moment, "It really is." Then she said, "It's so scary. We have such a tendency to believe that things are how they make sense to us. We can't ever stop doing it." She looked up at him and read his eyes. "Even the fact that I think this is scary shows how inclined I am to trust my own way?"

"We are indeed so small and frail. This is good for us," said Azshbir. He looked at the sky. "I think we should change the sails!" he called to the other men. "Take a nap," he said to Neah'ra.

"I know," she called over her shoulder to him– they had already begun to part.

"Shaelene and Shantee are watching the children. By the way, Shantee–" but her voice was lost to him in the wind and the voices of the other men.

He soon learned something about Shantee. She was engaged to a young man from Hasseleighton who had been thrown into prison for preaching to everyone. He had been tortured in prison, and continued to tell the Promise to everyone, warning people of the avenging judgment of the Creator on all who opposed His Conqueror and King and persecuted His people. He had been knighted a Knight of the Promise.

Several weeks later, they sighted a mass of darkness on the eastern horizon. There was cheering and screeching. Children sang and wanted to swim to the land. The mothers and older sisters were constantly busy, making sure that none of them jumped overboard. Azshbir called a meeting of the men. They would have to find a way to support themselves on the new land, which was probably Syrwe, since they thought it was in more or less the right direction. The sun passed across the sky in a different arc than that they had known on Camil. The north-eastern stars were bigger and brighter and they saw stars in that direction they had never seen before, but the north-western stars were slightly diminished in brightness. Only slightly. Reilia had told Azshbir a few nights before. Azshbir looked up at the stars and said, "I can't see it."

"I didn't notice it either, until Kira told me. She said Kellyth showed her. Try looking again," Reilia had urged him. Eventually, Della came out. She had the brilliant idea of having Azshbir compare two stars that had been the same in Camil. It took her and Reilia a while to show him which stars, but eventually he saw. After that, they tried to show him the new stars in the east and the north. It took hours to convince him, since he had never paid as much attention to the skies as his daughters apparently did. He asked them if they had showed Neah'ra. Della announced that she had told Neah'ra while Reilia struggled to tell Azshbir. Neah'ra had better eyes.

With a flash-back of pain, Azshbir had thought, *Or, perhaps, it might have something to do with the prisons of Ephezoa.* He shoved it aside and enjoyed the skies his daughters were showing him. It was also possible that Neah'ra was more interested in the stars or naturally had sharper eye-sight.

Now, he did not know how quickly they would approach the land. It was impossible to know how quickly the ship traveled. It was one of the issues some of the people had had.

A strange scent, simultaneously lovely and drawing and wild, strange, even repelling because of its newness, blew from the shores of the new land. It was light green and rippled, not unlike a very calm sea.

#90
Laughter on the Waves

Brisia sat down, leaning against the rail of the *Edgerunner*, and laughed, almost hysterically. She could not get the thought out of her head. "'He won't rescue you.' 'The Creator can't rescue you.' 'You're at our mercy. Your Creator is useless,'" she sputtered. She clung to the rail while she rocked back and forth, her body aching with laughter, some of her wounds, not yet completely healed, twinging.

"What is so funny?" asked Lalia.

Brisia was laughing too hard and was too out of breath to speak. She tried, but no sounds came out. Unable to stay put, Lalia moved on.

"Is something wrong?" Laekoorj asked.

"No… No… Not at… all," gasped Brisia, her voice barely audible. Laekoorj had to guess what she was saying, for the slapping of the waves upon the ship drowned it out completely. He knelt down next to her.

Brisia struggled to get control of her laughter. "It's just," she sputtered, "that they are so wrong!"

Laekoorj did not ask her who. She would tell him when she was able.

"I just clung to Him, and they said, 'He won't rescue you,'" she said, and collapsed into uncontrollable laughter again. She had not known that *laughing* could hurt this much. She wanted it to stop, but she could not stop laughing. Laekoorj was laughing a little too, just because she was, and it made it that much harder to stop, since whenever she began to stop she caught sight of him laughing, or heard him laugh in between the sounds of the waves, and laughed harder.

Finally, gasping, she said, "He did!" Laekoorj bent low, right next to her mouth so that he could hear her. "Sometimes, I wonder if He did just to prove them wrong!" She stretched out, still holding onto the rail. "He rescued us all… Oh my goodness… Besides, the Promise is our rescue… He *will* keep His Promise… But He rescued me!… I didn't even… ask!… But, they said He wouldn't… They know nothing… Hope they… know better… now."

They almost certainly don't, thought Laekoorj. *The Queen would never tell them she was rescuing us. She's supposed to be giving us over to even greater horrors.* He did not at all like the thought of his Brisia being hurt, though he had not yet married her.

When she stopped laughing for a while, Laekoorj asked her again. "Can you tell me more about what happened?"

"There's not much to say," said Brisia. "It really isn't interesting. I've already told you everything worth saying." She leaned over the rail and looked over the dull green side of the ship at the waves below. "I'm still not used to the way this monster rocks," she said, loud enough that Laekoorj did not have to be right next to her to hear. "It shakes me up. I always have to walk around using the rail."

He had noticed that.

She shook her head. "I still think it's ridiculous. They dared to tell me He wouldn't rescue me! It's totally hilarious." She was silent for a few moments, remembering. "Besides, it's them who need rescuing. I told them He's so big He doesn't have any size and could crush them so small they aren't human anymore." She shook her head again. "So stupid. So foolish. So ignorant. And, my brother. So sad." She gripped the rail so tightly her fingers whitened under her dark skin. "I wish…" she said.

"What was that?" asked Laekoorj, leaning closer.

"I just said I wish," she said, half-absentmindedly.

"Say that again. Louder please," requested Laekoorj.

"I didn't say ANYTHING," Brisia said. She hung her arm over the rail, vaguely wishing she could dip her fingers in the sea. "I wish people would see the truth," she muttered to herself. Even so, she could not get over what had happened. "He rescued us," she said again, overjoyed.

Somehow, Laekoorj heard it, though she had not spoken to be heard. "You told me so," he said.

She turned around and looked at him. "Do you know why Senise said she admires me?" she asked. "She's never told me that before. It makes no sense."

"Because you can laugh," said Laekoorj, knowing it was not the whole answer.

Brisia slapped him. "Lots of people can laugh. Senise can laugh. Besides, I've never laughed that hard before. I didn't know it could hurt that bad, so I *know.*"

Laekoorj stood. "I think it's my turn now," he said. "Nakar was on a crew, before he was thrown into prison, and he is working on teaching us all lots of things. I hear it is very hard work."

Lalia returned with Nahiza. "I see you are better now," she said, sitting down.

"Actually," Brisia teased, "you are better. You can walk around this thing without clinging to the railing!"

Lalia and Nahiza laughed.

Brisia was still thinking about Senise. She had been her friend. Nahiza asked, "So, what is so funny on this ship? I haven't seen *any*thing to make me laugh." She rolled her eyes dramatically. Brisia did not believe her and, even if what she said was true, it had not been that long and she could not possibly have seen everything.

"Anyway," said Brisia, "I was just laughing because it's so hilarious when people say 'The Creator won't rescue you,' and then He does! Because, they told me that, and He did! What they say just doesn't matter. Or maybe, He rescued me to prove them wrong!" She giggled again, mostly out of sheer joy at thinking of the attributes of the Creator. "He's so wonderful," she said. "It's sad, though. Them, I mean. They're all evil and dead and ruined and nothing. They're stupid and lost."

"Oh," said Nahiza. Brisia could tell neither of them really understood.

"I wish this ship would stop rocking, so I could dance," she said.

"She's going to marry Laekoorj as soon as she can walk around on *Edgerunner* without stumbling," said Lalia to Nahiza, showing off her great knowledge. "I heard them arranging it this morning."

Brisia ignored the twang of pain and threw herself on top of Lalia, tickling her. "Stop! Stop! You're killing me!" begged Lalia, trying not to laugh.

"I'm not *killing* you," Brisia said between breaths, "and you should probably use that word only when you mean it!" Ever since the younger ones were old enough to use words like 'kill' and 'murder' Brisia had been on their case for using them to mean what they did not mean. She was starting to correct Zsyinzjae for mis-using words now, too.

"We're too old for tickling!" said Lalia, trying to wriggle away from her. Nahiza just watched, as if she could not decide whom she wanted to attack.

Brisia let up, exhausted herself. "I only thought it was fair," she said, panting. "After all, I haven't tickled either of you in a year and a half."

"Something like that," said Nahiza, rolling her eyes again and standing so that she was above both of them. "We wouldn't remember. We can't tell the difference between a month and a year."

"You can tell by the new babies," said Brisia.

"She's right," said Lalia. She was sprawled out on the deck. "Athara has another, a baby girl, and her name is Taela. I think it's pretty, but she is so cute!"

"Taela is cute," said Nahiza. "I think you would like having babies, Brisia. Especially, since you like to tickle us so much."

Brisia shook her head. She would like having babies, she was sure. She missed Khiel horribly, though. Khiel had been so much a part of her life, all Brisia's thoughts and imaginings had her built into them, even if unconsciously. They shared everything. She knew there were a lot of things Khiel had not told her. She knew that Khiel's death fit in with her life. She knew that the real wrong, the real loss, the real horror was not in Khiel's death but in the hearts of her murderers. But, that did not change the fact she missed her. She looked out over the side of the ship.

"What are you looking at?" asked Lalia, sitting up.

"Nothing really," said Brisia, then corrected herself. "The sea. I wish I could feel the waves."

"I thought you hate feeling the waves," said Nahiza, standing over her.

"No," said Brisia. "I meant, I wish I could dip the tips of my fingers in them."

"Oh," said Nahiza again.

"The Queen told me that Taela means 'laughter' in the old language that used to be spoken by the desert people," said Lalia.

"There aren't any desert people," said Nahiza.

"There used to be," said Lalia, "but the desert got so dry and Avanzar got so big they moved out of the desert and became Avanzarin."

Nahiza rolled her eyes again. "Whatever, Lalia."

"It doesn't matter what Taela means," said Brisia. "It is a very pretty name, and it is just right for baby Taela. To me, Taela sounds like the name of a flower. Not a jungle flower, but a desert flower. Actually," she said, pausing, "desert isn't the right word, but I don't know a right one. I mean a dry forest, but it's not very thick like the jungle."

Nahiza rolled her eyes. Lalia looked like she was thinking in the same direction.

"There *are* places like that," said Brisia. "I actually prefer them to the jungle with all its biting bugs and dangerous animals. I hope wherever we are going is somewhere like that."

"Athara says she is worried that we are going to the bottom of the sea," said Nahiza, probably trying to even her score with Lalia. "But, we all know we can't live at the bottom of the sea, because you sing that song so much, Brisia!" Nahiza sang one of the lines in question. "Who has seen the halls in the depths of His seas, or touched the uttermost veil of His skies?" She hummed the next lines, and took up words again to sing, "The least of His works surpass us by far, the valleys of the sea where we cannot walk."

"You sing it very prettily, Nahi," said Brisia. "It's an appropriate song for being on a ship on the sea, isn't it?"

"Yes, it is!" said a new voice exuberantly. Kizyia had wandered into the conversation.

"Of course," said Nahiza, "Athara might think that it just means that we can't walk in the sea, and that no has seen the halls in the depths of the sea just because no one has gone there yet?"

"I don't think so," said Brisia. "You drown if you can't get up out of the water to breathe the air. You do know that, right?" she asked, looking around. They all nodded, more or less vigorously. One of them said, "Of course we know that!" Brisia continued, "I think the song is about how much the Creator has made that is beyond us. How much the Creator has made where we can't live, that we can't even get to. Like, the peaks of the mountains with the deadly airs?" She was speaking quietly, now. "I wonder… will we be able to? Death– and light. And, Kaarathlon was good, but neither we nor Kaarathlon was as good as it would be. Are we going to get to go everywhere and see everything? After the Promised One defeats death?" She did not know quite what she was thinking, but it seemed right. "Khiel," she murmured softly.

"We want to sing," said Kizyia, "but I don't sing very well. Can you help us?"

"I'm not sure I sing all that well, either," said Brisia, secretly thinking that she liked the way Kizyia sang; sure, she made up half of the melody even when she tried to sing something someone had written, but she sang with emotion and exuberance. "Athara is the best singer. If she's moping about how we are all going to go to the bottom of the sea, why don't you get her out to sing?"

Lalia stood. "I'll go get Athara."

"I'm going with you," said Kizyia.

Nahiza responded to the question in Brisia's eyes by shrugging. "I like bright greens, and purples sometimes," said Nahiza, irrelevantly it seemed to Brisia. "Kizyia likes glowing pinks and peaches." Brisia knew both those pieces of information already. So many things interested her, there was so much she wanted to see and know, but the favorite colors of the twins were not among them.

After a few moments, Nahiza got up and left. Brisia did not know whether to cry or laugh. Who could ever know that the Creator could rescue them? He had rescued them out of prison and torture. Surely, He could– and would– rescue them out of the sea. She had not thought about it in the prison– she had thought about very little in the prison– and it did not mean the life of any one of them nor was it clear that it referred to her or Khiel at all, but she knew that they could not all die. The Promise was supposed to come from among Hoobit and Sirifa's daughters. She wanted to cry because people were so ignorant, foolish, and stupid. She wanted to cry because there was so much evil in so many hearts. But, she wanted to laugh because the Creator was so good, so much more than good! She wanted to laugh because nothing stood in His way and He proved Himself, again and again. She wanted to laugh because the fears and doubts and evil intents of human hearts were so foolish, baseless, and vain.

#91
The Sign

"Arendellie!" said Vanesh brightly.

She stepped towards him. "Vanesh!"

He took her in his arms. "It's been months."

"It has been. I missed you, too," she said. "It was somewhat stressful."

"If you don't want to do this anymore, I would be so glad if you would stop. I'm sure we could make up a story to explain it," said Vanesh.

"Like that I got pregnant? Or the Undead Snow Queen is not in so much need of new subjects for the moment?" She shook her head. "It's a terrible, horrible story. I'm so glad it isn't true."

"I know," said Vanesh. "There is so much that is evil, but at least there is less wrong than there could be."

Suddenly uncomfortable, Arendellie stepped back. "I cannot stop. After all, to sit by and watch evil take place without doing anything is to be guilty of that evil, is it not?"

"Don't have this conversation with me," warned Vanesh.

Arendellie remembered Brisia's sorrow over her Dad and her brother. From her description, Vanesh was nothing like Dormik– if she correctly remembered his name– but, there was still the same problem. Vanesh was going down the path of ruin, and she could do nothing about it.

She could not wait to get to her scroll and read the passages Brisia had suggested.

Arendellie had finally snatched some time to read the scroll. She was reading the poem at the very end, and trying to understand what Brisia was thinking when she suggested it, among four or five others. She did not understand it, let alone how all its different parts and images fit together. Someone knocked on the door.

Arendellie rose and hid the scroll. "Come in. What is it?"

"A letter for your majesty," said the maid.

As soon as she left, Arendellie opened the letter up and spread it out.

"Nemor Tasanin, Warden over the Anores Prisons,

"To Her Gracious Majesty, the Queen Casarion,

"We have finally captured the trouble-maker, Neshekh of Ebrin. He is currently held in the first cell. If your majesty is interested, we would appreciate it if you would see him and give us any suggestions your majesty may have on how to deal with him. Given his prominence, we also would not want to completely ruin him if the Undead Snow Queen has knowledge of his powers and has requested him. We are all indebted to your majesty for all you do."

Arendellie let out a sigh. Neshekh? Neshekh Dasaran? The man she had been about to marry. A cloud settled over her. She did not know what to do. She figured she would see him, since they had known each other, and since she wondered what wisdom he might have, since the Creator had protected him so marvelously. She closed the letter, stepped outside, and summoned a few choice servants.

Arendellie had never seen a prisoner held so securely. Each of Neshekh's hands and feet were secured to the floor with two heavy-duty chains each. He was bound to the floor with several more chains across his body. Arendellie gritted her teeth. *O my Creator, when will this come to an end? How long must we all endure this? I feel like I am going to go insane. Please, tell me, is it time for me to take Aroch and Kathreen and go? Charter another ship and set sail?* In that moment, she decided to do so.

"Neshekh Dasaran," she said.

He opened his eyes. "Why are there women here?" he asked.

"I'm the Queen, and I wanted to see you." Arendellie motioned to her slaves to leave. "He is bound to the floor," she said. "There is no danger."

"He has escaped from bonds like these before," said one of them. "How do we know he won't do so again and assault your majesty?"

"You need not go far," she said. "If I see him struggling and breaking things, I will call you and I will run. He won't get out instantly."

"Okay," the male escort said, only partially assured.

When they were gone a little way, Arendellie spoke very quietly. "I am Arendellie, and I have some questions."

Neshekh tried to raise his head and sit up, but he could not. Arendellie flinched. Horror showed in his eyes, as he convinced himself that it was, in fact, her. "I thought you were called by the Creator!" he said, his voice low with horror and anger. "Instead, you are our greatest enemy. Araenyi, how?!"

Arendellie held up her hand. She wished she had asked Vanesh's permission. He probably would have said, 'no,' and then she would not be going through this pain. But, then again, she still cared about Neshekh and would not want him to suffer. "I'm not. It's a disguise. It is true that for a long time I did not care and was cruel, but now I believe the Promise. I don't hand you over to horrors; I rescue you and send you away."

The horror in Neshekh's expression did not diminish, but confusion was added to it. "I am so grateful, now, that the Creator took you away! I wondered why, and questioned Him in my evil and foolishness, but I now see and am so thankful!" His words were quiet, and he had to take breaths often, fixed in that position. Arendellie felt anger well up in her. It was an anger that she had thought she was getting used to, but she found it growing. Now and then she felt the horrible guilt, but more and more she was simply angry. She wanted to do more! She wanted to simply get the key, release the chains, and let him go free. She wanted to do it for everyone. This only doing what she could safely, in order so that she could continue to do it and over all provide more relief, was galling her. The word 'compromise' reared in her head. Evil was evil! It should be stopped. It should be defied. It should *end*. Foolish and juvenile thoughts, having to do with the dreams of children and fairy tales, unfit to the real world, below her, filled her mind. It would be wrong to do that! This hurt her and it angered her, but to give in would be to do less good, not more, to be less good, not more.

"I believe in the Promise," Arendellie said urgently. "I have been the Creator's instrument to deliver hundreds. It is good that we did not marry then, for I was evil then."

"If you believe in the Promise," said Neshekh, "you will say it! You will not hide in deceit, you will not consort with evil, you will not walk with the enemy!"

Arendellie knew he was in pain. She wanted to bury her head in her hands. She wanted to flee. "I believe in the Promise," she said. "If I do nothing against evil, I help evil. I am doing this because I believe in the Promise; I am doing this to help the People of the Promise."

"The Creator does not need your help!" said Neshekh.

Arendellie wondered. Doubtless, Neshekh had been delivered in marvelous ways. However, she had been the Creator's instrument to deliver Azshbir and many others with him, and Brisia and Sirifa and many others with them. Certainly, the Creator did not need her; certainly, He could have delivered in any number of ways without her– or anyone else. However, was that an excuse not to do what one could? Not to be used by Him?

Neshekh continued. "You should not try to help, by defying His clear commands."

"What clear commands?" asked Arendellie.

"To honestly proclaim the Promise and that the Promised Conqueror is your King," said Neshekh.

"But the Creator has used me this way," said Arendellie and then, overcome by sudden fear, "you won't tell them that I believe the Promise and am doing this not against you but for you, will you?" she asked. "Because, I can't actually lie about that."

"You said," said Neshekh, laboriously, "that you have some questions. My only answer to any of your questions is, stop working in deceit and darkness, and own the Conqueror as your King. It is the only way. It is the sign of the People of the Promise. You must do it; another cannot do it for you."

"Should I stay with Vanesh or–" Arendellie began to ask, then remembered that she had already made up her mind. She turned her back to Neshekh, determined to compose herself. He bothered her as no one else had. She thought she only needed her lie to last a little longer; she would ask El-Reiza to help her, and she would be gone. She knew that El-Reiza would help her. El-Reiza would be eager to help her; the last time they had met, in the Frostflower Mountains not far from Osilia, El-Reiza had told her so. She knew that, even now, El-Reiza was not far. She was still somewhat suspicious of the Elzari, but she had no other options and she trusted El-Reiza, even if she did not trust the rest of the Elzari.

When the servants asked Arendellie about Neshekh, she said that he was nearly out of his mind, and she would need a few days to know what should be done with him or whether the Undead Snow Queen wanted him. She tried to stay calm and steady, but her heart seemed to be pounding in her head and she could hardly think through it. She was disturbed and angry.

When she got to her quarters, she told everyone that she had fallen ill, something that had happened two or three times in all her years first as princess and now as queen. She sent a private message requesting El-Reiza to come, to which the Elzari Dragon-rider promptly responded. She had detailed how to come to her in a way that would not raise questions.

In the meantime, Vanesh pleaded with her to stop working so hard; she had probably gotten sick because of all her frantic work in the northern provinces. Arendellie, who actually did not feel well though she knew it had to do almost entirely with her anger, worry, uncertainty, and distress, told Vanesh she thought that would be a good idea. She wrote a letter, requesting that Neshekh be given to her, and explaining that she would not be working for the Undead Snow Queen much longer; the Undead Snow Queen would be willing to receive more gifts from Camil, but she was no longer in dire need of new servants. While writing the letter, she knew she would need to vomit, and asked a maid to bring her a bucket. It was the first time she had vomited since early childhood while not pregnant.

When Vanesh heard, he came to her as quickly as he could. He held her and whispered, "Araenyi, Araenyi, Araenyi," over and over again. "Are you okay?" he asked. "Please…"

"I'll be fine in a week or two," said Arendellie. "I got sick like this when I was younger." Her head did in fact throb. She felt torn by guilt. Vanesh loved her so much– in some ways, far more than she loved him, she knew– and it would break his heart to lose her. She worried that he might even die. Should she tell him what she was planning? Would he flee with her, or stop her? She used to be able to think of questions to ask and ways of putting things to get at least an idea of what his reaction might be but without letting on what she was doing, or even what she was thinking of doing. For some reason, she could not think of any of these questions or ways of putting things right now.

She wondered if she could have done things any differently, and so avoided this terrible situation.

The next day, after she had sent the letter to the warden, Nemor Tasanin, she was laying in the garden, feeling terrible, and thinking that the garden made her feel even more terrible, when El-Reiza came to her. She explained her situation and all that she wanted and feared regarding her children, her husband, and flight. El-Reiza listened, said almost nothing, and went away. Arendellie wondered if she had decided she was unwilling to help her, but El-Reiza had always been different and impossible to read. She began to fear that she had made a terrible mistake in trusting her, even so, and to try to think of some way to ask Vanesh if he was interested in fleeing with her and the children without letting him know until she knew what he thought.

He did not understand her question at all; it was the first time he had understood less than she had wanted to communicate, always excepting what she tried to tell him about the Creator, reality, and the Promise. It surprised her, since she usually had more trouble keeping things from him. She began to wonder how much he knew of what she was experiencing and planning even now. At the same time, Neshekh's words incessantly tormented her whenever she was not tormented by something else or frantically considering something else, so she thought and worried as much as possible. Nothing made sense to her anymore.

#92
Giant Mixing Spoons

Somehow, they managed to maneuver the *Last Watch* into a little cove. The waves rolled up to the shore and broke on it with foam. The sand and pebbles could be seen, distorted by the ripples in the water, lying on the bottom. They gently ran the ship aground. It was obvious, now, that the land was plains of tall grass waving in the wind. In his travels with Kathreen, Azshbir had seen a few places where grasses flourished, but never anything like this. The ground was very flat, so that from where the ship ran aground to the end of the water was at least a mile. Shantee's voice broke in on Azshbir's thoughts, speaking aloud what he was thinking. "The water looks calm. Some of us could probably swim, and by the time we would be very tired the bottom would be high enough we could walk the rest of the way. The problem is the children and those who never swam very much." Previously, when they had stopped at islands, they had stopped at the mouths of streams and the strong, healthy young men had climbed down and they had worked all day re-filling their water casks, using ropes to haul buckets and casks up and let them down. They had also gathered some wood and brought it up to use to cook the fish and birds they– and the dragons– caught.

Azshbir heard some scratching and scraping behind him. "We think this is a boat," said one of the women. "We found it in our cabin under the food and the water casks about a week ago."

"Yeah," said Azshbir. "It looks like it might be a boat."

Two boys, twelve and thirteen followed behind. "We found these under the boat!" one of them exclaimed. They held up two sticks with flattened and broadened ends.

Shantee laughed. "Why," she said, "would anyone need giant mixing spoons!"

"They're oars," said Azshbir slowly, trying not to laugh at her ignorance. "There were some in the bottom of the ship; that's how we grounded it here."

Shaelene, one of the women who had dragged the boat out, pulled her hair behind her shoulder. "So, that's what those were for! Shantee asked me what they were and if I knew what they were for, and I said, 'No, I have no idea what anyone would need giant mixing spoons for. Why don't you go ask somebody else.' Apparently, she never did."

"It didn't seem to matter," said Shantee.

The rest of the women were laughing now. "Oars! Where did you grow up and who were your parents that you did not even know oars existed?"

Shaelene blushed and looked like she wanted to hide. "A prostitute. I was a prostitute," she said.

"Well," said Azshbir, not wanting to further embarrass or humiliate anyone, "why don't we lower the boat– if anyone can figure out how to do that– and then lower people, and we can figure out how to use the giant mixing spoons to row to the shore." Then, after that, they would have to figure out how to survive on this new land. They would need to find water, too. They were all thirsty, since their water had been low, and rationed, for the last month, and was almost out now.

People collapsed on the ground in gales of laughter. "Giant mixing spoons!" someone exclaimed. "Let's get the boat– or, the thing we think might be a boat– down first," suggested Shantee, "and then the people and the giant mixing spoons down into it, and then while they figure out how to use the giant mixing spoons, we can laugh about it, until the giant mixing spoon comes back. Then, we repeat, until we and all our belongings are over there," and she pointed.

Azshbir let out a deep breath. Everything had been an adventure, from figuring out how to move the rudder to how to adjust the sails. Now, they were just about to keep on having adventures– the adventure of figuring out all the things they needed to do to survive in a new and almost completely different land. He had never seen more than nearly so much plain grass in one place before. Always, there were trees and other plants around.

Omaran was pointing to the boat. "I think we go and use the rope and we put it through the boat and lower it down the side. See, there's a hole on the boat right there and there to lower it. Someone, get me some rope! You, there, Nyezer, get me rope!"

When Azshbir finally made it to the shore, with Neah'ra and their children, he saw that it was even more unlike what he had imagined. The grass was almost as tall as he was. How on earth were they going to live here? There were no plants that looked edible. He had no idea what kinds of animals might live here and be good to eat. He knew how to hunt, but he did not have his bow and arrows or even a hunting spear.

It was late by the time everyone was on the shore. The last thing they did, that evening, was to gather some grass and use the last of their wood to build a fire. Looking at it, someone observed, "This won't last through the night and it's our protection. How about we take apart the railing of the *Last Watch?* We won't be needing the ship anymore, and we do need this!"

The next day.

Azshbir and two other men were making their way into the grasses, which were very thick and which appeared to be the source of the wild, nice, but strange fragrance. They had to work to walk. The good thing was that the grass, though it was still green, was drier than any grass Azshbir had ever known and they could tell what way they came because the grass was trampled down and parted, not perfectly but enough to tell, in that direction. Otherwise, they all knew they would be lost almost at once. They made a lot of noise walking through the grass, too, so they could hear nothing else. If something wanted to hunt man-size prey, they would all die. They stopped regularly to listen, but the grass rustled so much even after they passed that, assuming anything could get good at moving stealthily through it, they would not be able to know if something was hunting them and stopping whenever they stopped. When he stopped, he could still hear the shouting at their camp; many were angry, believing they were going to perish in this accursed grassland. Preposterously, they believed that if they had taken a crew they would have been better off, which made absolutely no sense. No crew would have known which parts of Syrwe were inhabitable and which were not. No one even knew quite where Syrwe was; only that it was somewhere in what was, from Camil, the north-east.

Now, Azshbir listened with his ears perked. He thought he heard something moving in the grass. He was almost completely still, but for his heart hammering in his chest. It was the same with the men with him.

A small, thin, wiry man, whose skin was an unnatural tan and whose hair was the color of poor soil, emerged from the grass in front of him, holding a bow and arrows. He touched his left hand to his right shoulder, dipped his head, and said something unintelligible.

Azshbir mimicked the gesture, assuming it was a greeting and not a challenge. If it was the later, he would be in big trouble. In the language he knew, he said, "Hello. We do not know this place," hoping that the man would know that he was not an enemy and did not speak his language.

Another man, likewise holding a bow and arrows, likewise unnatural colors, and likewise clothed in scant skins that hardly covered his body emerged from the grass. The scant clothing did not bother Azshbir; it was similar to what had been common in some regions of Ephezoa before Grale Casarion took over all Camil. Azshbir could not tell the difference between the two men, except that they stood in different places. The first spoke, seemingly to the second, explaining Azshbir-knew-not-what in their language. Then, the second man repeated the gesture and the greeting. At least, Azshbir thought that the unintelligible sounds that came out of his mouth were the same as those which had come out of his friend's mouth.

Azshbir tried to mimic the greeting again. He cast a glance at his friends, and saw them do the same.

A third man joined the first two, and the process was repeated. After that, the three men just stood there, occasionally exchanging a word or two in their language with one another. Azshbir did not know what to do. They seemed to be getting impatient. Eventually, one of them held out his bow and pointed to it. "Takak," he said.

"Ta'ag," Azshbir repeated.

"Takak," he said again, enunciating the word more clearly. After that, he proceeded to explain that the wooden part of the bow was s*mawi,* the string was *macgo,* when unstrung *tufi-sor,* and when strung *tufik,* and the arrows were, individually, *shokt,* and, multiply, *ashuktin.* Azshbir and both his friends found their words to be tongue-twisters. They explained that a knife was *nima* and two knives together were *namu,* and three knives together were *anamun.* Azshbir was very irritated by the waste of time, when one of his friends remarked, "Oh my goodness, this language is complicated!" The men went on to explain that dirt is *suto,* grass is *anrakat,* grass roots are *sab-rakat,* and the head of the grass is *artalra-sab-rakat.* Then, they seemed to decide that it was the dark men's turn to share their language.

The youngest, a boy about fourteen, took it up, sharing first his own name, Varast, and then his word for hand, finger, foot, and sky. Azshbir was totally frustrated. They could spend forever exchanging words. It had already been hours. He did not know if the Syrwens could learn Camilian, but he was almost certain he could not learn their language. However, they were sharing their names now. He actually tried to learn their names, even though he could not tell them apart. They were Sab-Arktikak, Asaubun-Ictushan, and Farat-Gutkralat. It took hours for Azshbir be able to remember their names, let alone keep them straight on his tongue, and he knew he did very badly. When he shared his own name with them, he made himself content with having it pronounced Isbir.

He turned to his friend. "I don't know about our friends, Sab, and Asaubun, and Farat, but we need to go back. We can't just exchange words all day."

Though it made them very uncomfortable, the light-people followed them, and the exhausting day was not nearly over.

When they saw their food, of which there was not a lot, one of them spoke quickly to his friends and then disappeared. After that, they would not tolerate a fire being built, but stamped it out and threw it in the sea, and the Camilians gave up. It was past midnight when one of the light men burst into Azshbir's tent, woke him up crying, "Isbir, Isbir," and then lots of words Azshbir could make nothing out of it, and thrust a strange growth of some sort in Azshbir's fact. The growth oozed sap, and the man pointed to it and held it up, and said, "Batish! Batish! Batish gumarnu! Gumarnu! Batish gumarnu!"

When he realized that his words and gestures were lost on Azshbir, he took a bit of the plant and stuffed it in his mouth. "Batish gumarnu, Isbir!" he repeated. "Batish farushim. Batish gumarnu. Batish Isbir-ni gumarnu."

Cautiously, Azshbir took a bite of the *batish*. He chewed it around in his mouth. It was not bad, but it tasted unlike anything he had ever had before. It was chewy, sticky, very wet, and a little bread-like. It had weird bubbles in it that popped when he bit down on them and produced an incredibly sharp and tangy taste in his mouth, then handed it to Neah'ra who had awakened and was trying to soothe her crying child while he talked with these strange people.

So, there was food of some sort around. Now, how would he manage to ask this man with whom he had no common words how to find this food?

"Batish," he said, and held the batish. He put the batish down where he had been sleeping and slowly pulled his hands away from it. He pointed. "Batish?" He went and buried the batish in the sand. He pointed. "Batish?" Then, he drew a shape of the batish and then another shape of the batish and another. He pointed. "Batish?"

"Inbutashin," the man said.

"Inbutashin," said Azshbir. He still had no idea how to ask for more inbutashin or how to find inbutashin. He hoped they would try to learn his language. He would never learn theirs.

Still holding Nourdë, Neah'ra appeared outside the tent. "It's food?" she asked.

#93
Deadly Place of Life

While helping Adaria watch her babies, Brisia had learned that the others, people the Queen had brought from Anores, had told them about Azshbir. These were people who had known and been friends with Azshbir; some of them had heard the truth of the Promise from him and those with him. It was he who had refused the crew Arendellie offered, and set sail from Anores. He and his wife, Neah'ra, had five children. Two twin daughters, two sons, and an infant daughter. Adaria was very happy about this; Brisia could hear it in her tone of voice. She thought she might even be hoping– though it was a wild hope– that they would land in the same region as her brother and get to meet him. She could not imagine how close Adaria and Azshbir might have been; she did gather that he was substantially older than herself. Thinking about it made her sad, wishing that Dormik could have been less evil– could have chosen the Promise and goodness instead of bitterness and revenge.

She and Laekoorj were married on the *Edgerunner.* They sang the songs that Khiel had written. Listening to the words and tunes and singing some of them herself, Brisia somehow found them more meaningful than ever before. The songs often seemed to rise into the sky on wings of their own. Somehow, beauty and light meant more to her than they had before; both defeat and victory seemed heavier– and lighter. She did not know what it was, but there was something new in her life or experience, except that it was not completely new. She could vaguely remember something like it, pieces of it, or a smaller it, from the past.

Now, she and Laekoorj stood on the poop (that is, the raised back) of *Edgerunner.* A few hours before they had launched out from a cove with a little stream. Above the cove, huge, ragged cliffs rose high into the sky. The waters that flowed down them were very cold. She could still see the pool into which the stream fell. As the wind blew it about, it turned into mists and rainbow mid-air. In fact, the cove was filled with an extremely light, fine rain because of this. Trees of kinds Brisia had never seen before grew in the cove. There was a fruit with a somewhat thick skin, rather unlike the skin of the jungle fruits. It was kind of flaky, kind of stringy, and kind of soft. On the outside, it looked like very soft orange bark. Inside, the fruit was made of many different pieces held together by the soft flaky, stringy stuff. There were other fruits there, too. They had re-filled their water, and brought lots of fruit on board.

"It's funny," said Brisia, "that we're floating on an ocean of water, and we have to get water from the dry land."

"Yes, it is," said Laekoorj. "The world is strange. It's amazing how the Creator made it."

Brisia nodded. She did not really care about the water that much; it was only a little amusing. She had her head craned back, staring up at the Frostflower Mountains. Unlike the Vinibra Mountains, they were full of rocks and mighty cliffs and they were covered in snow long before their brilliant white peaks touched the skies. From the cove, she had not been able to see it very well, but she had glimpsed them before. Now, however, if she looked to the east, she could see their end coming up at her. "I never imagined a place like that could exist," she said. "Could that be where the secret grove that Neemor and Eshaya climbed to, before the veiling, is?"

Laekoorj did not answer. So softly she could not be heard over the waves, Brisia said, "And, somewhere in there, Dormik... and the others... have gone."

She could, though, she thought, understand why they had made that decision. There was something about the Frostflower Mountains. The bare cliffs, some lighter, some darker. The forests, interspersed with cliffs, between the cliffs and the ocean. The snowy reaches, here and there dark cliffs showing through the snow. Above that, a dark mass of fluffy clouds hung about the mountains. Watching it, Brisia could see tiny white flashes of brilliant blue lightning. Above the clouds, snowy peaks showed against the brilliant blue sky. *I wonder what it is like, up there. I wonder if human beings can live there. I wonder if human beings can get there. I'm sure dragons could get there... unless the Creator won't allow it.* She knew that there were at least some places on the other side of the Frostflower Mountains where the Creator allowed humans to live, since there were the mountain tribes. She knew that the mountain tribes lived rather high up, because she had learned, from a young woman about her own age named Saria, that the reason that Grale– and after him the wizards– were believed not to have destroyed or enslaved them was that they fled far into the mountains, between narrow cliffs, into even narrower caverns, and into the regions of perpetual snow. In fact, the mountain tribes had long been mistreated, so they were used to fleeing and fighting in the mountains, so it was not really worth it. At least, that was what Saria said. She would not know anything about it.

Of course, Brisia thought, *they were thrust though the portal into Kaarathlon after they trespassed. The secret grove might not even be on this Kaarathlon in this time. Who knows?*

She felt a sudden stab of longing and sorrow. She missed Khiel! However right and happy Khiel's death may have been, it was sad, too. Sometimes, it still did not feel real.

Laekoorj put his arm around her and held her. She resisted the urge to wiggle away because it was slightly uncomfortable and a little ticklish. The movement of the ship still made her a little uncomfortable, and she grasped the rail with one hand, while wrapping her other arm behind Laekoorj under his arm. Sighing, she said, "I think I am going to get fat and weak, like this. Not literally fat, of course. No one wants to eat more food that they should, but all I do is cook when it's my turn, and jobs like that, that have to be done. It's not really that much. If I didn't mind the swaying of the ship, I could run around and things like that. The older children play a lot, and they can do lots of things. But I can't. If I tried, I wouldn't get very far before I fell over!"

"The children get in our way," said Laekoorj. "Besides, if you tried, you probably would learn."

Brisia shrugged. "Maybe. But, it's already been months, and I'm still not very good."

"You also don't try very hard or very much," said Laekoorj.

Brisia went on as if she had not heard him. "And, it's colder than I can ever remember."

For a long time, they stood saying nothing. Brisia leaned into Laekoorj, trying to get warm. The light-weight cloth used throughout most of Camil did very little to keep one warm, she now realized. It was as cold as any night in the Vinibra Mountains.

"The Creator has made so many things," she said, mostly to herself. "Things we could never imagine or come up with. Beautiful things. Hard things. It's wonderful, isn't it?... Even when the different things and places are uncomfortable." *How do You even invent it all? Oh, You are You! You really are bigger than size. Bigger than anything. Bigger and greater than all knowledge. You're the Creator! There are no words. None will do.*

After a while, Laekoorj said, "Remember that song you really like? The first tune Khiel wrote? It's appropriate. Look at the peaks of those mountains! They're in the sky. The bright, radiant sky that stings your eyes."

"It really does," said Brisia.

"The sea. The thought of how the sea is poisonous to us– we cannot drink it, even though it is water. And yet, all kinds of things grow in it and live in it, things that can only live in the sea. It gives new meaning to the parts about the depths of the sea where we cannot walk and the halls of the sea that we have not seen," continued Laekoorj.

"It does," said Brisia. She had not known that one could not drink the sea. She remembered, when she first got thirsty on the ship, asking someone, "Do you know how I can get some water? I can't get to the ocean."

The older woman had said, "It would not help if you could. Sea-water is salty, and you can't drink it. It's good for cooking, though. Let's try to find some water casks."

"Is the sea dead, then?" she had asked. "I don't know why, but I got the idea that lots of things live in the sea."

"Lots of things do live in the sea," the woman had said. "There are sea-plants and sea-trees. There are sea-animals. We would only know about the upper sea-fliers, but I'm sure there are low sea-fliers and sea-walkers, too. There's probably a whole sea-world. But we can't live there. It's a different kind of life than ours. I think the water casks are this way."

"That's annoying!" Brisia had said, much more loudly than necessary. "We need to take water from the dry-land onto an ocean of water, and if it runs out then we will die of thirst... while floating on more water than we could ever imagine."

"It's how the Creator made Kaarathlon," the older woman said. "I know there is a reason. A very good reason. This way is good."

"I know that," said Brisia. "The Creator does everything *right.*"

"But," the woman had responded, "you don't always accept it."

Brisia had resisted that piece of very accurate information. Still, she knew the woman was right. Laekoorj's words, tying the poem in the scroll and the deadliness of the sea together suddenly made sense. She remembered about the deadly radiance around the Creator. *There's something to an ocean of life being deadly to us. Being somewhere where we can't live, and upon which it is even dangerous to travel.* There had been great fear on *Edgerunner* a week and a half ago, when they had all seen a storm coming their way. Somehow, it did not harm them, though. It rocked the ship a lot, so that many were sea-sick and Brisia, though she was only barely sea-sick, could not even stand. It rained some, too. However, no real damage was done. Amazingly, the one experienced sailor with them said; Brisia would not have known whether it was amazing. It certainly felt scary, though.

"The peaks of the mountains and the sea… The heights and the depths," said Brisia. "That's what the poem focuses on, and how there is so much life and beauty that is deadly to us or that we otherwise cannot approach. Including the Creator!" *That's what doesn't make sense. He is so close, but He is more deadly and frightening and dangerous than everything else. Yet, He is so close and safe. We are promised that we will get to live with Him.*

#94
A Good Place

"We are sorry to inform your majesty that we are taking you into custody on the suspicion of treason," the soldier said.

In a moment of desperation, memories returned across decades. "This does not make sense!" Arendellie squealed, and moved quickly and subtly. In a moment, one of the soldier's swords was in her hand. She would not be fighting, but she had to gain time for El-Reiza to rescue her children. In a moment, the soldiers moved in on her, all their swords drawn. Hers flashed; it had been decades since she had held a sword, but the training she had received from Kathreen returned to her.

From the balcony above, El-Reiza saw a flicker of movement. She observed a couple strokes of the Queen's sword to be certain that she saw correctly. Her mouth widened in horror. She did not fight like an Elzari who had even begun training, but she fought like an Elzari child, untrained in swordsmanship but already initiated in the secrets of the Elzari. She certainly did not fight like even the best of Camilian sword-fighters. Mi'shael had understood and reported correctly! Someone had stolen the secrets of the Elzari. Nonetheless, she must take Kyil Kathreen and Aroch. She would have liked to kidnap the Queen; she should not be allowed to roam, teaching their precious secrets to others. What if the secrets fell into enemy or irresponsible hands? Worse, she was worried about the Queen. Did they know she had the secrets of the Elzari? Did they intend on interrogating or torturing her for them? Was that was this was about? Nonetheless, she must move quickly!

Meanwhile, Arendellie fought five soldiers at once. She twirled away and darted past them and pierced one fatally. Nonetheless, they captured her. One of them threw himself at her from behind, and there was nothing she could do. She let her sword drop.

"There's no way Hadac will make it!" called one.

The one who had captured her struck Arendellie on the head. "You killed my friend!" he said.

She only barely caught and slowly understood his words and the reply, "She's the Queen! Remember, our orders were to do her majesty no harm. After all, her majesty is only a suspect, and it's not good business to be arresting the Queen, let alone harming her."

They tied her hands behind her back and helped her stand. The whole way they argued to each other. "Don't bind her! Our orders were to take her with us peacefully!" said one. Another argued back, "What? And let her repeat that little stunt she pulled on us?" Another said, "It might not matter. That might have been a kind of wizardry. After all, she used to know that crazy wizard, Kathreen."

"Slave! Go to the door of the Queen's quarters. Do whatever you can to take care of the soldier, Hadac. He's bleeding. Real obvious," said another.

Arendellie was ushered into a room where the Council was gathered. The ropes immediately snapped from her wrists– by wizardry, she knew. A fear with which she was totally unfamiliar made her heart race and her stomach roil. Every half-second seemed to take an hour. A male wizard, named Koriel, clad in turquoise robes set with turquoises approached her, laid his hand on her head, and healed the damage left by the soldier's mailed fist. Meanwhile, another dismissed the soldiers. She looked across the room and saw Vanesh in orange and green robes. He looked so sad, so miserable, and so afraid. She wanted to comfort him. She tried to smile at him, but it was hard. She was so tense, so nervous, so uncomfortable.

"Take a seat, your majesty," said Valiana.

It took Arendellie longer than usual to slip into a seat. She would have gone towards Vanesh, but she saw that others sat directly on either side of him. She lowered her head. *O Creator, help me!* She did not know what was going on. Had Neshekh told them what she really was? Just that evening, she had been alerted that he had been executed. They did not want him to get away again, so they beheaded him. He had been tortured almost to the point of death before, repeatedly, and yet somehow healed and escaped.

The most prominent of the wizards, a man named Haradac, addressed her. "Is it true that your majesty has been caring for the treacherous ones who take the title People of the Promise and the title Knights of the Promise to themselves, thus rescuing them from the judgment we had determined for them and their kind and sending them away, where we do not know, and by thus averting from them the due consequences of their actions delaying their possible entry into the Creator?"

Arendellie was sickened by their religion. She risked a quick glance at Vanesh. He looked more miserable than ever. Nonetheless, she answered, "Yes."

Haradac turned to her husband. "What does your majesty say?"

"I did not know anything of this," Vanesh said. "My wife liked to take vacations and see new places. Her majesty greatly relishes all the comforts and extravagances royalty affords. She asked for funds and resources to organize these things and, somehow, what she was actually doing went entirely unnoticed. In fact, I am having a very hard time believing it. Until she replied in the affirmative to your question, I had suspected that a very clever thief was impersonating her, or whatever else the most plausible explanation might be. Possibly, a well-disguised enemy wizard."

For some reason, Arendellie was calmer now. She looked at Vanesh, but saw that he was not looking at her and that his face was contorted with anger and misery. Haradac turned his attention to her again. "Why did your majesty do this? Did your majesty not believe in the goodness of the Lord Casarion?"

Arendellie sat up straight and raised her head. "I am one of the People of the Promise. The Creator will yet send His Promise, to take our shame and give us His merits. The Creator is a terrible light and, far from us being able to become Him, His light is so real and so bright that unless He shields and strengthens us by His virtue He will become to us an intolerable torture, for, one day, His light *will* burn through Kaarathlon, and much sooner it will burn through our individual lives in death, and we *will* stand unshielded before the radiant burning of the Creator. Only in the Promised Conqueror is hope and salvation." It felt good. Too good. It felt better than anything she had ever done or experienced in her life. She wanted to dance, or run, or sing. She was so happy. Happy it had finally come to this. Happy she had finally *done* it.

"Will your majesty tell us where you have placed the People of the Promise?"

Arendellie looked up. Her eyes danced with happiness. "No," she said.

"You are the Queen," said Haradac, "and King Vanesh has begged for us to have mercy on you. Both these points put us in an uncomfortable position with regards to your majesty, since it would be improper for us to treat the Queen as it is proper to treat others. Can your majesty please be gracious and make this easy, either by telling us what you have done with the People of the Promise and where they are, or renouncing the Promise?"

Arendellie saw Vanesh imploring her with fiery anger and misery in his eyes. "Please, Araenyi," he said, his voice throbbing with pain. "Can it do any harm? Only renounce the Promise! Even so, you are worth more to me than their lives!"

Arendellie reached her hand across the table. "Vanesh!" she said, when Assea interrupted her. "You are not allowed to talk to each other right now, if you please, your majesties," she said.

Vanesh's misery just became more pronounced. Arendellie would not have known what to say to him anyways. She was happy, but she had already said all there was to say– many times over.

"If your majesty pleases," said Haradac again, "would your majesty please to be gracious to her subjects so that we will not have to do anything uncomfortable to us or unbefitting, and so that we will not have to waste our time and energy and life on understanding what is called for in this very unfortunate situation, but will your majesty instead please graciously renounce the Promise, or, if your majesty does not wish to do that, would she mercifully tell us what has been done with the People of the Promise and where they are?"

"By the mercy of the Creator, I will do neither," said Arendellie. She looked down at her hand on the intricately colored and traced table of green marble. She was almost weary of speaking. She was too glad for words. She was not even distressed by Vanesh's distress, nor did she even notice how far from all distress she was.

"This may be very unfortunate for others," said Haradac.

It took Arendellie a moment to process what he had said. She looked up. "What do you mean?" she asked. "Vanesh? It is very unhappy for him?"

The wizards looked at each other with surprise and mockery at her ignorance. Even Vanesh was surprised. Arendellie did not, however, notice. It took them a moment to respond. "Is it then a lie, your majesty, that many of your maids are People of the Promise who are looking for a Conqueror, even as your majesty is?"

"I can't tell you that," said Arendellie.

"Is that because you will not, or because your majesty gave to them the same mask you have given to us, and so they would be too afraid of your majesty to let you know, and so your majesty does not know?" asked Haradac.

Arendellie shrugged. "I will not tell you that, either."

Valiana leaned forward. Suddenly, the realization that they had once been something like loose friends– it was Valiana who had explained, as well as Arendellie could understand, how Grale Casarion had captured fire and why it had burned up his castle in Anores. Now, she was among the enemy. She only thought these things for a moment. "We already know," said Valiana, "that at least some of your slaves are such. For example, your first maid, Inshara. If they are not under the protection of your majesty, they are completely open to the various techniques that we use for the benefit of all. If we must deal with the troubles your majesty presents to us, you cannot possibly protect them."

For a brief moment, Arendellie understood what the Council was threatening. For the briefest moment, she thought, *Should I? If I tell them, how will they find and kill them? Send wizards out on dragons? How far away are they? Would it hurt?* Edgerunner *at least might not be too far away to reach. And, I just don't know.* Then, it was over. She could not do that. Neither could she lie and make up something that was not true but might pass as true. Besides, there was the group that had gone into the Frostflower Mountains. They were certainly within the range of these wizards. Besides, she did not even want to do so. It felt good to tell the truth and simply not tell whatever should not be told, and she could not have reasoned her way out of the happiness even if she had tried.

"Assea and Gamur, take the Queen to her room," said Haradac.

Arendellie stood. She turned towards Vanesh and smiled radiantly, but saw only misery and an intolerable, helpless rage in his face. "Please!" she begged him in one word. Then, the wizards took her out.

#95
The Healing

The cell was made of very light stone and it was clean. A single very small and barred window opened to the outside. If Arendellie had stood next to it, she could have just reached it with her finger-tips. She did not, though. At first, all she could realize was that it finally felt right. She felt good! It had been the most enjoyable thing in the world to simply do the good thing and tell the truth regardless of any consequences or any reasons she could come up with to not do so. Nothing had ever felt better. The only moment in her life that she could even compare to it– the only moment she could remember of anything like pure, exultant happiness in simple goodness– was playing with Kathreen and L'sa-moth, a few months after the purple and green dragon had hatched, one morning. They had both been children then. She had been what, six, maybe? But, even that was not like this!

She had long known the world was wrong. Now, it seemed suddenly righted. One reason for her gladness was that she was no longer the Queen of a country that committed untold atrocities, cooperating with those atrocities. She might still be the Queen in title, but she was now, herself, a prisoner of that country! She was no longer failing to do what she should: she had clearly confessed the Promise and who she was. She was no longer living a lie. She was where she belonged. All the pain and the wounds of being the pampered Queen and looking down on tortured and dying prisoners, that is, of being wrongly related to the world and to reality, were healed. She was on the right side of things! She was in the light. Suddenly, the meaning of Kathreen's words, spoken so long ago, about fighting and living in the light struck her. The Creator was light– or at least He dwelt in light. Certainly, His presence was light! She had told the truth– all of the truth that should be told. She had shed every lie, walked out of the darkness! She jumped and danced for joy, until her over forty-year old joints and feet ached and throbbed from impacting the stone floor.

Then, joy such as she had never known still coursing in her veins, she sat down against the wall and wrapped her cloak around her. She was just too happy! She wondered if everyone was this happy. If Brisia and Khiel and Azshbir and Neah'ra and Shantee and Adaria and Neshekh and all the rest were always this happy. She wondered if she found happiness so intoxicating and overwhelming because she had so long been a stranger to it.

Then, she realized her position. The wizards had not threatened to torture or kill her. They had threatened to torture and kill her friends to make her recant or tell them all they wished to know! Horror washed over her. She was still in a dreadful place. She was being made responsible for the suffering of others! On her choices, hung the death and torture of those with whom she was one. It was the same thing all over again.

Again, in a moment as thin as a hair, her perspective changed. She was not really responsible at all. The Creator was responsible. It was because of Him, His Promise, that they were all in this situation. She was here in obedience to Him. He was the Creator, and both she and they belonged to Him. He was mighty enough that nothing would happen unless He allowed it. So, it was not really her problem at all! Besides, she was, again, in no different a situation than they. She was not the first person, nor would she be the last, on whom the Council implemented their horrible method of torturing and killing others to gain someone's surrender. In fact, she had met some who had endured it, and more who had feared it.

Her mind flashed to the hundreds she had known who had suffered. She thought of Kyil, Yamië, Khiel, and Brisia, and many, many, many more. She flinched at the horror of what she had been, of where she had stood, but she knew it was not her responsibility to prevent the Council from committing their atrocities. If the Creator allowed it, what business did she have interfering? Far from not commanding her to stop them, He had forbidden her from doing what would be necessary to stop them. The Creator would know better than she. She had already seen that, in many cases at least, their victims were not destroyed. They told her that they had been *right*. Suddenly, a connection occurred to her. She, too, felt right here. Some ancient and hardly even noticed disease was healed, here. Perhaps, the Creator *did* do all things right? She had always believed it, at least in theory, but, really, actually? She knew, with absolute certainty, that however horrible the actions of the Council might be, their prisoners were well. They were in the hands of the Creator and, somehow, inconceivably, impossibly, but nonetheless in very actuality, it all came together for rightness and goodness. Were such people as Kyil even really prisoners? If there was such rightness, as Brisia called it, in these places, did she have any business using unlawful means to rescue people? She was already so grateful for what had just happened. Otherwise, how could she have ever known this happiness? How would she ever have stepped into the right relationship to light and darkness?

Gratitude washed over Arendellie. She knew the Creator had used her rebellion, her stubborn insistence on misery, to accomplish His will. He had promised that the Conqueror would first come among the daughters of Hoobit and Sirifa and in a distant land. Through her– yes, through her disobedience– that had come to pass or was even now coming to pass; she did not know which. She stretched herself out diagonally across the floor– it was the only way she could lie straight. "Thank You, thank You, a thousand times thank You," she sobbed dryly. "Even my disobedience brought Your will to pass, though You are in no need of any help from any of Your creation. Thank You, oh, thank You!" She could not have expressed her gratitude and joy. It felt like it would bubble up out of her or break her to pieces. She could not contain it, and yet she could not express it. "The worst thing You ever did to me is make me happy," she whispered. "Thank You, oh, thank You so much! I would never have done it by myself." She drew herself up and rocked back and forth on her legs. *Happiness,* she thought. *Happiness. I thought that, before I accepted the Promise, I had some vague understanding of where I was wrong, and then it was no longer vague, but very clear, yet I fought against it. Which was true. But, then I thought, 'Now, there is something wrong, and I am not fulfilled, but I have no idea what it is.' But I did. O my Creator, I did!*

Or, I could have if I had wanted. Thank You. She began speaking aloud again. "Thank You. Thank You. Thank You so much!" At the same time, she wondered how much she wanted to be fulfilled. It was almost as intolerable as misery. Misery... emptiness...fulfillment. These were the only three alternatives. They were the only three which could ever be, and yet they were all more– or less– than she could bear. Yet, she did bear it! "Oh, thank You so much," she whispered, and then words failed her completely. What could she say? She could only gasp in joy and gratitude, her entire being taken up into that gasp so that there was space for nothing else.

Then, she heard the door open and someone step in. She turned, and saw that it was Vanesh. He looked so miserable. He just stood there. She stood and curtsied.

"Araenyi," he said sorrowfully.

"Vanesh," she replied softly, her eyes downcast.

He stepped closer and lifted her chin. "You're... You're not happy!" he exclaimed in a whisper.

"But I am," said Arendellie.

"It's not possible," he said. "You know what they were threatening." She nodded. "These are the people you have worked so hard, driven by guilt and miserable compassion, to protect. How will you endure it? And, if you do endure it, how will I endure to lose you? I do not want you hurt. I know how much it hurt you just to see them, tortured and dying. How will you bear to see it done– and to know that you can stop it with a word? That it is directly because of you?" He himself seemed to tremble as he spoke.

She looked up into his eyes. She spoke quietly. "It is the Creator's responsibility; not mine. They do not belong to me." She wished she could share with him all that she knew now, but knew that she could not. He did not understand even the beginnings.

He gazed on her intently for a few moments longer. "I wish you would not. What made you tell them what you told them? Why could you not simply answer the first question with a lie, and our lives could go on?"

"It was the best– and the easiest– thing I have ever done in my life," said Arendellie. "That's why I'm happy now– I obeyed! I'm where I should be." She paused for a moment, seeing the anguish in his eyes and gathering her response. "You mentioned, just earlier, the guilt and misery I felt that drove my scant and miserable compassion and deeds? You see, that has all been healed, because I am now in the right..." Her words stopped dead in her mouth. She knew what she was about to say would hurt Vanesh dreadfully. "... the right relationship to the world... to reality... to the Creator... to His people... to *them.*" When he looked at her with a question in his eyes, she immediately corrected herself. "The Council."

"O Araenyi," said Vanesh. "You don't mean to say?"

She could not respond to that question. Then, he said, "Aroch and Kyil are gone, along with some of your maids. No one is happy about it...You knew about it?"

Arendellie did not answer.

"Do you know where they are?"

"No," answered Arendellie easily.

Vanesh did not question her further. She stepped into his arms. "I can't bear to lose you," he said. "I love you. Every time you look at me with your green eyes… Every time I see you move… Your voice… Even your stubborn and valiant insistence on doing what you want. Only, I wish you would drop that one. Oh yes, and the Promise. I really wish you would not make such a big deal out of the Promise. Araenyi… Araenyi… Araenyi."

Arendellie did not know how to respond. "I just wish you would accept the Promise, too. Then, you could share my gratitude and my joy!" she finally said.

Vanesh just held her tighter. She leaned into him. She loved him, too, she realized at last. She was glad that the Creator had not allowed her plan to work. Though she would have liked to raise Aroch and Kathreen, Arendellie was glad that her son and daughter were safe, and that she was here. It was so much more than she could ever have asked for or imagined. She wanted to cry for gratitude and joy.

Then, there came a knock on the door.

"I must go now," said Vanesh. His eyes pleaded with her, but he turned and left. At the same time, a slave entered carrying a platter of food. Arendellie smelled the delicious scents, but she did not feel hungry. Instead, she thought of Ellason and her desire to tell her the truth before she died. Of course, Ellason might have died. The prisons were no place to live a healthy life. However, there was a good chance Ellason was still alive. There was no reason she would be particularly likely to be tortured or killed more than anybody else, and it had not been more than two years. Arendellie said to the serving girl. "Do you know why I'm here?"

"You're a traitor, I heard," said the girl.

"The Creator is real," said Arendellie. "We will all stand before Him one day, because His light will destroy Kaarathlon." The slave cocked her head as if she were having a hard time understanding. "The Creator is completely other than us. His light is unendurable to us. That's why He gave us the Promise. The Promised One will bear our shame away and give us His merits, so we can live with the Creator. He will conquer death and make everything right."

The slave nodded. "I'm not really supposed to listen to you, but if your majesty wants anything, you only need to ask. Speaking of that, you are the Queen and you are a prisoner. Should I call you your majesty?"

"I'd rather you did not," said Arendellie. Even though the girl was not going to listen to her, she felt another wave or spike of unspeakable joy. "I would like it if you can find out if a prisoner by the name of Ellason Zaele is still alive. If she is, I would like to speak to her."

Sometime, half way through the night, she ate her food, which was now cold.

In the morning, two female guards brought Ellason to her, along with her breakfast. She shrank at the sight of Ellason. The tall woman was very thin and clothed in rags, through which some scars were visible. She looked completely miserable, but also like her entire existence was hatred, bitterness, and small cruelties. "You may speak," one of the female guards said, "but we will stay here the entire time. We cannot let prisoners converse unsupervised."

Arendellie nodded, inwardly rejoicing. She turned to Ellason and said, "I am one of the People of the Promise. I believe that none of us can live in the Creator's presence, because we have all fallen short and rebelled against Him. I also know that His light will burn through all things, so that one day we must stand naked in His light. He has given us hope and salvation in the Promise, for the Promised One will bear away our shame, so that we are not hateful and an enemy to the Creator and His terrible light, and He will give us His merits, so that we can live in His light and rejoice in what would otherwise be ceaseless and greatest torment. The Promised One will conquer and reign everywhere. Even death will be His realm, and He will lead His own people out, but His enemies He will cast into its dungeons forever." She noticed that the guards were very uncomfortable, as if they were not certain that this was allowed, but also did not know if they were allowed to do anything about it, and were worried about getting into trouble whatever they did.

Ellason was very upset. "I know this stuff already," she said. "I used to believe it." Then, as if she just realized something, "Was that why you were so upset with me? Because you weren't torturing them at all! You were rescuing them!"

"Yes," said Arendellie. "I should not have done it that way. I am grateful to the Creator that He is merciful and used my rebellion for good, but He does not want His people to lie or deceive."

"Your Creator is a weak, fairy-tale god," said Ellason.

"What if fairy-tales come true? What if the truth is both the real world and more than the real world and the fairy-tales and more than the fairy-tales?" asked Arendellie. That way of putting it had only just occurred to her.

"Well," said Ellason, "I can't believe you did what you did! To me, that is. I'm so glad you were found out– or fessed up to it, or whatever it was. I hope they torture you horribly to make up for what you did to me." There was glee in her voice. She had not experienced so much of the depraved and twisted forms of happiness she was still able to experience in a very, very, very long time. In her imprisonment, she had continued to nourish her hatred and envy of the Queen.

Arendellie smiled softly, not in mockery, but at things only she could see and that she would not have put into words if she had tried; she could not have even thought of trying to put them into words. After a few moments, she asked, "What of what you have done to us?"

"That doesn't matter," said Ellason. "What matters is that you have fallen."

Arendellie smiled even more. "Actually," she said softly, "I have risen. This is one of the best things that have happened to me."

"You're just trying to fight my victory. To believe that you're still on top even when it's obvious you're headed to the bottom of the sewer," said Ellason.

Arendellie did not respond. She looked up at the guards. "Unless Ellason has anything she would like to say, you can take her back to her cell, now. Oh yes, and give her my breakfast."

Ellason looked shocked. "The only thing I have to say is that I hate you and I'd like to suck your blood!"

#96
The Speaker

Finally, the people had accepted that there was no reason to think things would have gone better with a crew, and were getting along without grumbling or complaining. The insight that, yes, they *might* have landed in a different place which *may* or *may not* have been more inhabitable with the crew, but, then again, they may not have landed *at all* with a crew, but instead have all died of thirst out in the middle of the ocean helped a great deal. So did the fact that people were no longer so stressed. Asaubun-Ictushan, Sab-Arktikak, and Farat-Gutkralak had shown them how to find many different kinds of food, some of which most of the Camilians thought disgusting. It was not exactly pleasant; they could not drink the sea-water, and they were usually thirsty because the plants that grew were not as watery as they would have liked. That was until Kira figured out how to say she was thirsty. At this, Farat-Gutkralak– at least, Azshbir thought it was he, since he still had some trouble telling them apart and now knew that they were brothers– took some of the men out with him and showed them a kind of grass that was about two and a half feet taller than the anrakat– plural, sanrukitin– and spread at the top into broad fronds. He cut one of the stalks of this plant and, without delay, turned the cut side up. It was full of an ever-so-slightly whitish water that tasted strange. He then tried to explain to them that there were many intuarumin– singular, turam– so they should only do this when they were really thirsty. Then, they brought back the suromi.

Another adventure, and one that had occurred rather earlier, was convincing the three brothers that the dragons were not going to eat them. Azshbir still did not know who had succeeded in communicating that, or how it had been done, but when it had been done a greater problem emerged. Asaubun-Ictushan and his brothers took to worshiping the three dragons. They tried to offer sacrifices to them. They knelt and prostrated before them. They tried to do a worship dance around them.

Azshbir remembered Kira's response. She had leapt from behind Kellyth, with her hand held up, crying out in the foreign language. "Makdagak! Makdagak! Estumu ma oraulim! Estumu exiyralifin-ekundin." Amazingly, the three brothers understood her and immediately stopped trying to worship the dragons. When Azshbir asked her how she did it, she said, "I'd heard the words before, and thought they had meant that. All but *oraulim,* but they were shouting that a great deal. I guess Kellyth helped me put it together, so all I had to focus on was not twisting it up on my tongue." She laughed at that.

"You did really well," said Azshbir.

It was the next day that Kellyth flew the red dragon, Carneth. The three brothers all sat down on the shore to watch this amazing dance in the sky, with Kameth following behind. In the end, the dragons flew far out over the ocean to have complete privacy. "They catch the fish, but not right now," Azshbir said to the three brothers in their language. "Estamu ruktuk ansujin, orist-mal, nio."

For the Knights of the Promise, the problem was now how to communicate the Promise to the three brothers. Communication was halting and painful, but they were now able to communicate about a great deal. A couple weeks ago, when it began to get painfully cold for at least some of the Camilians, one of the brothers had understood, and Asaubun-Ictushan and Farat-Gutkralak had gone away. A couple of days ago they had returned with loads of animal skins and other materials, and all three brothers had spent the next days sewing the animal skins into clothing, enough for eleven of the Camilians to keep themselves much warmer. The brothers looked at them, laughed, and said, sometimes in Camilian and sometimes in their own language, that it was very funny for them to be wearing the clothes of deep winter in the mountains in late fall by the sea. Many of these words had been learned by drawing pictures in the sand. The men were about to leave again, when Kameth dropped a deer at the edge of the camp for them to see.

"She followed you," Azshbir said in his own language, hoping the men would understand. "I think she is saying, you do not have to go again. She will bring the deer. You skin them and make clothes. We all will cook and eat the deer."

The brothers beamed at him and at each other. They had obviously understood enough to be very pleased. Azshbir knew that they were also very pleased that the Camilians were now somewhat capable of foraging for their own food, though they were not one eighth as good as it as the Syrwen brothers. For a long time it had puzzled Azshbir, Neah'ra, and everyone else how they never left, unless the Camilians asked for something, and they seemed to want to be part of them. They borrowed their clothes to wear. They tried to cook like they did. They listened to all their conversations. While they sewed the skins, they had had more opportunity to simply talk, all of them together. It had emerged that, for some reason, the brothers had been exiled from their tribe and told never to appear among their people again– on pain of death, Shantee thought she understood.

Neah'ra, wearing a long tunic of animal skin over her Camilian dress, sat down next to Azshbir while he gutted a fish one of the dragons had brought. "We can tell them that there is one Creator of all things, can't we? At least, we can tell them there is one Maker of all things– who made all things out of no things? Do you think we understand enough or they understand enough?"

"Yes," said Azshbir, and rattled off a line in their language.

Neah'ra repeated it. "It's a shame," she said, "that they are so much more willing to talk to you men than to us women. They will hardly glance at us or say a word to us, though they will respond to our requests– if we can make them understand."

Azshbir looked around. "At least, they're far enough away they aren't likely to hear you unless you shout."

Neah'ra smiled. "I have Kgarjin watching Nourdë and Norden. Kuthreb is playing with the boys about his age."

Azshbir shook his head. Why was she telling him about that right now? She continued, "How would you tell them the Promise? Do we know their word for promise? Do they know what promise means? What about shame? Or guilt. Or merits? What about death? Or conquer? Or rule?"

"I think I could say that someone will hunt death– if I can guess how to say death instead of die or dead– and drag him back as a slave– but, that might actually be the word for pet? Or it might just mean my animal. You see, I could really mess this up."

"What about prison?"

"Well, I'm not sure how to say to vomit up, but I think I could say that death will eat those that his owner hunts. Always assuming I can figure out how to say death."

"I'm not sure if that's the right way to put it, but, why don't you tell me lots of the words again, and I'll see if I can guess? And if you agree… and everyone else agrees."

"I get what you're saying," said Azshbir. "It's a good idea."

"Besides," said Neah'ra, saying exactly what he was thinking, "if it's not an okay way to explain the Promise, we can try, do the best we can. Then, later, when we both– meaning us and them– know more words, then we can do better. Explain that we were really trying to talk about this. If they don't have a word for prison or dungeon, I'm sure we can describe it to them."

Neah'ra lay down on the sand. "I'm exhausted. Watching those children is so exhausting… And, I'm cold."

Azshbir glanced over at her. "A good thing you're not doing this job. I can hardly feel my fingers, and most of what I can feel is pain. Anyway, why aren't you wearing more skin-clothes?" He thought the skin-clothes looked dorky, especially over her Camilian dress. She even had a shawl wrapped tightly around her head several times to keep her hair against her face and her cheeks a little warmer.

"Everyone else is cold, too," said Neah'ra, "and we don't have enough yet. I let some of the other women and children borrow mine." She moved a little, trying to get as much of the warmth out of the sand as possible. "Sab-Arktikak and his brothers seem to think we are ridiculous for needing to wear so much."

Azshbir did not respond. She had said it about ten times already. He had told her she was probably right about three times. He was not in the mood for talking, either. He had to concentrate on what he was doing, especially since he could not feel his fingers.

The next day, Asaubun-Ictushan said, "In a sight-in-the-night, *rulm* speak to us. It was a tree-leaf speak. He said, 'Your *oraulim* speak to you, and the speak is not. People with night-hair and evening-skins walk on sea on bigger thing. They say to you who speaks and his speak is, who does his speak.' We told the sky-woman. She say, 'It is not.'" At this, Asaubun began to wave his hands around, and then to explain what he meant in his own language. Most of the words were far beyond the Camilian's limited vocabulary. The brothers finally seemed to decide that they could not say what they wanted to say. Then Asaubun-Ictushan said, "Sky-women and the little-sky-men. They say, 'You hear what is not. You *cusobarain* not-speaks. You go. Far, far, far. Or, we,'" at this they looked at each other and said some things, which were unintelligible to Azshbir. He thought they asked if they should use the word for hunt or another word he did not know, "'or, we hunt you. We kill you. *Oraulim* speak so.'"

It took Azshbir a couple moments to realize what they had just said. He rose and said, "We will tell you who speaks and what He speaks is. All that He speaks He will do. What He says He will do, He will do. In truth. He speaks truth." He took a deep breath. "First, I will tell you who He is. He made sky and earth and sea out of nothing." He repeated himself, as best as he could, in their language. He said, "He is the Creator. The one who made all things out of nothing. He spoke the things, and the things were. Because He speaks, the things are. The Creator gave us a Promise. Promise means He spoke something and it will be. He spoke something He will do, and He will do it. He spoke something that will happen, and it will happen."

At this, the brothers made it clear that they understood. "The Creator is the Speaker!" they said, then turned to each other and said, "Besgum Nalak-wathwarik!" Then, Farat-Gutkralak asked, "Where is His speak, Promise?"

"They mean, what, not where, I think," said a woman named Damiela.

Farat-Gutkralak repeated himself. "What is His Promise?"

"I don't know your words to say it," said Azshbir. "I don't know if you know our words to say it."

"Say! Say! Say!" said the brothers.

"All right. I will try," said Azshbir. "We cannot live with the Creator. We cannot walk with the Creator. We cannot be with the Creator. We did wrong. We did not live with the Creator. We did not walk with Him. Instead, we went our own way. Then, we did much hurt to ourselves and to everything else. This means the Creator does not look on us. The Promise is, He will send someone who will change this. He will take our shame– the wrongness in us that means the Creator does not look at us– away. He will give us His merits. Those are His rightness. Then, we will walk with the Creator. The Promised One will hunt all evil. He will make all things do what He wants."

Later, Azshbir was thinking about how strange this was. Communication was still extremely difficult, but certain things were by now very obvious. The Creator had, it seemed, specifically called these three brothers, for the purpose that these three brothers should know the Promise and for the purpose that they should be shown how to live in Syrwe by these three brothers. How perfect was the Creator's plan!

#97
The Twin

Nagi deftly pulled Arendellie's scroll out of the Queen's dresser and hid it under the folds of her dress under her belt. She twirled her blue-and-green shawl around and re-arranged it over her head, shoulders, and back to better conceal the scroll. Inshara had told her where to find it and sent her to get it, upon being alerted that the Queen's belongings were being sorted and moved; they all guessed that the Queen's allegiance to the Promise had been discovered and that she had not disowned it. What was now happening to her they did not know. It had been weeks since they had found the soldier dying in the visitor room. She knew, too, what had happened to Prince Aroch and Princess Kathreen and to Kalie and Aki'lam, who had been friends of hers. Vanesh had questioned them all extensively– and privately– but, as far as Nagi knew, they had revealed very little. She had not revealed anything. Vanesh did not pressure them; she knew he was driven only by concern for his Queen and for his children.

Now, she could hear other slaves and soldiers running around the place and moving things around. Hurriedly, she left the Queen's chambers and went out to the garden, where she busied herself trimming trees and cutting flowers. She tried to ignore the chaos and fear she heard from within. She heard cries of "No! Do not do this to us!" and, "Please, spare her!" and, "Never!" and many others things she could not hear very well. Her heart fluttered and her hands shook, marring her work. *There's one good reason for me not to go and see what's happening,* she thought to herself. *I am the keeper of the scroll.*

Nagi could not imagine what was happening. Slaves fled into the garden. Some of them were her friends; others she hardly knew. The Queen had had a great many. They cowered in corners and fled. She had no idea what was happening. She could hardly even grasp the tools with which she worked. She struggled to continue working. She could not think about what to do. She was only fourteen. She had been torn from her mother, a simple laundry-washer working for a lesser noble, when she was only ten. A couple years ago, while she was still being moved around and dreading the worst, the Queen had bought her. It was hard to think of it that way, now. Arendellie had been nice and personable. She said, "Please," which is what people said when they were asking someone who was at least close to their equal to do something. Now, she was afraid just at the thought of whom she might serve, now.

Right behind her she heard a man's voice asking, "Do you wait for a Conqueror?"

Nagi dropped her tools and turned. Her heart and limbs felt like melting jelly. She looked up into the man's eyes. "I do," she answered.

"I wasn't asking you," he said, as if he had not even noticed her. Relief washed over her, but it was short-lived. He must not have been thinking. The People of the Promise were always persecuted, wherever they were found. Sometimes, occasionally, someone was only forced to do hard and demeaning labor– made the lowest of slaves. More often, one was thrown into the dungeons to rot. One could be tortured. One would probably be executed. Other dreadful things might be done to one. Her heart melted at the thought. It had been foremost in her mind since Arendellie had been taken away. Surely, they would not do too horrible things to her, since she was after all the Queen? Why had she even been called Queen if she was to be tried before the Council? And, what about the other slaves, if they did overlook her?

The guards and soldiers left with almost all of Nagi's friends– all who had accepted the Promise. She stood on the garden path, watching them being marched away. Some had already been struck until they bled. One of the guards turned to her and asked, "What about her? Is she fine?"

"Yes, she's clear," answered the man who had questioned her.

Nagi struggled to speak. Her words stuck in her throat. Finally, she ran after them and cried, "I do wait for the Conqueror."

"You're fine," the man who appeared to be in charge said.

Nagi threw herself down on the ground to cry. This was the greatest disaster she could imagine after being torn from her mother. Aki'lam and Inshara had cared for her and helped her to recover. Aki'lam was gone, probably into safety. Inshara was being taken away, to die! She had spent hours crying and fearing about the Queen, and about what would happen to her now. Then, she realized she still had the scroll, one out of only three. She was a slave, sure to be sold and humiliated and moved around, to have nothing of her own, to be searched. How on earth could she possibly keep the scroll? If it were found, it would be burned. Would she be burned with it?

She felt someone patting her on the back. "It'll be okay, Nagi," said a familiar voice.

She just kept sobbing. "Arendellie... will die... Inshara will die... and... and... and..." She twisted around and sat up. Alitholiel sat down next to her. She burst into tears again. "And I will be sold to someone, and then I will be beaten and abused and burned!"

"Why?" asked Alitholiel.

"The Promise!" said Nagi, and buried her face in her hands and cried. "You haven't seen," she said, in between sobs, "what they do, but the Queen... brought me with her. I don't know what... what happened to you either... but, my mom, she knew the Promise and she... she taught it to me. That's why," said Nagi, and stopped even trying to talk.

"You're going to be my daughter's friend," said the noblewoman. "I and my husband have eight sons, but we have only one girl. Her name is Hariel. You were a favored personal handmaid of the Queen, so you can serve Hariel. Don't quarrel with her."

Nagi nodded. She was almost too terrified to comprehend what the woman was saying. However, a few hours later she was alone with Hariel in her room. She learned that the girl was two years younger than herself. It was the strangest afternoon of her life. "What's your name?" Hariel asked.

"Nagi," she answered,

"Well, Nagi," she said, "You are going to be my sister. We're twins."

Nagi's mouth dropped open. "What?"

"You are my sister. We are twins," repeated Hariel, "which means, I am going to do your hairstyle just like mine. Tomorrow, you get to do both our hairstyles. I am going to find a dress for you that's just like mine. Tomorrow, you get to pick the dresses, too."

It took Nagi a while to process what was happening. Meanwhile, Hariel put her hair up in a braided bun, and then ordered her to look through one set of dresses for something that looked kind of like the pink dress with yellow flowers sewn onto the edges of the sleeve and the hem that she herself was wearing.

After that, Hariel spent hours telling Nagi everything she could remember about her life and showing her all her toys and games and teaching her how to play them. There was one game that Nagi simply could not understand. Finally, Hariel threw it back in its box. "That's okay. You can learn that one another day. We have simply forever! It's your turn to show me something."

Nagi's head was still spinning from this recent change in her life. Her life was completely unbelievable. After being torn from her mother, she had ended up with the Queen, who was different from everyone else in exactly the way one would not expect from a queen. Now, all her friends were being tortured to death, and her new mistress had declared her to be her twin sister! Would Hariel's parents be okay with that?

"C'mon," said Hariel. "There's got to be something you want to share with me. Unless you had more sisters than you can count. If that's so, tell me about them!"

"No," said Nagi, overcome with sadness. "I didn't." An idea occurred to her. "But I do have this!" She got up and crossed the room to where the clothes she had been wearing were.

"Really?" asked Hariel, getting up and following. "Is your cloak that interesting?"

"Not my cloak," said Nagi. She reached in and took the scroll. "This," she said. "It is the true story of the world, from the very beginning to the last things, things that have not yet happened."

"Wow!" said Hariel. "Can you read it? Because I can't read."

"Yes," said Nagi. "Others of the Queen's slaves taught me. I'll teach you." So, Nagi found herself sharing the Promise with Hariel. It turned out that Hariel's parents completely accepted her new attachment to Nagi. The two girls quarreled much less than siblings normally would, since Nagi was both older and, when Hariel told her what to do, she accepted it, more or less graciously; after all, she was and always had been a slave. Hariel was not yet old enough to invent such nonsense as, "You must do it my way and my way must be the first choice you think of," or she was too thrilled to have another girl to play with all the time to notice it. She introduced Nagi as her "twin sister," to the other daughters of the nobility who were her friends, and, though Hariel did not seem to notice, Nagi knew that they looked down on her as a slave and looked down on Hariel for taking her for her twin.

One day, Nagi went to their room early, threw herself down on their bed and cried. Coming in half an hour later, Hariel asked, "What's wrong?"

Nagi looked up. She raised her arms, and her shawl made them look like yellow wings. "My friends are all dying! They were People of the Promise, too, and we were all asked. We all said who we were. They were all taken away to be tortured. For some reason, they looked over me, even though I told them many times who I was."

"Well," said Hariel, "I'm glad they didn't take you. If they had, then you would have been tortured and killed, too, and I would never have gotten to meet my twin sister. Don't you think that would have been pretty sad?"

"Uh, yeah," said Nagi. Then, a thought occurred to her. "Weren't you taught that the People of the Promise are traitors?"

Hariel scrunched up her face as if she were thinking hard about something. "Uh," she said slowly, "I think I *was*." Then her face brightened. "But, I'm not really sure. And, you're my twin sister. And, you aren't. At least, *I* say you aren't. I definitely am not a traitor, and you are my twin, just like me, so you aren't a traitor. So, that's fine. Let's play."

"I'm not in the mood to play," said Nagi.

Hariel cocked her head. "Why?" she asked.

"Would you feel like playing if you were thinking about the fact that your friends and your mom were in prison and being killed?"

"Your mom?" asked Hariel. "No, I wouldn't, but, tell me about your mom. Actually, it's not that way at all. You're my twin, remember? My mom is your mom."

"Well, she wasn't really my mom," said Nagi. She was finding Hariel hopelessly irritating. She would have preferred to simply be a handmaiden than this whatever-it-was Hariel had invented. Hariel roped her into explaining her sad past and, to make it worse, constantly interrupted by telling her how it was not true anymore.

Sometime after that, King Vanesh entered the house, and asked for the former slave of Queen Arendellie. Nagi's heart melted when she heard his summons. She had become amazed that, for some reason, in this household, she could speak all she wanted about the Promise and the scroll, and no one but Hariel ever seemed to even notice. Was she about to be tortured and the scroll lost? Upon hearing the summons, she quickly whispered to Hariel, "Take care of the scroll. You know where it is."

As it turned out, Vanesh had no intention of killing her or even keeping her from Hariel.

#98
An Inconsolable Longing

Brisia dug her feet into the sand and squished it between her toes. It felt like nothing she had ever imagined before. She had several layers of clothes on, but the wind still chilled her. She shivered. She took a few slow steps through the sand, feeling it under her feet and between her toes. It was a little– just a little– like the sand that sometimes accumulated on the sides of streams. "It's so nice to be on real ground again!" she called. A moment later, she started running up the beach. She had never run on sand before. She slipped through it and it took more effort to cross the same amount of distance than it should have. Still, she enjoyed it. It was so nice to be on land again!

She felt weight on her shoulders and then a pull. A moment later she was on top of Laekoorj. She gasped. "Ow!" she cried.

"Did I hurt you? Is it because of the baby?" asked Laekoorj, concerned. Brisia's belly was definitely swelling with the child growing within.

"No," said Brisia, wincing. It had twinged, once, while she ran. Now, it hurt so badly she did not know what to make of it.

"You really are hurt," said Laekoorj, moving carefully to lay her down. "Where?"

"Just... *scars*. There's no blood, is there?" she asked.

"Uh, no, I don't think so. Where?" asked Laekoorj. As she motioned vaguely with one arm, he asked, "Has this ever happened before?"

"No, it hasn't," said Brisia shortly. She sat up, wincing again. "I'm not that hurt... Not really." She closed her eyes for a moment. "It's just... well, scars were twinging more when I did things. That one where that kimmer bit me twinged sometimes. But... not like this." She closed her eyes. With an effort, she opened them again, looked around, and focused her mind on something else. "Are those *trees?*" she asked, pointing to the woods not twenty yards further in. "They have no leaves on them."

"No, I don't think you're bleeding," said Laekoorj.

"Well, it's already hurting a whole lot less," said Brisia. She looked around. "I'm fine, Adaria. Lalia, go and make sure nobody comes over here because they think I'm hurt." She stood up, a little carefully. She climbed up the beach to where the trees began. "They used to have leaves," she said, half to herself, looking at thousands of leaves covering the ground, of many shapes and sizes. "They really are trees."

Laekoorj walked with her, his arm around her waist. He nudged her gently towards the stream, where a tree, nicely covered in green leaves, grew. "They're shaped differently than the jungle trees!" Brisia exclaimed. "Kind of like the trees in the cove, and kind of like the trees from... Ebrin!"

"Here," said Laekoorj. "Why don't you sit down, and I will go work on setting things up."

Brisia wrenched free of his grasp, turned around, and planted her feet apart.

"I'm going to help," she said. "I need exercise. I'm finally on real ground. And just because I'm pregnant doesn't mean I can't do anything!"

"You're not just pregnant, you're hurt," said Laekoorj. "Both of those together means it's easier for you to hurt yourself, and maybe even the baby."

Brisia shook her head. The veil she had wrapped tightly around her head, entirely for warmth, began slipping off. "I'm not hurt," she declared.

"You shouldn't be doing this. We're all somewhat weak from poor food, you have a baby to grow in you which makes you more vulnerable, and you're obviously hurt. Otherwise, you wouldn't have gotten hurt the way we came down. I've done that to my sisters more times than I can count. But, I am so sorry."

"I'm not hurt! I can help."

"Fine," said Laekoorj, "but make sure you only do really easy things. Like untie knots."

"You know untying knots *isn't* easy," said Brisia.

"It won't hurt you," said Laekoorj.

When the men shot and brought back a deer, Brisia felt like she wished she could eat the entire animal herself. Everyone was cold, and the rain was also cold. They took apart the *Edgerunner,* and used its beams to build houses. They used the masts to make tents. The men made better bows and became better at hunting the animals of those places.

Finally, Brisia gave birth to her and Laekoorj's child. The baby was a girl, and they named her Mirla. About the same time, Esiri married one of the men who had come with them across the sea; they were becoming settled in Syrwe and learning how to thrive on the new continent.

Gazing on the face of her five-week-old daughter, after readjusting her to nurse better, while leaning into Laekoorj who had his arm around her, with Adaria and her children and Sirifa in the same tent-house, Brisia nonetheless felt deeply lonely. Even in the midst of those she loved and lived with, those she knew, those who had known her most of her life and the man she had married, with her child whom she loved and to whom she was so drawn, she felt lonely. She felt alone.

One day, in early spring, when the leaves were just forming and budding on the trees, when little wildflowers of all different colors peeked up from the grasses, when strings of white flowers flowed from the boughs of some of the trees, she and Laekoorj left Mirla in the care of their friends to go for a walk together. After nearly an hour, spent in silence, she pulled her clothing together, standing in a fresh, chilly breeze from the northeast. It blew her hair from her cheeks. Several minutes ago, they had stopped, and Laekoorj had held her for a long time. She did not want him to hold her now. She had felt like crying, and still did feel like crying, but she did not know why. She was not exactly sad, either. At least, she did not really think she was sad. She certainly had no idea what she was said about, yet she felt desperately lonely. Sometimes, she felt so happy she wanted to die, unendurably happy with a piercing kind of joy. She was not sure she did not feel this way now, but she wanted to break down and weep. She was so lonely she wanted to be alone.

Laekoorj spoke something, but she did not hear it. She was not listening, and the wind was blowing past them. After nearly half a minute, she asked, "What did you say?"

Laekoorj spoke more loudly, and she caught his words this time. "Is something wrong?"

Brisia did not know how to respond to that question. "No; I don't think so," she said. The wind was blowing past her, towards him, and he heard her words. She saw a bird flying in the sky above. She knew that the loneliness and the piercing happiness and the pain and the inconsolable grief were all one. She wanted home; Kaarathlon, beautiful as it was, dissatisfied her; she did not belong.

"Are you sure?" asked Laekoorj, moving closer to her and speaking more loudly.

Brisia's heart ached. She loved Laekoorj, but she wanted to be away from even him. "Nothing I could tell you," she mumbled.

"What did you say? I didn't hear," said Laekoorj.

Normally, the interaction would have infuriated her. As it was, the deep draining loneliness, sorrow, joy, prevented such a response or even the inclination to it. "Nothing I could tell you," she said again, deliberately raising her voice and turning her head to him, then away. She wanted to collapse and she wanted to flee. She wanted she knew not what. Somehow, the memory of standing at the stern of the *Edgerunner* watching the cove fade into the blue yonder and looking to the gleaming blindingly white peaks of the Frostflower Mountains was graven in her mind. "I want to be alone," she said quietly.

"Like this?" asked Laekoorj.

"No. More alone." She lowered her head, struggling. "Completely alone. By myself." She did not hear his response. She knew she was going to collapse. She was going to cry. A lump had already formed in her throat. She took a few shaking steps forward, struggling to contain herself for a little longer. She did not want even Laekoorj to watch, not that she thought about it explicitly, and still less did she think about why it was so necessary that she be absolutely alone. She shook, began to cry, and collapsed on the other side of a few trees, clinging to a bush for support or comfort. The tears flowed freely. She felt too weak to even stand; too weak even to sit. In a way, she felt too weak to live, too weak to draw breath– yet, of course, she did, and could not have helped but do so.

Brisia shook with sobs, until it was painful. She clung to the branch, leaning into it, enduring a deep pain. She wanted to stay here forever. She wanted she knew not what– a lifting of the burden, whatever it was, the burden of living– of doing– of trying? Her loneliness was not a loneliness that another could have shared, nor would it have been less lonely had another shared it, for many endure it, but the experience of another makes no one less lonely, less alone. Sometimes, it does not matter how many or who shares the same experience, the same weight, the same longing, the same joy, the same call, the same loneliness, one still stands alone under or before more than one can understand.

"O my Creator!" she cried out in a soft gasp.

After a while, she noticed that her breasts were full and hurt. Inexplicably, she felt like panicking. "Laekoorj!" She turned around and sat up straight.

In a moment he was with her. "Brisia!" he said.

She stood and swayed for a moment, feeling like she might pass out. When it passed, she said, "You weren't spying on me?"

"No, my dear Brisia, I wasn't. You asked to be alone." He stepped towards her and embraced her.

It hurt. "We need to go back," she said. When he did not respond at once, she said, "I need to nurse Mirla."

"All right," said Laekoorj, a hint of grudging in his voice.

"It's okay," said Brisia, trying to be cheerful. "We can do this again, sometime, except we can talk and be together, instead of me having a meltdown." She still felt terribly lonely– like some deserted place.

He took her hand, and they began walking back, in a much less round-and-about way than they had come. "It's not because you've been saying your mom's name all the time, calling our daughter that, is it?" asked Laekoorj.

Brisia shook her head vehemently. "Absolutely not! No! Not at all!" She lowered her head and took a few minutes. "It's been a long time, I think, since I first began to feel this. Before I was even pregnant."

"Your scars haven't been hurting you? That isn't the problem?" asked Laekoorj. He did not think that it was, but he was concerned for her and very protective about her, and simply had to ask.

"No! That totally isn't the problem!" Brisia insisted, feeling strangely embarrassed. After a few moments, she added, "I still don't want to talk."

A minute later, Laekoorj responded. "That's all right. We don't have to talk."

Sometimes, reading from the scroll interested her. Sometimes, it even seemed to interest her, to draw her, more than it ever had before. Other times, it was just so many words, worse, so many meaningless syllables in the air. She could struggle to think about what it meant, but none of it meant anything; did it even exist? It was with an effort that she made herself care for Mirla and help others watch their children from time to time, and yet she could not help but want to take care of Mirla. Bending down, she plucked a long piece of grass and began to twist it around her fingers with that same hand. It would not satisfy her. She dropped it carelessly.

When will it go? When will this sadness end? The thought words took on a rhythm, a beat, and a melody in her mind. *When will it finally come true? When will the dawn make glad our hearts? What is gladness? What is meaning? When will the ruin be healed? When will the far-spent night break? When will we see our hope? When will the promise flower? How long, how long? How long until the grief passes? How long until it finally comes true? How long until the dawn is more than dawn? How long until we see the meaning? How long until the wound is healed?* She could not cry anymore, but she still wanted to do so. Since the time of about Khiel's death, the deep pain and grief of the wrongness of the world had affected her, if possible, less than before. The joy and the rightness that came of and in it was near; she could reach out and touch it; she knew it. Yet this joy that was longing, this longing that was grief, this grief that was loneliness, afflicted her as it never had before, which is not to say that she thought these things out. She could not have thought these things out. She did not understand either the surpassing sweetness of a happiness, a sudden gladness, an inexpressible joy that seemed deadly or the inconsolable longing that went with it and was part and parcel of it, that was simply how she experienced it in a different mood or place, the terrible loneliness of a desire and knowledge that is not even known to the one infected by it and can never be told, the grief and pain of this loneliness and of both unfulfilled promise and incontainable– which is to say, impossible to keep or retain– joy. It was far too much for her and completely beyond her. Her heartbreaking lyrics were hardly an accurate representation of the cry which they were meant to express; they did, in fact, accurately express something in her life and experience, but only something on the side, related to that which they were meant to express as all things are in the last analysis, when reality is finally seen as what it is, and not in the fragmented and improperly connected way in which humans– and dragons– are compelled to experience.

#99
Fall of the Last Stronghold

"Unless your majesty will either tell us where you sent your so-called prisoners, or renounce the Promise and your treason, we will torture your maids for whatever information they have, and kill them."

"Do as you will," said Arendellie, without looking up from the marble under her feet. How many times had the wizards brought her in to question her and encourage her to tell them, and make increasingly less veiled threats, and tell her about all the things she could have if she gave into them, and question her about what she wanted but did not have that had caused her to engage in such rebellious, defiant, and finally counter-productive behavior? She had curtsied graciously and responded, "Thank you very much, but I have all I want. I am content. I am happier than I ever was before." It was true. She was used to comfort and luxury, and she was no longer young, and so sleeping on the stone floor resulted in aches and painful cricks in her body, and she also suffered occasional assaults of extreme boredom and a sense of purposelessness, but, all in all, she was happy and content. Something was right as it had never been right before. She was right where she belonged, and she was living like who she was. Right now, faced with their threats, she felt some sadness, but she also knew that it was not her problem to make sure what happened to whom. She was not in control. She was not responsible. She looked up, and her eyes met Haradac's. "After all," she said, "we all belong to the Creator. It is He who decides what you may and may not do, and how far He will allow you to disobey Him. It is not my job to disobey Him trying to keep others from doing so."

That night, Vanesh came to her, as he often did. They sat down facing each other, with their hands in each other's hands between them. Vanesh seemed even sadder than usual. After a long time, he asked, "Are you sure, Arendellie?"

"Sure about what? I don't understand."

"What you are doing," said Vanesh. "I'm sorry. I don't want to hurt you, but I want to be with you so much. I love you, Araenyi."

"I know," said Arendellie sadly. There was silence for a few minutes. Then she said, "I know I'm where I belong and doing what is right. I won't go back."

Vanesh nodded. Then he said, "Tomorrow, they are going to give you an opportunity to renounce in front of the entire city– or suffer." His voice sounded like he was going to cry. "This is it, Arendellie. I don't know why they think that you will. They seem so confident that you will. Perhaps, that you love me as much as I love you?"

Arendellie stood and took the two paces away that she could. She turned into the corner. "Vanesh," she said, sadly, "I don't even know what that means."

He rose also, came to her, and put his hands on her shoulders, but he did not try to force her around. She could feel the intensity of his love. She lowered her head and her forehead touched the smooth wall. "I don't understand you," he said. "I have heard of Ellason. Someone told me that every time you send her a meal she freaks out and screams about how she hates you and she would gladly drink your blood but she would rather die than ever receive a gift from you, but it's obvious that she has been taking it, since she is growing fatter. An exaggeration, I'm sure."

What is the purpose of this? wondered Arendellie. *I know it already.*

Vanesh's voice fell even further. "So many are going to die. So many die. I tried to explain to them that their way of governing is faulty and that they should let me try, since after all I *am* the rightful heir. It causes problems in some provinces. The People of the Promise are not the only who die. Almost all the dragons the Dragon Keeper left are gone, by now. I think there are only eighty-two dragons left living in Camil that are known. They kill anyone who has any loyalty to anyone except them. They separate families. They…"

"I know," said Arendellie sadly. She did. One of the reasons she had moved to have Ellason arrest Azshbir and those in Afteloan was because she knew of the plans already being put into practice in some parts of Camil and rapidly spreading. They were separating families to ensure that everyone had a broad exposure to the various climates and ways of doing things, so they could understand more about what helped their citizens to thrive. These plans had sparked rebellions in some regions.

Vanesh spoke in a low, strained voice. "I wish I could kill them with my bare hands. If they hurt you, *I will.*"

"No!" Arendellie cried softly, stiffening. She spun and moved away from him, landing in the far corner. It was an awfully small space.

His eyes glinted in the dim light. "I heard about how you fought the soldiers! Perhaps, that was part of what made the way you move so attractive. I saw it when I first set eyes on you." Arendellie cringed. Was that all he had ever seen or desired in her? No matter, was it not what she had been looking for, then? He stepped forward. "Why shouldn't I kill them?" he asked. "They torture thousands. They tear children from their mothers. They kill. They murder. They have already separated me from my queen for far too long. *Why shouldn't I?*"

"Please! I'm begging you not to!" cried Arendellie, trying to keep her voice down. "You will die! Please! I don't want them killed."

She heard the rage in Vanesh's voice. "Even though they torture children?" he asked.

She buried her head in her hands and began to cry. "No. Don't. Don't kill them. Let the Creator kill them in *His* good time."

He pried her hands away from her face and cupped her cheek. "My beauty. My Araenyi. My love. *Why?* What does the Creator ever do, but send His people to *die?*"

Arendellie wished she could get away from him for the moment. It was hard to think for some reason. Finally, she said, "He gives us *life.* He heals our wounds. He makes us *right.*"

"Nonsense," said Vanesh gently. "Because of Him, thousands die. He does not heal wounds. Because of Him, men, women, and children are covered in wounds and scars, *destroyed.* Right? What right is there in this world, except that I should kill the people who do this? His gifts are death and suffering, tortures and destructions, grief and sorrow, ruin and loss. Yet... somehow, so many love Him."

Arendellie did not know how to respond. How could she ever make this man understand? Perhaps, he did understand, only too well, and was fighting it, as she had done. Oh, how she prayed that was so, and he would one day turn, but it was just as possible that he knew nothing at all. After a long moment a thought occurred to her. "Are you like this because they are planning to torture me?"

"Who knows what they will do?" asked Vanesh in an anguished tone of voice. "Last I knew, they said nothing of it... Only the torture of killing *others*." He dropped his hand from her face. "If you don't want me to kill, then I will not kill for you. But, I *will* kill for others."

He cares? thought Arendellie, momentarily taken by surprise. She had not known he had cared for anyone in the whole world but her. "Please!" she pleaded. "If you must, go and visit other People of the Promise, and ask them what they would want done. Or, better yet, ask the Creator! If He wishes you to kill, then kill, but ask Him, for He is the King."

"What about those who are not His? Who care no more for Him than I do, or even than the wizards do? I will kill for them," said Vanesh. He was clearly upset.

"No," said Arendellie. "You will kill for yourself. And, you will die."

"I'd rather die than live a coward," said Vanesh. He sounded offended.

Arendellie buried her face in her hands again. She was already so tired. Why could he not understand? Why could he not seek the Promise? *There is no other hope.*

"One more time, together, Araenyi?" requested Vanesh.

Arendellie had never been in this place before. It was a kind of stage before thousands of people. She thought the entire city of Anores was looking at her, seeing the Queen for the first time, except that, though she had been dressed in lavish, jeweled clothes and crowned, she was Queen no more. She was a condemned prisoner, waiting for a fate she did not know.

She bowed her head. *Here I stand, Creator. I stand with Your people, below the world, waiting for Your Promise. I have no other hope, in life or in death. I stand with Your people, to suffer what they suffer and share in the reign of Your Conqueror. Forgive me for living away from You so long, defying You, living as a traitor and an enemy. Look down upon us, and have mercy on us all. Have mercy on Vanesh. Have mercy on Liesam. Have mercy on us all, O King.*

"What is your majesty's response?"

Arendellie realized that it was the end of a speech. She looked around her. "What?"

"These are your people. They are looking for your encouragement, from your favored position, to the attaining of triumph and oneness with the Great Lord, known to us as Casarion."

She held up her hand to address rank upon rank of citizens who were about to encounter one of the shocks of their lives– she would not say the shock, for while there had been comparatively less change in Hasseleighton than in the rest of Camil, some rather shocking events had already occurred. However, to the younger generation, to those aged like her son Liesam, this would really be a shock. She did not know how much she would be able to say. A wizard was amplifying her voice, but once he realized what she was saying he would almost certainly cut it. *My Creator, please don't let him make it be that I said what I will never say.* "The Conqueror will set us free! He will make us able to live before the light of the Creator! He will conquer death forever!"

At someone's command, a prisoner, a young man she did not know, was brought forward and killed. Arendellie looked up at the sky. "Creator, please," she whispered. "Please, do something. I know the Conqueror will not come for a long time yet, but, please, act."

"Next time," Assea said, "it will be someone you know. Will you take back your act of treason?"

Arendellie took a swift step backwards. "What about you? It is you who are the traitors! I am living in enemy territory. I know my King will come. Should I join the traitors, upon whom He will take swift and terrible judgment, or suffer to wait for His deliverance?"

"Another," said Assea.

Why? Arendellie screamed in her mind. *Why? Are they really this evil? This cruel?*

"Queen! Your majesty!" It was the voice of Alitholiel, a maid Arendellie had always despised. For a brief moment, joy spread its wings in Arendellie's breast. "You've come to the Promise?" she asked, turning. There was sheer terror and hatred in Alitholiel's eyes. "No! Mercy!" she cried, thrust to her knees. "I tried! I really tried! I spied! I told! I'm loyal!"

Another Ellason. She would have made another Ellason, thought Arendellie. She was not what she had been, though. She would have rejoiced in Alitholiel's swift execution before she believed the Promise. Serve her right, it was annoying, aggravating, and spies and snitches of that order deserved death. Even her torture would not have bothered her, as long as she had not been forced to be part of it. Even a year ago, Alitholiel's death would not have disturbed her. She would have been glad of her removal. Now, those thoughts were a million miles away from her mind. Every moment, almost, there was less resemblance between her and the life she had lived. "O Creator, have mercy," she begged, softly, as the snitch was slain; she could not do anything if she tried, standing between so many strong guards. "Have mercy. Please." Sudden terror arose in her breast. They were not going to kill Vanesh, were they?

"You do know," said Assea, "that you can stop this any time– renounce the Conqueror, and we will spare hundreds for you as your personal servants."

"Of course, her majesty knows that. Her majesty knows many things. However, she has contracted the disease, and we hope that we can cure her of it. When she proves that she is cured, we will have a celebration. Another."

Do something! Please! Let them all know Your Promise! That way, this won't be the end. Just a terror, on the way, and we will ride forth in triumph together when Your Promised One conquers. "O Creator, please, act!" she pleaded out loud.

"He cannot do anything; do you not know that? Is that not now plain?" asked someone.

Arendellie threw her veil and hair back. "He has spoken! He will come! He will reign! Do rebels say, in some prison where they are holding prisoners of war from the rightful King, 'Turn to us and join us in our rebellion, your King will never do anything, never win the war,' when they are all in terror, for they have but five thousand in their last stronghold, where they are killing prisoners, and the King is climbing the ramparts with an army ten hundred thousand strong, and will slaughter all who betray Him?" She took a deep breath and went on, ignoring their commands to go on killing. "I am the servant of a King in an enemy city. My enemy, a traitor to my rightful King, says to me, 'We will cast you into the dungeon, unless you swear fealty to us and serve us against Him; He can never do anything.' But, He holds the key to the dungeon. He rides on an army that can destroy you, a few scant rebels, in half an hour, and approaches quickly over the side of the mountain. Do you think I fear you? It is you who are in trouble!"

She wondered where Vanesh was. Certainly not watching, if he could help it, but he was king in name only. Who knew how much of his family power he still held? How much wealth or freedom? Who knew what he had been doing these past months, how many resources he had expended? Who knew where he would be, by the time this horrible day was over?

She did not hear it, but behind her the wizards were muttering about how something was not working. She stood and raised her hand. She was about to explain the Promise to her people. "The Creator, who is real and whose light is deadly to us, will send a Conqueror, who will bear our shame and–" she began, but at that moment she was thrust to her knees.

It was the nightfall and the daybreak in one.

It was the complete end of the struggle and the failure.

#100
The Shield of the Scroll

Of all who had ever served Arendellie, and who had not been taken away with her youngest children, only Nagi was not there. She and Hariel were playing, as usual. This time it was an annoying game of dress-up. Suddenly, Hariel turned to her and said, "You know what the really great thing is?"

"No," answered Nagi, confused.

"Most of the time, twins get separated, when one or the other or both of them is married. It won't be like that for us. We get to be together always!"

Nagi tried not to respond. How was she going to respond?

It was only a little while later that Hariel's mom, Signafri, entered with her husband. Signafri breathed a sigh of relief and sank down onto a couch. "This is one time when I am *soo* glad I have servants to cook and clean for me. It must be a great trouble to those who have to do their own cooking and cleaning, and to those who had to bring their servants with them."

"What happened?" asked Hariel, quickly going over to her mom.

"The Queen was executed, girl," said her dad.

"Why? Why would that happen? Isn't she the Queen? Her name was Arendellie, right?" asked Hariel. Nagi understood, though. She had questions too, but she would not ask them now.

"It was discovered that her majesty was actually a traitor, engaging in seductive practices in the dark, using her husband's resources without his knowledge. Her majesty spoke of another Conqueror and King who is coming and who will overthrow this city and this rule," explained her dad.

"My twin Nagi believes that a Conqueror is coming, but it won't be for a long time, and she definitely *isn't* a traitor," said Hariel.

Her dad glanced at Nagi, who was standing in the doorway, still dressed up to be a princess, and Signafri simply said, "Oh."

What is it? Nagi wondered. *I clearly confessed the Promise, and yet here I am. I still do, and nothing happens. Why? It's almost as if no one notices it… except for Hariel.*

Late that night, after they had all gone to bed, King Vanesh called for her again. She still did not know what to expect. He had wanted to see the scroll and read it, though he allowed her to continue keeping it. When she had not known how he knew about it, he told her that he had provided Arendellie the resources specifically knowing what she was doing with them, and that he knew both about her allegiance to the Promise and the scroll. He hated the fact that his wife did the things she did, but he did not hate that someone was doing them, only that it was his wife, and only because he knew it would lead to what was now happening– her imprisonment. He had not waed to talk much, only to say that he wanted his wife. She found being alone in the same room with him very uncomfortable, but there was nothing she could do about it. As, there was nothing she could do about it now.

The king looked so forlorn and so miserable. Nagi kept her distance, but she felt sorry for him. When they were completely alone, he said, "You are alive. I'm surprised."

Nagi looked up and met his blood-shot eyes. He looked like he had not slept for days. "Why?" she asked, her voice coming out in a croak.

"They searched out every other one of my wife's slaves. They tore them from households they were serving well in, and slew them all before Anores, regardless even of their loyalty to the new religion and to Camil Hasseleighton. They killed *everyone!* They killed every guard known to have served the Queen in her time in the cell. So, I sought out you, I don't know why, to make sure you were still alive."

"Why would your majesty care that I am alive?"

"I don't know," said Vanesh. "Araenyi is gone. I don't know anything anymore. I loved her. I wanted her. I wanted to live with her until I died. I am already growing old. I see no purpose anywhere. I don't know why I'm telling a slave this. Perhaps, because you are the only person I know of who knew my wife and who did not command her slaughter and who still lives. She begged me not to kill, but that's the only thing I know to do. If they kill me, they kill me. There is no other purpose for which I can live."

Nagi stood against the wall, frozen, not knowing what to say or do. It was hard for her to think. She was still constantly overwhelmed with a fear that made her mind and body feel like fruit jelly. She knew that how the king was thinking was wrong, but she did not know how to say anything. Finally, she stammered, "That isn't true."

Vanesh buried his face in his hands and turned away. "What isn't true?"

"Th-th-that there's nothing else you can d-do," answered Nagi.

Vanesh groaned. "What can I do?"

Nagi froze. She simply could not make the words form in her mind, let alone on her tongue. "Y-you kn-know," she stammered. Then, realizing how disrespectful that sounded, she said, "I b-beg y-your p-p-par-pardon, y-your m-majesty."

"It's okay," said Vanesh. "Like I care? About that kind of thing? Just nine hours ago, my wife was executed. She was in prison for months before it came to this. I don't know what they were thinking, but they were killing her slaves, and she spoke to them and to her people. When they could not stop that, they beheaded her... right there. I don't care. Prince I was. King I was called. Those who called me king took my wife, my queen, from me, and then they killed her. I will never see her again. I should kill them." Nagi could hear a few sobs in his voice; he was on the verge of crying. His voice was so hoarse that, when he first called her, she thought that he had been crying for hours. He took a deep breath, then said, "I don't really care what you call me. Don't insult me. But, as long as you don't kill my wife and aren't friends with those who did, I don't care that much. 'Your majesty' means nothing. Nothing means anything, anymore. Certainly nothing that they say and nothing that they touch."

Nagi nodded in acknowledgement. She still felt completely lost and bewildered. *Why? Why me? Why do I live? Why was I not taken to die?* It made no sense. She remembered running after those who had taken the People of the Promise to prison crying, "I wait for the Conqueror," and hearing one say to another, "She's clear." It was as if no one even heard her words.

After a while, Vanesh seemed to notice that she was still in the room, and sent her back to Hariel. Over the days that followed, Nagi observed the fear and distress that Hariel's friends and their parents were experiencing. Public executions were not uncommon, executions people were expected to attend happened, but nothing of this magnitude had ever happened before. It was almost unspoken, but many were desperately afraid– if they knew someone who believed the Promise, but did not even know it, they could be killed? If they knew someone who believed the Promise, and they reported him or her, they could be killed? Nagi herself continually wondered at her placement. She shared, more or less openly, that she believed the Promise and hoped for the Promised Conqueror, and yet no one seemed to notice it. Sometimes, people, like Hariel, or a few of Hariel's friends, or some of the other slaves in the household, heard her words and questioned her, but no one seemed to be capable of being aware at the same time of the fact that she was one of those who hoped for the Conqueror and the fact that the Promise of the Conqueror was counted as treason.

Vanesh never called for or visited Nagi again. Sometime later, she learned that Vanesh himself had been killed, and the crown prince, Liesam Casarion, had fled for his life– or so some said; it was also said that he had been thrown into prison or killed. The council had concluded, based on the unlikeliness of the people who seemed to be infected by it, that believing in the Promise was some kind of disease, and certain bloodlines seemed to be more prone to it. They were expending all their resources to exterminate all who had any connections to Ebrin, the village from which Kathreen Alarion, Arendellie, and Neshekh Dasaran had come, and also those who had lived with or known any Ebrinese. The torturings and slaughterings were seemingly endless and certainly senseless. There was rebellion in some parts of Camil, where the people decided they were not going to tolerate the rule of the wizards for any longer, since so many of their friends were killed simply for being associated with someone; in some cases, the person was a relative they had not seen in a decade or an employee they hardly knew. Nagi understood this from the other slaves and from Hariel's friends and their slaves.

However, the years passed and she and Hariel suffered nothing from the madness around them, even when Hariel married the son of the nephew of Koriel, one of the wizards. Somehow, they were protected from the insanity and tyranny. Always, she expected to be discovered, to be betrayed, and to suffer and die with countless others, most of them innocent of her crime which was no crime. However, it never happened. The scroll was never found or known by anyone hostile. In fact, long after Nagi's time and for more than two thousand years, it remained in the care of the slaves of the nobility, and now and then one of the nobility themselves, in the very castle of the tyrants, in the center of the realm of terror and horror. So, even in Camil, a few of those who waited for the Promise were preserved.

#101
The Gift and the Thanksgiving

Three years had passed, and Brisia had another child, a son, whom she and Laekoorj had named Dormik. She was so tired, tired of the weight and burden of life, of an emptiness and dryness that was worst when she was least physically exhausted. She diced herbs for stew while Dormik, still an infant, slept and Mirla played in the care of some slightly older girls and another mother with a few other children between a couple months and a year younger than herself. Sometimes she felt weighed down with the loneliness, the sorrow, the ache and desire, and other times she felt like a desert, deprived of all feeling, even the ache of longing, and yet needing– even desiring– something, though she could not desire. There was no meaning in anything. She cooked food, she cared for her children, she ate, her heart wrung when her baby screamed, but, beyond that there was nothing– only a dry, empty waste over which these things were a thin veiling, an appearance that told nothing of the empty space– or lack of space– behind. She ached with need and longing for meaning, for substance, for a rising well of joy, and the longing was the more painful because she knew no longing it was like a dry, racking cough or the spasms when one's stomach has nothing more to throw up and yet one is still trying to throw up. This alternated at times with the weight and pain of lonely longing for another world, and yet even that felt dry, transitory, shallow. She wanted– o, how she wanted– the swell, the joy, the fulfillment, what it had been like to read the scroll– or to sing– or to simply be alone and contemplate the Creator! Yet, it had been so long, and though she read the scroll backwards and forwards there no longer seemed to be anything in it– only jagged lines on a scroll that, strangely, bore only a few marks of use. She hated singing, for her heart would not sing. Conversations about the Creator grated on her ears, for she felt and saw so very little, and so ached for that for which she felt no ache of longing, because she was empty and dry. She wanted to flee from such talk and be alone, to see the shimmer of glory, but it did not come, and she hated that too. At first, she had now and then felt the stab of joy, of longing, of gladness, of meaning and fullness, of the Creator's glorious presence, but it passed, and even while it lasted, there was a sense of dryness, of shallowness, of which she became more and more painfully aware.

Late two nights ago, she had gone outside. She thought Dormik would stay asleep for a few minutes, so she stepped outside, under a night sky strewn with windblown, ragged clouds. A moist, warm air blew on her cheeks. There was nothing very remarkable about the night. She had stood there, feeling a deep sense of calm and contentment. For almost a day this peace had lingered, marred by her desperate clinging, by her fear of its departure. So many times she had destroyed a moment of joy, a thrill, a pleasure, by fear and clinging, by trying to keep it!

Brisia bowed her head as she diced the herbs. "My Creator and my Lord, thank You," she said. What motivated the action or where it came from, she did not know, but it sprung up from within her, deliberate and conscious. In this– in this moment–

in this struggle– in this depth– in this desert, she gave thanks. For this– this moment– this struggle– this depth – this desert, she gave thanks. To the Creator Himself and for the Creator Himself, she gave thanks.

If someone– say, Adaria, or the ailing Sirifa– had told her to give thanks, she would have shaken her head and said, "I can't." There was no feeling or real desire in her; there was no thanksgiving in her. It was true enough that she could not have given thanks. If someone had told her to give thanks for the lack, for the emptiness, for her very inability to really enjoy or to give thanks, she would have asked, "Huh? I can't. What is there to give thanks for about that?" She did not think about it, but, even now, if that question were asked, she would not have had an answer. She did not really know for what she gave thanks. She did not even really know what her thanksgiving meant or was. It was real; it was, perhaps, the most true thanksgiving of her life up until that point, but it was almost– but only almost– entirely unlike all previous thanksgivings. It was a true thanksgiving– a giving of thanks– an offering of gratitude, surrender, and love. It did not change the desert, the dryness, the lack of feeling, whether of gratitude or of love– which is not to say her love for the babies whom she had borne in her womb and whom she nursed, or for her husband, or for anyone else– or of joy, or even of contentment. Nonetheless, it changed it all completely.

Again, a few minutes later, Brisia found herself desperately reaching out, sinking back. Again, "My Creator, I praise You. I thank You," she whispered. Over the following days and weeks this pattern happened again and again– falling into moaning, weariness, and agonizing grasping of the fled feeling of joy, then, sooner or later, catching herself and giving a thanks she did not understand, a thanks she hardly even knew if she meant, a thanks the meaning of which she did not know, but, she did give thanks.

One day, Brisia sat and listened, nursing Dormik, while her husband read from the scroll to all of them. As Laekoorj read the words about the Creator and about His mighty deeds, words which Brisia had never understood, even in the days of joy and contentment, feeling and understanding, she was numb at first. Then, as he read the words, meaningless until that moment, there came a flash of what could only be understanding and yet was not like any understanding Brisia had ever known before. Perhaps it was only the sign of something else, something far greater, the sign of the Creator Himself. Then, the understanding of the meaning of the words, an understanding more like light than like understanding, slipped away. It slipped through Brisia's struggling attempts to understand, to know what it was, to understand what for the briefest moment she saw, to keep the sight, like a fish, and left her empty and dry. Finally, struggling against herself, she let it go. *I don't know why,* she thought to herself, *but I must let it go. I must trust my Creator and let Him give and take away. I don't understand, but I have to let it all go. I don't know why, but it's what honors my Creator. It's how I trust Him.*

Again, light and meaning shone upon what had until then been only words and nonsense to Brisia. She understood. With the understanding, with the meaning, came joy and peace, an almost burning, fiery joy. No, the understanding, the meaning was itself the glory of her Creator. Again, it was gone. It was like a flash of lightning, momentarily lighting up all reality and then swallowed up in the darkness out of which it came. She could not hold on to it. She let it go. She surrendered. *My Creator, only that You are Yourself– my Creator. Help me surrender. Help me give thanks. I give thanks to You!* she cried in her heart, throwing herself into a thanksgiving which, for that moment, she understood. It was the only way to surrender! But, the understanding was not understanding. Brisia was not spending any time thinking about what it was she was experiencing, seeing, and doing or putting words to any of it.

Then, Brisia knew. She stood before her Creator, she lived in His presence, as never before. Almost naked, she knew Him. He touched her, not through any created means, but by His own hand, through His very self. That was why this was the way it was! That was why she had nothing and could hold to nothing! That was why there was no keeping the understanding or the glory– for it was no mere understanding, no created glory, it was hardly even a glimpse of Him, but it was He Himself whom she knew, her Creator who visited her. All this time she knew no signs of His presence for He was giving Himself to her, not signs or sensations. All the time she felt nothing, for it was He who was touching her with His own hand and not with any lesser thing which was in some sense like herself or made for herself. She felt no wonder for it was the glory of the Creator, the Creator Himself, uncreated and beyond all mortal and created knowledge and things, who stooped to meet her. She felt no desire and yet was consumed with desire and parched with thirst because it was her Desire Himself who met her. Indeed, she had suffered so greatly not because it was her own desire, her own satisfaction and joy that was her desire or the desire of creation, the meaning and the everything, but because it was her Creator Himself who was the meaning and the everything, her desire and the desire of creation. She had realized and felt that everything else was nothing entirely because her Creator was present with her and to her as He had never been present to her before.

In that knowledge, swift, terrible, uncontainable, inconceivable, Brisia knew also– but without knowing or thinking about it– what was the reason of and the meaning for her thanksgiving: her Creator Himself.

When she continually let joy and wonder, knowledge and understanding, satisfaction and fulfillment go, she found that at every word and in every breath– almost– it flowed over her, in higher and higher wonders and joys, peace and satisfaction, in greater, purer, and truer revelations and visions of which, in some way, she was completely unaware, for the revelation and the vision was not hers and was not even revelation or vision, but the Revealed One, her Creator, Himself. When she grasped at it, when she resisted her inability to grasp, to keep, to hold, to know or understand, she found that she had nothing at all. When she let everything go, herself included, she found that everything continually flowed over and through her. It was because it was her Creator Himself, because it was everything, that was given her that when she tried to have it or anything at all, she found that she had nothing, not even desire.

Sirifa continued to ail, and two years later she died, several months before Brisia bore to Laekoorj their third child, another son, whom they named Kalimad after his mother's father. They had another daughter, whom they named Khiel, and after her a third son whom they named Shanner. Brisia continued to grow into her closeness to her Creator and found that she could say less and less of what she knew. Though she did not think about it this way, her knowledge of her Creator, her nearness to Him, had passed beyond not only language and human feelings but also human thought. She knew about the Promise and the Promised Conqueror that which she could not say. The words of the scroll, words everyone knew, words she taught her children, meant to her what no thoughts could contain, though even that she could not say. Her loneliness for Khiel was healed, and she was content though she still desired the repentance of her brother, whom she missed. It was her greatest and most piercing delight when she saw in the light of someone's eyes or heard in the tone of their voice that they too knew what the words meant and what no one could ever understand, though often this knowledge, at least in herself, could never even reveal its presence or show any signs that it was there. Once, she told Adaria, "Everything is different, but it is all the same. That the Promised Conqueror will bear our shame…" Very often, the meaningless and uselessness of words and thoughts pained her greatly.

She and Laekoorj had another son after Shanner, whom they named Ador. Ador was born in the same month as the eldest child and son of Mirla, now married herself, was born. Over the years, her children had caused her grief. Many times, Brisia wondered if her anguish over Daddy and Dormik was going to be repeated, since they did not understand and often acted in ways that she could not understand, but she remembered that she also had not understood and she also had acted in ways that she could not understand. From time to time, she still did not understand and still acted in ways that she could not understand. There was so much she knew, and nothing, perhaps, that she understood. That year, a few months later, Kalimad, who was seven, became sick with an illness of which no one among them had any knowledge. Many of them had been sick, more or less, but only Kalimad did not recover as the flowers opened and the ripening fruits were gathered. Brisia was tormented, nursing Ador and Shanner and watching and caring for Kalimad. After a while, he seemed to get better and played with the boys a little again, and Brisia was hopeful though still concerned while Laekoorj and some of the women encouraged her to relax, thinking he would be well, when he grew sicker again. Torn between her sons, all of whom she loved, Brisia scarcely slept or ate. She was able to sleep only because she was so exhausted. Watching Kalimad sicken and begin to die, it seemed like her own heart was being wrenched and that she was being torn apart. She continued to see her Creator, suddenly awe-struck– even if without a glowing physical feeling of wonder– by what she had never seen before and yet had seen again and again, sometimes in the words of the scroll, sometimes simply in a thought and quick breath, sometimes in the cries of her infant and toddler, in the moans of her now eight-year-old, in the torment of her own heart, and sometimes in water or a cluster of berries, the wings of a bird or the opening of a flower. She could not live without the Promise of the Conqueror, which seemed less far off as the days lengthened and as she grew more weary, pained constantly by a headache. Sometimes, she was not even aware that it had not come to pass.

Even when it was obvious that Kalimad was dying, Laekoorj tried to make Brisia eat and sleep, but it only tormented her more to be kept away from her children. He was distressed over his son, and this distress only made him more concerned for his wife. However, Brisia would sneak away to sit with Kalimad, doing all she could for him. Often, Khiel would come to her and cling to her, crying, and she tried to comfort Khiel as well. *Why?* she cried in the night. *Why, O my Creator? What is Your purpose in this?* Yet she never doubted her Creator's goodness and love.

Kalimad often asked her to tell him again about the Creator and the Promise and muttered increasingly incoherent sentences about the Creator and the Promise, though now and then he spoke amazing sense. Brisia realized that, were he to die indeed, it might be well– well as Khiel's death had been. It still hurt to watch him die, but somewhat differently, just maybe a little less.

Two months after Kalimad died, Brisia became sick and, a couple months later, also died. She tried to comfort Laekoorj and her children, along with her friends, with the assurance and knowledge that the time was right. Death was a wrong and an evil so horrible it could not be measured, but the Conqueror would conquer death– sometimes she found herself saying that He had conquered death– and, she could not really explain how, but there was light and life in her dying. Beyond death, beyond Kaarathlon, all the desires of the world would be fulfilled, every ruin would be undone, and all would be very good. It would be better and happier and fuller and more good in all ways than Kaarathlon had been when first the Creator made her. Brisia was as happy as she had ever been, she thought. In fact, she did not believe she could ever have been happier, more truly or completely happy. It was then, after she tried to tell him this, desperately wanting to comfort him and make him share her joy, that, once again, Laekoorj nearly pestered her to tell him about when she and Khiel were tortured together. "If you don't understand me now, you wouldn't understand if I tried to tell you what I cannot describe," she whispered. "In fact, I don't think I can describe anything." Brisia's grief was that few understood her and that she would leave her young children, Khiel, Shanner, and Ador. When she could do so no longer, her daughter, Mirla, nursed her son, Ador.

Five years later there was a drought and the river grew smaller and the surrounding land could not grow as much or support as much, and the village began moving up the river, to wetter and greener lands, year by year, until they settled in the place appointed for them, where the Promised Conqueror would one day come. The scroll passed into the keeping of Mirla and her brother Dormik, and then into the hands of their children. In the year after Laekoorj died, the river flooded its banks and the nearly flat plains around it, and the Knights of the Promises moved several miles away from it. They were a place where those who were fleeing from the tribes, skilled in the cruelty of the human race and worshiping gods and spirits, could find refuge, and also where those who had fled or were exiled and, for whatever reason, whether it was injury or lack of knowledge and skill, could not survive or care for any children they might have with them, could live and be protected. As the years passed, they became a small people, and Syrwe around them grew into a nation of Dragon-riders. They kept to themselves, staying away from the cities that began to grow up around them, but they continued to welcome any refugees who found their way into the woodlands and plains that were their home. As the years passed, they began to dwindle. A few among them bonded to dragons, and of these almost all left the Knights of the Promise to join themselves to the Dragon-riders of Syrwe. As the centuries passed, hardly anyone from the outside world came to them, and then no one came to them for many centuries. Many of their sons and daughters left to search for dragons eggs, and never returned, and they worked to teach and raise their children in such a way that they would not desire to go out into the world, but with little success at first. They found themselves having fewer children, and they diminished, but always they kept the scroll and held it in high esteem, reading it often and trying to find out the meanings of the various stories it told and the prophecies it foretold, though their pronunciation changed and they made copies which were easier for them to read as their language changed and melded with that of the peoples who had come to them for refuge, until the days of Y'landra, in which first the Conqueror, the Promise for which they had long waited, came to them, when there were left only a couple score of them, maybe fifty in all.

#102
Sal-Itshunrara-Miktkakar

Farat-Gutkralak leaned back on a pile of grass. In his arms nestled a two day old dragon. She was blue, purple underneath and with a purple knob on her tail, and her wings were red. Her name was Giyeth, and he had come across her egg, which had been laid months before by Kellyth, while searching for foods. "So," he was telling Azshbir and the others gathered around, "I was out in the woods, watching the moon set behind an arm of the mountain, praying to our *oraulim* and to our great *rulmya*, Aerakami, when I fell into a trance. I could sense great shadows moving around me, and, in the whisperings of the wind, a voice. What happened next, I cannot tell. It was like– what was it like?" he asked, looking down and into the whirling ruby eyes of his dragon who crooned. Her voice was clear, crystal, and warbled a little. "Well, I felt a presence that was very big and heavy. I thought to myself, 'It is greater than the *oraulim;* it must be the one who made even the *oraulim.*' I had heard many stories of meetings with the *oraulim*, and I had even met some of the lesser *oraulim*, but this was like nothing else. I knew. As I thought this, I felt very assured, but also very scared, *terrified*. I knew that I was right– the power somehow told me– yet I knew… Well, I guess the best word for it would be your *shame*. We have no word for it in our language. I guess I would explain it as when someone is exiled from the people, to wander around alone, but it is not even like that, or only half like that, and we don't have a word for it. We call it by the same word that we call death. *Ambaki."* He paused for a few moments and then said, "I knew that *iemausduil-rulmarya*, that he, wanted something from me. Here, my language is better. *Sarta. Sarta makgdakam rastari.* No. Even that is too weak. We have said it of our chiefs, at very terrible times. *Sarta amasduel-frandeulun-makgdakam iemusdoyel rastari-o.* That, I do not think, has ever been said before. It was terrifying, and I will speak no more of it. I have never spoken of it before." He gestured subtly.

Asaubun-Ictushan said, "I had something like that happen, Farat-Gutkralak. About a week later, all three of us were out hunting and we made a fire to worship the *oraulim* and Aerakami. The fire died down, and we were still hunting the next night, and this night we made no fire. Then, we all heard a voice. It said, 'The *oraulim* you have been worshiping are not so mighty as you believe. They cannot make their words happen. It is bad and for bad– *bitsnouwi*– bad things, that you worship them. There will come, on tents that ride the waters across the sea, a people with hair as dark as the night and skin like the shadows of dusk. They will tell you about the one whose words are always true and *sal-itshunrara-miktkakar*, the Promise that he will be.'" At Asaubun-Ictushan's words, Azshbir drew in a short breath. *The vision?* he wondered, thinking of what he had seen long ago and could never put into words. But, Asaubun-Ictushan continued. "We told the woman who speaks for the *oraulim* and in whose body they place their powers and meanings. She was angrier than anyone had ever seen her, and told us that we were deceived by the *auratilfaryim.* She and all the community put us out of themselves. It is like when one kills a beast and burns her flesh instead of eating her, to offer her to the *oraulim* to gain their favor, like when one kills a beast and burns her flesh to offer her to the *oraulim* to praise them and repay them, and like when one kills a beast and burns her flesh to offer her to the *oraulim* as a wall between one and their anger. We call it by all the words we call those. *Belarosh. Nimkarsh. Dhthralinkt.* In it, we become dead. If we return, they will kill us. It is horrible. It is *bitsnouwi*. We came here, and when we saw you, we knew who you must be, so we were very, very, very happy!"

Azshbir had long known that the religion of these brothers was very complicated and unlike anything he knew before. He had heard stories of *sal-itshunrara-miktkakar*– it was tongue-twisting just to think many of their words– which seemed like nonsense to him. Part of it might have been that they still had trouble with one another's languages, but, as they grew more and more comfortable communicating, it became more and more obvious to him that there was something very different about their ideas about the world. They seemed to have no trouble at all saying contradictory things, which was one of the reasons he could not even figure out how their legends began or how they ended. Of course, their legends were usually not about explaining a single thing in their religion– it was all too inter-connected for that. He was confused even by their *auratilfaryim*. He could not tell whether they were exalted gods, exalted men and heroes, exalted high priestesses, evil gods, evil men and warriors, or evil, rebellious, and fallen high priestesses– or all at once. He had heard legends that suggested any and all combinations. The *sal-itshunrara-miktkakar* especially fascinated him. It was the word the brothers had chosen for the Promise in their own language, and they had chosen it almost immediately. One legend explained the fact that it could never be broken by saying that anyone who took it and could not fulfill it then ceased to have ever existed– which made no sense. Another legend seemed to say that anyone who took it became whatever they swore, so that their existence and the fulfillment of their oath was the same, and they might die being their oath, but it would be fulfilled. Another seemed to say that the *sal-itshunrara-miktkakar* could only be taken by one who already had the power to fulfill that which he swore and was whatever he swore would be. Another said that only if something had already happened in some sense could it be sworn by the *sal-itshunrara-miktkakar*. Some of the legends were so confusing Azshbir had no idea what they might mean. Mostly they had to communicate in the language of Camil; Azshbir did not know whether he could not understand their language because the words and the ways the words could be changed or strung together was so complicated or whether it was because he could make no sense out of most of the concepts of reality on which their society and language were built, but they seemed to be better at speaking the language of Camil than he was at speaking their language, though their accent was so bad that it took a great deal of concentrated effort for him to understand them.

A year later, Farat-Gutkralak, the youngest of the three brothers, asked Reilia to marry him, in the ways of his own people. Though it still saddened him that he had not been there to watch his daughter grow up and to raise her while she was a baby and a little child, it was a great delight to him watching her turn into a young woman. Reilia would spend hours discussing the language and legends of the tribe of the brothers with him, where their concepts enhanced the knowledge the Camilians already had of the Creator and the Promise, and where the concepts were completely wrong. A year later, she had a daughter, whom her husband named Samwi-i-laktarath. That year, the plains were drier and there was less rain. The brothers explained to them that it happened often; their tribe moved from the plains to the mountains and back again depending on the weather and the cycle of the years. They would have to pass through the territory of his tribe to get to land that would offer them food and drinkable water in the coming years.

Several months later, they were shot and harassed trying to pass through the territory of the tribe. It was a long, fearful night. Azshbir was stiff and sore; he thought the cold had something to do with it. The eastern sky was white with dawn, and he was at a total loss for what to do. Some of them were wounded. "Have we lost them, now?" he asked Farat-Gutkralak, but he knew before the words were completely out of his mouth that something was horribly wrong. He could feel it in the air.

"No," he said. "We are surrounded. There is only one way. I and Reilia with go to them, with our daughter, and perhaps they will make peace."

"How?" asked Azshbir. "Will they not kill you?"

"We must go before the sun rises," said Reilia. Azshbir thought she was pale. Her voice was steady, but he thought he heard a quiver of fear. He could hardly see her though; it was still dark, and she was more a shadow of movement than a form. Something about her reminded him of his wife, her mother, Neah'ra. In her arms, Samwi cried, and she shifted, trying to keep the baby quiet. "I will explain it to you when I return, or Sab or Asaubun," she said. "You must instruct your people to remain silent, and get Sab-Arktikak or Asaubun-Ictushan to explain what you need to know in the time you have." He felt, rather than saw, her hand Samwi to Farat-Gutkralak, and lean forward to kiss him. "Look to the Promise!" she said. "Look to the Promise!" he repeated, as she took Samwi back into her arms. He heard and felt her and her husband climb up the ridge to the east, towards the rising sun. Their footsteps on the dry foliage on the ground were like hammers of dread in his ears.

The rest of that day remained a blur for Azshbir. He had been up, working and thinking under strain of physical fear for more than a day and a night, and as he grew older he grew ever more easily exhausted. Islands of disjointed memory remained: a volley of arrows arching in the sky, westwards he thought; a strange sound, like human singing and yet unlike any human singing he had ever heard before, wailing but not with sorrow, and mixed with the beats of drums and a stringed instrument; a red and blue feather he could not remember why he was holding; two pairs of blue dragon wings and two pairs of red dragon wings in the sky, crossing over the disk of the risen sun, again and again.

Then, Neah'ra speaking to him, but her face seemed lost in shadow and her voice in a cloud. "We must go, Azshbir! We must go. East and south, down to the plains. Now!" He thought he remembered her saying something about Reilia, but he could not put it together.

Finally, in some foothills, he remembered a chieftain, dressed much as the brothers dressed, standing before him. "Thank you for bringing to us the knowledge of *sal-itshunrara-miktkakar,*" Reilia translated for the chieftain. "We knew that the destiny of Kaarathlon was bound up with *sal-itshunrara-miktkakar,* and we thought that it would be lost into nothingness of hell, the curse and the crime, because there was no one. Now, you have brought us the knowledge which escaped in the revealings of our dreams. The many-ness of the one who will conquer the failure of the *sal-itshunrara-miktkakar* of the *oraulim,* of us, men, and be for us *sal-itshunrara-miktkakar.* We thank you for the knowledge of this one who will be the end and the rebirth of the *auratilfaryim,* the *belarosh,* the *nimkarth,* and the *dhthralinkt.* He is saying that the one is the *belarosh* of the person and of the community, and so also the *nimkarth* and *dhthralinkt* of the person and of all, though it's more exact than that, and I can't explain it all. He says that the true *sal-itshunrara-miktkakar* will make the failure, the deathness, the curse, and the crime into *amb'ruriar,* which is a life that comes out of the earth and makes the skies small and dark with its abundance. He says–" She looked around, and Azshbir could see the distress on her face. "I can't translate what he says," she said.

I can hardly understand her, thought Azshbir.

After that there was a feast, for which Giyeth, the blue and purple red-winged dragon of Farat-Gutkralak sang. Her song was soothing, and Azshbir wondered if it gave him more understanding of the concepts and thoughts of the tribe. Until that day, Azshbir had not known that Giyeth was a singer, though he realized that he should have, from the way that she crooned and little warbles in her call, but he did not know very much about dragons. None of them did. Shantee and Kira had raised their dragons, Kameth and Kellyth, alone, without the guidance or knowledge of other Dragon-riders. Kathreen had taught him many things, but whatever she knew of dragons she had not taught him. However, he remembered hearing a singing dragon in Afteloan, most days, until he grew too tired to notice or care in prison, and he had never head the dragon again after his release. He wondered if Kameth and Kellyth were the off-spring of the singing dragon of Afteloan, a male, if he recalled correctly, for the people of Afteloan were proud of their rare singing dragon, Jambelyth, and his rider.

Much of the tribe joined itself to the Knights of the Promise, but much of the tribe also rejected the Promise. Azshbir never understood what was the significance of the minutes before sunrise and a foreign woman and a child, but Farat-Gutkralak, he learned, had been wounded by members of the tribe who would not accept him, but rejected him as one of the 'dead'. Azshbir raised his youngest children, Norden and Nourdë. He died before either of them reached the age for marriage, having tried to give the leadership of the Knights of the Promise and the keeping of the scroll over to Omaran and Shantee. Nourdë never married, and she died young, at the age of about thirty, several months before Neah'ra died, almost two decades later. The Knights of the Promise preserved large sections of their scroll in their memory, and later wrote what they remembered down on parchments, but they made a vault in the stone of the mountain for keeping the one scroll. They kept the training of the use of the sword that had come down to them through Azshbir from Kathreen Alarion, who had it from Ishtailor, and when the nations of Syrwe grew up around them they bought more swords from them. At times, they fought with the tribes that, from time to time, invaded the place where they lived, and they never interacted with the civilization that grew up around them except to buy and sell goods, keeping the memory of Camil and what Camil had done to their ancestors alive in their minds and fearing Syrwe, for there was no land to which they could flee from Syrwe and no promise to guarantee that they would survive such a flight. In time, they had fewer and fewer children and disease took some of them, and they allowed some of their daughters to marry the pagans around them. They took the daughters of their daughters or the sisters of the men to whom they gave their daughters for their wives, and they cautioned their daughters not to share the Promise of the Creator with the families they married, lest the people turn not only against the women but against the Knights of the Promise from whom the women came. In this way, the Herald of the Promise was descended from them, for Ander's youngest sister, Rasira, was given to Meriloth of Spey. Her first child and son, Rasi Meriloth, married a woman of Spey, and his eldest daughter, whom he named Nourda, married Kezlim Palece of the near-by village of Dayle. She had only two children who survived infancy, Norden Jaryle Palece, the Herald of the Promise, the Promise who came to the descendants of Adaria, Athara, Senise, and Esiri, in the plains by the river Asagora, who was known as Sar-Emer, and a daughter, seven years younger than her son, Ameriasel. In this way, the two who were prophesied to come as the Herald of the Promise, the one who would see the things of the past and the one who would see the things yet to be, were cousins, Nathen and Jaryle.

By the time however, that the Promise, sal-itshunrara-miktkakar, Sar-Emer, came to dwell with Y'landra in Kaarathlon and that Kuthreb, father of Ander, who was grandfather of Nathen, and of Rasira, grandmother of the mother of Jaryle, was born, much of the knowledge of the descendants of Azshbir had perished. Little understanding even of the meaning of the Promise still remained among them, so that they remembered only that He would conquer and reign over all things, including death, but sal-itshunrara-miktkakar they had completely forgotten, as well as most of their scrolls and even the Song of Azshbir.

Glossary

- **Adaria Nan-reem** – sister of Azshbir and Knight of the Promise. Eldest daughter and third child of Sirifa and Hoobit.
- **Ador** – sixth child and fourth son of Brisia and Laekoorj.
- **Afteloan** – city in southern Ephezoa.
- **Akasdar** – dragon-rider in the Hasseleighton Army.
- **Aki'lam** – maid of Arendellie.
- **Aleria** – friend of Kathreen Alarion's mother and, later, of Mirla.
- **Alitholiel** – maid of Arendellie. Snitch.
- **Amrath** – pink and peach dragon; bonded to Audra, mate of Nameth.
- **Amria** – younger sister of Ellason.
- **Anasha** – village in the Enzenyar Mountains.
- **Andelf** – officer in Grale's army; responsible for Arendellie's entrance into the palace.
- **Anjis** – friend of Azshbir's.
- **Anores** – city in Hasseleighton. Home to Wizard Grale Casarion.
- **Arendellie Casarion** – once-friend of Kathreen Alarion, wife of Vanesh Casarion, queen of Camil Hasseleighton.
- **Aroch Casarion** – second son of Vanesh and Arendellie Casarion.
- **Asaubun-Ictushan** – one of three brothers from a Syrwen tribe.
- **Assea** – water and earth wizard, of the Lords and Ladies of Light after Grale Casarion's death.
- **Audra** – young woman from Northern Syrwe; Dragon Keeper. Feared as the Undead Snow Queen.
- **Avanzar** – nation in southeast Camil.
- **Athara Nan-reem** – sister of Azshbir and second daughter and fourth child of Sirifa and Hoobit.
- **Azshbir Nan-reem** – husband of Neah'ra, Knight of the Promise and keeper of a scroll.
- **Bemdar** – one of the People of the Promise. Future husband of Senise.
- **Brisia** – second child, oldest daughter of Mirla.
- **Carliet** – friend of Arendellie in Ebrin.
- **Carneth** – red dragon; mated to Kellyth.
- **Cavisto Argaddonn** – wealthy man in Afteloan, of the People of the Promise.
- **Daera** – ex-prostitute, friend of Neah'ra, killed by the Hasseleighton Regime.
- **Daffron** Katalonga – mother of Neah'ra and husband of Darnize.
- **Dallyth** – male dragon, bonded to Leairne.
- **Damiela** – woman with Azshbir.
- **Damil** – third child and second son of Kalar and Adaria.
- **Dardar** – son of Dorene.
- **Darloss** – city in Avanzar.
- **Darnize Katalonga** – farmer outside Afteloan, employer of Azshbir, father of Neah'ra.
- **Della** – one of the twin eldest daughters of Azshbir and Neah'ra.
- **Dinnessia** – wife of Cavisto; died in childbirth.
- **Dizzy** – Dorene's little dog.
- **Dorene** – friend of Mirla, Arendellie, and Kathreen.
- **Dormik** – Brisia's older brother; first child and son of Kalimad and Mirla. Also the oldest son of Laekoorj and Brisia.
- **Duhralra** – woman in Zunazra.
- **Dulu Mai** – Ephezoan hero.

-**Ebrin** – village of Arendellie.
-**Elanberry** – a very tart berry having roughly the size and shape of a large blueberry but reddish-pink in color. Grown in cool climates and watery, sandy soils.
-**Eliaeya** – mother of Vanesh Casarion.
-**Ellason Zaele** – older friend of Neah'ra.
-**Elzari** – a people with many secrets; skilled in something like martial arts.
-**El-Reiza** – woman attendee in the Hasseleighton Army, Elzari Dragon-rider.
-**Enzenyar Mountains** – north-south mountain range in southern Camil. Defines western border of Avanzar.
-**Ephezoa** – country in central Camil.
-**Eshaya** – the first woman
-**Esiri Nan-reem** – fifth child and third daughter of Hoobit and Sirifa.
-**Farat-Gutkralat** – one of three brothers from a Syrwen tribe. Dragon-rider; bonded to Giyeth.
-**Foretsth** – dragon of Audra.
-**Frostflower Mountains** – mountain range on the northern coast of Camil.
-**Gamur** – male wizard of the Council.
-**Girsa** – maid of Arendellie.
-**Giyeth** – purple, blue, and red female dragon; bonded to Farat-Gutkralak. Singing dragon.
-**Grale Casarion** – wizard, Dragon Keeper, king of Camil Hasseleighton.
-**Hadac** – soldier of Camil Hasseleighton.
-**Haradac** – lead wizard of the Council.
-**Hariel** – a daughter of nobility.
-**Hasseleighton** – nation in eastern Camil, home of Wizard Grale Casarion.
-**Hoobit Nan-reem** – father of Azshbir and Adaria. Knight of the Promise.
-**Inshara** – maid of Arendellie.
-**Jambelyth** – the male singing dragon of Afteloan.
-**Janya** – twin sister to Kalar; wife of Kuthrynd.
-**Jassie** – friend of Arendellie in Ebrin.
-**Kalar** – husband of Adaria, twin with Janya and older brother to Kavra.
-**Kalie** – maid of Arendellie.
-**Kalimad** – husband of Mirla, father of Dormik, Brisia, and Lalia. Also the second son, of Laekoorj and Brisia.
-**Kameth** – light blue female dragon; bonded to Shantee.
-**Kathreen Alarion** – dragon-rider, wizard, Knight of the Promise, once-friend of Arendellie.
-**Kavra** – younger brother of Kalar and Janya. Husband of Athara.
-**Kawina** – maid of Arendellie.
-**Kgarjin** – third oldest daughter of Shaelene.
-**Kellyth** – dark blue female dragon; bonded to Kira. Mate of Carneth.
-**Khiel** – friend of Kalar and his siblings, and of Brisia. Also the fourth child and second daughter of Laekoorj and Brisia.
-**kimmer** – strangler snake in the Vinibra Volcanic Mountains.
-**Kira** – second oldest daughter of Shaelene. Rider of Kellyth.
-**Kizyia Nan-reem** – youngest daughter of Hoobit and Sirifa and twin of Nahiza.
-**Koriel** – healing wizard of the Council
-**Kuthreb** – third child and first son of Azshbir and Neah'ra.
-**Kuthrynd Nan-reem** – brother of Azshbir, Knight of the Promise, and second son of

Sirifa and Hoobit.
- **Kyenth** – male red, blue, and purple dragon; bonded to Asaubun-Ictushan.
- **Kyil** – People of the Promise known to Arendellie.
- **Kyil Kathreen Casarion** – third child and only daughter of Vanesh and Arendellie Casarion.
- **Laekoorj Nan-reem** – younger brother of Azshbir. Third son and eighth child of Sirifa and Hoobit.
- **Lasaira** – daughter of Daera and adopted daughter of Azshbir and Neah'ra.
- **Leairne** – Dragon-rider from Camil; husband of Audra.
- **Leaoneth** – yellow and orange dragon hatched to Grale Casarion; formed a bond with El-Reiza.
- **Ledth** – dragon of Audra.
- **Lia** – young woman in Afteloan.
- **Liesam Casarion** – firstborn son of Vanesh and Arendellie Casarion.
- **Linjer** – a shrub-tree that grows in the thick shade and rich volcanic soil of the jungle forests in the Vinibra Mountains; makes some of the softest bedding, though it needs to be replaced every couple of months.
- **L'sa-moth** – green and purple dragon, bonded to Kathreen.
- **Marlekk** – youngest child and only son of Shaelene.
- **Minshi** – a maid of Arendellie.
- **Mieshor** – city in Ephezoa near the Vinibra Volcanic Mountains.
- **Mirla** – friend of Kathreen Alarion and Arendellie, mother of Brisia; killed by Hasseleighton torturers. Also, the oldest child and daughter of Laekoorj and Brisia.
- **Mi'shael** – Elzari Dragon-rider.
- **Nagi** – maid of Arendellie.
- **Nahiza Nan-reem** – youngest daughter of Hoobit and Sirifa and twin of Kizyia.
- **Nakar** – sailer; Knight of the Promise.
- **Nameth** – dragon of Audra, purple, male, mated to Amrath.
- **Neah'ra Katalonga Nan-reem** – wife of Azshbir.
- **Neemor** – the first man
- **Nemor Tasanin** – warden over the prisons in Anores.
- **Neshekh Dasaran** – once-fiancé to Arendellie.
- **Norden Nan-reem** – second son of Azshbir and Neah'ra.
- **Nourdë Nan-reem** – fifth child and third daughter of Azshbir and Neah'ra.
- **Nyezer** – man on board the *Last Watch*.
- **Omaran** – Knight of the Promise; husband of Shantee.
- **Osilia** – city in north-western Camil.
- **Prince Teka-Rok** – a hero in Ephezoan history.
- **Rathor** – cell-mate of Azshbir's.
- **Rattling Maroon Snake** – rare and extremely dead snake; somewhat aggressive. Capable of spitting an extremely harsh acid no farther than three and a half feet. Inhabits the Trinazee Mountains. Often maroon, though occasionally crimson or violet with maroon stripes.
- **Razi** – friend of Azshbir's, orphan street boy, murdered by the Ephezoan regime.
- **Regaleath** – purple and silver dragonspell-touched dragon, bonded to Grale Casarion.
- **Reilia** – one of the twin eldest daughters of Azshbir and Neah'ra.
- **Ringeth** – male dragon of Audra.
- **Roketh** – dragon of Audra.
- **Rothen** – oldest son and second child of Kalar and Adaria.

-**Sab-Arktikak** – one of three brothers from a Syrwen tribe.
-**Samwi-i-laktarath** – first child and daughter of Farat-Gutkralak and Reilia, daughter of Azshbir and Neah'ra.
-**Sanahi** – friend of Neah'ra and Ellason.
-**Saria** – young woman on *Edgerunner*
-**Saris** – Ephezoan heroine.
-**Seair** – younger sister of Lia.
-**Searth** – dragon of Audra.
-**Senise Nan-reem** – seventh child and fifth daughter of Hoobit and Sirifa.
-**Sephar** – country in eastern Camil.
-**Signafri** – noblewoman, mother of Hariel.
-**Shaelene** – ex-prostitute, friend of Neah'ra.
-**Shanner** – fifth child and third son of Laekoorj and Brisia.
-**Shantee** – oldest daughter of Shaelene, Knight of the Promise; married to Omaran. Rider of Kameth.
-**Sirifa Nan-reem** – mother of Azshbir and Adaria, Knight of the Promise.
-**Surra** – maid of Arendellie.
-**Skyith** – male dragon attached to Audra; gifted in language.
-**Taela** – daughter and second child of Kavra and Athara.
-**Uingalin** – easternmost and northern city in Ephezoa.
-**Undead Snow Queen** – a mythic undead woman who is supposed to come out of the north to slay and enslave the Camilians.
-**Valiana** – light wizard of the Lords and Ladies of Light.
-**Vanesh Casarion** – nephew of Grale Casarion, husband of Arendellie, prince and then king of Camil Hasseleighton.
-**Varast** – young man with Azshbir.
-**Veance** – younger sister of Dorene.
-**Venaria** – a plant that grows in the Vinibra Mountains. The flowers, pink strands with small heart-shaped petals growing off, can be more than a foot and a half long. They hang down from the vine's branches.
-**Vinibra Volcanic Mountains** – mountains in Ephezoa.
-**Yamië** – one of the People of the Promise, lied about by Arendellie.
-**Zimth** – dragon of Audra.
-**Zjathemph** – dragon of Audra.
-**Zsyinzjae** – oldest child and daughter of Kalar and Adaria.
-**Zunazra** – city in Sephar.
-**Zyimeth** – female dragon; mate of Dallyth; killed before she could lay their eggs.

Language

Aerakami – a goddess.
ambaki – dying or death
amb'ruriar – could be translated as salvation
anamun – three or more knives
anrakat – grass
artalra-sab-rakat – the head of grass
ashuktin – arrows
auratilfaryim – it is very confusing whether these are demons, damned men, or redeemed men.
batish – the seed-bearing vehicle of a particular plant
belarosh – a sacrifice that makes the gods happy with one, so that they are pleased and will give blessing.
bitsnouwi – a curse, bad luck, futile and vain, a horrible crime, or the world of the dead.
Besgum Nalak-wathwarik – He is the best, greatest, ultimate, mightiest Speaker.
Dhthralinkt – a sacrifice offered when the gods have been angered because they have not received their due to propitiate them.
Estamu ruktuk ansujin, orist-mal, nio – They catch fishes, but not right now.
farushim – delicious, good to eat
gumarnu – eat or food
inbutashin – plural of batish
intuarumin – plural of turam
macgo – sinew
Makdagak! Makdagak! Estumu ma oraulim! Estumu exiyralifin-ekundin – Stop! Stop! They are not mighty-spirit ones! They are human animals.
namu – two knives
nima – knife
nimkarth – a sacrifice whereby one repays the gods for their blessing and gifts, giving them thanks and averting the doom of improper repayment.
sab-rakat – the roots of grass
sal-itshunrara-miktkakar – an oath which binds the oath-taker to the action, outcome, or prophecy of the oath, or a person or outcome so bound, so that the oath-taker and the oath cannot be separated; the intricacies of the meaning of this oath would take many legends to explain; in short, that which is sworn, testified, or prophesied by the oath and the oath-taker himself are so united so that the oath-taker cannot even be forsworn but is identified with his oath, which must come to pass as certainly as he exists.
sanrukitin – plural of grass
Sarta amasduel-frandeulun-makgdakam iemusdoyel rastari-o – untranslatable; the best approximate translation might go, "I knew in the secret, unknown depths of my spirit that he most graciously demanded with the most, deepest, most plentiful authority which is because of himself that which he deserved without measure, and which I, in my inmost being, was unable to give, in the same way that he in his inmost being made it so that I give it." It is a very poor translation, having nuances which the english is incapable of carrying and lacking many of the nuances and senses which my english rendition implies.
Sarta makgdakam rastari – untranslatable; the best approximate translation would be, "I knew in the secret, unknown depths of my spirit that he graciously demanded from me that he completely deserved and which could not be withheld, but I could not give it."

smawi – wood
shokt – arrow
suromi – the upper portion of the turam stalk when severed from the roots.
takak – bow
turam – a tall grass, somewhat like a very small palm tree in appearance, with a stalk that can be cut and is full of sappy water
tufik – bow with string strung
tufi-sor – bow with string unstrung

CPSIA information can be obtained
at www.ICGtesting.com
Printed in the USA
LVHW051748240321
682333LV00004B/140